Wendy Bayne lives in Ontario, Canada, with her husband and four sons. She had been a registered nurse until retiring a few years ago. A passionate reader, she turned to a lifelong desire to write historical fiction with a twist. When not writing, you'll find Wendy most often curled up with a good book or on a walk with her husband wandering about the city, enjoying the sights and sounds along the Grand River.

I lovingly dedicate this book to my husband, Charles, and our sons, David, Matthew, Eric and Izaak, for their constant support and love, and for their help in making my dream come true.

# Wendy Bayne

## UNTITLED

CRIMES AGAINST THE CROWN

AUSTIN MACAULEY PUBLISHERS™

LONDON • CAMBRIDGE • NEW YORK • SHARJAH

A CIP catalogue record for this title is available from the British Library.

ISBN 9781528929462 (Paperback)
ISBN 9781528929479 (Hardback)
ISBN 9781528965880 (ePub e-book)

www.austinmacauley.com

First Published (2020)
Austin Macauley Publishers Ltd
25 Canada Square
Canary Wharf
London
E14 5LQ

A special thank you to my sons, David, Matthew, Eric and Izaak who supported and encouraged my efforts. To my husband, Charles, who read this book multiple times and loved it more each time. Special thanks to Eric, who wasn't afraid to criticise my work and who wouldn't let me give up.

And a heart felt thank you to Austin Macauley for taking a chance on me and for all their guidance.

# Chapter 1
## *The Abbey, Northumberland, England: April 1827*

My name is Clarissa Hughes, but I'm known to the people who care about me as Lissa. I am the natural daughter of General Sir Richard Hughes' deceased second wife, Charlotte the whore. At least that's how my mother was referred to in the private conversations, to which I was not usually privy. Our home is known as the Abbey where I live with my brother Samuel and my sister Irene, but it's more lovingly referred to by Samuel as 'that pile of stones on the edge of nowhere'.

Since my birth the General has taken little or no interest in either my education or welfare. His horses, brandy and my brother Samuel have been the sum of his interests in life, or so it seemed. Though I was never exactly sure of how he felt about Samuel.

Samuel has always been the handsome knight errant in my life, coming and going as he pleases, which isn't often, yet he always has time for me when he's home. Then there's my beautiful sister Irene who on the surface might appear to be meek and mild but underneath is an exceptionally strong and intelligent woman. I adore them both, as do the staff, our tenants and the villagers. Between the two of them they have been my protectors and the only family that care about me.

My place in our family is somewhat less exalted than Samuel or even Irene's, who the General treats no better than a servant. But at sixteen years of age there was little that was expected of me except to behave like a lady and stay out of the General's sight. I only wish that I had had some warning or an inkling that my life was about to change and that what I had taken for granted all my life was a lie.

The change came the evening Irene suddenly announced that she was marrying Samuel's best friend Colin Turner. It was a shock to everyone but Samuel. It was so precipitous that I assumed she must be marrying Colin to escape the General and the bleakness of our ancestral home. However, I was soon to discover that it was a love match and not one of convenience. I would find that between them there was a genuine and passionate affection. What had appeared to be a whirlwind courtship to me was in fact a love affair of long standing; that had survived many years of separation.

Irene had for all intents and purposes been a mother to me since the moment of my birth. Even though she had been only seventeen years of age at the time, it was widely known but rarely spoken of that I was the natural child of the General's second wife, a by-product of a drunken indiscretion during a school holiday, when Samuel and his friends had descended on the Abbey with only Irene and the General's young, bored second wife, Charlotte, in residence. The General himself was on the battlefield in France at the time of my conception and was still there at the time of my birth. So, it was to everyone's relief that my mother died as I came were considered prime catches by the mothers of every debutant in London, even though neither possessed a title.

I had so many questions racing through my head. What would Colin's parents think of me as his ward? Why was I not staying with them while Irene and Colin were away? Perhaps his parents were too old, I was a boisterous sixteen-year-old with one foot firmly planted in childhood and the other dreaming of a future with all its possibilities. I started to blink back tears as my thoughts overwhelmed me. Perhaps his parents disapproved of the marriage and wanted nothing to do with me. Perhaps they had disowned Colin because of me. I felt totally disheartened and lost.

Irene slid out of her chair to sit beside me on the floor, "What is it, Lissa? What's bothering you, my sweet?"

I turned to look at her with unshed tears in my eyes, "Who do I belong to, Irene? I have no one that I can call mother or father. Even you and Samuel are not really my brother and sister despite what the law says. And I know that the General can take that away from me any time he pleases with just a few words. Who will have me as a wife with no name and no fortune to claim as my own?" I sobbed, and the tears were now streaming down my cheeks. "What is to become of me?"

She reached out and touched my cheek, then pulled me into her arms, looking as crushed as I felt. "Lissa, you are only sixteen years old. Don't you think you are looking a bit too far into the future and borrowing trouble where it doesn't exist? Colin and I want you with us, my sweet child. You are our family!" My sister smiled while taking out her pocket handkerchief and wiping away the tears on my cheeks. She leaned forward to kiss me on the forehead before she got up, pulling me up with her. "It's time you were asleep, young lady." She rang the bell for Meg to come and help me get ready to retire. When she arrived, Irene gave her instructions to start packing my things in the morning.

Meg hummed as she combed out my hair and I sat glumly staring at our reflections in the mirror. She was eighteen which was rather young to be a lady's maid but then I was still too young to have a lady's maid. Her mother was the chief laundress at the Abbey and the district midwife, her father was our head gardener. Meg had been my only playmate when I was little, but when she turned twelve she became a tweeny, then at fifteen a house maid. I thought at the time I had lost my best friend forever. It was true that our play days had ended abruptly, but we still exchanged confidences and gossip whenever she could slip into my room. Though it was never the same, it was our friendship that had prompted Irene to select Meg as my lady's maid. According to Irene a good lady's maid was worth their weight in gold and it took years of training. So, in a way I got my friend back and Meg rose above what would have been her normal station in life. Irene's maid Beth was a distant relation to Meg's mother and became her willing teacher. So, it was with a sense of adventure that Meg willingly launched herself into the life of a privileged servant.

Her humming though was getting on my nerves which were so raw I snapped at her, "Why are you so happy!? You have a lot of extra work to get done and it all has to be ready for us to leave the day after tomorrow!"

She stopped humming, tilted her head to the side so I could see her in the mirror. Smiling at me, she responded, "Oh, not to worry, miss, I got a warning from Beth yesterday that we'd be on the road before too long and I've got most my work done already. I'm just saving some of the ironing which I'll get done up tomorrow." Meg had become very good at her job but her continued cheerfulness rubbed me the wrong way and I frowned at her reflection. Undeterred, she continued combing and added, "Isn't it exciting, miss, we're going to London!"

Meg's enthusiasm didn't infect me, but my lack of response didn't seem to bother her in the least. I admired and envied her for her sense of adventure, but I wondered if she knew that we wouldn't be returning to the Abbey. I would have to ask Irene in the morning. Meg might decide that she wanted to remain here with her parents. Then again it might have already been discussed and my asking would only be redundant. I sighed deeply making Meg stop brushing to squeeze my shoulder in reassurance.

I had too many unanswered questions floating around in my head and was fidgeting so much that Meg seemed ready to give up on my hair. One painful tug elicited an 'Ouch!' from me, "Your hair would make a proper rat's nest, miss! I suppose you've spent the day in the orchard running around like a wild banshee, never giving a thought to it." She tsked at me a few more times then finally got the last tangle out and plaited my hair into my night braid. As she finished she bent forward considering me in the mirror. "Cheer up, Miss Clarissa; this will be such an adventure, you'll see it'll be grand! I can't wait to see London. You'll see...it'll be wonderful."

As she helped me into my night rail she added, "You know how I know everything will be grand?" I shook my head no. She leaned close to me and whispered, "You were born under a lucky star!" Then she stood up and began picking up my discarded clothes, searching the pockets and shaking her head at the grass stains.

I arched a brow and glared at her, "Who told you that? I've never felt particularly lucky!"

She chuckled, "My mum says so and she was there when you came into the world, so she should know." She got a wistful expression on her face. "Da said I about drove him crazy back then, I missed her something fierce while she was gone to help birth you. He told me that it had seemed like ages before she came home with you and your mother." She giggled then added, "He was at his wits' end with me for sure." I jerked around looking hard at her, but she took no notice and continued. "Mum says that I'm ready to strike out on my own now. So, I can't thank you and Miss Irene enough for giving me this chance."

I tried to smile when she patted me on the shoulder as I rose and walked to my bed, climbing under warmed sheets. Meg banked the fire and blew out all the candles except for the one by my bed. "Goodnight, miss." she gathered up the remainder of my clothes from the floor and left, closing the door softly behind her.

My mind was a whirlwind, so much was happening so quickly. What did Meg mean that I was brought home to the Abbey? I had always been under the impression that I had been born here. I laid there watching the flames dance in the hearth, my final thought before I fell asleep was that I would find my answers in London.

The next day was mayhem. I decided the best course of action was to get out of the house and stay out, until I was either called for or the sun was setting.

I snuck into the breakfast room hoping to avoid an encounter with the General. Samuel was there and in high spirits. Apparently, he was looking forward to getting back to the city and all its pleasures. He regaled me with what we would do in London, where he would take me and what he would buy me. I just laughed at his stories. As brothers go he was almost perfect, except that I knew that half of what he promised me would never happen because somewhere along the way duty would call…it always did.

But there were things that I knew he wouldn't forget no matter where he was or what he was doing. They included books of every possible description, drawing and writing materials. I was a ferocious reader and fancied myself a keen observer of life, recording my observations of everything and everyone around me in my journals, including sketches to illustrate my words. Samuel hid these journals in his room to keep the General from finding them since everything of mine was to be made available for the General's inspection at any time. I couldn't bear the idea of him reading my personal thoughts and I was sure that if he ever found them, he would fling them into the fire just as he had done to a much worn and beloved copy of Gulliver's Travels. He had called it a frivolous piece of trash before flipping through it, then consigning it to the flames.

Samuel gulped down his coffee, grabbed a letter beside his plate, then standing he bounced it off my head. "Have a good day, Lissa, but you'd best stay out the house and out of trouble; it will be a bedlam here. I'll see you later, my sweet."

As he walked towards the French doors that opened onto the garden, the General entered the room by those very same doors. I quickly shoved a roll into my mouth and put two into my pocket then slipped out of my chair. I headed for the door that led to the hall just as the General bellowed, "Stop, both of you! Samuel, I wish to speak to you about your sister and this misalliance she has made."

Samuel puffed out his cheeks, whistling. He tried to look calm, but I could tell that he was annoyed that the General had blocked him from leaving. "Father, I really don't think there's anything else to be said on the matter. You already know that I support Irene completely." Samuel motioned for me to come around the table to stand next to him. Once I reached him he put an arm around my shoulders as if offering his protection. "I also know that you couldn't possibly have anything to say to Lissa. You barely acknowledged her existence. So, step aside and let us pass." He squared his shoulders taking a step forward and pulling me with him. "We're leaving tomorrow so you can fester here in this pile of rocks alone." I looked up at Samuel as he squeezed my shoulder. I was terrified that he was renouncing his own father on my account and what this might mean for him.

The General glowered, his face was crimson as he spoke, he was practically spitting he was so enraged. "You dare to talk to me in such a manner, boy! I could cut you off without a moment's notice, where would you find yourself then! You and your fancy life in London and on the Continent. How would you support yourself then, sir?!" Samuel tensed as the General smiled in triumph and continued. "Yes, sir! I know what you are about, you and that Turner. Carousing and gambling with the hoi palloi, making fools of yourselves in good society. It's well known that you're a wastrel. If it was only you I'd say good riddance and be damned. But that trumped up Turner is stealing my housekeeper!"

Samuel drew himself up to his full height looking the General in the eye, then he coldly but calmly said, "Your housekeeper, sir? Is that all Irene is to you? Might I remind you that she is your daughter and not in your employ!" Samuel's neck was rigid, and I could see the vein in his neck pulsing as he continued, "Never fear, Father, Irene has taken care of it. She contacted your sister who will arrive tomorrow to assume the duties of running this house. I'm sure that you'll barely notice the difference."

Then Samuel lowered his voice. "And as to what I do with my life, sir, that is my business. Go ahead and cut me off. It will make no difference to me. I have had private means to live on for some time. Or have your forgotten our mother's bequest to Irene and me?" He smiled as the General drew back as if Samuel had struck him, but Samuel was not done. "Grandfather was very bold when he tied up his capital so that you couldn't get your hands on it. It must have made Mother one of the wealthiest women in England at the time. And as for my allowance, sir, I haven't spent a penny of it since coming down from Cambridge."

The General seemed to age before my eyes as each of Samuel's words hit him. "It has been safely invested to benefit Lissa when she comes of age." He looked down at me and smiled, then looked back at the General with a stone-cold glare. "I knew that you would never make any provisions for her future."

Samuel made as if to walk around our father, but the General moved to block our way. His colour had returned to normal and when he spoke it was with less venom, "What of the family you may have someday?" Samuel looked down at me arching his brow. The General was gritting his teeth as he hissed, "Are they not to benefit from that investment?! Would you give it all to this—this person and deny your own flesh and blood?!"

Samuel laughed, relaxing, but his arm remained protectively around my shoulders. "Your memory has become exceedingly poor, Father, to have forgotten what I just said. Mother's bequest was exceptionally generous. And as for my family, when and if I have one and whether they are of my blood or not, they will never want for anything. But most especially they will never want for love." He smiled down at me. "Come, Lissa, what do you say to a ride across the moors."

I was so astonished by this whole dialogue, I could only nod. This was the first time I had ever witnessed Samuel openly defy his father. He took my hand as we brushed past the General who now leaned against the doorway looking as if he couldn't fathom Samuel. I could feel his eyes following us as we crossed the garden and headed for the stables.

We walked away quickly yet the General's voice still reached us as we ducked out of sight. "Nothing good will come of her raising! She should have died with her mother." From that moment on I knew that I wouldn't miss my life at the Abbey.

Samuel and I reached the stables and within seconds he had the grooms scurrying to saddle our horses even before the General's words had died in my ears.

# Chapter 3
## *Family*

Samuel took up a position by the hearth leaning on the mantel while I crawled onto my bed and the other ladies took the only two chairs available, then they all turned to face me.

Aunt Mary was the first to speak, "Irene, my dear, I know it's your story to tell but would you allow me start? I have a feeling you'd muddle it." Then looking up at Samuel, "Samuel, please get a chair and sit or I'll have a crick in my neck before we're finished."

Irene looked terrified, "But, Aunt, what about Colin?"

My aunt waited until Samuel returned with a chair and once he was seated she responded, "What about Mr Turner? Well, I believe that he's had his way for far too long and for no good reason other than his pride. This conversation is long overdue, the most important person in all of this is Clarissa."

Aunt Mary stared at Irene who looked horrified and Samuel avoided eye contact by inspecting his hands, so I spoke up. "I wish someone would tell me what is going on. For the last two days, I've felt like I've been standing on the edge of a precipice not knowing if I'm going to be pushed or I should jump."

Irene tried one more time beseeching our aunt, "Aunt Mary, please don't!"

Samuel shook his head. "Irene, let her, you were going to tell Lissa when you reached London anyway. But I think this may be better, it will give her more time to adjust. Go ahead, Aunt Mary." He smiled at me and I felt a little better.

My aunt cleared her throat and proceeded, "Clarissa, I scarcely know where to begin." She paused and clasped her hands, pursing her lips, then blurted out, "First, you should know that your parents are not dead."

I stared at her with my mouth open then quickly glanced at my brother and sister who both were looking apologetic. I didn't know what to think or say, so I sat there dumbstruck as she continued. "Lissa, ugh, who gave you that awful name? It sounds like a snake hissing when you say it." She glared at Samuel as he chuckled. "Just as I suspected! Samuel, I shudder for the children you will father one day." His mouth fell open in shock as my aunt pointed her finger at him. "Don't be fresh with me, young man. You will marry one day, and I imagine it will be even sooner than you expect. I just pray your wife has more sense than you do." She raised her hand to him to stay any argument. "Don't bother to protest, nephew, I know more about your life than you do."

Aunt Mary turned back to me with a self-satisfied smirk. "Clarissa, as you already know my brother is not your real father. But what you don't know is that your mother was not his wife Charlotte." I gasped and felt tears welling up as she continued. "Charlotte did die, though it wasn't in childbirth. Rather it was from a morbid fever and a condition of the lungs that made it difficult for her to breathe. She was with me and Irene in Cornwall when she passed way." She paused as if to gather her thoughts. "You see, I have a home there that belonged to my mother's family for generations. We had both hoped that the sea air would help her condition, but it didn't. Yet her health was not the primary reason for her being there. Rather it was to hide your mother's condition."

She paused as her eyes drifted towards the window collecting herself. "Charlotte was nothing like the woman that she's been made out to be. She was a kind and gentle soul, but she had a miserable life as my brother's wife. Once she became ill she knew that she was not long for this world, so she didn't care what people thought of her after she was gone. That included the opinion of her indifferent husband. My brother treated his horses better than he did her or his children." My aunt was suddenly overcome with emotion, removing her spectacles and pulling a handkerchief out of her pocket she dabbed at her eyes, Charlotte had obviously meant a great deal to her. She swallowed several times looking at Samuel then coughed. "I think we could all use a bit of that brandy now, Samuel."

His head jerked up, he'd been staring down at his boot tips all this time. "What? Brandy, oh, is that to include Lissa?"

"Yes, of course, it includes Clarissa." She emphasized my name and looked down her nose at him. He shrugged, got up and went over to the table that held the decanter. Then she added, "I think just a splash of brandy in some water will be sufficient for her." He prepared the drinks and passed them around. On returning to his seat he swirled it around in the glass, sniffed it then took a sip. I imitated his actions curling up my nose at the smell, it was dreadful, and Aunt Mary was watching me and smiled. "It's an acquired taste, my dear, and it's not something that ladies are usually offered, unless we've been under considerable stress or have suffered the vapours."

She took a sip before she continued her story. "It was easy for us to keep our secrets in Cornwall, it's very isolated there and I was an old friend to the neighbourhood and a generous employer. The locals trust me implicitly, having been the only family member to use the property in a generation. I also turn a blind eye to their bit of smuggling and I aided them when times were harsh. In turn, they don't gossip about what goes on in my home." She smiled, adding, "Remarkably loyal people the Cornish."

She took another sip of her brandy and as I listened to her I had to conclude that there might be more to my aunt than I'd realised. I was sure I'd find out even more about her now that she had attached herself to our party headed for London. At least she was willing to tell me the truth about my birth, so I was inclined to trust her for now. She repositioned her spectacles and continued, "Where was I? Oh yes…as your mother's time came closer I sent for a midwife that could be trusted, that being your maid's mother, Jennie Abel. You were delivered on a terribly stormy night which had delayed your father's arrival from France. But arrive he did, just minutes before you came into this world." She paused staring into space as if she was transported back to that night. "It had been Charlotte's deepest desire to see you before she died. She so wanted to know who she had sacrificed everything for. But as you came into this world, Charlotte passed out of it. She never saw you and tis a pity too, you were such a beautiful baby."

Lissa, hate me, not your father. He wanted to take us away when he came back from France and started to work for the Crown, but he was still gone a great deal. Besides the lie had gone on for so long I didn't know how to tell you." She slumped onto the floor and buried her face in her hands. "I didn't know what to do! Then the General came home, and I was afraid of what he would do if I tried to leave, I had to believe that it was better to stay here, that all would be well. Colin even spoke to the General the last night he was a guest here, he never told me what transpired except that he was forbidden from the house."

I plopped down beside her. "How could you live without him? It's been years!"

She looked at me seemingly choking on her words then she blushed. "We didn't live apart all the time. Whenever I could make an excuse to leave, I would meet him in Cornwall or London. Otherwise, we saw each other as often as we could whenever he came to the neighbourhood, I would ride onto the moors to be alone with him."

"But what about children you must have?"

"No." She shook her head and looked sad. "There are ways to prevent that, we were very careful. Colin and I would love to have more children; brothers and sisters for you." She wrung her hands together. "I want us to be a family, Lissa. We want you to get to know us as your parents but if you can't then perhaps we can be friends."

"I don't know, Irene, I have to think. I love you and I always will. Mr Turner was a good friend to us and he made me laugh, he was very kind. It made sense now why he never tired of me tagging along wherever he went, I'm sure he would very much like to have had a son though." She looked shocked and I rushed on, "Well, he did teach me lots of boy things like riding astride and using a pocket sling. Yet when we go to London, I will never be able to ride astride in public, nor use a pocket sling in the park." I tried to smile. "Excuse me for saying this, but I think you should give him a son as soon as possible." Then we both broke out giggling.

She gasped trying to catch her breath saying, "Colin taught you those things because he loved you not because he wished you were a boy. It was something he could do for you that no one else ever would." We both leaned against my bed while sitting on the floor. She sighed, closed her eyes then leaned her head back against my bed. "The night you were born the storm outside was awful and when your father arrived, he was drenched, exhausted and hungry. But the first thing he did in all his mud was to come to us. He took you right out of Mrs Abel's 's arms hardly a moment after you were born. He was the one who bathed you and wrapped you in a blanket before bringing you to me. I'll never forget as he leaned over to put you in my arms, you grabbed his finger and stared right at him. He introduced himself to you as your father and called you Clarissa. You were named after his maternal grandmother, a woman whom he loved very much. I thought Meg's mother would have a heart attack with him standing there talking to you and meanwhile a puddle was forming at his feet and your wrapping was getting wet."

She opened her eyes smiling like she could still see the scene before her. "Aunt Mary told him that Charlotte had died and that we'd need to accompany her body back to the Abbey soon, but she allowed us a few days together with you. In those days, you were barely ever in your cradle. Colin held you every minute that he could. He took you for your first ride along the beach when you were just a day old. I thought Aunt Mary would kill him when he got back." She leaned toward me and brushed a curl back behind my ear.

"He cried the day we left knowing it would be several months before we could meet again since we'd be in mourning. Oh Lissa, I have never seen anyone so devastated as your father. Colin followed us as far as he dared then sped off to London. He was even more determined than ever to make his own way and increase his personal fortune so that he could claim us one day. That day has finally come."

She looked deep into my eyes. "Can you accept us and all our faults? Can you forgive my cowardice when I wouldn't follow your father to the continent?" She hesitated and bit her lip before continuing. "I have rationalized my choices for years, Lissa, and I'm ashamed to admit that my entire motivation was fear. Fear that I would not measure up. That I wouldn't be good enough without all that the Abbey had to offer and that Colin would find me wanting as a wife and a mother…that you would end up hating me for it." She turned to me and stared into my eyes before continuing, "Lissa, I love you so very much and as for Colin, his love for you knows no bounds. He wants us to be a family in every way, that is if you can accept us. But if you can't, then Aunt Mary has agreed that you can live with her. I will not leave you here!"

I had no ready answer for her, what she seemed to be asking for was absolution. I had to think if it was within me to grant it. Could I harbour ill feelings towards my parents considering what they had sacrificed for me? They had never actually deserted or abandoned me. Rather they had cared for me and loved me in the only way they thought they could. Could I punish them for being young and afraid? I didn't know. I still loved Irene and Samuel and I had liked Colin very much at one time, maybe it wouldn't be so hard to love him too.

# Chapter 4
## *Farewell to the Abbey*

The morning dawned bright and beautiful, it was exciting to be headed for London, but I was still afraid of what the future held. In the breakfast room Samuel sat in his traveling clothes obviously nursing a headache, no doubt from the additional brandy that he had consumed before going to bed. Yet he still managed to smile at me while motioning for me to the sit beside him. Despite the state of his head it appeared that he'd eaten a huge breakfast which would delight our cook Mrs Croft who believed that my uncle never ate anywhere except the Abbey. Yet Samuel often missed mealtime at the Abbey when he was here because he was often out catching up with old friends, visiting tenants and no doubt stopping at the Sickle to treat them to a bite and a pint.

Irene was there as well, ready for the road but looking pale and subdued. She put on a strained smile when she greeted me, "Good morning, Lissa." There was a cup of tea and a sweet roll in front of her, both of which appeared to be untouched. Aunt Mary must have arrived just before me as she was only now reaching for the marmalade for her toast. I filled my plate with eggs and my favourite kedgeree but after a few bites, I had lost my appetite because of the atmosphere in the room so I spent the rest of my time pushing the food around on my plate, stealing glances at my travelling companions.

Aunt Mary had thankfully brought her own carriage, so we wouldn't need to borrow any equipage from the General. Much to my annoyance though I was told that one of the grooms would ride Jewel. Aunt Mary had deemed it inappropriate for a young lady to travel by horseback when a carriage was at her disposal and Samuel agreed despite my voiced displeasure. He hadn't even tried to argue on my behalf…the coward. But at least he had the good grace to grimace when he looked at me across the table. I was madly disappointed to say the least after having dressed in my old habit anticipating a vigorous ride. But instead of arguing as I normally would I decided to act like a lady and resign myself to the decision.

When Aunt Mary and Irene had finished eating, they rang for Mrs Burns then left with her to go over the housekeeping accounts and apprise her of the General's likes, dislikes and needs.

Outside everything was being loaded onto the luggage wagon by a steady stream of footmen and grooms. I dithered for a time in the hall watching the procession then wandered outside standing next to the doorway but well away from all the activity. Samuel was checking the horses as he spoke to the coachman, it was then that I noticed that not all the men were in my Aunt Mary's livery nor did they belong to the Abbey. These men were all armed and looked as if they would be extremely efficient in a fight. Samuel saw me observing them closely, perhaps too closely from his look of concern. Coming over he took my arm, walking me out of earshot and away from all the activity. "Lissa, I assume you noticed the additional men that will accompany us? They are members of your father's staff and for the most part, they're former soldiers or individuals who have unique skills that are useful to us in our work. I assure you that they are very loyal to your father…and to me." He waited, biting his lip and when I didn't respond, he lifted my chin with his hand looking me in the eyes, "They are here for added protection."

I raised my eyebrows then looked back at the men. "Do you expect trouble? Is that why even Aunt Mary's staff are armed?"

He took off his hat, ran his fingers through his hair and looked out over the lawn. "You, my dear, are far too observant for a young lady but to be honest you can never tell when or from where trouble may come. These are dangerous times to be on the road without adequate protection. Besides you and your mother are precious cargo." Tapping me under the chin he turned back towards the house. "Come, Lissa, we better light a fire under the other ladies, so we can leave, I want to reach our first stop before sundown."

Another carriage appeared from around the side of the house with Meg, Beth and Aunt Mary's companion Louisa already inside. Samuel's valet Dalton had ridden ahead to make suitable arrangements at the Inn where we would be spending the night. He had announced at breakfast that provisions for our stay each night would be made in advance at the Inns along our route to London and that we would not deviate from our route without his permission. It seemed that we wouldn't be wasting any time in getting to London.

Samuel collected Aunt Mary and Irene and assisted them into the carriage. Then he turned to me just as I was gazing longingly at Jewel. He stopped me as I made to climb into the carriage. "I promise that you'll be able to ride her before the day is done." I smiled and kissed him on the cheek then got in with his assistance. I resisted the urge to look back at the Abbey, it was no longer my home, I could feel the tears threatening but I was able to hold them back. I tried hard not to think about the fact that I was leaving behind everything I had ever known.

We made our way down the road and through the village. The people there stopped and stared as we drove past, some even waved. As we passed Ford's I saw Becky standing there with tears running down her cheeks; she fled back into the store when Samuel rode by without even acknowledging her. Mrs Ford remained outside of the store, smiling, and when Samuel turned to look back, he doffed his hat to her and she curtseyed. I chuckled a bit since it was obvious that they must have plotted this snubbing of Becky, it was for her own good. As we came to the smithy I saw Russell Biggles standing there with his arms crossed across over his broad chest and a grim expression on his face. But he nodded to Samuel and as we passed by Samuel yelled to him, "I wish you well, Russell! Feel free to name your first born after me!" Russell broke out in a smile, laughing heartily, and raised his hand in farewell.

Once we were on the open road Aunt Mary kept up a steady stream of conversation, listing the names of all the people we would have to visit when we reached London, including all those that we would have invite to luncheon and dinner, what kind entertainments we should host and so on. My opinion was not asked about the planning of these events, so I hoped that my participation would be minimal.

Irene was madly taking notes while occasionally glancing at Aunt Mary with a look of considerable concern as the list continued to grow. Aunt Mary finished just as Samuel signalled for the carriage to halt. We pulled over into a meadow to allow the horses some rest and for us to stretch our legs and take care of the necessities. There was a creek with some shade trees close to the roadway. The horses were watered as picnic hampers were distributed and blankets were spread beneath the trees for us to dine el fresco.

Samuel was in a better humour now as he stretched out, regaling us with stories of his last time in London. They were mainly about the theatre, balls and parties he had attended and how much Irene would enjoy them. He told me about the menagerie at the Tower and how he would take me there to see the exotic animals and that we'd go riding in Hyde Park every morning. I smiled that he still thought of me as a child or perhaps, he had no idea what a young lady of sixteen may or may not be interested in; especially when he was extolling the talents of an extraordinary doll maker he knew. "His dolls have porcelain faces that are so life-like you'd swear they could talk."

I shuddered at the thought of dolls talking. I hadn't fancied dolls since I had been given a French doll at the age of five with glass eyes that would open and close if you tipped the head back and forth. It had been very unsettling to my over-active imagination. "Don't you think I'm a little too old for dolls, Uncle?"

His eyes widened as he glanced at me like he was seeing me for the first time. "Hmmm…yes I suppose you're right. I stand corrected, Lissa, you are past the age for dolls. Perhaps a bracelet would be a better gift." Then he was off on a story of how he knew the perfect jeweller.

I rolled my eyes at him and changed the subject. "Now that I'm Mr Turner's daughter do you think that he will still be willing to teach me to shoot?" Samuel started to laugh, falling backwards, holding his hat over his face. Our aunt and Irene just looked at me with the most horrified expressions.

"He most certainly will not!" Aunt Mary was very flustered, almost forgetting the glass of wine in her hand that was in danger of spilling onto her skirts.

At the same time, Irene said, "Wherever did you get that idea, Lissa?"

Samuel stopped laughing, removing his hat from his face and rolled onto his side, so he could see us all. Then he cleared his throat. "I think I can answer that my, dearest sister, it was Colin that gave Lissa the idea and I wouldn't be the least surprised if he intends to keep his promise. Be prepared to be shocked, Aunt Mary, Colin has always been unconventional, and I expect he will remain so."

Aunt Mary was able to right her glass of wine just in time to avert a spill, tossing the remaining contents onto the grass as she sputtered, "But—but surely he can wait until he has a son!" Irene choked on her wine and turned crimson.

Samuel was smiling with an impish grin at the scene. "Oh come now, Irene, surely you know that Colin wants more children and so do you as a matter of fact. Besides he has the responsibility of begetting an heir and a spare, doesn't he? When his grandfather passes away, Colin will inherit. Don't you fancy being a countess?"

Aunt Mary tried to cover my ears unsuccessfully during this exchange, however, I escaped her attempts through a combination of her own restlessness and my squirming.

Without stopping to think for which I blame my youthful exuberance, I blurted out, "An heir and a spare? Why can't I be Mr Turner's heir?" Later I deeply regretted

36

asking that question, mostly because Irene looked hurt and once we were back on the road I received a lecture from Aunt Mary about hereditary primogeniture and a woman's place in society. It was enough to scare me into silence for the next several miles. And after giving it all careful consideration it seemed to me that unless you were widowed or wealthy and eccentric, a woman's place amounted to little more than the privilege of being a man's possession. I was determined that I would have to find a way to be wealthy but not married.

I spent the better part of an hour just watching the scenery go by as my aunt napped and my mother appeared lost in her own thoughts. Then Samuel suddenly called a halt to our procession. He rode up to the carriage window, "Would you care to ride, Lissa? I think Jewel is a bit restive, she needs a good gallop and you should learn how to handle her under those conditions." I readily agreed and to my aunt's horror the groom Jacob helped me out of the carriage then assisted me to sit astride, then I raced off down the road with my Uncle Samuel.

He slowed to a trot while we were still visible to our companions but out of earshot. "I couldn't help but overhear parts of the lecture you were receiving from our aunt." I raised a brow and pursed my lips glaring at him but we both grinned. "Her voice tends to carry when she's in a high dudgeon. So, I thought I'd rescue you before you made up your mind to be a confirmed spinster." He was chuckling then went on to say very seriously, "Lissa, you should know that there's nothing better in this world than a man and woman bonded by love. Believe me when I say that Colin and Irene will want you to marry for love."

I looked at him askance. "So I won't be bartered on the marriage mart?"

He grimaced. "You, my dear, will never have to worry about that. When Aunt Mary was talking about your season she was reflecting on how some marriages are arranged by an individual's parents. Basically, it amounts to two people being told who they will marry by their fathers, usually for the benefit of wealth or position. The individuals themselves may have some small choice in the matter but only in regards as to who has the most money, power or the best pedigree. Love in such matches is rare and when there's no love, neither party is ever happy." He looked very sad and I wondered if his own parents' marriage had been arranged or perhaps he'd been told who he could marry and could not marry. He broke out of his revere and continued, "Husbands and wives in those marriages will do their duty to keep the line going by having children but sadly it's often only the children that are loved."

"If that's an arranged marriage; then what kind of marriage do Mr Turner and Irene have?"

He smiled and looked over his shoulder to see that the carriages were still a distance away. "The best kind, Lissa. They have a love match. I have never seen, the like of their devotion to each other and you. Irene thinks she was weak by not following Colin to the continent. But Colin, Aunt Mary and I believe she did the noblest thing anyone could do, she gave up being with the man she loved to see that you were raised with all the privileges that were your birth right. It hurt her more than you know not to tell you that she was your mother or who your father really was. But until now I don't think you could have understood why they sacrificed so much. They love you a great deal, Lissa." He leaned over to look me in the eye. "Is any of this making sense to you?"

I nodded yes, and he patted my arm self-consciously then he suggested we turn back and join the carriage once again. As we walked our horses back I brought up the one question that was burning a hole in my heart. "I understand, but Samuel, Mr Turner, I mean my father, he left me, he stopped visiting and Irene never took me with her when she went to see him. How is that fair?"

He shook his head. "Colin never left you. After the General had forbidden him in our home, he came to the neighbourhood whenever he could and stayed at the Sickle or with Lord Gromley. He watched you from afar as you grew and bought you many of the gifts that I gave you, including Lotus and Jewel. He bought most of your books, writing and drawing materials. In fact, he would have me fetch your journals and drawings for him to see." Giving me a devilish smile, he said, "Why do you think I volunteered to hide them from the General? I want you to know that my best friend and your father loves you very much." He leaned towards me and lowering his voice mischievously said, "Now, not a word to your mother or our aunt but he will keep his promises to you, Lissa. He has never broken a promise that I know of. Not only that but he'll assure that you're better educated than most debutantes." Baron took a side step and tossed his head, Samuel calmed him with a word and sat up again, continuing in a more serious tone, "But more than anything he will always love you, never doubt that no matter how many brothers and sisters you might have." He turned and looked back the way we had come. "You should know too that Irene did take you to see Colin when you were a baby. But once you started to talk, she couldn't risk taking you anymore. It would have hardly been fair to expect you to keep such a secret at such an early age, it could have been disastrous for them."

Samuel reached out to swat my hat forward, covering my eyes, then he galloped off leaving me to straighten it and trot back to the carriage. Once there I was forced to dismount at my aunt's insistence and climb back into the carriage.

Samuel had made it very clear that we would be on the road for several days, a fact that our aunt was not at all happy about. She would have liked to break our trip in Lincolnshire for a few days with the Marquess of Exeter, an old friend of hers. Much to her annoyance Samuel insisted that we would be pushing through to London. He was emphatic that there would be no visits with old friends along the way. I thought that perhaps he was worried that the General would come after us.

We reached the Inn at dusk; road weary and hungry. Our grooms and footmen split into two groups, one group followed us into the Inn and the other went with the carriages and luggage. Samuel's valet Dalton met us at the door with the Innkeeper who took us immediately upstairs. Samuel effectively blocked my view of the common room as we climbed the stairs, but it sounded rather busy if not exactly boisterous for a public house in an insignificant town. The Innkeeper was in awe of Aunt Mary and kept bobbing like a robin as he showed us to our rooms. I would be sharing a large comfortable room with my aunt and mother while our maids and Aunt Mary's companion would share a similar room across the hall. Samuel and Dalton took the smallest room at the head of the stairs. The rest of the servants had accommodations next to the common room and in the stables.

In the private parlour, a table was already set for us to dine and a roaring fire was in the hearth, taking the chill out of the room. In a nook near the hearth, I spied a large feather bed stored to keep it warm for weary travellers. I thought it rather curious that Uncle Samuel immediately arranged at a significant cost for the parlour to remain empty for the entire night. The innkeeper was only too happy to accommodate us at a price I'm sure was well above what he would have normally expected from other overnight clients. With the arrangements made, he assured us that once we had washed off the dust of the road our repast would be ready.

Aunt Mary huffed at the little man as she slowly looked around but before she could start ordering people about Samuel jumped in and requested that as few of the Inn's staff as possible have access to our rooms or the parlour. They were to just bring the food up and we would serve ourselves. He also insisted that we all remain above stairs and talk to no one. The innkeeper nodded and seemed not the least affronted. Indeed my uncle seemed to be on familiar terms with him, but it was obvious that he didn't trust him completely. Samuel was worried about something and it was about more than just getting us to London.

After removing my pelisse and washing my face and hands I returned to the parlour to find Samuel standing by the hearth staring into the flames. He caught me watching him from the doorway and beckoned me to join him, then he whispered, "You, young lady, see far too much. I hope you have the good sense not to say anything to our aunt or Irene about what you suspect. It is of the utmost importance, Lissa, that you not say anything. I don't want them to be afraid, so not a word about anything. Do you understand?"

Before I could ask him any questions Aunt Mary walked in. "Good heavens, Samuel, are you trying to roast the child alive? Come here, Clarissa, and sit beside me. I'd like to talk to you about age appropriate activities for young ladies of your position."

I sighed, Samuel squeezed my shoulder, but I went reluctantly and sat with her. She patted my hand as she looked me over from head to toe. "You're a very pretty child and I think you'll blossom into a very beautiful young lady before too long." She took my chin turning my head from side to side. "Yes, you seem to have inherited the best features of both the Hughes and Turners. It's too bad that your eyes aren't blue; with your colouring, they would have been stunning. Well, we must all work with what God gave us." She had a faraway look in her eyes and I wondered if she was looking back at her own youth. Then she suddenly refocused on me, "Yes, I do believe you will be one of society's great beauties." I looked to my Uncle Samuel for help, but he only smiled as I grimaced.

Samuel went to the table and poured out a glass of wine then came over and handed it to her. "Aunt Mary, with all due respect, Lissa is only sixteen. She hardly needs to have her qualities evaluated just yet."

Our Aunt took a cautious sip then another, she seemed pleased with the wine. "Rubbish, my dear boy, it's never too early to start looking out for the girl's future." She held the glass up to the light. "If I didn't know better, I'd swear that this wine was French."

Samuel poured himself a glass and drank deeply, then filled his glass again. "It probably is, Aunt. Smuggling is one of the few vocations left to the people that is still profitable these days."

She grunted in disapproval, yet she took another sip. "Always has been, my dear boy, it always has been. Might I impose on you to ask our host if I could purchase a few bottles of this marvellous vintage before we leave?"

Samuel chuckled. "Consider it done, milady." He drank off the rest of his glass then poured another.

At that moment, Irene walked in hand in hand with a tall, dark-haired gentleman with a chiselled jaw and laughing brown eyes just like mine. It was Colin Turner, my father. He was looking exceptionally nervous as he stopped in front of me and in a voice full of emotion, said, "Hello, Lissa, it's so very good to see you again."

He turned slightly, taking Aunt Mary's hand and kissed it. "Lady Alford, thank you for watching over my family all these years. It's a debt that I can never repay you." She blushed as she looked at me then back at him. I felt a flutter in my chest…he had referred to me as family! His eyes were so like my own but his were filled with combination of fear and hope. No one seemed to breathe, and I could feel that everyone was waiting. He didn't touch me, but I could feel myself wanting him to hug me and never let go. Instead we just stared at each other, neither of us wanting to break the spell by moving.

My self-control finally broke and I threw myself at him. He caught me to him, hugging me close, rocking us back and forth, telling me all the nonsensical things I had dreamed a father would tell a beloved daughter. When he let me go, I realised that I was crying, he was crying, Irene, my mother, was crying and everyone else had tears in their eyes. He hugged me again then kissed both of my cheeks and called me his darling girl repeatedly. I felt like my heart would burst. Irene came to stand beside us then suddenly my father was hugging us both and laughing.

Aunt Mary cleared her throat and Samuel moved to pour wine for everyone just as Aunt Mary coughed again more loudly. "Good Heavens, Irene, Mr Turner, would you please try to control yourselves! Samuel gave me the distinct impression that we were to be circumspect and not draw attention to ourselves."

There was a sharp knock at the door just then. Samuel put down his glass as he pulled a knife from his boot with his other hand then he went to answer the door. My father turned quickly, facing the door, pulling me and Mother behind him. We all watched as my uncle opened the door cautiously. It was the innkeeper, his wife and daughter carrying in trays of food. Samuel stooped down, hiding his knife once again in his boot. Colin approached the man with a smile and laughter as they set the trays down. He patted him on the back, whispered in his ear then gave him some coins. The innkeeper smiled, nodded and left with his wife and daughter; but not before the daughter and Samuel had fully assessed each other's qualities much to the chagrin of her mother. Father locked the door after them, then turned around, smacking his hands together. "Well, I don't know about all of you, but I'm famished."

Samuel groaned. "Finally, we eat!" He practically raced to the side table and began heaping food onto his plate.

Aunt Mary touched him on the shoulder. "My dear boy, I do hope that you intend to leave something for the rest of us." He had the good grace to blush, yet he continued helping himself from the steaming dishes. The rest of us joined him. However, as the meal and conversation progressed I noticed that Samuel didn't attack the meal in front of him like anything near the starving man he claimed to be, in fact it seemed as if he had to force down every bite.

The meal was congenial and informal. Conversations included everyone, servant and master alike. Colin even made sure that I was included. At first, I was puzzled that he would ask my opinion about anything but when he noticed my perplexed expression, he explained, "Lissa, I want you to feel free to participate in our conversations. I want you to understand the world around you, to question things and never blindly accept something just because society or a man says you should."

He looked at Aunt Mary who rolled her eyes, but he wiped his mouth with a napkin to hide his smile while I bit my lip to keep from laughing. She knew what we were doing and looking over her spectacles at him, "Humph, Colin Turner, I never said that she should not be well-educated nor become a dog to society's dictates. I merely want her to know how the world works for most women, especially the place that's been assigned to us by MEN!" Then she looked at me smiling, "But there are always ways around men, Clarissa, and I intend to teach you every one of them, just as I did your mother."

Colin had the good grace to nod but Irene couldn't hold back a smirk and chuckle. Eventually Dalton, our maids and Aunt Mary's companion left to attend to their own needs and to prepare our rooms. The evening turned quiet as we helped ourselves to pudding and tea. Samuel appeared to have nodded off, but anyone could see that he wasn't. Suddenly he tipped forward in his chair, pointing to Aunt Mary, "No niece of mine is going to marry for the sake of money or position! No inbred titled lout shall have her." Slapping the table with his hands and almost losing his balance as he reached over the table to grab my hand, but he caught himself, saying very seriously, "You have my word, Lissa, that if you should ever become one of these boring society maidens or settle on some slug to wed, I shall spirit you away to the continent until you come to your senses."

Everyone looked at him like he was insane, but my father laughed out loud saying, "On that note I think we should all retire." He looked at my uncle whose eyes were closed, and his chin was resting on his chest. He reached over to remove the empty glass from his hand then kicked his foot under the table to awaken him, "Especially you, my friend. Up you get and off to bed."

Samuel looked up with a silly smirk on his face, giggled, then rose staggering to the door. He turned and bowed. "If you will excuse me, ladies, it seems that the rigours of the journey have caught up with me, so with your permission I shall retire." He fumbled with the latch to open the door then nodded to the footman standing outside, he turned left only to retrace his steps down the hallway in the direction of his room. I heard Dalton speak to him in the hall then a door closed and there was silence.

We looked at each other trying, to contain ourselves, but a series of chuckles eventually escaped us. Aunt Mary composed herself first and rose. "Well, Colin, now that you've arrived, what do you propose to do for sleeping arrangements?" Colin looked about. "I think we shall be very comfortable in here, Lady Alford."

Aunt Mary looked around and spied the feather bed in the alcove. Then she looked at Irene and smirked. "I dare say you both shall be warm enough, but I hope that you have the good sense to get some rest. We will be leaving early in the morning."

Colin and Irene both blushed and my father hid a chuckle with a cough, "Lady Alford, I'm sorry to say that I will not be accompanying you on your journey to London. Unfortunately, I have business in the area that cannot wait. But I shall meet you in London as soon as possible. Then we can put into action your plan to introduce my family to society."

Irene moved over to the alcove pulling out the feather bed as she looked pointedly at Aunt Mary first then at me. Aunt Mary raised her eyebrows and stood, "Come, Clarissa, it would appear you will not be sharing a bed with your mother tonight." She opened the door and motioned for me to go through. I couldn't help but look over my shoulder at my mother who was already in my father's arms. I wrinkled my nose and pursed my lips. Aunt Mary laughed. "Come, child, you will have to get used to that. Believe me when I say that they have no idea that we're still here." I walked out with her and the footman standing guard closed the door behind us then I heard the key turn in the lock.

Once we reached the door to our room I asked, "Should I fetch Meg and Louisa?"

"Not yet, Clarissa, I would like to speak with you first." She looked back the way we had come at the footman. "Murphy, is it?" He nodded. "Would you please ask Meg and Louisa to attend us in a few minutes and tell Beth that she will not be needed for the rest of the night." My mouth must have fallen open as we walked into our room. "Clarissa, my dear, close your mouth and come sit here beside me." She sat down graciously on the settee in our room and I took the place beside her. "Since our room abuts the room your parents are now sharing I think it only advisable that you... Well, that—" She was blushing as she paused to collect herself then she let out a breath and, in a rush, said, "Oh, damn it to hell they would leave this to me!" I was shocked to hear my aunt use such language, but it made her seem more human and less formidable. She took my hand and patted it. "Well, child, tell me what do you know of physical love? And I don't mean that stuff and nonsense in those novels that Irene lets you read." She eyed me closely, but I was at a loss for words and more than embarrassed. "Come now, surely you must know something having been raised in the country. Do you have any notion of what coupling is at least in animals?" Now I could feel the heat rising up my neck and was sure that my face must be crimson. "Well?"

I sputtered not knowing what to say. I didn't really want to think about what she was referring to in relation to my parents. Then suddenly the image of Rose Biggles and William Blaney down by the brook popped into my head. It had been three years ago this last summer. I had been daydreaming while sitting in the old Elm by the meadow near the Home Farm. Rose and William had come running through the field shedding their clothes. I was frozen to my branch in indecision but before I could make my presence known they were naked and wrestling in the grass, groaning something awful right under my tree. Yet neither one of them seemed to be in any distress nor did they see me though I was perched in the tree directly above them. Still I prayed that there was enough foliage to hide me from their eyes. I held very still and watched even though I didn't want to, but I had little choice since I had stretched out on the branch. I couldn't chance closing my eyes and losing my balance. Thankfully Rose had her eyes closed most of the time that William was on top of her swaying back and forth. Then after some time they both called out and lay still. They startled me so much that I almost cried out for fear that William had hurt Rose. But I was afraid to move an inch and was stiff from holding so still. In fact, I don't think I could have climbed down and run for help if it was needed. Suddenly, William rolled off Rose. I closed my eyes quickly but not before I had seen their exposed private areas. There was no blood, and both were LAUGHING! I kept hoping they would leave yet they stayed there for what seemed like forever, laughing and kissing. Finally, they got up, washed in the nearby brook, dressed quickly and left, walking hand in hand down a path that led to the Biggles farm. I sat up and once the feeling returned to my hands and legs I climbed down and raced home. I went straight to my room where I crawled under my bed and hid until Meg came to dress me for my evening report. I never told a soul about what I had seen but it was even clearer now what Samuel had meant about Rose and William having the honeymoon before the wedding.

42

Aunt Mary interrupted my thoughts as my eyes strayed to the wall of the adjoining room. "I can see from your face and that particular shade of red that I will not have to elaborate. Trust me, child, between two people who love each other there is no better experience, no matter how base and elemental it may seem." She took some waxy cotton wadding out of her reticule and pulled two pieces off handing them to me. "Place a piece in each ear, Clarissa; it will deaden the noise from next door."

Meg and Louisa appeared then as if on cue, assisting us to get ready for bed. Thankfully the day's excitement and fresh air had taken its toll on me and as I drifted off to sleep I was only vaguely aware of the sounds coming from next door.

I awoke in the morning just as Meg and Beth were pulling back the curtains. Irene was in the room in her dressing gown talking quietly to our aunt. She looked beautiful with her hair down and all mussed as if she had just risen from bed. I stopped my thoughts there as I hopped out of bed. They both turned to look at me. Irene stood up, blushing, "I shall go dress now. And you, sleepy head, had better hurry, or your uncle will make you eat your breakfast in the carriage."

The prospect of hot food made me move even faster. I wanted Meg to brush my hair and just tie it back with a ribbon, but she insisted on doing an elaborate plait to keep in under control in case I went riding.

My Aunt was waiting for me and before entering the parlour she informed me, "Since there will be no stopping you and your uncle from riding together, I have had the grooms unpack your side saddle. If you insist on riding, you will do so as a lady and not some savage." She didn't dampen my spirits if that's what she had hoped for, I had learned to ride side saddle before astride anyway and I was determined that nothing would make me unhappy today.

The rest of our journey was uneventful, if tiring. Colin, I mean my father, did not rejoin our group. In fact, he had left sometime in the early morning hours. I was disappointed, but my mother said his work was very important and that he wanted to get this local business taken care of before joining us in London.

Samuel became more morose and authoritarian the closer we got to London. At one point, Aunt Mary refused to leave an Inn where we had stopped for luncheon until she had a private conversation with him. It started out with raised voices that suddenly went quiet and it remained that way for a full half hour. When they emerged, it was obvious that his mood had not improved but that Aunt Mary's had.

I was not invited to ride with Samuel again after that day. Instead I was only allowed to canter along beside the carriage for half an hour each afternoon which neither Jewel nor I enjoyed. I was eventually tired of choking on dust, so after two days I relinquished Jewel to the groom Jacob for the remainder of our time on the road.

My mother was not unsympathetic being an avid horsewoman herself. Her mount Sheba had been left behind since she belonged to the General. I sat silently watching Jacob ride off through a field, letting Jewel have her head, when my mother leaned against my shoulder following my gaze. "Jewel most certainly seems to enjoy the open fields." I only nodded so she continued, "Lissa, life in London will be very different for you and for Jewel. She must become a town horse if you intend to keep her. You won't be able to gallop through Hyde Park anytime you please. In fact, you won't be able to gallop in town at all. Perhaps when we go to Somerset, you should take Jewel with you, she can live there instead of in London. We can always get you

43

another horse that's been bred for the town and is used to a life in a mews. It's up to you, darling, but perhaps you should discuss it with your father or Samuel. Though I wouldn't approach your uncle, he seems to be out of sorts these days." She reached out and patted my hand. "But it can wait, there's no hurry to make a decision."

We reached London in the dead of night. I saw nothing of the city as we approached except a smoky glow on the horizon. I had fallen asleep by the time we entered the city so when we reached our townhouse in Mayfair on the edge of Hyde Park, Samuel carried me inside. I listened to him cursing under his breath that I was getting fat so when I chuckled he called me 'Brat' and purposefully bumped my feet on the balustrade going up the stairs to my room. Once there he literally threw me on the bed then sat down beside me. "Okay, Lissa, I know that you aren't really asleep. So, if you will excuse the lateness of the hour, I need to apologize for being such a bas…a beast these past few days. I can't explain it, but I hope you'll forgive me. I promise I'll try to be a better uncle in the future." He got up, swatted at my feet and before he left, saying, "I'll see you in the morning."

Meg came in a short while later with hot water and the case with my night things. She looked more exhausted than I was so once she had my buttons undone and the pins out of my hair, I sent her off to find her own bed. I was tired but not enough that I could ignore the state of my hair, so I sat down at a beautiful Adams dressing table and brushed it out. Once I was done I washed my face and cleaned my teeth then I looked around my room. It was decorated in what appeared by candlelight to be shades of creams and blues. There was a comfortable four post bed with a canopy and dark blue silk curtains that stood against the wall facing the windows. The door to the hallway was left of the bed and there was another door to the right. I opened this one and found a huge dressing room, far too large for my current needs yet the only doors into it led into my room or out into the hallway. Back in my room besides the dressing table, there was a writing desk under one of the large windows that faced the back of the house which would take advantage of the natural light during the day and by the second window there was a chaise lounge and three chairs were arranged near the hearth. Partially filled bookcases were placed on either side of the windows and I wondered what I would find there when I perused the titles later. The paintings on the walls were all pastoral scenes, serene and reminiscent of Northumberland. But I was too exhausted to bother looking at them more closely, so I crawled into bed and let the cool sheets envelope me.

# Chapter 5
## *London: Revenge*

"Morning, Miss Clarissa!" Meg had obviously slept well, she was buzzing around the room chatting away; thankfully, I was not required to respond. "Oh, miss, you should see the house! Mrs Wren the housekeeper she took us around this morning, it will be a pleasure to work here for sure. Mr Hughes requested that you join him for breakfast and said for you to get a move on and to come down dressed for riding." She smirked as she ran to retrieve my new riding habit; this would be my first ride on Rotten Row!

Once I was ready I stood in front of the cheval glass. I looked at least eighteen dressed in the dark green riding habit, especially with my hair up under the little black hat. Meg stood behind me with her fists clasped together under her chin. "Miss, you look so growed up, I mean grown up. The family won't recognize you when you join them."

I smiled and thanked her then swept out the open door with my head held high and not paying attention to my feet, as a result I caught the toe of my new boots on the carpet and was just able to stop myself from falling. It was not the most auspicious beginning to my new life, especially when I heard Meg giggling as she closed the door to my room.

To assuage my bruised ego, I told myself I'd have that bit of carpet looked at later, but I gathered up what was left of my self-esteem and headed down the stairs. I had no idea where the breakfast room was, but I should have guessed that my Uncle Samuel would be waiting for me at the bottom of the stairs. He bowed from the waist and I curtseyed after stepping off the last riser, then he took my hand saying, "Miss Turner, you look lovely today." He escorted me into a beautiful yellow room where the sun was streaming through the French doors that looked out onto a riotous English garden. It was a dazzling room with the light bouncing off the crystal and silver set on the dark mahogany table, yet it felt like home, a comfortable setting for a family to gather.

Irene was already seated sipping on tea with a decent breakfast in front of her. She smiled and put down her cup as I came in on Samuel's arm, "Oh Lissa! You look beautiful." But I was aware that she was studying my hat with concern, tipping her head from side to side, "I'm not sure about the hat though, it ages you so much." I frowned, and she rushed to explain, "I only say that because I just realised how fast you're growing up, my darling."

I beamed at her, stooping to give her a hug and kiss on the cheek. "Thank you, Mother. I do understand what you mean, I feel like I've aged as well and it's still a little overwhelming."

Samuel grabbed a plate and was serving himself sparingly from the dishes on the sideboard. "Well, brat, you had better get a move on or we will be unfashionably late for your first ride. We can't have you starting off on the wrong foot looking like a rustic cousin come to the city." He sat down, grabbed his coffee cup and gulped down the scalding liquid in several gulps as if he was late for an appointment. I noticed though that his hand shook when he reached for his cup. I wondered if it was nerves or something else. He had become more withdrawn the closer we came to London though he insisted he was looking forward to being back in the city. Maybe it was just the after effects to much celebratory drink recently…yet I hadn't seen him take anything except for one brandy since my father had left our company. I shrugged mentally and went to help myself to some eggs, toast and tea. When I sat across from him, he looked up and grimaced. "Come now, brat, we don't have time for you to gobble all of that down!"

Using what I thought was a most haughty voice as I applied butter to my toast asking, "Uncle… Is it acceptable in polite circles for you to continually call me brat?"

He choked as he swallowed and spent the next minute or so coughing to clear his windpipe. He waved Irene off as she rose to offer her assistance. Instead she turned towards me hiding her bright smile from Samuel, "I admit, dearest, that your uncle uses that term without thought and far too often in front of family. However, I assure you it is not an acceptable form of address in company." With that she smacked Samuel on the back of his head and resumed her seat, taking a bite of toast, almost choking as she tried not to laugh.

When Samuel stopped gaping at me, he joined her in laughing. "By god, Irene, she is your daughter!" Mother gave him a quick disapproving glance and he responded, "Don't look at me like you don't know what I am talking about. You never once let Colin, or I, get away with anything when you were her age! I just hope that her tongue doesn't become as acidic as Aunt Mary's or as cutting as yours."

Irene beamed. "Lissa, my sweet, I think in the future I shall have to instruct you on how to cut an impudent gentleman."

Samuel raised his hands in surrender, "I give up since I am hopelessly outnumbered. Are you done, braah—Lissa? We need to leave now if we're to get our ride in during the fashionable hour." He rose heading for the door, so I drank my tea down, scalding my mouth. I grabbed another piece of toast which my mother took out of my hand as I passed her. We reached the door just as Aunt Mary entered so I stopped only long enough to enquire after her health before Samuel took my hand, practically dragging me out to the mews at a run.

I was out of breath racing after him in full skirts but thankfully the stable boys had our horses saddled and two grooms were standing by with their own horses waiting for us to mount. "Up you go, brat!" I laughed as Samuel threw me up onto Jewel. He mounted Baron and waited until I had arranged my skirts then signalled for the two grooms to follow us.

I looked back over my shoulder at our escort the one named Michael tipped his hat at me and when I turned back, I caught Samuel watching me, so I asked him, "Is it customary to always have grooms with us when we ride in town?"

He nodded. "It will be customary for you and your mother when you ride regardless of who else is with you."

I turned to look at the men, both rode like they had been born and bred in a saddle and I noticed that they were armed just as they had been on the road. As we came out onto the roadway the grooms moved ahead of us looking up and down the street before we crossed over to the park. "Samuel, I mean, Uncle?"

"Yes, Lissa?"

"Why are they armed?"

"It's your father's orders." I scowled at him because he should have known that his answer wouldn't satisfy me. He caught my look and huffed, adding, "It has not been so many years since footpads haunted these environs, attacking citizens by day or night. Besides, Colin is being especially cautious with his family, it's a wise precaution given our work."

I was shocked. I knew that my father and uncle worked for the Crown, but how could their work possibly put Mother and I at risk? "Are there people that would want to harm me or Mother because of what you do?" He didn't look at me but gave a short nod, it was all the answer I would receive.

We paused at the edge of the park, so I could look over its beauty with its expanse of green and the Serpentine just visible beyond. With the welcoming scent of grass and flowering trees, Jewel's head perked up along with Baron's as we trotted off to join the fashionable ladies and gentlemen on Rotten Row. Samuel seemed to know several people, yet he didn't stop to converse with them or to introduce me. I thought this was rather rude until I realised that I was only a child to him and my new status as his niece was not yet known to society. So, I relaxed and kept pace with him as we cantered, then walked, then trotted, then cantered again. Baron was well behaved while Jewel was a touch restive and shy of being close to so many other unfamiliar horses. I knew then I would have to seriously consider what my mother had said about sending her to Somerset. As we reached the end of the row and were about to turn around I caught sight of a man in a dark green coat partially hidden behind one of the trees on the right, just then he stepped out, raised his arm and pointed toward us. Jewel tossed her head nudging Baron and causing me to lose control of her for a second. Baron sidestepped when she bumped him just as a shot rang out. One of our grooms whirled around taking off at a gallop into the surrounding wooded area where I had seen the man. I looked behind me to find Samuel prostrate on the ground, bleeding heavily from his shoulder. The other groom Michael was tending to him, he yelled at me, "Miss! Get down now! Keep your horse between you and those trees." I jumped down quickly as a crowd gathered around my uncle. A lady screamed when she saw the blood and her horse shied, she was in danger of slipping out of the saddle, so several men raced to her assistance. The scene around me was one of chaos, yelling and screaming. I ducked under Jewel's neck to see if I could locate our other groom Jacob among the trees. Michael yelled for someone to send for the parish constable and the Bow Street Runners. No one paid me any attention standing there until Michael finally looked up and winked, he looked around before addressing me, "Miss, do you think you could ride home and roust the house?" I looked in the direction we had come and then back at him nodding. "Good, get them to bring the carriage here so we can get Mr Hughes home. He'll not be riding anymore today."

I was so terrified that I could only nod. I looked about to see what I could use as a mounting block since I would never be able to get onto Baron or Jewel without help. Just as I had spied a rock I thought I could climb Jacob returned shaking his head at Michael. He jumped down automatically, turning to assist me onto Jewel. We ignored the bridle paths and rode at a gallop across the park, heedless of the people around us. When we reached the mews, he pulled me down off Jewel, threw the reins to the stable boy while he yelled for the carriage to be made ready.

Turning to me he said in tone that was respectful but would brook no argument, "Miss, I need you to do exactly what I ask and without question." I nodded. "Go in by the garden entrance and find Mr Allan, tell him what's happened then have him take you, your mother and aunt to the library and lock the door. By no means let anyone in but Mr Allan, Michael or me. Do you understand, miss?" I nodded again. I could feel tears threatening but I held them back. He squeezed my arm in reassurance. "Mr Hughes will be alright, don't you worry none. I've seen him with worse and come up fighting. What's keeping him down now was getting the wind knocked out of him when he fell, and he hit his noggin hard. Now go on, do as I say." He turned then yelling at one of the stable boys, "Fetch Dr Jefferson, tell him that Mr Hughes has been shot."

Lifting my skirts, I raced for the garden door that led into the breakfast room just as Jacob was climbing up with the coachman directing him where to go. I found Mr Allan in the front hallway sorting the mail and asked him to take me to my mother and aunt. I wanted to run but I followed him at a sedate pace so as not to alarm the other staff as we passed. He opened the door to a small drawing room and I asked him to step in with me. Without hesitation, he followed closing the door behind him. I hardly knew where to begin so I started from the point where I had noticed that our grooms were armed. It didn't take me long to race through my story.

Irene seemed to hold her breath the whole time that I was talking, finally she let it out getting quickly to her feet and heading for the door, but Mr Allan stood in her way. "Ma'am, I must insist that you follow Jacob's orders. He has been with Mr Turner for some time and he knows what he's doing. I can assure you that Mr Hughes is in good hands. Please, let me escort you to the library then I will have Lettie bring you some tea after I alert Dalton to ready Mr Hughes's room."

Mother frowned but nodded. "Thank you, Allan."

He walked us to the library where he told my mother to lock the door from the inside. I was amazed that my aunt had not said one word since I had arrived. She sat down heavily on the settee by the fire while Irene locked the door and closed the curtains facing the street.

I looked about me in awe. This library could very well be my sanctuary. Every inch of wall space was covered with bookcases from floor to ceiling full of books from top to bottom. There were four windows in the room, two facing the street and two facing the side garden all with window seats; such a haven was the stuff of my dreams. My mother and aunt were so quiet I swear I could hear my aunt breathing. But it wasn't her breathing, she was crying. Irene sat beside her with an arm around her shoulders, so I went to kneel by them on the floor. Between her sobs she managed to say, "I promised you're your mother that I would take care of you and your brother and I've failed. Samuel is dead, and I was awful to him, arguing with him all the way here. I am despicable!"

I touched her knee. "Auntie, he isn't dead! He's just wounded. He had his breath knocked out when he fell off Baron. He'll be fine, you'll see. Michael and Jacob are bringing him home. They've sent for a Dr Jefferson, so he'll be here shortly too.

Samuel will be alright, I promise." I sincerely hoped that I was right, after all Jacob seemed to believe it.

Aunt Mary smoothed my hair back behind my ears and smiled. "When Alice died, she had asked for only one thing from my brother that he take particular care of your mother and Samuel. That was all she had asked of him, all that she wanted. But he was always so wrapped up in his own selfishness…and she knew it, so I agreed to watch over you both when she asked."

She shook her head. "Richard didn't like my interfering and when he met Charlotte at Lord Gromley's hunt six months later, he married her in part to be rid of me and because when he looked at her, he saw Alice. She wasn't anything like Alice except in looks. After they married he quickly lost interest in her and when she lost the baby he left her to care for his house and his children. He used the excuse that his country needed him because Napoleon was raging war on the continent. He just left her to wilt and die without a second thought. That bastard answered the call to war and abandoned his family." She turned and clasped my mother's hands. "Irene, if I had only been a better guardian, I should have been there to help Charlotte. She was a young woman without experience in child raising."

Irene pulled her close. "Please, don't torture yourself over the past, Aunt Mary! You were a widow; you had your own son to raise and an estate to run. Charlotte did her best with us but after she lost the baby she was so sick, and Father was no help. He was so angry that she had failed to provide him with another son, so he left us. Samuel and I understood that she tried to do all she could for us. But I must admit that neither Samuel nor I were easy to guide. Nanny was a wonder, but we tried her something terrible too and once she passed away from pneumonia we were impossible. Besides you came to us for all the school holidays and the summer." She smirked and tapped our aunt's hand, saying, "Even though you brought our cousin Dyson with you." Irene chuckled, and Aunt Mary smiled.

Aunt Mary sighed. "Yes…except for that one holiday when Dyson was being so difficult. If I had been there, you might not have…" Aunt Mary sobbed and Irene blushed.

Watching them both I felt a knot was forming in my stomach. I was twisting my gloves into a ruined mass of leather with my anxiety. Her unfinished sentence was killing me, so I said rather moodily, "If you had been there, I might not have been conceived."

Aunt Mary and Irene were horrified, both saying at the same time "Oh no, my darling!"

Aunt Mary pulled me to her. "Oh, my darling child, never! That's not what I meant at all. It was a promise that I made to your grandmother. She wanted Irene to marry in the church where she and generations of her family had been married. She wanted it more than anything, she begged me before she died that I'd see to it. But that damn vicar refused Charlotte's request, he wouldn't conduct the ceremony without my brother's permission. He also promised her that he wouldn't tell Richard, but he lied and he's the reason that Colin was forbidden the house. Once the General came home the little toad broke his promise and went right to my brother the first day he was home, telling him how he had thwarted the marriage. If I had been there with Charlotte, I could have done something perhaps to persuade the vicar or at least bought his silence, I'm sure of it."

Suddenly there was a lot of noise and yelling coming from the hallway, then someone was pounding on the door. We huddled together saying nothing. The door handle was tried then the pounding resumed as my father's voice called out. "Irene! Clarissa! Lady Alford!"

Irene ran to the door, turned the key then flung it open. "Colin, oh thank god! Samuel, he's been—"

My father stepped in, looked around then reached for my mother. "I know, my love."

Colin wrapped her in his arms, kissing her soundly. He stepped back looking at the rest of us saying, "Samuel is upstairs in his room; the doctor is with him now."

Aunt Mary made to get up, but my father motioned for her to sit. "He's awake but the language coming out of his mouth isn't fit for sailors to hear, let alone ladies. Let the doctor and Dalton deal with him first."

Lettie arrived with a tea tray that he took from her, placing it on the table in front of my Aunt. Then he smiled at Lettie as he walked her to the door. "Thank you, Lettie, would you please ask Mr Allan to bring Dr Jefferson to us when he's done?"

She smiled back saying, "Yes, sir," as she left.

Father closed the door then waited to hear her footsteps retreat before he coming to sit by my mother who was pouring out the tea. "Lissa, Michael told me that you were very brave today. I'm so proud of you, darling. But are you okay?! You know that it's alright to be afraid."

It was strange that until he had mentioned it I hadn't been afraid. I was worried and concerned but not afraid. "I'm fine, Mr Turner—" I stopped myself and stumbled on with "I mean, Father. I'm just worried about Samuel." He smiled, leaning forward to clasp my hand, but I pulled out of his reach. The look on his face was pained as if I had physically hurt him. But I had questions and I wanted answers from this man that I barely knew. "When did you get to London? And how did you know what happened?" I crossed my arms waiting for him to answer me.

Mother looked stunned. "Lissa, you shouldn't be questioning your father like this!"

Colin sighed, and Aunt Mary smiled at him patting his hand. "She is your child, Colin, there is no doubt about that. She has an inquisitive mind and notices everything. So, don't say that I never warned you."

He still looked sad when he responded, "Those are all good questions, Lissa. It's true that I have only just arrived, but I met the carriage just as it was about to cross into the park and Jacob called out as I passed that Samuel had been shot. I followed to help bring him home. Also, I spoke briefly with an Inspector from the Bow Street Runners. When I arrived, I was coming from the opposite direction of the park that can be confirmed by Jacob and Mr Cripps who saw me arrive. Also, I did not shoot Samuel."

Mother gasped. "Lissa! Samuel and your father are like brothers."

I pursed my lips together looking hard at Colin, my father, thinking of all the things that Samuel had said about him. Suddenly I couldn't believe that he would hurt Samuel. "It was only that I saw a man in a green coat much like yours just long enough to register that it was indeed a man."

My father leaned forward saying in a quiet voice that trembled with emotion, "Lissa, I'm so sorry that you had to witness that, but the Inspector will want to question you. Can you do that? We'll need every detail that you can recall for us to find out who did this to Samuel."

I could feel a blush rising up my neck and tried to smile all the while feeling ashamed that I might have thought him capable of hurting Samuel. Thankful that he wasn't treating me like a child nor was he trying to shelter me from reality. "Yes, I can do that, Father. But Mother and you will stay with me when I'm questioned…won't you?"

He stood up opened his arms to me with a hopeful look in his eyes. I went to him sliding my arms around his waist, hugging him tightly. He wrapped his arms around me cautiously. "Of course, my love, we'll both be there." As we broke apart he smiled down at me, then rubbing his hands together said, "Now how about that cup of tea and some of those cakes. I missed my breakfast on the road and I'm starving!"

Mother finished pouring the tea as I passed out the cakes. We all ate in companionable silence, waiting for the doctor to come to us. My father came to sit beside me in order to steal my almond cakes when I wasn't looking. We both chuckled at the silly game it was as if he were trying to make up for the missed years of my childhood. It was then I realised that I was starting to think of him as my father and not Colin. Mother and even Aunt Mary laughed along with us until Mr Allan finally announced a Dr Matthew Jefferson. I anxiously jumped to my feet and stood beside Father, facing the door.

Dr Jefferson was younger than I had expected and very handsome, he was tall with black hair, deeply tanned skin and deep brown eyes that seemed to twinkle. Darkly handsome, I envisioned him to be more of a pirate than doctor. Introductions were made, and I waited to hear his voice which to my disappointment was very English and very cultured, sadly he was obviously a gentleman.

Irene asked him to be seated, offering him some tea. "No thank you, Mrs Turner, I really must go. I left Mrs Clarence with the midwife and she was not too pleased with me. However, I wanted you to know that Mr Hughes will be fine. The bullet passed clean through, but it did nick a blood vessel and he's lost a great deal of blood. He should be fine with rest and the proper care. And as to his care I have spoken to his valet, he must rest and by that I mean he must stay in bed for several days." He paused to emphasize his meaning and appeared to be waiting for questions. When none were forthcoming, he continued, "I will be back tomorrow to change the dressing and check on him. However, if he bleeds through the one I just applied or becomes feverish, send for me. I have left Dalton with instructions as to what he can eat and drink." He paused and bit his lip as if making a difficult decision. "He may also have a few drops of laudanum if his pain is severe."

He turned and looked towards the door as if he was wrestling with what he wanted to say next. "I expect that you know he's going to be a difficult patient; nonetheless I suggest that you use the laudanum sparingly and only if he tries to get out of bed or becomes unruly then make use of it…but only if absolutely necessary." He looked as if he had something else he wanted to say but then changed his mind and remained silent.

Aunt Mary stood up, smoothed down her skirts and smiling at him she extended her hand which he took, bowing over it, "Thank you, doctor. I will go up to him now and organize the sick room and staff. I assure you he will not be left alone. Irene, my dear, perhaps you could speak to cook about making some beef tea and a light custard for when Samuel awakens."

Mother got up and moved towards the door but before either of them could leave the room, Dr Jefferson stopped them. "If you will excuse me, Lady Alford. I would advise you that Mr Hughes needs a more substantial diet than just beef tea and custard. I realise that is not the usual course of treatment prescribed by many of my colleagues, but I have found through experience that satisfying meals that tempt the patient to eat are more efficacious than a light bland diet."

Aunt Mary's chin came up and she opened her mouth to obviously argue while Mother and I cringed, waiting for her to say something cutting, but before she could utter a word the doctor continued with an impish smile. "He must also drink plenty of nourishing fluids to replenish what he has lost from bleeding. So, beef tea is an excellent idea, Lady Alford." Pursing his lips as if deciding on what else to say he continued, "And I strongly suggest no strong spirits. I'm sure I can count on you ladies to see that none is smuggled into him." He gave my father a sharp look then relaxed his face immediately when he saw me watching him. "He can have small beer with his meals and a very little red wine with water at dinner, nothing stronger until I say otherwise." Aunt Mary nodded approvingly.

Just then Mr Allan came to the door and announced that the Mr Spencer, the Bow Street Investigator, had arrived. "I have placed Mr Spencer from Bow Street in the small withdrawing room."

Dr Jefferson excused himself and took his leave after bowing to my mother and Aunt Mary. He nodded to me and shook hands with my father, both men exchanging a look of concern.

Aunt Mary, I observed, must have noticed their shared look as well since she now looked pale and worried as she stood there, twisting her rings on her fingers. But she shook herself and wasted no more time in sailing out of the room behind the doctor. My mother kissed Father on the cheek. "If you'll excuse me, darling, I think I will go speak to cook about Samuel's needs and arrange for tray to be sent up when he awakens. I'll also make sure another place is set for Mr Spencer for luncheon."

Mother smiled, but there must have been something in Father's face that made her hesitate before she reached the door. "Am I wrong thinking that you would like Mr Spencer to dine with us? I just assumed from the way you said that 'we' would need information about the shooting that you intended to involve yourself in the investigation. If so then you would need to enlist Mr Spencer's cooperation and indulgence, especially if you expect him to allow you access to whatever he learns." Father's face gave away very little, but the corner of his lip trembled as if he would smile or laugh. Mother arched her brow coyly, saying, "Or was I wrong to think that you intended to ingratiate yourself with the gentleman?"

To keep from giving himself away, Father focused on the carpet, pursed his lips, tapping them with one finger and only stopping after a few seconds then he put his arm around my shoulder and smiled at my mother. "You've read my mind, darling. Yes, I think I shall invite Mr Spencer to join us." Then he looked down at me, "Well, Lissa, shall we go meet this Inspector and size up his character?"

Mother looked puzzled. "So, you don't know this man?"

"Only by reputation, my love, but I think you'll find him a most interesting. If he's the man I think he is then his talents are being wasted in Bow Street, but we shall see." He paused to smile at Mother then continued, "Let Lissa and I reconnoitre our guest and satisfy his curiosity about the shooting. And as we dine, we can all take his measure." Mother shook her head, still smiling as she went off to speak to cook.

Father gave my shoulder a squeeze as we followed her out the door. "Come, my sweet, let's see what you can remember for our guest and we'll see what we might be able to find out from him."

Mr Spencer was standing by the windows looking out onto our back garden. At first glance, he was not at all what I had expected, indeed he was far from it. In fact, he appeared to be a gentleman. He was as well dressed and groomed as my father, he was tall and muscular, but his clothes fit him very well for such a large man. He turned around as we entered, Mr Spencer was indeed very respectable looking, he was clean shaven with a rugged countenance and a long, straight nose. He was considerably older than my father with grey at the temples of his dark blond hair. His most arresting feature though were his eyes, they were a deep emerald green. And from the way he looked at me I was sure he would know if I lied. He glanced first at me then my father and then quickly looked around the room as if he was assessing its contents, his eyes didn't seem to miss a thing. My father stepped forward and introduced himself, extending his hand, "Mr Spencer, I am Colin Turner."

Mr Spencer shook his hand while ignoring me. "A pleasure, sir, but have we met before? I seem to recall an occasion…" Father shook his head no. I wondered why I hadn't been introduced as I'm sure Mr Spencer was wondering. He waited a bit looking at me then back at my father before he continued, "An admirable home you have here, Mr Turner, very admirable." Mr Spencer thumbed his nose then caught me observing him, so he coughed taking another look around the room. "I take it that Adams was the architect." It was statement not a question.

My father indicated a chair and invited him to sit. "Please, Mr Spencer, have seat. Yes, the house was built by Adams. Are you a student of architecture or is there some other purpose behind your question?"

Mr Spencer smiled as he chuckled, it brightened his entire countenance and made him appear less threatening which was probably not an asset when dealing with criminals. "Touché, Mr Turner. You have undergone some significant changes since we last met for I'm sure we've met before though you may not want to remember the circumstances." He chuckled, and my father blushed. I would love to know what that was about. "So, Mr Turner, you can't fault me for being curious." Again, he looked around the room. My father was watching him closely, both seemed to be assessing each other.

There was a brief knock at the door and my mother entered, stopping behind our seat, she put one hand on my father's shoulder and one on mine. Mr Spencer stood up and bowed slightly as Father said, "Mr Spencer, may I present my wife, Irene."

For just a split second there was a flash of surprise in his eyes. "My pleasure, ma'am."

Then father reached out placing his hand on my arm, "And this is Clarissa."

Mr Spencer turned to me with a quizzical look then nodded "Miss."

My mother smiled graciously. "Mr Spencer, it's a pleasure to meet you. I can't thank you enough for coming to our home to interview our daughter." Again, there was that split second of surprise in his eyes, but he had better control of himself now and it was barely noticeable. I wondered if Father and Mother were trying to fluster Mr Spencer on purpose, if they were…it wasn't working.

He looked at all three of us through narrowed eyes before saying, "I thought I was here to investigate the attempted murder of Mr Samuel Hughes. So why do I get the impression that I'm being investigated instead?"

My mother laughed. "Mr Spencer, would you care join us for luncheon after you speak with Clarissa? I think there are many questions you will have for us."

He nodded at her but didn't smile, "And I believe that you have many questions for me as well, Mrs Turner." Nevertheless, he took his time before making his decision. He looked around the room again. "It would be my honour to join you, Mrs Turner. I don't suppose that Mr Hughes or Lady Alford will be joining us?"

Mother replied but seemed a little puzzled, wrinkling her forehead. "Mr Hughes will not be joining us. The doctor has confined him to bed. As for Lady Alford, I can't be sure."

He sighed as if saddened by that remark then turned towards me abruptly, "So shall we get down to the business of what happened in the park, miss? Then perhaps luncheon will be less uncomfortable for all of us." He took out a small booklet and pencil from his pocket.

Mr Spencer cleared his throat and began, "Mr Turner, I will need your ah daughter's full and legal name for my report." I squirmed at his implication, yet I should have realised that he would think that Colin was not my real father.

I was annoyed by his assumption, so I spoke up before my father could say anything much to the amusement of my elders. "My name is Clarissa Alice Charlotte Mary Turner. I am sixteen years old and the legal as well as the natural daughter of Colin and Irene Turner." Mother moved around to join us on the settee, clasping my hand tightly and smiling beautifully.

Mother and Father could barely contain a chuckle as Mr Spencer looked directly at me in disbelief and coughed, "Ah yes, well, thank you... Miss... Turner." He looked pointedly at my father who only nodded. Mr Spencer proceeded to query me about my morning and what had happened in the park. I gave as thorough an account as I could. I didn't omit anything even though he tried to fool me by rewording his questions. Nevertheless, my answers didn't vary. Father seemed impressed with how I was handling the interview since he had relaxed back into the settee. It's not that I wasn't nervous, but I knew how important it was that I be precise.

Mr Spencer finally finished with his questions. "Thank you, Miss Turner, I believe I have everything I need." He looked over his notes then back at me with a challenge in his eyes. "You have an excellent memory for detail."

I smiled and started to rise expecting to be dismissed by my father, but he motioned for me to sit. Mr Spencer and I were both surprised. He glared at my father before saying in an incredulous voice. "Mr Turner, what are you playing at? Has this young lady been rehearsed? If I recall correctly the last time our paths crossed, you were leading the life of a rich and somewhat debauched bachelor! And now you expect me to believe that you're suddenly a married man with a grown child? Would you care to explain?"

Father never moved a muscle, he was comfortable with the truth, you could see it in his demeanour and the tone of his voice. "I assure you, Mr Spencer, that Clarissa is my daughter. My wife and I married secretly seventeen years ago. It was against the wishes of our families, but we did so anyway with the aid of Lady Alford and my wife's stepmother. Clarissa was born approximately nine months later while I was on leave from France. The rest of our story is rather involved but I will be happy to share it with you after luncheon."

Just then Mr Allan knocked on the door and came announcing, "Luncheon is ready, madame."

Father stood up, offering my mother his hand, "Thank you, Allan, we will be right there."

She turned toward Mr Spencer, "Shall we?" Taking his arm, she started by asking him if he had any family as they walked out of the room.

Father offered me his arm but not before he kissed me on the cheek. "You were brilliant, my darling." then we followed my Mother and Mr Spencer.

Aunt Mary was just coming down the stairs as we reached the hallway when she called out. "Colin, you didn't tell me we were expecting a guest for luncheon."

Mr Spencer turned around quickly at the sound of her voice and with a wide grin on his face he bowed. "Lady Alford, it is a pleasure to see you again."

Aunt Mary gasped clutching her throat then practically ran down the rest of the steps "Arthur, my heavens, is it really you?! I knew you were with Bow Street, but I never expected to see you here." He nodded never taking his eyes off my aunt. Mother stepped aside as Aunt Mary stopped directly in front of Mr Spencer. She was so very tiny standing there looking up at him. He took her hand and kissed it, then he offered her his arm as they walked on towards the dining room totally oblivious to the rest of us.

Mother stood by my father with her mouth open. When the couple had reached the doorway, Aunt Mary looked back over her shoulder, "Irene, my dear, close your mouth, you look like a cod fish." Father shrugged and offered Mother and I each an arm.

At luncheon Aunt Mary and Mr Spencer's story dominated our conversation. Mr Spencer had never married because Aunt Mary was the love of his life. They had met in Cornwall one summer when they were both very young. Mr Spencer was a young captain who had just come home from the war in America. Aunt Mary had not yet had her first season in London. She had been ill the previous winter and was sent to Cornwall for her health with an elderly cousin as a chaperon. Mr Spencer was a dashing officer who was faced with a life on half pay. As the eldest son, he could have followed in his father's footsteps and run their prosperous farm and tin mine. But he had two brothers who were both married that could use the income that he would take from them both if he were to remain. Besides he said that he had no talent for farming and no desire to run the mine; while his brothers were well-suited to the life. So, he decided that he would rest and enjoy his family for a time before leaving for London to make his fortune. It was during that summer that he met Aunt Mary and they fell in love. He begged her to run away to London with him, but she refused. She knew that he wouldn't be able to support them both on a Captain's half pay and it would take time and demanding work for him to make his way in London. She feared that he would end up hating himself or her and she knew that her family would object strenuously to the match. They had enough influence to have any marriage put aside, her father was a ruthless mean-spirited man and wouldn't hesitate to ruin Mr Spencer and his family if he put his mind to it.

So, she gave up the love of her life to save him from ruin and he left for London devastated by her rejection. She cared very little about what would happen to her after that summer and eventually accepted an arranged marriage. It was a profitable match but without any love on either side. Her husband found consolation in a series of mistresses, but she had no one. She dedicated her life to her children, yet sadness had dogged her there as well. Her second son had died of scarlet fever in his eighth year and her daughter passed away before she was two years old of a wasting sickness. After her husband died in a hunting accident, her eldest son Dyson inherited and became a terrible trial to her. He took after his father being an ingrate and a bore. So, when her sister-in-law Alice died, she focused as much of her attention as possible on her brother's motherless children while trying to run an estate and raise her son.

I understand now why she had risked the General's wrath by assisting my mother and father to marry and for keeping their secret all this time. I could also see Aunt Mary's hand in my mother's decision not to follow my father to France. It was only now that I could appreciate how much my mother had sacrificed for me with only occasional stolen visits with the man she so desperately loved. At least she had had more than Aunt Mary did. My heart broke for them, they all must have suffered so much.

# Chapter 6
## *The Garden Gate*

Mr Spencer proved to be an entertaining guest. He knew London extremely well and knew several dubious characters that he called friends, acquaintances and snitches which interested my father immensely. After luncheon, Father and Mr Spencer adjourned to his study to discuss my uncle's shooting further and other business.

Mother and Aunt Mary went up to see Uncle Samuel, but I was forbidden to enter the sick room until he had passed his difficult stage. Knowing my uncle, that would involve a fair amount of swearing that young ladies should not be privy to. So, I was left to my own devices.

I went to my room where Meg helped me change into an afternoon gown. I must admit that London was going to try my patience sorely with the amount of changing of clothes that took place each day. And I was afraid that Meg would end up being exhausted with all the additional work, but she assured me that she was enjoying her work here. "Everything is very modern in the house and so many unfamiliar faces to get to know, it shall be a pleasure to work here, miss." She was so happy, in fact, that she was practically dancing around my room. "Can you imagine, miss, I have a room to myself here! It's none as grand as yours, but because I'm a lady's maid I don't have to share, and I have a key to it! I can even lock the door! I can't wait to write my mum to tell her about it, did you know that there's even indoor plumbing and heated water right here in the house! There is no fetching water from an outside pump or carrying tins of hot water upstairs for baths!" She picked up my discarded clothes and went off to do whatever it was that maids do.

The day was fair outside, so I grabbed my sketch book and ventured out into the garden. It wasn't large, but it had been beautifully arranged to create the illusion of space. The wall between us and the next property was high and covered with lemon and orange espaliers. I walked about looking for a place to call my own when I discovered towards the bottom of the garden a gate in the wall. I left my drawing materials on a bench under a nearby walnut tree, so I could inspect the gate. I tried the latch, but it was locked, I looked about for a key to no avail. One of the gardeners would surely know where the key was but with a quick glance around, none were to be found.

In my frustration, I jiggled the latch before walking away. Then a voice called from the other side of the wall. "It's locked."

I stopped to address the door, "I'm aware of that now!"

There was a muffled chuckle, "Sorry, I should have said that it's always locked. No one on my side has a key. What about yours?"

It was odd to be talking so casually to someone that I couldn't see and didn't know. I hadn't led a sheltered life in Northumberland, but I rarely had the opportunity to socialize with anyone of my own class.

The voice spoke again, "Hello? Are you still there?"

I furrowed my brow studying the locked gate and the wall. I suppose I could get a hand hold on the espalier but whether it would hold my weight was a concern; even then my skirts might get caught. I was good at climbing trees; however, an espalier was another matter. So, I stood there considering what to do as I examined the barrier.

The voice called out again this time, a bit plaintive and sad, "I say there Hello? Are you still there?" Before I could speak he answered his own question. "Well, of course not, you dolt! She's gone, and you probably scared her away." The gate rattled as if it had been kicked. I giggled, and he said, "I heard that! So, you are still there. Look, I'm sincerely sorry of if I put you off. It must be very disconcerting to have someone speak to you through a gate, especially with you being new here and all." He chuckled, the idiot chuckled. Then he began to ramble. "I talk to your under-gardener Jones sometimes. He could vouch for me being sane. Though we've never met face to face because of the gate, you see, and he tends to keep the conversation to gardening. Actually, he usually just says yes sir and no sir, Jones is not much of a conversationalist, but he seems a good chap. Did you know that he's very earnest about lemons and oranges? He's very particular about their soil."

I needed to see this person so taking a hand hold I started to climb the espalier, surprisingly it was holding my weight just fine. His voice called out to me a bit clearer as I was reaching for the top, "Ah, miss, what are you doing, are you alright? What's that noise?"

I had just pulled myself up onto the top of the wall as he'd finished talking. Looking down, I saw a boy with a mass of blond curls leaning his ear against the gate and smiled, "Hello there?"

He jumped at the sound of my voice and leaning back to look up at me, he lost his balance and fell onto his back, uttering, "Oomph". He tipped his head to look up. "Oh! Hello there!"

As I gazed down on him he got to his feet, brushing off his breeches and coat. He had tousled curly blond hair and very vivid blue eyes that dominated a tanned face that he could never have acquired in England unless he worked in the fields or spent considerable time at sea. I was puzzled when he didn't introduce himself, so I asked, "Who are you?"

He looked me over and smirked. "I might ask you the same? Mr Turner has never had any ladies as guests or otherwise at his home. So how do you come to be there?"

I felt panic for a few seconds. What should I say? Could I tell him the truth? Wasn't that what we were here for, to let people know who we were? I decided he was being rude, so I snapped back! "I'm Clarissa Turner. Colin Turner is my father."

He opened and closed his mouth a couple of times, finally surrendering himself to laughter. "Monk Turner is your father!" He spoke every word slowly and distinctly like it gave him immense pleasure.

"What do you mean by Monk Turner?" I was irritated that he might be calling my father a scurrilous name.

"Oh, it's just a nickname I gave him. My sister has been mooning over him since we moved here. Though he is exceptionally polite to all the ladies, he has never given her or any other a second look. Even father wonders at his celibacy. The word is that he doesn't go to bawdy houses nor show a preference for women or boys."

I frowned, balling up my fists till my nails bit into my palms. I was angry with him for talking like that about my father but before I could say anything, he continued, "Please tell me that your mother is still alive and living with you. This is going to be so rich. Maybe for once at dinner we won't have to listen to my mother's recitation of Colin Turner's better qualities."

I was balanced on top of the wall and while it was wide enough to accommodate me it was not very comfortable. There was no way for me to get down on his side, so I shifted from side to side pulling my skirts up under me for some padding. Just as I started to do so he reached up as if to steady me by grabbing at my leg. I quickly moved my feet out of his reach "No, I'm fine thank you." He pulled back looking slightly annoyed as I settled myself. "To answer your question, yes, my mother is alive, and she is here with Father and me."

He clapped his hands together and smiled. "Delicious!"

"You know my name, sir, but I don't know yours." I waited for him to answer me.

He stepped back to where I could see him better and bowed. "Your pardon, Miss Turner, my name is Ramsey Clarke. Late of Jamaica in the West Indies and now a resident of this glorious city; at least until I am sent off to Oxford next term." Now that I could see him better he appeared taller and older than I had first thought, perhaps eighteen or more. He had one of those faces that promised to be boyish for a good many years. Still blushing at my intense regard, he continued, "Can I assume then that Mr Turner is newly married?"

He was digging for information. I was annoyed by his regard and his questions and prepared myself to climb down from my perch, leaving him to his own devices. "Mr Clarke, you are impertinent! My mother and father have been married for seventeen years. Mother and I have resided in the country while my father was in France during the war and afterwards because his business often took him away for extended periods. I suggest that you call on my parents if you desire any further information for your amusement." With that I turned and jumped down from my perch. My landing was jarring and none too graceful, but no one was around to see me. I stood up and heard laughter coming from the other side of the wall. I clenched my fists again and almost stamped my foot. Then called out, "Mr Clarke, you are no gentleman. Good day to you, sir!"

The laughter continued but he managed to squeak out, "It has been a pleasure, Miss Turner, and I hope to see you again soon."

I retrieved my sketch pad and retreated to my room without anyone witnessing my fury and flung myself into the seat by the window, grabbing a book and furiously thumbing the pages as I looked out at the part of the Clarke's garden within my view. Ramsey was still there, seated on a bench with a book in his lap. I couldn't tell if he was asleep or staring at the gate. He infuriated me because he had implied that I was illegitimate. Then I only hoped that I hadn't unravelled any of my aunt's plans for our introduction into the Beau Monde. I knew enough about society that gossip often travels faster than the truth, so I decided that I had better tell my mother about my encounter. I put the book down and looked out the window once again to find that Mr Clarke had turned and appeared to be looking right at my window as if he had seen me stand up. I tossed the book onto the chaise and raced into the hallway bent on locating my mother as quickly as possible. Instead I ran straight into Aunt Mary.

Aunt Mary grabbed my arm and looked studiously over her spectacles at me, "Clarissa Turner! Whatever is the matter with you, girl?"

I was still stinging from Ramsey's inference, so I snapped, "I have to find mother or father. I might have made a mess of things after speaking to our neighbour, Ramsey Clarke."

Aunt Mary looked towards my open door. "Good heavens, child, how did you meet him?" Then she eyed my dirty hands and a grass stain on the hem of my dress. "Perhaps you should tell me what you have been up to and who this Ramsey Clarke is while you wash your hands and change your gown."

We entered my room and I pointed towards the window. "He may still be there sitting in the garden next door. He lives there with his parents and sister."

She moved to look out the window saying as she walked towards it, "I would not normally stoop to spying on our neighbours but under the circumstances…" She pulled back the curtain then dropped it immediately. "What an impertinent young man, he was looking right at me and saluted!" I clapped my hand over my mouth to keep from laughing. She glared at me then at the window. "Hurry up, Clarissa, don't dawdle. I would like to speak with Mr Spencer before he leaves."

"But I have to tell mother about Ramsey first."

"Your mother is resting." I must have looked disappointed because she added in a hushed tone. "I'll take you to your father, so we can both tell him about that young miscreant." I quickly washed my hands and changed my gown with her help. When we reached my father's study, the door was just opening, and Mr Spencer was taking his leave. He saw Aunt Mary and smiled. She took a step forward, laying her hand on his arm, "Arthur, if I could have a word with you in private please?" then she motioned to the library door across the hall. He nodded and they both left me standing in the hallway.

Well, so much for Aunt Mary helping me. I stuck my head around the door of Father's study and found him sitting at his desk. He appeared to be lost in thought but when he caught sight of me, he motioned me in. "Lissa, my dear, I'm sorry to have left you to entertain yourself especially with all that's happened."

"Actually, Father…" Then I changed my mind in mid-sentence as to what I was going to say and instead asked, "May I call you papa? It just seems, well, shorter and less formal."

He smiled and chuckled. "Yes, of course, you can, my dear. You may call me whatever you're most comfortable with." A feeling of warmth spread through me. I really did have a father who cared about me and perhaps even loved me. "Is there something else on your mind?"

I was wool gathering about having a father when he had asked me the question and was now patiently waiting for my answer. I shook myself trying to think, "Oh yes…well, umm, it's about our neighbours. I may have made a hash of things…but he just made me so angry."

He looked puzzled. "The Clarkes or the Summers?"

I cupped my hands in front of me, staring at my feet. Years of not making eye contact with the General had trained me for awkward situations. "Ah the Clarkes— I met Ramsey Clarke today by accident. I was afraid that by my talking to him I might have spoiled your plans for introducing Mother and I to society. If I have, then I'm so sorry, Father." I was terrified to look up and see his disappointment.

I heard a snort, then a chuckle followed with a full out laugh. "So, you met that rapscallion, did you? May I ask how this accident occurred? Or is it safe to assume that it involved your cat-like climbing abilities?" My head popped up. He was looking right at me with affectionate humour. "Oh, Lissa, my precious girl, come here."

He moved to a chair in front of his desk and motioned for me to take the one opposite him. I took several deep breaths while he tried to control his mirth. Then I told him about my encounter. He never interrupted me and continued to smile. When I finished, he said, "Well, it seems that we shall have to invite the Clarkes to dine with us. I had best warn your mama and Lady Alford to expect a call from Mrs Clarke and her daughter before too long. That should be a very interesting encounter." He chuckled again. "Perhaps I shall contrive to be there to witness your mother dealing with Miss Clarke's heartbreak."

I was astonished. "You know about his sister's infatuation?"

He chuckled again. "Yes, I have been aware of it for some time. Charity, the poor child, is not very subtle, and it has taken considerable skill to avoid her and her mother at social gatherings. It will be refreshing to have your mother here to act as my shield." I was rather perplexed by his statement and he noticed. He pulled at his ear looking rather abashed. "Lissa, my business has required me to do some things that I'm not particularly proud of but please believe me when I say that I have never been unfaithful to your mother and I would never do anything to hurt her. You and she are my life."

I stood up and hugged him. "Oh Papa, I know that. Ramsey told me that you were never anything but polite to his sister just as you would be to any lady. He even called you Monk Turner." Father looked surprised. "He can't wait to see his mother's reaction at dinner this evening when he tells her that you're married."

Father smirked. "I'm sure Ramsey will love telling them, it's rather nice of him to pave the way for us and by tomorrow evening everyone within two miles will know about you and your mother. Poor Samuel will hate to miss the excitement…he does love a good melodrama."

Suddenly I heard my mother's voice from behind me, "Lissa, you may have done us a great service." I looked over my shoulder to see Mother standing in the doorway. She was looking at both of us with a delicate smile and one arched brow as she addressed my father. "So, my love, who is this young lady that I am to shield you from…should I be worried?"

Mother had her arms crossed but she continued to smile at him. She looked beautiful standing there with the sun shining on her golden hair and her blue eyes flashing with amusement; she was radiant. I smoothed my skirts as my father took her in his arms and gave her a lingering kiss. Then they walked hand in hand to the settee. It still seemed strange to me that my sister was now my mother and that Mr Turner was my father, yet I couldn't deny our relationship. I was the female embodiment of father. Perhaps that was how my mother had survived being separated from him, she could look at me and see him.

Father took his time explaining to Mama what I had done. She laughed while smiling at me. "Then we'll need to prepare ourselves for tomorrow. Colin, you need to tell us as much as you can about the Clarkes; especially since they seem to know a great deal about you already. But before you start would you be a dear and ring for Allan, I would love some tea."

"That would be delightful." Aunt Mary had just stuck her head around the door. "In fact, I've already asked Mr Allan to bring it here." Father stood and motioned for her to come sit by the hearth in a chair opposite mama and papa. My father pulled me down to sit beside him and Mama as Aunt Mary looked over her spectacles at him and smiled.

While we waited for the tea, Father asked, "How is Samuel?"

Aunt Mary threw up her hands. "How do you suppose he would be, he's impossible! I don't see how we're going to keep him in bed without tying him to it. Dalton certainly has his hands full." Her lips puckered like she had tasted something bitter then she flicked an imaginary piece of lint from her skirt. "Colin, do you think Richards could give him a hand?"

"I'm sorry Lady Alford but Richards is in Cornwall."

Aunt Mary huffed. "Whatever for? We're about to launch your family into society and you have no valet!"

Mama chuckled. "It's hardly a disaster, Auntie. I'm sure we can manage without Richards for a time. When do expect him back, Colin?"

Father had been watching my mother, but he turned to answer Aunt Mary. "Never fear, Lady Alford, I shall not disappoint you. I've been used to dressing myself on many occasions and have never fallen short of the mark yet. But Richards should arrive here in a few days, he's been conducting some business for me to which his particular talents are better suited than mine."

Aunt Mary looked incredulous. "Preposterous, your valet is conducting business for you! What business could he possibly be better suited to than you?"

Father shifted his position and I quietly slid off the settee onto the floor to lean against his leg. Aunt Mary waved at me. "Heavens, Clarissa, get up! You cannot sit on the floor like a child." But before Father could answer her, Lettie arrived with the tea tray loaded down with scones, iced cakes and my favourite seed cake. Setting it down on the table in front of us she backed up, "Will that be all, sir, I mean, ma'am?"

Mother smiled. "Yes, Lettie, that will be all. Thank you very much and would you please tell cook that her seed cake looks delicious."

Lettie nodded. "Yes, ma'am, thank you, ma'am." She turned and left the room, closing the door behind her.

Aunt Mary watched the door close then turned to look at Father "She's very handsome but seems a bit out of place as a servant. Wherever did you find her, Colin?"

Papa cleared his throat. "Yes, well, she's Dalton's sister." He looked uncomfortable as she stared at him.

"Yes, I'd noticed the family resemblance." She left that hanging there waiting for a response to her original question. She now had my mother's interest piqued who had turned to look at him intently.

Papa's facial expression changed as he gazed at her with pleading eyes, he obviously didn't want to discuss Lettie. She reached out patting his hand, but I could see that she wasn't about to relent even though she was smiling. She turned back to pour the tea and asked, "Yes, my dear, wherever did you find her?"

He let out an irritated huff, crossing his long legs. He took a sip of tea after accepting a cup from her outstretched hand. It appeared to be too hot for his taste as he set the cup back down. Once we all had our tea, he clasped his hands in a semblance of pray, leaning forward resigned to finally answering. "Lady Alford, you might have guessed that my staff do not come to me through the usual channels of employment. They all have special talents over and above the positions that they occupy in this house."

Aunt Mary looked at him suspiciously, "What exactly does that mean, Colin?"

He ran his hand through his hair and sat back, taking mama's hand. "I suppose I should start at the beginning. When I left for France, I met an older gentleman onboard ship who worked directly for the Crown though I didn't find out in what capacity until much later. Sir Thomas Wiseman is his name and as it turned out he is the master of spies for his Majesty. It had been my intention that once I arrived on the continent to join a regiment, any regiment would have suited me since they all seem to be in desperate need of men. Being a gentleman, I had hoped to earn a battlefield commission since my father had refused to purchase one for me. He was dead set against me going to France in the first place since I'm his only son and heir and the only male heir to my mother's father. My only recourse was to join as a volunteer. To make a long story short by the time we reached Brussels Sir Thomas had convinced me that with my excellent grasp of languages, my status as a gentleman from an old respected family and my desire to serve my country made me an ideal candidate to be one of his assistants, or agents if you like. It turned out that my knowledge of languages was not the only thing that he found shall we say useful. I was accepted into society readily because of my pedigree, despite the lack of title, it won me invitations and favours that Sir Thomas being a knighted commoner could not hope to command. Also, my youthful exuberance and ability to play act as he called it made it possible for me to go about with the rougher classes with minimal assistance. A brief time later I recruited Samuel and we became his agents in Brussels. It was during those early years of service to Sir Thomas that I met Dalton and his sister. They were petty thieves that had accompanied the army across the channel. Dalton had apprenticed as a tailor but wasn't able to make enough money to support him and his sister. He had hoped to find a better life for himself and Lettie in the army, but he soon found that life as a dragoon was not any better than his life in England and his sister was attracting far too much of the wrong kind of attention from the officers utilizing her services as a laundress. So, he deserted taking her with him to live off the land and the pickings of war."

Aunt Mary choked on her tea. "You mean, excuse me, are you saying that your parlour maid and Samuel's valet are common thieves!"

Father laughed. "Not so very common, Lady Alford."

"Oh, for heaven's sake, Colin, stop calling me Lady Alford. I'm your aunt by marriage, you might as well address me as such. But please continue, you were saying that they're not so very common."

He nodded. "Thank you, Aunt Mary." She smiled over her tea cup as she took a sip. "They both entered my employ after trying to rob me in the street outside my lodgings in Brussels. The bulk of the army had moved on by then which meant Dalton and Lettie's opportunity for profit had as well. Dalton didn't want to take his sister onto a battlefield, he apparently had scruples about thieving off the dead. Once we had them cleaned up and fed regularly they proved to be exceptional mimics and picked up their new duties with very little effort." He sipped his tea to let that point sink in. Before continuing, Mother handed him a generous portion of seed cake. "In fact, Lady—I mean Aunt Mary, none of my staff have come to me as you see them today. The bulk of them have what you would call unusual pasts that were a result of necessity, not desire. It has taken Samuel and I considerable time to assemble them. They are not simply my household staff, they are also my business associates. It makes me far more effective in my position as Sir Thomas's agent that I can maintain a level of secrecy and anonymity by utilizing my own staff and working from my home is better than working out of a Ministry office."

Aunt Mary took a deep breath before saying, "Am I to understand that all of the staff in your employ are reformed criminals and that you, in fact, are a spy?"

He bristled slightly. "I am an intelligence officer, Aunt Mary, and not all of the people in my employ are former criminals." Smirking, he continued, "Some were soldiers that left the military to enter my employ. Some are disadvantaged individuals that had few prospects of their own but are highly intelligent, so they serve in various capacities inside and outside of our home. My man of business for instance is a Cambridge graduate whose family is impoverished, his father is dead and he supports his younger sister and mother. He's also a consummate forger which was how he paid for his education. Clarissa's French tutor is a young lady from France who lost her parents when their estate was confiscated by Napoleon's forces. She barely escaped with her life after being assaulted outside of the bawdy house where she had taken refuge working as a seamstress. Samuel found her in a nearby alley, he'd chased her attackers, but she was unconscious, and the madam of the house didn't want to continue housing her. When she had recovered, she had nowhere to go so we brought her back to England. Sir Thomas recruited her and had us set her up here in London as a teacher before we returned to the continent." He paused, seemingly to consider if he should elaborate. "Samuel has formed an attachment for her and is very protective of Mademoiselle Michaud." Aunt Mary arched her brows, opened her mouth to say something, but Father put up his hand to stop her. "She has her own apartments nearby here where she teaches French to genteel young ladies that are both English and foreign. In fact, the Crown pays for her accommodations, she in turn uses her talents to obtain information from those same young ladies and their mamas. It's amazing what men will say in front of women and children, giving them no credit for retaining let alone understanding what they've heard."

Aunt Mary frowned. "I'm not exactly sure how I feel about all this, Colin. Especially this Mademoiselle Michaud and the influence she could possibly have on Clarissa." She clasped her hands against her chest and continued, "A bawdy house, you say? I suppose you know what you're doing." She relaxed her hands and her face was placid once again. "I must give you credit, though from what I have seen so far your staff are extremely efficient." Aunt Mary selected a scone from the plate and took a small bite. I had finished my second piece of seed cake and was reaching for a third when my mother shook her head at me and nodded at my father, so I passed him the plate, it seemed like me seed cake was one of his favourites.

Father thanked me then addressed Aunt Mary. "I hope that you'll find my staff not only versatile but reliable as well, Aunt Mary."

Aunt Mary settled back into her seat again. "My dear boy, I intend to get to know all of them much better." She looked pointedly at both my parents in turn before saying, "Now to the issue of your neighbours. I saw a young man from Clarissa's window, he seemed uncommonly brown for an Englishman. Is there mixed blood there?"

"Not that I am aware of, Aunt Mary, Mr Markham Clarke and his wife Eugenia along with their daughter Charity and their son Ramsey have all been living in Jamaica for the last twenty some odd years. They've only recently returned to England so that Ramsey could attend Oxford and for Charity to find a husband. I'm told that they had owned a very successful sugar plantation there and raised horses. I'm afraid that is the sum of my knowledge regarding their history. Except that they have been in residence now for about three months. Their daughter Charity unfortunately seems to have formed an attachment for me since the evening I rescued them from a carriage accident. They were returning from the opera when I came upon them." He turned to look at my mother and continued earnestly, "But it was hardly a rescue. I merely offered them my carriage to return home in while I remained with their driver to assist him in untangling theirs from the wagon that had crashed into them. Despite my best efforts to discourage Charity she has remained persistent in her admiration. I can assure you that I have given her no cause to believe that her affection is returned." He clasped my mother's hands. "That is why I look forward to your eventual meeting with Miss Clarke so that she will finally see that my heart is irrevocably yours, my darling."

Irene blushed. "Surely you exaggerate, Colin. It can't be more than a young girl's infatuation but don't worry, my dear, I shall set things to rights in no time at all."

He kissed her hand. "I pray that you're right, my dear. She and her mother have tried everything to ensnare me." He turned back to Aunt Mary, "As for the young man Ramsey, he is I think eighteen years old."

I raised my eyebrows. "Really? I would have thought him much older. Perhaps it's just his tanned skin that makes him look older."

Father nodded. "Maybe he is older, Lissa, he has the kind of face that makes it impossible to judge an age accurately. I've never really conversed with him but by reputation he is a bit of a scallywag. Our gardeners tell me that he has developed a fondness for trying to gain access to our garden even though the gate in the wall does not appear to have a key."

Mother sipped her tea before saying, "Surely there must be a key somewhere?"

Father shook his head "No, my dear, the original owners of our home purchased the adjoining property for their son when he married. They had the garden gate installed to make visiting easier. When their son died in France during the war, his wife returned to her family. There was no gate key that came with either house to my knowledge, they must have been lost or misplaced by the previous owners."

Mother hated sad stories and I could see tears forming in her eyes. Father cleared his throat and changed the subject. "Aunt Mary, could you tell me what you have planned for my ladies? In light of recent events I feel that I'll need to make arrangements for an armed escort wherever you go."

Aunt Mary was affronted by the suggestion considering the look she gave Father. "Good God, Colin, an armed escort! Whatever for? Surely you don't think the man that attacked Samuel would come after innocent women?"

Father grimaced at her words, but he answered in a fashion that would brook no argument. "I'm not about to take chances with any of you." He raised his hands to stop her response. "But neither am I going to keep you prisoners here." He finished with a smile that didn't quite reach his eyes.

Aunt Mary capitulated and finally outlined our agenda of paying calls, going to dressmakers, teas, and soirées. I was exhausted just thinking about it. I was old enough now to accompany them and would have to meet the matrons of society and be assessed by my peers…my mind was numb with the contemplation.

Aunt Mary and Mother continued the conversation but once it veered into talk about fabrics, laces, gloves and boots Father quickly gave his excuses and made his retreat. Before they became too deeply immersed in their discussion I asked if I could go to my room and read and so I was dismissed with a kiss and a wave.

I had started towards my room but on a whim, I changed direction to find Samuel's room instead. Stopping at what I thought was his door I slipped in and found it led into his dressing room. The door adjoining his bedroom was ajar and I heard my father's voice raised in anger. "What were you thinking? What could you have possibly been thinking! No! Don't answer that for heaven sakes, Samuel, she could have been killed!"

Samuel mumbled something, but father shouted over him "GOOD GOD! Do you really believe they were aiming at you and not her?" I couldn't hear Samuel's reply, so I moved and stood as close to the open door as possible while Father continued. "I suppose you could be" He mumbled something then Samuel did as well. After a pause, I heard my father say, "Yes, I've talked to both Michael and Jacob and they agree with you." Again, I could only hear murmuring until father yelled, "NO!"

Then it got quiet when a third person close by my hiding place whispered "Hush."

Father continued, however, "I can't tell them about this, are you insane? No! We will go ahead with our plans. But there will be no riding in the park for anyone until we catch the bastard. I just got them back, Samuel, I will not lose them to that animal. I wish to god that I had never recruited him." Samuel's voice was still muffled but Father answered him, "We have to find him and stop him this time, one way or another. Did you believe him when he told you that your father is involved?"

More whispers then I heard my uncle say, "Are you prepared to kill him this time?"

There was a lengthy pause then a sigh. Finally, my father said, "Yes he's left me no choice."

Suddenly the door in front of me opened wide and Dalton was standing in front of me. "Hello, Miss Turner."

I smiled weakly, responding, "Hello, Dalton, I just thought I'd stop by and see how my uncle was doing. But I seemed to have come in the wrong door."

Over his shoulder I could see my father staring at me in shock. Samuel who looked awful was chuckling in the background and in a dry raspy voice said, "I warned you about her, Colin. Clarissa is not your average sixteen-year-old. She has spent far too much time alone, leaving her nothing to do but listen and watch everything that the rest of us were doing."

Father's face fell into a look of resignation. "Come here, Lissa. Tell me, how much did you hear?" Dalton stood aside as my father came and took my hand, leading me into my uncle's bedroom.

"Nothing, Papa, well, not much actually. Uncle Samuel mumbles too much."

Samuel was lying back against a mountain of pillows with a glass in his hand that I knew held neither small beer nor diluted wine. I was furious I couldn't believe that someone had ignored the doctor's orders! I loved my uncle very much and because I did, I let go of my father's hand and marched over to the bed taking the glass out of his hand. "This is very naughty, Uncle; you know the doctor's orders. NO spirits!" He cringed at my voice which I had raised to make my point.

Father and Dalton both laughed, and I spun on them. "Shame on both of you! Don't you want him to get better?" Both stopped laughing immediately. "Dalton, please remove this." I handed him the glass and the bottle sitting on the bedside table. "I believe cook has some beef tea and custard ready for my uncle, perhaps you could fetch him some." Dalton glanced at my father with the trace of smile still lingering. Father nodded, and he left the room.

I looked back at my uncle who glared at me with something between surprise and suspicion and with an edge to his voice said, "I see that you still eavesdrop whenever the opportunity presents itself."

I knew my face betrayed me. "How did you—what—I never did! I just came through the wrong door." I had been caught out and he knew it. "Oh, bloody hell."

My father coughed like he was trying to keep from laughing as Samuel continued. "I warned you, Colin, the brat has mad skills when it comes to sussing out information. She's one of the best eavesdroppers and observers I've ever witnessed at work."

I was incredulous. "Uncle Samuel, you knew I was there?!"

He was looking very pale, his eyes were dark and listless and when he chuckled, he flinched. He ignored me and continued speaking to my father. "I think you should put Lissa on the payroll. There isn't much that gets past her. I guarantee you that before the month is out she'll know everything there is to know about the staff and half of your neighbours as well. I've learned from experience that it's practically impossible to keep a secret from her." Then he flashed me a warm smile as he slid down on his pillows. "Now, both of you get out before Dalton comes back; I want to be asleep before he tries to feed me that beef tea." He closed his eyes.

Father put his hand on my shoulder and directed me towards the door, but I slipped out of his grip and ran back to my uncle's bedside to kiss him on the cheek. "Get better soon, I love you." Then I whispered in his ear, "I'll bring you an apple tart later."

His right eye popped open, he smiled and whispered back, "Thanks, brat."

# Chapter 7
## *Problems Galore*

Father escorted me out of the room and as we walked towards the stairs he queried, "Apple tart?"

"You heard me?"

He nodded. "It seems that you've inherited more than your eyes and hair colouring from me." He leaned over and whispered, "I'm a consummate eavesdropper myself." Nudging my shoulder, he smiled, and I couldn't help but smile back.

As we reached the hallway the footman Murphy was just closing the front door, he had a smirk on his face and a silver slaver in his hand. However, he immediately composed his face when he saw us and held out the slaver to father who took the cards off it. "Thank you, Murphy." Murphy nodded, putting the slaver down on a table near the green braise door and after a short pause to straighten a mirror, move a vase of flowers and then smoothed down the sleeves of his immaculate jacket departed through the door resplendent in his hunter green and buff uniform.

I was curious about all the staff and Murphy was a real enigma. It was unheard of to call a footman by his surname and he was more familiar with my father than most of the staff, yet he was formal to the extreme with the rest of us. I was beginning to realise that many things were unusual in my father's house, so I turned to him to ask "Father, Murphy's a very quiet man. I didn't hear him utter two words to anyone all the way down from Northumberland."

Father nodded as he read a card while tapping the others on the table. "Yes, he is a quiet, but he's suffered a great deal in life and there is nothing wrong with being quiet. I would hazard he just doesn't have much to say to anyone but he's good man. I know that you're naturally inquisitive but please don't bother him about his past. He lost someone he cherished when he was a younger, it's a very painful topic for him and is one of the reasons that he left Ireland."

"Doesn't he have any family?"

Father brushed my cheek with his fingertips. "He has an older sister still there, but his parents died when he was a young man and his younger sister died tragically. They were caught out on the streets in Dublin when the militia had been called out to break up a protest. He was just a boy then out with his sister, but she panicked when the mob charged down the street toward them. They were separated, and she ran in the wrong direction, fell and was trampled to death. She died before Murphy could reach her and he was almost hauled off by the militia when he was mistaken for one of the instigators. Fortunately, a priest had witnessed what had happened to him and his sister and vouched for him. He still regularly corresponds with his remaining sister in Ireland but has never gone back."

I was keen to know so I whispered, "Is he a rebel?"

Father shook his head. "Not really, Murphy would never take up arms to fight for home rule though he does indulge in writing pamphlets as a form of protest from time to time." My heart went out to Murphy, he was Irish and all alone in the England, it must be terribly lonely for him.

Father stopped tapping the cards in his hand and handed me one. I looked at the card. "Oh no!" I hung my head. "He's coming tomorrow." Father passed me the second card and all I could do was groan. "It appears that Ramsey really couldn't wait to tell his family about us."

Father replied with a chuckle, "So it would seem, Ramsey and Charity along with their mother will be calling tomorrow. Perhaps I'll spend some time with Samuel tomorrow that will give you a chance to get acquainted with our neighbours." I gave him a disparaging look but he merely smirked. "Let's go tell your mother, shall we."

In the study Aunt Mary was seated behind the desk with Mother standing beside her, holding several papers in her hands. They seemed to have just finished with whatever they had been planning so I handed Aunt Mary the cards as Mother looked over her shoulder. They simultaneously groaned, Mother dropped down into a chair and Aunt Mary closed her eyes as she pinched the bridge of her nose. "Well, Irene, there is nothing to be done for it. Beth must use all her considerable skill and make you a vision of loveliness tomorrow."

My father frowned, protesting, "She's always a vision."

Aunt Mary waved at him. "Of course, she is, Colin, but this is female business. We must rise to the occasion!" She looked my mother up and down. "I suppose diamonds would be a bit a much for you, my dear." Then shaking her head said, "Never in the afternoon in any case." She tapped her fingers on the desk as if an idea had struck her. "I have it, Irene, your jade would look wonderful with your pale green silk. It will make your complexion iridescent." Now looking me over from head to toe, "Clarissa, I will speak to Meg, but I think your cream dress with the peach floral print will be a perfect complement to your mother, it will bring out your hair's auburn highlights and she should weave a darker shade of peach ribbon through your hair. Yes, I think that will be perfect." Father was shaking his head and smiling.

My aunt was still deep in thought, but I couldn't curb my curiosity, so I inquired, "What are going to wear, Aunt Mary?"

"I, my dear, will be wearing my diamonds and a lilac gown." Mother arched her brow, but Aunt Mary just waved her hand at her. "I can afford to be eccentric, my dear, but I think the Clarkes will be very impressed with a Dowager Countess in diamonds. I'm hoping for them to be absolutely devastated by all of us. Now I must go to Samuel and bring him his beef tea."

I opened my mouth, but Papa shook his head as he said to her, "I was just with him, Aunt Mary, and he was asleep."

She puckered her lips then nodded. "Still perhaps I should check to see if he is feverish."

Father coughed. "I should have mentioned when we—I left him, he was sleeping soundly without a trace of a fever either. I assure you that Dalton has everything well in hand, but Samuel was very tired after making the effort of talking to me."

Aunt Mary glared at him over her spectacles. "Really, Colin, did you have to question him so soon. He's suffered a terrible trauma."

Father moved to sit beside Mother as he shrugged, "I had to collect information about the attack while it was still fresh in his mind. I've promised Mr Spencer that he could interview him tomorrow, so I suggest we let Samuel get as much rest as possible, Dalton is sitting with him."

Aunt Mary sighed, clasping her hands in her lap. "I suppose you're right, dear boy. Well, in that case I shall write a few letters before we dress for dinner."

I stood to follow her out...after all, I owed my Uncle Samuel an apple tart...so I excused myself by saying, "I'm going to read for a bit before I change my dress AGAIN for dinner. London life is exhausting." Mother and Father both snickered as I left the room and closed the door. I watched Aunt Mary walk down the hall and enter the small writing room, closing the door behind her. Now how was I going to steal a tart and get it upstairs without being caught?

I looked around no one was in the hallway, so I started to walk towards the braised door just as Murphy came through it, holding a small basket. "Here you go, miss, I heard that you'd be needing a few things for Mr Hughes, so I took the liberty of collecting them for you." He handed the basket to me and bowed slightly.

I peered quickly under the cover and there was the apple tart on top. "Thank you, Murphy! Thank you very much. But how did you know?"

"A message from your father, miss, whilst you were studying the cards left by the Clarkes." He kept a straight face, but the corner of his mouth was twitching.

Now I was perplexed. "A message, how on earth did he do that? I didn't see him give you anything."

"No, miss, you wouldn't, there are other ways to pass messages on without writing them down. It's a trick your father learned on the continent. It's very handy, miss." I raised my brow and stared at him thinking back to when I stood here with my father. I couldn't recall him doing anything unusual at the time. Wait the tapping, he had been tapping the other cards on the table while he told me Murphy's story. There was obviously more going on in this household than met the eye. Murphy was smiling kindly at me as if he had heard my thoughts. "Now you best scoot along before someone catches you, some may not approve of us seeing to Mr Hughes's comfort." Then he winked at me.

That made me immediately suspicious of what was in the basket. "Thank you, Murphy." He bowed and went off down the hallway. I climbed the stairs and at the top of them I pulled back the cloth uncovering the contents. Everything looked in order except for a silver flask tucked into the corner of the basket behind a book. I removed it placing it in my pocket. I would smuggle food to Uncle Samuel because Dr Jefferson said he needed to eat but I would not smuggle brandy.

I made my way to Samuel's room and knocked, there was no response, but I entered anyway. He was awake, just lying there staring at the ceiling. He turned his head slightly to look at me with one eye, then he went back to gazing at the ceiling "Do you know, brat, that there isn't a single crack in this ceiling, not one. My room at the Abbey is a masterpiece of cracks. When I inherit, I think I shall have all the ceilings re-plastered. What do you think...should I leave them as is or fix up that gothic mausoleum to be the envy of all England?" He turned his head on his pillow to look at me, he was sweating a bit and his colour was poor. He smiled but there was a glassy look to his eyes which shifted immediately to the basket and he licked his lips. "So, what have you brought me?"

I plunked the basket down beside him on the bed and pulled up a chair. He rummaged through the contents more than once. I knew what he was looking for, but I didn't let on that I had noticed. "Do you really care that much about the Abbey, Uncle? You always call it a mausoleum or a pile of rocks."

He ignored my questions to glare at me after rifling through the basket yet again "Okay, brat, where is it?"

I tried to look surprised. "Where is what?"

Now he looked angry as he held out a shaky hand, palm up. "Don't play games with me, Lissa! Give me my flask!" I moved back in the chair. I had never seen my uncle's anger turned on me. He reached out for my arm, but I withdrew even further. "Give it to me NOW!"

I realised then that my uncle had a problem with strong drink. He scared me, but I tried to be conciliatory. "Dr Jefferson said it would be bad for you and I don't want to see you become ill. You need nourishing food and rest."

"Blast it all to hell and DAMN Dr Matthew Jefferson!" He made a weak grab for my arm again, but I jumped out of my chair, knocking it over in the process to stand just out of his reach. Tears were starting to roll down his cheeks as he yelled yet again. "GIVE ME MY BLOODY FLASK!" He took the basket and flung it across the bed, hitting the wall behind me. I cringed as he screamed out in pain, grabbing his injured shoulder. Fresh blood was seeping through his bandage. Just then the door opened, and Dalton walked in. He quickly surveyed the room and the state of my uncle, "Oh my, what happened here, miss?" Before I could answer he reached back to pull the bell cord twice.

I quickly explained to him what had transpired. All the while Uncle Samuel was yelling obscenities at me. He was thrashing about in bed and had become tangled up in the bed sheets. I was sure that even as weak as he was if he could extricate himself, he would be after me. It was hard for me to hold back my tears.

Samuel stopped yelling finally and moaned. "Get the damn chit out of here, Dalton. Wait! First get my flask, she's hidden it somewhere. Search her!"

Dalton hesitated. "I think you should leave, miss. I'll take care of your uncle."

I heard someone running down the hall and my father came flying into the room followed by my mother. "What in the name of all that is holy is going on in here! Samuel, what in blazes are you screaming about man?!" He came to me, putting a comforting arm around my shoulders.

Mother went to my uncle's bedside. Samuel was trying to get out of bed again. Since she couldn't possibly restrain him, she reached out and slapped him across the face. "Enough, Samuel! Enough, I say!" She had caught his attention and he stopped. Then she gently pushed him back into the pillows. "Look at yourself!" In a softer but firm voice, she said. "This has got to stop!" She looked over her shoulder at Dalton. "Dalton, will you please see Miss Clarissa to her room? Clarissa, stay there, I will come to you directly." She turned back to my uncle, speaking to him in soothing tones like she did whenever I was ill.

I looked up at my father who was staring in disbelief at Samuel. He looked down and nodded at me then at Dalton. Dalton came to my side and I was ushered out the door. As it closed behind me I could hear raised voices again, my father and mother both seemed to be having a go at my uncle as well as each other. I wanted to stay and listen, but Dalton's presence prevented me, so he walked me to my room.

Meg was standing in the doorway wringing her hands. Dalton nodded to her then headed back to my uncle's room. I watched him go until Meg pulled me into my room, closing the door. "Oh, miss, such goings on. When Mr Hughes' bell rang twice, it was like everyone was called to battle. We were all told to report to our duty stations. Beth, Louisa and I had no idea what that meant so we felt that we'd better just come upstairs. If it isn't impertinent of me, can I ask if Mr Hughes is alright? He sounded very fierce when I walked by his door."

I had no words for her and just sat facing the door. I was heartbroken that my uncle had yelled at me and ashamed that I had taken it upon myself to correct his behaviour. I loved him, but I didn't want the drink making him sick. Tears rolled down my cheeks as I stared at the door waiting for my mother.

Meg sat with me trying to take my mind off my uncle, she chatted about the staff downstairs and the neighbours. She was very taken with Jacob even though he was at least ten years older. I tried to listen to her prattle on about how all the staff had colourful histories, that she had met Mr Crenshaw who was my father's man of business and that the cook was his aunt. She told me how modern everything was and how the staff at the Abbey would be envious of her and Beth. Then it dawned on me that at the Abbey I knew, every member of the household, the estate staff, tenants, villagers and all their histories. There was so much I needed to learn before I could really feel at home here.

It wasn't long before Mother walked into my room. She wasted no time putting her hand out palm up and in a flat voice said, "Give it to me, Lissa. I know that you have your uncle's flask."

I stood there wide-eyed with concern. She looked so despondent, so I pulled it out of my pocket handing it to her. She transferred it into her pocket then let out a huge sigh. "Lissa, I'm sorry you had to witness that but there is a good explanation for his behaviour which I think you deserve, however, Samuel must never know that I told you. Do you understand?" I nodded. "Good, now let's sit down and I will tell you why your uncle is so angry."

Meg went towards the door, but my mother stopped her. "Meg, you might as well join us. Lissa will only tell you anyway and the rest of the staff already know. But first if Mr Hughes ever asks either of you to bring him whiskey, brandy or any strong drink, please tell Dalton, Mr Allan, Mr Turner or me. Do not under any circumstances get him what he asks for."

Meg gulped then nodded. "Yes, ma'am."

Mother sighed and pushed a stray lock of hair back behind her ear. "Lissa, I think your father already told you the story of Mademoiselle Michaud, but Meg needs to hear this as well to understand why he is like this." Mother explained to Meg exactly what Father had told me. Then she paused for a bit searching for the right words. "What your father told you about Samuel being protective of Mademoiselle Michaud goes even deeper."

My mouth gaped open as I guessed, "Samuel is in love with her?"

"Yes."

I could feel myself smiling from ear to ear. "That's wonderful!"

Mother ran her hand across her brow. "One would think so, however, this is where it becomes complicated. Samuel would marry her today, but she keeps refusing him. She believes that when she was brutally attacked in Brussels that she was violated and may never be able to conceive a child. She feels that all that and being French would be an impediment to their marrying. Many people still harbour ill feelings towards the French, whether they were victims of the war or not."

I remembered Aunt Mary's lecture about the heir and a spare. "Does it really matter to Samuel if he has a son or not? It's not like there's a title to be inherited. It's just the Abbey, the home farm and the moors."

Mother rubbed her eyes and then tried to smile. "That's not all there is, Lissa. On our mother's side Samuel is the only remaining male heir to Lord Gromley's estates which are considerable. When his Lordship passes away, Samuel will become the Earl. If he married Emilie and they had no children, that would be the end of the family line, everything would revert to the crown on Samuel's death. Father and Lord Gromley have hammered this home since Samuel was even younger than you and he feels strongly about his responsibility but nevertheless his love cannot be denied." She pulled out her handkerchief dabbing at her eyes. "This time in London has been very difficult for him, especially seeing Colin and I together now. While we were separated he derived some consolation from knowing that he and your father were almost equally unhappy. I know that sounds silly but now that it's changed, Samuel feels even more acutely alone."

My uncle had been the only man until now that I knew loved me, I loved him dearly and he deserved to be happy. "If they love each other, there must be something that can be done to help them, Mama."

Mother smiled. "I don't know, dear, I can't help but think that there is more to this then either Samuel or your father is aware of."

Meg and I both stared at her. Then Meg say up straight and spoke up. "You think she's lying about not being able to have children!"

"Possibly."

I was perplexed. "Why would she lie about that?"

Meg pursed her lips and answered, "I think Miss Michaud is ashamed that she's lost her virtue. The only way a penniless girl can expect to make a good match is if her virtue is intact. That's why the likes of me and Beth don't step out with the gents. We haven't found anyone yet that values what we've saved for marriage. Most men these days just want a tumble and then it's a kiss goodbye. I can't imagine what it must be like for a lady with no family or fortune. She's too high bred even for the likes of Mr Allan and you are right, ma'am, her being French and a Catholic would stick in the craw of a lot of folks high or low."

"Surely Father and Samuel would know if she'd been...after all, they rescued her! They must have had a doctor care for her."

Mother shook her head. "Men can be very dense about these things, Lissa. Emilie was never examined by a doctor in Brussels, it was war time and there were none to be had at the time. They merely took her word for it. I'm not even sure if she was violated. Badly beaten yes, but by all accounts, Samuel was able to scare off her attackers before anything worse happened." She sighed heavily. I shook my head in disbelief as Mother continued, "You have to understand, Lissa, that Emilie would have been brought up in a very proper Catholic family, so she would never talk to Samuel or your father about what actually happened. But regardless she sees herself as damaged. The family and our staff know her story, however, it could hurt them both a great deal if they tried to keep it a secret from society and then were found out later."

Life could be so unfair; my circumstances may not have been ideal but at least I grew up knowing that I was protected and not alone. "Mama, there has to be a way to help them. I can't bear to see Uncle Samuel so unhappy! And I can't imagine how awful this must be for Mademoiselle. We have to help them!"

Mother patted my hand. "I'll speak with Aunt Mary first then we'll see what can be done. We must take this slowly, we won't get another chance to make this right." We both nodded. I felt deeply for Uncle Samuel.

I noticed that my mother was fiddling with the flask in her pocket. "Mama, are you going to give Uncle Samuel back his flask?"

She looked down at the hand in her pocket and withdrew it. "No, Lissa. He's been drinking far too much and for some time…if he continues, it could kill him. He needs to stop but it's going to be difficult for him. He will be very sick for a several days, so you must stay away from his room, Lissa. And no visiting without your father or me, this is going to take time."

# Chapter 8
## *The Clarkes*

The Clarkes came to call on us the following day. Mother, Aunt Mary and I were dressed to indicate wealth without being pretentious. My best manners were expected, meaning I had to act like most unmarried young ladies and speak only when spoken to.

Murphy had shown the Clarkes to the large withdrawing room that we rarely used. It was beautiful and decidedly formal which was why our family tended to use the library or small drawing room most days. I couldn't help but smile as I remembered Meg's description of the room as having been dressed up to impress. The walls were a pale green and the carpets and were a floral pattern in varying shades of pale blue, green and cream and the upholstery was all in a pale gold which explained Aunt Mary's choice for our gowns. We looked like we belonged in a cool glade, the room was the perfect backdrop…like a spring garden. Mother absolutely glowed, and Aunt Mary looked every inch the Dowager Countess. I had to admit that even I looked like the daughter of a rich and influential man. My peach gown was simple but elegant with capped sleeves and a modest décolletage. While the deep peach ribbon threaded through my hair enhanced the multiple auburn hews amongst my chestnut locks.

The Clarkes on the other hand may have money but they possessed little taste. Mrs Clarke's choice of a vile puce gown made her complexion look sallow and unhealthy. Her daughter Charity was in a beautiful pink dress that was far too pale washing out her already pale complexion. Plus, it was very girlish and didn't suit her older, more serious countenance. I wondered how Miss Clarke had kept her complexion so pale while living for so many years in Jamaica. Ramsey on the other hand was the epitome of a fashionably dressed young man if a bit over the top for my taste, the only things out of place on him were bleached blond curls and his deeply bronzed skin.

Conversation started out about the weather then moved onto gossip as is customary. I likened this conversation to feeling out your enemy while searching for their weaknesses. Miss Clarke spent a great deal of time looking about the room as if taking an inventory. It was very comical the way her eyes lit up whenever she spied something valuable. Still there was an air of sadness that seemed to cling to her.

Finally, Mrs Clarke who was rather gauche in appearance and manner broached the subject we had been waiting for. "Mrs Turner, I understand from my son that you have just lately come from the country. I do hope that it wasn't your health that was keeping you away."

Mother smiled graciously. "On the contrary, Mrs Clarke, I have always enjoyed exceptional health. It was the nature of my husband's business that kept me away, he travelled a great deal and I didn't want to raise our daughter in London, so I chose to remain in the country." I thought Mrs Clarke would choke on her tea. Miss Clarke looked startled while Ramsey just smiled and tried not to chuckle.

As if it had been perfectly timed, my father came in. The grand entrance could not have been better planned and I swear he'd done everything he could to make the most of his exceptional good looks from his doeskin beeches to his dark blue cut away coat with the high collar, his linen was as white as snow, his cravat expertly tied and his waistcoat the colour of butter with shining silver buttons down to his gleaming Hessians. Even Aunt Mary smirked as he walked into the room. He had obviously dressed to compliment my mother and they made a very attractive couple. Miss Clarke looked as if she might swoon, her eyes having a faraway look as she stared at my father. He took a calculated risk by ignoring our guests and going straight to my mother to kiss her lightly on the lips…in front of guests! The gasp that came from the Clarke ladies could hardly be ignored.

Father turned as if he had just noticed our visitors. "You must excuse me, ladies, even though we've been married for years I find that finally having my beautiful wife with me every day now tends to go to my head and makes me act like a new bridegroom." He nodded to each of the Clarke ladies then sat down close to my mother. She poured him a cup of tea working hard to control a smug smile, adding cream and sugar just as he liked it without asking. Then she took a plate and selected his favourite cakes placing them on the table in front of him. Miss Clarke who was watching her closely looked at them with longing as if she had been denied the sweetest treat. I suppose having been enamoured of my father for many months she now saw all that evaporate before her eyes. Yet she didn't seem to be angry, embarrassed or morose. I could see that she noted all the small touches and smiles between my parents that spoke more than anything as to how close they were.

Ramsey was slouched in his chair having a great deal of difficulty controlling himself. His shoulders were heaving with silent mirth as he watched his sister and mother.

Mrs Clarke finally threw convention to the wind. "Well, this is most unusual. I'm not sure I really understand what you mean, Mr Turner. Are you saying that you have lived apart for sixteen years or more?" She pointed to me like I was a piece of furniture. "And that you had a child. A child that everyone knows Mrs Turner's father has claimed as his own even though she is his late wife's natural child?" Father glared at Mrs Clarke as she continued, "You really want me to believe that you were able to keep this all a secret even from him? That is preposterous, sir! I think it is unkind and unfair of you to have played upon my daughter's affections these past months. This story is ridiculous!"

Ramsey was fidgeting as he closely watched his mother through narrowed eyes as if expecting her to walk out in high dudgeon, or perhaps she had said something she shouldn't have? It was obvious that we were the juiciest piece of gossip to come along in some time and Mrs Clarke seemed determined to squeeze every titbit of information out of us regardless of her daughter's delicate feelings.

It was at this point that Aunt Mary took over the conversation. She gave a wonderful performance playing the affronted dowager perfectly. By the time she had finished telling our family story you would think we were the stuff of a romance novel and fairy tale combined. She had Mrs Clarke apologizing to all of us while Miss Clarke's eyes were full of unshed tears.

Ramsey looked as if his self-control had reached the breaking point when he suddenly got up and walked to the far end of the room where he bent over a display of snuff boxes with his back to us. His shoulders were shaking but his fists were clenched. His mother noticed and at first appeared annoyed then her face melted into a look of admiration. Obviously, she was under the impression that Ramsey was touched by our story. But was he amused or angry he appeared to be trying to keep some strong emotion under control and I was not the only one that had noticed.

My father took pity on him and went to save the oaf. "Mr Clarke, would you care to come out to the stables with me; Clarissa has a beautiful mare that I'm not sure is suited to town life and I'd like your opinion." Ramsey was startled but had the decency to control his expression as he turned to look up at my father who continued, "I understand that your family raised horses when you lived in Jamaica and that you're quite knowledgeable yourself."

Ramsey relaxed as he glanced at his mother who was almost beaming at the notice he was receiving, and he appeared to be grateful for the rescue. "It would be my pleasure, Mr Turner." He turned with my father and walked towards the door, his face composed. Mother covered her mouth and I could barely hold back a snicker.

Father frowned at me. "Clarissa, perhaps you'd like to join us. You've ridden Jewel both in town and the country and know her better than any of the grooms." That was not exactly true since Jacob was the one who had ridden Jewel the most, but I was happy for the chance to escape. We had barely made it out into the garden before Ramsey burst into laughter and I started to chuckle. Father stood there with a smile on his face and waited for us to stop. Finally, we both sobered with Father standing there looking from one to the other. "I take it Mr Clarke that we can count on the ladies in your family to spread the word about my family?"

Ramsey coughed. "Mr Turner, I assure you that the streets will be running with tears of sympathy by the week's end. Please pardon me for asking, but my father will want to know if everything that Lady Alford related is actually true?"

My father patted him on the back. "Yes, as unbelievable as it may seem it's all true."

For a split-second Ramsey did not look pleased but quickly recovered himself. "Then, Mr Turner, may I say that you have an amazing family. Your wife is perfection, your aunt glorious and your daughter is a sweet child." I raised my eyebrow and fisted my hands.

Father caught my gesture out of the corner of his eye. "Ramsey, may I call you Ramsey?" He nodded his permission. "May I give you a piece of advice?" Father paused, and Ramsey nodded again. "If I were you, I'd never call my daughter a child within her hearing again. The women of this family can hold their own against any man, never doubt it. If you make any condescending remarks within their hearing, you will find yourself the recipient of their wrath in the future." Ramsey gave him a sceptical look as my father continued, "Even I have to keep my mind razor sharp around them. However, I can say that there is never a dull moment with them around." He laughed as Ramsey lost his smug expression. I relaxed my fists and flashed him a sweet smile. But when we made eye contact, his eyes were mere slits as if he was sizing me up as an adversary. Father started walking off towards the mews, so I moved to walk with him leaving Ramsey to follow.

We reached the stable yard and Jacob was there in the courtyard grooming Jewel. She was being shown to her best advantage in the afternoon light. I wondered, how did they do that, my father and these people that worked for him...they always seemed to know exactly what he would want and when. I peered out of the corner of my eye at my father as Ramsey examined the horse and Jacob calmly continued his work. Jacob caught my eye and winked like he had read my thoughts, it was a bit disconcerting; I must be giving too much away in my facial expressions. I'd have to watch that in the future. Then I turned my attention back to the conversation taking place with Ramsey.

"Mr Turner, may I ask how you came to know that I raised horses? I don't believe that it ever came up in any conversation during our previous encounters."

Father put his hand on his shoulder. "No, it never did. It was my brother-in-law who remarked that he'd seen you at Tattersall's the last time he was in town, conversing rather knowledgably with one of the grooms there." Ramsey pondered this obviously trying to recall the encounter he'd had with the groom as my father quickly continued. "I am to meet with your father at my club for a private luncheon on Thursday, I hope that you'll join us to discuss a business venture I have in mind."

"I would be delighted to, sir, but if you will pardon me, you never answered my question about how you knew that we raised horses."

Father only smiled evading his question. "I'm sure I heard it from someone I can't rightly remember now, it was probably from a mutual acquaintance. But I understand that you are frequently at Tattersall's when you're not engaged in trying to find a way to get through our garden gate."

They both laughed but I could tell that Ramsey was irritated by my father's evasive answer, yet he had to accept that he wouldn't get anything further in response. He turned his attention to Jacob, asking him questions about Jewel. All the while he continued to walk around and talking to her. Finally, when he was up at her head he closed his eyes and leaned his forehead against her. He remained that way for what seemed like ages, yet Jewel seemed to enjoy the contact. Then he abruptly turned and walked into the stables. Jacob, Father and I all looked at each other shrugged and followed him. We found him standing by a stall looking intently at Baron. He didn't touch Baron, yet the big stallion met his stare and stayed still under this scrutiny. Finally, Ramsey turned to us and sighed. "Regarding Jewel going to Somerset alone, it's already too late, they've formed a bond. To remove one from the other now would make them both very unhappy. Jewel prefers the country, but she will go wherever Baron goes and Baron will go wherever she does. Would Mr Hughes be amenable to sending this fellow to live in the country? I imagine that he would make a remarkable stud." Father shook his head no and I nodded yes. Ramsey looked puzzled watching us both before saying, "Well, it never hurts to ask."

With a look of scepticism on his face my father crossed his arms then asked, "Mr Clarke, do you mean to tell me that these horses have fallen in love? And they told you?"

Ramsey didn't flinch at my father's taunt, instead he looked smug again as he crossed his arms. "Yes, sir, they're mates, you can try to separate them but neither horse will do well without the other."

I looked at the faces of the men around me to see how this decree affected them. Even the stable boys had stopped to listen. Father was sceptical, Jacob was thoughtful, and the two stable boys looked to be caught somewhere between awe and mirth.

I was the one to break the spell. "I think we need to consider what is best for the horses, Papa. Perhaps you could start a stud! Baron and Jewel can be your first pairing." Father looked from me to Ramsey then turned to look at Jacob who quickly excused himself without comment.

Ramsey was smiling. "Mr Turner, that might just be the kind of business proposition that my father would be interested in. We were both saddened to have to sell off in Jamaica and not be able to bring any of our stock with us."

Father gave Ramsey a sideways glance and puckered his lips as if pondering something. "Perhaps we could discuss that with your father when we meet at my club. But for now, I would like to know more about how you ascertained this bond, would you care to join me in my study?" Ramsey agreed readily, it was obvious that neither of them wanted to rejoin the ladies.

Father looked at me with pity in his eyes, so I shrugged. "I know I should go back and join the ladies." I trudged off to rejoin my mother in the drawing room. But before entering I stopped to eavesdrop for a bit. My mother it seemed had taken Charity aside and was giving her a litany on the advantages of taking a young husband and grooming him to her liking rather than setting her cap on someone like my father who was already set in his ways." I almost laughed at the way she made Father sound like an old man though I was sure he would approve if it helped Miss Clarke to focus her attentions elsewhere.

Aunt Mary on the other hand was talking fashion with Mrs Clarke, being subtly manipulative. She expressed the value of having a good seamstress who knew what would suit you. "Those decisions should be left up to them, after all, what are we paying them for." Then all the ladies together started talking about the best haberdashers and milliners in London.

Without warning Lettie came up behind me and whispered, "Your mum and aunt will have your hide if they find you standing out here." I jumped and almost fell against the door. She smiled when I turned to glare at her, "Lady Alford and Mrs Turner have set the Clarkes up right and proper! Now they have them eating out of their hands. I imagine your aunt's seamstress Madame Price will be very busy with dress orders this season, especially once those two spread the word about her. It's very nice of your mum and aunt to do that for madam." I opened my mouth to ask why when she continued, "You know she's got a real talent, but it's hard to keep a business going with only a few repeat clients. This kind of help should set her up right and proper with her own shop."

I smiled at Lettie, "You were eavesdropping too!"

She didn't look the least offended by my accusation, "Yes, miss, you never know when you might hear something useful."

I was intrigued now. "How do you do it? You can't hang about the doorways all the time and not get caught."

"It's easier than you might think, miss, guests treat servants like we're deaf and blind. They'll say all kinds of things in front of us without a second thought like we're part of the furniture. Mr Turner knows the value of that kind of slip up so it's useful to him to have us very attentive to his visitors. Now these two here, they're lost in London society. I imagine that they used to be important people in the Indies. But I can tell that they want something from your parents, but I don't know what that might be…yet. I expect we'll be seeing a great deal of the Clarkes though." I loved that she didn't find my own behaviour scandalous. She nodded towards the door, "I think you'd better join them now, miss." As she walked away I noticed that her brow was furrowed like she was trying to work out a problem.

I opened the door then blushed when all heads turned towards me. Aunt Mary signalled for me to join her. As I walked towards her Mrs Clarke looked me over from head to toe while Mother had returned to her conversation with Charity. Mrs Clarke nodded approvingly as I sat down. "Yes, Lady Alford, I can see what you mean that less is more."

I arched one eyebrow as my aunt as patted my hand. "We were talking about colours, Clarissa. And how people should choose colours that suit them rather than what is popular. Peach for instance has not been fashionable for a few years yet on you it looks superb and not the least gauche. Yet any of the pale pastels favoured by many young ladies currently would be awful on you." I just smiled and nodded since my opinion wasn't needed. My mind drifted off to Lettie and why she had looked puzzled until I heard my aunt mention how much my riding boots and hat favoured the style worn by men. She had not approved at first but after seeing me wear them she thought that they were not only practical but very attractive. Mrs Clarke glanced at me quickly with narrowed eyes like I was a disagreeable bug. Further discussions included the advantages of training your own lady's maid and ended with where to obtain reliable staff; a point on which I almost choked knowing that my father's staff recruitment had been far from conventional. As if it had been timed Ramsey and my father returned and the Clarke ladies prepared to leave. For a first social call, it had gone on for an inordinate amount of time. Perhaps Lettie was correct that there was a deeper reason behind the Clarkes' attempt to make friends with us.

After the goodbyes and promises to return the call, Ramsey exerted his token influence as their chaperon to usher them out the door and into the street to return to their own home.

Mother collapsed back into her chair. "That was exhausting but I think beneficial." She looked at my father. "I'm sorry to say it, darling, but your deficiencies have been laid bare to Miss Hughes. I acquainted her with the pitfalls of falling in love with an older man, so I believe you will no longer be the object of her affections."

My father feigned shock. "Ah yes, the pitfalls of falling in love with an older man. Tell me, were you speaking from experience, my love? Should I be concerned?" He chuckled as he leaned down to kiss her forehead.

She reached out to pull him down beside her. "My experience with you, my dear husband, was enough. After all, I was very young when you swept me off my feet."

He wrapped an arm around her shoulder pulling her close. "There are only four years that separate us that hardly makes me an older man, my dear."

She squeezed his hand. "You goose. I was referring to my younger self as if I had met you as you are now."

He leaned towards her and whispered, "You would still have owned me the moment I saw you." Mother laughed and kissed him on the cheek.

She sat back ensconced in my father's arm. "I have longed for this day when we could sit as a family bantering and teasing each other. I must say that I finally feel free. Tomorrow, however, I must get down to the business of running the household."

My father gave her a horrified look. "What on earth is wrong with the household! Things have always been run to my satisfaction in the past."

Mother gave him a bemused grin. "My dear, that was fine when you were a bachelor. But may I ask you who keeps the accounts, who helps cook decide on the menus? When was the last time that the spare rooms were turned out or the rugs beaten? When was the last time the staff received new livery and uniforms or a raise in wages? What kind of allowance do you have set aside for them for emergencies? Do any of them have family in need that we could help, or do they have health problems we should be aware of." She turned to him. "Colin, running an establishment of this size as well as your property in Somerset requires a firm but compassionate hand. You call them your people and your business associates and from the sounds of it you may put them in jeopardy at times. We have a responsibility to take care of them…that's what builds loyalty."

He looked at her in a dumbfounded. "I go over the accounts with Mr Allan quarterly, but I have no idea who knows about all the rest. I suppose Mr Allan does."

She smiled leaning in to hug him with mischief in her eyes. "Exactly and while Mr Allan does a superb job there are many things that he should not be expected to deal with alone. The same goes for cook. You have no housekeeper for the girls on your staff to go to so who do they turn to when they need help or advice, that burden falls on cook. After all, you can hardly expect them to go to Mr Allan. Therefore, I will need to get to know the staff, their strengths and weakness and where we can help them. You yourself have said that none of them had been in service prior to working with you. I want to know that they fully understand their duties so that I might determine where we can help them the most. You can't just order people about and expect them to know what or how to do things, they need training, darling."

Father looked sceptical then amused. "I take it that things are going to change?"

Mother shook her head. "No, at least not much, we'll work this out together. But I'll need to know what the dual duties are for each of the staff as well. We cannot be clashing in our needs. Mine to run the house and yours to send Lettie off to the East End for information or Murphy off to Ireland."

He smiled a bit and mumbled, "I would never send Murphy off to Ireland." Mother rolled her eyes as he smirked. "You, my darling, are a treasure." But he sounded concerned as he added, "So starting tomorrow we will endeavour to put our house in order? Perhaps I should warn Mr Allan to pass the word along." Mother giggled and shook her head.

It was not exactly a meeting of minds and I'm sure that Father was probably terrified that his carefully constructed household was about to come unravelled. Mother sensed his concern and took his hand. "Colin, I promise that I won't change anything without your approval." He let go of the breath he'd been holding and relaxed.

There was a knock at the door and Mr Allan came in announcing Dr Jefferson. This time the good doctor agreed join us for dinner. Mr Allan poured him a whisky as he settled back while Aunt Mary asked him how Samuel was faring, he crossed his long legs, brushed off some imaginary lint from his breeches, "Tolerable, Lady Alford." He glanced at me and then my father.

"It's alright, Matthew, my daughter was the one that brought the seriousness of Samuel's problem to my attention. If it hadn't been for his reaction to her hiding his flask, I might not have believed my wife that Samuel is fighting a demon." He looked at me with saddened eyes.

Dr Jefferson sucked in his breath. "Very well, Colin, but this is not a new problem for Samuel. His symptoms are much too severe to have been from short-term abuse. Though I'm not surprised that you were unaware of it. He told me that he's hid his abuse from you by splitting his time between his travels abroad with brief periods in London, Cornwall and Northumberland. His man tells me though that he's been aware of it for several years now but was sworn to secrecy. I can treat his physical symptoms, but his abusive drinking seems to be a result of extreme melancholia. We have to get to the root of that problem if we ever expect to help him achieve any kind of recovery."

Father rolled his whisky around in his glass staring down at it. "And if we can't help him?"

Dr Jefferson didn't hesitate "Eventually, he will die."

"How can that be possible?! He eats, he gets exercise!" Father was distraught and angry about his friend.

Dr Jefferson took a deep breath. "I think your wife will tell you that she's been aware for some time that Samuel only eats well in front of Clarissa and that every bite is an effort. Sometimes he even vomits afterwards. He told me that Clarissa notices too much and he wouldn't worry her for anything."

I started to think back to the times that he had stayed at the Abbey. Those visits had never been for long. He had often gone out returning late, missing meals saying that he had eaten in the village. In the morning, I'd often meet him on the stairs as I was coming down he'd tell me that he had already breakfasted and gone for ride so that he was just retiring to his room to take care of his correspondence. As I started to think back the signs were there, including that he often looked ill on those visits and was vexed when questioned about his day.

I was deep in thought when my mother said, "Clarissa, are you alright?"

"What? Oh, I'm sorry I was just thinking about all the times that Uncle Samuel was at the Abbey and what he was like. I did notice things, yet I was too stupid to put it all together."

Dr Jefferson leaned forward, "Clarissa, you weren't stupid, your uncle was just very clever. For example, his morning coffee was apparently more spirits than coffee. Did you ever notice that he never took cream or sugar?" Both mother and I nodded wide-eyed. "Why should that alarm you when many people drink it black? Did he often leave the house on the pretence of business?" Again, we nodded. "His business was at a public house called The Sickle." He turned to my father, "Colin, when you dined together, did he drink to excess then eat very little?"

Father looked ashamed. "Yes, and often he would arrive late saying he'd eaten somewhere else. But he appeared to be sober, Matthew." Then he his shoulders dropped. "But he could drink me under the table on any given night."

Dr Jefferson nodded. "It's one of the cardinal signs of someone who is desperate to hide their problem, they can mimic being unaffected. Yet they suffer terrible side effects when they go without spirits such as shaking hands, headaches, being unable to sleep or eat and poor concentration. In your line of work, Colin, that's a weakness that can be exploited." Father looked ill and I knew intuitively that he wanted to say something to defend Samuel, but he couldn't think of anything.

The doctor continued, "As I said I can treat his symptoms if he's willing to give up the drink completely but there can be no half measures. It must be all, or he will not live long. And we need to find the reason for his melancholia if we're to have a chance of success. He needs to resolve whatever that issue is. Does anyone have any idea what it might be?"

He looked around at us, but no one seemed to be prepared to say anything, so I did. "Mademoiselle Michaud." My father sucked in his breath, Aunt Mary coughed, and Mother gasped.

Dr Jefferson chuckled. "A woman is his problem? You expect me to believe that Samuel Hughes has an issue with a woman? Now I've heard everything." He looked at my father who was at a loss for words. "Colin, he's one of the most inveterate womanizers I have ever met!"

I shook my head. "Oh, no, doctor, he is desperately in love with her and she with him! But she's rejected him because she believes she can't have children. She was brutally attacked in Brussels yet never saw a doctor afterwards, so it might not be true." Then I clamped my hand over my mouth.

I looked at my mother who was ghastly pale and pinching her nose. Father sighed, saying, "That's true, Matthew, there weren't any doctors in Brussels at that point in the war. We just assumed that she would know if she had been misused or not. But the ladies in my family don't believe it since Samuel chased off her attackers. She has repeatedly rejected him thinking that she has lost her virtue and would be an embarrassment to him and shunned by society."

Father looked at me with an expression of concern. "Clarissa, how do you know anything about this?"

I swallowed looking at my feet then at my mother. She looked my father square in the face. "I told her, you men honestly have no sense about these things! She's not a child, Colin, besides she would have eventually heard about it and you know it."

Father was bewildered. "But why would Miss Michaud lie to us?"

She sighed, "Oh, really, Colin, don't be obtuse. No woman is going to discuss anything like that with a man unless he's a doctor." Mother looked right at Dr Jefferson then smiled. "Matthew, is there an examination that you could conduct that would tell us if mademoiselle has been violated or if she can have children?"

He cleared his throat. "As to whether she has been violated, yes an examination would verify that. But as to having children, not precisely. Some women's physicality does present problems in conceiving though an examination would help me to make an educated determination if that should be a concern."

Mother smiled like a Cheshire cat. "Colin, I will need to interview Emilie before I allow her to tutor Clarissa, so I'll invite her to luncheon on Thursday while you're gone to your club. Matthew, do you think you could possibly time your visit to Samuel so that you could join us?"

Father looked aghast. "Irene! You can't possibly involve Matthew in whatever you're scheming."

Aunt Mary slapped her chair for attention. "Good heavens, Colin, I didn't take you for such a prude. This is Samuel we're talking about and I for one support any plan that Irene can come up with as long as I'm included. Well, doctor, can we count on your assistance?"

Dr Jefferson bowed his head in her direction. "With pleasure, Lady Alford, but only if the lady in question is agreeable."

# Chapter 9
## *Mademoiselle and Samuel*

Mother and Father spent the next day interviewing the staff and going over the household accounts. For several days after we made our rounds of our neighbours and my Aunt Mary's friends leaving our cards, attending at homes, visiting dressmakers and plotting how to bring a couple together.

Dr Jefferson came and went every day, he was pleased with how my uncle's wound was healing, however, he was concerned that his overall mood had not improved. During this time Dalton was treated for a head wound by the good doctor after my uncle threw a candle stick at him in a fit of temper, so all breakables and potential weapons were removed from his room or at least placed out of his reach.

I still wasn't allowed to visit him, but I wasn't sure that I wanted to under the circumstances. I could hear him at times during the day and night screaming gibberish followed by sobbing. Strangely enough it was his silent periods that worried me the most.

The weather had eventually turned cold and wet, so I spent a great deal of my time either riding about in the carriage with my mother and aunt or exploring the house. Father was busy with his solicitors or in meetings with Sir Thomas and I sorely missed the freedom of riding, but my father would not budge on his ban of anyone riding in the park. So, I went to the mews every day to visit with Jewel and watch the grooms brush her down after she had returned from her daily exercise.

During this time, I thoroughly inspected the library and found that at least half of the shelves were full of books in other languages. My father found me there one day and asked me to join him in his study. The study had become one of my favourite places, it was there that I felt an overwhelming feeling of love and safety. Something I had never identified with any room in my life. It was so unlike the General's study which had terrified me I had always associated it with discipline. But in this room, I discovered who my father really was; a warm, intelligent and generous man. He had an odd collection of nautical instruments as well as artefacts from his travels on display about the room. Books were strewn about the tables and on his desk both open and closed. The room was full of comfortable chairs and a large settee all of which smelled of paper, leather and my father's fresh woodsy scent. He was watching me intently as I gazed around the room then offered me a chair that I snuggled down into with the book I had brought with me. He begged my indulgence while he finished a letter he'd been writing so I read in silence for a time, the only audible noise was the scratch of his pen. I ignored my book and lost myself in visions of what life must have been like for him on the peninsula or when he was with my mother in Cornwall, it was all so sad and romantic.

When he finally put his pen down, the spell was broken. "Clarissa, I wanted to talk to you about a few things. You've grown up without me in your daily life and even though I know a great deal about you from your mother and uncle, it's not the same as being there with you and talking to you. I don't really know the person you are or who you want to be." I didn't move or blink, I sat there in awe of this man. We were both silent for a brief time, I suppose he was waiting for me to say something, but I was at a loss for words. So, he added, "I know it will take time for us to get to know each other but to start with what do you want out of life. How do you envision your future? I'd like to hear what your ambitions and interests are."

I stared wide-eyed at my father while I contemplated my answer. I wondered what kind of man asks a sixteen-year-old girl what her ambitions and interests are. For what seemed like the first time I took a good look at him and I saw much of myself in him. I also recognized that he was a handsome man, still young and vital just as my mother was still young and beautiful. I wondered what the future held for me in this household. I hadn't seriously considered that I might have brothers and sisters. Yet I wondered what it might be like if I did and what kind of a sister I would be. I warmed to the idea it would be nice to have someone to pass all my sisterly knowledge onto. So, I said quite blatantly, "I would like to be a sister, Papa. I know that you need an heir and a spare so two brothers at least would be nice." I smiled sweetly at him.

He looked shocked at first then he smiled as he passed his hand over his mouth to hide a chuckle. Finally, he burst out laughing. "I do love the way your mind works, Lissa, my sweet. But it's not just up to me, you know. I shall have to consult with your mother. Is there anything else?"

I grinned at him. "Yes, I'd like to work for you. I'm good at observing people and I'm an excellent eavesdropper. Even Uncle Samuel has said that I'm one of the best he's ever seen."

Pursing his lips and leaning forward he whispered, "I'm sure your mother would gut me if I were to involve you in my work. Shall we try for something more appropriate for now?"

My face fell. "But you're not saying never. It's just not right now, correct?"

He looked at me with respect. "That's correct, Lissa, it's a no for now." He hadn't excluded me from ever working for him, so that made me happy. Besides he might find that my skills as a sixteen-year-old could help him at some point then he'd call on me.

He was watching me carefully like he could see my thought processes. "So is there anything else that you'd like to do?"

I tried to think about the skills that would make me valuable to him in the future. "Yes, Papa, I would like to learn your silent code that you used with Murphy, and different languages like you, Uncle Samuel and Mother know. I'd also like to learn mathematics, so I can help my brothers manage their fortunes when I'm a spinster. Oh, and you did promise to teach me to use a pistol. I also think that by improving my sketching I could eventually do detailed portraits and drawings that might be valuable in your investigations."

Smiling at me, he leaned back in his chair to consider what I had asked. "Hmmm… That's quite a list on top of what a lady of good family needs to know." When I gave no response, he continued, "Are you prepared to study hard and pay attention to your tutors?" I nodded with great enthusiasm. "It will require considerable time and effort on your part. However, you must also still learn the skills of a gentlewoman."

My face fell a bit at this pronouncement, yet it would be counterproductive to my goal of working for my father if I was not welcomed into society. I had to be satisfied that he was even considering my requests. I jumped up, threw my arms around him giving him a huge kiss on the cheek.

When he hugged me back, I saw a single tear slide down his cheek. I reached up to wipe it away with my handkerchief then I leaned back so I could look at him. "Are you alright, Papa?"

"Yes, my angel. I'm better than I have been in a very long time. Having you and your mother with me has made me the happiest man in the world." He kissed me on the forehead then leaned back to look at me. He cleared his throat and asked, "I'd really like to know what this nonsense is about you being a spinster?"

I blushed and looked at me feet. "Oh, that. Well, mm."

Mother must have been listening to us since she came through the door and answered for me. "She got that idea when Aunt Mary told her what society dictates as a woman's place in this world."

Father looked perplexed. "Yes, but I don't understand why Clarissa would want to be a spinster?"

Mother rubbed the tip of her nose. "I'm afraid that's because Aunt Mary told her about arranged marriages and that for the most part a woman's place is dictated by a man's expectations, be they husband, father or brother." Then she crossed her arms and glared at my father.

I didn't want them to argue so I interrupted to explain. "Papa, I want to be loved the way you love Mama. I don't want an arranged marriage!"

My father rested his head in his hand, partially covering his face. Then he took a deep breath while looking at my mother with a glimmer of humour. "Irene, I would never ask any of our children to marry without love. I should think you'd know that. They will marry where their hearts lead them." She started to smile. "But I assure you that I will also watch out for their future as well as their happiness and I do my best to prevent a misalliance."

Mother glared at him almost growling, "Colin!"

Father smirked. "Just a minute, my dear, let me rephrase that. You and I will look out for their futures as well as their happiness and do our best to prevent a misalliance. In the end, the decision will always be theirs." She sighed, moving to his side to kiss him on the cheek.

I wasn't so easily convinced. "But isn't it true that anything I bring to a marriage becomes the property of my husband? And if at any time we do not suit each other, I cannot leave him because he will own everything of mine including our children and I will have nothing!"

Father motioned for me to sit with him and mother. "That's true, Lissa, but only if provisions aren't made to safeguard you in advance. Your Grandmother Alice had a very wise father who arranged for her inheritance to go only to her and then to her children; it could not at any time be touched by the General. My property will be your mother's should anything happen to me and I assure you that your mother and I will see to it that all our children will have independent means. As far as any children that you might have… I would hope that you would not choose a husband that you'd want to leave. So, my dear girl, there is an incentive to choose wisely."

He looked pointedly at me. "And if you are thinking that your mother and I were impulsive in marrying, you would be wrong. I have known your mother since she was twelve. Our love grew out of our friendship, we shared many similar interests and that friendship finally became a deep and abiding love."

Mother was smiling as she took his hand to squeeze. "I think what your father is trying to tell you is that desire and love are not the same things. If there is real love, then people will sacrifice anything to be together, including time. Waiting for the right person will not diminish the love. Lust lasts only until the object of your desire has been obtained, it rarely survives the test of time. It's an impatient and greedy emotion, Lissa."

I wasn't exactly sure what they were trying to say. "It sounds terribly complicated to me. How will I ever know the difference?"

Mother caressed my cheek. "Your heart will tell you, my darling."

Father chuckled. "Your mother is right…however, don't forget…" then he leaned over and tapped my head, "to use this as well."

I rolled my eyes, sighing. "I promise I won't forget what you've said and, remember, Uncle Samuel has threatened to take me to the continent until I came to my senses if he disapproved of my choice of a husband." I leaned against my father who put his arm around me and hugged me close.

Suddenly there was yelling come from the hallway, it sounded like my uncle and he was in a rage. The library door burst open, he stumbled in with only a night shirt on, his hair was wild, and his face was ashen with dark shadowed eyes. He was screaming nonsense, as spittle flew from his dry and cracked lips. He fell at my mother's knees taking her hand to his cheek all the while calling her Emilie and begging her to love him. Dalton was hard on his heels and flew into the room, followed closely by Allan. They both pulled up short when they saw us then they looked down at my uncle with pity as he buried his head in my mother's lap and cried.

Mr Allan cleared his throat saying that Lady Alford had sent him to locate Mrs Turner, that she was waiting with their guest. It was unusual for him not to announce who the guest was. Then I remembered it was Thursday and Mademoiselle Michaud was to visit. Father looked down at Samuel with distress etched on his face. He was due to leave shortly to keep a luncheon appointment with Mr Clarke and Ramsey, yet I knew that he wouldn't want to leave us with my uncle in such a state. Dr Jefferson was to dine with us, but he wouldn't be here for another half hour.

Suddenly from the doorway there came a shocked. "*Mon Dieu*, Samuel!" a petite dark-haired lady who I assumed was Mademoiselle Michaud was standing there with her hand to her mouth and her deep blue eyes wide open with tears rolling down her cheeks. She whispered in a hushed voice, "Oh, Samuel, no, no, my love."

Samuel looked up at my mother in confusion then turned his head to look at mademoiselle and quietly said, "Emilie?"

She immediately went to him down on her knees and pulled him into her arms, rocking him back and forth, speaking to him softly in French. The men in the room were looking anywhere except at the two people on the floor. Mother was smiling, and I was dumbfounded. Aunt Mary came in quietly and whispered to my mother, "Dr Jefferson should be here soon, my dear, I suggest that all we leave them alone." She turned to my uncle's valet, "Dalton, if you would be so good as to wait outside the door in case they need anything." Dalton nodded and headed for the door with

Mr Allan behind him. My mother and I trailed behind Aunt Mary when she paused and said over her shoulder, "Colin, I took the liberty of calling for the carriage. If you don't change now, you'll be late for your appointment with the Clarkes."

We all walked out leaving Samuel and Emilie in a pile on the floor, both crying and caressing each other, but I couldn't understand a word they were saying, it was in such disjointed French. Dalton closed the doors behind us and stood at attention to one side. Mother and Aunt Mary stood there looking at the closed doors as Father went up the stairs to change.

Dalton had a smile on his face as he glanced at us. "They'll be fine, ladies, don't you worry. Mr Samuel would never hurt Miss Michaud, never in a million years."

Mother looked sad now. "I know you're right, Dalton, but what good can come from this?"

Aunt Mary firmly interjected, "Actually I think they will be fine, my dear. After you left to find Clarissa, Mademoiselle Michaud arrived and I took advantage of my age and rank to set the young woman straight about a few things regarding my nephew; as well as what she had done to him because of her misplaced nobility. I also informed her that they had our blessings to marry."

My mother hugged Aunt Mary. "So you told her that they have our support and if there are any problems, we'll ride it out together as a family?"

Aunt Mary looked insulted and said with disdain. "I believe that's what I just said, my dear. Emilie has also agreed to let Dr Jefferson examine her. Though I assured her it was not a requirement for her to join our family, but I told her that she needs to know so it won't haunt her and Samuel, and she wants to give him the opportunity to reject her if what she believes is true. The poor thing is very naive and really has no idea if she was violated when she was attacked. She fainted during the beating. She's a remarkable young woman though and I think Emilie will suit Samuel very well."

Mother looked in awe at our aunt, "Is that why you sent me off on that wild goose chase to find Clarissa? You had me running all over the place; telling me you thought you saw her heading for the mews and if not then I should check the garden, the library and then her room!"

Aunt Mary merely nodded. I noticed that Dalton was struggling not to laugh until our aunt gave him a sharp look, "Have I amused you, Dalton?"

He composed his face and answered boldly, "Ma'am, begging your pardon but if you weren't a countess and me a valet, I'd hug you for what you have done for those two." He gestured over his shoulder with his thumb. "I've been telling him and telling him to talk to her, that something was not right about what she thought had happened. I saw her when he brought her home in Brussels. I was the one that undressed her but there wasn't any blood." He blushed before he continued, "I mean, down there where'd you expect it to be if she had been." He was blushing deeply by this point. "Well, you know what I mean."

Aunt Mary blurted out, "Good heavens, Dalton, you mean to tell me that you have seen Mademoiselle Michaud undressed?!"

His eyes got really big, "Oh, no, ma'am, just down to her shift. Our mother died before Lettie had started to bleed and our father was no help, so I've seen a lot and know more than I'd like to."

We all chuckled at his discomfort as he pulled at his neck cloth then he relaxed and laughed too. We all stood there just looking at each other. Murphy walked into the hallway; observing our tabloid, he arched his brows, smiled and disappeared back through the green braise door. Before it had closed completely, I heard cook say, "Well, it's about time!"

Aunt Mary linked her arm with my mother, "Shall we retire to the drawing room until Dr Jefferson arrives? Then we can have luncheon." Mother seemed reluctant to move as she looked at the study door. Our Aunt patted her arm. "I seriously doubt that mademoiselle will be joining us."

Mother still resisted leaving. "Should I have something brought to them?"

Dalton shook his head. "I'll look after them, ma'am. But from the sounds of it, it will be some time before either of them thinks about food."

Mother was flustered searching for something to say, "Dalton, Mr Hughes is hardly dressed to entertain a visitor!"

He smiled and shook his head. "True, ma'am, but I don't think its bothering either of them right now."

I started chewing my lower lip, this conversation was getting uncomfortably close to my memories of Rose and William. I tried to slip away but just as I was heading for the stairs I saw my father coming down dressed to go to his club. He was looking very smart in buff coloured breeches with a cream and silver striped waistcoat, white shirt and cravat, finished off with a dark green superfine coat. With his black boots and gloves he was the picture of a sophisticated and wealthy man. Once again, I realised that he was still young and handsome. Mother stared at him like no one else was alive which made my heart soar. I loved my parents and loved to see them like this. I waited for him at the bottom of the stairs and whispered, "Samuel is still in your study with mademoiselle!"

Father was smiling at my mother as he walked with me back to the study. When he reached out for the door, Mother grabbed his arm back then whispered, "Colin, Don't! Leave them be."

"And why should I, my love? Samuel never gave it a second thought about walking in on us."

She slapped his arm and rolled her eyes. "Really, Colin, we never had the problems to work out that these two have."

"Then may I suggest, darling, that you stop loitering in the hallway so that the staff can get on with their work." He turned her around, so she could see two housemaids who had stopped just outside the braise door, afraid to move.

With her hands clasped to her chest she said, "I'm so sorry, Betty, Grace please go ahead with your work. But leave Mr Turner's study for now, Dalton will let you know when you can go in there." The maids both bobbed and went into the morning room.

Father leaned over and kissed her on the cheek. "Well, darling, I must be off. I hope everything works out as you've planned."

"I've planned nothing, Colin! This has been all been Aunt Mary's doing. I wouldn't be surprised if she had stirred Samuel up in some fashion to get him to come downstairs in the manner that he did."

Dalton suddenly became very interested in the toe of his boot while Aunt Mary started to rearrange the flowers on the hall table. Father chuckled then clearing his throat, "Lissa, I'll expect a full report when I get back," and he headed out the door.

After he left we were still just standing in the hallway until I spoke up. "May I suggest Aunt Mary that you, mother and I adjourn to the withdrawing room and wait for Dr Jefferson? He should be here before too long."

We all took one last glance at the study door and crossed the hall to wait for Dr Jefferson. Aunt Mary took up some needlework. I still had my book with me and once I found my place, started to read again. Mother walked about the room picking up and absently studying various objects. She sat for a bit trying to concentrate on a portfolio of drawings but before too long she would rise again to pace in front of the windows looking out onto the gardens while wringing her hands. "What could they possibly be doing in there?"

Aunt Mary didn't look up from her work. "Don't be obtuse, Irene. What would you and Colin be doing under the same circumstances?"

Mother blushed and bit her lower lip; her only response was "oh". Fortunately, no further response was required.

There was a tentative knock on the door and Dr Jefferson entered. "Excuse me, ladies, for coming in unannounced, one of the maids let me in through the breakfast room." He smoothed back his hair and the straightened his sleeves, not that they needed them. "It's raining devilishly hard out there."

Mother looked puzzled. "What were you doing in the garden, Matthew?"

"Oh, I was in the mews actually, just checking on young Billy Phipps. It seems that Baron stepped on his foot. I met Colin as he was getting into his carriage and he asked me if I would go around and check on him."

Mother looked alarmed. "Is Billy alright?"

Dr Jefferson nodded. "Yes, he's fine, Mrs Turner. His foot is bruised but nothing is broken. Fortunately for him you provide good sturdy boots to all your staff or it would have been a very different story. I've given him and Michael instructions on how to care for his foot. He is currently sitting with it in a cold bath to take down the swelling."

Mr Allan entered, acknowledging Dr Jefferson with a nod then turning to my mother, "Ma'am, luncheon is ready."

"Thank you, Allan, we'll be right there. Would you see to it that places are set for Mademoiselle Michaud and Mr Hughes just in case they wish to join us? Oh, and please ask cook to prepare a posset for young Phipps? He's been injured and needs to rest for a few days."

Mr Allan didn't smile but his eyes twinkled when he responded, "The places are already set, ma'am, and cook has already sent a few extras out for the boy."

"Allan, you're a treasure." His facial expression never changed but his eyes continued to twinkle as he bowed leaving the room.

Aunt Mary put aside her needlework to offer her hand to Dr Jefferson which he kissed and then my mother's. He looked at me and smiled as I hid my hands behind my back. Aunt Mary stood up and walked to the door. "Well, I suggest that we go in. Cook hates to have a meal held back and I seriously doubt that Emilie or Samuel will be joining us. Besides I'm famished." She grinned, taking Dr Jefferson's offered arm as we all proceeded to the dining room.

# Chapter 10
## *Emilie*

Dr Jefferson made a pleasant addition to our threesome. A gentleman by birth with independent means, he had graduated from Cambridge and went onto the University of Padua for further medical training. Now in private practice he was a rare combination of both an accomplished physician and surgeon here in London. He was extensively published for such a young man, focusing on sanitation in the practice of medicine. His ideas were progressive but met considerable resistance from other members of the medical community. He regaled us with how he was keeping detailed records of his patients and the benefits of their strict adherence to his hygienic protocols. He was sure that some diseases amongst the poor could be eradicated just with clean water, proper hygiene and wholesome food. He went on for some length on the subject; mother seemed genuinely interested while Aunt Mary's eyes glazed over. I listened but not intently, instead I watched the rain lash the windows and dance on the windowsill.

We had progressed to the fruit and cheese when the door opened, and Mademoiselle Michaud peeked in, smiling, "May I join you?"

Dr Jefferson stood up to pull out a chair for her as Mother went to ring for meat and salad. "Oh, no, Mrs Turner, please don't bother, your brother and I have already eaten but we would like to join you for tea and biscuits."

Lettie responded to the bell and Mother asked her to bring the tea and cakes now. Then she turned back to mademoiselle and asked cautiously, "Emilie, where is my brother?"

She smiled shyly. "Mr Dalton has gone with him to his room so that he may dress more appropriately. He asked me to wait for him, but I felt that I must first apologize for my unseemly behaviour when I barged into your husband's study uninvited."

Aunt Mary reached out to touch her hand. "Oh my dear, that was entirely my doing, I encouraged you, after all. No harm done." She relaxed back into her chair assessing her through narrowed eyes. "I trust that some things have been worked out between you and Samuel?"

Mademoiselle blushed. "Yes, I believe they have Lady Alford. However, I would prefer to wait for Samuel before saying anything more."

Aunt Mary grinned, showing that she was obviously pleased with the answer. "Well, in that case let me introduce you to our family physician Dr Matthew Jefferson." Matthew bowed in her direction and Aunt Mary added quickly, "He's here to help both you and Samuel."

Emilie blushed and could barely make eye contact with Dr Jefferson. Mother went pale covering her face with one hand and I could barely control my chuckle trying to make it sound like a cough.

Dr Jefferson raised an eyebrow at our reactions as he sat down. Whereupon Samuel entered the room, shaved and dressed but he looked dreadful. It so shocked me that I felt my heart jump. He grimaced at my look as he took the seat next to Emilie, then smiled at me across the table. "Hello, brat. I understand that you've been forbidden to see me, I'm sorry if my current visage upsets you but I really haven't been myself." He took Emilie's hand, kissing it while staring at her, "But I expect to be on the mend very soon." Then he turned back to the table, gazing around at all of us, his brow furrowed as if he were in pain. "However, I will need to enlist everyone's help if I may be so bold to ask." He still looked very ill yet genuinely happy. His eyes glowed and his colour improved slightly whenever he looked at Emilie.

My mother started, "Samuel, it's so—"

Aunt Mary interrupted her while giving her a side glance then she fixed her eyes on Samuel. "Excuse me, Irene, but I have something I'd like to say." Samuel looked like he wanted to melt away, instead he sat up to look right at her. In a stern voice, she said, "Samuel Hughes, you have let this family down in the worst conceivable way." Everyone at the table gasped with shock. Poor Samuel looked like he had been slapped though he didn't cringe or get angry, he just sat there looking at my aunt, not moving a muscle as she continued, "You may feel that you have an excuse since you seem to have inherited your grandfather's addictive behaviour…after all, he was a known drunkard. But I must tell you that I consider it a weakness of character. Even your father is subject to the evils of its addiction, though he had the good sense to hide it better than you. I had hoped that you were made of sterner stuff, so it saddens me to see that I was wrong." Then suddenly her expression softened as she reached out to touch his hand. "But I am more saddened and disappointed in myself. I didn't see that you were suffering, and you obviously didn't feel that you could come to me with your troubles." She did indeed look solemn and concerned. "Samuel, we all need other people to help us make it through this life. There is no shame in asking for help. Nevertheless, you've asked for our help now so perhaps there is still hope." She smiled as he leaned over taking her hand and squeezing it.

Then she sat up straight batting him away. "And you look dreadful! So, the sooner we can start with the good doctor's regime the better." Samuel chuckled before she continued, "Dr Jefferson has kindly offered to treat you and he is going to instruct all of us in how to aid you. I think that Mademoiselle Michaud should be included since it's my understanding that you two have worked out at least some of your problems. I believe that you will be seeing a great deal of each other in the future." She clasped her hands in her lap and looked at them with downcast eyes. "As a first step in welcoming Emilie to the family I want you to know that you will have our full support. And Samuel, I must also beg your forgiveness for not recognizing the depth of your pain. You should never have had to carry this burden alone for so long. I will, we will all endeavour to never fail you again."

Samuel's eyes glistened, and he choked on his words before saying, "It was a hell of my own making, Auntie. If it weren't for the brat here exposing me, I would have eventually killed myself." He looked incredibly sad. Mademoiselle reached out touching his face with her finger tips, he smiled at her as he took her hand and kissed the palm. Then he looked up at Dr Jefferson "Well, Matthew what incredible tortures do you have in store for me? Bleeding, leeches, ice baths?" He tried to laugh but he looked terrified.

Dr Jefferson had been watching him closely, he had his hands clasped lightly in his lap while leaning comfortably back in his chair. "Nothing so extreme, Samuel. In fact, it may sound very simple, but I assure you it won't be easy. I prescribe fresh air, healthy food, and exercise."

Samuel ginned. "That is beyond easy; done, done and done!"

Dr Jefferson shook his head "Not so fast, my friend, first you must give up all spirits and I mean all! You cannot even take small beer."

Samuel's face fell, and his mouth hung open. "Good lord, man, what am I to drink then! My work requires me to socialize with people of many classes. If I'm not able to accept a drink it, will make people suspicious. I won't be able to perform my duties."

Dr Jefferson had his head tilted sideways taking in everything. "That shouldn't be a problem, just let it be known that you have a chronic illness and are under a doctor's care so that spirits are forbidden. You may drink lemonade, fruit punch, milk, even boiled water." He sighed leaning forward, "Samuel, this is most important. You cannot be left alone at social events for some time. You must always have someone with you that understands your needs in such situations. The call of drink will be strong, it will be a lengthy battle, perhaps even lifelong. But it's a battle that I believe you can win with help."

Samuel was shaking his head. "No, no, no, you have no idea what that would mean. It would impede my ability to—people would know that I was, that I'm unable to control myself. It would expose my weakness."

Dr Jefferson laughed. "You mean it would impede your ability to play the bachelor and dandy? Don't you think it's time to give that up and move on, my friend? I've already talked to Colin about this and he agrees, Samuel. It's the natural progression of things for both of you that your public personas change from bachelors to that of an engaged and married man. It will also explain how both of you have resisted the marriage trap for so long that both of you had already committed your affections."

Samuel opened and closed his mouth. Then mademoiselle spoke. "Samuel, you know that I already work for Colin, so we will be able to work together now. You must admit that there are many places that a bachelor cannot go that a married couple can. Besides did you think that as your wife—I would tolerate you acting like a carefree bachelor when we are married?" She arched her brow and pursed her lips. "I will not hide our marriage nor play the role of your mistress."

Samuel looked shocked. "Emilie, I would never! Wait... You'll have me! You'll marry me?"

She laughed, and it sounded like tinkling bells. "Was that not what I said to you in the study?"

Aunt Mary was smiling at my mother. "Irene, it looks like we'll be planning a wedding after all."

Mother's face fell as she looked at Samuel. "What about Father! Samuel, can he put a stop to this, do you need his approval?"

Samuel chuckled. "Not since I was five and twenty. Besides he's cut me off at any rate. He can't interfere even though he may try." Mother relaxed.

93

Samuel lifted Emilie's hand, kissing it again. "Irene, Aunt Mary, I want Emilie to have a beautiful wedding, anything she wants." Emilie looked terrified. He smiled saying, "But it doesn't have to be large, just beautiful and in a church."

Mother was chewing on her lower lip again. "Which church, Samuel?"

He looked at Aunt Mary who was chuckling. "You already knew, didn't you?"

"Oh posh, get on with it." She waved her hand at him.

"Emilie's family for generations have posed as Catholics to survive the Huguenot persecution in France. Even though it appeared to those outside of the family that Emilie was raised as a Catholic, it was tempered by her parents' protestant influence; she is more than willing to be married in the Church of England." He smiled, and it brought back the colour to his face and the light in his eyes. "This calls for a toast!" Everyone's eyes were on him as he went to the door to find Dalton standing there. "Dalton, would you ask Mr Allan for a bottle of champagne." There was a collective gasp, but he looked over his shoulder and smiled. "And a pitcher of lemonade." He walked back to Emilie to bend and kiss her on the lips before taking his seat again.

Mother reached out for Emilie's hand. "I'm so very happy for both of you. But, Emilie, are you sure you want to take him on? I grew up with him and there was never a more difficult child. Believe me he has not improved with age."

Samuel's face at first fell when she had started to speak, then he broke into a huge smile. "My dearest sister, may I remind you that I am four years your senior."

"I'm aware of that, brother dear, but being the eldest did not make you any wiser or more mature."

The conversation then descended into retelling stories from their childhood, their versions often differed considerably but were tremendously funny. Samuel, Emilie and I drank lemonade while the others drank champagne as toasts were made by everyone.

At one point, Dr Jefferson spoke briefly to mademoiselle aside from everyone else. Then he cleared his throat. "I hate to interrupt all of you, but I do have other patients to see. Before I go I need to exam your bandages, Samuel, and talk to your family about the plan to help you recoup your health. Mademoiselle Michaud has also indicated that she would like to consult with me before I leave. Therefore, to expedite things I would like to discuss Samuel's treatment first." Mother asked him to wait while she rang for Dalton and Mr Allan.

When they arrived, Mr Allan stepped out for just a moment to direct one of the maids to see to Dr Jefferson's requests for hot water, soap and towels for both Mr Hughes' room and in a guest room for mademoiselle.

For the next half hour, Dr Jefferson reviewed the restrictions he was placing on my uncle as well as a guide for his diet and exercise. He wanted all the staff and family to be aware of them so that my uncle wouldn't be able to fool any of us. Mr Allan and Dalton agreed they would speak to the other staff and that Mr Allan was to immediately lock up all the spirits in the house when we finished.

Dr Jefferson turned to me. "Miss Turner, I have a special assignment for you. I'm told that you will know who may have sympathy for your uncle and indulge him. I am putting you in charge of sussing out those miscreants then telling your father or mother, so their duties can be adjusted to keep them away from your uncle." I was happy to have a role except that I didn't much like the idea of being a snitch. But I promised that I would keep a close eye on him and anyone who was likely to give into his pleas for spirits.

Mother suddenly burst into tears, everyone was surprised except for me. Samuel looked ashamed and the others were just befuddled so I explained, "Mama tends to cry whenever she's happy or sad, this time I think she's happy." I looked at her closely and nodded. "See, she's smiling so she is definitely happy."

Father walked in just them greeting Dr Jefferson while eyeing Samuel and Emilie. He saw the tears still in my mother's eyes and that Dalton and Mr Allan were sitting at the table with us. Then he saw the bottle of champagne and glared at Samuel's glass. I picked it up and handed it to him. "It's only lemonade, Papa." He took the glass and drank off the remainder, choking as he swallowed. When he caught his breath, he smiled at my uncle exclaiming, "Well done, old chap!"

Aunt Mary moved to offer him champagne, but he declined with a shake of his head then looked at me, "So, Lissa, what's been happening? If I recall I left you in charge?"

I was surprised that he asked me instead of Mama, so I proceeded to tell him, "The short of it is that mademoiselle and Uncle Samuel are contemplating marriage and Dr Jefferson and all of us are going to help Uncle Samuel conquer his addiction to strong drink."

Father sat down beside Mother and with a wry grin said, "All this has happened in just the few hours since I left, how that is even possible?"

Samuel took Emilie's hand. "It's all about communication, Colin. I seem to have trouble expressing myself adequately around the only woman that I have ever loved. As for the doctor's plan, I know that I'm going to need everyone's help, I'm not strong enough to do this alone nor would I like to try." He took a deep breath then sighed. "I would also like to apologize now for being so difficult; even though I will probably continue to be difficult if not impossible for some time." He looked at me and winked. "So, brat, I will rely on you to tell me when I am. You're the only one I can count to tell me the truth, so you have my permission to put me in my place."

I looked at him with pride. "Agreed, Uncle."

He laughed. "Lissa, I think I might have just insulted everyone in the room."

I giggled. "It wasn't intentional. Besides everyone will try to be nice to you because you'll be struggling, so they might not tell you that you're being unbearable." I looked about the room then back at him. "But that isn't going to help you if you try to play on their feelings. You should be treated just as I am, if I do something wrong you and Mama would never let me get away with it, so I won't let you get away with anything either, Uncle Samuel." I smiled at my mother as she looked at me with pride.

Samuel came around to my chair then went down on his knees and hugged me, his whole body was shaking. "Lissa, I am counting on you to help me. I can only pray that I am worthy of your assistance and love." He kissed me on both cheeks then got up unsteadily as he leaned on my chair. "Well, Matthew, let's get the examinations over with, so you can be on your way to see to your other patients." He assisted Emilie out of her chair and they both left to go upstairs. I noticed as he tucked Emilie's arm around his that his hand was trembling, and he seemed to be none too steady on his feet and leaning rather heavily on Emilie. Aunt Mary and Mother followed them with Dr Jefferson, Dalton and Mr Allan behind.

Father looked at me. "Well, Lissa, perhaps you'd like to join me in the study and you can tell me everything that's happened while I was out in detail."

After we talked, I spent a quiet hour in his study reading as he worked at his desk. When he finally put down his pen, he stretched, got up and went to the window. I could see that it was still raining when he opened the curtains but not as hard as before. He stood there with his back to me, leaning his hands on the sill, apparently deep in thought. It startled me when he finally said, "Typical London weather, rain and more rain."

I looked at his back as I answered, "I thought that was typical for England, Papa, not just London."

He sighed. "You're right, my sweet. But there are times when I miss the continent. I remember the lovely sun and heat of Spain." He rubbed his eyes. "But I also remember how blasted uncomfortable it was during those days as well." Turning away from the window, he walked to the credenza. "Lissa, where's my whisky?"

"Sorry, Papa, Mr Allan must have already locked everything up. You'll have to ring for it from now on." I scrunched up my face waiting for him to get angry.

He just shrugged, "I suppose it can't be helped. I'll adjust eventually." He smiled as he rang the bell. Murphy answered the summons and went to fetch my father a whisky. "Lissa, I've been thinking about what Ramsey said about Baron and Jewel, we should consult with your uncle about what should be done."

My head popped up. "Are you considering sending them both to Somerset?"

He scratched his head, playing with a book on his desk. Murphy returned with his whisky on a tray, After taking a sip, he thanked Murphy as he withdrew.

He moved back to the window. "I talked at great length with the Clarkes today, both seem eager to re-establish themselves as horse breeders, but Mr Clarke would like to have a look at Baron and Jewel himself. I've put him off though until I could talk to Samuel about it. I'm just not sure if this is the right time or that the Clarkes are the right people."

He took another sip of whisky then stared into his glass and continued, "Setting up a stud may present us with an answer to a dilemma I have regarding our work. I've wanted to establish a legitimate and permanent presence somewhere near the coast closer to Cornwall. However, I'm undecided as to how much I should involve the Clarkes or who else would be able or willing to handle the responsibility?"

He ran a hand through his hair. "I'm sorry, this must sound confusing to you. I tend to think aloud sometimes. Yet this could be a perfect solution for Samuel and Emilie for a time. I must remain in London and available to Sir Thomas and Samuel right now is the only one that I would trust down there." He put his glass down turning his back to the window. "I need to think on it more, then talk to Samuel and Sir Thomas." He sighed and walked back to his desk fiddling with a book that was lying open. He picked up his glass, tossed back the whisky in one gulp and grimaced. "I think I'll go and see what the blazes is going on upstairs. Surely we should have heard something by now." He started for the door just as Mother walked in, looking very worried.

Her brow was furrowed, and she was wringing her hands. Father sat down hard in the chair behind his desk as Mother came and sat beside me. He reached over his desk. "Irene, are you alright? Is there a problem?"

She nodded. "Yes and no. About Emilie, it's just as we suspected, she was not violated and as far as Matthew can tell there is no reason why she can't have children."

Father started to smile. "Well, that's good news. Samuel must be very happy!"

Mother cleared her throat, but her eyes gleamed with unshed tears. "Samuel doesn't know yet. While Matthew was examining Emilie, he had a seizure." Father groaned and put his head in his hands as she continued, "He's awake now but very weak and disoriented." Then she burst into tears and between sobs said, "Emilie and Matthew are with him right now."

Father rose and headed for the door, but Mother reached out, touching his hand. "No, Colin! Matthew said he needs rest and quiet right now."

Tears were running down my cheeks. I wiped them away with my hand and asked, "Why, I mean what's wrong with him?"

Mother took my hand she had managed to control her sobbing though the tears were still streaming down her face. "Dr Jefferson believes it's a symptom of his body clearing out the toxins that are making him so ill. But he's still weak from the gunshot wound and coupled with the stress and excitement of all that has happened lately he feels it was just too much for him to handle."

Father ran his hands down his face. "Is he going to live?"

Mother frowned. "Matthew said it's just a temporary setback and that it probably won't happen again as he gets stronger."

She wiped the tears from her eyes and smoothed her skirts with her head bowed. "I've asked Emilie to come and live with us but she's adamant that you need her to stay where she is at least until they marry."

Father put his hand under her chin raising her head up and she continued, "I know it will look better if Samuel makes the appearance of courting her for a time. But I can't help feeling that Samuel would do better with her here." He held her hands and pulled her to her feet and into a hug. "We can have the wedding in three months, that should be enough time to satisfy convention, especially after Aunt Mary spreads the word of how they met."

Father smiled as he caressed her cheek. "And what story will she be telling people?"

Mother smirked, "The truth more or less…such as they became acquainted on the continent and fell in love. Then they were separated for a time and were reunited here in London, rekindling their romance. Does that meet with your approval, Colin?"

Father let go of her stepping back to look into her eyes. "Whatever you think is best for them, my love. In the meantime, I'll talk to Emilie about staying here. Let me think on how it can be done without causing a scandal."

He paused and took a deep breath before saying, "I might as well tell you that I met with Mr Spencer today after dining with the Clarkes. He's talked to all the witnesses in the park, Lissa seems to be the only one that saw anything clearly, so he has very little to go on. He's turned to some of his less savoury sources for information and from what he's been able to glean a former and rather unpleasant colleague of mine might be involved. The man in question is currently in London attached to a French diplomatic delegation so I have to tread carefully…but personally there's no love lost between us."

Father was not happy about any of this; he was clenching and unclenching his fists. He returned to his desk tapping his fingers on its surface and appeared deep in thought. No one spoke for a time my mother was still standing when he said, "Lissa, stay here with your mother. I must see Samuel."

Mother took my hand pulling me to my feet. "No, Colin, we'll all go. I can't have you upsetting him and besides Lissa has as much right as anyone to know what's going on. And she should see that Samuel is alright."

Father touched his pursed lips with one finger then sighed. "Alright, come then, let's go see Samuel."

Dalton was just backing out of Samuel's room and closing the door as we arrived. He was oblivious to our presence until Father cleared his throat as a warning that we were behind him. He jumped slightly. "Oh, sir, sorry sir!"

Father made to move past him when Dalton said, "The doctor just left so I wouldn't go in there right now if I were you. Mr Hughes and mademoiselle are talking about what Dr Jefferson had to say about her. She had to threaten to break their engagement if he didn't rest. She definitely seems to have the measure of him so he's resting quiet now."

"Thank you, Dalton, but this can't wait. Randal Browne is back in England. I'm sure you remember him." Dalton's expression didn't change so he obviously wasn't surprised. Father waited before continuing, "This doesn't seem to be news to you, would you care to explain?"

"Ah, no, sir, I think that would be better coming from Mr Hughes. But can it wait, sir? The doctor says that Mr Hughes' health is delicate."

"I promise I'll try not to upset him." He reached out and patted Dalton on the shoulder, effectively moving him away from the door and at the same time he reached around him to knock on the door.

Emilie answered, she took one look at my father's face and stood aside, "Perhaps I should leave." Everyone but me said "No!" She nodded, walking back to stand by the bed and taking Samuel's hand.

Father made sure that Mother was seated then asked Emilie to take a seat while I stood at the foot of my uncle's bed holding onto the bed post. Father walked back and forth between the hearth and my mother's chair with his hands behind his back.

My uncle followed him with his eyes. "For god's sake, stop pacing, you're making me sick. Just come out with it, Colin!"

Father stopped to cross his arms. "Did you know that Randal Browne was back in England?"

Samuel went pale as he rubbed his hand across his face. "Yes."

Father exploded, "And when were you planning on telling me! Have you talked to him?"

Samuel hoisted himself up on his pillows with Emilie's help. "You weren't available for consultation! If you care to remember you were riding around the southern coast gathering intelligence while I was preparing to bring your family to London!" Emilie patted his hand and shot my father a stern look.

Father ignored her. "That's not an answer, Samuel! You've not said a word about seeing him since I reached London."

Samuel was furious, his cheeks were cherry red now and his eyes blazed. I'd seen that look from the General and remembered it all too well. I was holding onto the bed post so tightly that my knuckles had turned white.

When Uncle Samuel responded, it was in a cutting and cold voice, "Well, let me see, Colin, if memory serves me right. When you met us on the road you were anxious to connect with your daughter and then bed your wife; then you left before dawn without a word! And once you were in London? Let me see, oh yes I was bloody well shot!" he was almost screaming now. "And I've been restricted to bed while trying not to bleed to death. What else? Oh yes, I've been trying to get rid of the bloody toxins caused by alcohol poisoning or addiction, whatever you damn well want to call it. So old man I'm so sorry that I've inconvenienced you and you feel out of the loop." He paused to settled back on his pillows. "Randal Brown is a lying blackguard! I warned you about him in Belgium. But he was a quick fix to a complicated problem that you and Sir Thomas had. I told you then that he would come back, and he did!" He ran a shaking hand through his hair and exhaled. "He sent word to meet him at the Sickle where he spent the entire time ranting at me about us staying out of his business and if we didn't he'd make us pay. I hadn't a clue what he was talking about, so I sent him off with a flea in his ear. If the old man finds out that he's still alive there will be hell to pay for both of us. This isn't just your bloody problem anymore, it's ours!"

Samuel slumped, he was exhausted now. Father just stood there looking at him tight lipped and white with fury. He relaxed a bit to rub a finger across his forehead then his shoulders slumped forward and in a quiet voice said, "I know, my friend, I shouldn't have let him go. He should have been just another causality of the war." Father was gritting his teeth. "So why is he here now? It's been years and Louisa's happy with Lady Alford. We both promised him to take care of her and we did. What other business could he mean?"

My uncle sighed with weariness. "Colin, it was never about Louisa. He used her as a pawn to spy for him. I've been wondering since his visit if he's involved with what's going on along the coast, why else would he threaten us? You've crossed him once by putting Louisa with your aunt and not taking her as your mistress. Can we even trust that he hasn't been in contact with her?"

I watched mother's expression change from a look of questioning to one of hurt. Father put out his hand to her and she turned to my uncle who was chuckling. "Irene, my dear sweet sister, Colin never had eyes for anyone but you. He never touched Louisa even in the line of duty, neither of us did. She was too enamoured of Randall and too wary and mistrustful of us." Then he chuckled again. "She was an exceptionally talented thief but a very stupid spy. I can assure you Colin has never been unfaithful to you." He sighed, squeezing Emilie's hand. "You were twelve and he was just sixteen when he lost his heart to you and it's been yours to command ever since."

My father held out his hand to my mother once again and this time she took them both, rising from her chair and going into his arms. Emilie was watching them with warmth then glanced back at Samuel who raised her hand to his lips and kissed it. Suddenly I felt uncomfortable and started to think about making my escape. My uncle noted my furtive glances at the door, so he sat up and pulled me from the end of his bed into a one arm bear hug then fell back exhausted with his eyes closed.

Father looked at him over my mother's shoulder. Emilie was leaning over him in concern but when he opened his eyes, grinning at her, he reached up to wrap his hand behind her neck pulling her down for a kiss. I closed my eyes at this point and crossed my arms.

I was finally rescued when Dalton knocked on the door. My father and mother broke apart quickly just as he came in. "Mr Turner, excuse me, sir, but Mr Spencer and an associate are here to see you. Mr Allan has shown them into the library since he felt that most of you would want to sit in on the meeting, it seemed the most appropriate choice; particularly considering the person he brought with him." Dalton said with the degree of distaste that he usually reserved for the stable muck on my uncle's boots.

"Thank you, Dalton. Would you let Lady Alford know that Mr Spencer is here?"

"She is already with him, sir." Then he withdrew.

Emilie plumped up Samuel's pillows and straightened his sheets. "You need to get some rest."

Samuel shifted his legs as if to get out of bed. "Oh no, I'm coming with you. I was the one who was shot so I want to hear what this Bow Street Runner has come up with."

Emilie pushed his legs out of the way and sat down on the bed. "You are going to rest and I'm going stay with you. I'll read you to sleep. Miss Turner, please pass me a book from the case?" I was puzzled at first as to whom she was addressing then I realised it was me. "I'm afraid that if I get up, your uncle will jump out of bed and I will not be able to restrain him."

I selected one from the bookcase and as I passed it to her, she looked at the title then clapped her hand over her mouth before showing it to my uncle. The look on his face was priceless, it was a treatise on the Jacobite rebellions, he groaned and closed his eyes. "Go with them, Emilie, and be my eyes and ears. After seeing that title, I think I'm asleep already." And he pretended to snore. We all laughed and left my uncle in Dalton's capable hands.

# Chapter 11
## *Not Quite a Gentleman?*

We entered the library to find Mr Spencer perusing the titles of my father's books while his colleague was sat by the fire. With the curtains nearest him drawn on an already a dull day, Mr Spencer's colleague sat in shadow, even though the fire cast light on him it did not illuminate the shadow across his countenance. He was the antithesis to Mr, Spencer appearing to be a small, wiry fellow that reminded me of a cornered rat with furtive eyes scanning the room while the rest of his body remained totally still. At first glance, he didn't appear to be much taller than me, but he was almost folded in on himself, so it was difficult to tell. His baggy clothes made him appear rail thin, but you could almost feel the coiled power within him. His eyes kept darting around the room like he was looking for a bolt hole and in a strange contrast his hands were very still and folded in his lap. He had long fingers with short nails that were immaculately clean unlike the rest of his person. He paid no attention to any one while he continued to look about him without turning his head. To my disgust he carried with him the faint odour of rotting vegetables and worse on his worn filthy clothes. His shoes were being held together with odd bits of mismatched leather and rags. But his eyes showed no signs of actual fear, rather they were full of curiosity and intelligence. He finally settled upon studying one subject, me; he looked directly at me and after a bit he tipped his head to the side, nodded then smiled. I admit his smile was at first unnerving until it widened then I saw that he possessed all his teeth and that they were white which was unusual for someone of his class. Then he spoke to me, "Hello, there. You must be the daughter that I've heard so much about. You impressed me with how you kept your head when your uncle was shot in the park, I admire that." His voice was cultured and educated; it held no hint of being an indigent from the East end or of the lower classes. I was astonished, my eyes wide and my mouth opened slightly. Noticing my reaction, "Surprised you, did I? Sorry for that, sometimes gentlemen fall, and I've fallen further than most; at least for today at any rate." He chuckled then shifted his gazed to my father.

Father had been watching him closely and Mr Spencer was watching him watch his colleague. "You know each other, Turner?" Father merely nodded. "Then perhaps I should make the introductions to the ladies. Lady Alford, Mrs Turner, Miss Turner and," he looked at Emilie, "I'm sorry, miss, but I don't believe that I've had the pleasure of making your acquaintance?"

The rat man stood up, I was shocked to find that his height was equal to my father's and that he looked remarkable lean and fit. Now that his face was in full light he had lost his rat-like countenance and was overall rather handsome despite the dirt that covered him and that his hair was a tad too long. "That would be

Mademoiselle Michaud if I could be so bold." Then he bowed, "Good day to you ladies, my name is Miles Johnson. Please excuse me if I don't make the customary obeisance; but when Mr Spencer found me, he wouldn't allow me the time to attend to my toilet to rid myself of these clothes and this noisome odour." He sniffed his clothes and grimaced.

Father stepped forward and shook his hand anyway. "Miles, what a surprise! I didn't know that you were still in London. I thought you had taken yourself off to Edinburgh. Hadn't London gotten a bit too hot for you?"

The man my father called Miles shrugged. "Edinburgh is a wee bit to provincial for my tastes, Colin, hence why I am still here. So, to stay out of the gaol I've been taking the more delicate assignments from this wastrel Spencer who seems to delight in sending me into the most odious places."

Mr Spencer smiled and laughed. "Why am I not surprised that you know his Lordship."

Mr Johnson grimaced. "Arthur, old man, please cease calling me his Lordship. My brother would be most distressed to hear you. Even though I am the eldest son and acknowledged by my father I do not merit a title having been born on the wrong side of the blanket," he finished with a sad smile. He had a very mobile face; in fact, he did not appear at all like the man who had sat before the hearth in the shadows with the light playing across his face.

Everyone was still standing so my father gestured that we should take our seats.

Mr Spencer remained standing until Aunt Mary took a seat then he joined her. "I look forward to hearing the story of how you know Wicker, it must be very interesting."

Mr Johnson sat up and raised one finger. "Arthur, do you mind using my given name in front of the ladies, Wicker sounds so plebeian."

Mr Spencer just shook his head chuckling, "Mr Johnson it seems just happened to be in the park the day Mr Hughes was shot. He and his companion decided to rest in the shade. And thus had a very good view of a gentleman near where the shot came from."

Father was watching Mr Johnson intently. Aunt Mary looked him up and down then shook her head, "Miles! For heaven sakes, can't you desist from this rakish behaviour! Good lord, you come from a perfectly respectable family. Your father and his wife accepted you as family and, yet you still try to make yourself look dishonourable. I seriously doubt that you intended go through with whatever you had in mind for, was it Miss Carter this time?" Mr Johnson looked amused but kept silent. "You forget, young man. that I knew your mother! She was a fine gentlewoman and if she were here now, she'd box your ears for that stunt. And don't give me any grief about your birth, I know for a fact that your father would rather you were his heir than Edward. Why do you try the man so?"

Mr Johnson's countenance had darkened, and he looked hurt. "But I'm not his heir, am I, ma'am. And once my dear papa is gone I will be out on the street as the bastard." He was angry, yet he controlled his voice so that it sounded almost conversational but dangerous. "I know that Lady Jane accepts me, but Edward isn't her son either and I'm deeply concerned for what will happen to her when my father is gone. I'm sure that Edward will waste no time in ridding himself of our stepmother and half siblings, let alone me. Pray Lady Alford who is going to care for them then and me without a pot of my own to piss in?"

He coloured slightly when Aunt Mary slapped the arm of her chair. "Miles, really!"

The tension was obvious in his clenched fists, yet his tone was soft when he replied, "Sorry, ma'am, I shouldn't be taking my ill temper out on you, please excuse my vulgar language. I know what you did for my mother by being her friend and I appreciate it more than I can ever say. I can only hope that Lady Jane's friends will rally around her when the time comes and not leave her to oblivion. Her parents are dead, and her brother is as useless and selfish as mine."

He ran his hand over the back of his neck then looked at my father. "Excuse me, Turner, I'm not here to lament about my family." He took a deep breath and his face relaxed back into a mask of laconic amusement. "So as for the shooting; I couldn't believe my eyes when I saw the two men riding away from where the shot came from. One of them was Randal Browne, I haven't seen him since I was on the continent after university. I was surprised to see him alive since I had heard that you had the job of putting that dog down during the war." It was interesting watching Mr Johnson, he was bemused but attentive and, in the light, he looked and sounded much younger than my parents.

Father rubbed his hand over his chin. Mr Spencer was watching him closely through narrowed eyes and Mother was biting her lower lip. It was Mr Spencer who finally broke the silence. "Excuse me, Turner, I feel like I've come into the middle of a story and if I am going to solve this case, I'd like to know what's going on." He pointedly looked around the room at the ladies. "But this may not be something that you want to discuss in front of your family."

My father looked at all the ladies then sighed. "Spencer, you may have noticed that I treat my family in a rather unconventional manner. I have lost too many years with them to exclude them now. In fact, they all work with me in a sense, since being a married man and a father now affords me avenues of investigation previously closed to me." Mr Spencer looked askance as he continued, "Just as you make use of the resources at your disposal, so do I. But I trust mine without reservation. Can you say the same?"

Mr Spencer nodded. "I see your point, sir; ladies, I beg your pardon. So, Mr Turner, would you care to enlighten me as to who this Randal Browne is and why he might have shot your brother-in-law?"

Mr Johnson sat back in his chair, crossed his legs and grinned mischievously. "Yes, Colin, I'd like to hear that explanation myself."

Father slumped down in his chair. "This could take some time; may I interest anyone in some refreshment?"

Mother rose and pulled the bell and Mr Allan answered promptly, "Allan, could you bring us tea and I think a decanter of Mr Turner's best whisky."

Mr Johnson cleared his throat. "Ah, ma'am, will there be cakes? Old Arthur here took me up before I'd eaten and it's getting rather late."

"Allan."

"I'll see to it, ma'am, and I suppose there will two more for supper?"

Mother looked at Father, Mr Johnson was all smiles as Mother answered, "Thank you, Allan, yes, there will be two more."

Father coughed to get Mr Allan's attention. "Allan, would you please find some suitable clothes for Mr Johnson. And have the china room prepared, he will be staying with us for the foreseeable future."

Mr Johnson stretched out and crossed his ankles. "Colin, you're a most generous host but I have my own rooms and clothes or at least I did. I should be able to reclaim them again shortly."

My father glared at him. "Miles, you're a trial to anyone's patience that has spent more than hour in your company. I'm not letting you out of my sight until this is settled. But if you don't behave while under my roof, I will ask Mr Spencer to entertain you in the gaol."

Once the tea arrived, Father started telling us about Randall Browne. He poured out whisky for the men as he talked and while Mr Johnson did his best to decimate the cake trays. "Randal Browne is a younger son of Lord Burley. He is well-educated and has been offered every advantage in life. But as a younger son he was expected to either join the army or the church. He chose the army as the lesser of two evils. Greed, however, has been the only thing that has ever motivated him."

He took a gulp of his whisky and grimaced as he swallowed. "I was dismayed when I found out that he was on the same ship with me bound for the continent. He had been a year behind us at school and a thorn in my side the entire time. Unlike my father his had willingly purchased him a commission in the Dragoons, hoping I suppose that it would improve Browne who had always been a useless sod and an embarrassment to his family. He soon found that army life didn't suit him. It was while we were in Brussels that Sir Thomas became interested in him for his ability to, shall we say to acquire things that others could not."

Mr Johnson laughed. "Oh, Colin, call it what it was—smuggling, black market, racketeering! Browne could procure or steal goods of any kind for the right price all the while he neglected his army duties. From what I've heard the man was a coward except if there was a profit to be made, then he'd take just about any risk without any concern for his or anyone else's personal safety."

Father looked cross and glared at Mr Johnson. "Miles, are you telling this story, or am I?"

Mr Johnson took a strawberry tart and held it poised to eat but instead he responded, "Oh, excuse me, old man! You just seemed to want to dither about the details. It's the details that make your friend Browne so interesting…and dangerous. Otherwise he just seems like any other wastrel of the upper classes; spending money, wasting time and doing nothing productive. When you come to think of it there isn't a more perfect persona for him to hide behind in his line of work."

Father interrupted him, "I can't see him stooping to murder!"

Mr Johnson became very serious. "Can't you, Colin? I can."

Mr Spencer then interjected. "Mr Turner, can we get back to your story? The answer may be as Wicker has said in the details."

Father rubbed the side of his face and sighed. "Yes, the details, you're right of course. Randall Browne is just as Miles has described him. My patron and superior Sir Thomas Wiseman was the person in charge of gathering intelligence from the disenfranchised French nobility, the upper-class Belgians and the visiting nobility of Spain. To do that he needed to entertain in a fashion that Brussels could no longer support. Yet Browne seemed to be able to get any luxury item you could think of, even things that had been in short supply for years and he seemed to know everyone that Sir Thomas wished to entertain. He also had a talent for charming information out of people and at the time, Sir Thomas was not particularly concerned with how he did it, after all it was war."

That is until one of the Spanish diplomats wanted Browne arrested for interfering with his fourteen-year-old niece. Sir Thomas has a daughter of his own and was not unsympathetic to the man's complaint. We had gotten about as much as we could get out of the people in Brussels and the war by this time had moved deeper into France and Spain, so he decided that he would turn Browne over the Spaniards. But somehow Browne got wind of it and took flight with the girl in question; her name is Louisa."

I gasped, and Mother looked pale. "Do you mean our Louisa, Papa?"

He grimaced and continued. "Yes, Lissa, Lady Alford's companion." Aunt Mary was glowering at him but said nothing. He took a sip of whisky and continued, "They'd bolted in the middle of the night and Sir Thomas sent Samuel and I after him but only because the Spaniards were ready to create a diplomatic incident which would have been very embarrassing to the British Crown. Can you imagine the scandal if it became public knowledge that a son of a peer of the realm was guilty of such a crime and while in the service of the British government? Samuel and I were told to do anything we needed to get Louisa back and to silence Randall Browne."

He cleared his throat, tapped his hands on his thighs then grimaced. "Sir Thomas's meaning was very clear, he wanted Browne dead. When we finally found them, we were stupid enough to walk right into a trap. It turned out that Browne had been working for the French all along. Everything that he had learned for us and from us, he had in turn sold to the French."

He sighed, took another gulp of his whisky then refilled his glass as well as the other gentlemen's. My tea had grown cold as had my mother's. Father had our undivided attention. Aunt Mary had continued to sip her tea watching us as if she had heard this story before.

Father resumed his narrative, "We found them waiting in a deserted barn not far outside of Brussels just as if he had expected us. Louisa was scared but unhurt. When questioned later, she told us that he had never actually touched her as her uncle had asserted. However, her mother had found a note from Browne in her room and jumped to the wrong conclusion. It appeared that the Spanish envoy had suspected his niece was being used as a spy in his household and wanted a reason to dispose of her. So, to avoid the embarrassment of admitting the truth to his government he chose to press the accusation of interference. Either way he made it clear that he didn't want Louisa returned; she was to be sent to a convent and they wanted Browne eliminated. He found out what they had planned but he didn't trust Louisa to remain silent, so he took her with him to use as bargaining chip if necessary and if not, he'd give her to the French."

He paused to collect his thoughts. "I didn't believe that Browne would kill her just to save his own skin. However, Samuel did, he was sceptical from the beginning of Browne's motives in taking her. When we entered the barn, Browne had a gun trained on Louisa's back. I had the better angle to shoot him, but I hesitated and missed my opportunity. He kept us talking so neither of us heard the French arrive until it was too late. He walked out of the barn assuring us that he would not betray our presence if we promised to take care of Louisa. I don't know if he told the French we were in there or if they didn't trust him completely. Maybe they'd seen or heard our horses though we had left them in a gully a fair distance away. Whatever it was, they set fire to the barn and left sentries at the door. We had to climb up into the loft and out a very small window. Climbing down was almost impossible for Louisa so we had to lower her with a rope from the loft. It was a narrow escape for us. She was unsure about leaving with us and fought us. I thought at one point I might have had to knock her out and carry her to keep her from running after Browne. It was a hard ride back to Brussels for all of us; we couldn't take to the roads with the French in the area and Louisa had no horse since she and Browne had travelled in a cart. So, I was riding double with her not at all cooperative."

Father stood up and walked around the room and refilled his glass again before taking his seat. Mr Johnson stretched and got up to help himself to more cakes. Aunt Mary had been watching Mr Spencer's reaction to all of this then she turned to my father. "Colin, you said you were told to eliminate Browne, but you missed on that opportunity. Did you have more than one?"

My father chuckled but without mirth. "Yes, a few weeks later I had him in my sights again. Sir Thomas had not been happy about the barn incident and in part that was the reason he decided to send us home. He couldn't use us as spies on the continent any longer since Browne knew us and was working for the French. He agreed that we could take Louisa with us back to England and find her a place as a companion instead of sending her to the convent. Her uncle was indifferent to what happened to her, he just wanted her gone. Apparently, her parents didn't even want her back, they were sure she had lost her virtue and therefore her value. Samuel and I weren't exactly in disgrace but neither of us were happy about being sent away when there was still work to be done." He put his glass down and stretched out his legs, still looking uncomfortable about what had transpired all those years ago.

"Instead of the continent we were to be assigned to watch the south coast of England for smugglers with an eye out for spies coming ashore as well as contraband. We were on the docks in Calais waiting to embark for the trip home when I saw Browne standing on the same pier a short distance away. Louisa didn't see him, and I was sure that he'd not seen us. It would have been simple to slip through the crowd then slide a knife between his ribs. But by the time I'd made up my mind to go after him he had disappeared. I assumed that he'd spotted us after all… I've not seen him since. So, you see I have no idea what he could have against me or Samuel that would enrage him enough to attempt murder." He flexed his hands as the tension slowly left his body and he relaxed once more. "The war has been over for some years now and he's been able to come and go with his French friends. Besides we have no actual proof of his treason so if he chose to stay, he would walk free. If anything, it should be Samuel and I shooting at him, not the other way around."

Mr Spencer spoke up, "I might be able to help you with the motive, Mr Turner. Over the last year there has been a considerable trade in French contraband goods here in London. We believe that there is an organized group of smugglers with significant connections in both politics and business on both sides of the channel. Mr Browne seems to have continued in his chosen trade of procuring things, but we have no concrete proof though he's been linked to some influential parties involved both in London and Paris. There's a great deal of money at stake and the quality of the goods is first rate. I've never seen the like of them before. But we never could track the buggers from this end. I assume that you haven't had much luck yourself on the coast, perhaps you're getting too close and making people uncomfortable."

Father sat back and contemplated what Mr Spencer had said. "You may have a point, Arthur, Samuel saw Browne before he came south with my family. They had words and Samuel he sent him packing but Browne told him that if we got in his way he'd make us pay."

Mr Spencer rubbed his chin. "Browne was in Northumberland? That's curious, I wonder why. The thing is, Turner, both of our resources are spread too thin. The only fellows we're catching are the little ones that make mistakes during the distribution of the goods. However, they don't usually talk and those that do don't know anything worthwhile. The one thing they all have in common is that they're so scared of these people that they'd rather face transportation than answer our questions. Whoever is behind this operation doesn't appear to make mistakes and has all of us working at cross purposes. There's no cooperation between the various jurisdictions over this matter. If we worked together, we could possibly make life very uncomfortable for them." He paused and clasped his hands tightly together then looked at my aunt before continuing, "But you could be putting yourself and your family at risk, particularly if this shooting was about your work."

Father groaned. "Good God, you make it sound like a war, Arthur."

Mr Johnson put down his glass and quietly said, "It is war, Colin. The worst kind of war; it's about greed and how far a man will go to satisfy that greed."

# Chapter 12
## *Confrontation*

Several days went by and during that time the Clarkes came to dinner and the horse stud was discussed at great length. Baron and Jewel were examined, and it was determined that they would make a perfect pair to start. Ramsey was smug for weeks after because he'd been right. Despite his sense of superiority, we continued our daily conversations over the garden wall until he informed me that he was leaving for Oxford the very next day. He seemed less than thrilled with the prospect and I was conflicted. It would be rather lonely in our corner of the garden after he left, I knew with him gone it would stop being one of my favourite places.

During the months that followed, I occasionally went to the theatre and dinner parties with my family. I also frequently went to the British Museum, the Tower and Hyde Park with Uncle Samuel and Emilie. Apparently, it was meant to broaden my education. But I learned more about the elements of courting than I did about art or antiquities…though they did try occasionally to enlighten me. I was also forced to meet some of my contemporaries; they seemed to fall into two categories, mean and milksop and all of them were insipid and boring. I found that no one of my own gender shared my interests, nor were they as well-educated as I was. Perhaps asking my father to challenge my mind had been a mistake since I was having trouble connecting with people of my age. Those that I could have carried on a conversation with if they had been so inclined were older than me and usually male. Behind my back, they called me an abomination which did not bode well for my future in the marriage mart. I tried not to let it bother me; after all, I had spent much of my life on my own without any friends from my own class. Ramsey was the closest that I had ever been to having a friend within the Beau Monde, so I refused to dwell on it and kept to my usual amusements supplemented by those I had found in London under the strict supervision of my family.

Thankfully Aunt Mary had been as good as her word and between her intervention and the Clarkes spreading our story, London society had accepted our family with minimal fuss.

Life at home was interesting, Uncle Samuel was temperamental for some time to say the least, resulting in Emilie and Dalton removing all the breakables from the rooms he frequented. And as expected, he was very ill for several weeks but he gradually started to look less hollow and grey. His wit returned, becoming more cutting as he got better. Father and my uncle went out often with Mr Johnson who was still our guest. And if I had to choose only one word to describe Mr Miles, 'Wicker' Johnson it would be intriguing.

My lessons had continued in earnest with Murphy teaching me the silent code and Gaelic. Mr Allan taught me History and etiquette. Lettie taught how to pick pockets and sought to improve my drawing. Michael was my arms instructor while Jacob surprisingly was assigned the responsibility of teaching me to improve my play on the pianoforte and horsemanship. Aunt Mary had a dance instructor come to the house twice a week and she aided me in improving my gentlewoman skills, everything from needlepoint to the still room. Mother taught me household management and with Emilie's assistance, they taught me several languages. Father had the harder task, he taught me dead languages as well as politics, both of which I barely suffered through. He enticed me to pay attention at least to politics by saying that to work for him I had to understand our system of government. Uncle Samuel was teaching me geography and all about smuggling. Dr Jefferson volunteered to teach me basic physic and wound care. The real surprise though was Mr Johnson, he decided that to combat his boredom as our guest he would teach me the art of disguise and lock picking.

We practiced our disguise in front of that family during evening theatricals since my father would not sanction him taking me out and about in London. With him I shared my love for literature, so he tried to direct me as to the books that I should and shouldn't read. Sometimes we agreed but just as often we did not which ended up in several heated debates and some name calling. Father was sceptical that I could keep up with everything but hoped that this would keep me busy and out of trouble. To be honest there were days that my head was so full, it ached, or I was so tired that I fell asleep as soon as my head hit the pillow.

My parents often went out in the evening to Balls and suppers with Samuel and Emilie who he was openly courting now. Many of these I could not attend since I was not formally out yet. But I loved to see them in all their splendid finery. I was in awe of Mother and Emilie sweeping down the stairs looking so beautiful that it took my breath away. While my father and uncle looked every part of handsome rich men of the ton with one exception, they could not feign the socially expected indifference of a husband for his wife…for they adored these women. Sometimes Mr Johnson would go with them but often as not he went out on his own, coming and going at odd hours.

On the rare occasions that Aunt Mary didn't have an engagement with Mr Spencer or old friends she would have me read to her or I would sketch her as she quietly sat with her needle work. When she was out for the evening Meg and I would day dream together and gossip. I'd tell her about the places that I had been, the clothes that people wore and the houses we visited. She was so intrigued that I insisted from then on that she accompany us on many of our daytime excursions around London.

I also convinced Mother to allow Meg to take a few lessons with me to improve her mind. She was after all intelligent and inquisitive, so we concentrated on improving her diction and she joined me for etiquette and French lessons.

Dr Jefferson was often a guest at dinner and accompanied us on many of our outings. I noticed that he had taken a keen interest in Louisa, my aunt's companion, since the day we had all gone to the Tower to view the menagerie. When we picnicked in the park afterwards, she sprained her ankle tripping over a tree root as we walked along the Serpentine. After that day Aunt Mary announced that she was sure she'd be looking for a new companion before too long and I was inclined to agree.

My father's valet Richards was the enigma in our household. I couldn't warm to the man, he had a sour and a deeply etched weathered countenance and always seemed to be angry. I wondered what made him so taciturn but more especially why my father even tolerated him.

I finally asked my uncle's valet about him one day when I passed him in the hallway. "Dalton, may I ask you a question about Richards?"

He pursed his lips and rubbed his forehead, looking like he wanted to vanish into the floor. He looked about him then dropped his shoulders. "Oh, miss, that is a topic best left alone."

I persisted. "But why? He hardly ever seems to be here and from what I can tell you take care of my father even when Richards is here."

He toed the floor and pursed his lips again. I thought he was going to refuse to answer me but finally he mumbled. "Your uncle is right about you, you see far too much."

I watched him closely while he appeared to be considering his options, so I pressed my advantage and all I had to say was "Is it that bad?"

He took a deep breath and in hushed tones said, "Richards is not a valet, miss, he never was, and that lout never could be. He's a smuggler that your father fished out of a gaol somewhere along the coast and gave him this position to make use of his vulgar connections and his knowledge of the smuggling trade. I don't trust him, miss, and you shouldn't either."

He moved forward to pass me, but I stepped in front of him. "What does my father think of him?"

I could tell that he was uncomfortable with my questions, but I wouldn't budge. "You'd have to ask Mr Turner about that, miss, but your uncle doesn't trust him, and I believe that your father has his measure as well. None of the staff like him being here, there really isn't any reason for him to be part of the household if you ask me."

I felt that I should offer him some sympathy after putting him on the spot, "It must make a lot of work for you?"

He smiled shyly. "Not really, miss, your father and uncle can be pretty independent, and Jacob can step in when I need him. He worked once for a ship's captain who fancied himself a bit of a swell. Now if you'll excuse me, miss, I need to see to these shirts." And he walked away with them over his arm.

I entered my room to find Meg waiting to assist me to change for dinner. She always knew the latest gossip in the household, so I broached the subject of Richards with her. "Meg, do you know anything about Richards or Dalton?"

She became very quiet and her eyes got very large as she looked around as if one of them would jump out of my dressing room. "Oh, my, miss, Mr Richards gives me the shivers. He doesn't talk much but when he does he's mean. He tries to put the rest of the staff down all the time and says we're to always call him Mr Richards, he puts on airs all the time and I've even seen him cuff wee Davey the boot boy for no good reason. He hit him so hard once that his ear bled. Cook wrapped his knuckles for that, she's the only one that's not afraid of him and she watches him like a hawk and keeps Davey close to her when Mr Richards is around." She sucked in her lower lip, her eyes glistening. "When Mrs Turner allowed me to take some lessons with you, he said I was being lifted above my station and that nothing good would come from it." She sniffed and used her handkerchief to wipe her nose, "None of the staff like him or trust him, miss. Mr Allan keeps our money and valuables locked up in his pantry whenever Richards is here. Michael, Murphy, John and Jacob watch out for the rest of the staff when he's around, especially the maids." Her lower lip quivered, and her hands were shaking.

"Meg, has Richards made inappropriate advances to you?" She shook her head no, but I could tell he scared her. "He sounds perfectly awful! Has anyone approached my father about his behaviour?"

"I don't rightly—I mean, I don't really know, miss. The staff here like to handle their problems in their own way, but it's always like that below stairs. Besides he goes on about how important he is to Mr Turner's work and none of us would want to upset Mr Turner."

I wondered if I should say anything to my father, perhaps if I asked Murphy or one of the others about him. I'd have to think about it and maybe ask my father about why Richards was so valuable to him. "Is Dalton well-liked?"

Meg brightened and smiled. "Oh yes, miss! Dalton is a hard worker and a real gentleman. Did you know that he trained as a tailor, but he wanted an adventure before settling down, so he joined the army? That's when he came into service with Mr Hughes." She grinned even wider and lowering her voice, so I knew she had some gossip for me. "I think he's sweet on Beth, but he's too nervous to ask her to walk out, I mean, court her. He's a fine man and would be an excellent catch for any woman."

I loved seeing people happy and in love. "Maybe we can do something to help him get her attention."

Meg chuckled before continuing, "Oh, miss, he has her attention! She says that if he doesn't get on with it she'll be asking him." I giggled then we started talking about how we could throw Beth and Dalton together and Mr Richards was forgotten for the time being.

I went down to dinner and for once I was not the last one to take my seat. That honour would be Mr Johnson's who looked a touch flushed as if he had been exerting himself. While Uncle Samuel poured some lemonade for us he asked, "So, Johnson did Lettie give you the slip again?" He cleared his throat then took a sip of lemonade as he chuckled.

Father rolled his eyes. "Miles, if you insist on toying with our female staff I'll have to find you other lodgings. Besides if you get too familiar with her Lettie is as likely to stick a knife in your gut and if not her then her brother will."

Mr Johnson looked embarrassed. "Come now, Colin, it was just a little misunderstanding…" He played with his wine glass then murmured "…on my part it seems. The girl has spirit though and I wager that there is more to her than meets the eye. You say she and her brother are from the East End?" Father nodded. Mr Johnson raised a brow. "I seriously doubt it, Turner. I'm positive that they have a secret that they haven't shared with you old man."

Father was obviously annoyed. "What the devil are you talking about?"

Mr Johnson smiled. "Have you ever heard her when she's angry? Her language is definitely not from the gutters of the East End, nor was she born to the servant class."

Father looked puzzled and glanced at my mother for a split second, but she seemed to be at a loss, so he tried to look bored when asking, "What do you mean by that, Miles?"

Mr Johnson took a sip of his wine but before he could answer the footmen entered with the soup. The conversation then veered off into generalities such as the weather, gossip and politics.

Aunt Mary took the advantage when there was a momentary lapse in the conversation to speak to my uncle. "So, my dear boy, when are you going to give Emilie a ring?" Samuel choked on his lemonade as Emilie blushed. "Come now, you've recovered enough from your illness that your natural urges must be exerting themselves. Don't you think that it's tempting fate with both of you living under the same roof?" My uncle looked shocked as he fumbled with something in his pocket then Aunt Mary turned to my mother. "Irene, my dear, do you think we can have a wedding pulled together in say three weeks? Nothing large, just family I think."

Samuel spluttered again, and Emilie just looked at her lap blushing a deep crimson. My uncle's face was beet red, but I couldn't tell if he was embarrassed or angry. Being put on the spot like that, he'd become almost inarticulate. "Aunt Mary, you, well, I of course, I have a ring!" He huffed and pulled his fist out of his pocket and through clenched teeth whispered loud enough for all to hear, "But it would have been nice to pick my own time and place!"

Aunt Mary put on a face of mock surprise. "Oh, come now, Samuel, romantic declarations in the garden under the moon are highly overrated. Besides it's raining. If I'm not mistaken, Colin proposed to Irene in the kitchen garden while she was pulling carrots and they're perfectly happy."

Mother and Father chuckled, and Mr Johnson leaned back in his chair with a bemused smile on his face. Turning to Emilie, Samuel took her hand ignoring the audible chuckling in the room, "Emilie." He took a deep breath then scowled at everyone before starting again. "Emilie, oh bloody hell! I had a perfectly good speech ready and now. Aunt Mary, really how could you ruin it!"

Aunt Mary just smiled. "Well, get on with it boy before the next course arrives."

He opened his fist to display a beautiful square cut pink diamond set in a gold band, Emilie gasped, "Yes, Samuel."

Samuel was taken aback. "Yes? You said yes! But I haven't asked you properly yet."

Emilie leaned towards him and in breathless whisper said, "You have asked me more times than I can count before today and my answer to you all of those times has been yes in my heart but now I can yes aloud."

My uncle smiled, took her hand and placed the ring on her finger. He kissed the ring then Emilie.

Aunt Mary smiled, picked up her spoon and started to eat her soup. I followed her lead as did everyone else except Samuel and Emilie.

The next several days were a whirlwind of activity, all involving the wedding. I noticed that most of the gentleman of the household frequently and conveniently disappeared whenever discussions veered into the preparations. Surprisingly Mr Johnson was the only one of them who remained behind to assist with some of the more masculine details. He arranged with a vicar of his acquaintance to educate and indoctrinate Emilie into the Church of England and he gave his input into the music and refreshments. All the while pointing out when things would start to get out of hand much to Emilie's relief. He noted that while Samuel was a man of means who would one day inherit vast estates, his wedding didn't have to be an elaborate affair, just tasteful.

Emilie was radiant during these days while Samuel looked terrified. It was not that he didn't want to marry Emilie but the responsibility of having a wife and possibly fathering children weighed heavily on him. He had informed the General by special post of his impending nuptials but not of the actual date since he didn't expect nor want him in attendance. Yet every time we were in the library and he heard a carriage or horse pass by his head would snap up.

We were gathered one day in the drawing room taking tea and discussing wedding plans while Uncle Samuel, my father, Dr Jefferson and Mr Johnson were playing cards and ignoring any questions that came their way. Mr Allan entered with the mail which he usually left in my father's study. Father looked up at him with raised eyebrows. "There is a something for you from the Home Office, sir, and something for Mr Hughes from the Abbey, along with the usual invitations and letters for the ladies." My father took the stack from him handing the invitations and letters out. He opened his letter, read it through quickly then leaned back in his chair tapping the letter on his leg while deep in thought.

Samuel read his while pacing in front of the garden windows. Then he threw the letter on the table near my father. "Good lord, he still thinks I'm a child to be bullied into doing what he wants. Well, I will not bow to his wishes. He can go to the devil. He's already cut me off so there is little else he can do to harm me."

Emilie rose and went to him taking his hand. "What is it, my love?" Father handed her the letter after reading it himself. She moved to the window for better light.

Samuel turned to look out the windows, but I could see the pulse in his neck beating, his face was flushed, and it was obvious that he was in a temper. He licked his lips and tried to look about him casually for something stronger to drink than tea but there wasn't anything available to him, there hadn't been for some time now. It was obvious that he was still fighting his demons. "God, I could use a drink." his shoulders slumped at this admission, but it was not the first time he'd said such a thing yet never with such desperation.

Aunt Mary and mother joined Emilie with my aunt reading the short letter aloud. The General's missive announced his imminent arrival in two days' time. He would be staying at Lord Gromley's town house and expected Samuel and his bride to wait on him there.

Aunt Mary returned to her seat and picked up her needle work. "Samuel, you and Emilie will go to see your father as will Colin, Irene and myself." She looked at me, "I'm sorry, Clarissa, but I think you should stay home." When I opened my mouth to protest, she added, "I promise that I will tell you everything that transpires."

Samuel was still in a temper. "Do you really think that I can't handle him alone, Aunt Mary!"

She never looked up from her needlework. "Of course, you can handle him, Samuel, that's not the issue. It's about making everyone else believe that we are a family, besides I wouldn't miss this for the world." She smirked. "I can't wait to see how Colin and Irene being there will put him at a disadvantage."

Samuel and my parents looked puzzled while Emilie smiled. It was my mother who spoke first, "Whatever do you mean?"

"Really, Irene, I should think it would be obvious. You and Colin, Samuel and his bride will be seen visiting my brother and what is more natural than that his own sister should pay a call along with her niece and nephew with whom she is residing?

113

To the world at large it will appear to be just a simple family visit to welcome the family patriarch to London. Richard will have to behave himself. If he doesn't behave, it will make the rounds of the Beau Monde like wild fire even before the next dinner party and that would not be pleasant for him… I will make sure of that."

She looked at each of us. "Good lord! Are you all dense?" She took a deep breath and continued. "You have all been embraced by London society! Do you really think that we have invested all this time in visits and dinner parties without a goal in mind?" She hastily bundled up her needlework and laid it aside. "First, we did not hide the fact that Samuel was shot by persons unknown for reasons unknown. Second everyone is aware that he has been ill with an addiction to alcohol because of his long-suffering love for Emilie and that he is under Dr Jefferson's care. It has become the romance of the season! Colin and Irene are now looked upon as if they are archetype hero and heroine from one of those romantic novels that are so popular these days. You're both living examples of a love match that works against all odds. Byron couldn't have written anything better. Your constancy and moral fortitude are excellent examples to their own children. Everyone loves a good love story, my dears, and this family has two. Believe me your father will think twice before causing a scene, though I'd love to have him try." She ended with decidedly evil chuckle.

I was puzzled as to why I was to be left out, I looked around the room for an answer. Mr Johnson sat staring at the fire and Dr Jefferson looked uncomfortable being privy to family business. Father was watching them both. "What is it, gentleman, you both seem to be disturbed about something." Dr Jefferson looked at me pointedly and raised his eyebrows Mr Johnson merely turned to give him a scornful look. Father licked his lips before saying, "Clarissa, my dear, would it bother you to have to face the General?"

Aunt Mary immediately glared at us both. "Colin! You can't possibly expect the child to confront her grandfather. He made her life hell!"

Father looked unsure but still said, "She must confront him at some point, ma'am, and I'd rather it happened when we're together than in a chance meeting. Besides aren't you the one that wants to catch him off guard and unsettle him? Clarissa has been established legally as my daughter, he has no claim to her now so what could be more unsettling to him than being out-maneuvered."

Aunt Mary glanced my way then back at Father. "Good point…what do you say, Clarissa?"

All faces were turned to me with anticipation except Mr Johnson who looked deep in thought, his brow was furrowed with lines of concern.

I gazed at him, willing him to look my way and when he finally did, he smiled giving me a slight nod. I had come to value his opinion over the past few weeks, so I answered, "In for a penny in for a pound." Mr Johnson was the only one who didn't laugh.

# Chapter 13
## *September 1827: The Visit*

Aunt Mary made sure that our other immediate neighbours, the Clarkes and the Summers, were aware of our planned visit to the General. The next morning, she informed us at breakfast that she had an express letter from Lord Gromley stating that he was coming to London hard on the heels of the General. She confessed to us that she'd a long-standing practice of corresponding with Lord Gromley to keep him apprised of what had transpired in our lives. This was a surprise to my mother and father; Samuel's attention was focused on Emilie, so they were both ignoring the conversation at the table and Mr Johnson seemed to be focusing on his breakfast, but I had no doubt that he was interested in what she had to say.

Mother was horrified. "Why? He's father's oldest friend, how could you?!"

Aunt Mary chuckled. "You're wrong, Irene, he was your mother's oldest friend. He only ever tolerated Richard for her sake and then yours." She took her time as she explained that Lord Gromley had willingly assisted in keeping the General away from the Abbey while we had made our escape. He had also provided affidavits to our lawyers that established my status as my parent's daughter and not the General's or Charlotte's child.

All of us were shocked to hear that Lord Gromley had only appeared to be a close friend of the General's for all these years. She informed us that he had been aware of everything that had happened between my parents from the moment of their first meeting. In fact, it was his Lordship that Charlotte and my aunt had turned to for advice when the Vicar had refused to marry my parents. He had been the one who suggested that they go to Gretna Green to marry. My father was obviously perplexed, and mother was astonished, but she asked. "Aunt Mary, why would he go to such lengths for Colin and me and yet act like such a close friend of my father's?"

My aunt sighed and there was a profound sadness in her eyes when she spoke, "Alex, I mean Lord Gromley, has never liked Richard. He knew him at school and thought he was a bore and bully even then. But they were forced to spend a fair amount of time together since their parents were good friends and neighbours. When Richard asked for Alice's hand and was accepted, Alex was furious." She closed her eyes and sighed again. The look on her face was so sad that she now had Samuel and Emilie's rapt attention while Mr Johnson continued to concentrate on his meal. "He was in love with Alice and would have married her himself if their families had not considered being second cousins too close a connection and therefore unsuitable. Alex always felt that Richard was beneath her, so he worried about her wellbeing. In fact, he argued hotly with the Blackwoods to find a better match for their daughter. They ignored his pleas believing that he jealous. Alex knew that Richard was just a self-serving egotistical beast but there was nothing he could do and therefore

116

resigned himself to losing Alice. But he wouldn't desert her. He was determined to watch over her no matter how much he suffered from it." She opened her eyes and looked at all of us before continuing, "She was the one reason that he could never bring himself to marry, much to his family's chagrin. You see the estate and title are entailed to the male line. Without any offspring of his own it would go to the only surviving male in the family, that would be you, Samuel. He always looked on you and Irene as the children he never had. I don't believe my brother ever knew the depth of Alex's attachment to your mother, even though he knew that they had always been close. When Alice died, I thought Alex would crawl into the grave with her or kill Richard." Aunt Mary wiped a tear from her eye and went on. "Instead he went abroad to India then to the America. Even during the war, he travelled to all the most dangerous places as if he courted death yet through all his travels he stayed in touch with me. At first, I thought he flattered me with his attention since I was a widow. Then I realised that he only wanted to continue to watch over your welfare even from afar. When he finally returned for good, he renewed his acquaintance with Richard and continued to watch over you. He did his best to influence your father regarding your education and well-being as much as possible. Richard never guessed that it was you and your sister that he was interested in and not in his own stellar companionship." Samuel and my mother were awe struck, while Father, the doctor, Emilie and Mr Johnson merely watched and waited. It appeared that we had an ally that the General was not aware of.

Father leaned forward, "Well, this is rich!"

Mother turned on him her face was flushed, tears glistened in her eyes. "Is that all you have to say?"

Father paused and looked sideways at Samuel with a grin on his face, "What else is there?"

Samuel started to chuckle, Mother reached over and slapped his arm lightly. "Stop it this instant the both of you! Doesn't any of this bother you at all? Our mother was in love with Lord Gromley, our whole life has been a farce, Samuel!"

He sobered immediately. "Irene, my dear sweet sister, our life has not been a farce. Our mother loved us dearly, I know that in my heart and in my mind as do you. Who she loved besides us was her own business. But it seems that Lord Gromley is the benevolent Uncle we never knew we had. I agree with Colin, this is rich! Surely you must see the absurdity of it all, Irene." Mother shook her head on the verge of tears.

Mr Johnson spoke up looking at my mother, "May I interject here. I think we have lost some of the plot of what has been going on. Mrs Turner, I'm sorry to diverge but perhaps lost loves can be discussed at your leisure another time." Everyone at the table glared at him for he was being unconscionably rude, but no one interrupted as he continued, "Mr Spencer has hit a wall in his investigation of the shooting. Randall Browne is missing and even his esteem father apparently doesn't know of his whereabouts at last count." Father's mouth fell open. "Sorry, Turner, I couldn't help myself. I glanced at the letter you received from the Home Office." My father rolled his eyes, but Mr Johnson continued, "Doesn't it seem strange to you that the General picks this time to come to the capital when he can no longer have any influence on anything that any of you do? I'm sure his solicitors have made him aware of the court's ruling in your favour regarding Clarissa as your natural and lawful child. He already knows that Samuel has private means and will not require his financial assistance now or in the future. So, let me pose the question again, why is the General here when he cannot change anything?"

Uncle Samuel look shocked. "Are you insinuating that my own father wanted me dead?"

Mr Johnson shrugged. "Perhaps not, but I do wonder if he knew about it. Exactly how far in debt is your father?"

Samuel looked haunted, his shoulders drooped as he sunk back in his chair. My mother glanced at Father while Emilie turned to Samuel. "What does he mean?"

My father slammed his cup down on the table as Mr Johnson rose and poured another cup of coffee for himself. "Oh, for heaven sakes, Miles, what are you getting at? Spit it out man!"

Mr Johnson sat back and crossed his legs, looking at my father with a crooked half smile. "I think you know, Colin, or you have had a suspicion for some time." Father looked like he was ready to explode. Mr Johnson then became very serious, laid his hands on the arms of his chair and sat forward. "I've been making use of my contacts just as Mr Spencer requested regarding the shooting. I've recently found out some very interesting things about the General, Mr Browne and your valet Richards." He paused for affect, letting what he said sink in before continuing. "Tell me, Turner…smuggling can be a very profitable business, can it not? Especially if you are willing to run the risks in dealing with anyone that gets in your way. True?" Father merely nodded. "Well then, it appears that you and Hughes may have interfered once too often in someone's ventures and the General seems to be one of those persons."

Mother looked stricken, Father was in deep thought while Uncle Samuel looked sick and angry as he snapped at Mr Johnson. "How long have you known this?"

"Not long." Samuel came up and out of his chair with his fists clenched.

Mr Johnson motioned for him to sit. "I only got word of it this morning when your fishmonger delivered a message to your cook for me from one of my contacts." He took a filthy piece of paper out of his pocket and passed it to father. "I think after you read this you may want to invite Mr Spencer to dine." My father took the paper, glanced at it then looked up.

Mr Johnson responded to his look. "Before you ask me, yes I've already sent a copy to Spencer. You can send that one to Sir Thomas if you like. Now would you like to tell us about the correspondence that you received from the Home Office? I take it from your late night with Mr Hughes, Murphy and Dalton you have a problem."

Father was outwardly calm, but his voice shook with suppressed emotion. "Damn it, Miles, if you were so bloody interested in my affairs and had information, why didn't you just say so."

Mr Johnson smiled and extended his hands toward my father, palms up. "I just did, old man. I had no idea what you were involved in and I had no information to give you until this morning. But I've had my suspicions about Browne for some time." He took a sip of his now cooling coffee. "As part of my service to keep myself out of debtor's prison Spencer has had me investigating a string of warehouse thefts that he and the River Police have been working on together. During my time on the docks I noticed that there is one warehouse that every thief in London takes a wide berth of." He turned to look at my uncle. "It belongs to your father Hughes. And who do you think I've seen coming and going at all hours from there—Browne and

Richards." He paused to take another sip of his coffee. "As that note says there is a huge shipment of French goods expected to arrive in London by ship, but here's the catch, the exact same shipment is also expected to land in Poole. One must be a decoy but which one? A smuggler's ship coming up the Thames to dock is rather unusual to say the least which seems to indicate that they are willing to take a greater risk this time." He ran his hand through his hair and sighed. "From what I've been able to learn all previous shipments of goods have been landed off the coast at various locations then hauled across country in wagons splitting up to take different routes to different sites. Once there the goods are then broken down into smaller loads before making their way to London and other commercial centres. However, your coastal patrols have been able to disrupt them lately costing them considerable profits in the last few months and apparently, some of their partners are very unhappy about that." He leaned forward with a very grave expression on his face. "Turner, if these people are who Mr Spencer and the River Police think they are, then you've made some lethal enemies not only in London but on the continent as well." He paused before continuing, "We know that Randal Browne and your man Richards appear to be running things but there are some other extremely well-placed but unsavoury characters backing them, I just don't know who. So again, tell me what was in the rest of your correspondence that had you up half the night?"

Father relented. "My contact in the Home Office has received word that a vast shipment of French goods was to arrive in London, however, he gave me no time frame except that a ship was headed to London. He also mentioned that my father-in-law was now a person of interest."

Mr Johnson seemed to contemplate this information. "How reliable is your contact, Turner? Can you be sure that you are not being deliberately being put off track?"

Mother interjected before they could continue, "My father is many things; but the head of a smuggling ring! I cannot credit it! I just don't see it…" her sentence trailed off as if she was at a loss for words.

Mr Johnson relaxed and smiled warmly at her. "I seriously doubt that the General is the head of this group, Mrs Turner. He may not even be a willing participant but rather just their puppet. If you wouldn't mind, I'd very much like to come with you to this family tea, perhaps in disguise as a member of Mademoiselle Michaud's family."

Emilie only arched an eyebrow and Samuel was laughing. "You have got to be kidding, Johnson! Emilie has no family."

Mr Johnson flourished his handkerchief like he was some sort of dandy and using a slight French accent continued, "I wasn't thinking of anyone in the direct line, perhaps a long forgotten and distant émigré cousin, one that has sought her out only recently. My own mother was a French émigré so it's not so farfetched."

My uncle was scanning the room again then with complete distain, he looked at Miles, "You are going to play the part of a French émigré, are you mad?"

Mr Johnson was not the least affected by his comment. "Come now, your father has never met me. Besides a person's French relations are almost impossible to trace with any degree of accuracy these days, he will never know, after all, I speak impeccable French. What do you say, Clarissa, do you think we can whip up a costume for an impoverished Frenchman?"

I smiled gleefully, already thinking of the costumes we had accumulated and what he would need to pull it off. He reached out his hand pulling me to my feet and we were out the door and on our way to the attics before anyone could move or object.

Once we reached out destination I stood there short of breath watching the dust motes float across a weak beam of sunlight that was coming through the window behind me. Mr Johnson was rummaging through the old wardrobes and trunks, looking for what I couldn't imagine. As I watched one piece after another being rejected a thought came to me that a costume might be a mistake in this case. He pulled out a ghastly coat which had to have come from a time before I was born and smiled at me looking for agreement. I knew my face must have looked like I had swallowed sour milk for his face fell. "No?"

I crossed my arms tipping my head from side to side before answering "Mr Johnson, that is a courtier's coat. It's very much out of fashion and it's hideous. I'm afraid it's all wrong." He stood there staring at me in the most peculiar way that I felt a shiver run up my spine, so I hurried on, "Besides it will be broad daylight, you can hardly pretend to be much older than you already are. You should pose as Emilie's younger cousin." He turned his back to me as if he was still looking in the wardrobe. "But I have an idea that will perhaps be more believable than any costume. Go as yourself."

He took off the coat and tossed it into the wardrobe. Then he faced me again with one hand on his hip looking at me intently, "You wish me to present myself as my father's bastard?"

"That's not what I meant, and you know it! You are a person of limited means, are you not?" He nodded. "Who earns his living through his wit and charm, am I correct?" He glared at me as I continued, "You are currently earning your way by teaching me about literature, the art of disguise and philosophy. That can be how you met Emilie in our household! After talking to her you discovered that you were distant relations. You already admitted that your mother was an émigré so how do we know that she wasn't related to Emilie's family?"

His dark brow arched, and a laconic smile spread across his face. "Philosophy, Miss Turner? I was unaware that I ever waxed philosophical when speaking to you." He chuckled in a low throaty fashion, more self-deprecating than amused. "Alright then, what else do you propose, poppet." I frowned at the word poppet. I resented the inference that I was a child. Then as if he knew my thoughts, he said, "Oh buck up, Miss Turner, it was only meant as a term of endearment."

I felt a flush come to my cheeks when it hit me that he was much younger than my father and mother. I tried to ignore the feelings well up in me and continued with my plan. "I think that as a gentleman tutor you would dress in immaculate if slightly worn yet sober clothes. Your breeding would show in all the little details like your current impeccable grooming and manners already do. The General despises weakness, so I think you should present yourself much as you currently are, a self-assured intelligent man and not as some French fop."

His face softened as he approached me. "Is that how you really see me? I must warn you that I have had several appraisals of my character before and none of them have been particularly complimentary."

He stood there looking at me, his face devoid of emotion yet there was a glimmer in his eye or was it a tear, I couldn't tell. I cocked my head to the side; he seemed to find this amusing, yet he remained motionless and didn't speak a word. "Well, Mr Johnson, you are a handsome man but not in the conventional fashion. Your hair is longer than most, your dark riotous curls give you the air of a romantic and your eyes are a beautiful grey." He chuckled as I continued, "You are very intelligent and have a ready wit. I imagine that women are attracted to you and men find you a charming companion. While you are kind and compassionate you are also audacious. Yet there is a touch of sadness that surrounds you, it's obvious that you have been deeply hurt." His eyes snapped, and he tensed with coiled energy or anger, I couldn't tell since his face remained impassive. "You're strong and fearless even though you attempt to hide it as much as you can. Still it's your eyes that are your Achilles heel, aren't they?" He raised an eyebrow as I went on, "Your eyes virtually crackle with intelligence, yes, your eyes must give you away on occasion. You really are so much more than what you appear, Mr Johnson." I sighed, gazing at him and continued, "How incredibly bored you must be with the people that you normally associate with." He was glowering at me now. I felt badly for laying him bare and apologized. "I'm sorry, I didn't mean to offend you?"

His features immediately softened. "No, you didn't offend me, poppet, rather you caught me off guard with how much you have observed. Children of your age…" I drew in my breath when he said children. "Excuse me, my dear, young ladies of your age rarely notice anything but the most superficial of qualities in others. You really do see far too much, Miss Turner. I shall have to beware of that in the future."

As we stared at each other the space between us became so charged that to relieve the tension, I replied, "Uncle Samuel often tells me that it's a shortcoming of mine."

"On the contrary, my dear Lissa." He paused then whispered, "But you should learn to not to share all that you see with everyone or it may prove to be your Achilles Heel." He was deadly serious and concerned.

Then he brightened as he pulled on his cutaway. "Come then, no costume or makeup will be required, we need merely to decide on how I am related to mademoiselle. My own father told me that no one knew much about my mother's family, so I shall claim my relationship through her. I agree that under the circumstances it would be unwise of me to pretend to be anyone but who I really am in case I'm recognized. Do you agree?" I nodded, and he smiled kindly at me. "We had best go back downstairs and work with mademoiselle on our story." He reached out and took my hand, leading me to the door where he stopped, he raised my hand slowly to his lips and kissed the wrist then palm, as he stared straight into my eyes with a peculiar look of intense melancholy. The moment seemed to go on forever, I felt my heart racing and I knew that I must be blushing when he said, "Heaven help the man that falls in love with you, Miss Turner, I fear you will lead him on a merry chase or break his heart."

We met with the family in the library and explained our plan. I sat back and watched them dissect the details, but they agreed that he shouldn't pretend to be anyone but himself. It was just the details of his mother's relationship to Emilie that needed to be determined. It was finally decided that Emilie should have been unaware of any relations that had survived the terror and immigrated to England. I didn't contribute to the discussion, instead I sat there and listened, so I wouldn't be caught out in a lie when we went for tea with the General. Every now and then, Mr Johnson would look at me as if for approval to which I would merely nod, and he would smile back.

Mr Spencer arrived shortly after and the men all adjourned to my father's study. Mr Spencer had made it quite clear that the ladies of the house were not invited to this meeting. I suppose he still suffered under the delusion that women could not keep a secret or that we were too delicate. I rose twice with the intention of leaving to eavesdrop, but I was foiled once by my mother and once by my Aunt Mary.

Mother and Aunt Mary were telling Emilie about the General to prepare her for the meeting, yet they still managed to keep a close eye on me. So, we sat and reviewed what had been decided about our visit including how we would dress.

Mr Spencer returned when the men were done to speak briefly to Aunt Mary then left. When my father entered the room, we all turned to face him. He walked across to my mother and took her hands. "It's worse than we expected, my love. Your father is very deeply in debt, in fact, he is in danger of losing everything. Fortunately, he cannot touch your or Samuel's inheritance from your mother and grandfather. But I'm afraid that if we don't stop him, he will lose the Abbey. If we do stop him then he will be disgraced, a ruined man at the very least and he could possibly face criminal charges at the worst."

Mother looked at him with anxious eyes. "What will you do? You can't possibly warn him, Colin, that would be wrong, and it would get you into serious trouble with Sir Thomas and the Home Office." She shuddered. "You have to stop him, my love! I left the Abbey to make my life with you and without any expectation of ever seeing my father again. But Samuel should not have to sacrifice his inheritance and honour to keep the General out of prison. If we —if you can stop him then you need to do it by whatever means is necessary." I saw the tears glistening in her eyes, but she smiled and kissed his cheek.

He looked at Samuel. "Well, old man, do you think we can weather the scandal that will result?"

My uncle was sombre when he responded "Really, Colin, do you think I care a fig about scandal. Sir Thomas might be able to cover up Father's actual involvement for our sake if nothing else, but I don't care. Whatever happens we'll ride it out. At least we'll do so on the side of the law. It won't make us very popular in some circles but at least we'll know that we did the right thing and for the most part we'll be respected for it. What we must consider is that this mess could expose our work for the Crown. Unless, of course…" and he looked pointedly at Mr Johnson.

Father didn't notice that Uncle Samuel had stopped talking, he was staring at Mr Johnson as well who glowered back at him, then flashed him a wicked smile. Father was busy tapping his fingers on his knee deep in thought. "There's no time to consult with Sir Thomas further but I—"

Mr Johnson interjected interrupting his train of thought, "Excuse me, Turner, I've never been known for my altruism, yet it seems like a good time for me to seek gainful employment. Perhaps as an agent for the Crown, what do think? Will Sir Thomas take me on to protect you two?"

Father looked up quickly and narrowed his eyes. "What exactly are you thinking, Miles?"

Mr Johnson spoke softly and with conviction. "Come now, Turner, I'm not a simpleton, from the looks you and Hughes are giving me I think the possibility has already been discussed between you two. But I have my own reasons for mentioning it. I told you that as soon as my father dies I fear that my sweet brother will disown not only me but my father's current wife and their off spring. I would like to be able to offer them some comfort and security but for that I'll need a profession and an income." He turned, sweeping his arm theatrically towards Mr Spencer. "Mr Spencer can vouch for my reliability and ingenuity if not my integrity." He glanced at me before continuing with a touch of rancour in his voice, "It's time that I looked to the future! As a bastard son, my prospects of finding a rich heiress on the marriage mart are negligible so employment is my only alternative. I know that my father will do as much as he can for me, but one can't count on what that will be."

Samuel was sitting beside Emilie, observing Mr Johnson. "You would do that to preserve our anonymity, Johnson?"

"Not for you, Hughes, though I have grown attached to your family. I am doing this for me. Someone recently observed that I must be incredibly bored with the people that I usually associate with and they were right." He stole a glance at me and winked. Then he continued very seriously, "I admit the added benefit is that your anonymity will be protected. It never hurts for people like me to have friends in high places." Then he brightened slightly and smiled. "Plus to my own amusement I just realised that my brother will be furious that the family bastard has a respectable position and one that he cannot influence."

Mr Johnson watched my father pace back and forth. "We haven't got much time to plan anything or for me to get in touch with Sir Thomas and hear his decision. Are you sure about this, Miles?"

He smiled looking around the room then took a deep breath. "Yes, I'm sure. However, there is one condition."

"What's that?"

"I want you to—" Then he closed his mouth looked towards me and frowned. My father frowned, and my mother squeezed his hand. Then Mr Johnson seemed to reconsider what he had been about to say. He chuckled finally saying, "I want you to get me a proper introduction to the delightful Miss Lettie."

My face fell, and Aunt Mary was startled, "Are you serious?"

"Oh, yes, ma'am, I'm very serious." He didn't look serious or even happy…he looked sad.

She snorted. "Well, young man, I'm not surprised given your reputation. But Miles, she is not of our class and I will not tolerate any tampering with her morals. Colin, you cannot possibly countenance his request."

Mr Johnson faked a shocked look, putting his hand to his chest. "Me? My dear Lady Alford, my intentions are nothing but honourable. And you're wrong about one thing, Lady Alford, I belong to no class." He grimaced at his own words and looked back at my father. "Very well, Turner forget, Miss Lettie, but this household has many secrets which makes for a very interesting place to live. Perhaps in the long run it might be best if I'm kept in the family so to speak." He smiled wickedly, my mother looked at him and then at me through veiled eyes. Suddenly his eyes changed, and he had that sad, faraway look I had seen so often before.

Mother sighed, saying, "We are an odd grouping. I just hope this works!" She glanced at me then Mr Johnson before saying, "Believe me when I say it, Mr Johnson, that if you hurt anyone in this household by your actions, I will not hesitate to kill you with my bare hands if necessary."

Father tried to hide a smile and Samuel choked back a laugh as everyone else just stared at my mother. Mr Johnson roused himself nodding to my mother and with a most serious expression said, "My dear Mrs Turner, I understand you completely."

# Chapter 14
## *The General*

The time finally came for our tea with the General, I was nervous but not afraid. Father and Mr Johnson were already mounted when we descended the stairs to the waiting coach. Jacob and Michael were likewise mounted behind them. A groom held Uncle Samuel's horse, waiting for him to finish assisting Aunt Mary, Mother, Emilie and me into the carriage. Murphy was up on the carriage box with Mr Cripps, our coachman. I noticed that everyone was armed including Aunt Mary and my mother, it had become the usual practice ever since Uncle Samuel had been shot.

We arrived at Lord Gromley's townhouse without incident and the door was opened promptly by a liveried footman and behind him and to everyone's astonishment stood Mr Spencer. He smiled congenially and asked us to follow him. We walked through a marbled entry hall whose floor resembled a giant chess board, the whole space had exceedingly lofty ceilings. The walls were a cool pale green and potted palms in black, glazed urns were positioned in the centre so that sunlight could reach them from an overhead sky light. Beautiful artwork was tastefully positioned on pedestals around the periphery or hung on the walls for viewing, none of it was out of place or overwhelming. There were also three niches which contained beautiful inlaid tables, on each sat an elegant candelabra. Otherwise the entire floor was open. The only visible doorway led into what was obviously the withdrawing room. Inside was an expansive and beautifully decorated room. This was a bachelor's home but there was a decided feminine touch in the decor. The walls were painted in a Wedgewood blue that was as pale as a summer's sky that was reflected in the polished oak floor. There were several seating groups of pale green and cream upholstered settees and chairs arranged atop floral Aubusson carpets in shades of muted rose, blue and green. Family portraits mixed with pastoral scenes hung above the beautiful cabinets and tables arranged around the room. A beautiful pale green chase lounge was situated in front of a bank of floor to ceiling windows. The most unusual choice in the room were the pale-yellow velvet curtains that hung on either side of the windows and French doors that overlooked the garden. Above the mantel hung a huge mirror reflecting the room back, making it seem larger than it was and almost ethereal. The whole atmosphere was of a garden transported inside. Aunt Mary looked around and gasped, "Oh my, I never realised."

Mother looked around with a troubled expression on her face. "It's truly beautiful. But it reminds me of something—something I saw once." She paused again closing her eyes. "It was a painting but I can't remember where I saw it."

Aunt Mary took mother's hand and her eyes glistened. "I remember it very well, my dear, it was one of your mother's." She walked around taking everything in.

Holding up a porcelain shepherdess, she remarked, "Even these ornaments are identical."

My mother's eyes were wide with disbelief. "Perhaps she visited here, and she was inspired to paint this room."

Aunt Mary shook her head. "No, my dear, this home wasn't built until after your mother died."

Mother licked her lips. "Then how did all this happen?"

Behind us the door opened and closed as we stood in awe of the room. A raspy voice full of emotion answered, "It was my doing. I took the painting from the Abbey when I was there for her funeral." Lord Gromley had just walked into the room. He looked smaller than I remembered, and his face was grey with obvious fatigue. He reached out with a shaky hand and sat down in the nearest chair and taking a deep breath, he continued, "In fact, I took almost all of her paintings and drawings with me. They have been the inspiration for most of the decor in my home. I've been saving them for you and your brother. And I thank God that I was able to save them from your father or he would have burned them all."

Lord Gromley shuddered and clenched his fists. "In fact, he was burning her things the evening after we had laid her to rest. I couldn't sleep and went to your mother's private sitting room to be close to her and my memories. It was there that I found him feeding her belongings into the fire. He was there with his filthy hands touching her possessions, burning her journals and paintings. I wanted to kill him that night just as he most assuredly had killed her. Instead I got him drunk, so drunk in fact that I had to call the footmen to carry him to bed. Then I packed up everything that I could, anything that reminded me of Alice or that she had cherished and sent them off to my estate. The next day your father crowed to me about how he had put her to rest once and for all so that her presence wouldn't haunt the Abbey at every turn. He thought that he had been successful in destroying her memory, so I let him believe it. He is…was a monster. I saved them all, children, they're here in the attics anytime you'd like to claim them…I saved everything that I could."

He waved his shaking hand about, taking in the entire room, his eyes glistening with tears as he looked around. "This is her vision. I used many of her drawings when I was having this house designed and decorated. But I find it difficult to spend much time here." A half smile graced his face, but his eyes were filled with pain. "I swear at times I can hear her laughter in the gallery and her footsteps on the stairs even though she had never been here. You see I loved your mother so very deeply that she haunts me still." Tears rolled down his cheeks as he looked at my mother. "You look so very much like her, Irene."

Aunt Mary went to him and kneeled at his feet with her hands on his knees, looking up at him and I saw a tear roll down her cheek. "She never stopped loving you, Alex. I know that for a fact; some of her last words to me were about you."

He looked at her hopefully as Mr Spencer quietly entered the room, no one took any notice but me. Lord Gromley covered her hands with his and whispered, "They were?"

Aunt Mary nodded and took his hands. "Yes, Alex." She smiled up at him and pressed their hands together. "She told me that she wished she'd had the courage to run away with you when you asked her. She always regretted her decision to bow to her parents' wishes…but she begged me not to tell you. She didn't want to hurt you anymore than she already had. I should have told you when I saw the pain you were in at the funeral, but I tried to honour her request. I wish now that I hadn't, can you forgive me?"

He patted her hand, rested his head back against the chair stretching out his legs like he was exhausted. "You are forgiven, Mary, and I'm glad you never told me, I don't think I could have handled the burden of that knowledge all those years ago and not kill Richard. It was hard enough as it was."

He closed his eyes, smiling slightly. "He knew how I felt about Alice, I'm sure of it since we could never be in each other's company for very long without picking a quarrel about something to do with her or the children. Just as I loved her, I hated him. I only wish that I had arrived here in time to do the deed myself."

Father looked up from where he had been seated, arched an eyebrow while looking directly at Mr Spencer who only nodded. My mother went to Father and reached out to touch his arm. Then she turned to look at Mr Spencer. "What do you mean do the deed?" then she shifted her gaze to Lord Gromley. "What do you mean, Lord Gromley?"

Mr Spencer stepped forward and Father wrapped his arms around my mother. Uncle Samuel came and stood by me taking my hand. "General Sir Richard Hughes is dead, madam. When he didn't come in for luncheon, the servants found him dead in the summer house. His throat had been slit."

Mother fell back into my father's arms in shock. Aunt Mary laid her head in Lord Gromley's lap while he placed his hand on her hair. Mr Johnson assisted Emilie to a seat then came to me pushing Samuel to go to her. It felt like someone had poured ice water down my spine. I shivered and before I realised what I was doing I said, "I want to see him. I want to know that he's really dead." I had no idea why, it just seemed to be profoundly important for me to know that it wasn't a charade.

My father assisted mother to the chase lounge then turning to me, "Lissa, I don't think now is the appropriate time." I frowned, and my brow furrowed, I could feel the anger starting to burn in the pit of my stomach. I wanted to scream at him, but I had no idea why.

Mr Johnson looked down at me. "I think she'll need to eventually, Turner, after all the man treated her abominably all her life. He is the thing in her nightmares. She should be able to look upon him and know that he can no longer have any control over her." I was amazed. How did he know that the General had always been the main feature in my nightmares? How did he know that I needed to make sure he was dead even though I knew Mr Spencer wasn't lying?

Father was distracted and upset as he assisted Mother to lay back on the lounge. Then he spun around and yelled, "DON'T YOU PRESUME TO THINK THAT I DON'T KNOW OR CARE ABOUT HOW THAT MAN TREATED MY DAUGHTER! Or how she feels about it! I'm the one that has had to listen to her cry out in the night since we came to London; not even sure if she would want me to check on her and offer her comfort. Before that it was her mother and uncle that did the same. When the time is right, I will make sure that she sees him. But good God man, not now...use some common sense." Mr Johnson looked complacent and didn't answer back.

Father was rubbing his forehead as he kneeled by my now seated mother. I squeezed Mr Johnson's hand to thank him then let it go and went to my parents. I leaned my hand on my father's shoulder and he wrapped his arm around me. "I would like it very much if you would comfort me when I have a bad dream, Papa.

And you're right, we will all see the General together when the time is right." I looked over to Mr Johnson. "Thank you for understanding, Mr Johnson."

He smiled at me and shook his head. "You have a remarkable daughter, Turner, I hope you appreciate that."

My father pulled me closer to him to kiss me on the top of my head. "I'm aware of that, Miles, I always have been."

Mr Spencer had been talking to Samuel and Emilie while Aunt Mary rang for tea. The universal cure all for the English was tea, it was the Englishman's answer to everything. I smiled at her when she looked my way and nodded back as she dealt with the maid who answered her summons. She then pulled Lord Gromley from his chair by the door and sat with him on a settee by the fire, holding his hand and talking quietly to him. The man still looked ghastly, but his colour had improved somewhat.

Mother sat up holding her head, she seemed a bit unsteady. "Oh my, I'm still a bit light headed, I'm sorry, darling. I'm afraid that the mention of what happened to father made me think of the amount of blood there would be and well I really haven't been myself lately."

Emilie came forward and sat by my mother, patting her hand. "It's alright, you'll be fine in a bit." Mother smiled weakly and glared at my aunt when she coughed.

Father stood up and looked at Mr Spencer. "Well, Arthur, do you have any suspects?"

Mr Spencer nodded at Lord Gromley who immediately went pale under his scrutiny. But he managed to stammer. "Oh God, no, I only, I only just got here myself, my good man! I will not mourn him, but I did not kill him."

Mr Spencer nodded. "I'm aware of that, Lord Gromley, it's been confirmed by your coachman, groom and the rest of your staff. Besides the footman that came after me told me that you weren't in London yet but were expected later today. He was just as surprised as I was to find you here when we returned."

He walked to the French doors that led out to the garden, "My men are canvassing the neighbourhood as we speak and searching the area. We found two sets of footprints leading from this door but none returning. We can only assume that General Hughes either knew his murderer or was followed into the garden."

Father crossed his arms. "That still doesn't answer my question, do you have a suspect in mind?"

Mr Spencer faced him then spread his hands wide. "Everyone and no one, Mr Turner. After considering the previous events such as Mr Hughes being shot and the things that have recently come to light courtesy of Mr Johnson, I believe that we can safely look outside of your immediate family. That leaves us with just the staff and any of his business partners. The servants have all been accounted for and no visitors were admitted by any of them. I would assume then that the murderer was someone the General expected and who he was not afraid of, at least not normally." He paused before continuing, "Where is your valet, Mr Turner?"

Father straightened to stare at Mr Spencer, his lips pressed tight together with suppressed anger. Mr Spencer repeated his question, "Mr Turner, I would like to know the whereabouts of Mr Richards!"

Father grimaced and sighed. "As would I, sir."

Mr Spencer proved to be unrelenting. "I have been unable to locate him, so I ask you again where is your valet?"

Father slumped. "I really have no idea, Arthur. He left the day before yesterday without my knowledge and I've not seen him since."

Mr Spencer walked back to sit on the other side of Aunt Mary. Mr Johnson was flipping through some papers on a table at the back of the room, but he spoke to my father over his shoulder. "Turner, your footman, Murphy, he's Irish, isn't he?"

Samuel groaned and answered instead of my father, "For god sakes, you already know that, Miles! What are you looking at there?"

Mr Johnson waved a pamphlet in father's general direction. "Just what seem to be a collection of political pamphlets on various topics."

Samuel glared at him and continued, "Before you ask, Miles, yes he writes pamphlets about Irish home rule now and again. However, he is not a rebel!"

Mr Johnson feigned a look of shock. "Oh, pardon me, but you did say that he's an Irishman and that he writes political pamphlets about Home Rule. Yet he's not a rebel. You know, Hughes, not everyone would see that in the same light."

Father walked over to him. "Alright, I see your point, but he doesn't advocate violence. Good God, he lost a sister in the Dublin riots. What are you implying, Miles?"

"I'm not implying anything, Turner, merely pointing out that these were left here for some reason and what better reason than to discredit not only Murphy but your family in the bargain." Mr Johnson stepped aside for my father.

He picked up one of the pamphlets and glanced over it then he slammed it back onto the table. "That is not Murphy's work! I know his style. For heaven's sake, I was the one that recruited the man and we've never found anything in his history that indicated he was violent, in fact, it's quite the contrary."

Mr Johnson raised an eyebrow. "He was a soldier was he not and did it well? Is that not being violent? And is his name not Aedan Murphy?"

Samuel growled. "Of course that's his name but you might note Johnson that he was fighting on the British side in the war and not with the French!"

Father picked the pamphlet up again, examining it more closely. "That's his name but those are not his words, as I said I know his style. Why would these even be here? My father-in-law was not a supporter of Home Rule to my knowledge." He looked at the settee where my aunt was sitting. "Lord Gromley, are these yours?"

Lord Gromley looked up. "No, son, they're not. While I sympathize with the plight in Ireland I have no influence in the house nor with anyone that does." He paused and reached out his hand. "May I see them?"

Father gathered them all up and brought them over to him. He examined the top one closely. "You're right, Colin, no Irishman wrote this! It's a decent attempt, I will give you that. But the Irish are a poetical and passionate people and they are very particular with their cadence when writing. The person that wrote this was only angry. I would hazard a guess that whoever did write it is well-educated and probably as English as either you or I."

Mr Spenser ran his hand over his hair and leaned forward. "But why, I mean why were they left here, what purpose does it serve?"

Lord Gromley pursed his lips. "Perhaps as Mr Johnson suggested to implicate this Murphy chap and thereby cast aspersion on Colin? You can see that these are hand-written and in fact appear to be drafts not yet ready for the printer." Lord Gromley pulled out another one randomly from the handful my father had given him. "Oh my, this is strange. Look at this one, it's about Catholic emancipation. It's been

128

a bone of contention in Parliament for some time now, but it would be the end of Liverpool as Prime Minister if any of the proposed bills were passed." He rifled through the others with a frown on his face and pulled out another one. "This one is about elections in the rotten boroughs and government corruption. Every one of these is on a different topic that touch the Irish or the poor and are very inflammatory to the present government. Look, you can see that they're all in the same hand and written with the same anger and language."

Then Aunt Mary spoke up, "What part could they possibly play in Samuel being shot or Richard murdered?" She looked about the room as if one of us could answer her.

Mr Spencer clasped his hands behind his back. "What about the General? Tell me, did he ever express any dissatisfaction with government policies on the Irish?"

Lord Gromley looked at Aunt Mary and shook his head as he answered, "Not that I am aware of. Richard never had much interest in politics. If the Tories were in power, he was happy. And I would swear that these are not written by Richard. Do you agree, Mary?" My aunt was reading one and nodded in agreement.

Mr Johnson snorted. "Colin, none of this makes any sense, do you think the General was going to try and discredit you or Samuel?"

Father shook his head. "No one knows what we really do for the Crown and besides we're not policy makers. Granted Liverpool has governed with an iron fist and it's made him unpopular in many circles, even within his own party. But our work has nothing to do with any of those issues. We're strictly involved with espionage and smuggling. We're servants to the Crown no matter who is in political power."

Mr Johnson was shaking his head. "Mr Spencer, might I suggest that the pamphlets were left here as a red herring to distract you from the case at hand or that they have nothing to do with the murder at all. I suggest that we forget the pamphlets for the moment and look at what we do know. First the General is deeply in debt, yet he owns a very large warehouse by the Pool of London which I might add was unknown to his family or his solicitors. So how does a man make such a purchase without anyone knowing and without any capital? Nor has he ever been involved in shipping or trade of any kind that we know of? Second, there is Mr Browne, a person of dubious ethics also deeply in debt and who has been seen coming and going from this warehouse with Mr Turner's valet who is a known smuggler." While the first two men are not particularly liked by their families or associates they have connections within society that the likes of Richards would not have. Richards on the other hand has the connections that could be of use to men in desperate need of money."

Mr Spencer rubbed his chin and bit his lower lip while flexing his shoulders. "I see your point. But I can't just ignore these seditious writings!"

Mr Johnson smiled. "I doubt we'll ever find who actually penned them. But are you prepared to embarrass Lord Gromley with these? The death of the General will be enough to bring an unusual amount of attention to him and to this house as it is. It's my belief that they were meant to be a distraction and to perhaps cast aspersions on Turner and Hughes."

Mr Spencer was grinning from ear to ear. "Johnson, Are you committing to assist in investigating this mess?"

Miles grimaced. "Yes, I suppose I am." Then he smiled and looked at my father in mock distress. "Turner, this is entirely all your fault! You've made my life far too interesting of late. Mr Spencer, I believe that I'm currently employed by his Majesty's government as an agent under Mr Turner's direction, therefore, am I correct in assuming, Turner, that these treasonous writings would come under the jurisdiction of Sir Thomas?"

Mr Spencer had his mouth open in shock, looking at my father with a steely glare as he asked, "Is this true! Is Wicker now in your employ?"

The tea arrived before anyone could reply. Emilie poured and passed the cups around. Once Father had a cup firmly in hand, he turned first to eye Mr Johnson and then address Mr Spencer. "His appointment is contingent upon approval by Sir Thomas. But yes, Johnson has agreed to act in the open as an agent of the crown in order that Samuel and I may maintain our anonymity."

Samuel had moved to stand by the windows, looking out at the garden. I wondered if he could see the summer house from there. There was a hesitant knock at the door and a little dark man with the most extraordinary gold earring dangling from his right ear stuck his head around the door. "Ah, there you are, Spencer. I'm done with my preliminary examination, the cart will be here shortly to remove the gentleman. You will have my report on your desk by tomorrow afternoon."

He started to shut the door but before he could, Samuel wheeled around and quickly asked, "Ah, sir, a moment please, Mr..."

The doctor answered, "Grimes. It's Dr Grimes."

"Yes, Dr Grimes. I was wondering if it would be possible to have our personal physician examine my father as well. Not that I would doubt your findings but for our own piece of mind. Dr Jefferson studied in Padua." He emphasized the word Padua as if that would mean something special to Mr Grimes.

And apparently it did, he initially stiffened then he bowed to Samuel. "As you wish, sir. I won't have all the equipment he may require but I would very much like to be in attendance when the—ah, examination is performed. It is after all Bow Street business." He smiled, and I saw that he was missing one front tooth which had been replaced with a gold one.

Samuel nodded. "I will arrange it. Thank you."

Dr Grimes bowed. "Your servant, sir. Mr Spencer will have my direction as to where he should come." And with that he spun on his heel and left.

Aunt Mary grimaced. "What an extraordinary little man! He looks more like a pirate than a doctor."

Mr Spencer laughed. "My dear Lady Alford, you have hit very close to the mark. Mr Grimes is a trained physician but when he was done with his education he signed on broad as a ship's doctor for a bit of an adventure. However, not being a sailor, he didn't realise that he had signed onto a merchantman headed for the West Indies. The ship was taken by pirates and it took him ten years of service to them to earn his way home. He's vowed never to board a ship again." He chuckled. "He has a comfortable practice now among the wealthy merchant class and supports a wife and family. He still has some interesting connections though among the more nefarious individuals that sail in and out of London."

He started for the door then as he put his hand out to open it, he added, "Gentlemen, since we will be working together on this perhaps you'd like to view the body before it's removed? Then you can examine the crime scene."

I walked over to my father's side taking his hand. He looked at me and shook his head no. "Lissa, I know that you're a very strong young lady, but I really want you to stay with your mother right now." I frowned until he added, "When we go out to the summer house, you may come with us." He squeezed my shoulder then left with the other gentleman including Lord Gromley.

# Chapter 15
## *Best Wishes to All*

We sat quietly waiting for the men to return, none of us moved or said a word. I knew that if I got up I would be told to sit but time was dragging on and it was so quiet that I could hear my heart incessantly pounding in my ears to the point that I felt like I would scream.

Finally, we were rejoined by everyone but Lord Gromley, so Mother asked, "Where is his Lordship?"

Father replied, "He's lying down. He's been under a great deal of stress and not been well lately, yet he left Northumberland as soon as he knew that the General was headed for London. It was not a comfortable trip for him and has taken its toll. I've sent for Dr Jefferson to attend to him. I believe he just needs to rest."

Aunt Mary looked pale and suddenly older. She started towards the door as if she would go to him, but Samuel touched her arm, redirecting her to Mr Spencer who wrapped his arms around her while she cried. In all the turmoil, we had forgotten that her only brother was dead and despite the person he may have been she had still loved him.

Father suggested that we all venture into the garden since Mr Spencer and his men had already been over the crime scene. My father, Uncle Samuel and Mr Johnson obviously wanted to go over everything themselves.

Mr Spencer gave us one order, "Please, don't remove anything." Father nodded. We left them in the drawing room and went through the French doors and stood looking down where the grass had been crushed but the warm day and mild breeze had dried up the rain from the previous night, making the prints barely visible.

The summer house was located at the bottom of the garden hidden from our view by a large willow tree next to an ornamental pond. Mother took my hand and we started walking towards it. Emilie hung back ghostly pale and she balked at following so Samuel went back into the house with her. I looked over my shoulder for my father and Mr Johnson who were slowly following and talking in whispers while looking about. We reached the pond where the sun sparkled on its surface when I caught the glint of something in the water on the far side as we passed but it disappeared as we got closer and was probably just a trick of the light. I followed my mother up three steps and into the shadow dappled summer house.

At first nothing there was nothing visible until our eyes adjusted to the dim light. Then I saw a large wicker chair with a reddish stain over one arm and pooling on the floor, beside it was a large glistening red puddle so thick that it still looked wet while the stain on the arm of the chair had already begun to dry, turning a reddish brown. The General must have fallen sideways in the chair for it to have collected on the floor like that. Mother gagged and immediately turned away then stepped back out the door. Father and Mr Johnson joined me as I stood transfixed, looking down at the congealed pool at my feet.

Mr Johnson walked around the periphery of the room, examining everything closely. "There doesn't appear to have been any struggle. And there's no trace of blood leading from the body. Whoever did this wiped off the murder weapon and took it with them." He held up a bloody lap rug that had been tossed on floor as evidence of the clean-up. He put it down then came and stood beside me, looking at the puddle and the chair. "Do you see it, Turner?"

My father looked frustrated and worried, "What are you talking about, Miles?"

He puckered his lips before responding, "There's no passion to this crime. It's very cold and calculated. Clearly our murderer has done this kind of thing before without compunction."

Father walked back looking closely at the entryway and the steps. "You're right, Miles, there isn't any blood leading out of here or anything that would indicate that someone was distressed and had run away."

Outside Samuel was standing at my mother's side speaking to her and just as we reached them, Samuel said, "I'm taking Emilie and Aunt Mary home, I think Irene and Clarissa should come as well." Mother nodded and stretched out her hand to me.

Father walked over to her and kissed her on the cheek. "I'll be home soon, darling, take Murphy and Jacob with you. I'll keep Michael with us."

We started towards the house just as the sun came out again and I saw the same sparkle again in the depths of the pond. I turned calling out to my father, "Father, you should check the pond. There's something shiny over there." I pointed to the far side of the water nearest the garden wall. He nodded so I turned and left with my mother and Uncle.

This time Samuel got into the carriage with us and Murphy rode his horse. He looked exhausted, but everyone looked drained as we sat there with our own thoughts. I wondered if his marriage to Emilie would be postponed now. Even though the General was not universally loved, he was my mother and uncle's father and it would be expected that we would observe a period of mourning.

My uncle rubbed at his nose and sniffed yet he didn't appear to be upset. Mother just sat looking out the window, her hands folded in her lap. The best way I could describe her look was numb. Emilie was shredding a handkerchief while watching Samuel. Aunt Mary had appeared to be deep in thought but finally broke the silence, "We have some decisions to make and quickly. Samuel, you must contact that minister friend of Miles and have him come to the house as soon as possible, the banns have been read so there is no reason that you can't be married tomorrow. I will not have this unfortunate state of affairs stop your wedding."

Samuel looked astounded, but he turned with a smile to Emilie. "Would you mind very much darling if we forgo the church wedding?"

Emilie took his hand, smiling, and looked up into his eyes. "Just so long as I am married to you I don't care where it takes place. But your father's death must be upsetting for you."

Samuel sighed. "He was my father though not an especially good one and I will mourn his passing. But what is most important to me is that I have you at my side as my lawful wife. I don't think that my mother would fault us for marrying in such a fashion. Though she is no longer with us, she has always been my guide for what is right and wrong."

Mother started to protest. "But the invitations?" Aunt Mary gave her a stern look and Mother took a deep breath, "Oh yes, I see, once people become aware of Father's death, they will automatically assume that the wedding has been cancelled or at the very least it will be family only. I'll have Allen take care of notifying everyone."

Aunt Mary touched her hand and smiled. "We'll get through this, my dear, it will be a quiet affair held in our home. Emilie's dress is ready, we'll have flowers from the garden, cook has the cake ready, it just needs assembling. Thank heavens we won't have to deal with all those dreary guests."

Samuel coughed, and all eyes focused on him. He looked grim. "What about the funeral? We'll be expected to do it in grand style, won't we?"

Aunt Mary pinched her lips together. "No, Samuel, I think not under the circumstances. It would be best if it was just a small family affair as well. People will understand and approve." She paused and looked out the window as a single tear rolled down her cheek. "I still find it hard to believe that he's gone. He was my brother and though I would never say we were close, I did love him." She sighed, straightened her skirts and continued after clearing her throat, "When Jonathan died, Richard came to the funeral. They had never gotten along, and lord knows we hadn't seen eye to eye for years but afterwards he took me aside and gave me the best piece of advice that I've ever received. So, I will pass it along to both of you. Don't mourn too long for a man that you didn't especially care for."

Everyone fell back into silence. I knew that I wouldn't mourn the General. But I would observe the essentials for the sake of my mother, uncle and Aunt Mary. We reached home, and Murphy jumped from his horse, escorting us to the door.

It wasn't long before the house was in an uproar trying to pull together a wedding and a funeral. Fortunately, the staff thought nothing of the extra work and they rose to the occasion.

Thankfully the Clarkes were away visiting Ramsey at Oxford and the Summers would never think of being so intrusive as to enquire on their own as to what was going on; they would rely on their servants to do that. Therefore, no explanations would be required from us as to what was happening. Sir Thomas agreed to keep the facts of the General's death quiet for now. But that would be no more than a day or two at best. He also approved Mr Johnson's appointment as an agent of the crown with great delight.

The staff did an amazing job of decorating the house and pulling together a wedding feast. I had no idea how they achieved all that they did without working around the clock. Emilie was stunning in a dress of the palest pink overlaid with silver lace and a veil to match. Samuel was immaculate and so handsome in his black evening kit with snow white shirt and hose and a waistcoat with thin silver stripes on a cream background.

Since it was to be only family Emilie had asked that all the staff be invited to attend the ceremony and to partake of the feast which they had worked so hard to make perfect. It had to have been the most unusual wedding in London that season. The Beau Monde would have been shocked to know that the cook and the boot boy sat at the table with the vicar, the master of the house and the bride and groom. It was really a marvellous party. The entry hall became a dance floor and the pianoforte was moved to the doorway of the music room to provide the accompaniment.

Mr Spencer attended as did Dr Jefferson who from the looks of it I assumed would be engaged to Louisa before the end of the year. It even looked like Aunt

Mary and Mr Spencer had come to some type of agreement. Everyone enjoyed themselves even though no liquor was served, which impressed the vicar and depressed many others. But the music and the food made amends.

Mr Johnson was able to dance with Lettie and was the perfect gentleman. I watched them closely, but Lettie had eyes only for Murphy who watched her intently as she glided around the room. Though she smiled at Mr Johnson, she barely said two words to the poor man. After the dance, he automatically returned her to Murphy's side and from the look Murphy gave him, he must have known that his cause was lost. Then he came over to me and bowed. "May I have this dance, Miss Turner?"

I quickly glanced at Lettie, but she was talking quietly with Murphy who managed to give me wink when he caught my eye, then I looked to Mother who nodded her approval. "I would be delighted, Mr Johnson, but what about your previous partner?"

"Ah, Miss Turner, it is never to wise to pursue a woman that is not interested in you. It only leads to heartache and I believe that she has already given her heart to the inestimable Mr Murphy."

"I'm sorry, Mr Johnson."

He smiled down at me. "Don't be, Miss Turner, some things are worth waiting for, especially love. And I can be a very patient man." He smiled at me then pulled me close and swept me into a waltz. It was the best night of my life.

The original plan had been for Emilie and Samuel to go to Somerset, but it was decided that with the General's death and the threat of a murderer still on the loose that we should all stay in London. Two days later the Times finally carried the story of the General's murder. Fortunately, Sir Thomas saw to it that the story of his death had been printed the same day as our request for the funeral to be a family affair. The timing of both could not have been better. Society would now understand and appreciate our discretion and once again the Beau Monde looked upon us favourably for our sensibilities.

It rained lightly but steadily on the day we buried my grandfather, Sir Thomas attended along with Lord Gromley, Mr Johnson, Dr Jefferson and Mr Spencer. I was surprised when Sir Thomas was pointed out to me, I had expected to see a wizen old man, but he wasn't even as old as my grandfather. At the graveside, he stood as erect and solemn as a soldier but once we arrived home I found that he was a man who smiled and laughed a great deal. He even quizzed me on my studies. Sir Thomas and Mr Johnson spent a great deal of time talking quietly in the corner of the room where there was no feasible way that I could eavesdrop on them.

Once the vicar left the general conversation turned to the dilemma of who shot my uncle and killed the General. Richards had never returned, and the French were still looking for Mr Browne who had not been seen since well before the General's murder, yet the French were positive that he had not returned to the France.

Later I noticed that Sir Thomas was speaking to my father and mother by the door as he was about to leave when he said loud enough for everyone to hear, "I'm sorry, Turner, but you'll have to go back, it can't wait. I know that it's not what you want, but this is important. Might I suggest that you escort Lord Gromley home at the same time. I know he hasn't been well and it will give you a cover story for leaving London so suddenly. And if my sources are correct, you'll find them both in

Northumberland. I know it's a long way to go but I need you to find the answers and soon. And Colin, take care of our problem this time any way that you can."

As he walked out the door, Mother reached for Father's hand and squeezed, he smiled weakly as he took her arm, turning to face our guests and the family. "We are required in Northumberland."

All conversation stopped, and faces became pale as he continued, "Sir Thomas has just informed me that the two people most likely responsible for the attack on Samuel and the murder of the General have been seen near the Abbey. The French are most desirous of laying their hands on Mr Browne and Richards is apparently with him."

Aunt Mary sighed deeply. "Colin, I won't be going with you. I refuse to make that trek again." Father opened his mouth, but she held her hand up to stop him from saying anything, so he paused and waited for her to explain herself. "I'm staying here in London under the protection of my husband." She looked up at Mr Spencer and moved towards him while he put his arm around her. "I have to introduce him to Dyson, the dreary boy is in town and I want to get his dramatics over with as soon as possible." I looked around the room, everyone was bug-eyed with their mouths open, including myself. "Oh, stop it all of you, yes we're married. I'm sorry we didn't tell you, but Arthur and I wanted to keep it a secret. We didn't want a fuss made at our age."

Mother sat down and was barely able to utter, "How—I mean, how long and when?"

Aunt Mary laughed. "A few weeks." She reached up and kissed Mr Spencer's cheek.

Father, Samuel and Emilie rushed to congratulate them both and welcome him to the family. I joined them by hugging Aunt Mary and welcoming Mr Spencer with "Welcome to the family, Uncle Arthur!" He smiled at me and kissed my cheek.

Mother was still in shock, but she rose to walk towards them, then suddenly turned ghostly white and fainted. Dr Jefferson and Father were at her side simultaneously. Dr Jefferson spoke first, "I was afraid that something like this would happen. There has been far too much excitement and stress for her the last few days." Father sat back, looking baffled. Dr Jefferson looked like he wanted to swallow his tongue. "Oh my god, she hasn't told you, has she?" He picked her up then as my father stood up and placed her in his arms. "Take her to her room, Colin, have her maid undress her and put her to bed. I will get my bag and be with you directly."

Father did as he was told without question. As he left the room Emilie, Louisa and Aunt Mary were all smiling. Samuel turned on them, looking totally perplexed, "Will someone please tell me what is going on?"

Emilie came to his side and whispered in his ear, he reared back like she had slapped him. "A BABY? Now! But how I mean, when—oh" Everyone but me and Mr Johnson started to laugh. Mr Johnson came to stand by me, "Well, poppet, you'll be a sister in due course. How do you feel about that?"

I looked up at him thinking for a second while holding his eye. "Well, I have only recently found out that I have a mother and a father, and I think I adjusted to that well enough. I'll have more time to think about being a sister, so as of right now I believe I'm fine." I smiled because I was actually pleased by the news. I wasn't worried anymore about my place in the family.

He smiled at me and squeezed my hand. "That child is going to be very lucky to have you as a sister."

I smiled and asked him, "Would you care to play a game of chess. No one is going to be of much use for anything until the doctor comes down, so we might as well amuse ourselves." I let go of his hand and walked towards the table where the chess set was arranged. I looked over my shoulder at him, his head was cocked to one side and had a faraway look in his eye as he watched me. "Mr Johnson?" His eyes came back into focus. "Are you alright?"

"Oh yes, yes indeed, Miss Turner. I'm quite alright." He gave me a crooked smile, joining me at the table and he immediately claimed black just as he always did, even knowing that it put him at an immediate disadvantage no matter who he played.

"Why do you do that?"

He cocked an eyebrow at me as I continued, "Do what?"

I nodded at the board. "That…why do you always pick black?"

"Do I?" He leaned back but kept his eyes on the board. "It must be a habit. My father taught me how to play chess and he told me that I might as well learn how to play the black pieces first." I didn't understand what he meant, I waited for him to explain. He looked at me finally, "It was an object lesson. No matter how much he loved me and my mother, in the eyes of the law and society I would always be his bastard, so I would always be at a disadvantage. Therefore, I had to learn to turn any disadvantage to my favour."

He looked sad and remote, but I was at a loss for what to say and blathered out, "It must have worked because I've never seen you lose to anyone and Dr Jefferson and my father are exceptionally good." I was mortified at how stupid I could be.

He smiled but there was still pain in his eyes. "Apparently, I did learn my lesson, poppet, as far as chess goes but I still have a tough time applying it to the rest of my life. But I'm working on it."

I watched him covertly throughout our game, but my skill was nowhere near being competitive with him. Yet he was exceptionally patient and ended up teaching me more about the game than playing. All the time we sat there he had a faraway look in his eye like he was looking back at the past or into the future.

Dr Jefferson returned but my father did not. "Mr and Mrs Turner have requested that I inform all of you that they are expecting an addition to the family in about five months." He raised his hand as people started to asked questions. He fidgeted and looked very uncomfortable running a finger around his cravat. "I can safely say that mother and child are doing well and that the father is a nervous wreck." Everyone gave a chuckle before he continued, "However, Mrs Turner has been under too much stress of late and she needs to rest. Under the circumstances, I have advised that she should remain here in London where I can look in on her rather than follow all of you off to the wilds of Northumberland."

Suddenly my heart stopped, that meant I would have to stay here as well. I looked at my only confederate, Mr Johnson, and I could tell that he understood where my thoughts had led me. But he didn't say a word as he turned his eyes back to the chessboard.

Mr Johnson and I had just finished our chess game when Father came into the room. He was grinning from ear to ear and accepted congratulations all around. Then he came to me, "Lissa, I'd like to speak to you privately if I may."

It wasn't really a question, but I could tell he wouldn't allow me to say no even if I wanted to. I followed him to his study and sat down on my hands to keep me from clenching them into fists. Father sat down behind his desk. My shoulders slumped forward, I knew he was about to tell me I had to stay here and watch over my mother. "Lissa, I'm sorry but I can't take you with me to Northumberland. Samuel, Michael and Jacob will be coming with me, but we need to travel light and fast. Lord Gromley is going to slow us down enough as it is." I inhaled deeply and bit my tongue as he continued, "I'm going to ask Mr Johnson to stay here to watch over you ladies so he's going to need your help and watchful eyes. Mr Spencer will stay here as well, but he has his own duties with Bow Street. It may seem an odd arrangement, but I want someone I trust here with you and your mother other than just the staff; I am not entirely convinced that London is safe yet."

My eyes went wide, and I asked, "You really think that we'll be in danger here?"

Father clasped his hands in front of him and sighed, "Intelligence is only as good as the man or men gathering it. And I'm not convinced that this latest intelligence is reliable. But it's Samuel's and my duty to go where we're sent."

Before I realised why, I blurted, "Father, do you trust Mr Johnson?"

He met my eyes and without hesitation said, "Yes, Lissa, strangely enough I do. Is there something that you know that I don't?"

"No, not really, except he does like to be a bit reckless regarding himself. I don't want to see him get hurt watching over us."

Father chuckled. "I suppose you're referring to the way he plays chess?" I nodded. "That doesn't mean he's like that in his day to day life."

I bit my lower lip and whispered, "I'm not sure that he would agree with you."

Father rose from his chair, came around the desk and sat in the chair beside me. I could tell from the look on his face that he thought I was being melodramatic. "Then I will expect you to keep him from doing anything foolish." I sighed deeply, as if a grown man was going to listen to an almost seventeen-year-old girl. But if I had to make him listen then I'd find a way.

"Poor Uncle Samuel, he should be on his wedding trip."

Father nodded. "Duty calls but we won't be gone more than a fortnight."

I nodded, and he hugged me closely. "Watch over your mother."

# Chapter 16
## *Call to Arms*

It had been two days since my father and uncle had left for Northumberland. Mother was confined to bed and it had rained every day. Mr Johnson and Mr Spencer divided their time equally between us and the outside world. Neither one of them could stay cooped up for long and convention dictated that Mr Johnson could not stay overnight in our home without a male relative present. So, he spent most of the day reading or playing chess with Murphy, Emilie or me, he could also be found in the music room where he tinkered with the violin. He usually left just before or just after the evening meal. I had no idea when he returned but Aunt Mary and Uncle Arthur had agreed to remain with us so that Mr Johnson would not have find other accommodation.

To keep our minds off what was happening in Northumberland we were quickly wrapped up in Aunt Mary's plans to make baby clothes. Beth and Meg were asked to join us and while they thoroughly enjoyed it...I didn't. I was good at sewing but the amount of time being devoted to it was excessive in my opinion and I found it difficult to keep my mind on the task. On the third day, I managed to escape to the library after having sighed enough for my mother to release me to find amusement elsewhere. I selected a book and tucked into the window seat that looked down towards the old garden gate. I sat there reading for some time, it had been an overcast day and the light was beginning to fade earlier than usual. I was about to close my book when I looked up, noticing a movement near the old the gate. It was standing open! Then I saw my father's valet Richards step through, followed by several other rough looking men. I wasted no time in leaving my book behind and racing to the drawing room. Mr Spencer had not arrived yet, but Mr Johnson was sitting in front of the chess board. I walked quickly to his side, "Mr Johnson, I just saw Richards with several other men in the garden, they came through the garden gate from the Clarkes."

He looked at me frowned then exploded into action. "Ladies, excuse me, but Richards and his men are in the garden. I need all of you to go to the library and lock yourselves in. Aunt Mary and Mother shooed Emilie and Louisa along as they left the drawing room." I turned to follow as he said, "Lissa, run to the kitchen and alert the staff. Tell Murphy and John to arm everyone that can use a weapon and then meet me in the hall." I nodded as I turned and ran for the kitchens.

I met Murphy coming through the green braise door, he was already armed. He explained that Mr Cripps had seen the interlopers when he came across from the mews for his dinner. Murphy and John had already passed out weapons and all the staff were assuming their positions throughout the house concentrating on the garden side. Beth came through the door with Meg, each carrying a crossbow and he sent them both upstairs. My eyes followed them with my mouth agape. Murphy spoke up, "They'll be fine, miss. It seems that having older brothers has its advantages. They were taught at an early age how to pick off hares in the fields. Where is Mr Johnson, miss?" I pointed to the drawing room just as he came through the door to the hallway.

Murphy passed me one of the pair of pistols that he carried in his belt. Mr Johnson walked across the hallway shaking his head. "Oh no!" He took the pistol from my hand. "Her father would kill me."

Murphy growled. "Gov, she's almost as good shot as her father and we need all hands."

The library door opened, and Aunt Mary peered around saying in a tone that would brook no argument. "Murphy, where are the keys to the weapons cabinet in here? I refuse to stand by and let those miscreants get into this house without being able to defend myself." She looked at the gun being extended towards me. "For heaven's sake, Miles, let the child have the pistol."

Mr Johnson waved his hand at Murphy, signalling him to go ahead and open the cabinet as he watched. My mother had been watching Murphy then turned her attention to Mr Johnson and me as he whispered, "Poppet, I need you to take your mother into the study and stay there." I raised one eyebrow and glared at him. "Don't give me that face. Who do you think they're here for? It's you and your mother! I need you to protect her and the study only has one window on the side of the house." He stood up and pointed across the hall, "Now go!"

As my mother walked towards me I grabbed her hand and pulled but she resisted, looking at Mr Johnson who shook his head no. Then she relaxed, putting her hands over her belly. She nodded to him then came with me. Once in the study I closed and locked the door and we sat down by the cold hearth. I stooped to start the fire, but she pulled my arm back and whispered, "No, leave it, Lissa, we don't want the light to draw attention to us."

"Should I pull the curtains, Mother?" She shook her head no and put a finger to her lips. The house was eerily quiet. I sat beside her and waited. She had pulled her little pistol out of the pocket in her gown then she took my gun and laid them both on the table beside her along with some additional powder and shot.

It seemed like we had been sitting there for ages when there was a sudden pounding on the front door, then a shot rang out and everything went quiet again. Mother's hands flew to her chest and she reached for my hand, writing the word Spencer in my palm. Oh my god, that must have been him! If he had been shot, then there would be no help coming. Our nearest neighbours were the Clarkes and they were away visiting Ramsey in Oxford and the Summers had left on holiday to the country. No one else lived close enough to have been aware of a shot being fired.

I saw a movement at the window but as I alerted my mother, she turned to look, and it was gone. Then we both heard a scratching sound at the window and we went stiff, but the scratching persisted, yet it didn't seem threatening. I moved away from my mother, she grabbed for me but missed. I crawled over cautiously and looked over the edge of the window seat. Dr Jefferson was there holding a bloody Mr Spencer. I stood up immediately and opened the window. Mother came to assist, and we pulled Mr Spencer into the room. He was almost insensible and bleeding from a head wound.

Dr Jefferson looked around, closed the window and pulled the curtains and knelt next to Mr Spencer. Mother had placed a cushion under his head and lap rug over him and Dr Jefferson quickly examined him then took his handkerchief out to bind his head. He opened his mouth and Mother cautioned him to be quiet, so he whispered, "It's just a graze but he hit his head when he fell, I had to wait for the ruffian that shot at him to move onto the mews before I could drag him around to the nearest window."

"What is going on here?!"

Mother leaned in closely to him and said one word, "Richards." He nodded that he understood, but he looked shocked, I knew he must be worried about Louisa.

He pulled out the pistol that he always carried concealed in his coat. "Is Mr Johnson still here?" I nodded. "Is Louisa here?" I nodded again.

He sat back on his haunches at Mr Spencer's side. "I'll stay here, it would be too risky to leave right now to get help. The house is surrounded, I take it?" I shrugged since I didn't really know but assumed that it was so we all sat on the floor and waited.

As we sat there, I realised that we had left our pistols by the hearth. I moved to get them just as a rock was hurdled at the window smashing it into a thousand pieces that rained down on Dr Jefferson and my mother. I turned just as a man came through the window. Dr Jefferson sprang at him wrestling him for his weapon as another man came in and grabbed for my arm. I screamed and tried to run for my pistol, but I was caught by the hair and whirled around into the arms of Richards. Noise was coming from everywhere now; inside and outside of the house shots were being fired. Men screamed in pain and there was pounding on the hallway door. Dr Jefferson was still struggling with the brute on the floor. My mother was lying beside Mr Spencer, she had been hit in the head by the rock. Richards growled when I kicked him in the shins, but he still dragged me to the window. I was screaming his name as loud as I could until he shoved a cloth into my mouth to silence me. Then he pushed me through the window to another man who put a rough sack over my head that smelled like dirt and potatoes. He gathered me up and tossed me over his shoulder then ran. While I pounded on his back I could hear the heavy footfalls and breathing of someone following us. That person yelled "Left", my captor abruptly jerked to the left just as shot rang out from the house, it was followed by a muffled grunt then a curse from the person behind us, but we kept running. Further behind us men continued to yell and scream.

The last words I heard before I passed out from lack of air in the sack were. "To Poole."

I woke to the sound of voices arguing. We were in some kind conveyance that was bumping over rough roadways. There was a decided lack of the normal sounds and smells of London. I was sure that I was no longer in the city but was anyone following? Was anyone left who could follow? My feet and hands were bound and each time I tried to sit up, I was shoved back down by someone sitting close to me. I finally worked the ties of the sack loose enough so that I could get more air and I was able to see my feet whenever I lifted my chin up but nothing else. I lay there listening, but I heard nothing more other than a man's muffled groans and the sounds of the coach moving rapidly. Sometime later I fell asleep and woke just around dawn. It was very hot with the sack on my head and I started to gag on the rag in my mouth. Once I started, I couldn't stop. I was so thirsty, and I needed to relieve myself. Suddenly the sack was pulled from my head and my hands and feet were untied. The sun was harsh, and I had trouble seeing at first, then a bottle was shoved into my hand. "Drink," he said as I stared into the pain racked face of Richards. I drank greedily from the bottle and to my surprise it was water and not ale. Richard's look was intense, but he said nothing as he just glared at me. He passed me a covered pot and said "Piss." Which I did since necessity ignored my loftier intentions of telling him what I thought of him.

When I was done, he took the pot and emptied it out the window. I should have kept my mouth shut but silence was not a natural state for me even though my mouth usually got me into trouble. "Mr Richards…no matter if you ransom me or kill me, my father won't let you live."

He made a snorting noise. "Humph! I haven't decided yet and as far as your father is concerned, he's been sent off to chase his tail around the moors of Northumberland looking for Browne and me." He chuckled but without mirth.

I looked out the window, but I didn't recognize anything. I had no idea how long we had been travelling. "Where are we headed? From the position of the sun I would say that we're traveling south. Perhaps to Poole?" That idea didn't make me at all happy knowing that we were moving further away from my father and uncle.

Richards moved his leg and grimaced. Obviously, he had been wounded during the altercation in London. I thought for a moment to offer my services since Dr Jefferson had taught me how to dress wounds, but at the moment I wasn't feeling very generous. He looked at me again, smirking, "You're too smart for your own good, missy. I told Browne we should nab your mother, but he thought you'd be easier to control. If you're so smart then you'll know that you'd better shut your gob."

My stomach growled before I could answer him and to my surprise, he tossed me a sack that contained a stale heel of bread and an over ripe apple. I bit into the bread and chewed before taking another sip of water then saying, "I heard you say Poole; I know Mr Browne's family has some property near there. But I seem to recall that he's not too popular with them seeing as how he is considered a traitor to many."

Richards reached out and smacked me across the face, "Shut it." He chuckled then grunted in pain because of the movement. "It's not his family we'll be meeting up with but associates of mine. And none of them will be too impressed with an impudent little bitch like you in tow. But that's Browne's problem. He'll have to do the explaining." Then he tipped his head back and closed his eyes.

I continued eating the bread and apple. I drank off half of the water and settled back to think about my problem. Richards thought I was a normal spoiled child of the Beau Monde, he knew nothing about my being educated in the ways of my father's world. The carriage we were in was none too clean and appeared to be hired equipage along with the horses. If anyone could follow us, I hoped that they would take that into consideration. Or perhaps the information would be forthcoming from one of Richard's associates that had been left behind if any were still alive.

We stopped to change horses and I was gagged again but at least no sack was placed over my head this time, but I was pushed off the seat onto the carriage floor. Towards dusk we turned down a lane that led to a large rambling Tudor farm house that looked abandoned. Moss grew on the roof and a retaining wall near an overgrown rose garden had crumbled into total disrepair. There was no light showing at any of the windows, but smoke could be seen rising from two chimney pots. The carriage stopped, and I was handed over to an even more disreputable looking ruffian than the one that drove us here. Richards required assistance from another man to climb down and to walk through the open doorway. As I looked back over my shoulder I saw that the carriage was leaving the way it had come. I was dragged by the arm and made to follow them into the gloomy interior of the entrance hall. As my eyes adjusted I looked around, the staircase leading to the second floor had a decided gap where the risers had fallen away into a heap of rotten timbers on the floor in front of me and moisture dripped down the wall nearest the door leaving a slimy green trail. Discarded bits of furniture were strewn about all in varying stages of disrepair and decay.

I had lost sight of Richards, so I assumed that I would be placed somewhere out of the way. I was taken back to the kitchens and pushed down into a chair. My jailor took a seat at the table while yelling for someone called Angel. A young girl about Meg's age came into the kitchen from what appeared to be a store room. "Get me some gin, girl, and something for this chit to eat and drink."

I merely looked at the man as he picked his teeth and sucked on what was obviously a rotten tooth. He had rheumy eyes that were bloodshot, greasy brown hair and he was unshaven. His hands were large, and workworn, and he was missing the tip of a finger on his right hand. Yet strangely his clothes while worn were in good repair and clean. The girl returned with a bottle and a mug setting them in front of him. The mug he ignored and took a long pull at the bottle.

Slamming it down on the table and wiping his mouth on his sleeve, he looked at Angel. "Well, what you are looking at? Get the brat something to eat before I gives ye the back of my hand." He raised his hand in a threatening motion and she scurried away. His eyes followed her and suddenly he looked sad. I turned away from him and looked around the kitchen which was large and immaculately clean with herbs, garlic and onions hanging from the low ceiling beams. A huge hearth dominated one wall where two settees were strategically placed for maximum warmth without being in the way of the cook or at risk of toasting yourself. Angel returned with some cold meat, cheese and fresh bread along with a bottle of cider then she fetched two plates and knives. The man took his bottle over to sit by the fire and put his feet up on the facing settee. Angel sat down beside me and started portioning out the food between us. This obviously was her dinner time as well. We ate in silence until the man by the fire started to snore.

I reached over and touched the girl's hand and wrote my name on her palm the way my mother had taught me. Angel just shrugged, she obviously didn't know her letters.

I leaned close to her and whispered, "I need your help."

She shook her head no and got up, taking the knives and plates away then she brought out a large cake. She removed the kettle from the fire and brewed a pot of tea. The man by the fire never moved and continued to snore.

When she sat back down to cut the cake and pour the tea, I tried again. "Please, I need your help to get away." She shook her head more vehemently, pointing at the man then ran her hand across her throat in a slicing motion. I nodded that I understood. She may understand my situation, but she was not prepared to risk her life to help me. "We can go together." She shook her head no again.

"Ere, what's going on there, stop that whispering." The man by the fire was awake now. "You," and he pointed at Angel, "get to bed." Angel scurried out the door.

My shoulders slumped as he stood up walking toward what looked like the pantry. Then Angel returned with a blanket and a pillow reaching out to hand them to me when the man grabbed them, tossing them into the room and pointed at me. "You go on, get in there." He motioned for me to move, I stood there defiantly so he grabbed my arm and pulled me towards the door.

I stumbled at the doorway and held on to the jamb taking a chance, "I can't, please! I'm afraid of the dark."

He grunted, rubbed his chin then looked at Angel who cowered behind him. "Give her yer candle." She passed me her candle. "Now git to bed." Angel turned and ran. He pushed me into the room and locked the door. I set the candle down on a shelf and looked around. At least I wouldn't starve to death, the pantry was well-stocked and just as clean as the kitchen had been. I picked up the candle and inspected the room, it wasn't large and seemed to be more of a small store room than an actual pantry, there was no window and the only door was behind me and locked. I looked for something I could use as a weapon, but nothing was at hand but food stuffs and a few dented pewter plates. At least the room seemed to be dry and warm, so I lay down wrapping the blanket around me. Before long, my eyes closed, and I lost all sense of time, but I woke suddenly to find my candle still alight and the sound of scratching at the door. I quickly looked around for mice or a rat. What I found instead was a piece of paper shoved under the door. Wrapped in it was a piece of charcoal and in the corner a crude drawing of an angel. I had no idea what I could do that she would understand. There was scratching again at the door then and a whispered, "Miss, are you awake? Please, miss, I can't stay here long."

I leaned against the door. "Angel, can you get me help?" There was no answer "Angel? Are you still there?"

In a tremulous voice that sounded only half convinced of what she was doing she responded, "Please, miss, just writes down who you need to come helps you. Then my brudder Robert will fetch them. He's going to Lon'on with Pa on an errand for the cap'n, he knows his way around, so he'll find your people. I told him and me mam about you and they said that it's our Christian duty to help you."

She sounded terrified. "Angel, I don't want you to get into trouble you need to go with Robert."

"No, miss, I can't! They'll hurt me mam if I do. Da's had some hard luck and he fell in with a bad lot. That's why he drinks so much, he's not a bad man, honest, miss. But me mam says I'm to get you to write it all down. Robert can read he'll get it to Lon'on for you. But hurry, miss, and stop arguing."

I quickly wrote down all the information I could think of starting with my mother, then Mr Johnson, finally Bow Street and even Northumberland. I shoved the paper back under the door and hid the charcoal in my pocket. Then I heard heavy footfalls. "Hey, what you are doing over there?"

"I thought I smelled smoke, Da. I didn't want her setting fire to our stores."

"Humph, I don't smell nothing but you're a good girl to check, my little Angel, now get yourself back to bed." I could hear him walking away when he spoke sharply. "Wait!" I held my breath afraid that he had seen the paper. "Tell—tell your mam not to worry, Robert and I'll be back soon then this'll be all done, and they'll be gone."

"I'll tell her, Da." I could hear her almost running out of the kitchen.

Then the door shook as if someone had leaned against it. "You better not be getting my girl into trouble, missy. I'm not doing this because I want to, but I mean to get me and mine outta 'ere alive." I hesitated as to whether I should answer or not and decided that not answering would be in my and Angel's best interest. "She's a good girl, my Angel, so you just stay asleep, missy, it's the best thing for you. I'll do what I can to keep them from hurting you. But I have my family to look out for too." He coughed and clumped away then I heard a door close. The candle was sputtering now so I blew it out and lay down to wait. Several days went by. I was left in the pantry and only allowed out for meals which I took with Angel. I asked about guards but all she would do was nod and look at the door that I had come through when I arrived and the other door leading to the outside. I pointed to the one remaining door, but she shook her head no when I moved to get up she clenched my hand. "No, miss, that leads to the laundry and other stores rooms, there ain't even a window let alone a door to the outside."

A fat ugly man who smelled of gin and manure came into the room glaring at Angel "Ere, who you are talking to?"

Angel's eyes got big and she swallowed before answering, "Just the lady. I told her there were guards all around and that ter ain't no way out."

He came over leaned across the table leering at me. "That's right, missy, you ain't going nowhere but where the cap'n wants. And if you try well you'd not want to find out what some of us would do to a fresh chit like you before we slit yer throat." His breath reeked, and I couldn't help but pull back which he assumed was from fear and not revulsion. He pulled me up by the arm and returned me to the pantry, locking the door behind me and I heard Angel scurrying away before he had the door closed.

And so, I waited.

# Chapter 17
## *Fight or Flight*

When the door opened again the light spilled across the floor, momentarily blinding me. I looked around and guessed that by the amount of light spilling through the doorway that it must be at least mid-day. Then I heard Angel's subdued voice. "Excuse me, miss, but the cap'n wants to see yer."

I untangled myself from the blanket then stood up, smoothing down my skirts. I swiped my hands through my hair and took a step forward when my upper arm was grabbed firmly by her father. He started to pull me towards the door leading to the front of the house and I looked back over my shoulder willing Angel to look up, but she refused to make eye contact with me. He closed the kitchen door behind us then loosened his grip and pulled me around to face him, "Here now, listen to me, missy, you hold your tongue in there, you hear." He pointed towards a set of double doors. "Both gents in there have been drinking an arguing a lot. So, watch your mouth." I was astounded to get any useful advice from this man who I had considered no better than a thug. "I'll try to see that you don't get hurt but I can't promise you nuffink if you rile them." He glared at me but despite his disreputable appearance, there was intelligence and perhaps a gentleness in this man that I would have denied existed in him before. I nodded as he grasped my arm lightly and led me forward.

I decided to at least try to appear a mild-mannered young lady, so I didn't resist as I he led me across the hallway to enter what must have once been a fine drawing room. It was a distinct contrast to the kitchen that was worn but homey and clean. Here was a mixture of decay and luxury. The walls were dingy, and dirt-smeared where the paint and paper were peeling. The windows were covered by rotting velvet curtains but the furniture while sparse and old was tasteful and immaculately clean. Mr Richards sat on a settee with his leg propped up. It was clear that he had a fever, his eyes glistened and tiny rivulets of sweat snaked down his face and neck. His lips were dry and cracked and his hand shook as he drank from a glass full of an amber-coloured liquid. He stared at me with obvious distaste; possibly because I was the reason that he was ill now.

The second man in the room had icy blue eyes that looked right through me. He looked me up and down then turned his attention to Richards. "So this is the chit you risked my men and your life for? She hardly looks to be worth the bother. But I suppose her father will think differently. Too bad we didn't have the pair of them; but I think it was best to take just the girl. You might have lost your life otherwise, Richards." He chuckled. "It's bad enough that you still have that ball in your leg."

Richards held out his glass to Angel's father who obediently refilled it. Richards took a gulp and glared at the other man. "Where is that damn doctor? You sent for him, didn't you, or was that lie too?" He coughed then snarled as he looked at my jailor. "Dawson, you prick. you had better not have messed this up! Where the hell are your son and that whore?" Dawson left the room at a signal from the second man.

The man with the blue eyes chuckled and responded, "Now, now, my friend, they'll be here shortly I'm sure. Dawson only just got back himself and ladies can't be rushed." With that there was a knock on the door and Dr Jefferson was shown in by Dawson. "See, I told you they'd not be more than minute or two behind." The doctor glanced at me, grimaced then scanned the room. The man with the blue eyes who I assumed was Browne was being loquacious when he addressed him, "I'm so glad you could join us, doctor!" he waved him towards Richards. "There is your long-suffering patient. But before you attend to him, please tell me it wasn't you that shot Richards? I imagine he'd want his revenge if it was and that wouldn't do at all, you're too valuable an asset to lose."

I was in shock! Was the doctor in league with Richards and this man? How could he have deceived us? I was usually able to tell when someone is a fake, but the doctor had always seemed so genuine and kind! I would never have thought that he had any evil in him. He ignored Browne and pulled back the lap rug and dressing gown hiding Richard's leg, then he removed the bandages and lint. He was positioned in such a way that I couldn't see the leg, but I saw his shoulders tense as he made his examination. Behind me I heard a scuffle in the hallway and a woman's scream cut short. Dr Jefferson spun on his heels and looked at the other man. "If you hurt her, Browne, I'll make you pay." Then it dawned on me that the doctor was here under duress.

"Hurt Louisa, why should I ever do that? She has been most useful to me. But I must admit that I'm surprised that she is still naive enough to believe that I saved her from the French by sending her away with Turner." He giggled like a mad man, adding, "I never dreamed that she would think she still owed me a debt when I sent her the note that I was ill and needed her to bring a doctor to me. But it was worth the try and safer than bringing in the local man. Are you sure, Jefferson, that you want to court such a gullible bit of fluff?" He made an unpleasant chuckling sound in his throat. Then he drank off what was in his glass and filled it again. "Oh, by the by I do hope that your journey wasn't too uncomfortable."

The doctor ignored him and bent to open his bag. "I'll need hot water, clean bandages and Miss Turner to help me."

Mr Browne banged his foot on the floor and the door opened behind me. He gave the orders for water and bandages. I had not been told that I could sit and since he continued to ignore me I waited.

There was a brief knock at the door and Angel came in with everything the doctor had asked for. She turned to leave but Mr Browne reached to block her, "Where do you think you're going, girl, the doctor needs your assistance." She turned around keeping her eyes down and walked back to the doctor then knelt at his side. She scrunched up her nose and closed her eyes.

Dr Jefferson said firmly, "I asked for Miss Turner's help."

Browne turned red and slammed down his glass, he obviously did not like his decisions being questioned and he gave way to his temper as his voice rose, "I heard you, doctor! But you will make do with what I GIVE YOU!"

The doctor huffed looking down at Angel. "What's your name, child?"

She opened her eyes looking up at him, "Angel, sir."

Richards had obviously had enough. "Shut it, both of you! This isn't a ruddy tea party, get on with it! Get the DAMN ball out of my leg NOW!" He was extremely pale and perspiring freely, I could even hear his raspy breathing across the room.

Dr Jefferson poured some of the water into a basin then he took a sliver of soap from his bag and started washing his hands slowly, slower than I had ever seen him do so before. He glanced at me once then at the window behind Richards' head. Mr Browne was examining his fingernails and hadn't noticed. Richards did though. "What the hell are you looking at?" He tried to look over his shoulder but gasped as he moved his leg. Then he screamed, "DAWSON! Get the hell in here!" My jailor appeared and looked down at Angel, worry clearly etched on his face. "Get outside and check the grounds!"

Dawson moved towards the door then hesitated, "I just came in from outside, sir, there weren't nothing nor nobody out there."

With a wave of his hand Browne interjected in his laconic manner, "Get out and look harder this time."

Dawson still didn't move as he looked at the window with fear in his eyes. I had a clear view but couldn't see a thing. Richards rose up on his elbows and yelled, "GO!"

Browne laughed, drained his glass and filled it again from the decanter on the table beside him. Then he turned in his chair to look at me. "Well, Miss Turner, what am I to do with you?" He looked at me through the liquid in the glass and smiled. "You are his daughter without a doubt. You know I'd always thought that your father and uncle might be lovers. Imagine my amazement when I found out that one of them was actually married and the other was in love with a French whore." He smiled unpleasantly when I tried not to grimace. "I was a good friend of your father's in France, did he ever tell you?" Browne chuckled almost spilling his drink but catching it before it overflowed the rim of the glass. "No, I don't suppose he would. Oh, wait I'm sorry…I'm thinking of the wrong father. I should have said your grandfather. It was your grandfather's idea to use Louisa to get information from the Spaniards because he had scruples about spying on the English allies himself. I, however, did not, money is after all money no matter who pays. But that's beside the point. Your grandfather had enormous gambling debts that he owed to people on the wrong side of the war. He really was terrible at cards." Browne waved his glass around miraculously not spilling a drop. "You see during the lulls in the action the senior officers of both sides would often meet on neutral ground for an evening's pleasure. Back then the only thing of value was gold or information and he didn't have any gold." He paused and waited for me to comment. I chose not to say a word. "You don't seem surprised or impressed by his treason, Miss Turner?"

He paused, and I noticed that his facial expression while talking had never changed then suddenly without warning he threw his glass at the wall behind me and screamed, "ANSWER ME!"

I looked at the doctor and swallowed, he had turned to look first at me then Mr Browne and back again and he nodded his encouragement to me before he returned his attention back to Richards. Could I trust him? Just then he dug into Richard's leg. Richards screamed so loud we all jumped. Browne started to laugh and got up out of his chair. He came towards me, grabbing me by the hair at the back of my head and leaned in close, his alcohol saturated breath was nauseating as he growled, "I said, answer me." When I didn't respond right away he slapped me across the face hard enough that everything blurred for a moment.

Tears of pain slid down my cheeks as I sucked in a breath and answered him, "The General was my grandfather in name only. He can burn in hell for all I care."

He reared back letting go of my hair and laughed like a maniac. "Good lord, you have spirit, girl, I like that." Then he leaned down pulling a knife from his boot and lurching forward, he grabbed me again, swinging me around and pulling my back to him as he placed the knife to my throat. "Doctor, are you done yet?"

Dr Jefferson was just applying the final dressing when he looked up. "Let her go! Are you insane?!"

He pulled my head back and pressed harder so that the knife was biting into my neck. He leered into my face saying, "I just need to know if my associate is fit to travel. There's a ship waiting for us in Poole, but I need him to be able to ride."

Richards answered him, "Get me up on the damn horse and I'll ride, you bloody bastard. Remember those are my people waiting and it's me that they're expecting, not you."

Browne smiled at him tipping his head to the side like a bird of prey, sizing up a kill; it was very eerie. Dr Jefferson stood up pulling Angel to his side and stepped away from Richards. Richards seemed to recognize the look and pulled a pistol out from beside him. "You think I don't know what you're thinking, Browne? I'm surprised you haven't tried to kill me before now." He glared at Browne but didn't raise the pistol, he was probably too weak to lift it let alone hold it.

Browne pulled me closer to him as a shield then sneered, "Oh, I've thought about it many times, my friend. You bungled getting Hughes in the park, so you should consider yourself lucky that I let you live this long. You botched that job, so it was up to me to silence the old man. I don't forgive things lightly, you should know that by now." He pulled my head back and looked at me, "I was astounded that the General suddenly grew a conscious when he figured out that we tried to kill his heir." He chuckled. "I'm even more surprised that he thought he could turn us over to Spencer and not have his own hands sullied. I was very disappointed in his lack of trust." He let go of my head while chuckling, but the knife was still pressed to my throat. "The cargo from France lands tonight and I'll be on that ship when it leaves with the tide, with or without you Richards."

Richards scowled. "That may be your ship, Browne, but the crew are my men. You won't be going anywhere without me." It was like the two of them had forgotten that anyone else was in the room.

Browne's grip remained firm, I could still feel the edge of the knife at my throat and his hot fetid breath on my neck. "Yes, I've been meaning to address that issue." Suddenly he let go and flung the knife with uncanny precision, it buried itself deep in Richards' chest. Richards made a feeble attempt to raise the pistol, but the light went out of his eyes before he could fire, and it fell to the floor. Browne grabbed me again holding me tightly around the throat as he called out "Angel, my sweet." Angel's eyes were huge, her lower lip trembled as she stared at Richards. Then Browne yelled "ANGEL!" His screamed deafened me as I watched the girl snap her eyes up to him. "That's better. Now bring me the pistol." She moved forward, shaking terribly, then bent to pick up the pistol but as she picked it up it discharged into the floor and she jumped back dropping it.

Browne sighed then casually said, "You're a clumsy little thing, aren't you. Now it's of no use to anyone. I don't suppose you know how to load one?" Angel shook her head no as he continued, "No, I didn't think so. Ah, doctor! Huh, no, I don't think it would be wise to put that in your hand. Hmmm, what a dilemma!" He looked over my shoulder at me, his face placid. "Well, Miss Turner, perhaps we should leave now. Have you ever been to Paris, my dear?" I didn't respond but he really didn't care if I did…he was clearly insane. "Angel, my dear, where is that father of yours? He should have been back by now." He took a deep breath but never relaxed his grip on me, "Oh, well, you'll have to do it then. Go and bring my horse around," Angel hesitated so I braced myself for him to yell again but he just said sweetly, "Go on, girl." Angel stepped forward then looked back at the doctor who nodded for her to go.

Then Browne's voice exploded in my ear. "Stop looking at him and GET MY DAMN HORSE!" Dr Jefferson took a step forward as Angel ran past us. But Browne saw him and gripped me tighter by the throat, "Oh no, doctor; stay where you are. I'm quite capable of snapping Miss Turner's neck before you could take another step. You just stay where you are." He moved his arms so one encircled my neck and his other hand rested against the side of my head. He grasped me tightly enough that I had trouble drawing a breath. So, we stood and waited. The doctor kept his eyes on Browne's hands and on the door behind me. My legs were getting tired, I had been standing for what seemed like hours, but it was nerves that was sapping my strength. Then an idea came to me that if I let my legs go out from under me like I was swooning it might be enough to break his grasp and I could get away. He had no other weapon on his person but there was another pistol on the table by his decanter nearer the doctor than Browne, had the doctor seen it there? Browne seemed to have forgotten about it. Yes, I could do this. I winked at the doctor and he bit his lower lip and I saw from the pleading look in his eyes that he didn't want me to risk myself. But I never got the chance.

Angel returned, and he pulled me back with him into the hallway. Dawson was nowhere to be seen. The front door stood open to the daylight and I could see a saddled horse standing there. He still held me by the neck, dragging me backwards out the door. We got to the horse and he threw me over the saddle then mounted up behind me. As he took the reins, Mr Johnson sprang out from behind the rubble of the garden wall, grabbing at the horse which had reared up at his approach. With the upward momentum, I slid off the saddle as Browne tried to regain control of the horse. I landed face-first on the drive with the gravel biting into my skin. My shoulder took a painful jolt and I rolled to the side to avoid the horse's hooves coming down on top of me though one managed to clip my arm. It all happened so quickly that I was unaware I had even been hurt. Then the pain exploded down the length of my arm. The last thing I heard before fainting was a shot being fired from the vicinity of the house and the words, "Bloody Hell."

# Chapter 18
## *Taking a Stand*

I woke up lying on one of the kitchen's settees under the painful ministrations of Dr Jefferson as he applied a splint to my broken arm. He smiled at me, "Well, Miss Turner, that was a spectacular fall, I must say. You've broken your arm, bruised your shoulder and have a few scrapes and scratches but you'll be fine."

"Thank you, doctor, but I believe it was the horse, not me, that broke my arm." I looked about the room. Angel was at the table chewing her fingernails with an older version of herself sitting beside her. A tall young man had his hand on the older woman's shoulder was whispering in her ear. She just patted his hand and nodded. Mr Dawson was seated at the end of the table nearest them and in his younger days he probably looked very much like the tall young man. Now he just looked grey and distraught. I didn't see Louisa or Mr Johnson and I wondered what had happened to Browne.

Dr Jefferson seemed to have anticipated my questions without my asking. "Browne got away, Mr Johnson has gone after him." I tried to sit up, but he pushed me back down. "You aren't going anywhere until I'm done, so lay back."

"And Louisa?" he stepped aside so I could see that she was sitting at the far end of the table with two pistols in front of her watching the Dawsons, her brow was furrowed and she was chewing on her lower lip. I was concerned that the Dawson family would be arrested, despite having aided in my captivity they had also facilitated my rescue. "Doctor, about Angel and her family, they've been most kind to me and they've only tried to help." Dr Jefferson looked rather dubiously at Mr Dawson and then arched an eyebrow at me, I understood his look of disbelief. "Well, Mr Dawson has been under a great deal of stress and he feared for his family's safety. He didn't hurt me and saw to it that I was fed and kept warm and safe." Mr Dawson's head popped up, looking at me in astonishment. I managed a weak smile in his direction.

The doctor looked back at the family. "If you say so, Miss Turner, but that man by his own admission was involved in your kidnapping. However, he did help his son Robert deliver a message to Louisa requesting a doctor's service as well as your message to your mother and Mr Johnson."

Louisa was glaring at Dawson when she said, "Mr Dawson should be under considerably more stress if he felt that he could play on both sides." What an odd thing to say but the doctor didn't seem to pay it any mind.

Mr Dawson hunkered down in his chair looking morose once again. The young man who was Angel's brother Robert licked his lips and spoke to Dr Jefferson "Weren't his fault, sir. He's been at his wits end since he lost his boat and he's tried to make a go of it anyway that he could to keep Mum, me and my sister fed and

151

I thought it odd that she kept referring to Browne by his first name when she was supposed to be in love with Dr Jefferson. I wondered if that was why the doctor looked so glum, was he jealous that she still might think of Browne as more than a friend.

Dr Jefferson took over the narrative abruptly, "I arrived and found young Robert with his father sitting on the fountain edge where I was supposed to meet Louisa. They explained to me what was really happening then gave me your message, Miss Turner. They accompanied me back to your home where we planned what we would do. We had no idea how many men we'd find so we decided that I should come and assess the situation before calling for the local militia. Johnson went ahead of us on horseback. After I gathered my bag, the Dawsons picked me up and Louisa was already in the carriage. She told me that she'd received at note from Browne saying she was to come with the Dawsons or my life was forfeit." He glared at her. "Johnson was well ahead of us but when we arrived, his horse was standing at the end of the drive. I was worried that he had been taken so I decided to stick to our original plan. But I had no time to convey it to Louisa. She was very anxious when we arrived and kicked up a bit of fuss when she was not allowed to follow me." He looked at her and she blushed. "Once I entered the room with Richards and Browne, she started to scream something in Spanish…I suppose she feared for my safety." He continued to look at Louisa intently, but she sat looking contrite with her head down. Then he continued, "But she stopped when Robert slapped his hand across her mouth." Louisa looked up and for a split second I caught her glaring at Dr Jefferson, but he pretended that he didn't noticed. Then Mr Dawson groaned, holding his head, he looked ill.

Thus distracted, the doctor changed the subject. "I assume Mr Dawson from the looks of you that you must have a massive headache?" Dawson nodded and grimaced as the doctor continued, "I'll give you some willow bark for that in a bit but giving up the drink will help more."

I just realised then that no one had asked about Browne? "What about Browne? Is he dead?"

Dr Jefferson shook his head no. "I missed him when I shot, and he got away."

He looked at Mr Johnson who was staring into his mug of tea. "You followed him, but Browne's horse would have been fresh…he must have out-distanced you easily." He only nodded. "I suppose then he must be on his way to France and good riddance."

Father was picking apart a piece of bread. "I'd still like to know why he kidnapped Lissa. None of this makes any sense! What did he hope to achieve?"

Robert cleared his throat. "Mr Turner, sir, Mr Browne was not right in the head. He hates you something fierce. He and Richards talked about you all the time, how it was because of you that he wasn't welcomed here in England and he'd been branded a traitor without proof. He said that he was going to fix you as bad as you fixed him. They talked about it all the time when they were in their cups about how much they hated you and a man named Samuel. Richards said once that your interference was upsetting their investors something fierce."

Uncle Samuel raised his arm. "For the sake of the narrative, I'm Samuel."

Robert glanced at him, forcing a weak smile. Angel giggled, and Robert gave her a sharp look then he continued, "You'd messed up Mr Browne's smuggling ventures and because of you he owed a lot of money to some really bad people. He's afraid of a big dark man what captains one of the smuggling ships but I don't know why. But the way he describes him I think it's the man who has come here a couple of times looking for him. But I don't know who he is."

My father leaned forward looking very interested, "What did he look and sound like, Robert?"

Robert looked wary. "Angel and Da were the only ones that saw him close up. I only heard him talk a few times. He had a strange voice, it was deep, and I've never heard nothing like it before." Robert turned to Angel who nodded but you could see that she was afraid. Mr Dawson had his head down on his arms, not looking at anyone. "Go on, Angel, tell 'em the story he told you."

I knew Angel was shy, so I reached across the table to touch her hand. We smiled at each other and she began speaking hesitantly. "He would come in here and most often I'd be cooking. He liked how warm it was in the kitchen…he didn't like the cold. He was a big man, bigger than anyone I'd ever seed and his skin was dark but not black. He had long dark curly hair, dark eyes, a long straight nose and a hard mouth. He scared me a bit, but he never laid a hand on me nor yelled at me. He'd just sit and stare into the fire and talk. He told me about how he and his wife had been captured by pirates and sold to some people far away in the Indies, but he'd run away from them and become a pirate." Her eyes became enormous when she said the word pirate. "But only because he needed to raise money to free his family. When he had enough he went to buy their freedom, but they were gone, nobody knew where they were. He was told that the owners had sold up and gone back to England. He was sad and wanted to find them, that's why he'd come to England. He wanted to find those people and make me tell him what had happened to his wife and children. And to… Ah," she paused looking for the right words and then she sat up straight and recited carefully, "and to get ret-tri-bution."

Father and Samuel didn't seem to note anything peculiar about the story, but I instantly thought of the Clarkes and wondered if they had owned this man and his family or was it just coincidence.

Mr Johnson just sat there while she talked, staring down at the table like he was deep in thought tracing the grain of the wood with his finger. He caught me watching him and the look he gave me was like he could see into my soul. It gave me a shiver and I wondered what he had on his mind.

Mr Dawson sat up straight, tapping the table in front of him to get our attention. "I think you all need to get back to Lon'on and the sooner the better. There has been murder done here and there's no telling what might happen if you're still here tonight when the goods from the ship start to arrive. It could be trouble! I might be able to talk some sense into whoever comes with the wagons but if Browne is with them, nothing good will happen. You need to go, and I want you to take my family with you. Please." He had tears in his eyes. "I need you to protect them; just get them to Lon'on. Promise me you'll take them with you."

Johnson looked at him in awe. "That's very decent of you, Dawson, you really aren't a blackguard after all. We can get them to London, but have you thought about what happens to them then?"

Dawson shrugged. "My Bess can manage with Robert and Angel and…well, they all be hard workers, they'll be fine." No one seemed to notice that he had not included himself in this plan to go to London with his family. Mrs Dawson looked close to tears, Angel looked terrified while Robert was staring hard at his father. I

155

could tell that he at least had no intention of leaving. I would bet that Mr Dawson would have a fight on his hands if he tried to make any of them leave.

Mr Johnson was tapping his lips and in a lighter tone, said, "You know I've been looking for a bit of property and even though this place is in a shamble, it has good bones. It's not that far from London and there doesn't appear to be an owner. It's ideal!"

Father rubbed his forehead looking puzzled then flinging out a hand in frustration, "What nonsense are you talking, Miles?"

Mr Johnson smirked. "I'm looking to establish myself, Turner. I can't continue to sponge off your charity and if my father dies any time in the next few years. I'd like to have a refuge for my stepmother and her children. Preferably one that can generate an income, so we at least won't starve. I think this place would do nicely. Of course, I'll have to approach the old man to fund this little enterprise and to help me refurbish it, but I'm sure he'll be amenable. At least it will be something that my dear brother won't be able to touch." He turned to Dawson. "Dawson, you did say that this was once a working farm, am I right?"

Dawson nodded. "Yes, sir, it was and a profitable one too with it bein' so close to Lon'on."

Father chuckled. "And what about the local smugglers? How do you propose to dispose of them, Miles?"

Dawson cleared his throat. "Well, sir, the local men, they be kinda scared of the place. Seeing as how Richards set it about that the place were haunted by the old lady what died here. But there ain't no truth to it, nope, not a bit. Besides it's too far from Poole for the locals to use the cellars for their bits and bobs and the barns are in no state to hide a stash of goods for any length of time. Richards only used this place because it's away from prying eyes and he could divide up the goods then send the wagons on their way." The Dawsons were all nodding.

Mr Johnson nodded with a grin, saying, "Well, there you have it, Turner. The property is deserted and haunted, it's perfect!"

Uncle Samuel leaned forward. "Miles, we still have Richards' associates to worry about or do you honestly think that he was the leader?"

Mr Johnson curled his fingers into fists then relaxed them as he glared at my uncle. "No, I don't believe he's the leader, Hughes. That's why I'm going to propose that you and I stay here with Dawson, we'll wait to see what happens. Turner can take the others back to London and report to Sir Thomas."

Father was shaking his head no while Samuel was nodding yes. "Samuel, in case you forgot, your bride is awaiting you and I can't leave you here with just Miles!"

Mr Johnson snapped an angry look at my father which he quickly concealed. "Thank you for that lovely vote of confidence, Colin. You trusted me to watch over your family in London, but you don't trust me here with your brother-in-law. Should I infer from that that you have doubts about my veracity? Or do you think I'm the mysterious leader of the smugglers that masterminded the kidnapping of your daughter?" His voice had been very cool and controlled but it thrummed with tension. My father looked astounded. Mr Johnson leaned forward, and I could see the blood vessel in his neck pulsating. His anger was obviously not under control. "Come now, Colin, SPIT IT OUT!" he pounded the table with his fist.

Dawson looked up, saying bleakly, "I already said that I'd stay. I know you have no reason to trust me but I'm staying to keep my neck out of hangman's noose and to save what me family has built 'ere." He paused, looking at his son and daughter with pride and love. "And maybe even for what the future holds for them."

Dr Jefferson cleared his throat. "If someone must go, it might as well be me. I can escort the ladies and the Dawsons to London then send help."

A long discussion ensued as to who would stay and who would leave. Mrs Dawson refused to go as did her children. It was finally decided that the open road was not safe for just a one man as an escort for all these people and it was not safe for only two men to stay behind with only a very recently reformed thug as their only support.

Louisa was very unhappy about it all, she wanted to leave as soon as possible and argued vehemently for a return to London by everyone. I watched her closely as she sat biting her nails and jumping at every noise. Then my mind clicked on an old axiom, 'Once a traitor always a traitor'. I was worried for Dr Jefferson. Louisa might still be a spy.

Finally, it was decided that we would all stay. Dr Jefferson, Mr Johnson and Uncle Samuel went with Mr Dawson to look for the most defensible positions on the property if it should come to a fight.

By now my mother would have alerted Sir Thomas so he would be aware that I had been kidnapped and that my father, uncle and Mr Johnson were here in Dorset and in pursuit of my captors, Browne and Richards. But would he send help in time?

# Chapter 19
## *Help Arrives*

I was supposed to be helping Angel and her mother in the kitchen, but they didn't need my help and with one arm I was only in the way. I walked out into the hallway and into the room where I had first met Browne. Richards' body had been removed and my father was there affixing storm shutters to the windows. He welcomed me with a smile and brushed his hands off on his breeches. "Lissa, my dear, I thought you were helping Angel and Mrs Dawson in the kitchen."

I gave him a weak smile as I ran my finger along the table that still held Mr Browne's empty glass. "I believe that I'm more of a hindrance than a help, Papa." He chuckled then turned to grasp another shutter. "Father," he let go of the shutter waiting for me to continue, "have you noticed how nervous Louisa is?"

He nodded. "It's only natural for her to be nervous, my dear. Mrs Dawson and Angel are both scared as well."

I pursed my lips. "It's not that kind of nervous, Papa. Didn't you notice that she argued very hard in favour of returning to London as if she knew that something terrible is going to happen?"

"She's probably right, Lissa. But I'm not sure what you're trying to say?"

I had braided my hair earlier with Angel's help and was now twisting the end of it, but I was too nervous to continue in case I was wrong. I was still feeling my way around having a father that I could confide in. "I just think that she knows more than she's telling us." He didn't move or say anything, instead he looked at me like he was seeing me for the first time. He waved me over to him and opened his arms. I walked to him putting my good arm around his waist; he hugged me close, kissing the top of my head. He was warm and comfortable, and I felt safe. I continued trying to make sense of what I knew intuitively. "I think she's lying, I'm sure that she's still working for Mr Browne."

He inhaled deeply, pulling my arm away from him as he stepped back cupping my chin, looking into my eyes he whispered, "We know, darling."

My mouth hung open. "What?"

He smiled sadly. "Samuel and I have never trusted Louisa. That's why I enlisted Matthew to help ferret out what she was up to. We've suspected that she was still working for Browne for some time, but we could never catch her in the act, it seems she's gotten better at spying over the years."

I was astonished. "You knew already? But Dr Jefferson, how could he—wait, he's working for you too?" I gasped with sudden realization. "So he isn't in love with her?!"

He laughed again. "Yes, Dr Jefferson is an agent but nothing of any romantic consequence has transpired between Matthew and Louisa…he is not in love with her. Louisa has a very low opinion of Englishman and believes that we lack passion, but she has a very high opinion of her charms, so she actually believes that Matthew is desperately in love with her which is exactly what we wanted."

He straightened up, glancing back at the shutters, "Matthew does have his standards. But you cannot let on that you know! We suspect that Louisa knows Browne's plan and that he'll come back here for his revenge. It's probably the reason that she wants to leave so we'd be caught out in the open on the road."

I had faith that he knew what he was doing but I was terrified for our family, what if Browne had confederates in London that would carry out a plan to hurt my mother. "You won't let Louisa leave, will you?"

"No, my darling, we won't." He pulled me back into a hug. "But I don't want you to be alone with her either; make sure you stay with the Dawsons. Do not under any circumstances go anywhere with Louisa, do you understand?"

"Yes, Papa." Then a thought hit me that I might be able to help defend the house. "May I have one of your pistols?" He chuckled but before he could answer we heard raised voices in the hallway. We both moved to the doorway and watched what was going on. The other men had just come back from their reconnoitring outside. Mr Dawson tipped his hat to my father then turned away, moving towards the kitchen, muttering to himself.

I watched the trail of wet footprints that he left as he walked away. Then I noticed the water falling from all their hats and coats, it had started to rain. Dr Jefferson came over to my father and said in a faint voice, "Where is Louisa?" Father looked to me and I shrugged. I hadn't seen her since everyone had left to assume their separate duties.

Robert came into the hallway carrying a load of peat for the fire, so father asked him, "Robert, have you seen Miss Louisa?"

He nodded. "She offered to go to the poultry house and gather the eggs. But come to think on it, that was some time ago and I haven't seen her since." Mr Johnson and Dr Jefferson both raced towards the kitchens. I looked from my uncle to my father then to Robert who just stood there looking in the direction where the other men had disappeared. Then he turned to my father, "No one told us that she couldn't be trusted."

Father nodded, stepping aside for Robert to take the peat into the room behind us. He patted his shoulder as he walked by. "You're right, Robert, that was my mistake."

Dr Jefferson returned. "One of the horses is gone."

Father groaned. "Where's Miles?"

"He's gone after her, she took his horse."

Uncle Samuel groaned this time. "Is he a fool?"

Dr Jefferson smiled. "Perhaps, but he said he could ill afford to lose the nag. Besides it had apparently gone lame on him when he went after Browne, so he doesn't expect to have any trouble catching her. He asked that we save him some supper." The doctor chuckled.

I was watching Dr Jefferson, but he didn't seem to be upset or concerned in the least about Louisa. Yet I wondered how he could purport to love someone and not feel remorse when they proved to be false even if he was only acting as an agent. Could he really be that detached? I was lost in thought when I heard Dr Jefferson address my concern indirectly. "I'm glad this charade is over, Colin. I don't know how much longer I could have pretended to love her. She said her uncle called her 'stupid'; well, he was right. The woman has no intellect and no sensible conversation at all. It's a wonder that your aunt has put up with her all this time. I seriously think we should consider sending her to that nunnery where her uncle wanted her in the first place." Then he and Samuel walked off chuckling, taking their dripping clothes with them while Father and I followed behind them into the kitchen.

The men had finished all the preparations they could make. But I was not given a weapon, instead I was assigned the coveted position of passing the shot for reloading to Robert. Neither of us were very happy with the arrangement since we both considered ourselves excellent shots. But my father would not be moved.

We just sat down to our evening repast when Mr Spencer, Jacob, Michael, Murphy and Dalton came through the door that led to the yard and the stables. Father jumped up at their entrance only to yell at them, "What the blast is going on! You were supposed to stay in London protecting our family!"

Mr Spencer stepped forward with his hands raised, "Calm down, Colin; do you honestly think I'd leave them without protection! Sir Thomas arrived shortly after you left and had the ladies pack up, he moved them all into his home. He left guards at your house and sent us down here to help." Suddenly there was a commotion coming from the partially opened door that included some loud grunts, groans and a woman screaming in Spanish with Mr Johnson yelling over it, "For god sakes, woman, SHUT UP."

Mr Spencer chuckled. "And that should be Mr Johnson with the Spanish hellcat. We found him fighting with her on the side of the road, so I take it that she finally showed her true colours."

Then there was the sound of Miles' voice raised in anger again. "That does it! I have never hit a lady in my life but for you I will gladly make the exception!" There was one ear splitting scream and then nothing. Mr Johnson walked in with an unconscious Louisa flung over his shoulder. "Is there someplace I can dump this— this person?" We all looked agape. "And bloody well make sure that it has a strong lock!"

Robert popped up grabbing a key ring hanging on the wall by the pantry, he was smiling and trying not to laugh. Mr Johnson was covered in mud, grass and other assorted filth and he smelled awful, Louisa was not any better. He glared at Robert. "You! Why didn't inform me that part of the stables is being used as a pig sty!"

Robert bit his lip. "It never came up in our conversation, sir."

Miles rolled his eyes then started to look around for somewhere to deposit Louisa, she must have had been getting heavy. Robert noticed so rattling the keys he pointed towards the pantry, but his mother jumped up, "Here now, you aren't putting her in my clean pantry. The old laundry room will be good enough for her. There's a hearth but no window and a strong door with a lock." She bustled forward crinkling her nose while taking a wide berth of Mr Johnson and pointing the way. Robert grabbed a basket of peat by the doorway and Angel went to the pantry retrieving the blankets and pillow that I had been using during my confinement, then they both followed their mother. Mrs Dawson peered back over her shoulder at Mr Johnson. "Well, come on you then, ye be dripping all over me clean floor; and you'll be washing off that muck before ye come back into my kitchen expecting to be fed."

Mr Dawson and I got up to retrieve more plates, cups and knives. Shortly we heard the thud of a solid door closing. Then everyone but Mr Johnson and Robert returned. I watched for a bit, but he didn't reappear immediately. Mrs Dawson caught my eye and winked, "He's sluicing his self off at the pump by the laundry." She chuckled. "It's a real pleasure to have water inside a house without having to traipse across the yard in all weather. My Robert is helping him, miss, so don't you worry, the gentleman will come back looking right and proper. Our Robert looks out for the vicar on special days."

When they finally returned, Mr Johnson was clean and brushed as well as could be expected under the circumstances. He patted Robert on the shoulder. "Have you ever thought of being a gentleman's valet?" Robert's eyes lit up as Mr Johnson looked pointedly at my father. "Colin, you're in need of a new valet, I believe. Dalton can't continue caring for both you and Hughes for much longer, especially since Hughes will be setting up his own household eventually. And I honestly don't have the resources to afford one. I'm sure Dalton would make an excellent instructor in the meantime and he'd probably be relieved not to have to care for you both." He gave Dalton a cheeky grin. "Wouldn't you, Dalton?"

Dalton's face lit up and he managed to splutter, "It would be nice, sir."

My father smiled at Robert. "Well, young man, would the idea appeal to you?"

Robert wasted no time. "Yes, sir, thank you! I would like that very much, sir."

Mr Johnson clapped Robert on the shoulder. "There now that's done, don't you or your brother-in-law get any ideas about the rest of my staff." He looked down at Mr Dawson "I understand from your son that you're really not suited to be a fisherman, rather you were raised to be a farmer on this very land." Mr Dawson nodded but didn't say a word. Mr Johnson didn't seem to take notice and continued, "Good then! I'll need your assistance to get this place on its feet again."

Then he became very serious as he looked at Dawson. "There are some conditions though, you have to be sober, man!" Mr Dawson nodded and gulped then he smiled a bit and nodded again. Mr Johnson addressed Dawson's wife and daughter. "You, dear lady, and your daughter, I will need you both as well." The family were beaming but he cautioned them, "I can't promise you more than a warm roof over your head, a full belly and a lot of arduous work to start."

Mrs Dawson looked him up and down then straight in the eye. "You keep that promise, sir, and we'll work hard for you. You'll have no complaint I can tell you that for a fact." With those words and a hard look to her husband, the Dawson family loyalty seemed to have been assured and I knew that Mr Johnson would be a man of his word.

Mrs Dawson waved us all to sit down as she and Angel fetched the rest of the food to the table. We ate a simple but delicious meal of a thick savoury stew, fish pie roast, fowl with hot root vegetables, fresh bread and cheese. Followed by a large apple tart. Yet she apologized for not having any cream to go with it. She was an amazing cook and her eyes danced as she watched the men consume everything in sight, exclaiming all the while that they loved her.

Uncle Samuel looked over at Mr Johnson as he ate his portion of the fish pie. "Miles, you never cease to amaze me. Here we are facing lord knows what conflagration tonight and you're making domestic arrangements as if nothing was amiss."

Mr Johnson put his spoon down and pushed his plate away, wiping his mouth and when he answered there was a bit of edge to his voice. "Well, Hughes, my father taught me to never ignore an opportunity when it presents itself."

My uncle merely agreed. "Right you are that's good advice." He chuckled and returned to his meal as did Mr Johnson, both men were smirking.

Finally, the meal was over, and my father moved away from the table asking all the men to join him in what had been the parlour. As they moved to leave, Dr Jefferson excused himself, saying he would join them shortly. Then taking down a plate from the china dresser he gathered some cheese, bread and fowl. Mrs Dawson walked over to him with a mug of hot tea in one hand and a club in the other. Dr Jefferson looked askance at the club, so she explained, "You open the door, sir, and I'll make sure that she doesn't get past you." She set down the mug and pulled the key out of her pocket passing it to him. Then they walked off together to check on Louisa. I helped Angel clear off the table and watched her as she started washing the dishes which was a new experience for me to even as an observer since I had never seen it done before. Angel was fast and efficient as she worked, and I watched in companionable silence for the most part.

Dr Jefferson came back and went to join the other men. Mrs Dawson in mean time inspected Angel's work and then set about making more bread and soup. "It's going to be a long night, Angel, girl; you and Miss Turner will sleep in the pantry tonight. I want you both close by and safe." Robert entered the kitchen dragging two large feather beds with a huge frown on his face when he looked at me. Uncle Samuel was right behind him with blankets which he deposited on the settee as Robert dropped his load by the pantry door.

Robert left, and Samuel sat down at the table then beckoned me over as Mrs Dawson and Angel arranged the bedding. "So, my dear, we seem to be in a pickle. Your father has said you're not to have a pistol while Miles, Murphy, Michael and Jacob all think that you should. That leaves your father, Mr Spencer, Dalton and Robert against you. The good doctor has abstained along with Mr Dawson, but he thinks you're a spirited young lady. The fact that you are a lady is why those other gentlemen are opposed to it, the feeling being that ladies aren't supposed to shoot people."

"Why does Robert have a say in this?"

"Because he's the loader he thinks it would unfair if a girl were favoured over him." I scrunched up my face ready to say what I thought when he stopped me by saying, "I have the deciding vote and I wanted to hear what you have to say on your own behalf. I know that Robert believes I will favour you. So, what say you, brat?"

I felt like this was an unfair test. I looked down at my arm in the sling then around the kitchen at the height of the windows. I grimaced and said with as much conviction as I could muster, "Robert should have the pistol, Uncle Samuel, not me." He raised his eyebrows in surprise but waited for me to continue. I pointed to my bad arm. "I've never shot at a moving target and he will have been hunting around here for years and besides I can't reload without assistance."

Uncle Samuel smiled then put two pistols on the table before him with powder and shot. "Robert will be back here along with Dawson and me." As he got up to leave he reached into his pocket and pulled out a pocket pistol, already loaded, which he put on the table and pushed towards me. "Use it only if it's absolutely necessary, you'll only get the one shot and it has to be at close range for that thing to do any damage."

We heard shouting coming from the front of the house and we all ran into to the hallway to see what the commotion was about.

Mr Dawson was standing there gesturing with his hands. "Then tell me, Mr Bloody high and mighty Turner, have any of you gentleman here ever been in a fight at night; without the benefit of captains and generals giving yee orders and all you're trying to do is just stay alive!?" He quieted down a bit when he saw us looking at him. When no one responded he looked disgusted, "I didn't think so. This isn't the bloody fecking army! The men coming here will kill you anyway they can they ain't going to march up ta the doors and let you shoot at them. If you think Browne hasn't told them what to expect then you're fools!"

Murphy stepped forward to stand beside Mr Dawson, "Sorry, Mr Turner, but the man's right. We need to be waiting for them out there as well as in the house. Those men will be coming armed and with wagons to hide behind. We need to be able to lure them to where we want them. Dawson and his son know this place better than any of us despite our having looked over the lay of the land and it always looks different at night, sir. Dawson knows how the land breathes at night and what it's like in changing weather. He knows this house and the outbuildings. Personally, I'd like to be heading back to London but here we are so let's make the best of the element of surprise…it's the only advantage that we'll have."

The entire plan seemed to change in a matter of minutes Dawson, Murphy, Michael and Jacob headed outside. My father, Mr Johnson, Dr Jefferson and Mr Spencer took the front of the house and my uncle, Dalton and Robert came to the kitchen.

Mrs Dawson had pulled out an assortment of knives and a bow. Dalton gave them the once over and tested the edge of one knife then he whistled when he drew blood. "These aren't kitchen knives, dearie."

Mrs Dawson smiled. "Not likely. They were me mam's knives, but they belong to me now. I'm good with a knife, have been all my life."

Dalton nodded and sucked in his lower lip before saying, "Right you are then, but that remains to be seen." He smiled like he didn't believe her as he picked up the bow testing the string. "And who is the bowman, the wee girlie?"

He chuckled and for his trouble Mrs Dawson picked up a knife, whipped it across the room, pinning his coat through at buttonhole to the table edge before anyone could move. "Yes, it's hers and my Angel's a fine shot with it."

Dalton didn't seem to hear her, he was too busy pulling the knife out and looking closely at it, the table and his coat. "Well, bugger me. I've never seen anyone but gypsy pull off that kind of trick!"

Mrs Dawson put her hand out for her knife as Dalton walked over and handed it to her. "I'm only half; my mam married an English soldier."

There was a rumbling outside in the yard and a commotion coming from the front of the house. Father came bursting into the kitchen with Mr Spencer and Dr Jefferson hard on his heels followed by a dark-haired boy who worked his way around the table only to race out the door into the yard. Robert took off to the front of the house. Father looked puzzled, "Mrs Dawson, it appears that relatives of yours have just arrived." She grinned from ear to ear and pushed past them out through the door with Angel running after her.

Dalton cocked one eye at my father and said, "Gypsies?"

Father nodded. "Gypsies. How the hell did she get a message to them? When did she get a message to them?"

Robert came back through the door from the front of the house with an elderly bent lady who he helped over to the settee by the fire as he said to my father, "That would have been me who got the message to them. This time of year, my mother's people can be found on Hampstead Heath, so before delivering my messages to all of you I paid them a visit."

Father looked suspiciously at Robert and crossed his arms, "They came to help us out of the goodness of their hearts?" Robert only shrugged.

The older lady cackled but there was a look of bright intelligence in her eyes as she looked my father over, "Hardly, Mr Turner. We did not know who would come to the aid of my granddaughter and her family so, we wait to see who stays to protect them."

"You're here to help us because of your family?"

She shrugged her shoulders just like Robert. "It has been a long trip, we lost much business by coming here so there are many things to be considered and talked about."

Uncle Samuel laughed. "If tinkering and horse trading on Hampstead Heath is that profitable, why did you all come? You could have just sent a few men."

The doorway out to the courtyard darkened as several men came in carrying weapons, bottles and bags. One of them had his arm around Angel's shoulder and she was beaming up at him. Her mother came in behind them, laughing and smiling. Mr Johnson came in with two young ladies hanging onto his arms and a very bemused expression on his face. "Turner, can you explain to me what is going on? There is a rather large Gypsy camp setting up in the meadow next to the stream."

The large man with Angel stepped forward, looking at my father and place his hand on his heart introduced himself, "I am Jibben." He looked at Mrs Dawson and continued, "Bita is family, but Robert has told us about the men taking your daughter and that smugglers were involved." He turned his head as if to spit but Mrs Dawson swatted him. Then he pointed at Mr Johnson. "Bita has also told me about this man's promises so I think you may be worthy of our help, English." He looked at Mr Johnson, frowning at the women holding onto his arms. They let go of his arms and stepped back through the door.

Mr Johnson nodded at Jibben and walked across the room to stand next to me. He smiled as he straightened his coat and cleared his throat. "Correct me if I'm wrong, Mr Jibben, but I assume what you are not saying is that you are expecting a share of the spoils of victory as payment for your assistance?"

Jibben looked at him puzzled as if thinking then he smiled, "No, no, no, my friend." He waved his hand to encompass his followers. "We will help you. Then we will take the wagons and goods off your hands. The smugglers will either be dead or your prisoners, you will have no need for the goods. Besides you don't have enough men to take the wagons from us." He paused and put a finger to his lips standing like a man deep in thought then announced, "But I will lend you some men to help you get any prisoners back to London to hang. That's a good deal, no?" He smiled but it didn't reach his eyes as he waited for a response.

My father covered his eyes with one hand then pushed his hair back off his forehead. "Those goods are proceeds of crimes against the King and therefore default to the Crown."

Jibben paced back and forth between the door to the yard where his followers where standing waiting for his orders. He pulled on his chin and grunted. When he came to a stop in front of my father, he was smiling. "Humph. Half the wagons and goods," then he stopped smiling, "or my people sit back and watch then we will take what we want from the winners and the losers. I think you are a smart man, Mr Turner." He pointed at me. "She is your daughter?" Father nodded. "She's very pretty, when you die, I'll take care of her. Maybe even take her back to her mother in London." He smiled evilly.

Mrs Dawson had moved to speak to the old lady in a whisper. The old lady stood up without assistance and walked over to Jibben, she smiled up at him, patted his cheek then she slapped him hard on the back of the head then calmly she said as she patted his cheek again, "You don't decide for us, Jibben." She turned around pursing her lips as she stared at my father, then she stared at Mr Johnson and pointed at him, "You, you will own this place?" She gestured to encompass the room and Mr Johnson nodded. She looked at him intently through shuttered eyes, "You are offering work and a home to my granddaughter and her family?" Again Mr Johnson nodded. She looked over everyone slowly like she was assigning a value to each of us. She motioned for Mr Johnson and my father to follow her into the yard.

The rest of us just stood there looking around at each other, waiting for them to return. Jibben and Mrs Dawson were having a heated discussion by the hearth in a language that I didn't understand. It was obvious that Jibben was furious, Robert and Angel joined her as the conversation continued. Suddenly Jibben seemed to give up arguing and turned to hug Robert and Angel.

The old lady returned to the kitchen with Mr Johnson and my father. They both looked bewildered. The old lady waved all her people out the door and then followed Jibben out. Uncle Samuel turned with his hands spread out wide. "They're leaving?"

Father rubbed his forehead. "Quite the contrary, they're staying and fighting with us. Actually, I should say that they will fight but they have their own methods which they will implement without our assistance or supervision."

Samuel sputtered, "But—but how? And WHY?"

Father pointed at Mr Johnson, "It's all thanks to him."

My uncle turned to him, "What?"

Mr Johnson chuckled. "I'm not sure how it happened but it seems I'm going to provide them with enough land on this property located near running water for their permanent winter quarters. In exchange, they will help us tonight and will assist me at planting and harvest time for a portion of what we harvest."

Uncle Samuel stood there with his mouth open. "You're lucky that you don't have any near neighbours. I'm not sure that the locals will be very friendly towards you once they find Gypsies are living on their doorstep for part of the year."

Father laughed. "That might be, Samuel, but Miles here drives a hard bargain. They have agreed that anyone caught thieving, cheating or involved in any illegal activities while in the district will suffer the consequences of the law and the whole camp will have to leave and forfeit the land. He has also insisted that all the children be taught to read and write. They can already do their sums better than any banker."

I could see that my uncle was on the verge of laughing but he collected himself and asked soberly, "Are you really going to honour that arrangement, Miles?"

Mr Johnson looked affronted and responded as such, "Of course, I will! Frankly, I'm surprised that you would even ask me. In the past, I may have given people the impression that I'm not reliable; but I assure you, sir, that I take my responsibilities very seriously." Then his voice became quiet and slightly melancholic, "Perhaps one day a lady may look favourably upon the bastard son of an Earl and agree to wed me." His gaze flick to me as he spoke.

The silence that followed was suddenly shattered by a blood curdling scream coming from the room where they had locked Louisa.

# Chapter 20
## *And They Come*

Dr Jefferson had been standing resolutely by the door to the hall listening to everything when the scream rang out. He gritted his teeth, closed his eyes then pulled the key to the laundry room from his pocket. "Would someone like to assist me? Preferable with a weapon in hand." He looked about the room, but no one would make eye contact with him.

Mr Johnson shook his head. "No, thank you, Jefferson. Wrestling that she-devil in the muck was quite enough for me."

No one else appeared to be up for the challenge, so Dr Jefferson started towards the hall where the laundry room could be found. My Uncle Samuel let out a sigh and took up the cudgel that Mrs Dawson had been holding out for any interested party. "Come on then. Let's get this over with. But I swear to God if she starts anything, Matthew, I will finish it—lady or not!"

Mrs Dawson chuckled as they moved toward the hallway as the screaming continued. She picked up her knife and began peeling vegetables and without looking at anyone said, "It's probably just Timber what's set her off."

I was curious by what she meant and since no one else asked I did, "What's Timber?"

She smiled "The cat!" and let out a burst of laughter. "He's the best mouser I've ever seen, keeps the whole house clear of vermin. But sometimes he likes to play with his catch for a bit before, well, you know, before he eats them." She laughed again this time a good deep belly laugh. "I imagine that's not something that would appeal to a lady." She was chuckling with a twinkle in her eye that belied what she said next. "I don't know for love nor money how he gets into the laundry, but tis one of his favourite places."

My uncle and Dr Jefferson both chuckled then set off on their errand of mercy. They returned with a white-faced weeping Louisa between them and a very large orange cat with yellow eyes following them, licking its chops as it plunked down by the hearth to wash. Louisa spied it, pointed and started to wail again; the cat ignored her entirely.

Mrs Dawson who had watched the parade with a smug smile suddenly moved into action. Stepping up to Louisa, she slapped her soundly across the cheek. "Shut your face, you bloody fool, it's just a damn cat! An if you don't behave, I'll have my man lock you in the wine cellar with the spiders and the real vermin." Angel's eyes went wide, she opened her mouth, but Mrs Dawson winked at her. I took that to mean that either there wasn't a wine cellar or if there was it was as clean as the kitchen and vermin free. Mrs Dawson pushed Louisa into a seat at the table. Then she grabbed a bowl, filled it with soup and thumped it and put spoon down in front of her. She tore off a chunk off a freshly baked loaf of bread, poured a cup of ale and placed them before her as well. "Now eat and not another sound out of you or I'll stuff a gag in your mouth myself."

While this was happening, I stepped to the yard door and looked out, but no one was there. It was as quiet as a church yard. The rain had stopped, and the wet cobblestones glistened. The only light outside was from the stars and the moon with clouds rapidly scudding across the sky creating strange shadows that almost looked alive. There was no sign of the gypsies, anywhere.

Angel was suddenly at my elbow. "It's wicked spooky out there, isn't it! Especially knowing that my mum's people are all around and you can't see nor hear 'em. It's like magic!" She snapped her fingers and gave me a mocking smirk as if she expected me to be spooked.

I told myself that it was only the quiet that was unnerving, "Not really, I'm not afraid. I know that they're out there, you can sense the difference." I could feel their eyes on the house and me and it gave me the shivers. "It's just that they moved everything so quickly and quietly."

She looked about her and smiled slyly, "That's the way of the gypsy. Now that Mr Johnson is gonna let them stay here I hope to get to know their ways better. My mum's a good teacher but we don't live like they do so it's not the same."

She made them sound so mysterious. "Do you want to live like them?"

She grunted, "Who? Me? Oh no, I'm too English for 'em and they're too gypsy for me. But I like the thought of 'em being around and helping to turn this place into a real home. Despite what people say gypsies are hard workers but they're cursed with the wanderlust. I want to make a good life for myself here with a good man and my own babes. Wandering about the country is not for me." She looked out into the dark. "It's just a dream I have to know their ways," she sighed and leaned against the wall, "it's just a dream."

Father came up behind us. "Ladies, I think it's time to close and lock the door. Murphy and the others just came in and said that they could hear movement on the road. So, let's get you two situated out of the way, shall we." He gently nudged us back into the kitchen then closed and locked the door.

I frowned at him. "I'm not going to hide, Papa. I can shoot, and Angel can load for me." He pointedly looked at my arm then at Angel who was shaking her head. "Oh no, miss, I'm going to be using me bow. Besides I've never touched a pistol, I don't know how to load one…my Da wouldn't allow it."

Father gave me a stern look. I could tell he was surprised at my attitude. "Lissa, we agreed and now is not the time to argue about this."

I felt in my pocket for the little popper Uncle Samuel had given me. "I'm not arguing, Papa, I'm just being realistic. You need everyone to help! If I'm going to die, I'd rather be with you then left behind in a locked room at the mercy of the winners."

Father opened then closed his mouth. He took a deep breath, rubbed his temple. "Fine, come with me. Angel, you stay here with your mother and brother."

Mr Johnson walked up to my father, grabbed his arm then he pulled him close and spoke in a very low hissing voice "You have got to be kidding. You can't bring her into the middle of a fire fight!"

Father shook his hand loose. "You've changed your tune, earlier you voted that she should be given a gun."

168

Miles grimaced. "That was for her own protection!"

Father was livid. "She's my daughter and she's made a convincing argument as to why she should be with me!"

Mr Johnson grunted with disgust. "Don't be ridiculous, she's a child!"

I bristled but before I could say anything my father relaxed his stance, "I know that you feel responsible for her being here, Miles. But she isn't a child and she isn't in London, she's here with me, with us." He put his hand on Mr Johnson's shoulder who still looked very disturbed. Father shook him good-naturedly to get his attention. "Miles, the fact that she isn't in London is not your fault! Good God man you kept my wife safe! If not for you she would have been here, and Lissa might have been dead. Don't you see that we would have still been here regardless? The truth is we really don't know what might have happened if things had transpired differently. I'm just happy that they're both alive! And I have you to thank for that."

Mr Johnson looked at me and sighed, "Well, poppet, it looks like you're with us." He bent close to me and whispered in my ear just as my father turned to the others and assigned stations. "That popper you have in your pocket is only good at close range so keep it safe and hidden until you need it. And pray that you don't need it." I stared back at him in surprise that he knew about the popper. I looked at my uncle who was talking to Dr Jefferson then back at Mr Johnson, his eyes showed fear and something else that I wasn't sure about. He bowed, gesturing towards the door with his hand, "After you, Miss Turner." I didn't know what to say so I went ahead followed by him and then my father.

The smugglers finally arrived just when it seemed like they wouldn't. It was well past midnight when they came silently and swiftly. The first sign was the sudden increase in activity of the wildlife which must have been disturbed by their movement. A shot rang out suddenly then the night was alive with flashes of light and the sound of weapons being fired, men screaming and wagons and horses moving. We were on a battlefield.

There was a scream from the back of the house and several shots were fired inside the house. I wanted to run back there and check on the people in the kitchen. But I couldn't leave my father and the others. Suddenly there was a terrible commotion coming from the hallway. My father left the window that he'd been defending and ran for the hall door. As he flung open the door, I heard a familiar voice, it was Browne. He was in the house! I felt in my pocket for the little pistol that my uncle had given me and ran after my father. I reached his side and saw Browne standing there with a pistol pointed directly at my father's chest. My father's pistol lay at his feet. I stopped in the doorway…my heart was pounding in my ears, but I still heard someone come up behind me and to my right, they were hidden behind the doorjamb. Browne was laughing at my father who looked extremely angry. Neither of them had acknowledged my arrival but I wasn't about to let that bastard kill my father. I pulled out my pistol raised my good arm to aim…I told myself that I could do this. Browne was a stationary target, he wasn't more than five feet away, I knew I could do this. All I had to do was aim and pull the trigger. Browne finally looked at me and laughed when he saw the little popper in my hand.

My father turned his head towards me, his face blanched when he saw my pistol and he yelled "NO!" But I could feel the resolve in my heart. I just had to make my hand obey. It seemed that I lost all sense of time and sound. I looked at Browne laughing, he had shifted his aim to me. Our guns went off simultaneously and two spots of blood appeared on his person. One was dead centre in his chest and the other was in the middle of his forehead. I hadn't even heard my pistol go off or seen the flash from the powder, I had been so focused on Browne. I watched him abruptly stop laughing and fall to the floor. I dropped the pistol and turned to my father. He pulled me to him, hugging me tightly. Then pushed me back to inspect me he was shaking as a tear slid down his cheek. "I'm not injured, Papa. I'm fine." Father nodded patting my shoulders while swallowing great gulps of air like he had been holding his breath. Then he reached down for his own pistol and went to Browne. He looked down at him then at the spent pistol by his body. Suddenly there was crash behind us and I turned to see Mr Johnson sprawled in the doorway, a small table had fallen across him. I rushed to him along with papa. He had been shot in the chest. He was very pale and seemed to have trouble breathing. He reached out to touch my cheek, smiled then closed his eyes. I heard myself screaming "NO!"

My father gathered me to him and held me tight. Dr Jefferson came running from the kitchen in response to my scream. He handed his pistol to my father as he knelt beside Mr Johnson then he turned to me, "Lissa! Go get Mrs Dawson and stay there with your uncle. He'll need you." Then he turned back to my father and shook him. "Colin, help me get him onto the settee," he pivoted on his heels. "Spencer, Dalton give us a hand here!" I heard the others coming but I couldn't look up at them. All the while I just stood there looking down at Mr Johnson. I couldn't tell if he was even breathing.

My father grabbed my hand shaking it to get my attention "Lissa! Look at me…" I turned my head towards him. "Go to Samuel. Miles will be alright, I promise." I looked in his eyes and all I saw was fear.

Panic set in, I decided that I couldn't stand there and watch Mr Johnson die so I fled to the kitchen as quickly as I could. Everything was quiet there. My uncle was sitting at the table with a cup of tea in front of him, so I went quickly to Mrs Dawson and explained what had happened. She gathered up the small kettle, a bowl and grabbed some clean linen for bandages then the doctor's bag and bustled out of the room.

I sat by my uncle as he poured me a cup of tea then push the cream and sugar towards me. It was so quiet! Eerily quiet. "Is it over?"

My uncle had been staring into his own untouched cup, he looked worse than he had when he'd been shot. "Yes," he said quietly, "it's over, thank God." He waved his hand towards the door. "According to Mr Dawson, our men are with the gypsies doing a clean-up." He rubbed his hand over his face like he was exhausted. "God, I need a drink."

I turned to take a good look at him and saw that there was blood on the front of his jacket, I jumped up, rattling the cups on the table. He saw me staring at him then looked down and scowled, he shrugged out of his coat folding it inwards, so the blood wasn't visible. "It's not my blood, brat, I'm untouched." He patted the seat next to him. "Sit and keep me company." He added more sugar to his cup then took a huge gulp. I sat with him taking his hand in mine, he squeezed it then leaned over and kissed me on the cheek. I took in the rest of the room, Angel was applying a bandage to Robert's head, he was awake and sitting so it must not be to serious. But I saw nothing to account for the blood on my uncle's coat. Mr Dawson was seated on the settee by the fire watching Angel and Robert with a slight smile of pride. Dalton, I assumed, had gone out with the rest of our men.

Then I noticed that Louisa was nowhere to be seen. I saw a pistol on the floor near Robert and my uncle had one close by him. Mr Dawson's was on the settee beside him. "Where's Louisa?"

My uncle swallowed hard, put his head down on his arms and groaned. The Dawsons were all looking at him with awe. It was Angel that spoke first. "She's dead, miss, she tried to kill Robert and Mr Hughes shot her."

My mouth was dry as dust as I looked at my uncle and all I could say was "Uncle Samuel?"

He turned his head to the side, so he could look at me. Then he closed his eyes. "We weren't paying attention to her. The shooting started so quickly that none of us saw her work her way around to where Robert was loading the pistols. She grabbed one just as he turned around with a spent one. She had it pointed at my back, but Robert lunged for her and it fired, grazing his head. When I turned around after hearing the shot, she was still standing there with the spent gun in her hand pointed down at Robert on the floor. It didn't register with me that she had already fired so I shot her before she could kill him. But she had already shot the gun. I killed her, an unarmed woman, I killed her, Lissa." He sobbed, turned his head and buried his face in his arms and cried.

I placed my hand on his back, I was at a loss for words. I looked at Angel then Robert for support, but they were looking at their feet. It was Mr Dawson that got up and sat down across from us. "I know you've taken the pledge to stay away from spirits and you're an inspiration to me just on that alone. But for what you did for my son you have my undying thanks." Then he plunked another pistol on the table. He reached over and shook my uncle's arm. "Here now, are you listening to me because it be important that you listen." Uncle Samuel raised a bleary eye to him and sniffed, pulling out his handkerchief he wiped his nose. Mr Dawson pushed the pistol towards my uncle who recoiled from it. "Now this here is the second pistol she was pointing at my boy, it's one of two that he'd loaded that were laying on the work bench. She'd took one of them after she tried to shoot you." He turned and pointed at Robert's feet. "That there one by his feet is the empty one that she dropped after missing you, she must have had it hid in her pocket. You killed the bitch what would have murdered me only son and for that I'm beholden to you."

My uncle reached out and took the pistol, looking at the priming that was still fresh. He looked at Robert who nodded and added, "Do you think that I'd have played dead like that if the pistol she was holding on me were empty? Not bloody likely! You saved my life, sir!"

Uncle Samuel ran his fingers through his hair trying to smile. He grabbed me and hugged me close. Then he leaned over and shook Mr Dawson's hand. He got up and walked over to Robert, "Are you truly alright?"

Robert smiled at him. "Dr Jefferson said I'd be right as rain. I'm just not to move to fast or bend over for a day or two."

Mr Dawson sniggered. "Sounds like you're just got out of any work around here for a couple of days. If that's the case, then you better find your bed and get some sleep, boy, and tomorrow you had better go down and see the vicar to tell him you'll be going to Lon'on. Maybe I'd better go with you, someone will need to explain to him that your ma's people will be here every winter too." He bit the inside of his cheek. "The vicar's a good head, he'll help us smooth it away with the folk hereabouts." He paused again, grimacing, "Maybe we'd better take Mr Johnson with us to introduce him too as the new owner and he can explain about your ma's people."

Suddenly my stomach flipped as Mr Johnson came to my mind. He was bleeding to death in the parlour. Stuttering, I said, "I don't believe that Mr Johnson...that he will be able to go with you—he—he's been seriously wounded." Mr Dawson's face fell as if he could see his future dissolve before his eyes.

Just then my father walked into the kitchen. I stood up wringing my hands, I could feel the panic building in my gut but he smiled and said, "Matthew thinks he'll make it, but he can't be moved for several days. Mrs Dawson is arranging bedding for him by the fire and Dr Jefferson and Michael will stay here with him while I get you and Louisa back to London."

He looked at my uncle's stricken face. "Samuel?"

"She's dead, Colin. I shot her; I had no choice, she was going to kill the boy."

Father nodded and sat down. He looked exhausted and older. He had once gone to the continent with the intent of becoming a soldier, but fate had taken him in the direction of intelligence gathering instead. And while that has its own dangers, it is in fact significantly different from the impersonal slaughter on a battlefield, and there was no doubt in my mind that this had been a battle. Father poured himself a cup of lukewarm tea and sat across from my uncle. "Browne is dead as well." He turned to me putting an arm around my shoulder, taking a deep breath he continued, "Lissa and Miles both shot him." My uncle's head shot up at this news. He looked at me as my father continued, "But Miles took a ball in the chest; he's lost a lot of blood. Matthew retrieved the ball and the material from his shirt so unless infection sets in, it will just take time. He was having some trouble breathing but Matthew was able to draw out the blood with a hollow needle and he's breathing easier now."

Uncle Samuel nodded then proceeded to tell my father what had transpired in the kitchen. Father only asked, "Does Matthew know?"

"Yes, he was the one that took her body outside when the gypsies came back to say they were leaving."

Father sat up, "Leaving!" He ran for the door to the yard just as Michael, Murphy and Jacob came through it. "The gypsies, where they are?"

Jacob swept his hand through his hair. "Gone, the big one, Jibben, said to tell you thank you for the spoils of the war. We couldn't stop them, sir, there were just too many."

Before Jacob finished Dalton came into the room from the hallway. "Sir, they're gone! All of them!"

"Yes. I know, Jacob just told me that they've left."

"Not the gypsies, sir. The smugglers, they're all gone!"

Father was angry and exhausted as he barked at Dalton, "What the devil do you mean all gone?"

Dalton sucked in his lower lip before speaking, "The bodies, any survivors, the Gypsies they're all just gone!"

There was a cackle and a hearty laugh from the behind us. "That's no exactly true, mister." Dalton jumped aside. Jibben was behind him with the old lady.

She shuffled over to my father, took his chin in her claw-like hand and pulled him down to her eye to eye. "You are an honourable man, Mr Turner. But there were no survivors; they will all be part of the bog soon, it's better that way."

Father looked at her first in horror then in awe. "How—how many?"

172

She shrugged and looked at Jibben who said, "Humph, about thirty, maybe more, maybe less."

Father rubbed his hands over his face, "My god."

Jibben shrugged his shoulders. "They were scum, you should not let it bother you. They would have slit your throat for a bottle of whisky. No one will miss any of them and if they do," he shrugged and surveyed the room, "...who here is going to tell them what happened?" He chuckled and then crossed his arms over his chest. "Your king will be happy we saved the gold and silver for you." He held up fingers as if to pinch something. "Of course, we took a little for our troubles along with the other goods. But I think your master will be pleased." He threw a thick packet of letters and documents on the table. "There is treason in those pages, Turner. I think your king and master will make you very busy."

Then the old lady and Jibben left. My father did not argue about the price they had exacted for their aid. He just sat staring at the packet before him and sighed as if the weight of it was more than his weary hands could possibly lift. Everyone else gathered around the table watching as he finally opened the first document and read it. Then he put his hands to his head and let the document fall back onto the table as he whispered, "Oh God."

# Chapter 21
## *London: December 1827*

We had been back in London for three months. My birthday had come and gone as we prepared for Christmas. Uncle Samuel and Father were often gone meeting with Sir Thomas and other government officials or on missions up and down the coast. Whatever had been in those papers that Jibben had given Father was never discussed within my hearing or even when I eavesdropped. Even Lettie said she knew nothing about what they contained or at least that's what she told me. Murphy, Michael and Jacob were often gone for days and weeks at a time. Mr Crenshaw, my father's man of business, was frequently closeted with my father and uncle. Apparently, part of his business now was in assisting to sort out the General's affairs as well as the business affairs of my father and uncle.

The Clarkes had decided against the idea of investing in our horse stud and were looking to move closer to Ramsey's university. Charity's first season disappointingly had not produced a husband. She had many suitors according to the gossips, but no proposals ever resulted. Her father suddenly felt that moving to Oxford would better her chances to find a husband among the scholars and academics. But Aunt Mary had heard whispers about Charity, it was nothing specific other than that she had not made the grade within the Beau Monde and was likely to be left on the shelf.

The General's affairs proved to be confusing as well as shocking to say the least. He was deeply in debt on one hand, yet he had hidden assets that were tied up in a trust for me of all people. Which upon his death was to be mine without restrictions but I wanted nothing to do with it and would have gladly given it all to Samuel to be applied to the debt levied against the Abbey. But Samuel wouldn't take the money, yet my parents didn't really want me to keep it either. In the meantime, it was decided to just leave it in Mr Crenshaw's hands to invest. My one and only question was why did the General do it? No one, not even the General's solicitors, bankers, or his former valet Appleforth knew of this trust's existence or why he had made me the beneficiary. He had used a different solicitor and bank to set it all up and my greatest fear was that the money had come from smuggling or some other illegal venture. Once the solicitors had finished tackling the many twists and turns of my grandfather's will Samuel was able to save the estate from bankruptcy by using a small portion of the inheritance he had received from his mother and grandfather. Thankfully it still left him well off, but the Abbey would have to start turning a profit as a working estate. The Home Farm was not large enough to bear that burden alone and while the orchards were famous for their fruit and cider production, the amount of money required to keep the Abbey solvent required more than what the farm alone could produce. My input wasn't asked for, but I felt like I had to think of something to help them find a solution.

Mr Johnson meanwhile had been our guest for only a very short time while he recovered from his wound. I was hardly ever allowed to see him and then for only brief periods. After we had been back in London less than a week his father had arrived to take him away to convalesce at his country estate in Devon. He corresponded with my father and after two months of convalescing he wrote to say that he was returning to Dorset with his father to purchase the ramshackle estate where he had been shot and that he had no immediate plans to return to London since he would be busy overseeing the repairs, renovations and improvements needed to make it a habitable home and a working farm once again. While there he would look into the smuggling ventures in the area for my father.

I was beginning to feel stifled and isolated... Aunt Mary and Emilie along with mother were busy shopping and sewing for the baby and life seemed to have settled into a pattern of predictable domesticity. However, I was still not allowed to venture out on my own as I had in Northumberland, so I was limited to the garden when unsupervised. Otherwise I was required to be in the presence of a family member or groom even then I could only go riding or walking in the Park at prescribed times of the day. My lessons had become disjointed with the frequent absence of some of my instructors. And the only contact I had with my father and Uncle Samuel was at meal times when they were home.

Even Meg had become distant. She had formed an attachment for Robert who had come to London with us to train as my father's valet. She was love struck even though Robert seemed to ignore her for the most part while concentrating on learning his trade. My mother's maid Beth assured me that the attachment was mutual but that the young man was taking his training very seriously and throwing all his time and energy into it, even Dalton felt he'd make a good valet.

Then one day I heard that Ramsey Clarke and his family had come to London during a school holiday. I rejoiced when I was told that they had been invited to dinner! Now I would really have some interesting conversation. But the discussion at the table for the most part was about horses and Ramsey's time at Oxford with much teasing by my uncle and father, who were both Cambridge men. Father tactfully tried to find out about their life in the Indies without mentioning slavery but didn't have any success.

Charity was not at all chatty and when the ladies adjourned to the drawing room her mother talked nonstop about Charity's success in Oxford. But whenever Aunt Mary or Mother addressed either lady about the Indies, they merely gave them a blank look then changed the subject as if they had never heard the question. Mother tried to press Mrs Clarke once and was met with cool reserve.

When the men finally joined us, I felt the tension in the room lighten a bit. I tried more than once to engage Ramsey's attention but without success. I noticed that he was in conversation with my uncle who was quizzing him about his Latin studies, but Ramsey looked decidedly irritated. It took me some time before I could speak to him and his response to my overtures when I finally had a moment alone with him was blunt and almost rude. "I must say that I was rather surprised to see you at table tonight, Miss Turner."

I was puzzled by his coolness, the Clarkes I had thought were friends, our dinners with them had always been informal. Yet I sensed that something was different now, that university had changed Ramsey. So, I asked him just as bluntly, "And why would you be surprised?" I tried to not let him see that I had been insulted.

His ears reddened, and he rolled his tongue around his mouth looking over my head…at least he had the good grace to be embarrassed or at least I thought he was. He took a sip from the glass he was holding and thus fortified, he regained his bravado saying, "Your parents do seem to be rather progressive and I suppose this gathering is a small informal affair, hardly what I would call a proper dinner party." He looked around the room while I tried not to clench my fists. Then he made eye contact with me and very pointedly remarked, "However, it is my understanding that in most households where young ladies have not come out, they are consigned to the nursery for dinner parties."

I felt like I had just been slapped in the face. I looked to see if anyone else had heard what had been said. Charity was the closest, but she turned away when I looked at her. Aunt Emilie was close by and she had obviously heard him, she was glaring at him and was starting to move towards us when I shook my head for her not to bother. I was barely able to hold back my tears, but I managed to look Ramsey in the eye and flung a retort in his face without malice. "Yes, Mr Clarke, my parents are progressive. But unlike some I earned my place at the table because of my ability to conduct myself civilly and with maturity." His mouth fell open and I was somewhat mollified by his shocked expression. Aunt Emilie kept her eyes on me as she told my uncle what had just transpired. He frowned and made a move as if to come over, but she grabbed his arm and whispered to him. I took a deep breath, nodded at her then smiled at Ramsey before I walked away from him and out the door.

In the hallway, I encountered Murphy and Lettie in quiet conversation and when they saw me they jumped apart. I tried to smile at them but didn't succeed so I waved to them and made my way up the stairs. I didn't go to my room where I knew Meg would be waiting. Instead I went to the nursery where Ramsey said I belonged. The ladies in my family had been hard at work making the space into a child's wonderland for my brother or sister. I sat down on the window seat looking out at the dark garden. Leaning back against the pillows piled there, and cried. My life had changed so much yet it was obvious that I had not adapted to sophisticated city life. I often dreamed of riding Jewel on the moor, sitting on a branch in the orchard eating sun warmed apples or just reading in the tall grass. I missed the freedom to come and go as I pleased, I even missed the village and all its familiar inhabitants.

I must have fallen asleep since it was a knock at the door that brought me back to reality. My throat was dry from my crying, but I managed to croak "Come in." To my utter astonishment, Mr Johnson walked in, dressed in full evening kit. He immediately noticed my tear-stained face and looked mildly distressed. I prevented him from asking me if I was alright by asking him, "How did you know I would be here?"

He smiled and pulled up a chair to sit by my seat. I sat up straighter and faced him. He looked at his hands interlaced in front of him, "I'm sorry that I was delayed and have only just arrived, but I met your Aunt Emilie in the foyer. She told me what had happened, she was on her way up to speak with you, so I asked her to let me talk to you instead. You see you and I have a great deal in common in some ways." He looked up at me with soft grey eyes. "I have had a great deal of experience with rejection and being on my own. I assumed this was where you went based on Clarke's comment."

I tried to reclaim my dignity but was a bit harsh, "I do not require any consoling, Mr Johnson!"

He tipped his head to the side looking at me with a smile, "I can see that, Miss Hughes. Would you then perhaps grant me the favour of letting me thrash young Ramsey on your behalf instead?"

I giggled and shook my head no, "That won't be necessary but thank you for the offer, I can manage quite well without Mr Ramsey Clarke in my life." I took a breath and waited for the jab of pain from the realization of Ramsey's rejection, but it didn't come. I wiped at my face with the handkerchief that Mr Johnson handed me and continued, "Other than my family I have been alone my whole life, Mr Johnson, it's not so bad. I will get used to it again."

His smile faded and was replaced with a wistful expression. "I suppose I should say that you are far too young to be so cynical. Except that I know exactly what you mean." He cleared his throat and quietly without irony said, "Miss Hughes, you are an inspiration to a reprobate such as myself." He hesitated then reached out and took my hand, "I would very much like to be your friend if you will let me. The seven years difference in our ages should not be an impediment to being friends and our life experiences I would say have made us sympathetic to each other. If I may paraphrase, someone that I sincerely admire, I think that we are both far too cynical and intelligent for the company of our average acquaintance."

I smiled at him and a sudden warmth invaded my heart as he took my hand in his warm and strong one. "I would be honoured to be your friend, Mr Johnson," knowing in my heart that he truly was my friend. "Perhaps you can help me with another dilemma." He raised an eyebrow and gave me a half smile, encouraging me to continue. "Can you tell me what it's like to be an older and more mature sibling?"

He laughed out loud then let go of my hand as he stood up, "Indeed, I can, Miss Hughes. Now would you care to join me and your family for some tea and cakes? I seemed to have missed dinner by arriving so late." I wanted to ask him who had sent him an invitation as I was not aware of him being on the original guest list, but I decided that it was none of my business, he was here and that's what was important.

He offered me his hand again as I stood up. "I believe that cook would be happy to put a tray together for you, Mr Johnson. After all, I've heard her say many times..." and I recited in my best imitation of cook, "I've a fondness for that Mr Johnson, a right gentleman he is. He knows how to appreciate fine cooking." I laughed and so did he.

"That sounds wonderful, Miss Turner." We left the nursery and proceeded downstairs talking about his place in Dorset and how the Dawsons were faring.

We were met at the foot of the stairs by my father and uncle. The Clarkes had apparently left in a flurry of high indignation after my father had heard about what had transpired between Ramsey and me.

Mother had already bespoke dinner for Mr Johnson, so he went to the dining room with my father and uncle, though he seemed genuinely reluctant to lose my company.

Aunt Mary had gone home with Mr Spencer so that left Aunt Emilie, Mother and I in the drawing room. Mother came and sat beside me. Thankfully she did not try to assuage my feelings with platitudes. Instead she tucked a few tendrils of hair behind my ears and looked at me as if with new eyes. "You've had to grow up very quickly, haven't you, my darling." She looked sad as she wrapped her arms around me. "I'm so sorry, Lissa. I feel like I've failed you. Perhaps—"

I interrupted her before she could go on about what she might have done differently. "Mama, I am very satisfied with the person that I am. In fact, I like who I am. I owe that to you and Uncle Samuel and to Father. I know that I'm loved that I have always been loved, that means a great deal to me! So please don't regret anything. I've had advantages, affection and liberties that most people my age have never had and that's because you sacrificed so much for me." As I was saying this to her, I realised that I meant it with all my heart.

She hugged me and leaned back in the seat with a heavy sigh, her back had been sore for days but today it was even worse. Dr Jefferson assured us that it was nothing to worry about and that he had never seen a healthier, expectant mother.

Aunt Emilie was smiling and came over to sit closer to us. But in a voice of that was full of innuendo said, "So, Lissa, Mr Johnson was some comfort to you?"

I looked towards her, smiling, but she wasn't smiling back. I felt like I had missed something, that she wasn't saying exactly what she meant so I stated with full confidence, "Aunt Emilie, Mr Johnson is my friend. He is a gentleman and an honourable man. I don't know what you are insinuating." Then I remembered the circumstances or her own life after she lost her family, so I assumed that she was thinking the worst. "Actually, I do know what you mean but this is not France nor Belgium at war time and I am not you."

She sat back quickly clasping her hands to her chest, her eyes glistened with tears, she reached out and took my hand. "You're right, Lissa, I'm sorry. He is a good man, I know it in my heart, please forgive me."

My mother grimaced placing her hands on her belly then she took a deep breath. "I think Mr Johnson is very much like your father, Lissa." She smiled weakly. "And you're right, he is an honourable man."

The gentlemen joined us and announced that we had been invited to Mr Johnson's home in Dorset for a short holiday at our convenience. Mother started to thank him then suddenly she braced both her hands on the seat and took sharp deep breath, calling out to my father, "Colin?"

Father looked at her calmly, "Yes, my dear?"

Her breath was coming in short gasps now. "I think you had better send for Dr Jefferson." And with that she gave a grunt and the seat beside me was instantly wet. I quickly stood up, my father's eyes were focused on my mother, but his only response was "oh!"

Mr Johnson looked in our direction, he placed a hand on my father's back, "I'll go, Colin, you stay with Irene." Then he turned and was gone.

Mama gave birth to a healthy baby boy that night and a month later he was christened James Thomas Ryerson Turner. The occasion of his christening should have been grand except we were still technically in mourning for my late grandfather. James and I got on very well, he seemed to either delight in my presence with smiles and giggles or found me boring and would fall asleep, Mama told me that I was a god-send.

Mr Johnson did not return to us after the night of James' birth and our holiday to his home did not materialize. It seemed that there was always some emergency on his property that required his attention, or he was away on business for Sir Thomas. But I did receive a Christmas gift from him. It was a silver locket that was etched with ivy and violets but when I opened it, it was empty except for the inscription 'Regarde Avec Ton Coeur' the translation was 'Look with Your Heart'. Father offered to have a miniature of the family painted to insert in it, but I declined. I felt that there wasn't any need to fill it at the present. Mother thought it was too lovely to wear every day, so it resided in my jewellery box beside the string of pearls that papa had given me on my seventeenth birthday.

Meg still had not made any progress with Robert except that he had admitted a deep affection for her. He asked her to wait since he was determined to supplant everything until he had learned his trade. My father's coming and goings along with my uncle's had kept both Robert and Dalton very busy which he enjoyed immensely but Meg was distraught every time he was absent.

When there were no lessons, I passed the time reading, drawing and practicing all that I had already learned. My drawing had improved considerably under Lettie's direction. So, I did a pencil sketch of every member of the family, staff, even Dr Jefferson and Mr Johnson. It was these sketches that I gave out as Christmas gifts. I didn't show the finished work to anyone, I felt that they were pieces that should be personal between me and the recipient. For the married couples, each received the picture of their spouse. Since I did the wrapping and labelling it was a surprise to all of them and in all cases, I'm pleased to say it had been a pleasant one. I also did one of James and me together to give to our parents from both of us. It was difficult and had to be done quickly by looking in a mirror while having James propped on a pillow beside me, but it turned out to be very handsome. Mr Johnson's portrait was the most difficult since I didn't have the actual person at hand to study. Instead I drew him from memory. As it came to life he materialised with the wistful expression from that night in the nursery. Lettie was the only one who saw it and was astounded at the likeness. I held onto it hoping that he would join us but by New Year's there was no news from him, so I sent it by post to Dorset.

We had been in London over a year since I had last seen Mr Johnson and my Aunt Mary and mother were busy planning for my first season, a fact that did not excite my interest at all. I missed my friend even though we wrote to each other frequently, sharing our day to day stories with each other. But the last letter that I had received from him had been almost four months ago, when he said that he had been important assignment from Sir Thomas and that he would not be able to write me for some time.

Christmas of had come and gone again as well as my eighteenth birthday and still no word from him. I knew my father was concerned about him though he tried not to show it. I devoted much time to eavesdropping on my father and uncle and was finally rewarded one day when I heard them saying that one of them would have to journey to Paris and look for him. That was also the day I was caught listening at the door for the first time. I had tried to scoot away when the study door suddenly opened and I heard my name "Lissa?" I raised my eyes and grimaced at my father who was standing before me with his arms crossed. Uncle Samuel was behind him obviously trying not to laugh.

I straightened up and tried to bluster my way through. "Hello, Papa! I lost a button and I'm just looking for it." I looked down at my feet and scanned the floor with great intensity.

Father relaxed his stance giving me a half smile. "A button, really?" He looked at me sceptically "You'll have to do much better than that, my dear, but not bad for your first time being caught." He leaned towards me. "However, when you hear news about someone you care about, you can't let it affect you to the point that you aren't aware of what is happening around you. Do you understand?"

I nodded. "Yes, Papa. But about Mr Johnson, what's happened to him?"

"We don't know, Lissa, but it looks like we'll have to go after him. Unfortunately, your uncle and I are well known by the French and no one from our staff would be admitted to the circles in which Miles was supposed to circulate."

Without thinking I blurted out, "Why can't we all go? No one knows that Mr Johnson works with you, just that he is a family friend. Besides you promised Mama a holiday and James is two years old now so he's old enough to travel. I can even practise my French. And while we're there we can look for Mr Johnson. Perhaps we can even ask Dr Jefferson to come with us and…and—" I realised that I had started to ramble, so I stopped in mid-sentence.

Father was shaking his head, I knew he was dismissing the idea, so I turned to walk away disgruntled. I was despairing that I would ever see Mr Johnson again. I looked up to see my mother coming down the stairs. She was smiling and had her head cocked to one side, giving my father a look like he had been a bad boy. "She's right, you know. Colin, you did promise me a holiday after James was born and Aunt Mary has been talking about wanting to go the continent soon now that Mr Spencer has retired from Bow Street. He could assist you in your search. I'm sure even Dr Jefferson would agree to come along, after all he's been working very hard lately and mentioned at dinner the other night that he's been looking to take some time off from his practice." She walked up and linked her arm with my father's, gazing up into his eyes. "And it would be most agreeable for me, darling. I've never been to Paris and you and Samuel know it so well."

She leaned to the side looking at my uncle who was frowning, "Don't you give me that look, Samuel. I know that you've promised Emilie that you would file a claim for her to be compensated for the loss of her family's estates and maybe even try to have them reinstated. I really can't think of a better time for us all to go." She smiled sweetly, patting my father's arm and flicking off an imaginary piece of lint in the process. "You can ask Sir Thomas about his views on it this evening." Father looked perplexed as she smiled sweetly at him, "I've invited him to dinner, my love." She kissed my father on the cheek then she strolled away walking towards the drawing room then she paused looking over her shoulder saying, "Tea anyone?" then she laughed and disappeared through the doorway followed shortly by a squeal of delight from Emilie.

My uncle was laughing out loud while patting my father's shoulder, "I told you when you said that you wanted to marry her that you'd have your hands full!" He gave him another firm pat on the back then followed my mother.

My father looked at me and blinked. "I understand that Paris is beautiful in the spring." He chuckled and followed my uncle.

# Chapter 22
## *Paris: April 1830*

Sir Thomas was delighted with the plan, the arrangements were made for us to leave by the end of the following week. We would be accompanied by Aunt Mary, Mr Spencer and Dr Jefferson. Robert, Dalton, Meg and Beth and Michael, Jacob, Murphy and Lettie were also coming. Lettie had become our nanny by default, my parents had been unable to retain anyone that would tolerate our liberal lifestyle or that could be trusted with James and with the comings and goings surrounding my father's business. Luckily Lettie seem to have a way with James like no one else and Murphy was thrilled that she would be coming with us, while Dalton on the other hand was not as happy, mainly because of Murphy.

Crossing the Channel was choppy but uneventful and everyone was relieved to reach Calais. We made it through customs with our dignity barely intact after having our persons and luggage searched for smuggled English goods. Our passports and official papers were taken from us to be sent on to the Prefecture de Police in Paris. Temporary papers were given to us for our journey and we were warned to report to the police immediately upon our arrival in Paris.

We pushed our way through the crowd on the quay while the surge of humanity seemed to be pressing us back. The sights, sounds and smells were overwhelming, and my head spun trying to take everything in. The port was so alive and according to my father very different now that the war was over. The soldiers of the emperor were long gone but you could still see evidence of them in some of the threadbare beggars haunting the dockside. While those officials of the re-established monarchy trying to maintain a semblance of order were sneered at or ignore by the general populace, there was a feeling of public unrest just below the surface, a palpable undercurrent of things to come.

We finally found the carriages that were waiting to take us to our inn hopefully without mishap. But only through the constant vigilance of our party had they kept the pick pockets and thieves at bay. Once we arrived at the inn we were shown to our rooms to freshen up before dinner. Then we adjourned to a private parlour to enjoy dinner which consisted of soup, two kinds of fish, beef steak, fowl, and meat pie. Followed by a gooseberry pie, cherries, strawberries, grapes and finally a light cake. We sat together, both servant and master, at the same table to eat. Our French host raised an eye over such an odd arrangement quickly making it known to his wife what he thought about eccentric Englishmen after assuming none of us understood French and none of us chose to correct that assumption until the next morning when we were leaving.

In the morning, Father went to settle our bill while our hostess saw the rest of us out to the carriages. As we waited for Father she made a disparaging remark to her daughter about our ignorant English palate. Aunt Mary immediately turned to my mother and they began conversing within earshot in perfect French until my father appeared. The lady of the house stood there with her mouth open and her cheeks scarlet. When we were all finally ensconced in the carriages, my father looked pointedly at our aunt. "Ladies, I don't suppose that you have any idea what happened to leave Madame Daniau so flustered or do you? Should I book another inn for our return journey?"

Aunt Mary looked down her long patrician nose at him. "Why, Colin, we we're merely discussing the quality of the wine at dinner and the croissants at breakfast."

My father raised his one eyebrow, "Do I want to know what was said?"

Mother shoved his shoulder with hers. "It was nothing, my love. But I think maybe we should avoid staying there in the future." She giggled softly so as not to awaken James who was sleeping in her arms. Father chuckled and reached out for my brother, taking him from my mother and laying him against his chest then he stretched out his legs and drifted off to sleep with his arms wrapped around my brother.

My aunt smiled as she watched him, and my mother's face shone with love. I looked at them both and wondered how my father could just fall asleep so quickly in a rocking carriage. Mother caught my puzzled look but mistook my curiosity. "It was the same with you, Clarissa. Your Papa would take you in his arms any chance he could. He'd even take you riding." She smiled shaking her head. "My god he scared me so many times when he'd ride with you along the beaches and cliffs of Cornwall. But he insisted that he needed to spend as much time with you as he could. He'd put you into an infant sling from the time you were a few days old and carry you all day long, relinquishing you only so you could feed. I swear he was better at changing your bottom than I was." It gave me a warm feeling to know that my father had loved me just as much as he did James. Mother was shaking her head looking at him, "I've caught him a time or two sneaking out with James recently for an early ride in the Park. But I must admit that I'm surprised he waited so long. We already have the reputation for being an odd family, so I couldn't imagine what else people could say."

"Why would him taking James be considered odd?"

She chuckled. "For one it was considered scandalous when I was caught out riding soon after giving birth. But your father carrying James in a sling as baby really set the gossips' tongues wagging. He even took him to his club recently to register him as a member." She chuckled. "Beth tells me that the gossip from other houses is that people can't decide whether we're all mad, or just unusually devoted? Personally, I think most of our acquaintances are leaning towards mad." She giggled again and then leaned forward to take my hand. "You and your brother are your father's greatest joy, Lissa, never forget that."

I grinned at her squeezing her hand in return. "I won't, Mama."
I caught my father smiling from under the brim of his hat as he reached out to take hold of my mother's other hand and James never moved a muscle. I decided at that moment that the society gossips were in fact correct, we were a very devoted family and perhaps just a touch mad.

When we arrived at the next posting inn for the night they were already waiting for us. The host's wife bustled out informing Aunt Mary immediately that the wine was the best from Bordeaux and that she would never find a flakier croissant this side of Paris. I whispered to my aunt, "How could she possibly know what you said in Calais?"

Aunt Mary shrugged but the hostess had heard me and explained in English, "Pigeons, mademoiselle, my sister and I send notes to each other by pigeons that we've raised."

I arched a brow. "What?"

"We raise homing pigeons, mademoiselle. It helps with our trade if we know who and what to expect in the way of our guests." She started laughing before she added, "But Adeline, she does not have a light touch with her croissants and her husband, Victor, he thinks maybe the English will not know their wine so much so he did not give you the best. They know better now!" she laughed out loud.

Mother looked at Father wide-eyed as he turned and said to the lady, "I had almost decided to alter my arrangements for our return journey. But perhaps we should give them a second chance."

She smiled and nodded enthusiastically, "You will get better wine next time but alas the croissants will not change." She chuckled spreading her hands out wide and inviting us to follow her into the inn. That night a storm moved in and with it came an assortment of odd characters that filled the Inn with both high born and low.

Surprisingly we had a whole floor of the inn to ourselves with a private parlour, but the men still went down to the common room after dinner to gather news and relax with a game of cards. Aunt Mary begged exhaustion and retired early. Then Mother sent me off to bed as well.

Meg was waiting in our room tapping her toes to the sound of the music that you could hear coming up through the floor from the common room. She loved to dance so I knew that as soon as she got me situated she'd be down the stairs with the rest of the staff, cajoling Robert to dance. There'd been no word about Mr Johnson though Father and Uncle had made enquires all along our route. He must have passed this way so perhaps some of the denizens of the common room tonight might have seen him or heard news of him in Paris.

Meg interrupted my thoughts with her excitement, "Oh, miss, I'm so excited being here in France, who would have thought it! My mother and father will be astounded when they get my letter. I must see about getting them a gift while we're here but I'm not sure what they'd like. They're not fancy people and Mum would scold me for spending my money on a fan or lace handkerchief."

I smiled at her as she finished combing and plaiting my hair, "I'm sure they'd loved anything you get them. Perhaps something that they can use every day, like a scarf or shawl for your mother and a new pipe or tobacco pouch for your father."

She tipped her head to the side biting her lower lip and sighed. "You're right, they've always been the practical kind." She looked about the room then leaned in to whisper, "Robert has promised to take me walking in the gardens of the Tuileries, do think I should? Will it be safe, miss?"

I wasn't sure. However, it was a public place like Hyde Park but in the current political climate it could be a dangerous place to venture to if you weren't careful. So, I erred on the side of caution, "I would imagine that as long as you stay on the main paths where there are lots of people, you'll be fine."

"Oh! so it's like the park in London," she sounded and looked disappointed.

"I'm afraid so but I understand that it's far more beautiful."

Meg beamed. "That will be fine then and thank you, miss, at least I'll know to what to watch out for."

She banked the fire in the hearth, ran the warming pan over the bed linen, snuffed out the candles then practically skipped out of the room. I watched her close the door then I picked up a book, took the candle by my bed and relit the others, so I could read. Meg would not be back for some time and she wouldn't tell anyone if I was still awake when she did come back.

But I fell asleep after reading only a few pages and was startled awake by a voice; the candles had burned themselves out and my heart was racing. I had been dreaming but all I could remember was darkness and a voice whispering in great despair 'Look with your heart'. I tried as hard as I could but couldn't recall anymore other than that it was dark and cold and that it was Miles' voice I'd heard. I was so unnerved that every creak of the floorboards startled me. Meg was not in her bed, so it must not have been terribly late. I got up, threw on my dressing gown then opened my door, the hallway was empty, so I padded down the corridor to my parent's room and lightly knocked on their door. Father opened it immediately. He was standing there fully dressed but Mother was already in bed. I hesitated but he took my hand pulling me into the room. "What is it, Lissa, bad dream?"

I hadn't realised I'd been crying until he pulled out his handkerchief and wiped my face. Mother was out of the bed and at my side immediately as they both ushered me over to sit by the fire. I hurriedly told them about my dream and that I knew Mr Johnson was in dire need of help. Father was pensive and bit his lip before saying, "Lissa, we had word tonight that Miles is a prisoner in the Conciergerie. He is being held for the murder of the French envoy Randal Browne."

I gasped, that was an outrage. "But that's not true, Papa, he was going to kill you. Besides I killed Mr Browne too! I mean I shot him as well!" I could feel the tears poised to run down my cheeks.

He put his arm around me. "Hush, Lissa, we'll take care of it. But Samuel and I must leave tonight. We'll ride ahead to our embassy in Paris to see what can be done. Knowing Miles, he probably hasn't asked for assistance from the Embassy. I promise you we'll get him released." He leaned over kissed my cheek and then Mama. "Perhaps you should stay here with your mother tonight. I'll let Meg know where you are." He left, and we climbed into the bed and Mother gathered me into her arms. We didn't speak, we just lay there immersed in our own thoughts.

I awoke in the morning with the sun shining through a chink in the curtains, I was snug in the warmth of my parent's bed and thankful the nightmare had not returned. I rolled over and gazed at a streak of sunlight creeping across the aged patina of the floorboards until the door was flung open and Lettie came in holding a gurgling James. She was followed by Meg and Beth, Lettie shifted James' weight and looked down at me. "Up you get, miss, we're all packed and ready to go, we're just waiting on you. Meg will get you ready then help Beth pack Mrs Turner's things while you eat your breakfast."

She sat beside me bouncing James on her knee as he laughed and drooled on a conveniently placed towel with which Lettie automatically wiped his chin. She shook her head as I gazed at them, "You'd never know that his lordship here is cutting a big boy's tooth but as long as he's got something hard to chomp down on, he's content to just drool." She touched his nose with the tip of her finger and he bubbled over with laughter. "He is the most exceptional babe I've ever seen. He's been walking and talking since before he was a year old…you're an amazing little man, aren't you, my Jamie lad." I laughed as she pulled out a rawhide bite block that Dr Jefferson had given her after removing a splinter from James' throat caused by vigorously chewing on a wooden spoon. James leaned over and gave me wet kiss and then wriggled to get down, then he ran for the door with Lettie after him. "We'll see you down at the carriages, miss, you'd better get a move on. Your mother and aunts were almost finished their breakfast." She grabbed James about the middle and swept him up into her arms and walked out of the room as James squealed with delight. Meg had me dressed just as Beth had finished packing, they were ready to leave so I gulped down a cup of chocolate and raced out to the waiting carriage.

As we waved goodbye to our hosts my stomach rumbled. Mother reached behind her and handed me a small basket. "Here, Lissa, I'm sure you didn't get enough to eat." I opened the basket to the wonderful aroma of fresh baked croissants and honey. I ate my fill to the point of bursting and sat back in my seat replete and ready to doze off.

We travelled at a brisk pace through a beautiful picturesque countryside dotted with quaint villages. But there was an underlying shabbiness and decay more noticeable in some places than others. I assumed it was the result of the current downturn in the economy and the tell tail signs of a once war ravage country that in many ways had still not recovered. The men in our party rode beside the carriages, openly displaying that they were armed and comfortable with their weapons. Mother, Emilie and Aunt Mary were also armed with little poppers such as the one Uncle Samuel had given me when we battled the smugglers. But my uncle had refused to return it to me after that night in Dorset and my weapons lessons had suddenly been curtailed because my parents felt that I might have been traumatized after killing Mr Browne. The fact is Mr Johnson and I had both shot him simultaneously but neither Dr Grimes nor Dr Jefferson had been able to determine who had fired the fatal shot.

I dozed and played with James off and on, but I was not allowed to ride outside because of the potential danger lurking in the surrounding countryside. Eventually we arrived in Paris and reported to the authorities. Once our papers were returned to us we made our way to the British Embassy as house guests of Ambassador Lord Granville and his wife. My father and Uncle Samuel were not present when we arrived, and no one had any idea when they might return. Lord and Lady Granville welcomed us warmly then after many fulsome apologies they left for a previous engagement. Though the adventurer in me wanted to explore the embassy and the city I was delighted when we were shown to our rooms. A light supper had been laid out in a second-floor drawing room and afterwards we sat there waiting for my father and uncle to appear. But it was not to be, I drifted off to sleep more than once and was finally sent off to bed along with everyone else but Mr Spencer who decided to wait up a bit longer.

Three days later my father and uncle had still not returned. Mother and Emilie were beside themselves, so Aunt Mary, Mr Spencer and Dr Jefferson met with Lord Granville to see what could be done. I was left to amuse myself by exploring the public rooms and the Embassy garden. The Embassy had been known as the Hotel de Charost before the war and was close to the Elysee Palace. Mr Spencer told us that in 1814 the Hotel had been sold to the Duke of Wellington for the use by the British government. With a grim chuckle, he informed us that some of the money from the sale may have made it into the hands of Napoleon while he was in exile on

Elba. The rooms were beautiful, and all the original furniture had come with the purchase, it was decidedly French in its elegance and decoration. Lettie and Meg accompanied me on our tour until James became fretful and Lettie returned to our rooms.

Meg and I found our way into the garden and sat down by a fountain. To distract my thoughts, I decided to spend some time trying to help Meg improve her French. Robert had planned to take her for a stroll in the gardens of the Tuileries and while he was very proficient in his French being a polyglot…meaning that he learned languages quickly…Meg didn't want to rely solely on his ability alone. However, neither of us had our heart in it, every noise that emanated from the Embassy had us stopping to stare back towards the garden doors. Finally, it was time for luncheon and as we entered the hallway leading to the dining room my father and uncle came down the main staircase. I ran to meet them and threw my arms around my father's neck, kissing him and then my uncle. "Where have you been?!" I asked anxiously. I stepped back and gave them both a long hard look. They were obviously exhausted and haggard. "Father, what's wrong? Is Mr Johnson—did you find him?"

He smiled at me and nodded. "Yes, we found him, Lissa. But he's extremely ill. He was treated abominably in prison and we've had him removed to a private estate that we've rented. We'll be joining him there as soon as we can pack. I warn you it will be sometime before he can return home, but we'll not leave him alone. So, my dear, your French is about to be put to the test." He smiled at my bemused expression. "None of the servants as far as we know speak a word of English."

I gasped. "Oh my, can they be trusted then? I mean the French were our enemies once and not that long ago."

Uncle Samuel chuckled. "Come along, brat, let us eat first then we can discuss what has happened and where we go from here." My father drew back frowning at my uncle.

Then he turned back to me to say with a troubled expression, "I suppose you might as well know what's happened, you'll find out soon enough one way or another."

Luncheon was a not exactly a jovial meal, but Lord Granville was heartened by the news that Mr Johnson had been found and freed. He was equally relieved to learn of our intent to depart the Embassy, thereby relinquishing the guest quarters.

We hastily packed our belongings leaving the Embassy to take up residence in a glorious country chateau. It was situated within a walled property of considerable acreage on the outskirts of Paris. The sweeping drive brought us past flawless lawns and a beautiful ornamental lake which reflected a mirror image of the château, a magnificent two storey building constructed from pink limestone with twin fairy-tale towers and huge sash windows. When we stopped under the portico, Emilie was the first to alight and practically run through the open door. Coming in behind her, she stood transfixed in the middle of the entryway speechless. Inside there were magnificent crystal chandeliers and beautiful parquet floors adorned with Turkish carpets. When she turned towards us there were tears streaming down her face. She ran to my uncle, hugging him and while still crying, she turned to us. "Welcome to my family's home. Samuel, how did you do this?"

My uncle blushed. "Mr Johnson filed the paperwork to start the process for your claim of compensation or restoration…he even managed to procure a lease for the property until your case can be reviewed. The additional information about your parents that he was able to gather should be helpful in moving your claim forward with the government."

Just then a very nervous looking elderly man came forward introducing himself as the concierge Monsieur Bollard. I assumed that he was the equivalent of our Butler in London. Then suddenly to my great surprise there was Mr Allan coming down the stairs smiling and welcoming us all to the chateau. Mother squealed with delight. "How on earth did you get here, Allan?"

"Mr Johnson's letter, ma'am." She looked perplexed as were we all. "He sent me a letter and said that if you all picked up and left for Paris at any time I was to come here and make this house ready." Then he stopped smiling. "Mr Johnson is in the room at the head of the stairs on your right, Dr Jefferson. He is in desperate need of your care."

Dr Jefferson detached himself from our group and Murphy passed him his medical bag then he raced up the steps two at a time yelling, "If Johnson keeps up this reckless behaviour and ever pays me for my services, I will retire a wealthy man."

Mr Allan watched the doctor retreat with a half-smile, saying under his breath, "Mr Johnson expressed the exact same sentiment." He caught me looking at him then cleared his throat. "Excuse me, now, if you will follow me," he gestured towards the staircase leaving a disgruntled Monsieur Bollard standing in the hallway.

Our rooms were huge and luxurious. The people who had cared for the property after Emilie's parents had been imprisoned did so with a loving hand. As far as Emilie could tell nothing appeared to have been damaged. Mr Allan informed us as to why this was the case when so many properties of the aristocracy had been looted and decimated. "Madame Hughes's family had been well-liked in the neighbourhood despite the revolution. So, when they were taken away the locals took it upon themselves to hide everything of value that they could from Napoleon's governors and tax collectors. It was claimed by one of Napoleon's confidantes during the worst times and therefore was protected until his demise. The intent now is for the current government to make a profit from the homes of the former aristocracy."

Emilie gasped. "Anais?" and looked hopefully at Mr Allan and he gave a sympathetic sigh but shook his head. "As to those servants from that time, none of them remain. You will find the current staff polite but subdued. Only the laundress is actually friendly and conversant in English."

He was correct that even when you came upon the staff unawares they were never smiling or humming, it was rather sad and unsettling. Meg and Beth had little to do with them, because of their status as lady's maids they had been assigned the vacant housekeepers retreat for their dining room and lounge, while Dalton and Robert dined with Mr Allan in the Butler's pantry. Mr Allan had insisted that he would not usurp Monsieur Bollard at the head of the servants table as much as he may like to. Mr Allan only worked with Monsieur Bollard to assure that our needs were being met since he found the man to be distasteful and untrustworthy. Lettie stayed in the nursery and when she could leave she ate with Beth and Meg. That left Murphy, Jacob and Michael eating in the staff dining hall. The food was good but according to Murphy the company was terrible. Monsieur Bollard apparently was not well-liked, and he kept the staff in a constant state of fear and subjugation. Beth and Meg began to feel the strain of meeting the needs of the ladies in our party especially with the invitations that kept coming in. I was eighteen now and was included in the all entertainments even though I had not had my first season in London. At breakfast, it was decided that our priority should be to find lady's maids for Aunt Mary and Emilie that would be willing to return to England with us. Lettie was asked if she would like the position but declined saying she preferred being the nanny and was not inclined to give it up. It was our nearest neighbour who by providence solved our problem.

Madame Baxter was the widow of a retired British Major who had once been a part of the army of occupation. They had stayed in France after he sold his commission because they fell in love with the country and the people. His intent had been to retire here with his family and enjoy the small estate he had purchased, restoring it to its previous grandeur. Once he had achieved all that he promptly caught a fever and died, leaving his wife and ten-year-old son the owners of a very successful dairy farm. It was now run by her widowed father who had come over from England to help when her husband had passed away.

I tried to get out of visiting Madam Baxter, but my mother insisted, I wanted to be close to Mr Johnson in case he asked for me but so far, the men were the only ones allowed to see him and all they told us was that he was improving. But it had been two months. Even when I sat outside his sick room waiting for Dr Jefferson to come out, he would only tell me that he was getting better slowly. Mr Johnson's father had written asking for Miles to be sent home, but my father assured him that he was being well cared for and couldn't leave the country yet with the murder charges still pending.

Madame Baxter thankfully recommended two village girls as lady's maids. They were the daughters of the former school master who had passed away a few years ago, the eldest had been a lady's maid in Paris but her mistress had recently died so she had returned to the village to live in gentile poverty with her younger sister. We were told that they both spoke some English, so it was arranged that she would bring them to the chateau to be interviewed.

Mrs Baxter's son Patrick turned out to be an entertaining child. He offered to take me on what turned out to be an exuberant tour of their farm, bouncing between French to English with ease. It was the first time since leaving Northumberland that I wasn't chaperoned, and the freedom was rather exhilarating. Patrick and I made our way into the orchard which adjoined our properties. He showed me his special tree where he had constructed a crude platform up in the branches. Even with my skirts I managed to climb up beside him to survey his domain. The platform gave us a clear view of the second-floor windows of the chateau. And as I scanned them I saw a man framed in the window of what I was sure was Mr Johnson's room. The man's hair was dark and long as he was wont to wear his, but something was wrong, it was not until he turned to leave the window that I saw the contrast of the bandage against the darkness of his hair, it covered his eyes. What was wrong with his eyes? I immediately felt ill and said as much to my companion. Patrick quickly scrambled down out of the tree guiding me back to the house where I pled a sick stomach, so I could return to the chateau. Patrick suggested to the company that the cause of my sudden illness may have been from eating a green apple…which I hadn't. He was a sharp lad and when I caught his eye I mouthed a 'thank you' for bolstering my excuse for leaving.

Madame Baxter was all concern and suggested a local tonic that even our doctor would approve of. Then she promised to send the young ladies to us soon. We said our goodbyes after extending a dinner invitation to her, Patrick and her father which was happily accepted since English company was a rare treat for them.

The journey home felt like it took forever. When we reached the entry hall I escaped to my room. Once there I dismissed Meg in a fit of temper after refusing any administrations from her, my parents, aunts, uncles and finally Dr Jefferson. I thought they'd never leave me alone. I knew that I had to see Miles, the picture in my mind of him at the window screamed at me to go to him or I may never have another chance. I don't know when I had stopped thinking of him as Mr Johnson but lately he was only Miles in my thoughts. I had taken to keeping his locket with me always wearing it when I could, keeping it in my pocket when I couldn't and under my pillow at night. When I listened with my heart as the inscription suggested it was his voice that I heard first and foremost. He was the one who always understood my pain when no one else could see it. In fact, I believe, he understood me better than anyone and I had come to have some very strong undefined feelings for him. I waited until I knew that everyone would be getting ready for dinner then made my way to Miles' room. I didn't knock before entering the room, I just opened the door. It was dark inside, the only light was coming from the fire in the hearth. He was not in bed but was sitting by the fire fully dressed, his face in profile. "If that's you, Dalton, go away. I told you that I wasn't hungry."

I felt a tear slide down my cheek and before I could stop myself and retreat, "I'm not hungry either."

He sat up straighter. It was then that I noticed the firelight bounce off the glass that he had held down by his side, it was half full of some deep gold liquid. He didn't turn towards me but hastily fumbled with the glass to set it on the table, spilling most of its contents in the process. "Miss Turner, you should not be here."

I stepped further into the room and closed the door. "Why?"

He was flustered, "It's…unseemly for a young lady to visit a gentleman's bedchamber."

I took another step forward, my hands nervously clasped in front of me. "I thought we were friends, Miles?"

He sighed then rose from his seat, but he didn't turn towards me. "Regardless you should not be here." He spoke sharply then his shoulders slumped, and his head fell forward. "But now that you're here I would dearly love to have your company." He waved his hand in front of him and ventured to take a step, bumping the table on which his glass stood.

I quickly went to his side, taking his hand and he gripped mine tightly as if not wanting to let it go. "Sit, Miles, please. I will take the seat straight across from you." We both sat down leaning forward, neither one of us anxious to let go of the other's hand. "How—I mean, do you want to tell me about what happened?"

"NO!" I flinched at the pain in his voice as he quickly dropped my hand. "Perhaps you should leave, after all. I'm not fit company for anyone."

I sighed looking for any signs of trauma other than the bandage over his eyes but there was nothing obvious. I felt another tear slide down my cheek. "No, thank you. I think I shall stay." I reached out and rested my hand on top of his, but he made no attempt to take it and I swallowed my disappointment. "I never got to thank you in person for the lovely Christmas present you sent me. It's so beautiful and far too expensive. Mother thinks it's too fine for me to wear all the time, but I want you to know that I keep it with me all the time regardless of what she thinks."

He smiled at that then he stiffened. "Are you sure she didn't tell you that it was an inappropriate gift?"

I smiled taking his hand in mine and writing in his palm the inscription as I whispered, 'Listen with your Heart'. He gave me a half smile. "I do, Miles, and my heart tells me that you are more than just my friend. I want to discover what that means." My words seemed inadequate, how could I say this without scaring him. "I mean that I want us to be more than just friends."

He sighed deeply, his hand lay still in mine, but the fingers of his other hand were clenched into a fist. "I doubt your parents would approve."

I was hurt that he would think that… so I challenged him. "Why? I don't see why they should object."

His head was bowed, and his shoulders rounded as he sat forward…as if he had given up. "Can't you? Do you think the matter of my birth would be of no significance to them? What about your uncle and Mrs Spencer, what would they say?"

I slid off my chair and knelt before him. I wanted to reach out and touch his face to make him raise his head to me but instead I continued to hold his hand. "Miles, my parents and family only want my happiness."

He removed his hand from mine to touch my cheek then pulled back like he'd been scorched. "But we can't, you would be shunned and lose your place in society, a place that is yours by birth."

I reached out placing his hand back on my cheek and held it there. "Miles, I have known no society that I care to be in but that of yours and my family. I would rather live my life with you in Dorset with the Dawsons and the gypsies than in the finest home in London." He sighed, shaking his head. I waited for him to respond but he didn't, so I left off my attack for the moment. "Now, are you going to tell me what happened?"

I laid my head on his knee and he placed his hand on my hair, gently stroking it as he told me about his incarceration and torture. The chief instigator had been Browne's younger brother Julian, apparently at the urging of his father. It was he who had laid the complaint with the Paris police using Randall's association with the French diplomatic mission as justification to seize Miles as a political prisoner. He had already bribed the police to confiscate Miles' travel papers and throw him into prison under another name where he was starved and beaten. Finally, when he couldn't take any more and in a fit of rage, Miles had killed one of the guards by snapping his neck. The other guard had thrown his lamp at him, splashing hot oil in his eyes. Then he was beaten again and left for dead without any care for his wounds. It took three days for my father and uncle to unravel the mess created by Lord Burley. And now with Miles having been charged with the killing of the guard it was a diplomatic nightmare since Miles was the son of an English peer. Dr Jefferson had done all that he could for his eyes, but he had no idea if Miles would regain his sight, all he could tell him was that time would tell.

As I sat on the floor with my head on his knee and his hand on my head I noticed the liquid that had spilled from the glass now sitting on the table. Being this close I caught the cloying smell of Laudanum. I recognized the smell from the Abbey still room, it was a preparation that my mother made sure was always available for the General after he had returned from India. "Miles, are you in pain?" He stopped stroking my hair but didn't answer. "Miles, I know laudanum when I smell it."

He sighed then shifted so that I sat up looking up at him. He had removed his bandages and opened his eyes looking straight ahead. "Can you live with this? Because I don't think I can."

I reached out and touched the scars that had formed around the edges of his eyes they were reddened but not disfiguring, his eyes were blood shot but otherwise looked normal. "Miles, your eyes look fine. Your skin and eyelids are inflamed but they'll heal. There are no deep burns and it's likely that there will be minimally scaring that will fade with time."

Leaning his head back against the chair, he said, "Don't lie to me, Lissa, please! I'm blind and I know what blindness from burning oil looks like! I've seen it!"

I reached out touching his face, but he grabbed my hand at the wrist pulling it away from his face. "I'm not lying, Miles. Your eyes are still a beautiful dove grey, they're not scarred." He moved his hands towards his face and dropped them just as someone entered the room behind us.

# Chapter 23
## *It's All in the Eyes*

Dr Jefferson and my father stood in the doorway to Miles' room and my father was obviously shocked, "Lissa, what are you doing here!"

Miles reached out for me and I took his hand as we both stood up. "Hello, Father. I'm visiting a sick friend." I arched my brow challenging him to questioning me further. He met my glare but said nothing more. I turned to Dr Jefferson. "Doctor, would you care to tell me why you haven't told Mr Johnson that his eyes are not scarred?"

Father stepped into the room nodding at Dr Jefferson, they both walked in and closed the door. The doctor sniffed the air and immediately came to the table beside us, he bent over sniffing the glass then tasted the liquid with the tip of his finger. He looked at Miles then at me and frowned. "It would seem, Miss Turner, that your visit came at a most opportune time. You prevented Mr Johnson from taking his own life, so it would seem." He looked at Miles with pity and a hint of veiled anger. I wasn't surprised, I already knew what had been in the glass. Miles' shoulders slumped, and he released my hand then lowered himself back into his chair.

I grimaced slightly as I saw the despair etched on his face, but I chose to ignore the seriousness of what the doctor had said. "What's important, doctor, is that he didn't, and we've come to an understanding that he won't be trying anything like that again."

Dr Jefferson smirked pointing a finger at my father. "I told you that he would respond to her and that she could handle him! She's not a child, Colin…as much as you'd like her to be." Then he turned back to me. "We've told him repeatedly, Miss Turner, that he's not badly scared. There is even a very good chance that he will regain his sight, but it will take time, but he doesn't believe us."

I pulled a chair next to Miles and sat down taking his hand in mind. "Is that true?"

Miles squeezed my hand and whispered, "Yes."

I tried not to sound upset, but I knew he could hear the concern in my voice. "Why, Miles?"

He stammered then whispered something that no one could hear and fell silent. My father came over and joined us. He brushed my shoulder with his hand then pulled up another chair along with Dr Jefferson.

I held on tightly to Miles' hand, my father noticed and sighed. "This is my fault, I wanted to separate you from Miles. I thought you were too young to form an attachment. I was in fact afraid, I was concerned that I was losing my little girl to another man."

Miles stiffened. "I agreed, Turner, to the assignment and your reasons for sending me."

I glared at my father. "Will both of you stop it! I'm not a child."

My father grimaced. "I can see that now."

My father bit his thumb and then sat up, "Lissa, if you're going to help Miles, I think you need to know what his assignment was. First, he was to collect additional information regarding the Samuel and Emilie's property claim and submit it to the courts. But he was also sent to track down Browne's business associates. He accomplished the first without any issues and the courts are already deliberating over the claim, but it could still take months.

"The second took him on a wild goose chase back and forth across the channel twice. He hoped to find out the names of the possible leaders of the smuggling operation at least here in France if not in England, but he doesn't remember what or if he discovered anything after being tortured and brutalized in prison. I believe he may have been getting close and that's why he was arrested and tortured. We just need Miles to remember!"

Miles let go of my hand, leaning forward with his head held in his hands and began to whisper, "I don't remember I don't understand why I don't remember."

I glared at my father for upsetting Miles and sent a pleading looked to Dr Jefferson "Colin, don't you think this can wait. The more immediate concern is the health of our friend." Father closed his mouth and nodded, and the doctor turned back to me. "Miles, do I have your permission to tell Miss Turner what we have discussed before." Miles nodded, and the doctor continued, "It is my considered opinion that Miles' continued blindness is a result of psychological as well as physical trauma that has affected his memory. Something horrific happened to him in that prison and to block it out he's blocked out everything including the information we want." Father opened his mouth as if to interrupt him, but the doctor put up his hand to stop him and shook his head. "I need to ask, Miss Turner, are you willing to help us with Mr Johnson…are you strong enough to help him?" He looked at Miles with sympathy but not pity and then back at me and I nodded. I reached out to touch Miles, but he jerked back and whimpered, crossing his arms tight against his body. The doctor looked disheartened. "He has moments even days like this where at times he's in a suicidal melancholia, he's not aware of where he is or who's with him." He hesitated to gather his thoughts. "It almost seems like he lives in a nightmare world where he's back in the hell where your father found him. You are the first person to bring him back to the point where he's been almost normal. We've often had to sedate and restrain him to keep him from hurting himself. That's why you haven't been allowed to see Miles, your father thought it would be too frightening." I stared at him with my lips pursed and my eyes wide. I was incredulous that they could think such a thing. He swallowed then continued, "But we need to change our approach, it's been weeks and our friend here needs to learn how to live again."

My father sighed, running a hand through his hair. "I agree but," he touched my hand to gain my attention, "Lissa, this could be a monumental task, you don't have to do this; you owe him nothing."

I was shocked that he was talking like that in front of Miles. "How can you say that! He has risked his life for me, for you! And you would leave him like this? Deny him help because you didn't want to frighten me! You may be able to do that, Father,

193

but I cannot, and I will not. He's family!" I turned my back on my father's surprised look. "Dr Jefferson, I will be happy to assist any way that I can. Miles will be whole again, I promise you that. I will not give up on him."

Tears were streaming down my face when my father pulled me into a hug and kissed my forehead. "You are your mother's daughter." I felt something warm on my arm, it was a tear and then another splash onto my wrist, looking up into my father's face I saw that he was crying too then he let me go, kissed me on the cheek and he and Dr Jefferson left the room.

I sat down on the floor again with my head resting on Miles' knee and waited. It seemed like forever before he reached out to touch my hair again, so we sat lost in our own thoughts until I heard my stomach gurgle and then his. I giggled, got up from the floor and pulled the bell. Dalton answered immediately as if he had stationed himself outside the door which I suspected he had. "Dalton, will you see that supper is laid out in the breakfast room for Mr Johnson and me. We won't require anyone to serve us." He smiled, nodded then left us.

Miles had turned towards the door listening to what I had to say. "I'm not sure that's such a good idea, Clarissa."

"It will be fine, Miles. Don't worry, I'll help you. You've been cooped up in this room far too long."

He gave me a weak smile. "But."

I smiled at the look of childish innocence on his face. "No buts…you can do this. I will be at your side the whole way until you no longer need me."

He set his shoulders straight giving me a shy half smile. "Alright, poppet, let's give it a try."

I went to him and took his hand as he stood up. I tucked my arm around his and we started to walk towards the door. He was obviously familiar with the dimensions of his room and the placement of the furniture since he walked without incident to the door. But when I opened it, he took a step back and shuddered. I hadn't considered that he might equate his room with his prison cell. He had been locked away for lord knows how long and this was just another kind of cell in an unfamiliar house, of course, it would be just as frightening for him to leave it. But I knew the real prison was the one that he carried in his mind. What had pushed him to the brink of wanting to end his life? It had to be more than being blind, there was something else. I let him relax then I took hold of his arm more firmly we counted out how many paces it took to get out the door and into the middle of the hall then to turn left to reach the top of the stairs. The stairs were slower going, he took the rail in one hand and my arm in the other and we moved down them one step at a time then slowly across the hall as I described what surrounded us. The family stood by the drawing room watching but not saying a word. Mother clutched a handkerchief to her chest with her eyes glistening. The others stood in mute awe. When we reached the breakfast room, Miles let go of my arm, pivoted and bowed in the direction of my family. I grinned at his cheekiness then walked with him into the breakfast room still holding his arm. I quietly closed the door behind us and guided him to a seat. As he sat down he chuckled. "Well, that was delightful. Now I know how the royal family feels when on procession." He leaned forward and buried his face in hands and shook his head.

"Miles, are you alright?"

He didn't look up but just sat there with his head downcast. "Yes, I'm fine. I just can't believe that you're willing to waste your time on me. I'm a wreck, poppet, half the time I think I'm still in prison. The rest of the time I don't know where I am or what I'm supposed to do."

I smiled then remembered that he couldn't see me, so I placed his hand on my lips and smiled. Then I sat down in my chair to his left. "One day at a time, Miles. We'll take it one day at a time. Now what would you like to eat?" I named off the dishes before me and we both made our selections. I served him then placed his plate in front of him and told him where the different foods were on his plate. He felt about the table for his utensils until I suggested that he use a spoon at first to which he merely grunted, giving me a disparaging look. Not surprisingly he refused, he eventually tried to cut his meat until he almost cut off a fingertip in the process at which point he threw down his knife and fork. "May I just have a sandwich it would be so much easier."

I giggled though he looked far from amused. "No, you may not have a sandwich. For heaven's sake, Miles, how have you managed up until now?" He raised his hands and wiggled his fingers.

In my sweetest voice but one that would brook no argument I said, "Well then practice will make perfect." I picked up his discarded utensils placing them in his hand. He sighed deeply and returned his attention to his plate.

After that it was one step at a time and occasionally two steps back. He suffered from frequent nightmares and I was the only one who seemed to be able to settle him without sedation. We both had many disturbed or sleepless nights, on those nights, we would sit side by side in front of the fire while I read to him.

He learned the layout of the house and after several weeks we began taking meals with the family. He was quiet and withdrawn at first, barely responding to even my overtures at times. It was my Aunt Mary who broke into this withdrawn retreat of his. "So, Miles, I have been in correspondence with your father he is most anxious to have you home but understands that under the circumstances you need to stay in France."

Miles turned his head in the direction of Aunt Mary's voice. "Thank you, ma'am. I would not want him here to witness my humiliation in court regarding the murder of the prison guard."

She looked at him long and hard. "That was not what I was referring to, my dear boy."

He looked puzzled as did everyone at the table. "Then you have me at a disadvantage, ma'am, to what do you refer."

She smiled sweetly. "Why that your courting of my great niece, of course! He's very happy for you and has assured me that he will do all he can to see you established. It's rather generous of him considering that I doubt that Clarissa would give a fig if you were a pauper or a king."

Both of us blushed to the roots of our hair. "Aunt Mary! Miles and I have agreed not to explore any deeper feelings than friendship for the time being."

"Oh, Posh Clarissa. You are both besotted with each other! You remind me of your mother and father."

Mother sat up her eyes were huge. "Aunt Mary, really!" She looked at Miles and I then she started to laugh and suddenly everyone started to laugh including Miles.

Miles reached out to find my hand then raised it to his lips. "We have been found out, my darling." And he beamed. It was the first genuine smile I had seen on his face since the night I had found him trying to kill himself. Then he became serious and addressed the entire company. "While my feelings for Clarissa have now been laid bare for everyone, she is correct that we have agreed to not commit ourselves to anything deeper than friendship now. I am still under the charge of murder as well as being a social pariah due to the circumstances of my birth. If that were not enough I am blind and—so I have no immediate means of supporting a wife, let alone myself."

I could see my father was ready to make some grand gesture that would only be a blow to Miles' self-esteem, but I was able to catch his eye and shook my head. He closed his mouth as he took my mother's hand in his. Miles sat up looking in the direction of my father. "Thank you, Colin, for not speaking your mind right now. I know you would be generous to a fault where it concerns Lissa but now is not the time to discuss our future beyond today." If there was ever a way to stop the family from trying to take charge of our lives without being offensive, he had just found it.

Miles was expected in Paris at the end of the week for the hearing into the death of the prison guard, so we were spending as much time together as possible. I knew that he was still concerned that he would be convicted of the murder and spend the rest of his days shut away from the sun. Therefore, we spent much of our time together outside. We often met my young friend Patrick Baxter on our walks which always seemed to lead us to the orchard and away from the prying eyes of my family. Patrick was delighted with Miles who treated him no differently than he treated anyone else. They became fast friends after Miles advised him on the proper construction of a kite. He was even able to assist Patrick in its construction by checking the dimensions and quality of materials using his heightened senses.

Finally, the day came for him to leave for Paris, he had been adamant that I should stay here in the country, but it was my mother who insisted that we all go. Father and Miles met with Lord Granville as soon as we had settled in our hotel. It had been suggested by Dr Jefferson that Miles should wear a bandage over his eyes while in Paris as a sign of his infirmity. As such he would be given due consideration in the court and by the citizens of Paris when he was outside of the familiar confines of our suite. Miles bristled at this idea, but he eventually agreed.

When the day of the trial came, my father wouldn't allow the women to attend and it seemed like they were gone forever. In fact, it was well into the evening before they returned to the hotel laughing boisterously. Miles had been cleared of the charge of murder. The other guard had mysteriously come forward to confess that Miles had killed the guard in self-defence when the guard had tried to slit his throat. He also attested to the fact that Miles had not tried to escape as he had first reported. The door to Miles' cell had been left open when he ran for help, but the prisoner had not attempted to flee and was still in his cell when he returned. He denied though that he was the one that had beaten Mr Johnson or hit him with the lantern. The fact that Miles had already killed the guard before he had been hit was overlooked in the relief that the French courts would not have to put the son of an English nobleman on trial.

Miles seemed less than content that he was no longer faced with a murder charge so when I caught him in the small writing room in a pensive mood I asked him what bothered him. "It's a small thing, poppet, but I cannot forget it, in court they insisted in referring to me as milord. The French do not look with disfavour on the bastard

196

sons of their nobility and often the same rights and courtesies of legitimate heirs are extended to those born on the wrong side of the blanket. To be honest it rattled me that our own country never lets you forget the sins of your father." That was the all he said before he kissed my hand and walked out of the room, stumbling against the door jamb. I had no answer for him, so I let him go believing the wisest course of action was not to intrude on his desire for solitude.

I was relieved as was everyone that he had been vindicated but wondered why the missing guard had suddenly reappeared to testify. I assumed that my father had found him and coerced him into testifying but at what cost. On one of our daily walks Miles remarked, "I wonder how your father found the guard and how much the bribe was to get him to turn on his murdered comrade? Not that the thought of bribing him to tell the truth matters. But now I am further indebted to your father."

I sighed. "Miles, can you not simply accept the fact that justice has been served? You were wrongly accused, and the prime witness came forward to do his duty. Does it matter that he was bribed? He spoke the truth and that's what counts."

Miles pulled me to a stop to face him even though he couldn't see me. His face was still careworn and tired, but his wounds had faded to the point that only the lack of spark in his eyes was evidence of the trauma he'd suffered. "My sweet, poppet, it's not the bribe that matters so much but now I owe your father once again. How am I to repay him when I'm not a whole man?" He sounded like he was resigned to a fate worse than death. I pulled him down to an arbour bench, his shoulders slumped forward and rubbed a hand across his face.

I had been hoping that without the stress of the murder charge hanging over him that his sight would come back but it hadn't. There had been some slight improvement over the weeks since I had taken charge of his recovery, he could see shadows in brightly lit rooms but not enough to distinguish individuals yet. He had also started to remember more of his time in prison and it came to light that there had been more than just the two guards in his cell. This third man had stayed in the shadows while Miles was questioned. However, he never spoke loud enough for Miles to hear him clearly. Yet it was only in his presence that Miles endured any torture.

We stayed in Paris long enough to attend the Granville's dinner party on Friday and for my mother and aunts to do some shopping. Miles and I only wanted to return to the chateau or to go home to England, but my father insisted that there was much that he and Samuel needed to take care of here in France before we could return home. But I was hardly in a party mood especially after Miles insisted that he wasn't going to attend. His decision was supported by my mother and Dr Jefferson much to my chagrin and despite my attempts to beg off, I was not given a reprieve. It was made clear that I was expected to attend, even Miles was against me in this.

Aunt Mary had insisted that I dress in my best finery and had her new lady's maid Adele dress my hair in the latest Parisian fashion. She also insisted that I wear her pearls to complement my pale sherry gown, but I refused. Instead I wore Mile's locket as my only decoration on a ribbon identical to the one woven through my hair just a shade darker than my dress. I went to Miles' room, knocked and entered. I found my father with him, they both looked worried but neither had looked up as I came in. "Excuse me, I only came to say goodnight before we left." Then I saw that Miles was dressed for an evening out. It was thrilling to see him in his evening kit again and I suddenly forgot about their stressed expressions. "Miles, are you coming after all?!"

Father inhaled deeply arching his brow at Miles as if he could see but Miles merely nodded. So, my father explained. "It seems that a couple of surprise visitors will be at the dinner tonight. It was therefore prudent that Miles attend."

I gasped. "Father, how could you insist that Miles attend this evening when he has no desire to! And who are these new arrivals that would require his presence?"

Father cleared his throat. "They're not exactly new arrivals if my information is correct."

I was disappointed having hoped for some excitement. "Oh... I was looking forward to some new conversation from home."

Miles stepped forward reaching for my hand. "Tired of me already, poppet?"

I sighed. "That's not what I meant, and you know it, Miles. But the Granville's entertainments tend to be boring after a while with the same people always in attendance."

Father laughed. "Lissa, the Granville dinner parties are the talk of Paris; you're too young to have become so jaded, my dear!"

Then he bit his lower lip, "The newcomers are Miles' brother Edward and his friend Julian Browne, Randal's younger brother."

I held on tightly to the back of the chair in front of me and asked, "Why are they here?" I was concerned for Miles, I knew that his brother held no love for him and Julian Browne had every reason to hate both of us.

Father stood up and straightened his waistcoat. "We have no idea, Lissa, but with Browne here it can't be good. Miles feels that his presence will rattle them enough that we may find out. Therefore, he will be seated beside you and across from those two gentlemen at dinner."

I looked at them both thinking about how difficult this might be, "But Miles?" I sighed taking in his look of resignation, "All right then but I don't think you should wear the bandage. The scars are barely noticeable, and your eyes are as clear as ever. Let them guess how much of your vision has returned."

Father took my hand, drawing me around to sit beside Miles as he explained, "There is more to this, Lissa, than just unsettling them by Miles' appearance. It was Julian Browne who brought the charge of murder against Miles on behalf of his father, he came here for the trial and Edward is reportedly lending his support to Julian. They were old school chums who seemed to have renewed their friendship considering what they see as a common enemy...Miles. I find it strange since from all reports there had been a significant falling out between them after school. I might add that Edward's coming here was unbeknownst to Miles' father so I'm not sure where Edward fits into all of this and until we do find out we cannot trust him."

Miles laughed. "My poor brother has been robbed of his entertainment. I'm sure he would have loved to have seen me swing but I can assure you he is here for himself as much as for Browne."

There was a knock at the door and two older gentlemen entered. One was a startling older version of Miles and must be his father. The only exception to his looks were the shape and colour of their eyes. His were bright blue while Miles' were grey. His dark curly hair was as thick as Miles but was laced with shots of pure white. Beside him was a gentleman that bore no resemblance to either man except for the eyes, they were the exact shape and colour as Miles.

Both men were smiling as the Earl came forward, taking my hand in his, he bowed over it. "It's an immense pleasure to finally meet you, Miss Turner, I am Miles' father."

I curtsied saying, "It's a pleasure to finally meet you, Lord Shellard."

I looked at Miles, but he didn't seem the least surprised at his father's presence. The Earl turned to the other gentleman and introduce him. "May I present to you the Marquis Du Quenoy." He then said in a much softer voice looking only at his son. "He's your uncle, Miles, your mother's brother."

Miles jerked his hand out of mine and went white as sheet. "What game are you playing, father! Mother told me that all her family were dead." Father showed the Marquis to a chair directly across from Miles. The Marquis was still smiling, and he couldn't take his eyes off his nephew.

The Earl however looked angry and sad at the same time, "You were very young, Miles, and misunderstood what your mother said. She told you that she was dead to her family. I assure you that Charles is your uncle," and the look on his face would brook no argument. "Mr Turner has apprised me thoroughly of everything that you have been through. As to why you did not see fit to contact me for help, we will discuss at another time." He paused clasping his hands in front of him. "I came here to aid you with the charges against you but instead I found that Mr Turner had already taken care of that. It was my good fortune to run across Charles when I arrived and together we have implemented a plan that I hope will right an old wrong."

Miles looked confused as did we all. "Father, there is nothing you can do, you can't roll back time."

The Earl sat down beside the Marquis. "Please son, this has nothing to do with your incarceration. I must confess a truth that I have kept from you for far too long. You have been the innocent victim of a cruel plan that was perpetrated by my father and my previous wife's father." Miles sat stoic and showed no sign of emotion.

As the story unfolded I was amazed and horrified that people could be so calculating and cruel. Miles' paternal grandfather had agreed to an arranged marriage of his son to his best friend's only child. It would unite two old and powerful houses with connecting properties leaving a good portion of the Devon and Somerset borderlands in their combined control. But Miles' father had begged to go on the grand tour after finishing Cambridge and before committing to marriage. It was the habit in his day that wealthy young Englishman would take a tour of the continent to sow their wild oats. However, he never made it further than Paris, having been caught up first in the electricity of the city and then in the urgency to get out after the French Directory had been overthrown by Bonaparte. People were afraid…they still remembered four years prior the mass executions ordered by Robespierre and coupled with the fact that the economy was in a shamble, the country was ripe for another revolution…Bonaparte on the rise and no one knew what to expect from the new order.

"I had met your mother during that time, we fell in love and married against our families' wishes. Your Uncle Charles was the one exception but then he is a romantic at heart, so he helped us to wed and was the only family member present at our nuptials." He looked at his friend who was still drinking in Miles. "When I was finally able to bring my bride home to England, we were already expecting your arrival. My father was furious when he heard of my marriage and even before we had reached London, he had spread a vicious lie that your mother was my French mistress and that I was still destined to marry Carolyn. He was a cruel greedy man who was not about to lose the power that would come to him through my marriage to Carolyn…and I was a young fool."

He sighed looking at Miles as if for absolution but since Miles couldn't see him he sat there expressionless as if carved from stone. His father looked down to his clasped hands and continued, "When you were born, your mother and I were so very happy." Thankfully, Mrs Spencer and your mother had become friends and I appealed to her to watch over the both of you while I returned to Paris to obtain the proof of our marriage. By then the war between our two countries had escalated and I was detained as a foreign national suspected of all sorts of crimes against the people of France and espionage. I would have appealed to Charles for help but by then his father the Marquis had been imprisoned and the rest of the family had disappeared. I was finally released and given three days to leave the country, barely enough time to make it to the coast."

The Earl impressed me with the control he showed while telling his story, but he was detached, living outside of himself as he relived the events that had declared Miles a bastard. "But I didn't leave, I searched for the priest who had married us, but he'd died in a riot that had destroyed his church and the church records were nowhere to be found. The new priest said that someone who helped to fight the fire that had destroyed the church had taken them, but he didn't know who he was. My time was running out and I was just able to escape back to England by bribing a fisherman to take me across the channel before the French authorities caught up with me. When I got home I wrote to everyone, friends, diplomats, anyone I could think of to help me locate Madeline's family. I had heard rumours while in Paris that they had gone to Italy, but they seemed to have disappeared and no one knew if they had even reached their destination."

He bit his lower lip and glanced at Miles. "When I returned home, my father threatened to cut me off if I didn't marry Carolyn. I didn't care about the money or title, I was already married, and I loved your mother and you more than anything. God, I would have lived in a hovel with your mother and grown turnips, I didn't care. Your mother did care for my sake and yours, she felt that a half-life with me was better than nothing, that we had to think about your welfare. She knew that I would always love you both even if I could not give you my name. you would at least have everything else that I could give you." He coughed to clear his throat. "Maria insisted that in France bastard sons were often raised in the home of their father right beside their legitimate children. Frankly I was appalled and refused to even contemplate it, but your mother was just as headstrong as she was beautiful and fragile; she had such strong pure soul. The fact that she had been estranged from her family weighed heavily on her, especially living in a foreign country with only one loyal friend. Your mother decided that she would not see me likewise estranged from my family, as if I cared." Tears welled up in his eyes. "But family was very important to her and she still loved hers very much. When we received news that her father had been executed, she became deeply depressed. The only person that could rally her was you, Miles." He stopped looking at his son and concentrated only on his clenched hands. "I remember she would sit with you in the house or the garden just watching you play and telling you stories only in French. But time was running out for us, between your mother and my father I was being pressured to marry Carolyn.

I continued to put them off…the last thing I wanted was to marry her. She was a few years older than I and I had hoped that her father would grow impatient for her to marry and produce grandchildren. But greed motivated both of the old bastards." He glanced up at me. "I beg your pardon, Miss Turner, what I meant was that they held fast to their contract with each other. Your mother tried everything she could to convince me to marry Carolyn, but I continued to refuse."

He sighed, and I could hear the pain in that one breath. "Finally, my father cut off my allowance. I had to borrow heavily on my name alone and the prospect of my future inheritance. But we were deeply in debt and my creditors were pressuring me at the bidding of my father. Finally, I had to go to London to see to my affairs, it was about the time of your fourth birthday. It was then that Maria went to see Carolyn without my knowledge. The weather was miserable the day she ventured out, it was very cold and rained constantly. On the journey back from seeing Carolyn your mother took chill and fell ill. When I found out what she had done, I was furious. She never told me exactly what was said between her and Carolyn except that Carolyn had agreed for you to be raised as one of the family and that she would recognise you as my natural son."

His voice shook with emotion, he paused trying to control himself. "Your mother never recovered from her illness and she died a few weeks later." He was so overcome I didn't think he would be able to continue but he did, "Carolyn and I were married six months later. Surprisingly she never went back on her word. I brought you home with me and she never said a word of reproach nor of love. However, when Edward was born, she did everything she could to poison his mind against you and me. She refused me her bed after his birth which was the kindest thing she had ever done for me." It was incredible how much these men had endured, and it had all been motivated by greed and revenge. "Believe me, Miles, I have grieved the loss of your mother every day since she passed away. And even though I care deeply for Jane, it has never been the same for me. Jane and I are more companions and friends than lovers. The children she has given me are a joy but not to the degree that you have been, Miles. Edward on the other hand is Carolyn's son, even though he is of my body he has never been mine."

Miles sat with his head in his hands I could tell by the tension in his shoulders that he was furious. "I am your legitimate son and heir and, yet, you never saw fit to tell me!"

The Earl was decidedly uncomfortable. "I'm sorry, Miles, I should have told you when you were older but I had no proof to legitimize you. I thought it would cause you unnecessary pain. That is, I had no proof till now."

Miles head snapped up. "Proof." He swung his head from side to side like he was trying to see the people seated across from him. "What proof?"

The Earl leaned forward as if to touch his son but sensing it Miles sat back out of reach and the Earl withdrew his hand. "From Charles, he was a witness at our wedding and is more than happy to provide affidavits as to the legality of my marriage to your mother."

Miles in a temper barely controlled his response as he turned on his uncle. "Why wait so long to contact my father, sir?"

I was ashamed of Miles for being so abrupt. "Miles!"

The Marquis bristled slightly then relaxed. "No, mademoiselle, I understand his anger." He looked at Miles with the same steely grey eyes but there was still a softness in them. "I had no reason to think that my sister was not happily married and living in England. I was angry that I'd no word from Maria since the day she had kissed me goodbye in the church and left with your father as a married woman. I wrote to her in England, I sent my letters to your father's ancestral home, but she never wrote back. I had no idea that she didn't live there. Your father assumes his father destroyed them."

The Marquis' demeanour relaxed somewhat. "Then my father was executed, and our family barely escaped with our lives. Suddenly I was the head of the house with bigger problems than corresponding with what I thought was an indifferent sister. Thankfully my father had seen the unrest developing in France and had transferred most of our fortune to Switzerland. We had very little of value with us when we left France and instead of heading to Italy as we had told people we went to Switzerland to stay out of the grasp of Bonaparte. Once there we had only our French papers to prove our identity and to access our money. We couldn't travel as French citizens, or we would have been arrested by Napoleon's troops so once I could gain access to our money we adopted Swiss identities. It was not an easy task to establish our family there. I had to find a way to maintain and if possible to increase our fortune. I had been raised to the life of a Marquis, to manage a vast estate." He chuckled and looked at his browned hands. "Fortunately, I'm a quick learner and there were opportunities in the vineyards that surrounded the village where we lived. Now I am now a successful vintner and wine merchant.

"Since the defeat of Napoleon, I have ventured back into France to find new markets. It was here in Paris that I heard amongst my colleagues that there was an English wine connoisseur who had just arrived in Paris on family business. I always thought England could be a lucrative market, so I decided to ask for an introduction with the idea to beat out my competition and perhaps establish my son in London. When I found out this connoisseur was William, I rejoiced hoping to be reunited with my sister. I was saddened and shocked to hear what had befallen her and you." He glared at the Earl as if it was all his fault then he relaxed, and his eyes were a soft dove grey once more. "I have promised to provide affidavits and to help him find additional evidence to support your legitimization. We intend to appeal to the French courts before moving onto the English courts."

The Earl jumped in. "This will take time, son, but I will see that you are made my heir before I leave this world, of that I have no doubt."

# Chapter 24
## *Deadly Dinner*

When we were ready to leave, I walked down the stairs with Miles while my father, the Earl and Marquis Came down behind us. I whispered to Miles as we descended, "You don't have to do this. You've had a lot happen today so if would you rather not go you can stay here, I'll even stay with you."

Miles chuckled before saying, "Technically, poppet, I am still an agent of the Crown, so I can't allow personal issues to distract me. Whatever happens in that regard to my father's machinations is out of my control, but I dearly hope that I have my sight back if the old man ever has to tell my beloved brother he's been deposed as heir and is now the spare." He sounded a tad bitter though he tried to make it sound light and laughable.

The rest of our party met us in the hallway, all of us looked splendid in our finery. It was a short carriage ride to the Embassy where we alighted at the prefect time, neither to early nor too late. I took Miles's arm and with light pressure signals that we had been working on he was able to negotiate his way to the reception room. At this point, Dr Jefferson joined us passing Miles a pair of dark spectacles. "Here you go, my friend, just as you ordered, just dark enough that others can't see your eyes. Lord Granville and his wife have been told that while your vision has returned, you are overly sensitive to light, it should take Lady Granville no time at all to let her guests know." He chuckled and looked at me with surprise. "My word, Miss Turner, you look enchanting tonight!" Then he glanced at Miles. "I'd keep her close, Johnson, if I were you and luckily there won't be any dancing tonight or Miss Turner's card would be full."

I glanced around the room, several people were looking at us and whispering. I smiled shyly at the doctor. "Why thank you, Dr Jefferson but I think there will be several young ladies speaking to Lady Granville about getting an introduction to you."

He laughed. "Touché! Then I had best join your father's group and talk politics." He bowed and tapped Miles on the shoulder. "Good luck."

Miles smiled, "Thank you, Matthew." The doctor patted him on the shoulder and walked off to join my father and some acquaintances.

The Earl and Marquis came to stand with us bringing Miles a glass of champagne and a lemonade for me, we stood about making small talk until the final guests arrived. Miles' brother Edward and his friend Julian Browne both entered the room laughing loudly which drew everyone's attention as I'm sure they intended it to. Once they were the centre of attention they apologized profusely to Lady Granville for arriving so late. She grimaced at how loud they were but assured them that it had been no imposition. Her Ladyship moved on while they stood there looking around them until they saw our group and made their way over to us. I tensed and tapped Miles hand in the silent language that Murphy had taught me. He squeezed my hand turning towards the two smiling men. Edward grimaced, and Julian hesitated with surprise but they both continued to our side. Edward glanced at me then looked at the Earl. "Hello, Father! I had no idea that you were coming to Paris. Did my brother contact you for help yet again?" Miles tensed.

The Earl's face was expressionless when he addressed his son, "No, Edward, he didn't. But I came anyway, he is after all my first born and I would not desert him to the caprices of the French judiciary. May I ask what you're doing in Paris? The last I had heard from you was that you and Julian were going shooting at your Uncle Angus estate in Scotland?" He raised a brow and waited for Edward to answer.

Edward went pale and Julian glared at Edward sharply then he turned to the Earl, answering after raising his chin and almost hissing, "Rain, sir, there was nothing but rain. That tends to make for a miserable shoot, the birds are not fond of rising when it is pouring down rain."

The Earl looked down his nose at Julian and with icy voice said, "Really, that is odd." He looked pointedly at Edward. "I had a letter from your Aunt Millicent just before I left. She invited me to join their hunting party, but she made no mention of you or Julian having joined them and said that the weather had been crisp and clear for weeks."

Julian was livid, and Edward was at a loss for words, then finally with an edge to his voice, "I believe, Father, that I am of an age that I don't need to explain my every move to you. Besides I doubt that you would want us to discuss in public the sport which kept us in town. Let's say that we were better entertained there than at a dismal shooting party in the wilds of Scotland." The gong rang for dinner and Edward held out his arm to me which I ignored as I continued to hold onto Miles. Lady Granville came to claim the Earl while her sister claimed the Marquis, leaving Edward and Julian to their own devices.

I bristled with indignation and whispered to Miles, "How rude, neither one of them spoke to you or acknowledged your presence."

Miles shrugged but he looked puzzled. "Nor did they ask for an introduction to you or my uncle. But it's typical behaviour from Edward where I'm concerned, and Julian seems to be cut from the same cloth. Please don't let it ruin your evening, poppet. Besides from what I've been hearing from the people around us it's true then, I am the luckiest man here with such a beauty on my arm."

I blushed, slapping his arm. "You shouldn't eavesdrop on other people's conversations!"

He grinned. "This advice is coming from a consummate eavesdropper? Now that is rich." he chuckled as we entered the dining room.

I ignored his repartee and concentrated on the signals he needed to help guide him to our place at the table. I read the menu quietly so that he could make his selections with relative ease and in his usual self-deprecating manner, he said, "By any chance are there any sandwiches on the menu?"

I moved to slap his leg, but he caught my hand before I made contact. I was shocked and whispered, "Miles! Did you see me move my hand?"

His brother and Julian were making their way to the table with their dinner partners and Miles seemed to be watching them, he answered, "Yes, well no. I sensed or rather heard the motion, but I saw the blur of your hand moving towards me."

I was piqued that he hadn't told me that he had regained more of his eyesight, but I was excited for him. "Why haven't you said anything? I feel like a fool guiding you around when you can see."

Then he leaned towards me and his lips grazed my ear, "You're no fool, my sweet, it's only been for the last few days and it comes and goes at the most inconvenient times. I find I can see blurred images when things are close and there's enough light. Each time it happens though it's been longer and clearer, but I really must concentrate. I have to admit that I'm terrified it won't last or that it won't get any better." He squeezed my hand under the table. "Besides I like holding your hand." I blushed and squeezed his hand back.

We were starting to draw the attention of our dinner companions when Edward sat down across from us and leaned forward. "Tell me, brother, who is this delightful tidbit that you have attached to your arm."

Miles frowned. "That's poor manners, Edward, even for you. But if you must know, this is Miss Clarissa Turner, the daughter of Colin Turner."

Edward was obviously annoyed but managed to nod. "Your servant, ma'am." He couldn't insult me openly with so many witnesses, but Julian chose to say nothing and merely glowered at us both.

Conversation with our table partners was sparse since they only spoke French and appeared more interested in their food and wine. Miles had one of his moments during the fish course when he lost his vision, fish was a not a dish that a blind person should eat without someone having picked out the bones first. He had obviously felt a bone in his mouth and rather than try and swallow it, he coughed it into his napkin then declined to eat anymore. It was a painfully quiet meal with Julian and Edward glaring at us and ignoring their own dinner companions.

After the meal there was a musical evening; Miles and I sat with my family, the Earl and Marquis. During the intervals, we discussed our plans for the next few days. We would not be leaving Paris anytime soon since we had all been recruited to find additional evidence of the Earl's marriage to Miles' mother. And as Emilie and Mother reminded their husbands they had not been shopping yet. Edward and Julian remained together throughout the evening avoiding our party, but I could feel their eyes on us. Edward must be perplexed as to who the Marquis was. He would walk around the periphery of our group between entertainments and appeared to be trying to eavesdrop. However, we spoke exclusively in French, not only for the sake of the Marquis since his English was not as good as his Italian or French but because Edward's French was atrocious. The Earl and my father discussed how the Marquis could go about establishing a foothold in the London market and Miles seemed comfortable enough with his uncle now to ask him about his mother. We heard stories of her beauty, her love of literature and then finally about her love for the Earl. Unfortunately, the Marquis had been the only one to support the Earl's suit and their marriage behind his parents' back. He said that he would have regretted his support if he had known what her life in England would be like. But he was very happy to meet her son. He was thankful too that she had at least been safe from the troubles in France. Miles' grandmother had not survived long after the death of her husband. The journey to Switzerland had been arduous, taking its toll on her especially in the high mountain regions. When the news of her husband's execution had reached them, it was more than she could bear.

Starting a new life, one of which he had been unprepared for was difficult since he had been raised to run an estate, not to start a business venture. But it had worked out and over time he found that he had a talent for trade. His sister Jeanne was now married to their nearest neighbour and his onetime competitor. After Jeanne's marriage, it was decided by her and his wife that working together between the two families was more profitable and made for happier family events so he and his brother-in-law were now partners. Jeanne and her husband Philippe have three children, two girls and a boy. He himself had three children, two boys and one girl. He attributed his youngest son Anton's wanderlust to the fact that his wife Eloise was pregnant when they had fled France and it was Anton who he wanted to establish a foothold in London.

As his tales continued my attention strayed towards Edward and Julian. I felt like we were being stalked, as if they were assessing our strengths and weaknesses like predators. I kept an eye on them while whispering my concerns to Miles. But he was so caught up in hearing about his French family that he merely nodded when I spoke to him. Edward and Julian finally lost interest and drifted out of sight much to my relief and so I excused myself to take a breath of air. My mother rose to come with me. "It's alright, Mother, I just want some air, the press of people in here is suffocating."

She smiled at me. "I would like some air myself."

But I could tell her mind was elsewhere. "You're missing James, aren't you?"

She laughed. "It shows that much? I do miss him but it's only one evening. Lettie is a wonderful nanny but as he gets older and more inquisitive I worry more." Then she giggled waving her fan energetically. "And I must admit that one of Lady Granville's entertainments a month is more than enough for me." We slowly made our way through the crowd to the garden doors that had been thrown open to relieve the heat in the room as the evening progressed. Mother was stopped by Madame Janvier who was desirous to talk to her about her infant daughter's colic. Mother was more than happy to stop and tell her what Dr Jefferson had recommended. She seemed determined to singlehandedly further the good doctor's reputation among our French acquaintances.

I soon grew tired of their conversation, having heard it before, so I made my way outside to stand near the terrace stairs with my hands on the railing. I looked off into the darkened gardens where fairy lights had been strung. You could just make out the moving forms of couples that were looking for some privacy. Suddenly my elbow was grabbed, and an arm was wrapped tightly around my waist, I was propelled forward and down the stairs. When I had collected myself enough to scream, the hand move from my elbow to my mouth and I only managed a strangled gurgle. I was forced across the uneven ground stumbling several times and eventually catching the toe of my shoe in the hem of my dress, feeling it tear as I fell to my knees. "Get up, bitch! I know what that bastard and your father are trying to do. I'm not going to let them undo what my brother established to replenish our family fortunes. I'll not let them ruin everything now!" He pulled me up and kept pushing me forward. Several people saw us but withdrew into the shadows. I hoped that one of them would recognise that this was not a lover's quarrel and come to my aid or go for help. He chuckled. "I told my brother that killing the old man would be a useless gesture. None of you cared enough about him to heed it as a warning. Your kidnapping was useless as well…he should have listened to me and just killed you and your mother, but he was too soft."

I caught my breath and tried to slow my pace by feigning a limp so that I could kick off one of my shoes. At one point when I stumbled, he slapped me so hard that I felt my lip split and blood run into my mouth. Then he suddenly stopped and tensed, considering the shadows surrounding us as if he had heard something. He leaned so close to me that I could feel his hot breath against my neck. "I'm only sorry that your mother didn't follow you out onto the terrace as she had planned then I could have slipped a knife between her ribs." He was slowly walking me forward when he paused again twisting from side to side, "Did you hear that?" He jerked me around in a circle peering into the darkness. "I'll find a way to get to her later but maybe your dead body will be enough to stop Turner."

Now he seemed to be talking to himself. I could only catch the occasional word but thankfully he had slowed his pace. I had no idea where we were going except it was away from the house and the stables. The gardens were large, but this was Paris, not the countryside, and we would eventually come to a roadway and then what would happen.

Then I heard it! At first, I thought it was a bird or squirrel; but it was tapping and there was a pattern to it that was repeated over and over. It was something very like my father's secret language, but my head was still spinning from the slap, making it hard to concentrate. Then it came to me it was one word repeated over and over, it was 'duck'. I looked around, but I didn't see any ducks then as the cloud lifted from my mind I realised that they meant for me to duck! I dropped to my knees which pulled Julian forward when a shot rang out from the trees nearby. Then Julian fell over me, pulling me down the rest of the way. He ended up half sprawled on me and very dead. I lay there staring up into his eyes watching the blood drip from a hole in the middle of his forehead. Then out of the woods at a dead run came Dr Jefferson, my father and Uncle Samuel. To the right of them, Miles came walking out at a much slower pace with a pistol in his hand.

Dr Jefferson reached me first. "Miss Turner, are you hurt?!" I shook my head. By then my father and uncle had reached my side. Father rolled Julian off me then picked me up in his arms and started to walk back the way they had come. The doctor followed, asking me questions, but I ignored him as I strained to see Miles. Uncle Samuel had gone to him and took the gun from his hand while clapping him on the back then I lost sight of them.

We entered the house through the conservatory. It was dark in there but lighter than it had been outside. Father placed me on a chase lounge as the doctor brought a lamp from a nearby table to examine me by its light. Finally, he pronounced me fit to walk. My father left then to speak with Lord Granville, Miles' father and his Uncle Charles. After he made our excuses to Lady Granville he went about gathering up the rest of our party while the doctor retrieved my cloak and escorted me out to the carriage. I waited inside as my father and the doctor explained to our party what had happened to the best of their knowledge. The doctor warned them that I was not to be pestered with questions, that I was most likely in shock. I hadn't notice till I heard him say shock that I was shaking and very cold, I tried desperately to quell the feeling. By the time everyone had climbed into their respective conveyances I had calmed down somewhat.

My mother sat with her arm around me, assessing my face and looking very concerned while my father was across from me. I leaned towards him and asked, "Where is Miles?"

Father looked at mother. "He had to stay behind, Lissa. He may have been the one that shot Julian."

"That's impossible!" I tried to recall what had happened and I was sure that Miles had come out of the woods after the shot was fired I was sure of it. "He couldn't have, his vision has been blurry at the best of time how could he possibly shoot a man in the dark with that kind of precision and at a distance?"

"I don't know, my darling. We all went in different directions searching for you. The last time I saw Miles he was in a heated conversation with Edward when he couldn't find you." He took a deep breath and his eyes glistened in the light from the carriage lamp. "It was the shot that alerted us to where you were." He sighed leaning forward to touch me as if to make sure I was real. "We thought Browne had killed you! I have no idea how Miles managed it but I'm so thankful that he did."

I sat back allowing my mother to fuss over me. Her attention was welcomed but I was worried for Miles, he would never survive another incarceration and the French were likely to arrest him because of the previous charge and I wouldn't be there to tell them that he had saved me. "Father, the police! Miles can't...he just can't, not again."

He shook his head. "Lord Granville will have to notify them eventually, but Julian was shot on the Embassy grounds, Lissa, and therefore on British sovereign soil. He's is a British subject; as is the victim so it shall be dealt with under British law."

"He's in trouble, isn't he?"

Father bit his lower lip. "Not if his father and I can help it. I promise you that nothing bad will happen to him, we'll see to it."

We arrived back at the hotel and gathered in our small drawing room where my ordeal was recounted then dissected. Uncle Samuel, Dr Jefferson, the Earl and Marquis had stayed behind with Miles. Mr Spencer asked me several questions repeatedly, I assumed he wanted me to be prepared for when or if the French police came to question me. I was tired, cold and my brain was mush. It was Aunt Mary who finally put a stop to it "That's enough, I think, our morbid curiosity has been more than satisfied." She looked down at Emilie. "Emilie, my dear, I think it's safe to say that Samuel will not be returning tonight and, Arthur, I'm sure the Ambassador will be calling on your services tomorrow, so you'll need all your wits about you to deal with the French. I'm sure we're all exhausted, I know that I most certainly am."

I suddenly wanted the comfort of my mother, yet she had gone to look in on James as soon as we had arrived home. Suddenly I was jealous of my little brother then as if by magic she came into the room. "That is enough, everyone. In case none of you can see it, Lissa is still in shock." She took my hand, kissed father on the cheek and pulled me towards the door. Father had a slightly bemused smile on his face. Emilie and Aunt Mary both sighed and smiled as they got up, following us out and leaving father and Mr Spencer alone.

Aunt Mary and Emilie had preceded us up the stairs after biding us goodnight. But my mother held me back until they had turned towards their rooms. "Are you truly alright, my dear?"

It was only then as she looked down at my gown and brushed the hair behind my ears that I noticed my state of dishabille. I gasped when I realised what she was referring to. "Oh, no, Mother, he merely slapped my face and dragged me through the garden. I resisted moving so I fell several times but otherwise he didn't hurt me. He was in a terrible hurry to get me away but to where or for what purpose he didn't say. I don't think he intended to kill me, at least not right away." I lied about that, but I could tell that she already realised that I would not have been held for ransom, rather my dead body was to serve as a message to my father.

We reached my room and found Meg half-asleep in the chair by the fire. Mother woke her up and sent her off to bed. She helped me to undress and we said nothing more until I climbed into bed. "Mother, I'm glad that you didn't come out on the terrace with me." She gave me a quizzical look and I swallowed hard, but she needed to know. "He would have killed you if you had, I'm so glad that you stopped to talk with Madame Janvier about babies."

She looked as sad as she caressed my cheek. "Whenever you seem to need me the most, my darling child, I'm never there."

I was horrified that she thought I was blaming her. "No, Mama, no, there was nothing you could have done. I'm just so happy that you're safe. That we both are."

She sighed and pulled me into a hug. "I'm just glad that Miles found me and asked if I knew where you'd gone. I should have known when he had that reprobate brother of his in tow that all was not well. When I told him that you'd gone out on the terrace, he shoved Edward into your uncle's arms saying, 'Tell them' then he turned and practically ran out to the terrace. I was surprised that his eyesight had improved so much."

I grimaced. "As of dinner it hadn't, he was still just seeing blurry images and only when there is sufficient light."

Mother looked perplexed. "But your father told me that it was Miles who shot Julian Browne. How could he possibly have shot him in the dark?"

"I don't know. But I feel like I'm forgetting something, it all happened so quickly." I tried to remember what had transpired in the garden even though I didn't want to, but I replayed each step in my mind. "I'm sure that he didn't shoot him, he couldn't have, when he stumbled out of the trees he was to father's far right with the pistol in his hand. He was looking around as if unsure of himself. I don't think he even saw me. He couldn't have fired!"

"Are you sure, darling?"

"Yes, I am." I moved to get out of bed. "I must speak to Father."

My mother rose. "Sit, I'll get him. You aren't running around after what you've been through."

She left immediately, and it seemed like forever before she returned with my him. Before he had even closed the door, I asked "Did Miles say that he shot Julian?"

Father looked puzzled. "He didn't say anything other than wanting to know if you were okay. But of course, he shot him, Lissa, you saw him with the gun in his hand."

I was getting frustrated. "How do you know it was Miles? If he didn't tell you, how do you know?"

Father scratched his brow. "I suppose we assumed he had a gun and Browne was dead."

"What did Miles look like? How was he behaving? You saw him after we got back to the Embassy, I didn't. Please, Father, this is important. Did you see the pistol? Had it been fired?"

Father raised his hand. "Just one question at a time, please, and let me think a minute." He paused apparently collecting his thoughts. "He was a dreadful mess, from the looks of him he must have fallen several times while looking for you, but it was dark. He didn't seem to hear anything we asked him. He just kept asking about you, Matthew said he was in shock and needed to rest. But no, I didn't see the pistol. Samuel gave it to Lord Granville and he locked it away." He settled back on my bed while my mother leaned against him. "Why all these questions, Lissa?"

I explained to him again about my journey through the garden in every detail just as before, but I had forgotten to mention the tapping so when I told him, he rang for Murphy.

When Murphy arrived, Father went out into the hallway with him, but he wasn't gone very long. "I've sent Murphy to the Embassy to tell Samuel what you've just told me. It's late and nothing can be done at this hour so try and get some sleep."

# Chapter 25
## *Shadows*

I was tossing and turning with my dreams and in them I saw shadows coming out of the dark some of them were Miles, some were Randall and Julian Browne. But mostly they were just shadows. But I had the pervasive impression that there was someone standing just behind Miles in those shadows. The person was indistinct, all that I could envision was a beard as black as night with vivid white teeth that shone as he smiled just before he disappeared in a puff of smoke. I finally got out of bed. It was sometime just before dawn, so I lit a candle and sat down to sketch my vision of the man from the murkiness of my dreams. As I drew the dark man I had the distinct impression that he hadn't been alone, but I couldn't grasp the other image.

I returned to bed and slept soundly until Meg came into my room, slamming about in the wardrobe. Obviously, something was wrong, so I sat up just as she yanked back the curtains allowing sunshine to spill across the room pushing back the shadows. I watched her stomp about lighting the fire and getting down my riding habit. It appeared that someone had told her that I would be going out and apparently, we would not be taking the carriage. Finally, she left and brought me back a cup of chocolate, her face was pinched, and her eyes were red. "Whatever is the matter, Meg?" I looked at the chocolate dubiously, I preferred tea in the morning as Meg knew so something had put her off.

Meg huffed. "It's the new maids, miss, the ones for Mrs Hughes and Mrs Spencer. Beth is taking them in her stride and being senior, it's easier for her. But they mean to drive me crazy!"

I wrinkled my brow as I tried to figure out what it was she meant. "Meg, I'm confused. You were so happy that you and Beth wouldn't have to do double duty any longer and now you're unhappy?"

She stopped and crossed her arms and huffed. "Not exactly, miss. The extra hands are welcomed but if I hear 'it's not done like that in Paris' one more time from that Gwen, I'll scream the house down! That's practically all she says, miss. And what kind of name is Gwen for a Frenchie anyway!"

I set my cup aside. "I can speak to Emilie to talk to her or to her sister Adele, she seems to be very nice."

Meg sniffed and pushed a stray bit of hair behind her ear. "There's nothing wrong with Adele, I suppose. Except Jacob and Michael might come to blows over her one day."

I smiled as I came to understand what might be wrong. The new maids must be creating some unrest. "Is Robert paying too much attention to Gwen since she arrived?"

Meg stood there fighting back tears. "Not so that most would notice. But he seems to be around a lot when I'm showing her how Mrs Hughes likes things done and how we do them back home. He whispers things to her in French that I don't understand; then she blushes, and he blushes; it's making me sick, Miss Clarissa."

I thought about it for a second. It didn't sound like Robert at all. He had been very focused on learning his duties as a valet for my father and he seemed genuinely fond of Meg. There had to me more to it. I'd have to find out what it was one way or the other or my maid was going to drive me mad. But right now, I had other problems. So, I decided the best advice would be the easiest advice. "Meg, just talk to Robert."

She looked up at me with hurt but puzzled expression. "Talk to him about what, miss?"

I bit my lip. "Just ask him if he is sweet on Gwen."

Then she blushed to the tips of her ears. "Oh NO! I could never be so forward."

She composed herself eventually and helped me to get ready. When I left the room, I knew she would be crying while she straightened everything up. As it was I almost ran into Robert coming out of my father's dressing room. I glared at him and he recoiled at my look, then stammered, "Good morning, Miss Turner."

I continued to walk down the hall without responding, then I spun on my heel and walked right up to him. "Robert Dawson, your flirting with Gwen is breaking Meg's heart! If you don't have feelings for her any longer than you should tell her so." I stood there with my arms crossed, daring him with my eyes to speak up.

He stood there with his mouth open. "Me and Gwen, miss? I—I'm not sure where Meg got that idea."

"Oh really, so your hanging around when Meg is teaching Gwen things and both of you blushing as you speak to her in French means nothing?"

He furrowed his brow then his eyes lit up. "Oh no, it's not me, miss! It's Michael, honest! They're sweet on each other and he asks me to pass messages along for him…which I'd rather not. But I found out from him that her English isn't very good and she's afraid to ask Meg to speak French since Meg's still learning French. Gwen's afraid she'll lose her position if anyone finds out so when she's with Meg, she asked if I could interpret for her and I get to spend more time with my Meg. But Gwen thinks Meg hates her and she's afraid to ask her why so I'm helping her with her English but frankly, miss, it's all exhausting." He grinned sheepishly.

"Wait a minute but I thought Gwen was fluent?"

He pursed his lips. "It's her sister that is fluent, miss. They didn't want to be parted so Adele lied about Gwen's English knowing that Mrs Hughes is French and probably wouldn't mind speaking French most of the time. She is working on it though and doing well. It's just that Meg makes her real nervous 'cause she's so good at what she does. Gwen's never been a lady's maid before but she's a quick leaner."

I started to giggle. "Is that why she says, 'it's not done like that in Paris' all the time?" He blushed and nodded. "Then you better speak to Meg today or your next day off will be spent playing cards with the grooms." His eyes got big and he looked behind him at the sound of my bedroom door opening. He immediately turned and walked up to a very tearful Meg, took her arm and walked her back into my room. I smiled to myself and made my way downstairs, happy that another crisis had been averted.

At the bottom of the stairs stood my Uncle Samuel, "Come along, brat, we haven't got all day."

My voice caught, and I was barely able to squeak out, "What are you doing here and where is Miles? You didn't leave him in prison, did you?"

He laughed. "You wound me! Do you think me so callous as to leave your paramour in a jail cell? Actually, he's still at the Embassy." I sucked in my breath and he backed up. "Don't get upset with me! Matthew is with him, he was exhausted and had a terrible headache, so Lord Granville invited them to stay there. I came back to the hotel to be with my wife. I didn't think you'd begrudge me that much."

I sighed. "I'm sorry, it's just that I've been so worried. Oh my god, my sketches, I must get my pad. Something came to me last night." I spun around and started for the stairs just as Meg and Robert were running down the stairs towards us with my sketch pad in hand.

Meg was breathless. "Miss, oh miss!"

They reached the bottom of the stairs and Robert took the pad from Meg's hand. "Miss Turner, this man, you've seen him?"

Samuel came over and took the pad in hand and pointing at the picture. "Who is this?"

"I don't know, Uncle, I vaguely remember seeing him last night just before Julian was shot. He was part of my dreams last night and to exorcise him I got up and drew this picture. I could swear that he was standing behind Miles and I had a sense in my dream that he wasn't alone." I threw up my hands. "I don't even know if he's real or a product of my exhausted mind."

Robert cleared his throat. "Oh, he's real, miss. He's the dark man my sister told you about."

Samuel looked stunned but quickly recovered. "Lissa, we'd better show this to your father. And, Robert, I think you had best come along as well." Meg was left standing in the hallway biting her fist. I smiled weakly at her and followed my uncle and Robert into the one of the hotel's private dining rooms.

It was decided based on my drawing that we would leave for the Embassy right after breakfast. Once on the road we walked our horses at a sedate pace as if we didn't have a care in the world in case we were being watched. I wanted to race to see Miles, my heart was pounding, and I was impatient to get moving. Robert was positive that my sketch though incomplete was the dark man that he had seen on several occasions in Dorset. Was it true then that the man was not only a pirate and smuggler but perhaps a murderer? My stomach was tied up in knots just thinking about it. I couldn't even enjoy the sights on the way to the Embassy. Father dropped back to ride at my side interrupting my musings with a chuckle. "Lissa, you need to keep up darling."

I looked about me and saw that I was well back from our group. The reins of my mount were slack in my hands and my horse was wandering off the road to take a nip at the nearby grass. "I'm sorry, Father! I guess I was lost in thought."

He smiled at me as I grasped the reins more firmly and pulled the horse's attention back to the road. We caught up with the others as they approached the drive to the Embassy. Father spoke to me again, this time his tone was very serious, "I expect you conduct yourself as a well-bred lady and not throw yourself at Miles. It would be embarrassing for him in front of so many people."

I glared at him then I smiled devilishly to let him know I was not angry. "And embarrassing for you as well, I suppose?"

He didn't look at me, but I could see his grin. "You are about to get a lesson in what it's like to be in company where young ladies do not openly express their opinions. Please don't make it difficult for yourself." I bristled but relaxed when he added, "I need you to watch, listen and learn. If you ever expect to work for me in any capacity at all, following orders is paramount to success." Then he said under his breath with hint of amusement, "I'm sure that was a waste of my breath," then he chuckled quietly. Uncle Samuel came up beside him and asked if everything was all right. Father merely smirked and tipped his head toward me which made my uncle likewise grin then wink.

I was thoroughly put out by them, so I decided to demonstrate that I could be the perfect lady in every way. After all, I had been raised to be one, it was only within the confines of my family circle that I took liberties.

I arrived at the entrance with my father, Robert, and Uncle Samuel, they all jumped down and proceeded towards the door. Michael came to gather my reins along with the other horses while he waited for Lord Granville's grooms to take charge of our mounts. But he hesitated and cleared his throat loud enough to make my father looked back at him, then up at me still seated. Pinching the bridge of his nose, Father came back to assist me down from my side saddle as he would any lady, "Well-played, daughter, but I suppose I deserved it."

I merely smiled. "Thank you, Father. And yes, you did deserve it." I straightened my skirts and proceeded towards the steps.

He caught up to me and spoke into my ear. "Don't be so cheeky, miss." We both laughed and climbed the stairs just as the door opened.

We were taken into Lord Granville's study where he sat behind his desk with his secretary at his side. He stood up smiling when we entered but frowned when he saw me enter the room. Mr Dunhill his secretary saw his Lordship's frown and spoke up, "Perhaps you daughter would like to take a turn in the gardens or visit with her Ladyship, I believe she is in the conservatory."

My father ignored him, addressing Lord Granville instead, "If your Lordship will excuse me, my daughter was traumatized in those gardens, so I would prefer to keep her at my side. Besides she has presented us with a very interesting alternative to Mr Johnson as the killer."

Lord Granville pulled at his chin. "Come now, Turner, I've already had this conversation with the lad's father and frankly I don't see who else could have done it when none of you other gentlemen were armed."

Father took a deep breath. "May I see the weapon that was taken from Mr Johnson?"

His Lordship wasted no time taking a small key out of his pocket to unlock a drawer in his desk and retrieving the pistol which he handed to my father. Father then pulled a piece of fresh white paper in front of him and unloaded the gun in front of Lord Granville. No one in our party was surprised but his Lordship was shocked, and his secretary looked angry. Lord Granville swallowed several times before saying anything. My heart fell as I was sure he was about to tell us that he had given Miles over to the police. Finally, he found his voice, "I'm should have checked the weapon myself, but things have been rather chaotic since last night. I'm relieved that it's not Johnson. His brother the Viscount has been insisting all day that he should be arrested and his father the Earl has been after me let him go free. I cannot tell you how relieved I am." He did look relieved then concerned, "But that still leaves us with a murderer at large." He rubbed his forehead and grimaced. "I suppose I shall have to turn the case over to the local authorities now."

Father moved forward in his seat. "May I beg a favour from you, Lord Granville? Don't do that, at least not yet." Lord Granville drew himself up to argue, then Father pulled out the picture I had drawn of the dark man and placed it on the desk in front of him. "My daughter thought she saw someone behind Mr Johnson last night. This is the image of the person she saw but as you can see, it's incomplete. Yet my valet recognized this man as a smuggler he's seen several times near Poole in Dorset." His Lordship glared at Robert who looked like all he wanted to do was disappear into his chair. "He is only known as the dark man in that region, but he has an unusual accent. I thought at first that he might be from the British West Indies but from his look perhaps he's Spanish. Have you ever seen him?"

Lord Granville took the sketch and moved over to the window, he sucked on his lower lip looking up several times at his secretary. "Are you sure about this, Turner?" he tapped the picture looking sharply at me before turning back to my father. My father nodded. His Lordship took a deep breath and moved back to his desk and sat down. "Then we have a problem. This looks very much like the nephew of Don Francisco Martinez de le Rosa. But I'd heard that he had died at sea."

Father looked amused. "Perhaps he didn't. Can you tell me anything about him?"

He pointed at the sketch. "Gabriel was a younger son and from all accounts a hellion from a tender age. His father decided to send him to the Indies to a relative's plantation, hoping it would be a sobering experience. But his ship never made it. There were whispers for some time that his ship had been captured by pirates and that the young man had been sold into slavery. His family tried to locate him and almost created a diplomatic incident with England, thinking that he was being held in one of our colonies. I assume that they eventually gave him up as lost. That's all that I know except that his uncle is living in Paris right now.

"Don Francisco is not a popular man in Spain currently but don't think for a moment that he's powerless." He leaned across the desk and pushed my drawing back to my father. "I don't know how long I can postpone involving the police, especially in light of this news. I don't know how long I can give you, Turner, too many people already know about the murder."

Father was losing patience; he would never make a diplomat or a politician that much was obvious. He was a man of action. "The murder, yes, but not this new development," he pointed at my sketch.

The door opened amidst a protest from a footman and in walked Dr Jefferson, right behind him was Miles. I almost stood up, but I remembered my promise and remained seated. Dr Jefferson smiled and bowed towards me. Miles did nothing, he didn't even look in my direction. I opened my mouth and closed it again as he came forward with a cane in his hand, obviously using it to look for obstructions. He turned in our general direction. "Hello, Colin, Samuel and," he tipped his head to the side inhaling, "Robert?" Then he looked in my direction and grinning from ear to ear bowed. "Miss Turner, that rose scent is far too heavy for you. I prefer the vanilla and lavender that you usually wear."

I gasped and almost answered him back as I normally would have but thought better of it. "I will keep that in mind, Mr Johnson."

The Ambassador looked uncomfortable as he turned to my father with a questioning look then shrugged his shoulders. Dr Jefferson interjected at this point. "Your Lordship, I am positive that Mr Johnson did not fire that shot last night. He assures me that he heard someone nearby laugh and another person cautioning them to stop it."

Lord Granville gave only a throaty "Humph".

But the doctor was not to be deterred by the lack of response. "I distinctly remember the position of Mr Johnson to Mr Browne's body when I arrived within seconds of the shot. It would have been nearly impossible for him to make that shot given the condition of his eyes and the lack of light."

His Lordship smiled and tapped the picture on the desk. "I'm inclined to agree with you, doctor, since Miss Turner has recalled seeing someone else in the woods. In fact, she drew this." He pointed at the drawing still on his desk. "Do either of you remember seeing this person in the vicinity or sulking about at the party perhaps?" He slid the paper toward Miles then he grimaced. "Excuse me, Mr Johnson, I forgot that the reports of your returned eyesight were greatly exaggerated, after all." He glared at the doctor who bit his lip and looked down at his feet. "Dr Jefferson, do you recognise this man?"

Miles worked his way towards me while the doctor examined my drawing. He went to sit down beside me but snagged his cane in the skirts of my riding habit and fell forward surreptitiously, kissing my cheek. Then he pivoted with complete grace to sit down, landing directly on my riding crop and in the process of removing it he took hold of my hand under the folds of my skirt as he righted himself. No one paid us any attention except for the secretary who watched Miles' every move very closely. I think I had discovered who was Lord Granville's eyes and ears at the Embassy.

The conversation continued as they argued back and forth as to what should be done or if it should just be left to the authorities in Paris which the only course of action that Mr Dunhill supported. It was finally decided that my father would lead the investigation and that Miles was exonerated. My father handed me back the sketch but asked that I duplicate it for Lord Granville and the Paris police as a matter of courtesy in case they knew the man in question. The conversation had stopped, and his Lordship pointedly glared at me while Father merely cleared his throat. I took the hint and excused myself to visit with Lady Granville.

I was taken to the conservatory by a footman and announced to her Ladyship. I curtseyed and made my apologies for interrupting her. She had on a large canvas apron over her gown and gardener's gloves. "Miss Turner, it's so nice to see you again," she stood smiling at me as she pulled off her gloves then turned to the footman. "I'm a little thirsty, you must be too after riding here in all that dust." She looked over my shoulder smiling at the footman. "Simon, two glasses of lemonade, please." Waving him away with a hand she took a seat and motioned for me to take the seat across from her. "I must say that I admire your recuperative powers. Most young ladies would have taken to their bed for days after enduring what you did last night." She paused cocking her head to the right as if assessing my appearance. "And yet here you are today, the picture of health. I assume that you have questions that you'd like to ask me." I must have looked surprised which, in fact, I was. "Come now, my dear, we all know that most men would never think to ask a woman about their observations, let alone their opinion." She chuckled briefly lowering her eyes.

"I must confess though that I feel like I already know your family. My sister is Mrs Eugenia Clarence, she lives in Mayfair very near to your home. I've heard a great deal about your family from her." I knew Mrs Clarence as the nosiest woman in Mayfair and Lady Granville was watching me closely and laughed. "I know Miss Turner that my sister is an inveterate gossip but having one baby after another tends to make her thirst for any news, so she cultivates the worst gossips in the Beau Monde as her closest friends."

I swallowed and thought of the only polite thing I could say. "I believe that Dr Jefferson is her physician."

"Yes, he is. But it's her ability to ferret things out without seeming to venture out of her home that makes her such a delightful correspondent. I must confess at times that I feel like I'm back home sitting in her drawing room listening to the latest news when I read one of her letters." Our lemonade arrived so we chatted amiably about London for a few minutes. "Well, my dear, I'm sure you're in a hurry and I must get back to repotting these orchids, so ask me your questions."

I pulled the drawing out of my pocket, unrolling it before her. "Have you ever seen this man before, Lady Granville?"

She barely gave the sketch a look when her face became expressionless. "Why?"

I inhaled, deeply surprised by her lack of expression. "I've found that as you say women and even children often see and hear things that their male relatives would never give a second thought to." She narrowed her eyes like she was trying to weigh my veracity then she leaned forward to gaze at the picture for a short time.

She finally arching a brow and looked directly at me. "Yes, I did see him. He was here last night. I don't know who he is though, we were never introduced. I assumed that he was a guest of one of my other guests." It was my turn to look sceptical and she smiled. "You know how it is at large parties, some invited people don't come and others that were not invited show up. But in my position, I have to protect the identities of my guests."

"Did you notice who he came in with?"

"No, my dear, I'm sorry but he does remind me of someone however, but I can't think of who. I only noticed the gentleman because he was so tall and dark, and his skin was a deep bronze which is most unusual in Paris or England any time of the year. But I did see him standing by the doors to the conservatory talking to a slight young man with a mass of blonde curls. You'll have to excuse me but as the hostess I was constantly on the move dealing with dozens of competing priorities." We chatted about the other guests, but she couldn't remember anything else, so I thanked her and took my leave.

The men were just coming out of Lord Granville's study as I came into the foyer. Father looked at me with a quizzical eye, but I merely smiled, and he nodded back. "Miles and Dr Jefferson will be accompanying us back to the chateau in the Ambassadors' carriage, Clarissa." I desperately wanted to ask if I could go with Miles, but my father gave me a warning look.

While we stood outside waiting for the carriage and our horses to be brought around, Miles stood beside me whispering, "I take it you found out something that we did not?"

I looked about to see that no one was paying us much attention. "Yes, but how did you know?"

He shrugged his shoulders. "It's like a vibration in the air, the staccato of your step across the marble foyer, the sudden tension in your father and his intake of breath. It's little things like that that I feel or hear since my eyes have failed me; maybe it's a sixth sense." He sighed and relaxed. "I don't know how I do it, I just do."

I brushed my hand against his as the horses and the carriage arrived. Then he took my hand and squeezed it tightly before I let go and walked over to the mounting block. There with the aid of Michael I mounted and rode off with the others with the carriage rumbling out of the gate behind us.

# Chapter 26
## *Secrets Revealed*

We returned to the hotel and packed immediately to return to the Chateau. Once we arrived there were urgent dispatches from England that needed to be attended to and Dr Jefferson wanted to examine Miles' eyes more closely. I went to my room to change then to the nursery to visit my brother. When I entered, Lettie was there along with Emilie and my mother. Mother was singing to a smiling James who was trying desperately to stay awake. Emilie was watching Mother with a look of longing on her face as Lettie was setting things to rights in the nursery. Suddenly, Emilie asked, "Lettie, when do you think you and Murphy will marry?"

Lettie turned beet red but didn't look up. "I don't know what you mean, ma'am?" Mother and Emilie both smiled at her, Lettie smiled slightly but then it vanished. "He has asked me, ma'am. But I haven't given him an answer yet. After all, Master James still needs me and well..." She paused biting her lip, I could see she was struggling with voicing what was on her mind.

Mother leaned forward to prod her into speaking, "Yes, Lettie?"

Lettie looked up tears glistening in her eyes. "What would become of us if we did marry? I know that most gentry don't employ couples in childbearing years and I'll need to work, ma'am, to help support us outside of the household. Then there's our work for Mr Turner, I just don't see how it can be done."

I felt a breath of air on the back of my neck and looked over my shoulder into the face of my Aunt Mary who was standing there ramrod straight with her lips puckered in disapproval. She nudged me into the room then came in behind me. Mother blanched after seeing the look on our Aunt's face and Emilie pretended to be interested in fringe on her shawl as Aunt Mary walked over to Mother and asked, "How is my great nephew today?" I chose to sit down in a chair by the door in case I needed to escape before Aunt Mary launched into one of her lectures.

Mother looked down at James and in an overly cheerful voice said, "Splendid! He's such a happy little boy."

Aunt Mary almost smiled but instead she just made a grunt of approval then she turned to look around the nursery still with that sour look of disapproval on her face. She stared at Lettie as if assessing her qualities. "Lettie, I had my doubts about you becoming the nanny to our young James, but I was wrong. You have done an admirable job for one so young, so I don't think that I would be out of order in saying that I hope you will remain in the position for some time to come." She was struggling to keep her face composed but I could see her sucking in her cheeks to retain that look of intimidation. Then she glanced down at Mother and continued, "Especially since I believe there will be at least one more brother or sister for Clarissa and James soon." My mouth fell open and my mother turned scarlet while Lettie looked downcast. Emilie reached out to touch Lettie's hand in commiseration.

Aunt Mary walked over to the window, she just stood there looking out for a bit with everyone's eyes on her back. I couldn't believe that she could be so unfeeling if she had heard what Lettie had said before she made her presence known. Without turning around, Aunt Mary said, "Irene, my dear, you already have a reputation in the world at large for being eccentric. Yet despite that people are in awe of how you inspire loyalty in your staff. Therefore, I see no reason for you to change now and bow to convention." She turned to look at my mother, still grim-faced, "Do you?"

Lettie and Emilie both looked puzzled, but my mother looked inspired. "Oh yes! I see what you mean, Auntie! What do you think of the old carriage house in London and there are cottages in Somerset that aren't being used?"

Aunt Mary nodded. "I believe that would do admirably."

Mother continued, "In fact, Colin, and I have talked a bit about the possibility of our staff wanting to marry and what could be done for them and still be available for his work. It would be a benefit to all of us in the long run." Mother was excited and James' eyes were wide open watching her. "Of course, I thought that it would have been Beth and Dalton first. But I see what you mean, Aunt Mary, married staff living on the estate would be eccentric but with them being agents for Colin, it will be very convenient." She was obviously warming to the idea. "Besides it's so hard to find staff that can adapt to our unconventional comings and goings. I think it's a wonderful idea!"

Aunt Mary stood over Lettie looking down at her, "So, child, do you and your beau wish to marry here or in London? I understand that you only have your brother and that Murphy has a sister, but she lives in Ireland, yet he may wish to have her present."

Lettie looked up at Aunt Mary as if she was about to be eaten alive. Then James whimpered, and she jumped to her feet, Mother was clutching him too tightly, so she relaxed her grip and he settled leaning against her chest, so he could observe his kingdom. Lettie looked down at him with a smile and he smiled back at her. "I don't know, ma'am. We've tried not to discuss it because we thought we'd have to leave. And then there is my brother and well, I don't think he'd be too fond of the idea seeing as how…well, he just wouldn't tis all."

Aunt Mary sat down. "Lettie, don't you think it's time that you tell us the secret that might be an impediment to your brother's approval?" Lettie's eyes got huge, her colour drained away till she was as pale as the curtains on the window, but she remained silent wringing her hands. I had never seen Lettie disconcerted. So, Aunt Mary continued, "My dear, I know very well that you are not from the East End of London, would you care to explain?"

Lettie gasped. "Oh, I can't, ma'am. Dalton would—"

Aunt Mary arched her brow. "Leave Dalton to me, my dear. This is about your future and I think you owe this family complete honesty, let's start with where do you come from and who are your parents."

Lettie sat down with a thump as if totally defeated, she looked at the floor then drew in a deep breath. "We're from Whitstable, ma'am, in Kent. Our father was a successful merchant dealing in dry goods. Our mother was a vicar's daughter. Neither family approved of their marriage, so they made their way on their own. Our parents never spoke of their families, so we assumed they'd disowned them. I still have no idea if any of them are even still alive or where to find them if they were.

"Dalton was the only son and our father expected him to follow him into his business, but he wasn't interested. He wanted to be a tailor." She smiled. "He does love fine clothes and he's good with a needle. Anyway, he apprenticed himself to Mr Ireland, our father's tailor. Father was outraged feeling that being a tailor was beneath Dalton. But it's what he wanted so our mother supported his choice. Dalton was very good at it and he was a fast learner. But the tailor had a son who was apprenticed at the same time so there would never be a chance for Dalton to take over the shop or work as his assistant. But this didn't bother him, he was sure that he'd be able to talk our father into setting him up." Aunt Mary raised her brow clearly impressed with either Dalton's drive or their father's wealth.

Lettie paused to take a breath before continuing, "Then our mother passed away suddenly when I was only thirteen and our father was never the same. He loved her dearly and missed her so much that he started to drink heavily. Finally, one day he just didn't come home. We never knew what happened to him. The constable figured he'd just run off." Tears were in her eyes and her shoulders slumped forward. "Dalton had almost finished his apprenticeship when it happened, so we lived on in the house for a bit. But he didn't make enough money for its upkeep and we eventually had to give it up. My father's partner said he'd help us. But since our father hadn't been declared dead he couldn't give us any money from the business without our father's consent. And since we had no proof that he was dead the shareholders would never approve. Therefore, Father's assets had to remain in the business." Aunt Mary clicked her tongue. Lettie sat up straight and held her chin up. "We didn't know any better, ma'am. We thought that he was our friend and we had no family that we could turn to. He told us that he'd help us get set up in London with a friend who was looking for someone to take over his tailoring shop. He promised to send us our father's annual dividend share when it came due, so we set off to London together. But when we got there the shop he'd spoke of was closed, the owner had died nearly a year before. Dalton wrote to our benefactor and while we waited for a response he tried to find work because he knew that the money we had wouldn't last long in London. But without references he had to do hard labour which was something he hadn't been used to, ma'am. I tried to get work too but without a character no one would take me on as a maid and Dalton wouldn't stand for me working in an ale house or factory. We wrote to my father's partner several times, but he never responded. Dalton finally found a tailor who hired him on. But the man was a drunkard, he was only looking for what amounted to slave labour from us. Dalton and I both worked there, me in the front of the shop and Dalton in back and the owner rented us a couple of rooms above the shop to live in. It was hard work and Dalton was the only one doing the cutting and sewing even though the owner had a good clientele of gentry. So, when the shop closed for the day I would go back to help him. Mr Parsons the owner made it clear that he wanted me to listen in on the conversations of the gentleman who came into the shop. I was to tell him what they said, I didn't know at the time why he wanted to know but I'd assumed he was for no good."

She pulled out a handkerchief dabbing at her eyes then her nose, finally she balled it up in her fist before she continued. "Then one day just after the shop had closed Mr Parsons laid his hands on me in a very personal way. He was deep in his cups and could hardly stand but he was strong. Dalton came out front when he heard me scream and he pushed Mr Parsons away from me. He staggered and fell, hitting his head on a table corner that blackened his eye. He screamed abuses and threatened to set the bailiff on us just before he passed out, so we fled that night."

She hiccoughed while tears were streaming down her cheeks as she relived those bleak moments. "Our money only lasted two weeks even with us just taking only one meal a day, we had to sell our few possessions just to live. Eventually we ended up sleeping in doorways and begging for food." She wiped her cheeks on the back of her hand and Emilie handed her another handkerchief. "Then Dalton met up with a sergeant in the pub where he was sweeping the floors and he offered Dalton the King's shilling to join up and fight Napoleon's hordes. We were starving, and the sergeant assured him that I would be welcomed as well since that they always needed laundresses for the officers. I should have known what he meant but I soon learned once we were on the continent."

She took a deep breath and composed herself before continuing, "We hadn't been there long before, I had to start fending off the wandering hands of the officers while Dalton was about his duties. When he was there, they'd leave me alone. Then after about two months I had to fight an officer off, I marked him with my nails and he said he'd see me hang for attacking him, so I ran and found Dalton on picket duty. He would have killed the officer, but I convinced him it was better to just leave." She wiped a tear off her cheek. "He wasn't cut out for soldiering anyway and we weren't any better off in the army than we'd been in London. That's when we took to picking people's pockets and petty theft." Aunt Mary raised both eyebrows.

Emilie's mouth was hanging open. "How did you manage to do that?"

"It's not difficult and hunger is a fast teacher to a willing pupil. We stole only from those that had the means. I mean only those that wouldn't miss it, ma'am! We lived on the fringe of the army for a time stealing food and living off the land. But then the army moved on to do battle and Dalton refused to take me there. He said that no matter how far we had fallen, we wouldn't stoop to take pickings off the dead. We made our way to Brussels where Mr Turner ah came to know us."

I was almost in tears; Emilie and my mother were both sniffling and James looked at all of us in bewilderment with his lower lip trembled as if he wasn't sure if he should join in as well.

Only Aunt Mary was dry-eyed. "Well, my dear, I don't think there shall be a problem. Murphy is extremely lucky to have won your affections. I just hope that he appreciates the fact that he is getting better than he deserves." Lettie looked askance, and Mother huffed as if she was perturbed. Aunt Mary was bewildered by her reaction. "Good heavens, now what? He's a penniless Catholic and a radical, isn't he?!"

Lettie giggled. "Oh no, ma'am, he's not really."

It was Aunt Mary's turn to look perturbed "Rubbish, young lady! I don't know what he's been telling you, but he most certainly is."

Lettie tried to look contrite. "I'm sorry to seem contrary, ma'am, but he isn't. That's just a story he's told the other staff, so they won't think less of him for being of better birth than the rest of us."

Aunt Mary pursed her lips glaring at Lettie over her spectacles with narrowed eyes. "You'd better explain yourself, child."

222

Lettie smiled and started in, "His mother was an Irish gentlewoman whose father was a country squire. His father was a gentleman who was secretary for Lord Grant. He comes from better people than I do, Mrs Spencer. Plus, he has no religion, ma'am, his parents were followers of William Blake, they didn't support any church, but they believed in God and taught him the Bible. It wouldn't bother him a wit where we married. But you're right, that he is a radical in so much as he believes Ireland should be free, but he doesn't support violence to achieve that end. He lost a sister in the riots and it affected him deeply."

Aunt Mary sat with her mouth open. Then she shook herself. "Well, he can hardly stay as a footman if he is to marry our nanny and future governess." She turned to my mother. "Well, Irene, what do you think?" Mother was chewing on her lower lip and bouncing a once again happy James on her knee.

Emilie also appeared to be deep in thought, so I spoke up. "When we were at the Embassy today we met Lord Granville's secretary, I wonder if—"

Aunt Mary interrupted me. "Splendid idea, Lissa! Yes, I believe that would work. Mr Murphy could be Colin's secretary." She looked sharply at Lettie. "But is his name really Murphy?" Lettie smiled and nodded yes. Aunt Mary closed her eyes and clasped her hands as if to pray. "Oh well, I'm sure Collin will make the best of it." Then she looked over at Mother. "So, Irene, my dear, we'll leave it in your capable hands that by the time we are back in London Mr Murphy will have been transformed from footman to secretary."

Mother still looked uncomfortable. "Aunt Mary, I know that you mean well but think about the trouble this may cause for Murphy and Lettie with the other staff."

Lettie frowned. "Ma'am, if you let Murphy and I tell Mr Allan our story and ask his advice about what to do, it might sit better with the others hearing it from him instead of just whooshing Aedan into a new position. You know that once we tell Mr Allan he'll feel obligated to tell Mr Turner and Mr Turner will turn to you for your opinion. Then you can present him with your plan." She looked to my mother with a hopeful glance but it all sounded rather complicated to me.

Mother looked at Lettie with a great deal of sympathy. "Did the staff give you a great deal of grief when you became the nanny?"

"A little, ma'am," she giggled. "But I made a grand fuss about it being a burden to have to care for the little master just because we needed to keep secret what we do for Mr Turner. The others quickly became sympathetic. Besides Master James has them all wrapped around his little finger now and they all like Murphy. I think Jacob knows something about Murphy's origins, he does get a bit morose when in his cups, especially around the time of his sister's death. So, he may have said some things but Jacob's a good friend."

Aunt Mary laughed. "I told Colin there was more to his staff than he knew. Tell me, Lettie, are there any other hidden gentry among the staff that you know of."

She chewed on her lip looking down at her feet. "Not that I'm aware of, ma'am. I think Murphy and I are the only ones that I'm truly sure about."

Emilie burst out laughing, all eyes shifted to her and Aunt Mary raised one eyebrow. "You find this humorous, Emilie."

She shook her head. "No, Mrs Spencer, but it's just that I remember hearing Billy Phillips reciting the alphabet in Latin not so long ago. I think there are more secrets to be found out, ma'am."

My Aunt smiled. "Emilie, please call me Aunt Mary, after all you are a member of this family." She turned to look at my mother. "Well, Irene, you interviewed all of the staff, is there anything else we should know about Billy?"

Mother took a deep breath. "Colin has given him access to the library, despite being an orphan Billy came to us knowing how to read and write and has an inquisitive mind. His mother taught him while she was alive, but he has no idea who his father is. Given his mother's profession he could be related to just about anyone, even someone we know."

Aunt Mary took off her spectacles. "You mean to tell me that Billy's mother was a prostitute?"

Mother swallowed. "She was more of a courtesan actually than a street person."

Aunt Mary cleared her throat and tried to sound nonchalant, "I take it that she catered to only the best gentlemen." Mother merely nodded. My Aunt sighed then stated emphatically, "So, it is unlikely that anyone will come forward to claim the boy? How did she die?"

Mother looked serene but sad. "She died saving Billy, he was pushed into the street in front of a wagon by a passerby. She got to him just in time to throw him aside, but she was trampled to death. The house where they had lived would only keep him if he was willing to umm…" she looked at me and my eyes went wide. I knew that I must have turned beet red. "Suffice it to say that he refused so they literally tossed him out into the street almost under the wheels of Colin's carriage. The rest is as they say history and Colin took him into his service."

Aunt Mary barely suppressed a sad smile, and then Emilie cleared her throat. "Shouldn't we try to find out who his father is? In France, the illegitimate children of the upper classes are cared for and schooled; why even…" and she glanced at me and I frowned at her knowing that she was thinking of Miles. She abruptly shut her mouth just as James let out a loud burp and started laughing, then we all laughed relieving the tension in the room.

A shadow darkened the doorway that I was seated next to and I looked up to find Miles and Dr Jefferson standing there, both smiling and looking inquiringly into the room. Miles didn't seem to notice me, but Dr Jefferson did and nodded. I reached out and took Miles' hand he smiled and squeezed my hand. Then he let go, stepping into the room followed by Dr Jefferson. "I hope we haven't interrupted, ladies, but I've been told that cook will not hold luncheon one minute longer, so the good doctor and I came to rescue you from her wrath."

He turned looking straight at me and winked. My heart skipped a beat as he reached out his other hand towards me. I rose to take his arm and whispered, "Miles, can you see me?"

He tapped my arm. "Not really but it's better. I can see outlines now and at least distinguish male from female and a chair from a table. It was your laugh that told me where you were seated." I noticed that everyone was listening to us and they seemed to be holding their breath.

Aunt Mary then ventured an idea. "What about spectacles?"

The doctor interjected, "Unfortunately, there is no lens maker that I know of that could make spectacles that would help him. But I still have hope that his vision will return completely, if slowly."

I smiled up at Miles. "So you won't be rid of me as your assistant any time soon." I noticed that Mother and Aunt Mary shared a look that gave me the distinct impression that they disapproved of my friendship with Miles.

Not surprisingly it was Miles who seemed to sense my tension and broached the subject. He turned to face my mother and Aunt. He bowed towards them. "Mrs Spencer, Mrs Turner, I can assure you that my intentions towards Lissa are entirely honourable. Even though I may never be legitimized as my father's son in England, I still intend at some time to speak to Mr Turner about his daughter. Until that day comes, we're just friends."

Aunt Mary became flustered and was at a loss for words when my mother spoke up. "Mr Johnson, I can assure you that my daughter has already made up her mind about you and rest assured neither her father nor I would dream of standing in your way. But I do appreciate your candour. Now then shall we eat?" She smiled beautifully at Miles as she handed James off to Lettie. Then she smoothed out her skirts and walked ahead of us, Dr Jefferson offered an arm to Emilie and Aunt Mary and I followed with Miles.

My mind was spinning, I felt hot and cold at the same time as Miles held my arm tightly against him and we navigated down the hallway. But I had forgotten my role as his other pair of eyes as a result he drove his knee into a cabinet, he swore under his breath but never let go of my arm. "I'm so sorry, Miles."

"Perhaps I should speak to your uncle about improving the lighting up here once the estate is returned to his wife." He gave me a lopsided grin. "Just for safety's sake in the future." Then he chuckled as I moved us into the middle of the corridor where he walked with greater confidence.

At luncheon, we reviewed all that we had discovered and talked about what action we could take. I broached the possibility that the young blond man that was seen with the dark man was Ramsey Clarke, but my father dismissed the idea out hand. However, I wasn't so sure Lady Granville's description seemed to scream Ramsey to me. I tried to explain that it felt like the Clarkes were always just on the periphery of everything that had happened to us. What their connection could possibly be was a mystery to me though. My father and Uncle Samuel were dead set against any such wild speculation and insisted the answer was among the guests at the Embassy that night. After saying my piece, I sat quietly and listened to the rest of them. Miles contributed very little to the discussion, he didn't even voice an opinion when I mentioned the Clarkes. But he hadn't dismissed me either as my father and uncle had.

Mother was watching me closely and Aunt Mary was whispering to Uncle Arthur. Emilie just looked around the table while Dr Jefferson concentrated on eating. I laughed inwardly watching him, he always ate like it was his last meal, yet he never gained any weight. Looking at my own plate it was obvious that the cook had gone out of her way to prepare English dishes. I knew she hoped that we'd take her back to England, she had family there and was tired of the life in France.

I finally turned my attention to my mother since she was still staring at me, but she noticed my attentive gaze, blinked and turned to my father. "Colin, I don't think you should dismiss Clarissa's idea regarding the Clarkes."

Father had continued talking over her but must have heard her since he stopped talking to smile at her indulgently, "Yes, my love... Do you honestly think there's merit in her speculation?"

Mother gave him a half smile. "Lissa has always had extraordinary powers of observation and I've been trying to think back over last night about what and who I saw and realised that I rarely pay attention at these events as to what is going on around me. Have you even asked Mr Johnson what he may have experienced? Dr Jefferson has made it quite clear that his other senses are sharper with the loss of his sight. He may have picked up on things that we didn't." I could tell that Father was about to reject this idea, but she continued before he could say anything, "I just think we all need to search our memories and examine them for things that seemed out of order or that we may have dismissed at the time. Fair is fair, Colin; Lissa's insights could have merit."

Father turned to me and raised his eyebrows. "Alright then, Lissa, what makes you think the Clarkes are involved?"

I was quaking inside biting my lower lip as Father waited with everyone looking at me, so I ventured, "Did the Clarkes move into their London house before or after you?"

He looked puzzled. "Well, I've owned the property for some time, but the Clarkes only moved in before you and your mother joined me."

"But how long had they been there?"

Dr Jefferson cleared his throat. "It was two months." Everyone looked at him confused. He cleared his throat. "Mrs Summers is a patient of mine, she lives in the house on the other side of the Clarkes." He closed his eyes tightly like he was trying to remember something. "Very observant woman, Mrs Summers. She said it was strange that they barely had any trunks or furniture when they arrived and what they did have was rather shabby. She rarely saw Mr Clarke, but the ladies were always out and about in the neighbourhood. At first, they were somewhat of a curiosity being new and exotic having recently come from the Indies. The lad was seen occasionally but he was not very sociable apparently. She personally didn't care for them, they never returned dinner invitations and were often not at home when calls were returned." He wrinkled his brow like he was trying to recollect his thoughts. "Oh, and the men that had brought their household goods stayed with them for a time. She found it odd to say the least, they were a very rough sort for servants and they were coming and going as they pleased until you moved in, Turner. It was then that Mrs Summers said the Clarkes got themselves a proper staff and some better furnishings but not enough for such a large house and she knew for a fact that the previous owner had left very little behind."

Father turned to me. "All that proves, Lissa, is that we both moved in within months of each other?"

I grimaced at his tone responded sarcastically, "Alright but how did Richards gain entry to their house and then through the garden gate into our yard?" I turned to look at Mr Spencer. "Uncle Arthur, do you know if the Clarkes' house showed any signs of forced entry?"

He looked down at his hands and frowned. "No, there was no sign that they had forced their way into the house."

I tersely continued my questioning, "It had been raining a great deal for days so was there any sign that that they came over the garden wall? Were there any footprints or trampled plants?" He shook his head no.

I focused back on my father, "Then there is the issue of the garden gate. It wasn't broken down nor was the lock picked according to the police report, so a key must have been used. Even though you had never found one. The Clarkes could have lied about not having one?"

"Then there was the horse stud they were so enthused about it but suddenly pulled out because they wanted to move closer to Ramsey. How does Mr Clarke make his money if he can move so frequently? Charity's season was a disaster because something was not quite right about her. Is it because she can't pass muster among the dowagers and mothers of the Beau Monde?" I looked at Aunt Mary for confirmation and she nodded. "So, they suddenly move to Oxford to find her a husband among the academics. But did any of us see them move? I didn't. I suppose we can ask Mr Allan if any of the staff had remarked on it. Yet they came to our dinner party on the pretence of it being a school holiday, didn't it seem like an odd time for a term break?" I looked at my Uncle Samuel who nodded as did my father. "And before I spoke to Ramsey that night, Uncle Samuel had been quizzing him about his studies. You spoke to him using some simple Latin phrases, yet he didn't seem to understand you. Didn't you find that a bit strange especially since he'd have to have at least some Latin to even be admitted to Oxford?"

Father held up his hand to stop me. "Point taken, Lissa, there are too many coincidences for it to be random. But that still doesn't mean that the Clarkes are in league with this dark man or have anything to do with the smuggling business."

I huffed. "But, Father, there's the dark man's story that he told Angel Dawson, how he had escaped from a place in the Indies where he had been enslaved and when he had gone back for his family the owners had sold up and moved back to England. And now he's come to England in search of them. What if those people are the Clarkes?" I stopped, I could see I wasn't making any impression on my father or uncles.

I bit my lip again and looked to Miles, he, of course, didn't see me, but he seemed to understand my silence and spoke up, "Colin, I have a question for you. If the dark man is the ringleader of the smugglers, why would he shoot Julian Browne if he was in league with him? Why not shoot me since I was so close to him. They could have still made off with Lissa since I was the only one armed in our party. In fact, wasn't it that shot that alerted the rest of you to her whereabouts?" He shook his head. "It makes no sense to kill Julian if the plan was to take Lissa all along to deter you from further investigation. There is a great deal going on that we don't know." He sighed and continued, "We need to stay here until we find out everything we can about this dark man at the Granville's soiree. Though I'm afraid it could mean interviewing everyone who was there. But we simply don't have the manpower and I'm not sure that Lord Granville would even give us his guest list."

Uncle Samuel was nodding his head in agreement, but his eyes were bright with an idea. "If we didn't notice the dark man or Ramsey Clarke then I seriously doubt that any of the other quests remember them or gave them a second thought if they did. However, the Embassy staff are quite another matter! They might have noticed something that was out of the ordinary inside and outside of the house."

Father nodded. "But we'll still have to get his Lordship's permission to interview the staff, especially when you consider what they may have noticed that the other guests would like to have remain private."

Uncle Samuel agreed and then Miles leaned forward, "Yes, but that kind of information could be of value to Lord Granville. Especially if we tell him all that we find out it may be of use to him at some point. As a diplomat, you can never have too much information, Colin."

Father paused and took a sip of his wine. "That may work, Miles." He looked around at everyone at the table. "Alright then... Arthur, Samuel and I will speak to the staff."

Miles coughed, and my father glared at him. "You have something else you'd like to add?"

Miles grinned then became serious. "I think that would be a mistake, Colin." Father bristled. Even though Miles wasn't smiling I could feel the vibration in his arm from the laughter that he was trying to hold back. "The good doctor and I would be able to do a better job."

Father pinched the bridge of his nose barely containing his irritation, "And why do you think that, Johnson?"

Opening his hands to the room Miles said, "We're nonthreatening. The good doctor has been trained to make keen observations while keeping people at ease as he questions them. And with my heightened senses I can tell a good deal about people and being blind, I'm not someone they'd find intimidating." Father began pulling on his signet ring and turning it around on his finger.

Miles didn't give up though and demonstrated what he meant, "You're playing with your signet ring right now, Colin. Mr Spencer has a stone in his shoe and has been rocking his foot heel to toe under the table trying to dislodge it. Mrs Spencer's digestion is a bit upset but rather than speak to Dr Jefferson she has been taking peppermint water. Mrs Turner has been distracted all evening and seems concerned about something that she will need to discuss with you later." Father looked at Mother sharply then back to Miles. "...she has been practically shredding every hanky she possesses for the last week. And Samuel, you've been finding it difficult to sleep at night and often get up to sit in the library." We all looked at him askance. "My room is at the head of the stairs and Samuel's gait is a touch heavier on the left side than the right, not that anyone would notice except in the middle of the night. Plus, the library door sticks and makes a slight popping sound when you open it. However, Samuel, your wife is aware of your nocturnal wanderings." My uncle looked at Emilie and she blushed at having been found out. Miles was unaware of this exchange and continued. "She gets up and follows you only to sit at the top of the stairs until I assume she sees the light go out in the library. Then she scampers back to your bed. I'm surprised you've never noticed how cold she is." He noticed Emilie and my uncle both stiffen. "Sorry old man, but perhaps you should chat with Matthew about your insomnia." He smiled, and I thought Uncle Samuel was going to throttle him.

Emilie leaned across the table. "Thank you, Miles, I think that is excellent advice." My uncle blushed to the tips of his ears but as far as I could see no one was making eye contact with anyone else. Emilie giggled and then Aunt Mary finally laughed.

Father huffed. "Very well, you and the good doctor may have the honour of interviewing the staff. Samuel, Arthur and I will look about the grounds again and speak to the local authorities about strangers that have recently arrived in Paris. Arthur, I hope that we can count of your Parisian contacts and their assistance in this."

Uncle Arthur smiled. "Of course, you can."

# Chapter 27
## *The Embassy Interviews*

I desperately wanted to go with them the next day. But my father said no, and my mother agreed when I would have argued. However, immediately after my father left with my uncles my mother turned to Dr Jefferson and Miles. "Matthew, Miles? Lissa, Aunt Mary, Emilie and I will be accompanying you." Dr Jefferson opened his mouth to protest but she put her hand up. "You gentlemen will do fine with the male servants but what of the female staff? They will have noticed a great deal more about the men and women that attended the reception then the male staff, especially if it involves a handsome man. They'll remember not only what a man looked like but what he was doing and who he talked to…maybe even what was said. They will also take note of the women to a similar degree; whereas most men will hardly countenance another man." She waited for a reply, but none was forthcoming. She shook her head looking pointedly at both. "And no woman is going to speak candidly to either of you gentlemen, you are both far too…distracting! Admit it, you need us."

Miles and the doctor both burst out laughing. It was Miles that spoke up first, "I concur with your assessment and bow to your wishes, ma'am. But you will need to hurry, the carriage has already been ordered along with a few, shall we say necessities."

Mother laughed. "You mean bribes? Well, we have a few of our own necessities as well." Having said that Beth and Meg came down the stairs each with bags containing scented soaps and candy.

Dr Jefferson looked at Mother and then at the bags, smiling devilishly. "And how, Mrs Turner, do you plan on explaining all of this to Lady Granville?"

She smiled as she took her hat from Beth, pinning it on then pulling on her gloves. "I don't have to. It's a token, Matthew, it's expected of the guests to acknowledge the staff in such a way after exemplary service. Besides I have already sent her Ladyship a large case of English goods that she can't obtain in France when we first arrived. It never hurts to be prepared, she'll have no objection to us interviewing her staff but just in case I sent a request to her ladyship last evening for permission to interview them unchaperoned and she agreed." She smiled sweetly at him and walked out the door.

Miles leaned towards Dr Johnson, "Tell me, Jefferson, does Turner know that his wife is a force onto her own."

Dr Jefferson raised one brow then opened his mouth to reply when Aunt Mary answered for him, "Of course, he knows, my dear boy, and it causes him no small amount of concern, as well as pleasure." Then she glanced at me. "So be forewarned, young man."

It was my turn to laugh as I took Miles' arm. "Shall we?"

When we arrived at the Embassy, Lord and Lady Granville were both conveniently out and were not expected back for some time and their butler had been told to cooperate with us to the fullest. Once we arrived, I noticed Mr Dunhill was lurking by the door to his Lordship's study with a look of stern disapproval, so I called out to him, "Good Morning, Mr Dunhill." He now had no choice but to acknowledge us much to his apparent chagrin.

He came forward made the customary abeyances. "Good morning." He did not smile nor looked pleased by our presence as he bowed to my aunts and my mother. His eyes were heavily lidded as if he mistrusted us, yet he said in a friendly enough manner, "If I can be of any assistance today, please feel free to have one of the staff alert me. But I'm afraid that you are on a fool's errand. The staff have been thoroughly questioned by myself and no one saw anything out of the ordinary." He started to turn then seemed to think of something else to say, "I would hope that you will exercise the greatest discretion about anything delicate that you may discover regarding his Lordship's guests. I would have advised the staff of that duty if his Lordship had seen fit to warn me earlier of your visit. But I will remind you that I know his Lordship's mind that it would upset him greatly to have his hospitality abused."

Aunt Mary looked like a thundercloud as she stepped forward. "Mr, uh, Dunhill, is it?" He nodded with a self-satisfied smirk. She smiled back like a cat that had trapped a mouse. "Might I remind you that I have known Lord Granville since we were children and that Lady Granville and I have been friends since they married. I know them both very well and I am sure that they will appreciate hearing of how you have reminded us today of our duty. But please don't let us keep you any longer." She had effectively put him in his place and dismissed him as only a former Dowager Countess could, it was hard not to giggle as he turned and walked away from us flushed to the tips of ears and with his fists clenched tightly at his sides. Aunt Mary was still angry as she whispered, "Pretentious little prig."

The butler Mr Fraser was standing next to my aunt with just a trace of a grin. Then he seemed to recollect himself and turned to our group, "Ah, gentleman, if you would follow Thomas here, he will take you to my pantry where you may interview the inside staff. However, I took it upon myself to assume that you would prefer to interview the outside staff in the stables where they would be more comfortable, therefore the factors office has been made available for you when you're ready. The tokens you have provided have been distributed as you requested, and might I say that the pocket knives will be greatly appreciated for being of such an exceptional quality. Regarding the refreshment that you provided it has been decanted and will be in place as you directed but I have but one request, gentlemen. The men are not generally used to strong spirits so if I may take the liberty, I'd like to ask you to be liberal in the use of the water to dilute it, especially with the younger ones. I would greatly appreciate it personally and so will they in the long run."

Dr, Jefferson nodded, "Of course, Mr Fraser. Our intention is not to get them drunk I can assure you."

"Thank you, sir." Fraser visibly relaxed then he signalled to a footman who stepped forward and led them through the green baize door. Then he looked back at us and pursed his lips. "Ladies, I have set up the small sitting room on this floor for you to conduct your interviews. I take it there will be no spirits required?"

Mother smiled. "No, thank you, Fraser, just tea and some nice cakes if you please."

He raised an eye. "Might I suggest, Mrs Turner, that the staff will not be used to such niceties and that mugs of tea and buttered bread will be more to their liking."

She nodded. "You may be right normally, Mr Fraser, but I want this to be a special day for them so tea in china cups and nice cakes if you please."

He sighed. "As you wish, madam."

As he turned, Mother reached out and touched his arm to get his attention. He looked back at her as he casually took a step away from her hand. "Mr Fraser, before you go I'd like to thank you for all your assistance and preparation. I know this has been an imposition for you and all the staff. You have my sincerest gratitude." He smiled warmly and from the look he gave my mother you would have thought the compliment was worth more to him than anything else. He bowed then and led us to the sitting room.

I turned to Mother after he had left assuring us that tea would be brought in shortly, "That was so nice of you to compliment him like that, Mother, he seemed to genuinely appreciate it."

Mother smiled and caressed my cheek. "It wasn't the compliment that made him smile, Lissa. It was the acknowledgement of the disruption this would cause the staff in their daily routine. It's something that more employers should be aware of when they ask staff to alter their routine on a moment's notice."

There was a tentative knock at the door and the tea was brought in. We had decided since the room was large enough that we would invite all the female staff in at once as if to a tea party. Then we'd see what we could glean from their chatter and hopefully they would put each other at ease. We just needed one statement to prime the pump to get them talking. The cook was the last to join the group then Aunt Mary set the tone. "Madam Reynolds, I must say that your dinner last night was exquisite! I think I have rarely been served consommé so clear or veal so tender, not even at the King's own table. I would love to get your recipes for my own cook, that is if you would be willing to part with your secrets." I was shocked when Madam Reynolds spoke with a clear Cornish accent as she blushed and smiled, acknowledging the compliment and agreeing to write them out for her. Intrigued by her accent Aunt Mary asked her how she came to be in France. "My husband were a French smuggler, ma'am. I met him on the beach by my da's place in St. Agnes. I went for a sail with him one day, but a storm blew us out into the channel and we ended up here in France during the war. We were caught, he was pressed into the French Army and died on the battlefield after we'd only been married a month. His colonel took me on when he found out I could cook. I'm a fast learner, ma'am, I can cook English, French, Italian and German food; don't care much for the German stuff though, ma'am."

She had set the other staff at ease and they all began speaking of their own experiences and how they came to be at the embassy and it became just an informal group of ladies taking tea. It was a large household but thankfully everyone relaxed in short order and by the time we were done and the presents of scented soap and candies had been handed out, we had a great deal of information. We'd have to sift through it later and decide what was true and what was not or at the very least what had been exaggerated. But I didn't feel that we had gathered much that was useful despite our best efforts.

All the staff had left, and we were gathering our things together when a tentative knock came at the door. I opened it to two girls of about twelve years of age. I invited them in and they introduced themselves as Renee and Odette, the tweenies. They eyed the cake tray and the pitcher of lemonade with longing. Mother looked at them and asked if they'd like to take some tea with us. I gave my mother a quizzical look but took my cue from her offering them each a plate and telling them to help themselves while I poured out two tall glasses of lemonade. I sat them down at a table since they clearly didn't know how to balance a plate and a glass. Mother leaned forward once they were settled and asked why they hadn't come with the others. Renee was the only one that could speak English, yet they both seem to understand it.

Renee sighed after finishing a bite of custard tart. "They thought we wouldn't know anything because we should have been in bed, but we wanted to see the fine ladies and gentlemen, madam. We hid in the conservatory and watched from there, but we heard from the others that you were asking about a dark man and a young Englishman with blond curls?"

Mother waited while Renee finished her tart and took a sip of lemonade and asking for permission to have another tart. "Go ahead, my dear, please both of you help yourselves." She moved the cake tray closer to them. "Yes, we are asking about them. Did you see or hear anything?"

Odette and Renee both nodded with their mouths full and it was a bit before Renee said anything. "Yes, madam, the blond boy called the dark one Gabriel. The boy was very young and very angry, he wanted to know what Gabriel intended to do. I could not hear everything they said but Gabriel was also very angry, he said it was none of his business; except that he would put a stop to what they were doing soon. Then he said something having to find what that they had both been looking for before he could stop them…but I didn't hear what it was that they were looking for. Then Lady Granville came into the conservatory with two other ladies to show them her orchids, so we hid. When she left, she closed and locked the door, so we had to go outside and around to the kitchen door to get back in the house." She looked at me with a worried countenance. "That is when we saw mademoiselle…" she nodded at me, "with the nasty Englishman that had tried to kiss Inez. He slapped Inez very hard when she tried to push him away, but Lady Granville caught him, so he let her go and walked away. I was so afraid that Inez would get into trouble, she is very pretty and very good too, but Lady Granville is a kind mistress and told Inez to stay in the kitchen and help there."

Mother nodded. "It sounds like you have a good mistress." They both nodded. "Did you see anything else?"

Renee looked at Odette. "*Oui.* The dark man was in the garden too, he was hidden in the shadows by the fountain and when the nasty man and mademoiselle walked past him, he followed."

They both shrugged when Mother asked if they saw anything else. Emilie grinned and spoke to Odette and Renee in French, so we pretended that we didn't understand them however that was all that they seemed to know. Neither knew what had happened to the person I thought might be Ramsey. Nonetheless, it was more than we had gotten from all the other staff combined, including Inez who hadn't told us anything about being abused by Julian. The girls looked at the remaining cakes, so Emilie got up, wrapped them in the tissue from the candies and handed it to them "You can take the rest them to your room."

Odette looked a Renee and shook her head no, Renee smiled. "That is very kind, madam, but Lady Granville is a good mistress and taking those would be unfair to the others."

Aunt Mary opened her bag of scented soaps and candies then smiled. "You do indeed have a good mistress, but she would want you to have these gifts as a thank you for helping us." She pulled out two bars of soap, and two bags of candy and passed them to the girls. They squealed with delight taking the gifts while thanking her. Then they curtseyed to my aunt and to rest of us and left.

Dr Jefferson and Miles were waiting for us in the morning room with self-satisfied smiles on their faces and the look of having imbibed a bit too much whisky. Aunt Mary clicked her tongue and shook her head, "Well, gentlemen, I suggest we leave before that odious toad Dunhill seeks us out."

As if on cue there was a tap at the door and the odious toad came into the room with two grooms. "I'm afraid that I cannot allow you to leave, Mrs Spencer, until I know what you were told by those two children."

Miles and Dr Jefferson both rose and stepped forward to put us behind them with Miles saying, "I beg your pardon, Mr Dunhill, but your tone is most offensive. I suggest that you apologize to Mrs Spencer and the other ladies then we'll be on our way."

Dunhill pulled a pistol out from behind his back and pointed it at Miles. Both footmen seemed shocked and stepped away from him, moving back to either side of the door. Mr Fraser then stepped into the room with pistol of his own and cocked it. Mr Dunhill looked over his shoulder at the sound, "You can leave, Fraser, I have this under control. These people were trying to abscond with state secrets, I saw them coming out of his Lordship's study."

Mr Fraser blinked slowly looking at the two footmen and motioned towards the door and they both left without hesitation. Fraser took a deep breath. "I seriously doubt that, Dunhill." He took a step closer to him. "Mrs Spencer, please excuse me, ma'am, I should have told you about the tweenies, but I had no idea that they had been downstairs. They only just now came and told me what they told you and to confess their omission." Mother looked startled then confused. "You see they didn't tell you everything, ma'am, for fear of reprisal from Mr Dunhill. But they also saw him speaking to the murdered man." Dunhill was looking around the room licking his lips, a small trickle of sweat ran down the side of his face as he took a step towards my Aunt. Dr Jefferson suddenly moved, grabbing at the pistol in Dunhill's hand, in the struggle he dropped the pistol and it went off. The shot missed everyone burying itself into a portrait over the mantel. Nevertheless, Dunhill continued to fight back but he was no match for the doctor who finally knocked him down with a punch to his gut. Miles picked up the pistol that had landed at his feet and Mr Fraser moved to the door calling for the footmen. They came in and took charge of Mr Dunhill, leading him out at Mr Fraser's direction. Mr Fraser laid his own pistol down on a nearby table as he sat heavily in the chair nearest him and pulled out his handkerchief to wipe off his brow. "Oh my, I haven't done anything like that since the peninsular war."

Dr Jefferson went to the table taking up his pistol. "Sir, this pistol is not loaded!"

Fraser looked up at him with an inscrutable face. "I know, sir, I had no time after I saw that piece of dung come in here. Oh my," he was very flushed, and his hands were shaking, "I do confess that I make a better butler than a foot soldier."

Dr Jefferson knelt beside him feeling his pulse then loosened his neckerchief. "May I send for some water or perhaps something stronger?"

Fraser's head popped up. "Oh no, sir, but thank you. I can't have the staff seeing me as anything but omnipotent." He chuckled then he leaned back in the chair as his colour improved.

My aunt sat down near him and reached out to touch his hand but drew it back. "Mr Fraser, what you told us, did they hear anything or only see Mr Dunhill speaking to that man?"

"No, milady, the children didn't hear anything. But I've been keeping my eye on him since he was hired on." He turned his attention to my mother, "I knew your father, Mrs Turner, from the war and a crustier man there never was; but he knew how to spot good men and foul and I learned a good deal from him in that respect." He took a few deep breaths and seemed to relax a bit more. "I haven't trusted Dunhill from first moment I met him. But oddly enough his Lordship hired him based in part on a recommendation from your father apparently vouching that he knew him well and valued his abilities. What alerted me to something perhaps being wrong with the recommendation was that the General empathized several times that Dunhill was a good Northumberland man, born and bred. I immediately knew that for a lie. The folk in the North Country don't speak regular English, ma'am, as you well know coming from there yourself. Even if you only speak posh English like yourself you can still understand the common speech; but not him, never. I knew then that the General felt he was a man that merited watching."

Dr Jefferson poured out some brandy from a decanter sitting on a marquetry table by the door. He passed it to Mr Fraser who hesitated then tossed it back and coughed before proceeding. "My mother was from Northumberland and she spoke the Geordie and I learned it at her knee as I learned my posh English at the end of the vicar's cane. But Mr Dunhill doesn't have any Geordie at all. Even with his posh English he shouldn't be able to hide a Northumbrian burr completely. I pointed this out to his Lordship, but he still wasn't satisfied that he'd made an error in hiring the man, so he contacted the Home Office. It wasn't long before he received a letter from Sir Thomas Wiseman asking him not to dismiss the man but to keep him under observation until at some point Mr Turner or his representative arrived and then he could discuss a course of action with them. But with all the ruckus with Mr Johnson's incarceration and then the shooting here at the embassy, the occasion never presented itself."

Miles sucked in his breath. "I was supposed to meet with Lord Granville when I first arrived in Paris, but I met with my misadventure before I could call upon him. Mr Fraser, may I ask what exactly you did in the peninsular war?"

Mr Fraser grinned widely. "Intelligence of a sort, sir, I was with the Duke of Wellington, of course he wasn't a Duke then."

Miles chuckled. "Then you were no common foot soldier either, sir."

Mr Fraser smiled. "Just common enough so as not to have questions arise if I were caught."

"I take it, Mr Fraser, that you come with the Embassy and are not a personal servant of Lord Granville?"

Mr Fraser grinned. "You have the right of it, Mr Johnson. I am loyal to my country, the Crown and to the Ambassador, whoever he maybe just so long as he too is a loyal and honourable servant of the Crown."

Aunt Mary sighed and smiled. "We owe you a further debt of gratitude, Mr Fraser, is there anything we can do to show our thanks?"

Mr Fraser stood up and straightened his neckerchief. "Not for myself, Mrs Spencer. But there is something I would ask on behalf of all of us...please solve this crime quickly. I'd hate to have any of my staff leave because of this incident. The Frenchies are a nervous lot to begin with working for the English and now they're afraid of their own shadows, seeing murderers in every dark corner."

We arrived back at the chateau well past luncheon. However, Emilie ordered up a traditional English high tea which included beside the usually cakes and sandwiches a pigeon pie and Welsh rarebit, a decidedly British treat. We had just sat down to eat when my father, uncles, Lord Shellard and the Marquis joined us.

We ate as we discussed our time at the Embassy. Nothing of use had been found on the grounds and as for the Paris authorities they were not as cooperative as my father had hoped. They were still aggrieved at having Miles removed from their custody, whether it was right or not. But the Marquis came up with an alternate strategy and invited the Prefect of Police to accompany them to a wine tasting of a new vintner that the Marquis was very impressed with and apparently so was the Prefect. After several glasses of Perrier-Jouet's champagne the Prefect was happy to tell him everything that he knew had transpired while Miles had been in their custody as well as who they were currently watching as persons of interest in Paris. I was appalled that men would rely on spirits to loosen tongues, but I had to admit that it was effective in this case.

According to the Prefect, Lord Burley had sent his son Julian accompanied by Miles' brother, Edward, to lay a complaint of murder against Miles. Miles had also been accused of treason in an affidavit written by General Sir Richard Hughes who requested that he be arrested and turned over to Julian's custody and returned to Great Britain. However, the Prefect was suspicious of their credentials and while he did arrest Miles he would not release him into their custody. He could not, however, ignore a writ from the French Minister of the interior granting them full access to the prisoner for questioning until they received confirmation from England that he was indeed a suspect in these capital crimes.

The Prefect assured the Earl and my father that he'd not been aware of the methods employed during their questioning or he would have put a stop to it. But he became nervous when asked why Lord Granville had never been approached to confirm the charges against Miles or why he had never been made aware of the arrest of a British subject. The Prefect insisted that he had informed his Lordship but that he had never received a reply. We agreed that it was safe to assume that Mr Dunhill had intercepted the message and that the Prefect did not care enough to follow up with the Embassy. Uncle Arthur had shown the Prefect a copy of my picture and was sure from the man's reaction that the he recognized the dark man, but he denied having seen him.

Despite the excellent champagne he did not divulge any further information but he suggested that they might like to speak to the Minister of the Interior. So, the Earl requested an appointment which surprisingly had been granted for tomorrow afternoon.

Then Miles and my Aunt Mary brought them up to date on what we had found out from the embassy staff, that the dark man was called Gabriel and that it was still possible that the blond man was Ramsey Clarke.

# Chapter 28
## *A Picnic*

Nothing more came of the meeting with the Minster of the Interior, he would not even admit that he knew anything about Gabriel, only that this person could perhaps be the nephew of Don Francisco de le Rosa. The minster had detailed notes on every member of our party including James and shared that information with my Uncle Arthur as a form of intimidation to stop us from poking around and asking uncomfortable questions. Yet after seeing my sketch of Gabriel, he had the gall to ask if I had really been the one to do it and if so would I consider a commission to sketch his wife. Uncle Arthur started to tell the minister what he thought of him when the Earl apparently jumped in and said that he thought that I would be delighted and that my parents were sure to be agreeable being very sensible of the honour, so he offered to arrange it on the minister's behalf.

I looked at the Earl in shock opening and closing my mouth several times at a loss for words. He merely smiled at me, "Come now, Miss Turner, you are very talented. I've seen the sketch you did of Miles that hangs in his Dorset study."

Father rubbed his chin looking at me with an expression of restrained amusement. "Well, Lissa, you ladies proved today that women are more observant and hear more than the average man. Would you care to try your hand with the minister's wife?"

Aunt Mary made a throat-clearing noise, "Colin, she cannot go alone, it wouldn't be proper. I suggest that Emilie accompany her."

Emilie sat up wide-eyed. "Me, but why me?"

Aunt Mary looked at her over her spectacles. "Because, my dear, you are French, and you speak the language flawlessly and you are attempting to regain possession of this grand estate, in such cases it never hurts to make friends in high places." Father opened his mouth to speak but before he could say anything my aunt continued, "Besides the rest of us would only put the Minister and his wife on guard. But a gift for the minister at the same time would not be out of place. Monsieur Marquis, perhaps you could recommend a vintage that would make the minister more amenable to answering my nieces' questions. I should think a case would not be too extravagant."

In any event the proposed gift proved to be very practical when we received an invitation from the minister's wife for all us to join them for a picnic on their estate. Uncle Samuel seemed delighted with the idea since many of the legal and judicial men of power were sure to be there. Mother was happy since James had been invited which meant that Lettie would be able to lend us her talent for eavesdropping. Murphy would also be in attendance having been elevated to the position of my father's secretary, much to the amusement and pride of Mr Allan, Michael and Jacob. The invitation had also included the Earl and Marquis.

The French apparently loved dining el fresco, but their idea of picnic was obviously very different from the English. It seemed as if the inside of the minister's home had been recreated outside with a huge buffet set up on tables with chairs and chase lounges scattered about the grounds in groupings, encouraging conversation and insuring privacy, fortunately it was fair day. The Marquis' selection of a gift for the minister was superb according to our host, it was much-appreciated especially since he would not have to share it with the company today; it still needed to age for a few more years. The case of Scotch whisky was a most unusual choice for a Frenchman, but the Earl had agreed that it would appeal to the minister for its uniqueness.

The minister's wife was as lovely as the minister himself was homely. It was rumoured that she was once considered the most beautiful woman in Rennes and that she had been a rich titled widow who'd lost her first husband to madam la guillotine. Yet she had somehow avoided arrest or the loss of her considerable fortune. She had a smile that projected a pervading sense of peace with just a touch of melancholy. When it came to choose a place for her to sit for her portrait, we settled on a glade where we were surrounded by untamed nature rather than a formal garden setting. It seemed much to her liking and removed us from the overwhelming presence of so many guests. The minster seemed pleased with my choice and left Aunt Emilie and I alone with my subject. Madame asked us to call her Marie Esther as she explained to us how she had met her current husband and married. As I had suspected her first marriage had been the love of her life and his death was the cause for her underlying melancholy. Her current marriage as she said was based on the mutual admiration of two clever people who had weathered the storms of war with their heads and fortunes intact, but it lacked passion even though he was totally devoted to her.

Emilie in turn shared her story about her own family and her quest to regain the family property in France. Marie Esther scrunched up her face as if she found the subject distasteful, but she was also sympathetic and sent a footman after her husband who came to her side immediately. "Jacques, my love, Madam Hughes has a case before the courts to reinstate her family's property to her. Would you be a darling and whisper in the right ears? I like her and would love to see more of her. I think we will be good friends." She beamed at him and you could see that he was totally under her spell. "Besides you've said that the English make excellent neighbours and her husband," she looked about her, and spotted Samuel then pointed to him "…over there is very English." As an afterthought she waved a hand at me saying, "And this sweet talented young lady is his niece. Do you think you can assist them in this matter, my love? Even if it's just to have the case moved forward?" She smiled and batted her eyelashes bringing his hand up to her cheek before kissing his palm. I had never in my life seen anyone so outrageously manipulated and not even notice it. He was totally at her mercy and she knew it.

To give him credit he pursed his lips for a bit and appeared to be considering it before answering. "With pleasure, my dear, I will speak to Monsieur Hughes and find out the particulars." He kissed her cheek then looked over my shoulder sucking in his breath and beaming with approval, "*Mon Dieu est si bon!*"

I looked up at him and smiled as sweetly as I could, "Thank you, Monsieur Comte." I was delighted that he liked what he saw. Now I was determined to apply all my skill to this drawing in hope of winning his favour for Emilie and my uncle.

When he left, his wife smiled, "I hope you don't mind my presumption of calling you a friend after such a short acquaintance, but I have vowed to myself never to be without a place to retire to if ever our country is turned on its head again. She looked at my aunt with nervous anticipation."

Aunt Emilie smiled, recognizing that fear of being disenfranchised, "You and your family will always be welcomed in our home here or in England."

The comtesse sighed with relief, reaching out to clutch Emilie's hands. "*Merci, Madame Hughes...*" A tear glistened in her eye and they both hugged. It was then I that realised her survival during the war must have been a near thing.

I returned my attention to the drawing while Emilie talked away in French they had finally, as in all conversations between women, got around to gossiping. Emilie ventured to ask about the dark man. "Madame Comtesse, there was a very attractive man at the Embassy party the other night, perhaps you've met him. His first name I believe is Gabriel. He's very tall, dark hair and eyes and dark skin...I believe he may have come from the Indies or even Spain."

She crinkled her brow before answering "Ah yes, Gabriel, the dark angel of Paris! All the women find this man broodingly handsome and mysterious." She licked her lower lip then shrugging continued. "But he accepts very few invitations yet seems to appear at all the best parties and salons without invitation. No one knows what his name is other than Gabriel. He can be very charming when he wants to be and very how should I put it, cruel? Yes, that is it, cruel... like he hates us all." She brushed at her gown as if to remove bits of debris. Then she continued, "But for the most part he is quiet, he watches everything and everyone like he is searching for something."

Emilie took a leap of faith and posed a question, "Do you know if he's related to Don Francisco de le Rosa? There seems to be an uncanny resemblance."

Marie Esther pouted as she played with the rose she held in her lap. "I do not recall ever having seen him in the company of Don Francisco. The Don attends even fewer parties than Gabriel and they both seem to prefer gentleman's clubs to mixed company."

I interrupted her, "Madame la Comtesse, there is also a young Englishman with curly blond hair in Paris, his name is Ramsey Clarke. Have you seen or heard of him at all?"

She nodded frowning with dislike. "*Oui, mademoiselle*, I hope that he is not a particular friend of yours."

I grimaced noticeably so she would see my own distain. "He is a former neighbour, but we lost touch with him and I would prefer to keep it that way."

She still looked at me sceptically. "He is a nasty young man! His French is deplorable as are his manners. Do you know that he begs for invitations! He says he is looking for his sister that she was spirited away by a man to Paris and that he has come to take her home."

I blinked and thought back to what the tweenies' had told us about Gabriel and the blond man, "Do you believe him, madam?"

She shook her head making the curls by her cheeks dance. "No, of course not! He is just ah how you say it in English, a wastrel. If he was here looking for his sister, then why did he not apply to the Prefect or my husband for assistance?"

I nodded this time. "*Touché*, madame." She smiled, and it lit up her face. She was indeed very beautiful with the porcelain complexion and colouring of Raphael's Madonna and Child right down to the large deep liquid brown eyes that are so unusual in blondes. I turned back to my sketch when it became apparent that there was nothing else she could tell me about Ramsey. Emilie continued to gossip with her and to slip in a question about Gabriel every now and then.

But all she had to say was that Gabriel just appears and disappears at a whim. Then she stopped speaking, tipping her head to the side like she was trying to decide if she should tell us something. After looking around for her husband she reluctantly whispered, "But that man Ramsey? He did meet here with my husband once when he first came to Paris. It did not go well, I'm afraid, both men were very angry." She paused and looked around her again. "When I asked my husband about it, he said that Ramsey was a man of business from the West Indies who was looking for new markets in Paris for his sugar and coffee, but he was impatient and wanted my husband to expedite the permits for his warehouse. Jacques is a very proud man and he took offense at the attempts to bribe him." She bit her lip and looked around pinpointing her husband then she sighed and continued. "But I don't believe that was the first time they had met, it was the way that they spoke to each other, it was too familiar for them to be new acquaintances."

Emilie's eyes widened with surprise. "You eavesdropped on them?"

Marie Esther rolled her eyes. "But of course! Every good political wife does! How else can you be a helpmate to your husband?"

Emilie let out a breathy chuckle. "Your husband cannot be bribed, that is very admirable!"

Marie Esther laughed. "Oh no, my dear, he can be bribed! But there are ways to do it that do not insult the recipient. This Ramsey did not understand this, he was in too much of hurry. Jacques was so insulted that he sulked for days. He even thought of having him arrested but was concerned that he might anger someone powerful by doing so."

Emilie leaned forward, "Who was he afraid of?"

"He wouldn't say."

Emilie looked at me and we both grimaced. I finished my drawing and presented it to the Comtesse who was delighted with it. She called over her husband and he quizzed me about painting his wife, but I told him honestly that my skill in oils and watercolours fell short and that I could not do the Comtesse justice. Truth is I was not disciplined enough to practice in either medium.

After I packed up my materials and asked Michael to return them to the carriage I went looking for Miles who I found deep in conversation with his father, uncle and an older gentleman. The older man was a formidable looking standing ramrod straight as if he was a soldier on parade. I momentarily thought of my grandfather the General who had been a similar type of man. But this man had olive-toned skin, a long narrow face with a strong patrician nose. He turned as I joined them raising an eyebrow and looking down his nose at me as if I had no business being there, it was a look made to discourage me joining them, but I didn't feel disposed to give him the satisfaction. When I didn't leave, there was a momentary shadow of sadness in his eyes which was soon dispelled. In fact, he looked instead like a man who was used to giving orders and having them obeyed without question much like the General. I had to wonder where men like them learned such arrogance. Miles raised his head turning towards me, smiling as he reached out his hand. "Clarissa, you're done with the Comtesse already?"

I took his arm, smiling up at him. "Yes, she was the perfect subject."

Miles turned back to Don Francisco and introduced me. The Don was not impressed and made it known. "Perhaps Miss Turner should join her mother and the other ladies. I'm sure our conversation would only bore her." He sneered at me giving me a barely perceptible bow as he turned his back to me.

I smiled back as genuinely as I possibly could when he looked back to see if I had left but I was sure he could see the insincerity in my eyes. "On the contrary, Don Francisco, my father encourages me to open my mind to new and complex ideas."

He arched a brow and frowned. Making use of his considerable height he turned back to me and without hesitating said, "Then I beg to differ with your father, Miss Turner. Everyone knows that educating women is a waste of time and resources since you have neither the capacity to retain or process information like a man." I bristled at this attack on my father and the insult to my gender.

Miles obviously felt me tense and spoke up before I could, "In that case, sir, I think our conversation is over. Excuse me, Father, Uncle, if you will excuse us, Clarissa and I shall adjourn."

Miles tugged at my arm, but I remained firmly planted, glaring at the Don who had turned his back on us both and was speaking to the Earl and Marquis. I was livid at this point and answered him back, "It seems that your, nephew, sir has better manners than you despite him being a smuggler, pirate and a murderer."

He stopped talking to look over his shoulder at me then at Miles, "I suggest, sir, that you take your English *juguete* elsewhere and school her in the art of silence."

Miles looked murderous as his eyes narrowed trying to see the Don clearly. He took a step forward, but I wouldn't release his arm. I knew him well enough that he would strike the Don for calling me a toy.

His father stepped to Miles' side potentially to restrain him just as my father joined us. Both fathers looked like they were about to thrash the Don, but it was the Marquis who spoke first. "Don Francisco, I think it is in poor taste to insult the daughter and son of emissaries of the King of England. You should remember as a diplomat yourself that you never know when you might need the good graces of those who have the ear of the English King." It was a bit of an overstatement, but his point had been made and he grinned pleasantly at the Don.

Don Francisco glowered at us and took a deep breath before responding, "Indeed, my friend, you are correct." He looked at me nodding. "My apologies, mademoiselle, I am not used to ladies being so outspoken, it's a failing of an old man who is not attuned to the new ways." He tried to smile but it looked more like a grimace. Then he spun on his heel and left with his head held high and his back stiff as if he would literally march out of sight.

My father and the Earl looked astounded, it was the Earl who found his voice first, "Charles, that was bloody marvellous! But can you afford to offend a man like that!"

The Marquis reddened then smiled watching the Don disappear around the corner of a high hedge. "Maybe, maybe not. But I do so enjoy putting his pompous ass in place." He bowed to me. "Pardon my language, mademoiselle." I tried to hide my amusement, but I still giggled a bit until I saw my father's expression change from puzzlement to worry as he looked to where the Don had disappeared. Then I noticed that it was not the Don but Miles' brother Edward that had caught his attention, he was standing by the hedge watching us. Then he too turned about and walked away.

Father took a deep breath turning his attention back to us. "Charles, I appreciate you defending my daughter but are you sure that was wise?"

The Marquis waved his hand around his head in a very French gesture of dismissal. "I have known him for a very long time, we were once rivals for the same fair hand." He laughed out loud. "She threw us both over for a fat Italian cloth merchant. We ended up getting drunk together that night. Bah, I'm not worried about Francisco, he has very little influence in my kind of commerce." Tapping his nose. "He has no appreciation for a fine vintage, so his opinion is not respected in my circles." He covered his mouth as he coughed and laughed at the same time.

The Earl was distracted during this conversation looking towards the hedge, so I assumed that he had seen Edward lurking there as well. He was pulling at his chin as if mulling over a course of action, then he seemed to come back to himself looking at all of us. "If you'll excuse me, I need to speak to some gentlemen about my petition regarding Miles. Charles, would you care to join me? I think we need to expedite this venture." Then he spoke exclusively to the Marquis as if the rest of us weren't there. "I would just as soon get a judgment taken care of as quickly as possible and get back to England." He licked his lips then looked quickly at my father and Miles. "When I return to England I have decided to appeal to the King directly instead of pursuing a route through the courts."

Miles looked shocked and reached out to his father to touch his arm. He looked at Miles, heartbroken. "I can't abide this any longer, Miles. I think Edward is aware of my intentions by now, so I need to get this done before he attempts to prevent it." He looked at my father, "Has that Dunhill chap been removed from the embassy? I'd like to send some letters home in the diplomatic mail."

Father nodded. "Yes, William, but surely you don't think Edward would attempt to harm you or Miles?"

The Earl made a derogatory noise. "I don't know. He is his mother's child, not mine." And with a touch of pain he added, "He has never been mine. Carolyn was a ruthless and spiteful bitch, he learned those same lessons at her teat!" He blanched as he realised what he had said in front of me. "Excuse me, Miss Turner, that was an unfortunate choice of words no matter how accurate."

I smiled at him. "No offense taken, Lord Shellard."

The Earl looked at Miles and his eyes softened. "I have my heir at my side and I will do everything in my power to make it official. But Miles, should I fail, you should know that not all my assets are entailed. You will inherit a considerable estate." Miles' eyes widened. "Don't worry, my solicitors are aware of my wishes and have been working with your own solicitor under my employ to make sure that there can be no challenge to my will." He chuckled then. "Edward made a vital mistake when he shifted his business to Lord Burley's solicitor and banker, otherwise he might have had an ally in Jameson and Jameson. I have even suggested to those gentlemen that they should take on your Mr Phipps as a junior partner to ensure your good graces in the future." He sobered then looking up at the sky which had become overcast as he continued in a subdued voice, "You will be a very wealthy man, Miles, with considerable property even without the title. Your brother will find that once I'm gone his circumstances will have improved but not near to the extent that he has envisioned."

He patted Miles on the shoulder. "Be careful, Edward can be as spiteful as his mother." He put a hand on Miles' shoulder. "Also, my boy, you don't have worry about your stepmother. She and the children are well provided for as well. The only thing I ask of you on their behalf is for you to be there to give them your counsel and support. But for heaven sakes don't let Willy go to Oxford! And he's NOT to be allowed to enter the Navy under any circumstances. If he insists on serving his country, then buy him a commission in the Horse Guards, anything but the Navy!" He shook his head and laughed. "The boy has it in his head to be another Admiral Nelson, it would kill her with worry if Willy ended up in that branch of the service." Then he turned away, "Come, Charles, let's go speak to the justices, shall we?" He and the Marquis both left chuckling and in an amiable mood.

Father glanced at Miles with concern, "You don't think that Edward would do him harm, do you?"

Miles grimaced. "I think my brother is capable of just about anything in the right temper. But to kill our father? I don't think so, but I really don't know."

Father gave him a half smile. "I should tell you that we've been looking at Edward for the past year regarding Lord Burley's smuggling operation." Miles' face was a mask of conflicting emotion, so Father continued in a rush. "But there is nothing that points to his involvement. He and Julian seemed to have only recently renewed their friendship at Lord Burley's behest. Did you know that Lord Burley was a good friend of Edward's mother? He's lost two sons and he might be using Edward because you became an agent. I cannot emphasize enough that anyone who gets in their way may have cause for concern." He bit his lip before saying, "Miles, do you know where Lady Jane and the children are right now?"

Miles tensed, and the strain was obvious in his voice. "My father has nothing to do with our work, why…" he paused letting his thoughts catch up with what his father had said, "you think that Burley discovered my father's intention to make me his heir and he's using Edward's anger to enlist his aid in having me imprisoned and tortured?" He rubbed his eyes letting out a heavy sigh. Before my father could answer, Miles continued, "I suppose it could be, they know that I am working for the Crown. But do you honestly think Burley would harm Lady Jane and the children?!"

Father shook his head. "I don't know, Miles, but my family has been repeatedly attacked." He looked around him and I followed his gaze. I noted that Murphy was standing close by watching everything and everyone. While Michael and Jacob were in view doing the same thing as they stood near Lettie, and my mother with James and my aunts. Father was worried, it was evident from the lines of concern in his face and the alertness in his eyes. I saw him watch as Dr Jefferson and Uncle Arthur broke away from a group of men to make their way over to us. Father turned back to Miles but suddenly he looked exhausted and frustrated as he said quietly, "I think he's capable of anything, Miles."

Miles jerked like he had been slapped. "I have to speak to my father, Colin, he must return to England as soon as possible."

The tension and worry that exuded from them was palpable and bone-chilling. Father grimaced. "I don't agree, Miles, I believe that your father is safer here with us. Leaving precipitously would only cause Edward or Burley to take steps before we can determine what they might be up to, but Edward's motivation I'm sure is more about the legitimacy proceedings than Burley's business."

Uncle Arthur and Dr Jefferson had reached us just in time to hear what my father had said to Miles. Uncle Arthur leaned towards Miles, touching his shoulder to get his attention, "I spoke to an old friend of mine, he's one of Paris's top solicitors it seems that Edward has been busy trying to muddy your father's petition and the evidence. But oddly enough Don Francisco has been working aggressively against Edward. He has even presented additional documents to the court to support your case. I have no idea how he managed it, but he has the registry from the church where your parents were married."

Miles just stared at him then shook himself. "Does my father know about this?"

Uncle Arthur pointed behind Miles. I turned around and saw the Don speaking to the Earl and Marquis along with the chief justice. I told Miles what I could see happening when suddenly the Earl and the Don embraced, and everyone shook hands all around. Miles was breathing quickly and had his head cocked to the side as if he was listening for something. Suddenly he yelled, "FATHER, DOWN!" Murphy was near at hand and knocked the Earl to the ground as a shot rang out. My father and Uncle Samuel ran off in the direction of the shot followed by Murphy with his pistol drawn. Dr Jefferson ran to the Earl who was being helped to his feet by the Marquis. General chaos pervaded on the grounds with the women screaming as they ran towards the house, most of the men were calling for their horses and weapons as the servants were dashing about grabbing the silver and crystal that was strewn about the grounds. Michael ran to us suggesting that we all retreat to our carriage. Miles was torn between staying with his father or going with us.

I made up his mind for him. "Mother, I'm staying with Miles and the Earl."

Knowing that Miles needed me as his eyes, she nodded as she handed James to Lettie, she hugged me then slipped her little popper into my pocket. I watched them all disappear around the hedgerow then I took Miles' arm and went to his father's side.

The Earl was on his feet brushing his sleeves off but when he saw Miles, he took a step forward and wrapped him in a bear hug. I stepped back so as not to be crushed. Don Francisco was directly to my right and he leaned to whisper to me, "Miles' mother was a very beautiful woman; he looks somewhat like her."

I was taken aback that he spoke to me in such a sociable manner. "You knew his mother?"

He nodded. "Does that surprise you, Miss Turner?" He was chuckling, it was a rasping sound and I wondered if it was from a lack of use. "She spent some time in Spain visiting her mother's family when she was very young, my family were neighbours. She was very fond of singing and had the voice of an angel." His eyes looked off into the distance as if he could see her and hear her voice.

"You loved her?"

He laughed, "Oh my, no, Miss Turner. I was too busy pursuing a career in politics when I knew her. I had no time for young ladies. It was merely her voice that enchanted me."

It just came to me. "Oh! You mean she was already in love with someone." I eyed the Earl.

The Don nodded and smiled, this time it did reach his eyes. "Yes, to an English Viscount who was so persistent that her father had sent her away. But then the world went mad, she returned to France and I never saw her again. I heard that her father had been arrested and, so I came to Paris determined to locate her and see what I could do to help her and her family. But they were gone. During my search I found the church where she had married her Viscount. I had hoped the rest of the family had gone with her to England. The priest there was a good man, he became my confessor while I was in France we became good friends. But he was old and not well, he was very afraid that the madness sweeping the countryside would engulf his church and that it would be looted like so many others. So, he gave into my care the church registries and much of their plate. Then a few weeks later the church was set fire by marauders. I went to help and pulled the old priest out then helped to put the fire out. The priest died from exhaustion and I think a loss of heart a few days later. He asked me to keep the registries and plate safe until the church was rebuilt one day. Shortly thereafter I was forced to leave for Spain, so I took them with me."

I was puzzled and asked him, "But why bother?"

He sighed taking a step away. "Would you believe I couldn't bear the thought of anymore of this beautiful country's history being destroyed. The names in those registries go back hundreds of years, the plate is from the time of the crusades. Just think of all the families that have been married, buried and christened in that one church, what would have happened to those documents? The locals may have saved them or used the pages to wrap fish and the plate would have been taken from them. I'm a writer by desire and a politician by circumstance, Miss Turner, any written record of our lives is worth saving for the future. Wouldn't you agree?"

I turned to face him in awe of his words, he genuinely meant what he was saying. his face was like an open book while he spoke. But then the shutters went down again, and he was the dour Don Francisco once again. But I responded to the man inside that façade, "You amaze me, sir. I would not have counted you among the sentimental."

He looked down at me with the hint of a smile which lightened his face for a moment. "You are so lovely and so very young." Then he looked around him saying in a more sombre voice, "What you see of Paris today is a mere shadow of what it once was. It was arrogance that brought it to the brink of irrevocable destruction and became instead an apoplectic storm that ravaged this country. We have a duty, my dear, to preserve our past, so we can understand our future and not make the same mistakes. But more than anything the people who have lived and died here do not deserve to be forgotten."

I was so struck by his words that I felt a tear roll down my cheek. "No, they don't. They should be honoured and remembered." He raised a hand and wiped away my tear with the tip of his finger. He bowed to me, took my hand and kissed it then he straightened up looking me in the eye, "I may have been wrong about you, Miss Turner." He smiled then he walked away towards the Comte's house.

Miles was speaking with his father and Dr Johnson was standing by them staying alert while the Marquis stood smiling, watching the father and son. Uncle Samuel returned looking concerned "Is his Lordship alright?"

"Everything is fine, Uncle. In fact, I think everything may be perfect." I looked over his shoulder but there was no sign of anyone with him. "Where's Father?"

He sighed. "The Comte called out the militia and we met them in the woods they're demanding answers from your father about who would want to shoot Lord Shellard, so he asked me to come back and see everyone home." I tensed and thought about going after him, but my uncle seemed to have read my mind. "Don't worry, Lissa, Murphy is with him and the militia just wants to talk to him so let's gather up the strays and go home."

# Chapter 29
## *Autumn 1831, France: Lost and Found*

Two weeks later the gentlemen were in the billiard room celebrating the news that Miles' legitimacy had been confirmed by the French courts. I smiled to hear them carrying on, I wanted so much to go to Miles, but this was a time for him, his father and uncle to be together and not a someday possible fiancée.

My mother needed me at her side, she was worried about my father because he had not returned from the Comte's home. He had sent several messages that he was aiding with the investigation and we were all to stay put. He was the one who sent the message and the documents concerning Miles' confirmation and assured us yet again that he was okay. Today, Mother had gone to the nursery to be with James, this was her routine now, she refused to come down taking her meals there because the windows had a sweeping view of the surrounding countryside and the drive leading to the chateau. I feared for my father thinking back to when Miles had been incarcerated. But it hadn't been the French that had tortured Miles; it had been our own people, the French merely facilitated it. Still my heart was pounding in my chest when I finally heard my mother running past my door.

I followed her to the head of the stairs just in time to see my father coming through the door as my mother raced down the stairs and threw herself into his open arms. He laughed, pulling her back and looking into her eyes that were swollen from days of crying. "My darling, whatever is the matter?"

She gulped for air and stuttered, "I—I didn't know."

I was poised on the bottom step by then. "Papa." I was going to mention that she had been afraid because of what had happened to Miles, but I changed my mind. "I'm glad you're home." I smiled, and he reached out an arm for me pulling me into a hug with my mother.

Then mama pulled back smiling up at him then at me. "We have cause to celebrate today! You're back! Miles' case has been decided in his favour and now we can go home to England."

Father rubbed his cheek. "Not yet, my dear, there is still the question of Julian's murder and my promise to the ambassador. But if you want to go home, darling, I'll make the arrangements for you and the others." He reached out to brush a stray hair behind her ear.

She took his hand, kissing his palm then shook her head, "Whither thou goest so shall I," and then she chuckled. "No, my love, we'll stay. There are still a few dress makers and shops that I haven't visited." She chuckled with delight as my father groaned.

That evening the celebration for Miles was cautiously optimistic, there was still the English Crown to approach. But with the marriage registry in the Earl's possession it seemed to be of less concern now. However, there was still a murder to solve and the ambassador's patience were running out. And there was still the mystery of the person involved in taking a shot at the Earl, but the Minister for the Interior insisted that it was now a matter for the French authorities and he would brook no interference from us. Father had been questioned thoroughly and repeatedly and after initially assisting the authorities he'd been told to go home and warned to stay out of the investigation.

Miles was enraged but there was little he could do on his own, being almost sightless. The Earl and the Marquis had moved from Paris to the chateau much the to the minister's chagrin. He would have preferred them to remain in the city, but he eventually relented after realising that the Earl's security would then be our problem and not his. The Earl on the other hand was loath to hide but he obviously enjoyed the thought of being with his son and I knew that at least some of Miles' anxiety would be relieved with him residing here. In addition, it afforded them time to plan their approach to the King once we returned to England. I didn't spend as much time with Miles as I had in the past with his father here. Instead, I visited with Mrs Baxter and Patrick almost daily and rode around the chateau's domain with Emilie and Jacob.

Father, Uncle Samuel, Jacob and Michael were often gone for hours on end every day until they came home one day worn out and bedraggled. They had finally found Gabriel or rather he had found them.

Gabriel was a large angry-looking man, but I wasn't as much surprised by his appearance as I was by who came with him. It was Charity Clarke dressed in men's clothes. "It was you at the embassy not your brother."

She smirked but stood closer to Gabriel taking his hand as she swallowed before saying with a great deal of venom, "Yes, it was me, but Ramsey is not my brother and the Clarkes are not my parents!"

I looked at her with scepticism, not knowing if she was lying or telling the truth.

She drew herself up with her head held high. "If you must know, I am Gabriel's wife! We met on board a ship bound for the Indies, but it was captured by pirates. They killed everyone else and sold us as indentured servants."

Gabriel squeezed her hand and she stopped talking and he glared at me, "Our personal history is not relevant to the issue at hand." He turned to my father, "You asked for information in return for my wife's protection."

Father looked to my mother who had just come into the hallway along with Emilie and Aunt Mary. It was Uncle Samuel who turned to Emilie, "My dear, it appears that we'll be having additional company staying with us."

He looked beseechingly at Emilie who smiled at him and with an underlying tone of mirth to her voice said. "Of course, my love, shall it be one room or two?"

No one made a sound until Charity broke out in a resounding laugh that dispersed the tension. "One, Madame Hughes, Gabriel and I have been married for seven years; only three of which we have spent together." And then in a bitter undertone, "Thanks to the Clarkes and their scheming thieving ways."

I could see now why Charity hadn't done well in the London marriage market, she was obviously not from the upper classes, there was a slightly rough edge to her. She was perhaps from a gentile family but not from the upper crust and most importantly she was already married. She was very self-assured, but it was obvious that she took her direction from Gabriel without question. I suppose that was a wife's duty, but I couldn't help but wonder if Don Francisco would approve of his niece.

Gabriel was eyeing me up and down in a manner that I didn't care for at all, but I refused to lower my eyes. Miles came out of the library stepping up behind me and laying is hands on my shoulders. I reached up to touch him and saw Gabriel raise a brow then quickly avert his gaze. Father suggested that they retire to their room to freshen up and change then we would meet in the salon. The footmen came in with their worn luggage, our group broke up and our guests followed Mr Allan up the stairs with the other gentlemen close on their heels. I went with my mother and Aunt Emilie to the salon where we were joined shortly by Dr Jefferson, the Earl, the Marquis and Miles.

Miles stretched his legs out rubbing his hand across his forehead and then his eyes, he had been complaining of flashes of light and headaches for some time now. The tinted spectacles the doctor had procured for him helped but he refused to wear them most of the time. I walked over and jerked the curtains closed on one side to shelter him from the bright sunlight and on returning to my seat beside him he took my hand giving it a squeeze. Emilie had called for refreshments, so we sat in silence for a few minutes, I looked about me and noticed that Aunt Mary was not with us nor was Uncle Arthur. I looked to my mother and she seemed to understand, nodding towards the Earl.

The Lord Shellard chuckled. "Mrs Turner, your family's ability to communicate without a word is extraordinary or are you all mind readers?"

Mother smiled at him. "It's merely a mother-daughter talent, my Lord."

He grunted and looked at me. "Are you sure, Mrs Turner? Your daughter seems to be able to read my son's mind very well."

She laughed out loud. "That is an entirely different talent, Lord Shellard, I assure you." Everyone laughed.

I frowned glaring at my mother but decided I would not let them distract me. "Lord Shellard, do you know where my Aunt Mary and Uncle Arthur are?"

The Earl nodded. "They're packing, Miss Turner." I couldn't believe that he felt that answer would be sufficient, but I bit my tongue as he gave me a crooked half smile "They are doing me a service by taking my petition to legitimize Miles to His Majesty; by doing so we hope to keep Edward here and out of England. Then they will collect my wife and children and take them out of harm's way to Cornwall for a holiday."

"But, my Lord, doesn't that expose both you and Miles to further danger here from Edward? And now that we've taken in Gabriel and his wife, can you be sure that you're safe here?"

The door opened and instead of the refreshments as I had expected Gabriel and Charity walked in. They both looked exhausted, yet Charity had apparently been listening at the door with her chin held high, scanning the room and effectively challenging anyone to interrupt her. "His Lordship is safe from us, Miss Turner, we are no friends of the Brownes. It was not my husband that shot Julian Browne…it was me! My husband followed me into the woods at the Embassy, not you."

The room was stunned silent. Gabriel moved forward sitting down and pulling his wife along with him. Charity sat holding so tightly to Gabriel's hand that her knuckles were white. He opened his mouth, but she interjected. "Gabriel, this is my story to tell." She let go of his hand first smoothing her skirts then folding her hands in her lap. "After the death of our father my brother and I were to journey to the Indies where he had procured a job as a factor on a coffee plantation. Gabriel and I met on the merchantman Windswept out of Portsmouth, he joined us on the ship in Bilbao where we had stopped to off load some cargo. To say the very least he was a charming shipboard companion." She shifted her eyes to glance at him briefly, he was watching her like she was the only person in the room.

She blushed at his scrutiny then continued, "My brother didn't trust him though. He had been warned by the captain that Gabriel had a most inappropriate reputation when it came to young ladies which was the paramount reason why he was being sent away by his family. Thus, we weren't allowed to be alone very often."

Then her face changed and her eyes watered. "A few weeks after leaving Spain my brother contracted a fever along with four of the ships' company. He was the only one that died, he didn't linger long but we had sailed too far for the captain to put into a port anywhere, so we buried him at sea and continued our journey. I was now unchaperoned, unprotected and with no prospects. I was at the mercy of the captain and crew, but Gabriel stepped in and became my protector. He promised to take me with him to his family's plantation and once there he would help me return to England or find a suitable position for me in the Indies. I'm a country gentleman's daughter, my education is sufficient for gentile village life but not for employment even as a governess. So, during the voyage Gabriel undertook to improve my languages, mathematics, geography and literature.

"When we were within a few days of reaching our destination, our ship was attacked. The crew were killed, and the ship was sunk. Gabriel and I were the only survivors, it was during the attack that he proposed we pretend to be brother and sister if captured. We found out later after listening to the pirate crew that the whole point of the attack had been for the English owner of the Windswept to collect the insurance money for the loss of its cargo. Most of which had already been off loaded in Bilbao. And to capture Gabriel and ransom him so our ruse that he was my brother protected him as well as me." She swallowed and looked to her husband.

Gabriel smiled at her and took up the narrative, "We were discovered hiding in the hold before they sunk the ship and were brought before the captain. The man who had found us was able to convince him that we would be of more value to him alive since there was little in the way of plunder on the ship. I told them that the man they were looking for had died of fever and had been buried at sea. The ship logs confirmed that there had been a death, but the captain had neglected to enter a name, it was a lazy clerical error that saved us. Even though his employer had wanted no witnesses, the pirate captain was not averse to making a bit of personal profit. He sold Charity and I as indentured servants to the Tarlsons, an English couple who owned a small coffee plantation on Bermuda. Our sale had not stipulated our relationship to each other, so we told the Tarlsons that we were engaged and had planned to marry once our indenture was over. We had hoped to escape from them and to find my family but as it turned out that was not so easy. We were surrounded by jungle and had no money plus we were more than a thousand miles away from my family's planation in Cuba. Mrs Tarlson as it turned out was a woman of strong moral convictions and insisted that she could not condone us living in sin, so we were married. I decided then to try and enlist their aid and told them our story. Unfortunately, neither she nor her husband believed us. I think they were afraid to let us go and lose their investment. It was obvious that they didn't trust their slaves and they looked on us as added protection, so we lived in the main house with them as privileged servants. The Tarlsons were rather isolated and had few visitors and in a very short time they began to treat us almost like family. They promised us that in seven years we would earn our freedom and would then give us enough money to buy passage to wherever we wanted to go, but I still wanted to try and escape. I had made plans to do so but within a few months we discovered that Charity was with child and I couldn't leave her, she gave birth to our twin sons as an indentured servant to my eternal shame."

He sighed, and I noted that his hands were shaking with suppressed rage perhaps from self-loathing. He took an offered glass of brandy from the Earl and drank it off, then started again, "Then," his voice choked with emotion, but he continued, "then one day when I was in the fields overseeing the workers, the Clarkes came with a band of raiders. They killed the Tarlsons and all the house slaves. When I heard the shots, I raced back but the only weapon I had on me was a machete and a knife. Charity met me halfway telling me to run. But she couldn't leave our boys, they were only two years old. It was impossible for me to save them, but I promised to come back for them in the night. When I returned she and the boys were already in the hands of the Clarkes and being held captive in the big house and surrounded by the raiding party."

Gabriel became overwrought, so Charity took up their story, "It became clear that the Clarkes were looking for someone. Their employer Lord Burley had found out that the captain had sold two survivors, one of them fitting Gabriel's description, they were hunting for him. They told me they knew he was there because he had been seen in town with Mr Tarlson, the description matched that of Gabriel de Bearne. I knew if they suspected me of being Gabriel's wife my life and those of our children would be forfeit. So, I lied to them about who I was. I had never been off the plantation and none of the neighbours knew me, so I pretended to be the widowed daughter of the Tarlsons who had come out from England with my sons to live with them. I told them that the girl who had been with Gabriel had died. They didn't believe me and I was beaten for information about Gabriel. They even threatened our boys but all I told them was he had been in the fields and must have run off when he saw they had come. Search parties were sent out looking for him. The remaining slaves that hadn't run away were terrified, but they didn't give me up." She chuckled. "They were more afraid of me because my twins were considered bad medicine; they thought I was a witch.

"Then one day Ramsey Clarke came back from town with a letter telling them to stay put that someone would be arriving to take charge. So along with their son the Clarkes took up residence waiting for this person to arrive. It had been over a week and the other raiders were getting restless talking about taking their share of the plunder from the Clarkes and leaving. But before they could Ramsey and his father killed the ring leaders in their sleep. The next day the others took whatever they could carry and ran. Finally, Randall Browne and his brother Julian arrived. They were very upset that the Clarkes had not found Gabriel. The Clarkes wanted to kill me and the boys but Randall said no, that he thought Gabriel would come after me. The Brownes suspected that I wasn't who I said I was, so they ordered the Clarkes to sell up and establish themselves along the coast as a respectable family with property. I was to remain their hostage as an enticement for Gabriel to come out of hiding. The Brownes had a property picked out for them where smuggled goods and contraband could be off-loaded and hidden from the authorities but where they could keep an eye and an ear out for Gabriel as well."

After they left the Clarkes took it into their heads to pass themselves off as landed gentry they could pass well enough in the hills as gentle folk but closer to town it would be obvious that they were hardly quality, they needed me to teach them how to behave. Following Browne's instructions, they sold the plantation along with all the slaves and settled on the coast where they established a horse stud. They knew horses and did well but the market for horses is small in the Indies and the Clarkes liked to live well beyond their means." She reached out to Gabriel taking his hand in a tight grip and sighed.

Gabriel picked up the story, "I did run, but not far. I was hiding in the jungle. I followed the Clarkes to the coast, but I had no means to earn money, so I joined the crew of a smuggler's vessel that plied the coastal waters between the Indies and America. At the time, I had no idea that the ship was one of Burley's but thankfully no one knew who I really was, but they instinctively knew that I was not of their class, it wasn't held against me so long as I worked hard. Thankfully my time spent associating with rough characters in Spain gaming and whoring stood me well with my fellow crewmen." He coughed and looked embarrassed. "I was able to fit in with them for the most part, but it was difficult to bow to another's authority, that was never my strong suit."

He leaned back and crossed his legs looking more confident now. "The irony was not wasted on me when I discovered who owned the ship and so for almost four years I kept track of Charity and the boys as best I could. Our meetings were few and short. I had no means to care for them, so it was better that they stayed with the Clarkes where she and the boys at least would live in a better style than I could provide." He rubbed a hand through his hair and sighed as if in telling the story he was releasing all the anxiety he had built up over the years. I should have tried to locate my family, but I was on a British ship and things were not shall we say easy between England and either the Dutch or Spanish settlements in the area.

"Then last year the storms came battering the coasts, they were devastating to many including Burley. He lost a great deal of money with his shipping, both legal and illegal. Our vessel the Horseman encountered a hurricane off the coast of Hispaniola, we lost the captain, first mate and many of the senior crew. Nevertheless, we limped into a Spanish port of call where I assumed command mainly because I spoke the language. If I hadn't taken command the Spanish would have seized the vessel and arrested the crew. But by the sheer force of personality alone I saved the ship and crew. We made repairs quickly then set about increasing our fortunes under my leadership.

"As it happened many of the ships we plundered belonged to Burley, it was more by accident then design but it made me rich if not happy." He laughed heartily for a bit. "At the time, it was bittersweet to know I was improving my fortune at the expense of an enemy. It was only by a quirk of fate that I had slipped through Burley's fingers. My first thought once I was my own man had been to contact my family in the Indies, but I was unsure of what kind of reception I would receive. I'm not the eldest son and I had caused considerable trouble both socially and politically for my parents and uncle. I was still unsure if it had been Uncle Francisco who had arranged for my abduction to dispose of an embarrassing nephew on behalf of the family. After all, it had been my uncle's idea to send me to the Indies.

"When I finally returned to spirit Charity and our sons away, I found that they were gone. The story in town was that Clarkes' money had been running low so to escape their creditors they had sold up and headed for England with Charity and our sons. But in fact, Lord Burley while not happy with their failure in the Indies had another use for them in England. I found out through associates of Browne's that he had no love for Turner and that Charity was to be used in some scheme to get close to him. It seemed that you were making things difficult for his Lordship's endeavours in England and France. But Browne wasn't about to stop there, he intended to exploit any advantage he could, including your father, Mrs Turner. He knew about the General's weakness for playing cards with the French officers during the war and there were unsavoury rumours about him when he was in India. But his fraternizing with the French would have been considered a treasonous act by many and could ruin a man like your father and his family with him. So, Browne wanted Charity to get close to Turner either as his wife or mistress, he didn't care which, but he intended to ensure her cooperation by holding our sons hostage." He paused to see if my mother had reacted to this revelation; she did not. "Your husband was immune to her charms, so they decided to look elsewhere among the influential and men of power. My love made it difficult for them though by telling potential beaus that she was not a virgin. Naturally no man of the beau monde wanted a scandal attached to them, so they did not pursue my wife. But Burley and the Clarkes had already separated Charity from the boys when they had first arrived in England and she had no idea where they were."

He clenched his fists, glared down at the carpet as if it had offended him. "I approached the Browne's factor in the Indies when I heard that they needed a new captain to make the Atlantic crossing. The previous captain had met with an unfortunate accident on the docks and had his leg crushed. Once I arrived in England I found Charity here in London and I reluctantly agreed that she needed to stay and play her part, hoping to find out the location of our sons." There was a coldness in his eyes that made me shiver but then he came back to himself and the look vanished as suddenly as it had appeared. "I sailed in and out of Poole as captain of the Brownes' most successful smuggler mainly because of my talent for languages and my beard." He gave a self-satisfied smirk. "The Brownes never knew who I really was."

He stretched and held out his glass for a refill, after taking a sip he continued, "The only respite I ever had was stopping occasionally at the old estate outside of Poole that I believe Johnson now owns. The young girl that lives there with her parents is a kind soul, she would listen to my ramblings with a sympathetic ear." He sighed then chuckled. "And her mother was an excellent cook but had an acid tongue. You may not be aware, Johnson, but I was on the ship anchored off Poole the night when most of my crew didn't return from their altercation with you. I heard about what happened from the few that did return, and I must say that you have some most unusual friends."

His tone suddenly changed from bemused to angry. "I came looking for the others when they were overdue and found the gypsies burying the bulk of my crew in the bog. They wouldn't tell me a thing other than my men and my business associates had a fatal disagreement with the wrong people. I was surprised to find that even gold wouldn't buy me your names. That kind of loyalty is rare, Johnson." He turned and looked at Miles, unaware that Miles could not see him. "For the most part, my crew were good men just trying to survive in a cruel world. But I don't hold you or Turner responsible for their deaths; that is on Burley's head."

He took up Charity's hand to kiss it again. "After that I made my way to London and watched you for a time, it was difficult to speak to Charity except in crowded reception rooms and the notes we contrived to leave in the park. It wasn't long before the Clarkes moved to Oxford and I could no longer meet with her privately, but she had discovered that the boys had been moved by Julian and his intent was to bring them to Paris. It was then that Charity ran away with me to follow Browne. But that nuisance Ramsey came after us and he alerted Browne to my probable identity." He clenched his fist again and slammed it on his knee. "They still have my boys somewhere in Paris."

Aunt Emilie with her kind heart asked, "Why would they bring the boys to Paris?"

Gabriel shrugged. "To ransom them to my uncle perhaps or to lure me out into the open? They are a very suspicious family and believe everyone is as dishonest as they are. I did manage to discover that my uncle isn't working with Burley, in fact, he is living here in exile. Still I felt that I couldn't go to him and put him and my family at risk. It would be a terrible scandal for all concerned if I were to reappear after all these years…a pirate and a smuggler. Besides I need my anonymity to find my sons." He stopped and looked around the room, my father and Uncle Samuel had still not joined us, and I was puzzled as to their absence.

The Marquis was scratching his head then ventured to say, "That's an interesting story, monsieur, but it still does not tell us why you shot Julian Browne."

Charity looked him in the eye saying one word, "Revenge." She bowed her head and, in a whisper, said, "I heard Julian talking to a mousey looking man at the Embassy party who said that the Spaniard's brats would have to be disposed of, because you people were getting too close. Browne told him that he'd have Ramsey take care of it that night but first he had a bit of unfinished business with Miss Turner. The other man was not happy about it and said that his Lordship would be most displeased. But Julian told him that he had more important things to worry about than his father's displeasure." She sobbed as she continued, "They knew that the boys were Gabriel's children…and they were going to kill them!" She sobbed but continued, "I had to stop him before he spoke to Ramsey!" She was visibly distressed, but Gabriel put his arm around her and glared at us, daring anyone to challenge their story. It was clear that they both were under considerable stress.

There was a knock at the door signalling the arrival of the refreshments and with them came my father's valet Robert Dawson. He looked nervous and never more so than when he saw Gabriel. But he turned to my mother and Aunt Emilie who was seated beside her, "Begging you pardon, ladies, but Mr Turner and Mr Hughes will not be able to join you as they've been called away on urgent business." Mother thanked him as did Aunt Emilie. Robert made to leave the room and as he moved towards the door, Mother asked, "Robert, do you happen to know who called them away and to where?"

Robert gulped and nodded. "Yes, ma'am, I do. My Uncle Jibben sent him a message and asked to meet them in the town's marketplace."

Mother leaned forward. "Really! What is he doing here and what does he my want with my husband?"

Robert gulped and took a step forward. "He's here with a couple of my cousins on a bit of business to arrange marriage contracts with the local Roma. But he said that he had come across someone's personal property while in Paris that he hoped Mr Turner and Mr Hughes would take off his hands and see it returned to its rightful owner. He also has some information about a person of interest and needed to speak to them." He shifted his gaze to Gabriel who bristled at the look and seemed ready to accost Robert.

Mother pursed her lips. "Robert, what do you think your uncle meant?"

Robert had inched his way still closer to the door. "Well, ma'am, my uncle's surprises generally have strings attached if you get my meaning and as you well know he never gives information away for free, so Mr Turner took a heavy purse with him." He paused and then took a step back into the room. "The master will be fine, ma'am, he has certainly sussed out the way to deal with the Roma and besides my uncle actually likes him. Don't worry, ma'am, my uncle would never hurt him…except maybe in the pocket." Mother smiled and thanked him. Robert quickly left with one last glance back at Gabriel, only this time with a slight smile and a nod.

Mother huffed and looked at the assembled company. "It appears we're are on our own once again, Emilie. Gentlemen, perhaps you'd like something stronger than tea, Mr, ah, I'm sorry but I cannot continue just calling you Gabriel."

He smiled and nodded, "De Bearne, madam, Gabriel Antonio Tomas Eduardo de Bearne."

"Thank you, Mr de Bearne, oh excuse me but do you have a title that I should be aware of?"

"No, madam, just money." He chuckled. "My father was a younger son, but a very successful younger son. He has a talent for making money that he passed onto his sons, even a reprobate like me, though my methods in recent years have been rather unorthodox."

With this the Marquis perked up, "De Bearne you say? I believe I might know your father. He and my father once discussed investing in a business venture in England before the war."

Gabriel smiled and nodded. "Papa has always longed to establish himself in England as well as in the America. But it's a risky venture and he is far too cautious. The English can brew spirits such as this whisky and ale with great skill. But their wines, well, they really cannot produce a decent vintage, not enough sun and too much rain. Even you must agree that God created Spain, France and Italy for making wine." All the gentlemen agreed.

The conversation dissolved into talk of wine and England, it was clear that many of us were homesick. But much to my surprise no one had broached the topic of what to do about Charity; after all, she had murdered Julian Browne and I was loath to bring it up myself.

Aunt Emilie and Mother had moved to sit with Charity and I could tell they were talking about children just from the look of wistful longing in Emilie's eyes. I was starting to feel out of place, so I walked over to look out the windows at the garden below. I picked up a book of water colours thumbing through it then finally I just stood there holding onto the open book lost in my own thoughts looking out at the view but not really seeing anything. The garden had changed since our arrival. The blossoms were gone, and the trees were now in full leaf. Autumn was upon us. I heard rather than saw my Aunt Mary and Uncle Arthur leave without saying goodbye. A brief time later I saw Mrs Baxter, Patrick and her father Mr Hillsborough arrive in their delivery cart with a load of dairy products. With them were two small dark-haired boys who were helping to unload the cart. They were so similar in appearance that at first, I thought it was only one boy racing back and forth to the kitchen door. Then one of the boys looked up at me, Gabriel's face was perfectly etched on those cherubic features. I gasped and dropped the book, everyone's head turned to me as I stood rooted to my spot. I could only point at the window, so Dr Jefferson and Gabriel came to my side and looked down. Suddenly Gabriel was pounding on the window next to me almost shattering it, then he turned and raced from the room with the doctor hard on his heels. Patrick looked up and seeing me waved then pointed at the two boys laughing. Charity came to the window and when she saw the boys, she reached out to touch the glass then promptly fainted. The Earl and Marquis came to her assistance, carrying her to the settee. My mother and Aunt Emilie attended to her as I stooped to retrieve the book I had dropped. I looked out the window once again, this time to see Gabriel running across the lawn calling out to the two little boys who were racing towards him.

Mr Hillsborough was smiling from ear to ear as he stood there with his arm around Patrick. Mrs Baxter was at his other side holding onto his arm. I fumbled with the window's latch and opened it then yelled down inviting everyone in for refreshments.

# Chapter 30
## *Reunion*

Charity recovered from her swoon quickly and rushed out to meet Gabriel and their sons. From my place by the window I could see the de Bearne family grouped together on the lawn, experiencing the joy of being reunited. They were totally oblivious to the groom taking the cart and horse to the stables and all the gardeners working around them.

Dr Jefferson escorted Mrs Baxter, Mr Hillsborough and Patrick to the salon. I greeted them while remaining at the window, watching the numerous gardeners below. Allan followed them in with a cart loaded down with cakes, sandwiches, cheese, fruit, lemonade and champagne. He nodded at Emilie. "Beg your pardon, madam, for taking the liberty but I witnessed the reunion and thought that additional libation and cakes were in order." He blushed and almost smiled when Emilie rose, thanking him with a kiss on the cheek.

Mr Hillsborough settled in, delighted to be able to tell us how he came to be in possession of the two de Bearne boys. "I was in the market after having made several deliveries to some of our larger customers. You see I like to deal with them personally, it makes them feel important when I give them the personal touch and sometimes it puts me in the way of new customers. Plus, I'd promised Ida that I pick up a few things for her and Patrick on my way back." He stopped and took a sip of his tea after swallowing a tart whole, once he'd washed it down he continued. "So, I'm in the marketplace and who do I run into, Mrs Turner, but your husband. He was in a hurry and a bit flustered. Both he and his horse looked as if they'd just run a steeplechase. Then Mr Hughes comes up with a gypsy walking two equally winded horses and on top of one of them sat two little boys, the spittin' image of each other. Anyway, the little mites looked fit to drop. But before I could ask what Mr Turner what he was about, he begged me to bring the boys here to their parents but secret-like."

Mother was wringing her hands. "And what of my husband, Mr Hillsborough?"

Mr Hillsborough looked abashed when he answered her, "Why he and Mr Hughes climbed back up on their horses and rode off with the gypsy like the devil himself was after them. I'd not had any time in which to ask them anything. I might say that I was surprised somewhat to see them with a gypsy, though for all the man acted like he was Mr Turner's equal. If I'd known that any were about I'd have bought some liniment for me old bones from them, they do have knack for making fine potions and liniments." Mother and Emilie looked anxious for him to get on with his story, but Mr Hillsborough took no notice and continued. "So, to make a long story short, I stowed the boys in the back of the wagon wrapped up in the new feather bed that Ida had me buy and the tykes went right to sleep. Then I picked up

Ida and Patrick to come along with me since Ida's been complaining that she needs to get out of the house more and I still needed to make your delivery anyway." He looked at his daughter and grinned. "Really though I knew Ida would want to hear about my adventure, but I couldn't stop to tell her since I promised Mr Turner I'd bring them right here. But being a woman, she couldn't wait for me to come back."

Mrs Baxter reared back glaring at her father. "Is that so! Well, I seem to recall you not being sure of how to deal with the lads once you got them here if the family didn't want them. They were that scared, Irene, they were holding onto each other and crying…and it was you father dear that asked me to come along and with Patrick to keep them amused."

She turned beaming at my mother, "It seems from what the boys could tell me that they were lured away from their prior home by someone promising to take them to their mother. But instead they were brought here. They were so well-behaved on the way here, but they clung to each other with all their might, the poor things."

Mother knew that Mrs Baxter wanted to hear the story about the boy's parents and usually she wasn't shy about satisfying her curiosity, but she let it go this time. I looked out the window again, the little family were gone and so were the gardeners. My heart leapt into my throat when I heard voices and the sound of footsteps coming down the hall, Charity, Gabriel and the boys entered the room. Introductions were made, and Mr Hillsborough had to tell his tale again much to his delight. It was obvious that the boys were in no condition to tell us more. Allan saw to having the adjoining room to their parents prepared for the boys so after a few handshakes and a whispered thank you, Charity and Gabriel excused themselves. Naturally they wanted to be alone with their boys so without a word from anyone they walked out the door.

Mrs Baxter was smiling at them as they left, "Well, Mrs Hughes, you seem to have a full house."

Emilie raised both brows and sighed, "So it would seem."

Mr Hillsborough was getting fidgety, I'm sure he was wanting his supper and he said as much. "Well, Ida, I think we should be away. These wee cakes and sandwiches are all very nice but they're not very satisfying." Patrick who had his face buried in a jam tart looked up at his grandfather as if he had lost his mind.

Mrs Baxter shrugged, rising to her feet. "I suppose we'd better be going before you have to turn to eating your shoe leather and Patrick gets a belly ache. Come along, my brave knights, let us adjourn to our own castle." Mr Hillsborough waved his hand at his daughter to move along but bowed over my mother and Aunt Emilie's hand then bowed to me and the gentleman in the room and left.

Patrick came to me mimicking his grandfather by bowing over my hand then he bowed to the both sides of the room. It brought a smile to my face when he ran up to Miles and told him that he had it on good authority that it would be prime weather conditions tomorrow afternoon for kite flying if he was available. Emilie brightened at the idea and suggested that weather permitting we should all enjoy an English picnic the next day. Patrick grinned while asking, "Will there be tarts?" Emilie laughed and nodded. His mother put her arm around him, lecturing him on manners as she exited the room to catch up with her father.

Before long, Mother and Emilie were in full planning mode for the picnic, they hardly needed my input. Dr Jefferson had been speaking to the Earl, the Marquis and

Miles quietly but when I took a seat by Miles, the conversation stopped. "Please, gentlemen, don't let my presence prevent you from continuing your discussion."

Miles laughed openly as he took my hand. "Dr Jefferson, my dear, has a mind to invest in my uncle's London endeavour. So, you are more than welcome to join in."

The Earl looked sharply at Miles but quickly veiled his eyes, the Marquis sat with his eyes downcast. The good doctor as always gave nothing away. I knew he was lying and pursed my lips, I was on the verge of giving them a piece of my mind on men and their ridiculous ideas about a woman's intelligence and specifically regarding their need to shield women from unpleasant truths. But I decided to forgo it when Miles squeezed my hand as if he knew what I was planning. Instead I smiled blandly to convey my displeasure. The doctor and the Marquis both coughed into their hands, but the Earl looked right at me and laughed. "Miles, you were correct, Miss Turner misses nothing and if I'm not mistaken has decided not to chastise us for lying to her just now."

Miles sighed. "I see that marrying an educated and curious woman will cause me no end of problems."

The Earl nodded. "And endless delights as well. Your mother was just such a woman. Perhaps that's why my subsequent choices have been less than satisfactory in the matrimonial line."

Miles sat back looking curiously at his father, "Even Lady Jane?"

The Earl clasped his hands together pursing his lips before saying, "I care for her a great deal, son, but her head is as empty as a cracked egg. She's pleasant enough company, is an efficient housekeeper and an excellent mother, but she could never replace your mother. Maria was the love of my life. While Carolyn on the other hand meant less than nothing to me. I shouldn't have, but I married Jane for purely selfish reasons in a desire not to be alone. And before you ask me, yes, she is aware of my reasons for marrying her. I have always been honest with her." He sighed, looking sad. "Romantic feelings don't seem to run deep in Jane. She is happy with her situation and as far as I am aware has never harboured a grand passion for anyone. Perhaps when I'm gone she will discover that with someone. I sincerely hope so; the girl deserves it, but I don't believe she has it in her." He smiled at me. "You're shocked that I am so pragmatic about my wife. But some women are like that, Miss Turner, they are pleasant people, but they have no passion. Carolyn was cold and empty, she married me only for my title and wealth. Whereas Jane is content within herself, but she is a good friend and a willing listener. She told me before we had married that she had accepted me because it was expected that she should marry and since she had no means to support herself independently I seemed to be an appropriate choice…I ticked all the boxes. But she didn't expect me to love her. I believe she thought I would be kind and not too demanding. Her father was a martinet and a calculating opportunist, he never gave a care to his daughter, she was left with nothing when he died." I smiled at the Earl and at his honesty and looked forward to meeting his lady one day to see if what the Earl said was true…men, after all, are terrible at understanding women.

"Miss Turner, I hope you will forgive us for excluding you. We have in fact been discussing how to go about apprehending both my son and this Ramsey Clarke and return them to England. None of us trust the French to deal with Ramsey effectively and if my son Edward is behind someone shooting at me then I want him in an English court and not somewhere that he or Burley could buy his way out." The Earl looked careworn except whenever his eyes drifted to Miles then they would light up showing the deep affection which he harboured for his son.

"Your concern for justice does you credit, Lord Shellard. But perhaps my father and Uncle Samuel are better suited to the task of apprehending them."

The men laughed, and Miles said, "She has you there, Father. Neither you nor my uncle is of an age to be racing about the countryside looking for miscreants and criminals. While the good doctor is capable he has his instructions to stay here at the chateau to watch over the ladies since I'm still incapacitated with my affliction and can hardly provide them protection without assistance." He voice was a little bitter though he tried not to show it.

Emilie rose from her seat and joined us, "Excuse me, gentleman, Lissa; Dr Jefferson, could I speak with you in private for a moment?"

"Of course, Mrs Hughes," the Doctor bowed and escorted Emilie out of the room.

Mother I noticed was leaving as well but as she reached the door, she said, "Lissa, I'll be with James if you need me, dear." She left with a touch of a smile on her face.

The Earl watched them leave then glanced at me, "I think we can expect an addition to the Hughes family in the near future." I was stunned by this I knew they had been trying but so far had been unsuccessful much to Emilie's disappointment. I could feel the heat rising to face and knew that I was blushing. He chuckled, "My dear, I have been married three times and am the father of five children, I am well aware of the cardinal signs by now." He became reflective suddenly looking back into his past. "I enjoy being a father for the most part. I have four children that I am proud of and I only wish that I could reach out to Edward, but he was never my child, he was always Carolyn's. Perhaps if I had tried harder to counter her influence…" his voice trailed off. "No, I don't think that there was anything that I could have done differently. He came out of the womb poisoned against me." There was profound sadness in his countenance and he looked extremely tired for a moment. Then he shook himself and continued, "With the de Bearnes here and Julian dead, Burley will be seeking his revenge if I know him. Perhaps we should see to the defences of the chateau while we're here, gentleman."

The Marquis grimaced, "Does he have any more sons?"

The Earl made a throaty sound. "Yes, Charles, he has two sons remaining. There is Justin, his heir, and Alexander, his youngest who can't be above twelve years of age. I doubt that he would risk Justin. But he does have two sons-in-law and there is no reason to believe that they aren't involved in the family business ventures."

The Marquis looked deep in thought but did not appear to be paying attention to what the Earl said. He came out of his reverie looking squarely at Miles. "Miles, my boy, has anyone interviewed the staff here at the chateau? I know it's not my place but I'm not sure that they can be trusted."

Miles brow was creased. "What makes you think that?"

His uncle ran his fingertips over his eyebrows. "It maybe be nothing, things have changed so much since I called France home but when I was in the garden yesterday there was very little actual gardening happening, it was more like the gardeners were studying the chateau. Then there was the footman who called them to luncheon rather than the scullery maid. That's rather unusual for a superior servant, don't you think?"

Miles stiffened at my side. "How many gardeners were there, uncle?"

The Marquis bit his lip. "Six, but one was just a boy and the only one who was actually working, he was on his own in the kitchen garden."

I spoke up. "That's Jean, he's the laundress son, he's not here every day. His mother sends him to the village school three days a week. She wants him to be a priest and he wants to be a farmer." I chuckled recalling his plan to fail at Latin to sabotage his mother's plans.

Miles reached for my hand. "Lissa, do you know if he's here today? Did you see him anywhere in the gardens as you stood by the window?"

I smiled because he had been aware that I had been standing by the window but of course he would know, I had called out when I saw the de Bearne boys. "Yes, I did but he's probably in the laundry with his mother now. Miles, there were five gardeners were out there when the de Bearne boys arrived but they're gone now."

Lord Shellard rose to ring the bell. We waited but no one answered. Miles turned to me. "Where are the weapons kept on this floor?"

I hesitated as I slowly realised what he was asking, "This floor but—"

Miles shook my hand. "Lissa, I know your father, even in a strange house Colin and Samuel would be prepared." He called out as the Earl was ready to pull the bell rope again. "Father, please don't pull the bell again. I don't want anyone downstairs to think that we suspect anything. Lissa, think, where are the weapons."

I looked up as the doorway opened and my mother came in with Lettie. "You'll find them in my dressing room in the wardrobe with my ball gowns, it has a false bottom. No one is answering any summons and all the outside staff have disappeared. I've sent Robert to see what's happening below stairs and to locate Mr Allan and Michael. Murphy and Jacob are with the de Bearnes in the nursery already. I suggest that the third floor offers the best means of defence with only one stairwell it is the old fortress part of chateau. Where are Emilie and the doctor?"

"Here!" Emilie called out as she and the doctor came rushing into the room. The doctor looked to my mother, "Michael has retrieved the weapons from your dressing room cache."

Mother calmly directed us to collect blankets, portable refreshments and fuel for the fires as if she expected us to be under siege. As we made our way along the second floor Meg, Beth, Dalton and Emilie's maid Gwen joined us. Huffing up the stairs behind us came Mr Allan with one of the kitchen maids, both fortified with sacks of food stuffs. Mother looked over their shoulders. "Mr Allan, did you see Robert below stairs?"

Mr Allan looked hesitantly at the sullen maid beside him then answered, "Yes, ma'am, he sent the French boy and his mother to the Baxters to bring back help." The maid gave him a withering look as she swept pass us into the nursery.

When we entered the nursery, Gabriel was facing the doorway with a loaded pistol in one hand and a throwing dagger in the other aimed at us. Charity and their boys sat behind him in the corner with James, they were showing him how to stack his blocks. It seemed like an age before Gabriel finally lowered his weapons, so I had to wonder whose side he might be on, if anyone's.

The kitchen maid took over the care of the children and Charity joined Michael as he checked over and organized the weapons. Lettie, Meg and Beth loaded up their crossbows and put them well out of reach of small interested hands. Emilie and Gwen sat with the kitchen maid and the children. Mother loaded several rifles and stood them by the windows while the Earl and Marquis were doing the same. Just then

Robert came stumbling into the room gasping for breath "Oi! I think I found the rest of the staff, but they're locked up in the cellars. I couldn't get to them, there're armed men all over the house." He paused when he saw the kitchen maid giving her a queer look then shrugged as she turned her back to him before he continued to tell us all that he'd seen. Robert reported that there were at least ten men in the house that he had counted and more outside.

Miles had been standing by the door listening and when Robert was done he wasted no time in speaking up, "Gentleman, may I suggest since there is considerable heavy furniture in the hallway that we move as much of it as we can to block the stairwell." Everyone moved immediately to follow his orders.

After that was accomplished I was engaged in sorting ammunitions and loading the pistols, I couldn't help but think back to my kidnapping in London at the hands of Randall Browne then my rescue by Miles followed by the subsequent attack that Brownes had led against us. That time we'd had considerable help from a band of gypsies who sadly were not available to us now. I was worried about Jean and his mother, had they made it to the Baxter's and what could they do? Mr Hillsborough had always been a country squire and though Mrs Baxter had been married to a major I could hardly expect her to lead her workers to storm the chateau and secure our safety. The most we could hope for was that she could rouse the local militia. But as an Englishwoman would she even be able to convince the authorities to send out the militia to a property whose ownership was still in dispute between the people of France and the surviving member of a deposed aristocratic family married to an Englishman. I thought the chance of her rallying any help was less than abysmal.

I don't know what I expected as the time passed, perhaps an attempt to breach the barricades across the stairway, a bombardment of the outside walls or a siege. But nothing happened, so we sat primed and anxious. Emilie and the maids amused the children until James fell asleep. The de Bearne twins became bored with their company until Emilie found a horde of toy soldiers for them to play with.

Miles was sitting by the door listening and fidgeting which was not a good sign; a bored Miles was a dangerous Miles. I walked over to distract him. "What are you doing?" He didn't respond so I changed my question. "Miles, what are you planning?"

He still appeared to be deep in thought and I'd seen that look before, impaired eyesight or not he was not a man to sit idly by. "Humph," he said then looked up at me with a grin. "Remember how dark it can be on this floor?"

I shivered recalling it, "Yes."

"Well, I extinguished all the lights once the furniture was in place. With my heightened senses, I would know if anyone was coming up here long before they could see me." I reared back in shock at what I thought he was proposing, "Miles, you can't possibly go out there!"

He cocked one brow at me. "My eyes are not a handicap in the dark, my dear." He reached up to caress my cheek. I knew he could discern people as male and female and large pieces of furniture in the light. But could he really tell where people were just by listening? "Lissa, please don't argue with me, I have to do this."

I clasped my hand over his holding it in place, "Argue with you! How can I argue with you when I don't even know what you're planning?" I tried to keep my voice down but was failing miserably. The doctor and Murphy came over to stand with us, they had obviously heard some of our conversation and were looking seriously sceptical.

Murphy clapped the doctor on the shoulder saying with hushed bravado. "You'll need to stay here, doctor, in case we need you to put us back to together again. Lettie would never forgive me if I got myself killed." Then he grinned at Miles. "Come then, Mr Johnson, what's the plan before I get cold feet."

Miles smiled. "I can't think of a man I'd rather have at my back Mr Murphy and I do mean my back. I'm the one with the advantage here so I lead, there will be no heroics from you, my friend." Murphy nodded grinning from ear to ear. Then Miles sat up straight, he looked like he was listening intently. "Lissa, is my father staring at me?"

I looked over my shoulder the Earl was glaring at Miles and from the looks of it he was ready to come over and say his piece. I whispered, "Yes he is, and he's headed this way."

Miles sighed stood up and reached for a pair of pistols on the table beside him, shoving them into his waist band. "Lissa, would you please get Murphy a rifle as well as a couple of knives for me."

I knew there was no use arguing with him, so I grit my teeth and as I passed the Earl, said, "Good Luck." The Earl walked up to Miles leaned forward and whispered in his ear. What was said I couldn't hear and Dr Jefferson and Murphy had moved away to give them their privacy. The Earl finally clapped Miles on the shoulder. "Good luck, son." I was astounded! That was all that was it! I had picked up the rifle and a set of throwing knives then carried them over to pass the knives to Miles as I about to hand the rifle to Murphy, the Earl intercepted it. Murphy's empty hand was still extended when the Earl said, "I'm sorry, Mr Murphy, but this will be a father and son expedition only. I taught him how to hunt and track, we've worked together many times in hills of Scotland going after more skittish prey than these louts." He checked a pistol that he'd taken from Miles, then the rifle and lastly, he loosened a knife in his boot.

Miles moved to open the door, but the Earl grabbed his arm then he looked at me with a grin on his face, "Go on, give him a kiss for luck." I stood with my mouth open then looked at my mother and she nodded. I went to Miles putting a hand on his shoulder then I suddenly found myself in his arms pressed close to his firm body with his soft lips against mine. I stop thinking, letting him lead me where he wanted. Someone coughed, and Miles' father cleared his throat. "Miles, son, ah son I think the young lady would like to breathe." Miles lifted his head and chuckled, I did feel lightheaded, but it wasn't from lack of air. He let go of me, opened the door and ducking down low he left, followed closely by his father. The doctor pulled me back shutting the door on them.

I shook off the doctor's hand and pressed my ear against the door until Murphy came to me, "Miss, you'll not hear much through that, it's solid oak, so I suggest for your safety that you at least step away. Mr Johnson would be most distressed if he found you damaged when he returns."

I looked at him through tear-filled eyes. "But what if he calls for me, Murphy, what if he needs me."

He answered me honestly, "He won't call for you, miss, but if he does then it's already too late."

I leaned forward resting my forehead against his chest to steady myself then took a few deep breaths before saying, "I'll just sit here then and wait." I saw Mother and Aunt Emilie were watching me with concern as Murphy assisted me to the seat by the door. He handed me a pistol which I found oddly comforting as I cradled it in my lap. I turned sideways on the chair and leaned my head against the wall straining to hear anything I could from the other side. But there was nothing, not a sound, not even that of a discharged pistol or an angry voice. Surely, I should have been able to hear something. Then I remembered when I had first met Miles he had appeared a menacing dark creature folded onto himself sitting in the half light of the fire after having been brought to our home by my Uncle Arthur. Miles was a man of many faces and temperaments, he had often used subterfuge and disguise to blend in and outwit his enemies, but how could he manage it being almost blind. Then it came to me; this would not be a fire fight. He would not attack from a distance he would use the dark and his heightened senses to find his target and eliminate them quietly so as not to alert the others. He would use his bare hands and a knife. His father was there not to fight but to provide him with cover if he should be discovered or possibly to retrieve his body if he failed. I was sick with worry now, I needed some occupation to relieve my mind of these terrible thoughts. I felt like I was going to be sick.

It was then that Lettie came to stand by me to ask for my advice, I was rather shocked that she would come to me of all people. She pulled up a chair noticing my reluctance to leave my seat and began "It's about Murphy. He's not known to be a patient man and he'd like to get married as soon as possible but I'd like to be wed back in England. We have friends back home and they've become like family." She paused then moving as if to look back over her shoulder but resisted. "I'd like Aedan's sister there as well but that's not my biggest problem. You see Murphy and his sister both have a bit of money and property from their parents and even though Mr Turner has promised to help Dalton with the case of us being robbed of our inheritance…" She fiddled with her shawl as she seemed to pause to gather her thoughts, but she refused to make eye contact.

I patted her clasped hands, "And you feel that you're not bringing anything to the marriage at this point, you want to wait so that you'll feel like an equal partner?"

She nodded and sighed. "That's it, miss. Our father's company is still thriving, and Dalton and I have a right to some of that since our father's shares were never sold. If my father hadn't vanished things would have been different. I would have come to marriage with the dowry that I was raised to expect. So, what I'm asking you is can you help me convince Aedan to wait until it's settled?"

"If I do that, Lettie, he may think that you don't love him or that you don't think he's good enough for you."

She gasped and grabbed my hand, "Oh, my lord, NO!"

I looked over her shoulder and smiled at Murphy who was watching us, he smiled and nodded back. My heart felt heavy remembering my own situation with Miles. "I know that's what I thought when Mr Johnson rejected me based on his lack of prospects. But the heart wants what it wants, how much money you bring to a marriage means very little when you marry for love. Besides it's not like you will ever be destitute or unemployed. But I think your idea of waiting to marry in England is a fine one. Then we can do it up right." She smiled at me then I looked over at Murphy again and suddenly realised that they had intentionally distracted me. I leaned in and hugged Lettie. "Thank you, Lettie, I think I'll be fine now."

She patted my hand. "But what I said is true, miss, and I thank you for your advice; though I don't think Aedan will be appreciative when I tell him that I want to be married at home." She chuckled as she blew him a kiss over her shoulder. "After all, I only plan on getting married once so I might as well do it right."

Just then there was an explosion outside as if cannon had gone off.

# Chapter 31
## *Rescue*

The Marquis was by the window motioning for us to join him, "Come! Come, everyone! Our rescuers have arrived." A bullet hit the window sill and a stone chip flew up, cutting his cheek. He stumbled back but the doctor caught him, assisting him to sit so he could examine it. It wasn't deep and wouldn't even require a suture. Everyone stepped away from the windows at Michael's suggestion, so we had no idea who or how many had arrived. The Marquis said all he had seen were men riding into the stable yard. All we could hear were distorted shouts from below, some clearly in French followed by gun fire. There was still no sound from the hallway, perhaps those in the house had retreated to help their friends or had they overcome Miles and his father and were planning to hold us hostage.

Gabriel stepped forward grabbing a rifle and stood in the alcove of one of the windows. Charity looked no less fierce standing in the one next to him when she yelled, "Gabriel, it's Ramsey! I can see him down there to your left behind the hedge row."

Gabriel shifted around to look in her direction. "How can you tell?"

Through clenched teeth she growled, "I'd know that blond scum anywhere. I'm surprised he's still standing, he doesn't usually join in a fight, he's a coward...he'll run soon."

Gabriel raised his rifle and eased open the window saying, "Not this time." Taking aim, he fired. "Got him." Charity gasped then threw herself away from the casement reaching out to Gabriel who ignored her hand. I could only assume that he'd hit his target since he was absorbed in the sight below. He turned his head looking past Charity to my mother, "It would seem, Mrs Turner, that your brother and husband have arrived and with help." There was even more shooting and yelling coming up from below, it was clearer now that he had pushed the window wide open. Then another explosion went off. Gabriel chuckled. "Your gardeners will not be pleased, Mrs Hughes. The new arrivals just threw a grenade into your Greek folly."

Emilie's head shot up. "Really?!" She grinned. "Then it had to have been Samuel, he hates the thing," she giggled.

Robert ran towards the window, Michael pulled him back, but Robert was persistent and broke away to get to the window. "Hush! People! Listen. Do you hear that?"

The doctor seemed to be straining to hear as well but shrugged. "What?"

Robert grinned from ear to ear. "That's not French, it's Romani, it's them! It's my uncle!" Robert chuckled. "There's nothing that Uncle Jibben likes better than a good fight. Though he prefers to do his fighting close up with a knife and his fists."

Murphy came up to slap Robert on the back. "Why on earth would the man prefer that? There's always a chance that he'd go down first."

Robert bit his lip and said in a sombre voice, "He says that for every life taken there is a weight of responsibility that comes with it. Therefore, you should feel the weight of that action with your own hands and see what you've done in their eyes." He shrugged then said in a bit brighter voice, "That's what he tells the children, but I really think he just likes a good scrap, it keeps him in practice with his knives." I was astonished by his uncle's philosophy that he could be that intellectual about such brutality. All the men nodded as if the whole thing made perfect sense to them; while the women had a mixed reaction somewhere between bewilderment and shock.

As the yelling and screaming continued outside I returned to lean my ear against the wall. I wondered how many men Ramsey had come with. Charity had called him a coward and didn't seem to think he was the type that other men would follow. Yet they were still fighting.

Mother was watching Gabriel who was keeping an eye on the battle below. He stiffened when Charity whispered to him, grabbing hold of both his arms as if to restrain him, his hands were fisted, and his jaw tensed. Mother came to sit by me. "Gabriel's angry and I'm afraid for his family, he may try to go out there."

I asked. "Why?"

"If I'm right, he missed Ramsey and now he's gone."

I watched Gabriel standing with his arm around Charity, both were looking at their boys. I shook my head "He won't leave his family, Mama. Not after just being reunited with them. Besides if he tried, we'd stop him."

She sighed then reached out taking my hand as if to anchor us both in our chairs. I knew what she was feeling, the man she loved was out there in the middle of the battle and the man I cared about deeply was doing lord knows what in the hallway while essentially blind. She squeezed my hand. "Have you heard anything, Lissa?" My mouth was so dry that I couldn't speak but there was really nothing to say so I only shook my head no.

James woke up from his nap, he toddled towards my mother with a huge grin saying, "Bang, bang loud!" he was oblivious to the tension in the room. James made an abrupt turn towards the pistols on the table. Mother gasped as he reached out for one then said with delight, "Guns, Lissa, they go bang, bang!" and before anyone could pull him away he withdrew is hand saying, "Papa say NO to Jem!" then giggled to everyone's delight and turned back to my mother reaching up to her, "Papa was loud." Then he looked at me and asked, "Why you sad, Lissa?"

I had stopped listening for noises from the hallway since James had awakened so I jumped when there was an audible thump against the wall next to me. I was up and at the door with my hand out when Murphy pulled me back and whispered, "No, miss, he wouldn't want you out there." I drew my hand back looking at the door with my hands clenched at my sides. The door handle moved then stopped…then it moved again. Murphy was at my side immediately pulling me to stand behind him. Then the Marquis and Michael joined him to stand in front of me. Allan and Dalton stood to either side while Jacob, Gabriel and Robert stood in front of the other women and children. Suddenly I felt lightheaded then realised that I had been holding my breath. I took a deep breath as we waited, it seemed as if time had stopped. I noticed the Marquis wipe his hand across his brow and that the scratch on his cheek was red and angry looking. Michael and Murphy made identical gestures of dragging their knuckle across their lips as if in anticipation of what was on the other side of the door. Allan and Dalton had both been former soldiers, one a deserter and one an aid decamp, they shuffled nervously from one foot to the other but appeared no less determined than Murphy or Michael. There was another hard thump against the door then the sound of something or someone sliding down and hitting the floor, then silence. Murphy edged towards the door and as he reached out there was the sound of a gun being fired at close range very near the door. He automatically jumped back motioning for us to step to either side and away from the doorway. Finally, I heard a voice, "Lissa, let us in! My father needs the doctor." There was a gruff muffled retort followed by some equally gruff mumbling. I ran to the door before anyone could stop me and jerked it open.

Slumped against the doorjamb was Miles, his father was leaning heavily on him and both were dripping sweat and covered in blood. Yet they were grinning and chuckling like fools. Both sounded incredibly wheezy as if they barely had a breath to spare but they continued laughing as the other men helped them into the room. The Earl looked at me with a smile nodding towards Miles, "Can you believe it, Miss Turner. He stabbed me! The boy actually stabbed his own father!" Then he let out a hearty laugh as he extended his arm for me to see the blood dripping down his arm. The doctor stepped forward and assumed command of the situation.

Miles turned to me smiling, "I told him to stay behind me but he's so used to being in charge."

From a seat by the window the Earl retorted, "Ha! It was two against one, you think I was going to stand back and watch one of them slice you open!"

Miles slumped to what had been my seat by the door. I examined him as closely as I could without him being aware but found no evidence that any of the blood was his. "I had it under control, old man." He took a drink from the bottle that Murphy handed him, grimaced then said, "Besides if you were so concerned, why didn't you just shoot him instead?"

The Earl turned away from the doctor as he tore open the sleeve of his shirt to get a better look at his arm. He grimaced sucking in his breath before answering, "What! And let you have all the fun. It's been a while since I've fought in close quarters, it was exhilarating!" He bit his lip and grunted as the doctor probed his wound, making it bleed more. "I was thinking that perhaps we should resume our weekly fencing matches at Whitley's when we return to England. What do you say?"

Miles was emotionally and physically exhausted and concerned about his father, but he chuckled a bit, passed his hand over his face before saying, "Father, in case you've forgotten in all the excitement I am basically blind, and you want to fence?! Don't you think that would give you an unfair advantage!" then he laughed and gulped down the rest of the bottle of ale.

The Earl gasped as the doctor poured brandy over his wound to clean it. The Earl jerked the bottle from the doctor's hand and took a quick drink from it before he passed it back to him with a bleak smile. But he still answered Miles back, "Ha! That didn't stop you out there and besides the rapiers will be buttoned. Perhaps Miss Turner will join us? I hear that she has some skill."

Mile pursed his lips and shook his head, "Doctor, do you think perhaps you could sedate my father?"

Dr Jefferson gave him a sharp look. "I hardly think," then he saw the smirk on Miles lips as he tried to contain his laughter, but it was the doctor who barked out a laugh as he bandaged the Earl's arm. The Earl glared at Miles but finally couldn't help himself and started to chuckle as he picked up the brandy from the table beside him.

Then Miles let loose with a belly laugh and the tension leeched out of his body leaving him exhausted, but at the same time elated. He had proved to himself that even without his sight he was still of value, still a man. My heart ached for him and I prayed that his new-found sense of self-worth wouldn't dissipate so that he'd slide back into despair because of his infirmity.

He finally sensed my presence nearby and held out his hand out to me. I sank down to the floor leaning my head against his knee. He ran his hand over my hair as he leaned back in the chair and sighed. No one was in hurry to look out into the hallway, but the doctor felt obliged to venture out to see if anyone might still be alive, Gabriel accompanied him. They returned grim-faced and somewhat awed, Gabriel spoke out in disbelief, "There are six dead men out there!"

The Earl shook his head and mumbled from his position leaning against the window, "Damn! Two of them got away."

Gabriel's mouth hung open then he snapped it shut. "But how?"

Miles sat up and put his hand on my shoulder. "Stealth mainly; my father and I make a good team."

I looked at him puzzled. "I thought your father was supposed to stay behind you."

The Earl barked out a laugh. "He knew there was no chance of that happening. Besides where do you think he gets his stubborn streak from." He grinned at his son then became instantly sober. "We fell into an easy tandem of covering each other, it was reflexive." He sighed deeply then, "Doctor, tell me is it night vision or his hearing that makes him so accurate? It was really remarkable; he could pick out their hiding places in mere seconds." Then he looked long and hard at his son who was slumped back in his chair with his eyes closed and spoke quietly while watching him, "Still to take a life is no small thing no matter how justified, it numbs the soul." I looked up at Miles, his exhaustion was apparent but there was a sadness there as well which was the proof of his father's words.

Mother had been looking intently out the windows, suddenly she was pounding her hands against the glass. I got up and raced to her side, on the lawn far below us my father was approaching a hedgerow where Ramsey was crouched taking aim at my father. Then suddenly a shot rang out, the report was so loud I would swear that it had come from this room. All I could look at though was the smoke from a shot below and my father lying on the ground, not moving, and Ramsey had disappeared. Gabriel jerked out of the alcove where he had been and grabbed two pistols, ramming them into his waist band, then took a rifle with him as he ran out the door. He was followed by Murphy, Michael, Dalton and Robert, all armed to the teeth. Mr Allan closed the door behind them. The Marquis was explaining to Miles what had happened while I had turned back to the windows to see my father regain his feet with no apparent injury. Uncle Samuel raced to his side then pointed up to our windows. It was then that I noticed Charity stood with a spent rifle at her side, her sons holding onto her skirts as she blankly stared out the window. I willed her to look at me, but she didn't, she merely said as if she knew I was watching her, "I saved your father, Miss Turner, but I missed my chance to kill that bastard Ramsey. I hope you appreciate what that cost me."

269

Mother reached out and took her hand. "I do, Madam de Bearne. Thank you."

Charity cocked her head as if she hadn't heard Mother correctly, then she smiled slightly and knelt in front of her boys. "Mama has to help clean up in the hallway…you stay here with Mademoiselle Rennet." She pointed to the kitchen maid who was pulling biscuits out of one of the sacks. "See, she is making a snack for you already!" The rest of us followed her out leaving Emilie, the Earl and Miles behind.

Miles had suggested that we store the bodies in one room and sort it out later which we did. Mother, Meg, Beth and Gwen cleaned out a box room at the head of the stairs, they moved the luggage and boxes from there into the schoolroom next to the nursery. Charity, Lettie and I searched the bodies for anything to identify them, they were all strangers except for the one footman, none of the others were chateau staff. Suddenly I had a flash of an image cross my mind, the look on Robert's face when he had seen the kitchen maid. My heart leapt into my throat immediately as it hit home, Robert's look had been one of momentary confusion, was that because he didn't recognize her, or did he wonder how she had escaped capture? Suddenly a shot rang out and then a crash came from behind us. My mother, Charity and I ran for the nursery. The snack items were scattered all about the floor and Miles stood over the kitchen maid with a gun in one hand and a knife in the other, a spent pistol was mere inches from the maid's side. The de Bearne boys were standing behind Miles holding onto Emilie's skirts and James was in her arms. Mother immediately went to Emilie and took James, cuddling him so tightly that he started to whimper till she relaxed her grip. The maid was in the corner with her back against the wall. She hissed and spat at Miles as he questioned her in French.

Then we heard people pounding up the stairs yelling our names.

Mother raced to the door and yelled back, "In the nursery, Colin!"

Father and Uncle Samuel raced into the room pulling their wives into their arms, making the rest of us blush from the intimacy of their embrace. Michael and Murphy restrained Mademoiselle Rennet, leaving her seated in the corner.

Father went to stand over the maid, "Well, mademoiselle, you are in a great deal of trouble. I understand from the local militia that you and your band have been being causing enough mayhem in the district that they're ready to hang the lot of you without a trial." He paused but she only looked at him with utter contempt. "If you have anything to say in your defence you should say it now because after what happened here today I wouldn't doubt the commander's words for a second." Her eyes got very big and a single tear slid down her cheek. He loomed over her with his hand against the wall and a knife in his hand. My father was a man of infinite patience for many things but an attack on his family was not one of them. "Who hired you?"

She bit down on her lip looking from side to side as if she hoped one of her confederates would come to her rescue. Then she smiled smugly and shook her head. "You will get nothing out of me, English pig!" She spat at my father's shoes.

Uncle Samuel approached her from the opposite side to lean in. "You have a younger brother, I believe. His name is Gaston?" She was sweating now as she looked from my father to Samuel and back again. "He works here in the stables, doesn't he? He's been badly hurt, mademoiselle." Her eyes became wild as she strained at her bonds, kicking and thrashing.

Father reached out and smacked her across the face. I recoiled taking a step back to grasp Miles' hand. Then he spoke to her in a very soft, concerned tone, "Listen to me, mademoiselle, he's badly hurt and may die if he is not cared for. I can have the doctor take care of him." She closed her eyes refusing to respond. Then my father shouted, "MADEMOISLLE!" Then lowering his voice he said in a threatening tone, "He is suffering unspeakable pain and I don't care if he dies. But you do." She glared at him then spit in his face, catching him on the cheek. She chuckled as he wiped it away with his sleeve. He reached out grabbing her by the hair, banging her head against the wall then he slapped her again. "Well?" She turned her face away from him. He inhaled deeply, "Fine, he dies!" He walked away to one of the open windows signalling to someone below.

Mother called our sharply, "Colin, you can't!" But he ignored her,

Uncle Samuel looked down at the maid "He'll do it...he'll have one of the gypsies put a bullet in Gaston! Your brother was not part of the plan, was he? He was supposed to have gone to the farrier's in the village, but the head groom went instead. Your brother had no idea what was happening. Do you know that he fought on our side? He was hurt by one of your men, Marion...it's serious."

Father turned back to her with a look that was so cold it chilled me. "Come...look, he's in the yard." Samuel helped her to her feet but before she could move my father looked back to the window, "My men will shoot on my signal."

Samuel helped her to walk to the window. I looked out the one near Miles. Gabriel was standing over someone who was lying on the ground. Marion looked down and screamed then tried to kick my father. I understood now why she was afraid, it was because it was Gabriel standing over the boy. She knew that he would not hesitate to kill her brother. She licked her lips looking at both my father and uncle then standing up straight, "You wouldn't! He's an innocent, that would be murder! The captain of the militia will take a dim view of the..." then she spat the next words out... "an ENGLISH murdering a citizen of FRANCE!" She ended it by cackling like a crone.

Father grabbed her by the neck forcing her to look out the window as he pointed down. "His death will be on your head, not mine." He raised his hand and leaned out the window to shout, "Gabriel!"

"NO!" She yelled.

He stopped to look down at her. His face was devoid of emotion until he smiled, but that smile never reached his eyes. "Who hired you?"

She struggled for a bit, "I don't know."

Father looked at her with contempt and yelled, "LIAR!" turning back to the window.

She whimpered, "NO! Please monsieur. The money, it came from Ramsey, but the plan was not his. He is too stupid, he was only the messenger. There was another man, but I never got a good look at him. He came to the tavern only at nightfall and stayed in the shadows. He would go straight to a private parlour where Ramsey met with him then he'd leave before dawn, but I never saw his face, he was always cloaked."

Father came within inches of her face. "Do you expect me to believe that you never had him followed? You've been at this far too long, Marion, to be that sloppy." She drew back from him, obviously shocked so he continued, "The militia captain knows a great deal about you, mademoiselle, he would love to catch you and your band. It seems you've been terrorizing the citizens of France as well as travellers in this region for some time. He expects me to turn you over to him." He paused to let that sink in, "That is if I capture you."

She glared at him and in a sceptical voice said, "Now who is the liar."

Father laughed. "Your band has been decimated, Marion. Those that we didn't kill, or capture, have run, and I doubt you'll ever see them again. So, tell me what you know."

She sighed. "I want to see my brother first."

My father looked at Dr Jefferson. "Can you see to the boy, please?" The doctor nodded and gathered his things together. "He's not in any condition to be brought up here and you, my dear, are going nowhere until we have our little chat." Her eyes followed the doctor as he left the room with his bag. "The doctor will take care of him, you have my word." Marion looked over her shoulder at my Uncle Samuel and he nodded. Then her bravado dissipated before my eyes she was no longer the leader of a band of cut throat thieves, she was a defeated woman worried about her brother."

Miles stepped forward and whispered to my father who turned red to the ears and nodded. I couldn't tell if he was angry or embarrassed. Then I followed his eyes as they looked around the room, all the children were terrified. Charity knelt holding tightly to her sons who looked on the verge of tears. James had his head buried in my mother's shoulder, sobbing, Emilie looked like she was about to faint. Meg, Beth and Gwen were nearly in tears and Lettie stood next to Murphy white-faced holding tightly to his arm. Then I realised what Miles must have said that this was not the place to conduct an interrogation. I looked down, both my hands were fisted. I could feel my nails biting into my palms and my knees were shaking. Dalton and Robert returned speaking briefly to my father and uncle then they took Marion by the arms and led her out of the room.

A short while later as we were trying to sort out what had happened below, Jibben entered the room with another man that looked like he belonged on the deck of a pirate ship. Suddenly I recognized him, he had been a pirate! It was Dr Peter Grimes, the coroner for the Bow Street Runners. He was a dark little man with a gold tooth and an extraordinary gold earring dangling from his right ear. He was laughing as he entered then abruptly stopped and bowed when he saw us. "Good afternoon, ladies, it's a pleasure to see you all again."

# Chapter 32

## *Negotiations*

Aunt Emilie stepped forward. "Welcome to our home, gentlemen, and thank you for your timely intervention below."

Jibben chuckled then bowed in a most courtly fashion with the grace and ease as if he had been born to it. He looked around at the company assembled then laughed out loud when his eyes fell on the Earl. "Ah, William, it is good to see you again, my friend! Thank you for the stables and barn you have built for my people at our winter home. Grandmamma was very impressed by the gesture, you will always be welcome at our fires." He arched an eye when he saw the Earl's bandaged arm but remained silent.

Then he turned to my father. "Turner, my men are cleaning up outside, but the authorities have arrived." Father frowned and took a step toward the door when Jibben reached out and grabbed his sleeve. "Not to worry, they are pleased that we have dealt with everything. They've taken the prisoners and the bodies. They have offered to take the boy home to his mother, so he can tell her what happened to his sister." My father only nodded, he was obviously upset by what he had been forced to do to Marion by using her own brother. Then I noticed Jibben staring long and hard at Miles with a very quizzical look, touched with compassion.

Miles' face was complacent when he said, "Stop boring a hole through me, Jibben, it makes my skin crawl. And before you ask, I've discussed it with my father and yes you may have access to his stone quarry to build more permanent homes on the site. I suppose that my neighbours will raise an objection but as the saying goes in for a penny in for a pound. However, you cannot divert any of the streams, do you hear me! I would prefer to maintain some of my neighbour's goodwill. But you may dig a well. Hopefully that will keep you from mucking up my stable yard drawing water. Remember the same rules apply to those that stay behind during your travelling season. I hope that we are clear on that. It means that all your people remain responsible for their actions and everyone will suffer the consequences of any violations." Miles couldn't see Jibben's changing expressions, but he ran the gamut from anger to humour as Miles continued, "I promise though there must be irrefutable evidence of guilt and not just suspicion for me to evict you. So please don't betray my trust. I rather not have to leave my home or be burnt out." Miles flopped back in his chair as if that speech had exhausted him.

Jibben chuckled but continued to watch Miles closely. "I would expect no less from you, Miles."

Then suddenly his attention turned to me. "Miss Turner, you have grown into a lovely young woman. If I was not already promised to someone I would take you as my wife." He looked back at Miles, grinning, "But I have many young men with me who are still looking for wives so if you do not intend to claim her, Miles, I cannot be responsible for their conduct." Miles sucked a breath in through his teeth and glared in the direction of Jibben. Why was he baiting Miles? "She needs a whole man," he paused to look Miles up and down then grinned, "one with eyes that work."

Miles stood up with clenched fists while everyone else stood by and watched the scene unfold. Jibben remained relaxed and unconcerned and Miles said nothing, he just turned on his heel and stormed out of the room barely missing the doorjamb.

I walked up to Jibben and moved to slap him, but he caught my hand leering at me. Murphy, Dalton and Robert moved towards me, but my father put up his hand and they stopped. Jibben dropped my hand. "Your father has told me and my cousin," he pointed to Dr Grimes, "about what happened. He has listened to your father and uncle talk about his affliction and he thinks his continued blindness might be of the mind and not physical."

I was outraged. "How dare you say that Miles is feigning his injury."

Dr Grimes shook his head at me. "Not feigning, Miss Turner. It could be that his brain truly believes that he is blind. He was severely traumatized while in prison with no reason to believe that he would ever leave there alive. What he went through has taken its toll and it may have been too much for him to endure so he became blind. It is much the same as a hysterical paralysis where the body cannot move even though there is nothing physically wrong. In short, Miss Turner, he is afraid to face the world again. I would like to try and help him if I can."

I wanted to stamp my foot and yell that he was truly blind but instead whirled on him, "Miles is the bravest and kindness soul I know. So why—why would he do that to himself; why?"

Dr Jefferson had returned and interjected, "Lissa." He paused searching for the right words. "Miles was tortured horribly, there are forms of torture that a man like a woman cannot abide. He is haunted by it and feels like he is less of a person because of it. He's experiencing a devastating shame because he believes that he might have done something to deserve it. Miles still has nightmares, does he not?" I nodded. "Yet he has never shared the contents of those dreams with you, has he?"

I shook my head. "No, but," then I realised what he was hinting at. I whispered just loud enough that others heard. "He was raped?" The doctors both nodded.

My mother came to me wrapping me in her arms. I was fused to the spot. "Who—who did this to him?" I was getting angry, I could feel the heat coming up from my gut. I wanted to lash out at that person, to kill them!

Father took my hand and pulled me to sit down. I looked at the Earl and Marquis, they were both grim-faced. I looked back at my father. "The guard from the jail couldn't describe the man in any detail other than that he was English with dark hair, so it was probably either Julian or Edward."

I pulled my hands from him. "And Miles knows this?"

Father nodded his head, "Yes."

"Why didn't he tell me, I have to go and speak with him." I stood up pushing my way past those near the door and ran after Miles, not knowing where he had gone and not listening to the shouting behind me. I searched everywhere I could think of until it came to me that he wouldn't go to any place where we had been together; not with those dark thoughts from his days of imprisonment as his sole companions. I stood at the foot of the garden and looking around at the torn flower beds, grass and shrubs. Then I stared out towards what was left of the folly that my uncle so detested.

I saw a flicker of movement within the ruins and ran to it. He was there, sitting on the one remaining bench, his elbows on his knees and his head in his hands. His shoulders were shaking in silent sobs. I walked over to him and sat down. When he didn't turn to acknowledge me, I reached out and gathered him into my arms. We sat together with my arms around him while we both cried together for his pain, the pain that I had been too shallow to see. We sat there until the sun started to go down. I was without a cloak and was freezing but I would stay with Miles for as long as he stayed there. He finally wrapped his arms around me and we continued to just sit there, not speaking a word to each other. There was enough warmth within the circle of his arms to sustain me, so we leaned on each other.

Finally, he kissed my hair and let go of me, standing up he offered me his hand and we returned to the chateau hand in hand. We went to our rooms to clean up and change our clothes. And when we returned to the foyer Allan was there to greet us. We followed him to the breakfast room even though we could hear voices coming from the main dining room. He smiled at both of us. "The others said for you to take your time and join them later if you wish." Allan opened the door and we were greeted by warmth and the succulent smell of hot food on the table. We say across from each other then he looked at me for the first time since I had joined him in the folly. "I suppose you want an explanation."

"No, Miles, you don't have to explain anything to me."

He shuddered then whispered, "So you know?" I could barely hear him, but I knew what he had asked me.

"I know now, the doctor told me." He just sat there with his head bowed looking at the plate in front of him. "Miles! I love you, I always have, that's not changed, it never will! But you need to talk to someone about it. You need to let the anger out or it will consume you, my love."

He hesitated then with barely contained fury yelled, "My ANGER? You talk about anger! WELL WHAT ABOUT MY SHAME!"

His yelling startled me, but it got my ire up as well. I was angry at Edward, Julian and at Miles. But I tried to be composed. I didn't succeed as I heard my own voice raised, "DID YOU CONSENT to this violation! DID you ask for IT?!" then at just above a whisper I added, "Could you have fought back, or did you choose not to?"

His face was a mask of incomprehension then he looked shocked, "NO! No, of course not. I fought but I wasn't able to stop it...you can't."

Reaching across the table to him I took his hand in mind, "Miles, I don't expect you to get over this quickly, if ever. But you cannot let it define who you are. I'll help you any way I can, I swear!"

His shoulders slumped forward saying my name like he was a child, "Lissa."

I grabbed his hand hard willing him to look at me which he finally did and in a hushed voice full of my love for him, I said, "I love you, Miles, we are meant to be together. I know that in my heart. Are you trying to tell me that you don't feel the same way?"

His facial expression almost broke my heart. "Lissa, I am not the man I once was. I'm...I'm damaged."

Once again, he managed to enflame my ire, so I shouted at him, "This is beyond ridiculous! You are NOT damaged! You have been terrorized and violated, but you are still Miles Johnson!" I closed my eyes, I was so incensed I needed to concentrate and not let my temper get the better of me. But I lost that battle and through clenched teeth hissed, "I swear to God that I could kill Julian and Edward with my bare hands! I will not let them take you away from me!" Then I found my calm centre, it was Miles, he was looking at me with the most compassionate expression, so I squeezed his outstretched hand, "Just talk to Dr Grimes, Miles…he believes he can help you. Please, for our sake." Miles came around the table and pulled me from my seat, holding me in his arms, anchoring us to each other then he bent his head and kissed me.

When he finally released me, he said with a touch of humour and pain, "You have more spirit in you than I realised, poppet. I can see that a life with you will never be dull!" He pulled me back into a hug full of love. "Julian is dead, let's leave him dead and as for Edward, he's mine to deal with."

We both turned at a noise from the doorway where the Earl stood. "No, Miles, Edward is mine. If he did this to you…he is mine to deal with." The Earl stood there at rigid attention and his look brooked no discussion.

I opened my mouth, but the Earl put up his hand, "A death, Miss Turner, comes with a price and no one here will pay that price. Instead, I shall take away everything that means anything to him. Society will shun him when I'm done with him. I doubt that even Carolyn's family will take him in once I'm finished. He can live in Wales with Carolyn's cousin, they're of the same ilk, they can ruin each other with the little money that I will leave Edward with." His features melted when he looked back at Miles. "I hope though to live a sizable number of years and last long enough to see my children and your children grow into adults." With that he walked back out the door and left me standing beside Miles.

Miles stared at the doorway. "Does everyone know what happened?"

I nodded and whispered, "Yes."

He held himself up straight fingering his caveat as if it was too tight. "Well, then, I won't have to worry about baring my soul to the whole company, thank God. You're right, my love, I will follow your suggestion and talk to Dr Grimes, I would very much like to get my sight back." I burst into tears and flung my arms around his neck. He bent down and kissed the top of my head. "I think we should join the others now. I'm not very hungry, are you?" I shook my head no. Then he made a choking noise in his throat. "I think I had better face them all now before I lose my nerve, it will be easier than dealing with them one at a time." I agreed, and we walked hand in hand into the drawing room.

Jibben, Dr Grimes, Father and Uncle Samuel were at a table with a map, arguing over of all things shares and a smuggling ring. Jibben saw us come in and waved us over, "Johnson, can you please explain to Turner and Hughes that my people are not militia to be ordered about at his whim and that we do not recognize his authority!" Then he looked back at my father's stern face. "If we are to help him with the smugglers then we must be allowed to take our SHARE!" He exploded on that last word and waved his arm around.

Father was equally incensed. "I have never heard of such an outrageous proposition! You stole from the crown before, Jibben, and the crown was willing to let it go then, but not again!"

Jibben continued in a growl. "So we must wait for the King to grant us compensation! Why should we when the compensation would already be in our hands! Bah, you English." He turned to pick up a glass that I assumed contained

276

brandy and drained it in one gulp. Then slamming the glass down on the table, he glared at my father looking like a blood-thirsty pirate.

Father was looking almost as equally affronted, "May I remind you, sir, that you are English too."

Jibben slapped his chest. "I am Roma! Not English!" He looked as if he was going to spit and changed his mind at the last minute when he caught sight of Aunt Emilie.

Miles ran his finger down his nose clearly trying not to laugh. "Jibben, if I'm not mistaken you were born in Wiltshire and your father is an English gentleman, that makes you English in the eyes of the crown."

Jibben fish mouthed for a few seconds. "Then the crown is blind! I am Roma first!"

Miles managed to only just choke back a laugh. "Be that as it may we have had this discussion before about the law and how it applies to you. If you were to take anything not allotted to you that would be stealing and the law takes a very dim view of that." He cleared his throat just managing to control his mirth as he continued. "However, I'm sure that you and Colin can come to an agreement for compensation that can be taken at the time."

Jibben pointed at Miles and called out, "HAH, you see, Turner, this man understands!"

My father pursed his lips and Miles raised his hands to stop anyone from saying anything untoward, so he continued, "Jibben, that would be with the expectation that there would be no further compensation forthcoming in the form of reward or recognition later."

Jibben slapped him on the shoulder. "You see, Turner, that's how you negotiate. You English never dicker, that is why you always make bad deals." He spat in his hand and held it out to Miles. "My hand, Johnson, take it and we have a deal."

Miles snorted then nodded in the direction of my father. "I don't have the authority to bargain, Jibben. That would come under the jurisdiction of Mr Turner." Jibben eyed my father up and down then slowly held out his hand. Father looked from Jibben to Miles who made a spitting action into his hand. Father's eyes became enormous then looked back at Jibben with scepticism. But to his credit he took a deep breath spit into his hand and held it out to Jibben and they shook, then Jibben laughed heartily, pulling him into a bear hug!

Father grimaced glaring at Miles and when Jibben released him, Father whispered to Miles as he was wiping his hand off on his handkerchief, "How much did I just agree to?"

Miles shrugged. "It depends on the goods and how valuable they are to Jibben's people and what is the inherent risk of the plan you got him to commit to."

Jibben was standing with a huge grin on his face while Uncle Samuel laughed and offered Jibben another drink. My uncle took up his glass of lemonade and they toasted the partnership. Miles then adjourned to speak to Dr Grimes. The Earl and Marquis were sitting over a chess board engrossed in their game, Dr Jefferson had moved away from Dr Grimes to watch the chess game only to be called over to the map table as it was cleared, and a deck of cards appeared.

Mother and Emilie stopped talking when I sat down. I looked at them suspiciously. "There is no need to stop or did I interrupt a private conversation."

Mother patted my hand. "Not really private, my dear. But it's something that we don't want to burden your father and Samuel with."

I knew I looked puzzled and Aunt Emilie was looking around cautiously. "We don't want to tell them yet. Dr Jefferson knows, of course, but—"

Then it dawned on me and I had to restrain my reaction, "Oh my god, Emilie, the Earl was right, you are expecting!"

Emilie smiled and nodded then quickly glanced at the card table, but the men were completely engrossed in their game. "But how did the Earl know?"

I smiled. "He told me that he knows the signs after being a father five times."

She giggled looking at him. Then she turned her smile on me, "Not only will you be an aunt, but you'll be a sister again too."

My mouth fell open and I looked at my mother. I could see the blush on her cheek and that both ladies were a bit fuller in the face, then I remembered that they had not always looked their best at the breakfast table recently but seemed to bloom as the day moved on. I leaned in and kissed them both on the cheek. "When will you tell them?"

They both looked at each other and shrugged then Mother said, "So much has been happening lately we didn't want to throw them into a panic."

"Mother, you do know that something is always happening in our lives. Look at Papa and Uncle Samuel, they both look care worn, perhaps some good news would make them feel better."

Mother looked around. "Not now!"

I shook my head. "No. But maybe later when you're alone?" She smiled and nodded in agreement.

"Lissa, are you and Miles—I mean, is Miles—"

My heart clenched because I wasn't sure what she was asking but I answered as best I could, "We'll be fine, Mother. It will take time and hopefully Dr Grimes can help him. I think he'll be better now that what happened to him isn't a secret from the people that care about him and love him."

Mother yawned and decided she would go and check on James before retiring for the evening. Aunt Emilie was going to check on the de Bearnes, they had retired right after dinner to spend time together as a family and to bond with their children once again. That left me as the sole female in the room a prospect that would put me at a decided disadvantage in any conversation, so I rose with them to retire to my room. All the gentlemen expressed their sorrow to lose our company and at the same time there was an undercurrent of childlike excitement that ran through them. Let them plan their war against the smuggling ring. I knew that there would be no place for me in the confrontation to come.

As we left we met Gabriel walking across the hallway making for the drawing room. "Ah, ladies, is everyone retiring?"

My mother smiled, "No, Mr de Bearne, you are still in time to join in the fun."

He seemed taken aback, "Excuse me, Madame Turner?"

"I'm sorry, I shouldn't make light of what my husband and brother are planning."

He looked at the three of us and quirked one eyebrow, "And what are they planning?"

It was my father who answered him from the drawing room doorway, "A raid on Lord Burley and his smuggling ring."

Gabriel whistled through his teeth. "Indeed!" Then he smiled ear from ear, "May I be of assistance?"

Father gave him an appraising look. "I would have thought you'd seek out your uncle and return to your family in Spain."

Gabriel laughed. "My uncle knows I am alive and there will be much to discuss with him eventually. But my family has thought me dead for some time, so a little while longer will not hurt." He stopped smiling and became deadly serious. "Besides, I owe the Clarkes and Brownes my undivided attention. I only ask that you keep my wife and sons under your family's protection while I assist you in this business."

Father was partially in shadow, but I could see his frown and Gabriel could as well. He responded with a challenge in his voice, "You need me, Turner! I know how they do things." Then he relaxed losing some of his bravado but none of his anger, "I need to be part of this, let me assist you. I promise you will not regret it."

No one spoke for a time as if we were all frozen in that moment. Father looked at him sighing, "De Bearne, I can't afford to have you to go off on a personal vendetta and jeopardize our plan."

Gabriel shook his head. "You have no idea how deep this operation runs. It's not just Burley, he uses people, powerful people through blackmail and threats much like he did Mrs Turner's father." He stretched out his arm and pointed at my father, raising his voice, "But you and Hughes have proven to be his only stumbling block." He lowered his arm and his voice. "Even Hughes' drinking problem was not sufficiently embarrassing to use against him since he openly acknowledges it. Neither you nor he have any other vices to exploit. Even the Earl is an open book just as is the Marquis. There is nothing in any of your pasts that will serve his purpose. So, it has come down to who will survive—you or him. Beware, Turner, he will stop at nothing to destroy you, your family and friends."

Father was watching him closely and had not interrupted or changed his stoic expression. "Mr de Bearne, you're telling me nothing that I'm not already aware of, so how do I know that I can trust you?"

Gabriel laughed out loud and his laughter brought the other gentlemen to the doorway. "I have asked you to protect my family. Do you honestly think I would leave them in your hands only to betray you? You have to take a chance at some point, Turner, and I'm offering my services to enact my revenge."

Father stood unmoved just watching Gabriel, the tension kept building, it was my mother who finally stepped forward. "He's right, Colin, he won't betray you. He needs your help as much as you need his information." She looked pointedly at Gabriel. "Otherwise, his revenge would be murder." Father appeared to be considering Gabriel's offer as Mother walked over to him and took his arm. "Colin, you know that you would do exactly the same thing if you were in his shoes." And with that she kissed him on the cheek then went up the stairs followed by Emilie.

Gabriel walked over to stand beside my father as I looked on, "You have a remarkably astute wife, Turner, and she's right, we need each other."

# Chapter 33
## *Loose Ends and Going Our Separate Ways*

Over the next few days, things did not progress as swiftly or exactly as we would have liked. The ambassador wanted an answer he could live with regarding the murder of Julian Browne, so the plan was to tell him the truth with just a few essentials left out. The de Bearns presented themselves with their children to Lord Grenville and they explained their story in detail that they had followed Julian to the Embassy party and then followed him outside. When they saw him walking away quickly with a woman who seemed to be resisting, they were torn between going after him and going back for help. They chose to follow and attempt to aid the lady. But before they could catch up with him they heard a shot. Mr Johnson was standing ahead and to the right of them with a gun at his side, but they were positive that the shot hadn't come from his gun and they would swear to it. When other people came to assist the young lady, they left without knowing that the shot had been fatal. It was close enough to the truth that it stood up to cross questioning and verification in as much as my father and uncle were willing to provide. Lord Granville was walking a diplomatic tight rope and that he was not in possession of all the facts. But he was wise enough to know that it was probably a good thing particularly since Gabriel's Uncle Francisco was on the verge of being called back from exile and into the position of a potentially powerful ally to England. Julian on the other hand was a proven kidnapper as verified by the de Bearne boys and my father plus he had attempted to abduct me. My Father pointed out that this could be a huge embarrassment to England and the ambassador, so he suggested that the official story should be that Julian had been shot attempting to prevent my abduction by one of the gang of thieves terrorizing Paris and the countryside. The ambassador decided without prompting that the de Bearnes wouldn't be mentioned in the official report. It was not a neat nor clean story, but it was acceptable to all parties. The death of Julian Browne was labelled as death by misadventure in the attempt to save me. I wondered how ironic it would seem to Lord Burley that the very people he sought to destroy had saved his family's name from being sullied.

Mr Dunhill was also on the list of things to be dealt with, he had not been cooperative when questioned until Gabriel appeared with my Uncle Samuel. It turned out that he had been blackmailing many of Embassy guests and they were very happy to discover that he was under arrest for treason. The disposal of his case was left up to the ambassador to handle through normal channels. No one felt he would survive long in prison if he even made it there. But the ambassador had masters to answer to just as my father did and they may consider it easier to dispose of Mr Dunhill than to try his case in a court of law.

Ramsey Clarke was still missing though Charity swore she had at least wounded him but by the time Gabriel had arrived on the scene he had disappeared, leaving his confederates to take the blame for his crimes as well as theirs. When Marion, the band's leader, was questioned, she insisted that she didn't know where Ramsey had gone. Her brother told us that Marion had often met a blond man at a nearby crossroads tavern set back off the road and when Uncle Samuel and Gabriel questioned the owner, he was willing to say anything for a price. But the barmaid told them that Ramsey had been there about three times to talk to Marion and once he had come with another man, but she couldn't give us a description since she only saw his back. On that occasion Ramsey had insisted on a private room in which to meet Marion and it was Marion who served them. They returned to Marion with this additional information, but she wanted to bargain for her release or at least for her life if she told them what she knew about the man. Father said he couldn't promise her anything but that he would speak on her behalf. So, Marion told him, "He didn't speak except in a whisper to Ramsey and always in English. He sat in the shadows never taking off his hat or cloak." She swore that was all that she could tell us. My father subsequently issued a plea for leniency in her judgement, it was all he could do for her.

Then our attention was turned to something of a more personal concern, the claim for the chateau was before the courts a process which the Minister of the Interior had promised to accelerate. True to his word within a week the chateau and all its properties were returned to Emilie with no fanfare. The papers were merely delivered by the minister's personal secretary with a bow to Emilie saying that the people of France welcomed her home. The Marquis who had been instrumental in assisting with the vagaries of the French system became aware through a friend that there was a considerable sum in back taxes that would be assigned to the new owners in the next quarter. He told my father that it was likely an attempt to regain the control of the property. The sum would be considerable burden and with neither the chateau nor the Abbey turning a profit and it could ruin my uncle.

Miles came to hear about it as the Marquis and my father tried to determine the best way to let my aunt and uncle know and came to me explaining the dilemma. He knew that I wanted nothing to do with my grandfather's legacy and suggested that if I still wished to give my uncle the money that I had inherited from the General that this was the perfect opportunity. I agreed, went to my father and mother who heartily approved of the scheme and with my father's help and the Marquis, I was able to use a sizeable portion of my inheritance to pay off the back taxes before the papers were turned over to my uncle and aunt. The only stipulation I made was that they would never know what I had done. Emilie and Samuel were ecstatic that the property had been returned to her, but it meant that they could not return with us to England right away. The estate had been cared for but not very well. They needed to hire someone they could trust with the running of the property, so it would turn a profit when they were not in residence. Even with my help they could not afford to just have it stand empty between visits. It was Lady Granville who approached us with a possible solution. The Embassy often ran into issues with providing adequate quarters for visiting dignitaries and she proposed that the Embassy rent the chateau when the family were not in residence. That way the staff could retain their employment and the house would not sit empty between their visits. Before accepting Emilie wanted to discuss the possibility with the staff to see if this would be an acceptable arrangement for them and they still needed someone to oversee the house and the estate. It had once been a successful working farm which had stagnated from mismanagement. There were vineyards that had gone wild and Samuel and the Marquis thought there might be the possibility of producing wine in the future.

So, while the men were about their business of tying up all the loose ends from our adventure in France it was Mrs Baxter who offered the solution to my uncle and aunt's dilemma about the chateau.

Mrs Baxter was seated in the blue drawing room taking tea with us when she asked, "Tell me, Mrs Hughes, is it true what I heard in the village that you'll be renting the property to Lord Granville when you're not in residence?"

Emilie laughed. "News travels quickly, I see…yes, it's true." Mrs Baxter pursed her lips, opened her mouth then shut it again. Aunt Emilie looked puzzled about this sudden interest. "Do you foresee a problem with that, Mrs Baxter?"

She grimaced, looked out the window then clasped her hands in her lap and sighed. "I don't suppose you've hired a factor or a housekeeper, have you?"

Emilie responded with good humour. "No, we haven't actually. My husband was going to advertise in the papers."

Mrs Baxter looked horrified. "Oh, my dear, you'll get nothing but charlatans and thieves with an advertisement."

She raised her chin and pursed her lips again. "Now, I don't mean to tell you your business, but I think I can help you there. Andre DuPont was our factor before my father came to live with us. The Major was never raised to be a farmer even though he loved to think that he could do it but he left most of the decisions to Andre. Andre knew how talk the Major out of the things he shouldn't do and into what he should. He still works for us, but my father says that his talents are really wasted, and we can't pay him as much as he's worth. Positions such as he's trained for don't come along very often so he's stayed on as my father's assistant. I thought I would recommend him to your husband for the position at the chateau." She paused for a breath.

Emilie looked flabbergasted. "Mrs Baxter, that's wonderful! Even though my husband was raised to run a large estate, our family seat in England will require most of his attention, we may not be in France as often as we'd like. Plus, he has his work for the Crown, so I am afraid," Mrs Baxter looked totally dejected and was biting her lip as Emilie continued, "he would have to do most of his consultation here with Mr DuPont by correspondence and would rely heavily on that him to make decisions without his input. Would Monsieur DuPont be comfortable with that?"

Mrs Baxter beamed and nodded. "Oh, my, yes, he is a most capable man and his English is excellent!"

Emilie looked extremely pleased. "If you can spare him, could you please have him come to the chateau tomorrow? He can have luncheon with us and he can discuss the particulars with my husband."

Emilie sobered and sighed. "Now if you could only find me a housekeeper! After looking at the accounts I'm sure that that odious concierge has been robbing the estate blind."

Mrs Baxter smiled and reached out to pat my aunt's hand. "I don't have to find one for you, my dear, you already have one!"

Emilie sat back stunned. "I can assure you, Mrs Baxter, I do not have a housekeeper at present."

Mrs Baxter smiled. "Of course you do, it's Bridgette your laundress!" Emilie looked at a loss for words. Mrs Baxter laughed. "She is little Jean's mother! And before that weasel of a concierge was installed by the local magistrate, she oversaw the house and did an excellent job too. Has your Mr Allan not told you how the staff always turn to her for approval whenever he issues an order? It's not just because he's English, Mrs Hughes."

Emilie sat forward sensing a story, "But why did the magistrate replace her if she did such a decent job?"

Mrs Baxter sat back in her chair and took in a deep breath. "Because of the tavern owner's wife. It was a case of pure and simple jealousy. Even though the ways of the old regime are dead not everything has changed, such as the pecking order in the local social strata. Here as in many villages the people from the big houses have more status than the people in the village. So, Madam Toulouse used a trumped up charge that the chateau's housekeeper had not paid them for services rendered. The local magistrate at the time was her brother and she won her case. But the magistrate found that there was not sufficient evidence to remove her from the chateau altogether so instead of dismissing Bridgette he only demoted her to Head Laundress."

Emilie clearly didn't know whether to laugh or cry. "That is outrageous…how can I right this terrible wrong?"

Mrs Baxter looked like the cat that swallowed the canary. "Just hire her back, this is your home now and the concierge will be leaving since he is a government appointee. It was never proved that the tavern owner was cheated, and the chateau's books were in perfect order. That's why she was only demoted just to shut up the tavern owner's wife. The only person in the village that will be unhappy about her reinstatement will be that shrew."

Mrs Baxter was very pleased with herself, but Emilie looked worried, "Mrs Baxter, where is Bridgette's husband, does he not have a say in this?"

"She has no husband, Mrs Hughes."

We all started at this. "But what about Jean, her son?"

She shook her head, "The poor waif is not hers. She found him lying in the orchard sick as a dog; he couldn't have been more than four years old. The pitiful thing had been living off the green apples from the orchard, he was rail thin, filthy. She brought him back to the chateau and cared for him. We all searched for the child's family, but no one knew him nor claimed him, so she raised him as her own and as far as he is concerned she is his mother."

I could tell Mother was thinking of James as a tear ran down her cheek. Mrs Baxter changed the subject as she looked at me. "Now that that's settled when you are and your young man going to marry?" I must have turned a bright red for I could feel the heat creeping up my neck and I wanted to hide my face before she could see my blush.

It was my mother who surprised me by saying, "I think in the late spring when it's warm, but not too hot, all the flowers will be in bloom then. I would love for her to be married in Northumberland in the old church where her grandmother was married but I'm not sure she really cares." She smiled at me, but I could see her mind churning. I expect that if she had her way the old vicar would be grovelling next spring. "But there is a lovely chapel near our country estate in the south as well. I'll leave that up to Clarissa, but I think the spring would be perfect."

I felt better and not as red, but her support puzzled me. "There is one problem with your plans, Mother, he hasn't asked me." Mrs Baxter recognized my discomfort and before my mother could say anything else she asked after Emilie and my mother's health. I let my mind wander seeing in my mind's eye Miles asking me to marry him. He had hinted at it and intimated his intentions to my father. But he had never actually asked me.

After several days all the loose ends at the chateau had been taken care of. The factor had been hired and the housekeeper restored to her rightful position. The staff were all happy and the cook was delighted that she would be returning to England with us to work for Emilie in their London home. The undercook at the chateau was ecstatic for she would finally be promoted to the position of cook, a promotion well-deserved and was heartily approved by the outgoing cook.

Everyone seemed excited by the thought of going home. The Marquis had already left to return to his home with a promise that he and his family would visit England next spring. Of course, the men were anxious to leave and act on their plan to bring down Lord Burley's smuggling ring.

Gabriel and my Uncle Samuel for some unknown reason had fast become friends, they could often be found in what they called the practice yard, challenging each other in archery and sword play. Father would often join them for hand to hand combat that Gabriel was proficient at, he turned out to be an exceptional instructor. Charity and my mother and Emilie were all caught up with the talk of children, their education, nutrition and all stages of development. I was the template and James as the ongoing experiment. But I was always on the periphery of these conversations and activities. Charity and I did not bond, we were still wary of each other, yet she seemed to have made friends with the other ladies.

Our staff were busy packing and saying their goodbyes. The reinstated housekeeper had things well in hand and Emilie was very pleased. Mr DuPont was hired as my Uncle Samuel's factor and found that they were of the same mind as to the farm and the potential winery as they rode out together almost every day to survey the chateau and assess the needs of the farm and tenants.

Miles however was avoiding me, he was often closeted with Jibben or Dr Grimes and sometimes Dr Jefferson or his father, otherwise he just disappeared. I was left mainly to my own devices. Thoughts of what might have happened to cause his distance between us caused me all kinds of anxiety due to my over-active imagination. It was on our last day at the chateau that I was finally able to speak alone to Miles. I was walking slowly back over the fields after saying goodbye to Mrs Baxter and Patrick when I caught sight of him watching me from edge of the orchard. Even when I came to him he stood there looking straight ahead, his face full of sadness. I wanted to reach out and touch him, but I didn't, nor did he make any attempt to touch me. He looked down at his feet still not saying anything, so I was the first to break the silence. "What is it, Miles? I assume you have something you want to tell me without the others around."

He said quietly but clearly, "I'm leaving."

I refused to understand what he meant but my heart was in my throat, my voice was touched with hysteria, "We're all leaving, Miles!"

He jerked his head up glaring at me, "Don't be obtuse, Clarissa, you know what I mean. I won't be going back to London with you."

My brain registered what he said but my heart was on the verge of breaking. "That's all? Don't I deserve any kind of explanation?"

He reached out as if to take my hand then pulled it back. "I'm a liability, poppet, to any of your father's plans at this stage. I have nothing of value to contribute to anyone as I am."

I made a choking sound somewhere between a sob and laugh. "Don't call me that ridiculous name if you're so anxious to turn your back on me! I should have been prepared for the day that you no longer wanted or needed me."

This time he did take my hand then pulled me to his chest. "My sweet silly girl you'll be with me in my heart as always. That's what makes this so difficult, Lissa. I would marry you today and take you with me. But I can't, I have to do this myself."

I looked up at him in shock. This is the first time that he had ever told me that he would marry me. "Why? We can run away and get married?"

He leaned down and kissed me on the forehead... I had never received such a tender kiss. "We can't, my beloved. Dr Grimes believes he can help me, but he's also promised to help Jibben with his part of the plan, so he has agreed to take me with him. The place we're going to is isolated and it will be a hard journey, we'll have to live rough at times...there'll be no place for you with us."

"Nonsense, I can stay nearby in a village." He was already shaking his head no. "Surely there must be some place...I want to help you!"

Miles crushed me to him. "Please, Lissa...please understand. The Brownes know who you are, and a lady would look out of place where we're going, you would be at risk. Dr Grimes insists that I cannot not take you with me, you would be a distraction and would impede what we need to do."

I was furious and rested my clenched fists on my hips. "Oh, he does, does he! Well, we'll just see about that. Where is the good doctor, I'd like to speak with him?!"

Miles chuckled slightly even as a tear escaped his eye. "I warned him about you and told him that he should wait for me in the village to escape your ire." I made to move pass him, but he pulled me back, looking earnestly into my eyes. "He's waiting for me, I have to go."

I didn't know what to do but I couldn't let him leave without me. "Then I will come that far with you."

Miles held me close to his chest, "No, we have say goodbye here. I'll write as often as I can, my love. Promise me that you'll keep safe or at least try to stay out of harm's way. I know how you like to be involved in your father's schemes. But please don't take any chances without consulting him first." He bent and kissed me thoroughly enough that I had no retort for him other than my tears when he let me go. He immediately turned his back on me and walked back to the chateau, making his way carefully around the trees until he disappeared. I sunk to the ground and cried. Not earth-shattering sobs but a steady quiet flow of tears, I would not distress him by sobbing aloud and have it carried to him on the wind.

Once my tears were done I just sat there pulling out the grass and throwing it into the wind. There was a dull ache in my heart and a weighty lethargy in my body. I just wanted to lie down and never move again. I watched a line of ants marching past my feet in single file, carrying assorted items back to their nest. Without warning a pair of boot tips appeared, how they could have crept up on me without my noticing I had no idea. I looked upward shading my eyes from the sun to see my father. He held out his hand to me which I took, he pulled me up from the ground and into a hug. He smoothed my hair back behind my ears then cupped my face with his hands, "You'll survive, Lissa, your mother and I did, and you will too. Miles is luckier than I was though, I want you to know that I have no objections to him marrying my daughter."

I wasn't sure I had heard him right, "What do you mean?"

He hugged me again as he turned me towards the chateau with his arm around my shoulder. "Miles asked me for your hand in marriage this morning and your mother and I gave our consent."

I started back away from him. "What!"

Father looked confused. "Did we do wrong?" The vindictive side of me would like to have said yes but I couldn't. "I thought it's what you wanted?"

I shook my head. "It would have been nice to have been asked first." Father looked at me askance then I realised Miles had already asked me in his own way and that I had said yes in my own way. It was obvious that we'd never be a conventional couple, I chuckled, wiping my nose with my handkerchief.

"I'm sorry to confuse you…he did ask me in a way and I agreed. It's just that I like to be celebrating my engagement with my fiancé and family. Instead he's gone off with a retired pirate as his only companion!" I threw up my hands and huffed. "Have you ever noticed that our family attracts the most unusual people?"

He laughed. "Yes, my dear, I have noticed. It's part of what makes life interesting; your mother and I wouldn't have it any other way." He paused…then smiling to himself, "Did she tell you yet?"

"Tell me what?" Knowing full well what he referred to but I did not want to spoil his pleasure in telling me, so I tried to look perplexed.

He was beaming and looked younger and happier than I had seen him in some time. "We're to have another child. You and James will have brother or sister sometime in the new year."

I smiled up at him. "Then you may finally have your heir and a spare." he smiled and clasped my hand tightly as we reached the gravel drive.

He paused and cleared his throat, "You'll also have a cousin about the same time, Samuel told me this morning that he and Emilie are to be parents." He was still smiling but it gradually darkened as he turned to look down at me then in a very sober tone said, "Lissa, we'll be returning to London soon and there will be some very dark days ahead of us and I'll need your help to keep our family safe. With that in mind your weapons training will resume a soon as we reach London."

I brightened at the thought of being included and agreed readily "Whatever you need of me, Father." He patted my shoulder as we walked companionably chatting about our expanding family and his plans for a pony for James and a tree house.

As we passed into the courtyard, "I suppose Miles told you that he and the doctor will be infiltrating the smuggler's ring?"

I stopped moving, everything stopped, time, my breathing and my heart all stopped and in a whisper of desperation I managed to say, "No!"

# Chapter 34
## *England: October 1830*

The crossing to England was a bit rough but uneventful. Edward was on the same ship accompanying Julian's body back home, but he kept his distance, rarely speaking to anyone even to his own father. He genuinely appeared to grieve for his friend, so I couldn't fault the man as much as I had detested Julian.

I spent a great deal of my time on deck watching for England's shoreline and feeling a weight on my chest because of Miles' absence, knowing that he was willingly walking blind into danger. His only companion would be Dr Grimes and how much benefit there would be from infiltrating a smugglers ring remained to be seen.

I had made any number of plans to go after Miles and discarded every one of them. It always came back again and again to my father, asking me to care for our family when he and Uncle Samuel were away. Besides I barely knew how to get about in London let alone how to get to another part of the country without assistance. What really stopped me though was that I knew Miles would rebuke me for coming after him; I knew nothing about smuggling except that these men could be dangerous which would only make me a liability.

Father came up beside me as I was musing on the immediate future. The sun was starting to set, and he told me that we would see land at first light. It was getting colder, but he stood there with me holding onto the railing as the ship rolled on the waves. I stole a look at him, but his eyes were glued to the horizon, his mind seemed to be somewhere else. Finally, he moved to rub his hands together to restore their warmth then he rubbed his nose then with one finger and turned his head to look at me. "Lissa, I want you to know that I would not have let him go if I thought he wasn't capable of dealing with whatever comes his way and I trust Dr Grimes as his companion."

Why did he have to mention Miles being gone, everyone had tacitly avoided the topic since the day he'd left. I bit my lip trying to hold back a sharp retort and failing miserably, "Well, thank you so much, Father, for those words of comfort! But in case you hadn't noticed the man is for all intents and purposes BLIND! Yet you trust Dr Grimes! Do you even know him well enough to say that?! Is he trustworthy? Will he care for Miles or leave him to fend for himself if things go wrong? Is this a way to get rid of Miles so he won't sully the Turner name by marrying me? After all, in England he is still considered the Earl's bastard."

Father clenched and unclenched his hands; his face was red and expressionless. Now I knew who I got my temper from. I waited to feel the sting or the barb of his tongue as I glared at him. It was not long in coming he grabbed me by the upper arms turning me to face him, "ENOUGH! Do you hear me, Lissa, that is enough!"

Tears were streaming down my face, they were the first I had cried since Miles told me he was leaving. My father looked at me, huffed then pulled me to his chest hugging me closely. My arms gradually wrapped around his waist as he spoke quietly, "I couldn't have stopped him, Lissa, it was better that he went with my blessing so that I was at least aware of what he, Jibben and Grimes had planned. If I hadn't, you know that he would have gone without my approval, this way I can at least try to protect him. I do have friends that can watch out for him and Grimes." I nodded and sniffed. He pulled back to place his hands on my cheeks then he kissed me on the forehead. "Miles left a message for you."

I looked up at him. "And you're just telling me now?"

He smiled. "He asked me to deliver it when I thought you were ready to hear it. You weren't ready until now."

I snorted, swiping my hands across my eyes then crossed my arms standing up straight and looking him in the eye. "Well?"

He pursed his lips shaking his head as he looked out over the choppy grey water of the channel with one arm around me then he looked down at me. "He said 'don't let her search for me, I may not be able to save her if she gets into trouble. Tell her that I will write when I can and that she needs to keep her eyes open when she pulls the trigger and'," he paused and rolled his eyes of all things, "and finally he told me 'tell her to look with her heart'."

I was astonished. "That's all?"

Father chuckled then became very sad, "Well, no, that wasn't all but you'll have to ask your mother about the exact wording. I'm just not comfortable expressing another man's emotions. Let's just say I know how he felt leaving you behind." He dropped his arm, pivoted and walked away.

I saw my mother come up on deck as he moved away from me, she stood there waiting for my father then she reached out, hugged him, kissed him on the cheek then she turned and came towards me while my father walked on without looking back. I raised a brow at her as she approached me with a smile. "Well, Lissa, I see that your father is still intact, nothing missing, no bleeding or broken bones."

I was breathless for a second. "Whatever do you mean?"

She chuckled. "I doubt that there is a person on this ship that didn't hear you yelling at each other."

I looked around and yes people were staring at me, one or two of the crew were even laughing and I heard the word 'shrew' as they passed by. I was mortified and hid my heated face in one hand while holding onto the railing with the other. Mother smiled again then held out a letter and I immediately brightened as she passed it to me. "It's not from Miles, well, not directly. It's his words I just put them down on paper for you. Aunt Mary did the same thing for me when your father left us for France, there were things he found he could say to her that he couldn't say to me. It was the same with Miles, he could say certain things to your father and I that he was afraid to say to you." She took my hand away from my face and placed the letter in it. "It's on sturdy paper so it should last but don' cry on it or the ink will run. Then I suggest you let it go." I didn't understand her, and she knew it, but she patted me on the cheek and went to join my father. I watched them go arm and arm down the deck as did many others. They were so close that you would be hard pressed to slip a piece of paper between them. I had never thought about what all those years of them being apart and what must have been like for them. They had spent years where they had only been able to meet occasionally for a few days here and there. My pain and fear were real but the only two people I knew that could understand that were my own parents. I was ashamed of lashing out at my father, but he seemed to know and accept that I needed to, and I knew he wouldn't hold it against me. I looked down at my hand that held Miles' last words for me. I held it tightly, but I couldn't bring myself to read it. Miles had told me in the orchard what he needed to tell me, and I wouldn't spoil that. I would wait for him to come back to me to tell me what he could only say to my parents. I looked back at my mother where she stood by the rail with my father, she was watching me, and I smiled at her as she nodded out to sea. Then I knew what she must have done with a similar missive that Aunt Mary had given her. I could picture her so clearly standing at the top of a cliff in Cornwall looking out to sea towards France after my father left. So, I let my letter go, it dropped towards the water, was caught on a breeze that lifted it up to fly past me just out of my reach. My heart clenched when it swooped back toward the ship, it fluttered in front of me again before it plunged back down to the water where it floated within sight for a time and then it was lost in our wake. I looked back at my mother, but she had turned away, her head resting on my father's shoulder both looking towards England and home. I stood fast as well looking for home and I promised myself that I would do everything I could to help my father ensure Miles' safety.

My parents argued all the way to London as to whether we should all stay in London, or that the women should go to Somerset or Cornwall. Since Aunt Mary and her guests were already in Cornwall he felt that we would stay in London for a brief time then join them. I know in my heart that I wanted to be as close to Miles as I could since my father had finally told me where he had gone but would going to Cornwall put him and us at risk?

Home at last, Meg unpacked as much as I needed for the night and the next day. I told her the rest could wait, she was clearly relieved since the sea trip and carriage ride had exhausted her. While changing for dinner I asked how things were with Robert. She pushed out her lower lip and tears glistened in her eyes. "Oh, miss, he wants to get into your father's business, like Dalton and the others. I don't see why he can't be happy with just being who he is."

I looked up at her as she dressed my hair. A few days ago, I would have felt the same way about Miles. I didn't know what to say to make her feel better, so I told her the truth. "He wants to be more than just a valet, it's important to him."

She cocked her head sideways as if genuinely perplexed by my answer. "What?"

I clasped my hands in front of my face as if in prayer, "It's like you becoming a lady's maid after being a tweenie. You didn't ask for it but you were given the opportunity to better yourself and you took it. But you still wanted to improve yourself even more, so you started taking lessons with me. Then in Paris you wanted me to help you improve your French because you didn't want to rely on just Robert translating for you."

She nodded her head. "Yes, miss, but my learning French isn't likely to get me killed. So, what's that got to do with Robert?"

I tried to keep from grinning by pursing my lips before continuing, "You've grown and changed, Meg, since you became my maid. You've learned new skills that most lady's maids wouldn't know. You ride almost as well as I do, you are deadly with a cross bow, you have a delicate touch on the piano and your French has improved." She blushed. "I've heard you conversing with Emilie and her maid sometimes, you really are getting quite good. But Robert came to this job already having a promising idea what was expected of him and he's a fast leaner just like you and he's good at it. But he wants more. He sees the other men in the house doing more than just their position within the household and he wants that, Meg."

She took a deep breath nodding then slipping into her below stairs English with a smirk, "I seed he wants to better his self so he don't feel so out of place just like I wanted ter talk better once." She was watching me to see if I would correct her but all I could do was laugh and she laughed with me. "I think I understand now, miss, but I don't have to like it."

I looked down at the locket around my neck, touching it with one hand. "No, Meg, you don't have to like it. You just have to love him, look with your heart." My nerves were now on edge thinking of Miles and the last thing I wanted was to join my parents and the de Bearnes in a meaningless conversation.

But I finished changing then went down to dinner, everyone had gathered in the drawing room. It seemed odd that Uncle Samuel and Emilie were not with us and Aunt Mary and Uncle Arthur were in Cornwall and the Earl had returned to his London home to prepare to join his wife and younger children in Cornwall. Dr Jefferson had to check in on his partner and their practice. And Jibben had disappeared presumably to join his family again on Hampstead Heath. That left Gabriel, Charity, my parents, and myself. The de Bearne boys who never strayed far from their parents even for meals were absent. They had been so exhausted by the trip to London that they were already asleep in the nursery with Lettie watching over them and James. When I came into the room, Father had a decanter in hand pouring Gabriel a drink and talking quietly. Mother and Charity looked up and beckoned me to sit with them.

Charity seemed upset about something and wouldn't make eye contact with me. I faced my mother and queried her with my eyes. She nodded to Charity. I didn't particularly like Charity, I could not forget her deception and arrogance and I still remembered how rude she had been when she was with the Clarkes even if she had only been playing a part. So, I swallowed my negative feelings and ventured to engage her "Mrs de Bearne, I—"

She put her hand up. "Please, Miss Turner, hear me out. When we came to dinner the night that Ramsey was so terribly rude to you, that was my doing I'm afraid. I encouraged him. It was the Clarkes' intent to still plant someone in this house and your attraction to Ramsey seemed to be something that they were desirous to exploit. I couldn't let that happen! He is an awful person and would have treated you abominably. So, I coached him on what his behaviour should be like towards a young lady of your social standing. I told him to be standoffish, even rude to you, that it would make him seem irresistible. I had hoped that you would detest him. At first, I was so pleased that he had taken my advice. But then I saw how hurt you were when you left the room that night. I felt badly. I must apologize for that. I can only hope that you will understand that what I did was with the best intentions."

I disliked her a little less for her confession because it was that episode that had brought Miles to me in the nursery. That part of the night was as fresh in my mind today as if it had happened just yesterday. I smiled at her briefly before saying, "Of course." She reached out and touched my hand, my first reaction was to withdraw but I didn't.

My mother had been watching me closely. "Lissa, Mrs de Bearne has asked for our help." I sat back and waited for her to continue. "She was not born to the world that her husband was and is nervous to meet his family. She would like us to help her learn what she needs to know to fit in. I think we'll start with a visit to our dressmaker then I'll work with her on the aspects of household management. She has a very good ear for languages and figures, she plays the piano very well and is an excellent horsewoman so that won't be a problem."

I tried to muster a smile when I looked at Charity, "My mother is an excellent teacher but a hard task master." My response had no warmth, but my nerves were on edge since my thoughts were with Miles and not the complexities of maintaining a home.

Mother cleared her throat. "I would like your help with her introduction into society as Mrs de Bearne and not Charity Clarke. We will, of course, have to come up with a story that adequately explains her change of status…"

I was speechless at first and without thinking interrupted, "And how exactly am I supposed to do that?"

Charity looked hurt and my mother was annoyed. "I would have thought that considering the difficulties that you experienced in your own life that you'd be more understanding and extend her the hand of friendship."

I felt like I had been slapped in the face and responded with anger, "You mean when you and Father didn't own me as your daughter and allowed me to grow up in the shadow of innuendo that I was a bastard and subjected me to the parenting of the General?" Then the harshness of my statement hit me. Mother looked devastated and Charity embarrassed. Father and Gabriel stood with their mouths open, staring at me. My mother with tears in her eyes reached out and slapped me across the face. I jerked back, placing my hand on my cheek then stood up and raced out of the room without a thought of where to go. I ran out into the street and crossed into the park. I continued to run and finally slipped on a wet patch, falling to my knees in a copse of withered bushes. There I buried my face in my hands, but I didn't cry, I was too ashamed. I finally looked about to discover that I was off the normal paths and that I was utterly alone no one had followed me. My gown was already filthy, so I sat down and pondered what I should do, how could I return and apologise not only to the de Bearnes but to my parents.

Then I heard a chuckle and a "tsk, tsk," I looked around me but there was no one there. Suddenly the branches of the hedge nearby parted and there stood Jibben. "Such a mess you have made of your pretty dress, Miss Turner. You really should not be out here alone. You are lucky that I saw you run from your parent's home. It's such a foolish thing to do."

I glared at him. "What do you care?"

He laughed, spreading out his coat and sat down beside me. "I don't. But I care about my cousin and your Mr Johnson. If the wrong people caught you out here, they could use you against Johnson and that could hurt my Peter…to you he is Dr Grimes. I don't suppose you'd like to go home right now?" I shook my head no and looked at him, praying he would just leave me alone. Instead he stood up, grabbed my arm and pulled me up. He wrapped his coat around me. "I didn't think so. I'll take you to see Grandmama, maybe she can help you. Women's problems just confuse me." He pulled me towards the roadway and away from my home. His tinker's wagon was at the side of the road, the horse was quietly munching at the long grass, but it looked up to give Jibben a withering stare. Jibben patted the mare and laughed, "Don't look at me like that, Rosa, blame this young lady. I promise you when we get back to camp, I will give you some extra oats." He patted her again then helped me up to the high seat and jumped up beside me and we started to move off.

He walked the horse through the streets slowly. "Your parents will be worried."

I wrapped my arms around my waist like I needed to hold myself together. "I don't think so."

He grunted. "That bad, hmmm." I only nodded then we didn't speak again for a while. I shivered and pulled his coat tighter around me, it smelled of wood smoke and peppermint.

I didn't want to talk but my curiosity got the better of me, "What were you doing back there by the park?"

He chuckled. "I'm a tinker, among other things, so I was plying my trade. The Mayfair cooks like sharp knives and no one is better than me and they know it. Plus, it's a good place to find out things. Most people think servants know nothing, that they're deaf, huh! If those maids and grooms only knew what to do with the things they tell me they would all be rich." He paused and chuckled. "Well, maybe not I am not rich yet, but then I'm too generous, I tell your father and uncles too much for free. But when I give information to them or to Bow Street Runners, they leave us alone for the most part, so it has its value." He pulled a sack out from behind him reached in a pulled out a bread roll tore it in half and passed me a piece. "Here, eat, thinking is hard work and you look like you have a lot of thinking to do." We passed the rest of the trip in silence, once we reached the camp Jibben took me to his grandmama's wagon and left me with her after saying, "She is troubled, fix her, please."

Jibben's grandmother just looked me up and down then walked around me. She opened a trunk pulled out a shirt of a bright magenta silk and a skirt of darkest indigo shot through with threads of silver and a shawl to match passing them to me, "Dress in these." Then she left the wagon with a tea pot. By the time I had changed she was back with a plate of stew and black bread that she set down on the table and pointed at it as she motioned for me to sit on a stool as she set about brewing the tea. I ate the stew with relish, it was excellent, and the bread was fresh with a slightly bitter taste, yet it was a nice compliment to the stew. Every movement of my companion was accompanied by a soft jangle and when she finally sat down and threw off her shawl, I saw the multiple chains and bracelets of silver and gold coins dangling from her neck and wrists. She watched my eyes take it all in and remarked, "You like?" She shook her wrists and pointed to her many necklaces of coins. "This is my fortune. It goes with me everywhere." She smiled then gestured for me to drink my tea. There were thin almond biscuits to go with it that melted in my mouth as soon as I took a bite. When I was almost done, she took my tea cup swirled it around three times then turned it upside down to drain it, when she righted it she stared into the cup then looked at me intensely. She rose and walked to her door carrying the cup and called out, "Jibben!" Then she wrapped my dress up in a bundle and handed it to me.

Jibben popped his head in through the door, "Yes, Grandmamma?!"

She waved her hand at me. "Take her home. She has work that she must do."

Jibben looked sceptical "What of Peter and Mr Johnson?"

His mother had her back to him, but she spoke loud enough for us both to hear. "She will be in trouble again...but they will be fine." She turned back, handing me a small soft leather pouch, it smelled of lavender and something else that was sweet, but I couldn't place it. "Keep that with you at all times and at night under your pillow, it will protect you."

I wanted to laugh but the look she gave me would brook no laughter. "How, I mean, what does it do?"

She leaned close to me. "It will warn you of the things that are a danger to you and those you love."

I wanted to ask her how, but she raised her hand to stop me as if she knew what my question would be, "You will know when it happens." My heart sped up and I swallowed hard. Then she moved around the table walking past me and went out the door, brushing Jibben aside.

Just then I heard horses arrive in the camp and my father's voice shouting for Jibben. He scrunched his facial features as if in pain. "I think I will not have to take you home. Your father is here. Tell me, little one, did the amulet work?" I looked at him puzzled then nodded yes, my heart had sped up just before I heard the horses and my father's voice. He grinned from ear to ear. "Good! No one is better than Grandmamma! Keep that near you, Miss Turner, it could save your life." I heard my father call out for Jibben again and he answered this time, "Over here, Turner, she is here."

# Chapter 35
## *Troubled Minds*

My father's head and shoulders appeared through the doorway, he glared at Jibben who laughed at him then left. Father came into the confined space towering over me looking worn out and beaten, glancing around, holding his hat in hand he sat on the stool where Jibben's mother had been sitting. He looked ridiculous with his knees bent up almost touching his chest. He tossed his hat on top of a trunk, took a deep sigh and in an angry voice hissed, "Sit!" I opened my mouth, but no words came out and he repeated "Sit" but less forcefully. I looked down at my costume blushing as I saw him taking it in. He pinched the bridge of his nose between his thumb and forefinger then clasped his hands on the table before him. "Well, Lissa, I hope that you've got it out of your system. Honestly I've been waiting for this to happen." He looked at me and could see my confusion. "I mean the euphoria of being part of a family has finally worn off, it took longer than I thought it would."

My heart constricted. I was afraid of what he might say next, so I tried to stop him, "Father—Papa."

But he raised his hand to stop me. "Lissa, your childhood was not what I would have wished for and you have every right to be angry and hurt. Your mother and I were young but more than anything we were afraid. If the General had never come home, I'd like to think that our lie might not have been so bad. But he did come home, and our lie became a nightmare for you. I should have walked in and claimed you and your mother, be damned with what came next. But in truth I was a bigger coward than your mother or your uncle for keeping the truth from you. I deserve your hate, Clarissa, not your mother. I can't tell you what our life might have been like if I hadn't left you in that place. I just know that I should have tried."

He pulled a folded piece of paper out of his pocket it was a sketch; at first, I thought it was the one that I had done of James taking his first steps. But it wasn't, it was older, and it was of a girl, it was me. He laid it out in front of me. I noticed smudges here and there as well as some water spots, there was even some blood on it. He smiled down at it. "This reminded me so much of the one you drew for me of James. It was from your mother. When I was on the continent I carried it with me everywhere. Whenever my mail caught up with me there would be another sketch of you doing another first or in a new frock or one of you sleeping." He chuckled. "I used to talk to you or rather to the pictures, I called you my dumpling. I'd tell you stories about my adventures and my hopes for the future. I showed perfect strangers those pictures and told them that you were my daughter and how very much I missed you. Then I'd tell them the things that your mother had written to me about you, just as if I had been there. My heart was so full when I could talk about you and your mother. I thought I'd drive your uncle insane. But, Lissa, it was your smiling face that kept at bay the horror of the things I'd seen and the things I had done. Without your picture in my pocket I don't know how I might have changed; but you kept me from the darkness and for that I can never repay you, except to be the best father that I can now." His eyes glistened in low light and I could already feel the hot liquid of my own tears running down my cheeks. I reached out over the table taking his hands in mine, we held onto each other tightly with the picture of me lying between us. We sat there not speaking and not looking directly at each other. Then he stood up not letting go of my hands but pulling me up with him. "Will you come home with me to your mother? Can you forgive us?" I stepped into his arms and he pulled me to his chest whispering, "I love you, my little dumpling."

I looked up at him and knew that my face must be a fright with my nose running, my reddened eyes and tear-stained cheeks. He pulled out his handkerchief and offered it to me then motioned towards the doorway and ushered me down the steps. He had brought his curricle for us to ride home in and the matched bays pulling it were being admired a little too closely by Jibben and his cousins. Father handed me up and tossed a shilling to the boy that had been holding them as he climbed up beside me. He looked down at Jibben and extended his hand, "Thank you, my friend." Jibben looked at his hand with suspicion but reached out and shook it, my Father grinned before he let go. "We will talk later. Come by my home tomorrow for lunch and bring your grandmother."

Jibben let go of his hand and stepped back wagging his finger, "I think you are a little bit crazy, Turner. But we will be there."

Father gathered up the reins. "Oh and come to the front entrance when you arrive."

Jibben looked shocked. "I take that back, you are very crazy, Turner."

Jibben's grandmamma came up behind him and slapped the back of his head then said to my father, "We will be there."

Then she walked away into the darkness, leaving Jibben rubbing the back of his head as he said, "We'll be there, Turner."

The drive home was quiet and peaceful. I asked only one question, "How did you know where to find me."

"Jacob followed you, but he kept his distance and saw Jibben collect you." He smiled down at me and pulled me closer.

When we arrived home, Mother met us at the door and pulled me into hug that almost choked me. She finally released me just as I was starting to see stars before my eyes. "Lissa, I'm sorry."

I kissed her on the cheek. "So am I. That was a hateful thing for me to say. Father was able to explain things to me with a great deal of clarity."

She smiled and pushed a tendril of hair behind my ear. "He told you about the pictures, didn't he?" I nodded, and she took from her pocket a miniature of her and my father. It must have been done when they were first married, they were so very young. I held it in my hand and it was warm from her carrying it. "I'm going to have it enlarged and painted in oils, but I would like to incorporate that picture of you taking your first steps if I may."

I raised an eyebrow. "But who will you get to do it? Both you and I are more than adequate at drawing. But truthfully my attempts at painting have been abysmal and to invite an outsider into our lives to do this wouldn't be wise right now, there'd be too many questions."

Charity came out of the shadows to look over my mother's shoulder. "I would love to do it, it's one talent that I do possess, Miss Turner. I'm good at painting and it will help keep me occupied while Gabriel and your father are off on business. I don't have your hunger to be involved in adventure nor your mother's talent for piecing together bits and pieces of information. But I can paint."

I was annoyed at her for interjecting herself into this family moment but then I realised that she had, in fact, quelled the tension. So, I decided to give her a chance to prove that she had a place with us. "I think that would be a wonderful, Mrs de Bearne. Thank you."

Mother stepped back smiling at both of us. "I have the original drawing that the miniature was made from. It has a great deal more detail in it then you can see here." My mother must have anticipated my question about who had done the original miniature. "Both the drawing and the miniature were done by Charlotte, my stepmother. She was a very talented artist just like my mother, Alice." She paused looking down at the miniature that I had given back to her and she ran a finger over it, almost caressing it.

"I think that was the reason my father married Charlotte. She had so many of mama's qualities and talents and she was a kind soul too. But she never had my mother's vibrancy. I think that's what my father held against her the most and why he left her alone so much after their son was still born, she didn't have Mama's spark. Charlotte was only ever a shadow of Alice Blackwood. He could never appreciate the person that was Charlotte Thorne." She spoke in a very soft voice as if afraid of disturbing the memory of the two women that had shaped her. At least I had been fortunate enough to have always had my mother at my side as I grew up. Even if I hadn't known she was my mother, she had always treated me as I would have wanted a mother to treat me.

Father came in and Gabriel joined us, throwing more light into the hallway from the open door to the library. He bowed to me. "Miss Turner, I am delighted to see you safely returned. While you were gone, and your parents were busy, a letter came to me from Dr Grimes, it included a missive for you." I crinkled up my brow not understanding why Dr Grimes should be writing to me or sending it to Gabriel. His brow crinkled as he flashed me an amused smile. "Ah yes, you're not aware that Dr Grimes and I know each other." He grimaced then chuckled reaching out to clasp Charity's hand. "Dr Grimes was the pirate that discovered Charity and I hiding in the hold when our ship was attacked on the way to the West Indies. It was shortly after that raid that he returned to England. But he has kept his hand in the business you might say in a small way. Being a Bow Street Coroner with a small private practise doesn't always pay well. At least not enough to maintain his life style and his work amongst the poor. We connected with each other again after I arrived in England through a mutual business associate. That's why he's gone with Mr Johnson, he has connections along the coast." I frowned at him and he glared back but then smiled and chuckled, "Piracy is not always about profit, Miss Turner, it can also be a tool that governments use to subvert their enemies. But it's a small and very exclusive brotherhood…one that you can never really leave."

I was peeved by his answer since it added fuel to my current anxiety. "But why not address a letter directly to me?"

He smiled indulgently but was very frank with me, "Because you are the daughter of a known agent of the British Crown, that could get him and Mr Johnson killed."

He put his hand in his pocket, pulling out a thin letter that couldn't be more than one sheet and handed it to me.

The only seal was a daub of plain candle wax. I looked at my parents who both nodded, so I raced up the stairs to my room shooing Meg out who screamed in fright when I came flying in dressed like a gypsy. I grabbed a branch of candles and huddled by the window so that by the moonlight and candlelight I sat and read Miles' letter. The handwriting was hesitant at first and there were several blotches of ink but nothing bad enough to obscure what he had to say.

*October 9, 1830*

*We have arrived safely and are currently ensconced in a small Inn by the seaside. Surprisingly we have been welcomed by the locals as the good doctor seems to be known to them. The doctor has put out that I am his erstwhile assistant even though I am essentially blind. Fortunately, I have been able to prove my worth to Dr Grimes that with a heightened sense of smell I've developed the ability to differentiate between suppurating wounds and gangrene in the initial stages; thus, the good doctor has been able to save more than one man's limb on this trip. I also seem to have a talent for calming nervous individuals which has helped not only with his practice of medicine and tooth pulling (from which he is making a tidy profit) but also when trying to gather news about the region.*

*We have even supped with the commander of the local militia. As a result, the doctor and I have been introduced to the community at large as gentlemen despite the doctor's appearance. However, our penchant for visiting low taverns and having late night meetings with unscrupulous individuals has made some people wary of us. But neither smuggler nor militiaman believe that they we're supporting their enemy's endeavours. Instead we are viewed as friends of the common man on one hand and eccentric Londoners on the other.*

*Since news from London and the world at large is like gold here we have been feted by the local gentry, half of which dabble in the smuggling trade themselves. Even if being nothing more than a knowing customer. It is only with half a heart that many of the gentry side with the militia and customs officers to quell this illegal trade and usually only when it has threatened to undercut their own business interests. I have found it all very amusing since most of them were aware of each other's activities both in their business and their personal lives. However, it is always the lack of proof that has limited the number of arrests made.*

I could hear Miles' voice in my head with his wry sense of humour, but towards the end of his letter his tone became more serious.

*The doctor and I make rounds during the day to see patients and to care for those in need by bringing food and fuel to them. At night, we can be found in dark coves observing a ship anchored off shore watching them unload their smuggled goods. Or too often we have stood shivering on shore with the locals watching a ship sink in high seas or crashing upon the rocks only to wait for the refuse to wash ashore and be plundered by the people of the surrounding villages to augment their meagre stores and incomes. The doctor and I do what we can to protect any survivors of these catastrophes and to watch over the bodies of those washed ashore.*

He ended with hastily scratched M at the bottom of the page, there was no other salutation, sentiment or return direction. I could only assume that it was safer that way. Folding it and holding it close to my chest I opened the window. I kissed the tips of my fingers and blew the kiss to my beloved wherever he might be.

There was a gentle knock at the door and my mother came in. "I was just going up to check on James and thought I'd better check on you first." I nodded, and she came in and closed the door. "I assume the letter was from Miles?" again I just nodded and handed it to her. "Oh no, Lissa, that's not why I came."

I tipped my head sideways to rest it against the window. "It's alright, Mother, there's nothing personal in it. I even wondered how Mr de Bearne deduced the letter was for me."

Mother laughed faintly. "Smell it, Lissa." I looked at her perplexed by such an odd suggestion. "Go ahead, indulge me."

I held the letter up to my nose and inhaled. "I smell fish and salt and…" then my eyes widened, "and Miles' cologne of spice and sandalwood. How did you know?"

"Just a guess, your father never sent me love letters and only in the vaguest of terms would he tell me about his work. It was when he talked about the everyday life around him that I knew he wished I was there with him. And he would always drop a bit of his cologne on the paper and seal it."

I looked at the letter in my hand as if I had Miles' heart in my hands. "What an extraordinary man my father is."

My mother smiled. "I know. But your father didn't tell Miles to do that, Lissa. I just think that they're both extraordinary men. Now if you'd like to preserve the smell, put it in the bottom of your jewellery box, it will hold the scent, including the fish smell." She got up and I rose with her then the light caught the silver threads in my costume and mother gasped. "What beautiful fabric! It looks like a fall of shooting stars. Did you get that from Jibben's people?"

I looked down and swished the skirt from side to side to see the threads twinkle and sparkle. The blouse was unremarkable, but the skirt was beautiful, I picked up the shawl that complemented it perfectly, it looked like moonlight on falling snow. "It is, isn't it?"

Mother fingered the shawl and its softness. "I must speak to Jibben's mother about acquiring some of this. I hope she'll be willing to sell us some of the material." I bit my lower lip, I was sceptical that my mother had ever haggled with a gypsy in her life. She blushed, "I can see that you have no faith in my ability to bargain." I cocked an eye at her and she nodded. "Well, perhaps you're right. I'll take your father with me." Then we both laughed, and Mother asked me to join everyone downstairs for the rest of the evening. I looked down at myself and she said, "There's no need to change," and with that she left to check on James.

I rang for Meg to help me change despite the beauty of the clothes. I felt out of place in them in these surroundings. I just couldn't envisage myself in the drawing room taking tea while dressed like a fortune teller. That reminded me that Jibben's grandmother had read my fortune in the tea leaves but had never shared it with me.

I fingered the scented leather pouch in my pocket as I walked to my dressing table and placed Miles' letter under the bottom tray of my jewellery box. Then I pulled out the pouch with the intent of depositing it into the same space, but something stayed my hand. I felt anxious again and my heart raced, I'm not a superstitious person but I convinced myself that it would insult Jibben's people if I didn't carry it with me just as she had admonished.

Meg came into my room noticing what I was holding in my hand. "What's that, miss? Is it a sachet of some sort?" She sniffed. "It smells lovely, I can put it in your clothes press if you like."

I shook my head. "No, thank you, Meg. This was specially made for me by Jibben's mother."

Meg's eyes became huge. "Gypsy magic?" I saw her make a sign against evil that was commonly used by the village people back in Northumberland. "Oh gosh, miss, shouldn't you burn the evil thing?"

I was surprised at her since she loved Robert and he was part gypsy, she'd need to get over these little prejudices, so I was annoyed when I spoke, "No, Meg! She made it for me as a protection amulet."

Then Meg looked in awe. "Ooooh, protection, Robert's got one of them too and it's saved him many a time from mortal danger." I had to keep from smirking but who was I to doubt its power. She nodded as if she could read my mind, "Miss, you never know so you'd best keep it with you after all." I held it out to her, but she put her hands out as if to push it away. I smiled at her child-like fears, but at least I could be sure that my amulet would be safe from my maid.

I quickly changed and ran downstairs. Mother had arrived just ahead of me along with the tea. I was starving despite having been fed at the gypsy camp. The de Bearnes had gone up to check on their sons and had sent word that they were awake and would sup with them in the nursery. But Dr Jefferson had arrived and was a welcomed addition. Mother was smiling from ear to ear and I wondered what was on her mind. Then I looked at everyone else and they too were smiling. "What have I missed?"

Dr Jefferson accepted a cup of tea from my mother and cleared his throat. "Well, I find myself, I mean that I've… Oh, damn, I'm engaged to be married."

My mouth was hanging open, all agape. "Who? I mean how, no I mean who and when?"

He chuckled. "As to how, Miss Turner, in the usual way. I proposed after speaking to her father. As to who, it's Miss Isabel Wiseman."

I almost dropped the cup of tea I was holding. "Sir Thomas's daughter?!"

He nodded very pleased with himself. "Yes, the very same."

I sat back totally amazed. "And Sir Thomas approves her marrying a sometime agent and a physician?"

Mother gasped. "Lissa, that is rude. Matthew, please excuse her, we've been at odds today." She gave me a very disgruntled look and nodded at the doctor.

"I'm sorry, doctor, I just mean that I know how unusual life is in this family, will you be giving up your work with my father."

He shook his head still smiling. "Actually, Miss Turner, I think it was my being an agent that was a major point in my favour with both Miss Wiseman and her father."

Now my interest was piqued, and I wanted all the details. "But how did you ever meet her?"

Father started laughing. "Go ahead, Matthew, tell her." He sat down crossing his legs at the ankle and continued laughing out loud.

Dr Jefferson glared at him then looked at me and smiled, "I unintentionally bumped into her and she fell into my arms."

Father almost choked as he sipped his tea, so I swivelled in my seat to look at him. "My god, man, you pushed her into a fish pond!"

I looked back at the doctor wide-eyed, surely he would never do anything of the sort. He was blushing and pulled on his lower lip before answering. "I did not! It was an accident, at a masquerade we attended before we went to Paris. I was taking a stroll in the garden for some fresh air after the press of the ballroom when I saw Miss Wisemen, she was dressed as a huntress and was with a fellow who looked at first like he was demonstrating how to use her bow, but as I was passing by he seemed more intent on doing her harm."

Father called out. "Oh, that is rich. Let's face it, old man, you were stalking her. Her companion was Eckersley, you've never liked him since he joined Sir Thomas's staff." He paused to see that we were all paying attention. "Eckersley fancies himself an adventurer and lays it on rather thick at times, particularly with the ladies. In reality he's little more than a trumped-up gentleman messenger. He inherited a tidy sum from a maternal uncle with a nice property in one of the Home Counties and envisions himself as taking over from Sir Thomas one day and frankly the old man does seem to like him. He's been trying to court Miss Wiseman except that our Matthew here has had his eye on her since he treated her for an ague last Christmas, but Miss Wiseman took her time in expressing a preference."

Dr Jefferson sighed, "Alright, Colin, that's enough. If you all must know, yes, she did charm me while I cared for her and when I saw that weasel set to put his arm around Isabel, I pretended to stumble into them and they broke apart. It was dark and Eckersley thought I was attacking them; anyway, he reached out to grab me, but I side-stepped him and ran right into Miss Wiseman who had moved to come between us. She lost her balance and fell into the fish pond before I could prevent it." Then he started to laugh out loud. "Eckersley scurried off like a rat on a sinking ship and I remained to assist Miss Wiseman out of the pond. Thankful she hadn't screamed and came out of the pond laughing to my delight. She has a very musical laugh." He stopped and stared off into the space.

Mother looked amused. "Then what happened, Matthew, what did you do?" Dr Jefferson seemed lost in a pleasant thought. "Matthew!"

He came around and looked at my mother. "Oh, we, ah well, I mean I helped her sneak back into the house and change. I mean I didn't help her change, I acted as her look out while she went to her room to change. She is such an intelligent young lady and fast thinking, when we returned to the party she explained her lack of costume saying she had an entire of glass of wine spilled on her by someone when they bumped into each other on the terrace." I looked at him and wondered how anyone could believe that story. He smirked and shrugged. "Well, it seemed reasonable at the time the party was rather crowded and there were several intoxicated individuals milling about the crowd. That my dear, Miss Turner, is how I won her fair hand. She stopped paying attention to Eckersley and turned her affections to me though apparently, I wasn't immediately aware of this change."

Father hid his face in his hands and was laughing again then amidst his merriment he managed to choke out, "Matthew, you are so obtuse. The girl practically threw herself at you! I've never known her to visit her father as often as she has in the past eight months, just happening to be there whenever you were. She all but fell into your lap, man. It's a wonder that she wasn't the one to propose. Frankly I didn't even know that you were paying her court, it seemed all rather one-sided to me." Mother rolled her eyes and slapped his hand.

Dr Jefferson gave my father a very disparaging look. "I'm not accountable to you for my free time, Colin."

I was smiling at their easy banter, I too wondered when Dr Jefferson could pay court to Miss Wiseman with the amount of time he seemed to spend with us and his practice, but it was none of my business. Though I did venture to ask, "So there will be an engagement party soon?"

He brightened up considerably. "Yes, indeed, there will be. In fact, it's part of why I'm here. I have come to bring your invitations to a dinner party being hosted by Sir Thomas."

"Will your family be attending?" As soon as it was out of my mouth I knew I had been mistaken to ask. His countenance darkened, and his hands curled into fists. Then he looked up and smiled. "My Aunt Elizabeth will be attending, she has cared for me since I was a babe after the death of my mother. My father will not be there, we have not spoken for a number of years."

"Oh, I am so very sorry."

He relaxed while taking a sip of his tea. "Don't be. My father and I have not seen eye to eye since I was a youth and he expected me to follow in his footsteps, being a useless gentleman with no occupation other than waiting to inherit his estate. It bothers him to no end that he cannot control me since I need neither his approval nor fortune." I would love to have asked how he came by his own fortune since it was obvious that he was a man of considerable independent means over and above what he earned as a physician and agent to the Crown. But his eyes reflected a pain that went deeper than just the estrangement from his father. There was more to this than he was prepared to tell. Mother evidently knew because her face couldn't mask the concern that she felt for Dr Jefferson and the pain he so obviously felt.

To lighten the mood, I addressed my mother, "Do you think Emilie and Samuel will be back in time for the dinner party and should we see madam about new gowns?" I looked to my papa for his response to the last question.

Father raised his hands. "No new gowns! I haven't seen you in half of what you both bought while in Paris, young lady!"

Mother laughed at him then looked down at the invitation that Dr Jefferson had handed her. "Matthew, this invitation is for the end of this month! How long have you been engaged?"

He looked down obviously embarrassed. "Ah, since this morning but it would seem as far as Isabel is concerned we've been engaged for much longer than I thought." He chuckled. "It was often alluded to but never formalized before I went to Paris. Her father was quiet put out with me for not asking his permission before I spoke with him this morning."

Mother was laughing. "Oh, Matthew, you never had a chance, poor man. However, Miss Wiseman is an accomplished young lady, I think you two will suit each other just fine." Mother was about to add something when there was a pounding at the outside door. My father made for the hallway and the rest of us followed closely behind. Michael had just opened the door and a bedraggled Viscount Tinley stumbled in or as he was known to the family Edward Johnson, Miles' brother.

# Chapter 36
## *Actions and Consequences*

Edward was soaked and filthy as if he had ridden long and hard, he was gasping for his breath as he asked, "Is my brother here?"

My father looked at him with something akin to loathing as he stood there, dripping a puddle on the floor in front of us and he looked in no mood to respond to him. But he gathered himself, "You had better come in to dry off and explain to me what is going on." Michael whispered a few words to my father who gave Edward a sharp look.

Edward looked anxious and he was obviously very upset. "I need to speak to my brother." He gasped for another breath then fell face forward onto the floor.

Dr Jefferson and Michael raced forward and with his assistance they were able to get him into the library, remove his soaked great coat, boots and stockings. They laid him gently on the settee by the fire. Michael then went for Dr Jefferson's bag which he thankfully took everywhere with him. We left the men with Edward and moved to the other end of the library while the doctor examined him. In short order, he pronounced his collapse to be from exhaustion."

Michael nodded, saying, "To be sure, doctor, his horse is near dead, but the grooms are caring for it now."

Edward started to come around and Father moved to hand him a glass of brandy, but the doctor stayed his hand. "No, Colin, he needs something to eat first then the brandy." Food was called for and in short order Mr Allan arrived with a plate of sandwiches and a fresh decanter."

Edward reached for the brandy in my father's hand, took a gulp only to choke and splutter. "My brother. I need my brother, where is he?"

Father looked down at him disdainfully as Edward took a huge bite out of the sandwich in his hand. "He's not here at present. Actually, I have no idea where he is."

Edward laid down the sandwich then leaned forward, his head in his hands and groaned. "No, the one time I've needed him and he's not here."

Just then there was a commotion in the hallway and Edward's father came storming into the room. "What the hell is going on here! Edward, what have you done now! You come to my club ranting that you need Miles and then without waiting there for me you race to my home accost Brentwood apparently screaming for Miles. What on earth is going on?!"

Edward started laughing uncontrollably. "You have no idea, old man, how angry Lord Burley is. He's ready to eradicate our entire family."

The Earl looked down at his son with disgust. "That should make you very happy. Are you looking for you brother to give him up to Burley? Why am I not surprised that you'd turn against your own family to save your hide? You disgust me."

Edward sat back and gulped down the brandy. "Well, Father, be that as it may. Both you and Mother instilled in me the idea that family is everything and without it you are a lesser man. But where you differed, Mother was full of vitriol while you spoke about honour and love. I learned that the hard way in Paris." He was crying now in great sobs. "I know you think it was me that hurt Miles, but I was never in the cell with him, it was Julian. I was disgusted when I found out what he had done and if he hadn't been shot at the Embassy ball, I would have done it myself that night. Who do you think gave Miles the gun! Believe me, Father, no one can loath me more than I do myself right now."

The Earl stood there, fish mouthing. Edward pointed and laughed at him. "I made that exact same face the day you told me that you were proud of me finishing university—even though I didn't do as well as Miles—and I said—"

The Earl blanched. "You said 'I love you, Father'. I'm sorry I didn't know what to say to you then until after you had turned away and left...yet you have continued to hate me and your brother."

Edward shrugged his shoulders. "Mother was an effective and merciless teacher, it's hard to see through that kind of hate. But I realised that day that no matter how badly I treated you that you would always be kind to me and that you would never treat Miles better than me...even though Mother said you did. I hated that you spent more time with him but now I know it was Mother who kept me from you, she was poison. In fact, she ruined most of my life, she hated you so much there was no room in her heart for love, not even for me." He looked at the sandwich in his hand then threw it back onto the plate. "I must find Miles...but thank you for your hospitality, Turner."

Gabriel had come into the room and remained standing in front of the door at my father's signal. "You're not going anywhere until we know exactly what is going on." Edward fell back against the settee and Mother came forward to sit beside him, she picked up the plate and held it out to him. "First, I think you need to finish these, now eat." He tried to smile at her as he reached out to take back the sandwich he had been eating and wolfed it down.

Father was rubbing his forehead and then motioned for us all to take a seat. "There is little that can be done tonight so I think it best that you tell us what is going on."

Edward looked at his father like he was begging for understanding. "When I took Julian home, news of his death had outpaced me. Burley already knew and was under the impression that Miles had killed Julian, he was furious. He wouldn't listen to me that Miles had nothing to do with it or about how depraved Julian had become. He's mad with grief and hate, he ranted about how much he hated you and that I should have been his son. I had no idea that my mother was even in love with him or that she was his mistress so now I'm not even sure if I am your son."

The Earl reached out to him. "You're my son in every way and Lionel Burley is a liar. Your mother told me that she and Burley were lovers. She had sought to lash out and hurt me, to make me think that you weren't my son but when she realised that would hurt you too, she told me that she had only taken him as a lover after she was sure she was pregnant with you. In her own way, she did love you, Edward."

Edward had tears trailing down his face. "And how—how do you know I am not a cuckoo, Father, how do you know that I am not Burley's son?"

The Earl grabbed hold of his hand. "Because you are here, because you have been looking for Miles, because I know in here." He laid his palm against his chest. "From the moment you were born I knew you were mine. Besides you have my eyes and the Johnson nose...no one has a nose like ours."

Edward drew back his hand, half sobbing half chuckling. "Why did she do this to us?"

The Earl sat back and sighed. "Because I loved you, but not her." Edward's head snapped up. "Edward, all my children are dearer to me than anything in this world. Even though you and Miles have made me exceptionally angry and occasionally disappointed, I have always loved you both, as I do all my children." He looked around I supposed for a drink. Gabriel was in the process of pouring one and brought the decanter over to the table, pouring brandy into everyone's glass. The Earl drank off half of it then continued. "Burley knows that, son, so he's trying to turn you against me. Just as he's always tried to make things as difficult as possible for Miles at every turn. But he's failed this time. Mr and Mrs Spencer have presented my petition to his Majesty and they are confident that Miles will be confirmed as my heir." I searched Edward's face for anger or hurt but all I saw was relief. The Earl smiled at him and raised his glass to him. "You'll finally be free of a burden I know you've never wanted, Edward, and free to pursue your own passions." He paused then looked directly at Edward with a smile, oozing pride, "You're quite good, you know."

Edward looked up at his father cradling the glass in his hand that Gabriel had placed there. "Who told you that I paint, Miles? I wouldn't be surprised if it was, he caught me painting by the lake last summer."

The Earl shook his head. "No, it wasn't Miles. I know that you don't go to my sister's in Scotland to hunt or fish. She's very proud of you, you know, just as I am. Millicent says that you have a real talent and she would know since she's exceptionally gifted herself. Do you know that she sells her paintings under an assumed name?" Edward looked up as his father nodded. "Not that you will ever need money. Edward, with being my younger son there would be no stigma attached to you being an artist, you may be considered a touch eccentric but nothing worse." Then he laughed, and Edward looked at him puzzled. "I just want you to be happy! Millicent has told me how miserable you've been at the idea of inheriting and I know you have no talent for estate management." He stopped then looked about at the rest of us then saying to Edward who was still looking at his father with astonishment, "Now what is Burley up to, can you tell us anything?"

Gabriel suddenly leaned over Edward's shoulder. "And if you are or have been lying or do anything to hurt this man, your brother or these people may not hurt you, but I will skin you alive." Edward had turned to look at him and Gabriel's grin made me shudder. Edward went ghastly pale then Gabriel clapped him on the shoulder. "I think we understand each other." No one but the Earl and my mother looked at Edward with any compassion.

I thought back to the garden party and the attack on the Earl. "Did you try to kill your father in Paris at the garden party?"

Edward glared at me, but his expression quickly softened. "No, but I saw who did. It was Ramsey Clarke, he and his parents are apparently distant but poor relations of Burleys."

Then Edward coughed and squared his shoulders. "Burley has serious financial problems, he has for as long as I've known him, but he's always managed to stave off his creditors and debtors' prison. At one time, he had counted on marrying my mother for her fortune to help him clear his debt but when she married my father, he started investing in risky gambits that I heard included smuggling, but I've only found this out since reconnecting with Julian. Burley had been heavily in debt to several people that would think nothing of killing him then he married Lady Burley, even though he loathed her. He ran through her considerable fortune in no time while the poor woman bore him four sons and two daughters in rapid succession. You know that she drowned when Alexander was only two years old and that it was whispered that she killed herself. I had initially become a friend of the family through my mother, but I didn't really know Randall, he was more Miles' contemporary, but Julian and I had been good friends at school for the most part."

His father leaned forward. "What do you mean for the most part?"

Edward turned a brilliant shade of red and sighed. "He had perverted sexual appetites." Wringing his hands and chewing on his lower lip, he continued, "We parted company for some time after he almost killed a whore. But then Randall died, and I felt that I should write him to express my condolences, so we became reacquainted.

"I had no idea that Miles had been instrumental in Randal's death but neither Julian nor his father said a word about it until Lord Burley heard that Miles was in Paris. I'm so ashamed now that I listened to them. He told me that you were working with Miles to have me declared a bastard and he led me to believe that I was his son and not yours. He told me you planned to leave me destitute out of revenge but that he would care for me if I helped him." Edward wrung his hands looking at his father. "I'm sorry, Father, but you were spending so much time with Miles and when not with him you were with Lady Jane and her children. I was stuck on the estate trying to understand what Wembley wanted to teach me about the estate accounts and I didn't care. Lord Burley's words poisoned me just as Mother's had."

The Earl reached out taking his hands in his. "Edward, all you had to do was talk to me. I'm sorry that you felt like you couldn't."

Edward pulled back and waved him off. "It makes no difference now."

He sniffed and then turned his head to look at me. "Anyway, Miss Turner, I believe you actually wanted to know if I had any idea what Ramsey had planned? I didn't at the time. It wasn't until I brought Julian's body home that I found Ramsey and his parents staying with Lord Burley. I was informed then that the attempted assassination of my father had been in my best interests so that I might inherit quickly. It was at that point that I knew Lord Burley had been using me to get his hand on the Johnson fortune through me. I was even foolish enough to change my banker to his. But that first night back from Paris he talked about an eye for an eye at dinner, he was looking for revenge. I felt like I had reached the end of my usefulness to Burley and I feared for my family, so I left after everyone had retired. I went home but Lady Jane and the children were gone, and no one knew where they were. I know that Tyler knew there they were, but he refused to tell me, so I went to Miles' country home, then finally here to London. He means to kill or ruin us all."

Edward truly broke down into heaving sobs. My mother moved closer to him and wrapped her arm around him, drawing his head onto her shoulder.

Father jerked forward reaching out, but Mother shot him a glare, challenging him to make a scene. He knew better than to cross my mother especially when she was being maternal. Normally she was a woman of decided opinions but her maternal instinct was ten times fiercer when she was with child.

The Earl smiled at her then got up and paced the room. Father, Dr Jefferson and Gabriel moved to the other end of the room to talk in whispers. I poked up the fire while watching my mother. Charity who had been hovering behind the door came in and bent down to whisper in my ear, "Do you believe him?"

I pursed my lips glancing back at my mother and Edward. Mother was looking at me and shook her head, she didn't believe him entirely, so I decided to be truthful. "It is a good story and has a ring of truth to it. But you asked, do I believe him entirely?" I shook my head. "No. There is something he's not telling us." The Earl had paced around the room then joined the other gentlemen, he listened to what they had to say when they reached an agreement they came back to their seats.

It was my father that spoke despite that the Earl looked like he wanted to. "Mr Johnson."

Edward's head snapped up. "That's Lord T, oh, I suppose it might not be anymore."

Father's face was composed but his eyes were hard as he leaned forward in his seat. "Precisely. You have given us an idea of what to expect from Lord Burley, but we had already reached that conclusion ourselves. Do you have any other information as to his plans?"

Edward flinched then glared at my father, "You don't believe me, do you?!"

Father sat back, crossed his legs at the ankle, assuming a very relaxed posture. "On the contrary, everything you have told us is probably true. It's what you haven't told us that concerns me the most."

Edward sat up straight, shrugging off my mother's attentions. "What?! Do you think I'd still betray my family after all that I've told you?" Edward looked at his father who bowed his head rather than make eye contact. Edward was madly chewing his lower lip, looking at all of us in disbelief. Either he was a very good actor, or he was telling the truth.

His father grabbed his glass of whisky and drained it. "I don't know, son, there is so much so much history between you and Miles, you and me. I love you, but I don't know if I can trust your words."

Edward suddenly deflated, the colour drained from his face and he flung his head back. He looked up at the ceiling then closed his eyes. "Alright...I'm being followed. I'm supposed to find Miles and lead them to him or they'll kill me!" He opened his eyes and looked back at his father then in a bitter voice said, "Miles can take care of himself; he's always been able to do that. Hell, he works for you, Turner! And God, he most assuredly knows better than to trust me. Miles will see them coming before they even get close to him. He's a crack shot and deadly with a blade of any kind... My paint brush isn't much of a weapon, I can't paint them to death, Father."

I was livid, my head and heart were both pounding. "He's blind, you fool! He can't defend himself."

Edward choked on his drink. "What—no, he can't be. I saw him in Paris, he was—he was—he only needed those dark glasses after prison and the lantern accident."

I stood with my hands fisted. "How did you know about the lantern accident?!"

He looked panicked. "I—I don't know. Julian, yes, Julian told me."

I screamed at him. "LIAR!" I took two steps towards him, I wanted to beat on him with my fists. Charity grabbed my arm and stopped me.

Father looked from me to Edward. "Well, do you care to address that accusation?"

Edward took out his handkerchief and wiped his brow and upper lip. "I went to see him, don't know why or what I intended to do. But Miles was like a mad man, the one guard lost control of him and Miles killed him, but it was in self-defence the guard was beating him to death when I arrived with the second guard. I didn't know what Julian had done to him. Then the guard I came with flung the lantern at him and I ran."

The Earl glared at him. "You were there, and you did nothing to help him?"

Edward grabbed his hair. "What could I do? He was under an arrest warrant arranged by Lord Burley! They weren't going to let me take him out of there! Julian would have killed me if I tried."

Charity stepped forward. "Then what about my children? Don't tell me that you knew nothing about them! You had to know what Julian was going to do with them!"

Edward now looked totally lost. "What children? I don't know what you're talking about!"

Father looked over at Charity. "The boys never saw Edward or heard of him, Mrs de Bearnes." She slumped and sat down in a chair near the hearth.

I was still standing and seething. "You could have gone to your father! He could have gotten Miles out of prison."

Edward rolled his head and rubbed his hands down his thighs. "How was I supposed to know that Lord Burley's charges weren't legitimate?" He looked at his father pleading in his eyes. "You never told me anything about what happened. All I knew was what Lord Burley and Julian told me. I didn't even know that you were in Paris until Miles had been released. But then you and I haven't exactly been on speaking terms, have we." Suddenly he stood up and became very agitated, rubbing his face with his hands. "Lady Jane, the children, oh my god…he must have them by now!"

The Earl stood up and grabbed him by the shoulder. "What are you talking about?"

Edward was beside himself now pacing the room. "Burley forced me to go with him to our estate. He wouldn't accept that no one knew where they'd gone. I got away from him there, but you know him, he would have gotten someone to tell him."

The Earl was pale and scared. "Fisher! It would be Fisher; Lady Jane would never go anywhere without telling Nanny Fisher where she was going! Why didn't I think of that?"

Edward was distraught now, he pounded his head with his fist "STUPID, STUPID! God, what have I done. I never thought of her. I should have told Tyler to get her away."

Father looked at Dr Jefferson. "Care to take a trip to the Earl's estate, Matthew?"

Dr Jefferson sighed. "Well, someone should, it might as well be me. This nanny, does she live in the big house or somewhere else?"

Edward just looked at him dazed as the Earl answered. "She was my wife's nanny, she came with her when we married as she had no other place to go. She lives in one of the gardener's cottages on the estate Jane and the children are quite fond of her. Give me a minute and I'll write you a letter to Tyler, our butler, he can help you."

Father seemed at a loss. "Wouldn't Lady Jane have taken the nanny with her?"

The Earl shook his head. "Nanny Fisher was also her mother's nanny, she must be close to ninety now, she'd never agree to leave the estate."

Father asked, "Would she have told this nanny where she was going even though you told her not to."

The Earl looked worried. "I don't know."

"You don't know! Good God, man, she's your wife!"

The Earl growled at my father. "Precisely, Turner, does your wife do everything you tell her to?!"

Father blushed. "Well, no…but she—wouldn't have told the old nanny if I told her not to."

Mother rolled her eyes. "If you'll excuse me, Lord Shellard, by your own admission Jane is not a particularly sensible woman. I assume that you didn't tell her that there was any danger." She pointedly looked at the Earl and shook her head as he looked embarrassed and nodded. "Regardless of what you did or didn't tell her, she'll know now; Aunt Mary and Uncle Arthur will have apprised her of the danger even if you didn't."

Father nodded when the Earl appealed to him for confirmation. "She's right."

All eyes returned to Edward when Gabriel asked, "Who exactly is following you?"

Edward didn't hesitate. "The Clarkes."

Gabriel reared back. "All three of them?"

Edward nodded. "Eugenia is worse than her husband and son put together, if there're any brains between them she has them all. They dance to her tune and she is vicious, it seems to be a trait of the Burley family."

Gabriel grinned and approached my father. "Charity and I can help with this, let me have them."

Father looked sceptical until he looked at Charity and saw what I did, she'd go after them even without my father's approval. "How many men do you need?"

Gabriel paused before answering. "Give me the footmen, you'll need the others when you go to Cornwall."

Now it was my turn to snap a sharp look at my father and he sagged noticeably when he looked my way. "I don't suppose I can ask you stay home with your mother and brother, can I?"

Before I could utter a word, Mother jumped in. "No, you can't because we're all going. And don't start, Colin, you know very well that you're going to need us all. I'm not going to sit here at home waiting to hear what's happened."

The Earl had been writing the letter for Dr Jefferson and had just sealed it when he said, "I think that is a fine idea, Mrs Turner, a family excursion. What an ideal way for me to get to know my future daughter-in-law. Edward and I will come along with you."

Edward looked sick and his father chuckled. "You didn't think that we'd just leave you to your own devices, did you? You still have to earn our trust, Edward, so you're coming with us."

# Chapter 37
## *Cornwall*

Mother organized our departure with the help of Murphy whom we still call Murphy even though he had been elevated to a position that should have engendered a Mister to go with it. He claimed it made the staff feel more comfortable about approaching him when reporting to him about their assignments.

Our footman John and his twin brother would go with Gabriel. John's brother Richard had accepted the footman position vacated by Murphy. Richard was still in training, but Mother was determined to keep him since she would be the talk of the Beau Monde with identical twins as our footmen. Father was happy to have him on staff because of how quickly he grasped the details of situations. And he had an encyclopaedic knowledge of the less savoury parts of London from working in the local distilleries. Richard was not sure that he wanted to be a footman, being done up in fancy dress as he said was not appealing to him, but the chance to be with his brother and earn a better living was enticing.

Gabriel and Charity would be staying in our home with their boys and Lettie while we were in Cornwall. It had been hotly debated with my father that James should be left at home too, but mother won out exploiting my father's fear of the Clarkes gaining access to our home and James.

We were to leave right after breakfast and Gabriel was to ride out dressed in Edward's clothes on his horse just before our departure. Edward was coming with us, but he couldn't be seen. Father had an idea on how to achieve it which had made the Earl chuckle and Edward sulk. Gabriel hoped his deception would lure at least one of the Clarkes into following him. His size and hair colour were about the same as Edward, but he had a much darker skin tone. I was the only one to notice this, so I raced to our closet of costumes to find Miles' makeup kit and returned with a large cloak that he could wear over his own great coat and with the aid of makeup, I was able to lighten his skin while Allan prepared his saddle bags to look ready as if for a long journey. At a distance the Clarkes would be hard pressed to tell it wasn't Edward.

The Earl arrived with his carriage and offered to take me and Edward with him thereby leaving more room on our carriage for my rambunctious brother and so my mother could rest comfortably. I was not really pleased that Edward would be traveling with us, but I was determined to make the best of it. I had my popper in my reticule and another pistol under my pelisse, as well as a small dagger that Miles had given me in Paris, it was close to my body and held in place by my garter just as Miles had instructed. The Earl I noticed was well armed as well. I nodded at the twin Scottish dirks he carried cross wise on his belt, "Is one of those for Edward?" I was not keen on the idea of him being armed since I still didn't trust him.

The Earl looked down. "Oh no, these are a match pair and stay with me."

"They're lovely."

"Aye, they are…lovely and deadly. They were a gift from my sister, Millicent, she married a Highland Lord or as they say Laird, she's gone native and embraced the culture completely. She hopes to get me posing in full Highland kit for a portrait one day." He laughed. "At least her husband Angus and I agree that it will never happen. An Englishman dressed as a Highlander would be considered tantamount to treason by both the Scots and Englishmen but for entirely different reasons." He patted the dirks. "But these little stickers have been my friends since the day she gifted them to me, they are perfectly weighted and balanced. I don't think I've ever travelled without them on my person except at sea, never want to have a weapon like that too close to," he blushed, "well, let's just say it could be quite painful if you slipped on deck." He chuckled then leaned forward to take one of my hands. His hands were warm and callused which surprised me. Into my hand, he placed a ring. I was surprised when I looked down to see it was a women's signet ring with the Shellard crest. I moved to return it to him, but he shook his head no and closed my hand around it. "I want you to have it, my dear, it belonged to Miles' mother. Maria would approve of you, she had spirit like you and knew exactly how to get her way, she made me very happy. I think you'll do the same for Miles." Just then the coach lurched as the final trunk was loaded in place. The Earl met my eye and we both smirked. "That'll be Edward." He chuckled. "It'll do him some good to be locked in that trunk until we're sure we haven't been followed."

Gabriel came out on his mount while the baggage was still being loaded, he bent to speak briefly with my father then raced away in the opposite direction from the way we would be travelling. Not soon after two men, one distinctly blond, the other older, followed him. As my father passed our carriage window he said, "It looks like Mrs Clarke and whoever she has with her will be following us." Charity was watching from the nursery and signalled something to my father, but I was at the wrong angle to see what it was. Father turned back to us. "Are you both armed?" I nodded and so did the Earl.

The Earl whispered, "When do you think Edward can be released?"

Father pursed them as he tried to hide his smile. "I had air holes made in the trunk but I'm afraid he will have to wait until we are well out of London." The Earl arched both brows in surprise. "But there's no need to worry, my friend; Irene put some laudanum in his coffee so he should sleep most of the way."

"What a remarkable woman," he looked at me and shook his head. "Does Miles know what he's getting into marrying you?"

Father chuckled and answered for me, "Oh yes, we've had that conversation already."

Now I was astounded. "Father! When? I mean why?"

He smiled at me. "When he came to ask for your hand. I felt I owed it to him to explain exactly what he was getting, he seems to think that you'll make life interesting and I had to agree. And don't give me that look, Lissa. It was by no means a biased evaluation, after all, your mother was there and she didn't offer up an argument, quite to the contrary she agreed with me." He chuckled at my expression and then pulled on his gloves. "Well, we've given Gabriel enough of a head start so we can be off now." With that he turned and mounted his horse. Since Michael and Jacob were coming with us, it was decided that Murphy would remain behind to manage things at home with Lettie. Mr Allan was coming because father would be lost without both Murphy and Allan. We would be on the road for about four days over less than hospitable roads, at least the weather was fine and hopefully it would stay that way.

The Earl sat back looking out the window as we journeyed through London. The traffic was slow as usual with riders, wagon, carriages, phaetons and foot traffic moving in all directions. The noise was almost palpable with drivers, riders, costermongers and shop keepers yelling all at once, it was impossible for us to carry on a conversation, so I let my thoughts drift; and my mind wandered back to a previous long road trip from Northumberland to London when I had ridden with my Uncle Samuel over the meadows and hillsides. I had not seen Jewel in some time since she and Baron had been sent to Somerset. But she had been delivered of her first foal by Baron, a fine colt that was apparently the image of his father. By all reports both animals seemed to be happy and healthy and Baron was making an admirable profit for them as a stud.

I was doing everything I could to keep from thinking about Miles but thoughts of him kept creeping into my mind. I had one hand deep in the pocket where I put his letter, it was as much a talisman for me as the amulet Jibben's grandmother had made which rested in the same pocket. For some reason I felt that the two belonged together, that if the one was meant to protect me then perhaps it would also protect Miles through his letter.

Once we were outside of the city the Earl straightened up in his seat and leaned forward. "Miss Turner, may I ask you how old you are?"

I smiled. "I'm almost nineteen, Lord Shellard. Is there some reason that you ask?"

He pursed his lips I assumed pondering if he should continue. "It doesn't bother your parents that you are so young, and that Miles is seven years older than you?"

I sighed and stopped smiling. "My parents have no reason to object. My mother was seventeen when she married my father, granted he was only four years older but none of their parents approved. May I ask, sir, how many years there are between you and Lady Jane?"

He smirked and sat back again. "You, Miss Turner, are impertinent, but I do not disapprove of you. Miles is a man who knows his own mind, I just wanted to be sure that you are woman and not a child. I hope you won't be insulted by this, but I don't want Miles hurt by anyone, even someone he loves; he has already had enough pain in his life." He sighed looking out the window before he continued, "He told me about your life before you were reunited with your parents. It couldn't have been easy for you."

I folded my hands in my lap and willed him to look at me. "Your Lordship, I know what it's like to live with the stigma of being labelled a bastard. But you loved him and cared for him as your son and I know that my parents suffered by not being together, just as you did having your true wife labelled as your mistress."

He jerked back like I had hit him. "*Touché*, Miss Turner, *Touché*!" He licked his lips. "Dr Jefferson told me what you did for Miles in Paris, how you stopped him when he attempted to kill himself. You gave him a reason to live and helped Miles to become more independent with his affliction." He relaxed and looked out the window. "Dr Grimes believes that his blindness is emotional and not physical. But I still can't help worrying that he will never recover; so are you prepared to tie yourself to him, he will need a strong helpmate if he should remain blind."

I cleared my thoughts while attempting to control my temper. "Lord Shellard, I am not tying myself to anyone. I am marrying your son because I love him, and I will take him however I can have him. But before you question my motives I was committed to Miles in my heart long before I knew he was your legitimate son and before he had any hope of being recognized here in England as your heir."

He laughed out loud. "Direct aren't you, Miss Turner! I like that, you and Miles will do well together, and I suspect he's right that you will make life interesting."

I looked at him in disbelief. "Was this a test as to my loyalty to Miles?"

He shook his head. "No, I was truly just curious. I worry about my son, but I have only his best interests at heart. Your parents had already informed me about the depth of your feelings for Miles and I know their story from your Aunt Mary. I just wanted to make sure that they weren't exaggerating as parents often do." He glanced back out the window. "It looks like we are finally out of the city."

My father had dropped back to ride by our carriage. He leaned towards the window and tapped on it for the Earl to lower it. "There is a stand of trees just over this next rise, I think it would be an appropriate time to pull over, stretch our legs have a bit of refreshment and perhaps extricate your son from his cage." Father chuckled and moved on before we could reply. As if on cue there was a thump and a string of curses from the rear of the carriage where Edward was being held in the trunk.

When we pulled off to the area indicated by my father, the trunk was unstrapped, and the lid of the trunk opened. Edward was to say the least extremely disgruntled, especially when he required the assistance of Michael to get out of the blasted thing. It was then strapped back into place on the carriage while Edward stood there ranting at the treatment he had received. Mother bore down on him with a bottle of ale in her hand. "Oh, for heaven sakes, Edward, shut up and drink this. She thrust the bottle at him and he reluctantly took it from her." She watched him take a cautious sip and rolled her eyes. "It's not drugged if that's what you're thinking. If you behave, I'll even see that you get some bread and cheese to go with it."

Edward straightened after taking a healthy gulp then inquired, "Am I your prisoner, madam?"

Mother looked back over her shoulder. "Heavens, no!" Edward smiled smugly then she continued, "You're my husband's prisoner." Edward opened his mouth to respond but Mother beat him to it. "He wanted to drug you again, so remember this, Mr Johnson, you are out of that trunk only on MY whim. If you misbehave, my husband will have you back in there without the benefit of sedation." Then she walked over to my father and patted him on the arm as he tried very hard not to laugh.

Edward glared at Father as he approached him, "I'd listen to her if I were you. If you do one thing that I think might jeopardize anyone in this party, you'll be lucky if I only dump you in the trunk, instead of slitting your throat which I admit would be my first inclination."

Edward blanched then tried to laugh but it came out more like wheeze. "You wouldn't dare! My father—"

He looked directly at Lord Shellard who was drinking his ale and watching the war of words transpire. "Don't expect any help from me, Edward, you're a grown man. But if you let your arrogance dictate your actions then I shall assist Turner in returning you to the box…but I would not countenance him slitting your throat." Edward looked dumbfounded and I had to turn my back to the whole scene along with the others to keep from laughing in his face.

Once we settled down we sat quietly on a hillock watching a pair of riders approach over the crest of the hill. We were hidden from their view but not the carriages. The lead rider peeled off to ride toward us while the remaining rider continued up the road.

Father pulled his pistols as did Michael and Jacob. Lord Shellard had his at hand and stood firm watching the rider approach. Edward was frantic and dove into the nearest carriage to huddle on the floor. I quirked an eyebrow at the Earl who shrugged. "He's as good a shot as Miles, but he lacks the fundamental courage to shoot at a target which is likely to shoot back. He doesn't have the killer instinct." I merely nodded.

Once the rider came close enough to be identifiable my father lowered his pistol and everyone else followed suit. It was my Uncle Samuel. Father stepped forward as he came to a halt and jumped down from his horse. "Glad we caught up with you, you're being followed by the way. I think it's Ramsey but he's a skittish little bugger. I haven't been able to get close enough to be sure it's him." He looked around as if he might be lurking in the bushes. "Sir Thomas had a communication today that the house in Cornwall is currently occupied by people other than just Aunt Mary, Spencer and his Lordship's family. It seems that Lord Burley is paying a visit with a few of his friends and holding them hostage."

Father slapped his thigh swearing a blue streak. "Damn, it's going to take the carriages three days at best to get to Cornwall, but I can't leave them unguarded. Maybe they should return to London and we'll push on." Just then I heard music and turned to see a gypsy caravan coming over the rise with Jibben in the lead.

Uncle Samuel looked over his shoulder then back at my father. "Sir Thomas was at your home just as Emilie and I arrived, and he advised me of the situation with the Clarkes. So, I um took the liberty of picking up an escort and some help."

Father sighed, running his hand across his eyes. "How much is this going to cost me?"

Samuel clapped him on the shoulder. "Courtesy of the Crown to be paid in full by Sir Thomas."

Father looked shocked. "Well, that was rather generous of the old man."

Samuel chuckled. "I was surprised he acquiesced so quickly to my demand, but he rather likes the idea of having a band of gypsies on the payroll so to speak."

Father smirked and nodded toward the band. "Do they know that?"

Samuel laughed out loud, "Oh my god, NO! If they did they'd be camping out on the palace grounds."

Father nodded. "So what of Gabriel?"

"That's who was riding with me. He has gone on to the Inn where we'll be staying tonight and looking for that sneak Ramsey along the way. Gabriel capped old Clarke, but Ramsey got away. Mrs Clarke attempted to gain entrance to your home by stealth, but Murphy told me that Charity took her down handily and Murphy got her cohort. When I left Sir Thomas's men had taken them off to Newgate." He looked around at our group. "Where's Matthew?"

315

Father explained what had transpired while my Uncle had remained in France. "And what the duce are you doing back here already?"

Samuel laughed. "It was Em and Mrs Baxter's idea. Mrs Baxter hasn't been back to England in some time and wanted to bring Patrick for a bit of vacation. She's thinking of sending him to school here, I wish her the best of luck on that one. Personally, I think they were just feeling lonely after everyone left. Oh, by the by I was paid a visit by the local tax collector before we left, he had some documents for me to sign and during our conversation I found out that there had apparently been some issues with the chateau's back taxes but that they had been taken care of before I received the transfer papers. You didn't have anything to do with that, did you, Colin?"

I grimaced inwardly waiting to hear my father's response. Without missing a beat, he said, "No, my good man, I had nothing to do with it. Maybe the Minister of the Interior Monsieur Corbière made them disappear for services rendered. It would be very French of him not to say a word till later when he needs a favour."

Samuel arched a brow and said in a drawl looking suspiciously at my father, "Yes, it would be very French of him."

Father was saved from saying anything else with the arrival of Jibben who dismounted in one fluid motion to stand beside my father. He placed an arm across his shoulder. "Ah, Turner, so we work together again for his Majesty! I hope this will be fun, my men are bored, they need something that will stir their blood and that our women will sing songs about! They were disappointed that our raid on the warehouses was postponed." Then he spied my mother and walked over to her to take her hand and kissed it like a courtier. "Mrs Turner, may I say that impending motherhood becomes you!"

My father looked furious but Mother only blushed. "Why thank you, Jibben." Uncle Samuel watched my father with a rueful smile as he went over and removed my mother's hand from Jibben's grasp.

Then Jibben turned on his heel nonplussed and grasped the Earl's hand. "William, I am so glad to see you again, my friend. Are you and the beautiful Miss Turner becoming better acquainted? A word to the wise, my friend, when you negotiate the marriage contract it should be noted that she is very headstrong and disposed to fits of temper." I stood there with my mouth open, I couldn't believe that he'd said that to the Earl then he had the nerve to look at me and wink.

Father, Jibben, my Uncle and the Earl walked off to speak with Michael and Jacob then Robert drifted over to join in the discussion. The coachmen were busy with the horses when the cavalcade of gypsy wagons finally reached us. Jibben's grandmother was in the front wagon biting down on a pipe as she brought the horses to a stop. She removed the pipe while keenly observing our surroundings then shook her head motioning for Jibben to come to her. He walked over, jumped onto the wagon and bent down to listen to her. When she was done he got down and she began the process of turning the wagon around with the others following suit. Jibben walked up to my father. "Mama says you picked a terrible place to stop, it's too close to the city and Ramsey is up in the hills behind you watching." He pointed to the distant hillocks as if he could see him there himself.

I spoke up. "How does she know; did she see him?"

Jibben pointed to his forehead. "She sees him in here. Mama refused him a reading once after touching him, she sensed that he is without a soul…pure evil, she can feel that same evil up there now."

I ventured to look after her wagon then back at him, but he was grinning at me. Then he became serious and said in a very cultured voice, "Remember, Miss Turner, 'there are more things in heaven and earth than are dreamt of in your philosophy'." He was quoting Shakespeare to me like a gentleman in a London drawing room, then he grinned, turned away and walked back to the men.

Mother with James, Meg and Beth following her ventured over to me and we moved to sit on the blanket covered grass watching the men discuss strategy. I wanted listen in, but I knew I would not be welcomed so I distracted myself by playing with James. I sat with him watching a troop of ants march past us as he tried to divert their course; but they remained ever true to their destination and merely went around or over whatever road blocks he placed before them.

Father finally came over to us and knelt, James immediately forgot the ants and walked over to my father. "Papa…here!" He presented him with an ant on his sticky finger. My father fell onto his back laughing and lifting James above his head with James laughing and kicking his legs as he screamed out, "Papa, papa, papa!"

My father smothered James with kisses and I felt bereft as I wondered what I had missed out on as a child. I felt my mother's concern rather than saw it. She reached for my hand and squeezed it. Then my father sat up holding James, they looked so much alike, both were grinning from ear to ear as he looked at me, "You were just as inquisitive as this little mister at the same age." Then he blew on James' belly who returned the attention by shrieking in Father's ear. But Father was still looking at me and smiling, "One day you'll know the same joy," then he went back to blowing on James' belly.

I looked at my mother for confirmation that I had indeed known him as papa once and had called him such, she nodded with glistening eyes. I felt a warmth in my heart as I realised that we had really been together as a family whenever we could in those first few years. But then I had lost him and forgot him, but he had never forgotten me. How painful that must have been for him to come to our home before my grandfather had returned and to treat me as the younger sister of his best friend; the agony that must have caused him. I would not begrudge him these moments with James since I had once had them too.

# Chapter 38

## *The Journey with Gypsies*

James tired of playing and fell asleep on my father's lap so he handed him to Meg while he spoke to us, "I was ready to send you all back to London but Jibben and Samuel believe that Ramsey would only turn around and follow you back there and while I have my reservations about all of us pushing forward I'd rather have you close by."

Mother looked puzzled. "Close by, where will you be?"

He looked back at Jibben and Samuel. "I'm going with them, the Earl has agreed to stay with you along with Michael and Jacob. You'll be traveling with the gypsies, but you'll stay at inns during the night and travel with them during the day for safety's sake."

Mother did not look pleased. "And where will you be staying at night, sleeping rough under a hedge?! That is not acceptable, Colin! How will it look to whoever has been following us if you suddenly run off?"

The Earl came up behind us. "She has a point, Turner, and you'd be taking a number of the able-bodied men from the gypsy camp with you, are you willing to leave them with just myself, your two grooms and your valet?" Father glared at him. "I am fairly competent with a pistol and sword and I'm sure your grooms have more skill than I from the look of them, but Robert is just a lad and Allan is your butler!"

Samuel joined us and coughed. "You know, Colin, you can't always be in the thick of things and with James, Irene and Lissa here I think they might feel better with you staying with them. We're only going to reconnoitre when we get there anyway. We'll meet up with you before we take any action. By then word might have reached Miles and Dr Grimes. I'm sure Burley is aware that we'll be coming, he just doesn't know who or how many."

I looked at my father waiting for him to make a decision, so I asked, "What about Gabriel? He's gone on ahead, do you trust him?"

My father wasted no time in answering me, "Yes, I do. This is about his family; he needs them to feel safe, so he has to eliminate those that threatened their safety."

I bit my lower lip and pointedly glared at my father then my uncle, "And what if you get in his way, are you going to condone murder then turn around and give Gabriel up to the Crown? I don't think he deserves that, Father."

"I agree," the voice came from the copse of trees directly behind me. Gabriel stepped out. "Ramsey got away again," he looked back over his shoulder at the hillock behind us. "If we are discussing our next move, I suggest that we all travel with the gypsies and we should stay in their camp at night. Burley wants to break us up, I can feel it in my bones."

318

Jibben was not far off and approached us to say, "This Lord Burley sounds like a man that doesn't like to take chances, Turner, you may be wise to listen to this one and my friend William. As a great General once said, 'If your enemy is secure at all points, be prepared for him. If he has superior strength, evade him. If your opponent is temperamental, seek to irritate him. Pretend to be weak, that he may grow arrogant. If he is taking his ease, give him no rest. If his forces are united, separate them. Attack him where he is unprepared, appear where you are not expected.'"

Everyone stood in awe of Jibben for a few seconds then the spell was broken when Meg of all people said, "That's a quote from The Art of War by Sun Tzu!" Jibben grinned and nodded while the rest of us stood gobsmacked looking at Meg.

Father ventured, "How did you know that?"

Meg blushed as she was brushing down her skirts, "Not me, Mr Turner, I got it from Billy Phipps, he loves that sort of stuff. He told me the man he thought was his da used to talk to him about things like that all the time, just like he was a man and not a brat like the other men that came to see his mother."

Mother grasped Meg's arm. "Billy knows who his father is?"

Meg looked terrified now. "Well, he isn't sure, that's why he's never said anything. But he did tell me he's sure that he's an officer in the army. He thought he might have recognized him at that dinner party you held for Mr and Mrs Spencer after they got married."

Mother clasped her hands to her chest. "Good heavens, Billy's father is one of our acquaintance?!" Meg only nodded. "Did he tell you who?"

"No, ma'am, he said that he didn't want to cause a fuss, but I think he really didn't want the man to deny him. He did say that his mum never told him who his da was though, but he thought that the Major at your last party had the look of the man he thought was his da."

Mother shook her head. "Colin?"

Father raised both of his hands before him. "Yes, I know, dear, but one crisis at a time please. It could be Hopewood, I'll investigate when we return to London. But it may be better to let the thing alone, Irene."

Mother blurted out. "How do you know it's Hopewood?"

Father smiled. "He's an acquaintance, I met him through Sir Thomas. He was a major who recently resigned his commission in the Coldstream Guards after his father past away. Billy looks a bit like him and has the same interests...so it's possible."

Mother clasped her hands together, she looked excited. "Do you think he'll claim the boy if Billy is his?"

Father was reticent. "It's hard to say, Irene. He's not married and spends a great deal of time on his estate. He's not too far from us in Somerset, I promise you I will address this when we are done in Cornwall."

Mother smiled and kissed him on the cheek. "I know, darling, we have other priorities."

Father turned to Jibben to change the subject, "Don't you think it's about time that you gave up the halting English accent and gypsy bravado and tell us who you really are?"

Jibben's eyes grew dark, he fisted both hands then he relaxed and bowing to my father he spoke with a perfect English accent, "I see my bravado as you so aptly put it has finally been my downfall. Grandmama always says that I lay it on too thick."

He smiled and bowed to my mother then me saying, "Stephen Thomas Jibben Locke at your service, ladies."

Father and Samuel both stood with their arms crossed staring at him, it was my uncle who spoke up first. "Oxford, I take it? Especially since I don't remember hearing of you at Cambridge and we would have heard of a fellow like you."
Jibben scratched his head and sighed, "You have me Hughes."

Samuel continued, "Why the facade?"

Jibben shook his head. "It's not a façade." He pointed back over his shoulder, "Magda is my real grandmother. My mother is part Roma and my father's a gentleman farmer in Devon."

Samuel smiled. "Your mother is only part Roma?"

Jibben shrugged. "A youthful indiscretion of Granmama's, she liked Englishmen in her youth…but not so much now." He coughed and looked at the ladies. "I must apologize, ladies." Mother nodded "My mother had no desire to follow the Roma way of life and lived with her father. She met my father at a local Assembly room and the rest was history, from that moment on they had eyes only for each other. My mother wanted me and my sister to know both cultures, so I have travelled with Magda almost every summer since I was a boy. My mother said it gave me the chance to get over my wild streak. Otherwise you'll find me at home for the planting in the spring and harvest in the autumn. I have done so every year of my life since I could mount a horse except for my time at Oxford. Magda wanted to make sure that I had a good education and she insisted that I attend my father's old school though I had wanted to go to Cambridge because I heard you chaps had more fun. But one does not defy Grandmama."

I was puzzled. "So Bita is your half-sister?"

He chuckled. "A cousin, her mother is from Magda's gypsy husband. My sister married well and lives in Devon with a very English husband and a brood of children. Their oldest come to see Magda in the summer and go wild for a few weeks each year. My sister is very talented with herbal medicines and cures. She can deliver a calf and set a bone better than anyone I know. She loves to dance and has the voice of an angel…her husband is quite proud of her."

Father was taking this all in then he stopped Jibben before he could say any more, "At least now I know I can safely invite you to my club even if you are an Oxford man. But would you care to tell me why you suddenly decided to quote Sun Tzu? I'm sure you had a purpose other than unmasking yourself."

Jibben stopped smiling. "Turner, you are walking into a trap, you must know that if you split up your party it would be suicide; you're going to need all of us. The Roma will fight for William and for Miss Turner since she is the betrothed of their benefactor. But you only have me on your side. If you send your women home under the guard of your valet, butler and the Earl, the Roma will follow them. I cannot command them, all I can do is ask them to collect your bodies when Burley is done."

Samuel arched an eye at Jibben. "So you have military experience?"

Jibben actually blushed. "Yes, my father is a retired Colonel in the 1st Dragoons and as I said my parents meant me to savour both cultures, so I served as well. But the army did not agree with me or me with it. We parted company on amiable terms only after I had read every book in their library."

Father smirked. "The 1st has one of the finest military libraries in the country."

Jibben nodded. "Yes, they do. I was a mere lieutenant who had a talent for riding fast and winning at cards. Neither talent ingratiated me with either my commander or the aristocrats that felt the regiment was the domain of only blue bloods, so I spent a great deal of my time with either the horses or their splendid library."

Mother cocked her head at him. "Yet you have never married, Mr Lock?"

Jibben sighed. "Not yet, if I did I'd have to give up one of my lives and I'm not prepared to do that just yet." His smile was wistful but because he did not turn towards the caravan I felt his heart may lay in Devon. Then he shook himself and addressed my father, "We need to stay together, Turner, they already know that we're coming with you and we're being watched so there's no advantage to us splitting up."

Father grimaced and chewed on his lower lip and looked towards the caravan, then the carriages and up and down the road. Then he cupped his face with both hands and massaged his eyes while he thought. "You're right, Lock...as much as I hate to say it."

We were soon on our way once again this time followed by a gypsy caravan. It was twilight before we reached the Inn. Mother, myself, Meg and Beth were taken upstairs by the Innkeeper's wife who was followed by two maids with hot water.

There was no private parlour so once we had washed and shaken off the dust we adjourned to the common room for our evening meal. The meal was plain but hot and filling. There was a stew of some kind no one was sure the source of the meat, but the gravy was thick and savoury, and the meat was tender, there was also roast capon with vegetables, a sharp cheese and crusty bread. Pudding was a tart with thick cream. Everyone ate heartily but I noticed that our company drank sparingly from the Inn's wine and not one of them had any ale or small beer which made the Innkeeper suspicious at first until my father overpaid him for the meals. Uncle Samuel was drinking from his flask and when he caught my eye he leaned over and handed it to me. Inside was pomegranate juice which we had both developed a fondness for when we were in Paris. I smiled and took a sip. The mood of the common room around us was subdued, several patrons had come in, had only one drink then left after furtively casting their eyes over us.

We adjourned to our rooms and within a few minutes we were called to congregate in my parents' room. It was Robert who spoke after father nodded to him. He stepped forward rubbing the back of his neck. "I forgot Mr Turner's shaving kid and went out to the stables to get it out of the carriage. I chatted for a bit with the grooms when I noticed that Lord Shellard's coachman Greene was talking to two men and when I saw them step into the light I knew them at once."

Uncle Samuel interrupted, "Who were they?"

Robert licked his lips and bit his thumb. "They were two of the men that came and went from the common room after one drink and giving us a thorough once over."

Father looked around at all of us. "Robert, did you see where these men went?"

Robert swallowed. "Yes, sir, I watched them leave before I came to you. They rode out hell for leather down the road headed south in the direction we've been travelling."

The Earl stepped toward the door. "Let me go speak to Greene."

Robert called out. "No! I mean please don't, my Lord, I don't think that would be wise, a gentleman of your stature shouldn't venture out to the stables at this time of night. I spoke to Mr Greene, but he didn't give us away, but he does think something bad is afoot, my Lord, and I...we both agree that the Innkeeper has been paid to keep silent. When I came back through the kitchen he was right nervous. He was well into his cups when he grabbed my arm as I passed him, but he didn't say anything to me, just shook his head then let me go."

Father ran his hand across his brow. "I think we had better leave now. Michael, Jacob and Robert, just take what we need in the way of luggage out to the carriages, we'll leave the rest here. Samuel, Lord Shellard I suggest that we carry our valuables on us."

Mother spoke up. "No, Colin, give all the valuables to the women, we have deeper pockets and they'll be safer with us in the short term."

Father only nodded. "I'm going down to speak to the Inn Keeper."

Uncle Samuel looked concerned. "Are you sure that's wise?"

Father hefted a leather purse in his hand. "If his silence and cooperation can be bought then I believe we have the deeper pockets." When he returned he still had the purse and handed it to my mother. "He's already dead to the world on the kitchen hearth, his wife was covering him over when I walked in. She wouldn't take the whole purse only enough to cover our expenses plus storage fees for what we leave behind. Now we need to move quickly, I'll slip out and rouse Cripps and Greene they'll have the carriages and horses ready. Remember, take just what you need and any valuables." We all scrambled to our rooms banked the fires and grabbed our things then went out through the kitchen to the stables. Everything was quiet, and we left without being seen and made for the gypsy camp, Jacob had gone ahead to alert the gypsies.

Magda and Jibben were there waiting for us and insisted that it would be safer for everyone if we travelled as one of them. Jibben pointed over the hills. "There is an abandoned barn over that rise where, you can leave your equipage and ride the horses back. Then we will drink and think." Several of Jibben's people went with our men to hide the carriages. In the meantime Magda had us arrayed in gypsy clothing and James was sleeping soundly in a large wagon that had been vacated for my parents, our maids, Uncle Samuel, myself and James. The other men were assigned to different wagons within the camp.

The next days on the road were interesting but not uncomfortable which surprised me. Feather beds had been supplied for sleeping and the food while seemingly exotic was delicious. The community embraced us after Magda's endorsement.

We all had chores to do like everyone else and it was funny to see Greene and the Earl's grooms running around trying to finish their work as well as Lord Shellard's. Finally, he assigned himself the duty of huntsman and went out with several men from the camp to bring back meat. One day he downed a nice buck that would feed the whole camp and then some, he was the hero of the day. The women immediately fell on it to clean and skin it, nothing would be thrown away. Gabriel and my father were very competent fishermen while the other men including my uncle were good with small game and traps. Allan settled in showing off his culinary skills which I had had no idea he possessed, he even impressed Magda who had been the most sceptical. Meg and Beth fit in quickly with mending and beading; mother and I seemed to pose a problem for Magda, she felt we were above being put to work. So instead she decided to take us under her wing and show us how to make her herbal medicines, one in particular that she gave my mother for her morning sickness that worked amazingly well.

Mother insisted that Magda could make a fortune selling it, but she wasn't interested in vast wealth. "I have all I need here and in Dorset. Family, that is everything, no man or woman is richer than the ones with a loving family and good friends." You couldn't argue with her logic, so mother worked at compiling a medicinal booklet, drawing the plants used and recording the recipe.

It would take us almost two days longer travelling in this fashion since we stopped in villages and towns along the way for the gypsies to ply their trades and wares, but they were amazing at hiding us amongst them without us being noticed. Once Gabriel and Jibben got close enough to the two men that Robert had seen to hear them talking, Burley's name was mentioned at least twice to the effect that he was waiting in Cornwall at the house and expected to make his stand there and not on the open road.

What he hadn't counted on was my father knowing the area and terrain so well or that Samuel was with us, they both knew the house and the people in the neighbourhood even better. Once we reached the outskirts of the village of Pulruan we made camp on the bluffs. My father and Samuel went to the public house under the cover of darkness to see if they could find additional allies or gather any information about what was happening at the house on the cliffs. Shortly after they left an agitated Jibben came to my mother and crouched down by our fire. "Gabriel and Robert are missing."

Mother looked alarmed. "What do you mean missing?"

Jibben flung his arms out and motioned with his hands. "They are just gone. They took horses and..." he made a whistling noise "...they have gone...they left the camp."

Mother was getting angry. "Where did they go?!"

Jibben sat back on its heels looking very perplexed. "I don't know! They're your people, I have my own people to worry about."

I sucked in a breath. "Miles! Do you think they've gone to find Miles? Gabriel would know some of the same people that Dr Grimes does, they have both worked with the smugglers on this coast. Would he betray them...would Robert betray us?"

Mother looked shocked and Jibben ran his hand across the stubble of on his cheek making a rasping sound. "Robert didn't leave with him... I think he is following him."

Mother's brow was furrowed in worry. "How do you know that?"

Jibben smiled. "It's what I would have done, he's very loyal to your family, Mrs Turner, and to Mr Johnson, he will not let anything bad happen to them if he can prevent it."

I was afraid for Robert. "But what can he do against a man like Gabriel?"

Jibben slapped his chest. "He is Roma like me, Miss Turner. He's been trained and knows how to walk with the shadows and quiet his horse. Bita and I have taught him well...he will be safe. Besides we don't know that Gabriel has gone to betray anyone yet."

Mother interjected. "So we just wait to see if Robert comes back?"

Jibben laughed. "NO...Magda and Bita would cook my bullocks and eat them in front of me. I have sent three men to follow Robert. He will return safe."

We continued setting up camp and making supper, the Earl joined us along with Michael and Jacob and they all accepted bowls of stew and bread. The Earl cleared his throat. "Jibben just told us about Gabriel and Robert he assured us that Robert knows what he's doing."

Mother just sat there stirring the stew in the pot not making eye contact with anyone. Suddenly she stood up, "I'm going to check on James." I made to get up and go with her, I wasn't hungry, but she pushed me back down. "No, you stay here, I won't be gone long." She rose and disappeared into the darkness.

I was worried about what was happening out there beyond our little camp; the Earl sensing my concern reached out to take my hand. "My dear, I know that telling you not to worry is an exercise in futility but try." I smiled at him, then just sat there staring into the flames. Michael and Jacob went off to find Meg and Beth to take them to the big fire for the evening's music and dancing. I had no heart to attend and excused myself as Jibben came to sit with the Earl.

I made my way to our wagon and opened the door; inside sat Ruth, one of Magda's many grandchildren. she was watching over James and beading an intricate design onto a shawl. I looked about for my mother, but she wasn't there. Ruth looked at me with concern as she handed me a note from my mother. All it said was 'I have gone to the village.' My heart sank into my boots as I turned around and jumped down from the wagon and ran back to the fire with Jibben and the Earl. I waved the note under their eyes; the Earl took it to read out loud.

Afterwards Jibben waved his hands over his head and yelled, "Why can't any of your people just stay put!"

# Chapter 39
## *Surprises*

Jibben was furious as he pointed at me, "YOU! You will stay here or I'll—I will tie you to a tree." There was a low throaty chuckle that was just audible coming from the darkness behind him. Jibben sighed and turned, "Grandmama, I assume that you have something to do with Mrs Turner's disappearance?"

Magda came to our fire, stirred the pot of the stew then sniffed at the contents. She patted me on the back smiling as she sat down beside me. "Jibben, it is good that you and the army did not like each other, or you would be dead by now." She took up a bowl and spoon then gestured at me to ladle some stew into her bowl. She took a mouthful, chewing thoughtfully, then swallowed. "This is good stew." Her compliment made me smile and I felt privileged that she thought it was good. Then she regarded her grandson across the fire saying in her raspy voice, "Use your brain, Jibben! We have been followed! A trap has been set with the hope that you men will lead us into it. They expect us to come charging down on the house, but their plan will fail. I sent Irene to Old Jessica, she will know what to do." She ate a few more spoonfuls as Jibben gawked at her in disbelief. Then using her spoon, she pointed at him. "Women are the secret to success…you men know nothing! Who cooks and cleans for those people in the big houses who can come and go and be treated like they don't even exist…it's the women!"

Jibben considered it then grinned, "That's brilliant, we can dress the men like women!"

Magda looked at him like he was an imbecile. "Sit, Jibben! Dress a man like a woman, pah! Have you not been listening to me? Give a woman a weapon and we can out manoeuvre them without them even knowing it. Meanwhile those that were following us are now following Mr Turner and Mr Hughes."

Jibben rubbed his hand over his face. "And when exactly where you going to talk to me about this plan of yours?"

Magda spit into the fire then took a drink from a flask that she pulled from her pocket. "Why should we talk to you? You might be a favoured son, but you are too English."

Just then Michael and Jacob came back to our fire with Jacob asking, "Where's everyone gone? None of the women are dancing tonight?"

Jibben crooked an eyebrow at Magda who shrugged, "We have better weapons than most of the village women and we know how to use them."

Michael sat up and opened his mouth, he'd obviously caught on very quickly while Jacob was still puzzling it through. Michael punched him in the arm. "That's what happened to the crossbows, Beth and Meg took them!"

Jacob looked sick when the Earl gave him a stern look, then he turned his attention to Magda to say, "And what do we do, ma'am? Just sit here!"

Magda was still eating stew but after she swallowed she looked at the Earl, "I think you should go to the village, William; your sons will be there by now."

"My sons!"

"Yes, I sent Gabriel and Edward to find my Peter and your Miles."

The Earl was flabbergasted. "Oh God, madam! Did you not realise that Edward cannot be trusted?"

Magda smiled. "Yes, you can, you will see."

Magda finished her stew, stood up looking down at me. "You should go with these men to the village. I will watch over James; he is a sweet child…maybe he should come to us in the summers after he can ride a horse. I will talk to your mama about this." Then she shuffled off towards our wagon.

I turned to the Earl, but he was grinning at the fire. "Well, gentlemen, Miss Turner, I think we have been set a task and I'd very much hate to disappoint the lady."

Jibben ran both hands over his face and groaned then whispered loud enough to hear, "I hope I don't live to regret this." The Earl laughed and clapped him on the shoulder.

"Perhaps it's time for you to find an English wife and settle down…that is if you live through this." Jibben groaned again. The Earl laughed heartily, saying wistfully, "I think after this is over I'll spend some time on my estate teaching William, John and Diana how to fish or maybe I'll take them and Jane to Paris. Jane has never been abroad, I think she'd like the shopping." He chuckled but I noticed that his fists were clenched, and his smile did not reach his eyes, he was worried, and I think more than a little afraid.

Jibben was silent and withdrawn as he left with Michael and Jacob to assemble our party and saddle the horses. I went to our wagon to change, Magda was there cooing to a happy James who squealed and called out to me with his arms up, "Issa!" I took him out of Magda's arms, kissing his fat little cheeks. He puckered his lips then and gave me a very wet slobbery kiss in return. Then he laughed at the smacking noise he had made with the kiss. I smiled at him and he reached out to pull my lips up wider. "Mama, Issa? You tell me story?" He smiled and looked back over his shoulder at Magda. "Magda…story?" Magda nodded so I put him down and he went willingly to her, James never waited long for an answer to his questions, he was a happy child and ready to settle with anyone that would tell him a story.

I asked Magda if I could borrow a riding habit and she laughed, "You think I have room for English clothes in here? You wear what you have on."

I raised my eyebrows. "I can't ride astride in these." I swung the full Gypsy skirts from side to side. "My legs will show; these skirts aren't heavy enough to stay down when I ride!" She laughed and just waved me out the door. James was laughing with her and stomping around saying, "Legs, legs, legs." There was nothing I could do but ruffle James' hair, say goodbye and leave.

I found the Earl and our companions waiting with the horses, Michael gave me a foot up; my lower legs were uncovered immediately but none of the men said a word but Jibben smacked a couple of his younger cousins for gawking at me before they mounted up. I tucked my skirts under my legs as firmly as I could, then we were off. I had never been to Cornwall, but the sound of the sea was always with us even as we rode into the wind. We had not gone far when my skirts slipped even further up my legs. I chose to try and ignore it though my face was red for reasons other than just the wind. Nothing was said about my state of dishabille, but I would be much happier when we reached our destination.

We had arrived on the outskirts of the village, Jibben and his men wandered off in groups of two and three and the Earl and I followed Magda's directions to the home of Old Jessica. We found my mother there along with about a dozen gypsy women, Meg and Beth. She was deep in conversation with a villager who was drawing a map for them in flour that was spilled across a table. She looked up at me smiled then continued talking. Some of the gypsy women were apparently already making their way towards the house on the cliff to gather information and lure away any sentries from their duties.

Mother looked shocked but the wizened old lady who had just informed her about it laughed, "Don't worry, Elsa knows what she is doing, or Magda would not have sent her ahead. The rest of you will leave in in a few hours. The cook, Mrs Rook, insisted that she will be there which is good since the men there know her on sight. The other maids, scullery workers, washer women, and dairy maids have been promised compensation for a lost day's wages while our gypsy friends take their place. I hope, Mrs Turner, that your husband is a man of honour; these people have a hard-enough life as it is without being cheated out of a day's wages by the gentry."

Mother reached out her hand covering the old woman's. "Never fear, Miss Jessica, he will honour my promise."

We sat waiting for it to be time to leave, some people dozed, and others spoke quietly. The Earl chatted for a time with my mother and Old Jessica, he was not happy being told that he was to remain behind. Then just before dawn Miss Jessica saw us out her back door two and three at a time all taking different routes to the house on the cliffs. Mother and I mounted our horses to ride along the cliffs. We were halfway there when four men reared up out of the bracken, Mother pulled her pistol and aimed. I yelled, "STOP!" before she shot. Standing there on the path were Miles, Dr Grimes and two other rough looking characters.

I rode up to Miles as he stepped forward smiling and calling my name, "Lissa!" he reached out touching my leg then quickly withdrew his hand like he had touched an open flame when he felt only skin. Dr Grimes and my mother both laughed at his reaction. The other men with them merely stood there with their mouths open until Miles collected himself and helped me dismount then held me tightly against him and whispered in my ear, "I have missed you so much, my love."

Dr Grimes assisted my mother down from her horse and took the reins of both horses, casually handing them to the other men who promptly mounted and raced away. Mother turned in shock and was ready to object when Dr Grimes put his hand up quickly. "It's best that we go on foot from here, Mrs Turner. Burley has taken the house, and no one is allowed in or out except for servants."

"That's very good to hear, Dr Grimes, it means our surprise should be in place." He looked perplexed as did Miles who just shrugged. "Did Gabriel and Edward find you?"

Miles grimaced. "Yes, they did and said there was a plan to take the house, but where Colin is?"

Mother shrugged. "I don't know, somewhere in the area, I imagine. Do either of you have weapons?" Dr Grimes pulled back his coat to display an array knives and pistols in his belt, Miles only nodded. "Good, then we need to get to the house and be in position."

Miles was used to the machinations of my parents and didn't seem so much perplexed as curious. "Then what exactly is supposed to happen, Mrs Turner?"

We had started walking towards the house as she answered, "All the servants have been replaced with women from your gypsy troop, Mr Johnson." He stopped dead in his tracks.

Dr Grimes merely chuckled. "Ah, this sounds like a plan of Grandmama's." He turned and started walking ahead leaving us to follow.

My first sight of the house was as the sun rose, it was a two-story rambling edifice of indeterminate age with several outbuildings. Smoke was rising from most of the chimney pots and people were moving about in the yard. Once we got closer I could see the attraction of this place, the view was magnificent! The surf was pounding on the sandy beach below with sheer granite cliffs on either side. There were seals down on the surrounding rocks barking and cavorting in the surf. The trees close to the cliff were almost bent back on themselves and their growth had been stunted from the constant sea breeze. We approached as close as we dared and took cover behind a Cornish hedge made of field stone and earth near the side yard. From there we had a clear view of the back of the house and stables. Shortly after we were in position the maids were in the yard feeding the chickens, milking the cows and starting the wash. Suddenly this pastoral scene was interrupted when the stable door was flung open and out came a rush of horses sending chickens and geese squawking across the yard. Then several men came running around from the sides of the house and garden heading towards the stable. Smoke was now pouring out the stable door. Panic set in among the men who started screaming at the women to abandon their work and start drawing water as three of the men entered the stable and the other six went off to retrieve the horses. An older man with aristocratic bearing came out of the house and stood in the middle of the yard gazing around as water was drawn and an efficient bucket line formed to run water into the stables. He didn't so much as give the stable a single glance, he seemed intent in scouring the area beyond the out buildings. A younger man dressed as a gentleman came to the door and gestured urgently for the older man to come inside. It was impossible to discern from this distance what either man said but the older man turned, walking swiftly to the door and before entering looked once more over his shoulder directly to where we were hiding. We were well-hidden and watched through chinks in the earthen mortar, still my blood froze, and I held my breath, it was as if he was looking directly at me. Then he shook his head and entered the house, slamming the door behind him. I finally took a deep breath. "Who let the horses out?"

Dr Grimes smiled and pointed to an area just visible behind the stable. "That looks like young Robert and Gabriel." And he chuckled. "Jibben must have found them."

Mother shook her head. "I think it was more likely Magda who sent them, she seems to have orchestrated this whole plan. I suppose we should just sit back and watch."

Dr Grimes and Miles both grinned. "*Au Contraire*, Mrs Turner, we can now head into the yard." I noticed that the women had stopped drawing water and the men that had gone into the stables hadn't come out. Then I saw one woman look right at our hiding place, waving at us to join them, so we quickly scrambled over the wall.

Berta, one of Magda's daughters, took us aside and explained that the outside guards had all been captured. I looked to the stables, the smoke was still floating out the door as she explained that the fire had been only a smudge pot quickly fired up and put out, but it would smoke for some time yet.

We ventured close to the house avoiding the windows. One of the scullery maids came out the kitchen door with a huge pan of dirty water throwing it across the yard then she turned towards us and held up three fingers and then five. Berta nodded and signalled to the other women in the yard to draw their weapons. Besides Berta and the four of us there were three more women that joined our group. The others remained on guard in the yard assuming positions that would conceal them. I looked back over my shoulder as the scullery maid gestured for us to follow her inside, I couldn't see a soul anywhere, but I knew they were there.

We all entered the scullery and stood quietly as the maid went back into the kitchen. From our vantage, we could hear three men talking as well as the sound of cutlery on plates. At which point my stomach chose to rumble. Miles put his hand on my shoulder and a finger to his lips. I glared at him as if I could control my stomach. He gave me a smirk, nudged my shoulder and as much as I wanted to continue to glare at him I couldn't help myself and I smiled back. Mother was staring over my shoulder with a blank expression on her face. I turned to see what had her attention and saw my father's hat and coat tossed on a barrel, both were considerably worse for the wear and one sleeve was almost torn and covered in blood. I was worried that she would swoon but as I moved to towards her she caught my eye and shook her head no. Miles was looking in the same direction and knew what had upset her. He reached out and squeezed her shoulder while she gave him a weak smile in return. It was then I suddenly realised that Miles could see again. I grabbed his hand and wrote the word 'eyes' in his palm and he nodded to me. I wanted to know right away what had happened. How he was cured? But that would have to wait, our families were in dire need of our assistance.

Suddenly the sounds of breaking crockery and falling cutlery came from the kitchen then someone whistled. Dr Grimes pushed us from behind and we all fell into the kitchen amidst broken plates and three men sprawled across the large central table with the cook, her assistant and the scullery maid standing behind them, each holding onto a large iron skillet. Miles and Dr Grimes took rope and linen from one of the maids and started binding and gaging the men. When this was accomplished they were dragged into the pantry and the solid oak door was locked behind them. My stomach growled, and I rolled my eyes heavenwards just as I caught sight of Miles who tossed a warm roll to me. I caught it perfectly and devoured it in four bites. The cook, Mrs Rook, knew my mother on sight, she had refused to abandon my aunt when she had been approached by Old Jessica.

Mother spoke kindly to her but was dancing around the obvious question, so I interjected, "Mrs Rook, we've never met but I assume from the hat and coat over there that my father was taken prisoner? Do you know what happened and if he's alright?"

She pursed her lips and smiled. "I'm sorry about that, miss." Mother gasped, and I could feel tears forming. "But I swear Mr Turner's head is made of Cornish granite. He came skulking across the yard just as I was about to go out and gather the eggs…it weren't even light yet. But this bunch what is staying here eats constantly. And as I gathered up my basket I saw your father through the scullery window; he was only a dark shadow, so I took the cudgel that I use for knocking out pigs and whacked him on the head. I didn't know who he was until we pulled him inside…so I stuck him in the second pantry. It's nice and warm in there but I'm afraid he's still out, he's breathing easy, ma'am, but I'm afraid he'll be missing all the fun, miss."

I clasped my hand over my mouth, I didn't know if I would laugh or cry with relief. Mother smirked, took a step back then went down the two steps into the room where my father was. She came back, "He's sleeping like a baby; James is definitely the spitting image of him." She took Mrs Rook's hand. "But where is my brother?"

The cook looked at a loss. "I don't know, Mrs Turner, I never saw him."

Mother huffed but there was nothing that could be done about it, we would find him sooner or later.

Dr Grimes and Miles in the meantime had taken up guard by the door leading into the main house. Listening proved to be useless there was nothing to hear so they relied on my mother and the cook to tell them the placement of the rooms and all the points of access. There was only the main entrance at the front of the house and fortunately the foyer was not large. Back here our door led into a small service corridor that gave access to the back stairs to the upper floor. Then there was a back hallway to the outside and to the right of this door you would find the writing room, billiard room, and the summer parlour. Off the main foyer were the library, morning room, dining room and the main drawing room. The conservatory, study and winter parlour were down another hallway at right angles to the main, one just past the billiard room running behind the main staircase.

Mrs Rook whispered, "Everyone should be gathering to eat shortly." as she looked back at the maids preparing the trays and serving dishes. "Now the Spencers and Johnsons are served all their meals on trays in their rooms as well as the guards on that floor. The other henchmen eat in the main dining room; the ones from outside usually eat here in the kitchen and we've already taken care of all them."

Miles smiled, "What about Lord Burley?"

She cleared her throat. "Ah, yes, well, his Lordship and the young dandy with him would normally eat in the library, that's where they've taken all their meals. But his Lordship came out to see what the ruckus was in the yard then the dandy came rushing through here and called him back. They both went upstairs, I can't say though what's going on up there, ma'am." When she realised what she had said, bit her lip and looked very worried.

Dr Grimes stepped in front of her and the cook's eyes got as wide as saucers taking in his appearance, but he gave her a beautiful smile. "May I enquire ma'am as the to the health of the families?"

She smiled shyly back at him. "Well, the wee girl, she has a cold, poor thing, and Lady Jane, she was looking a might piqued when she first arrived, but she got roses back in her cheeks once we got her stomach settled down if you know what I mean."

He nodded then gave a knowing look to my mother who was blushing. Mrs Turner, given your condition I would prefer it if you waited here with Mrs Rook. With Dr Jefferson absent on this adventure I would prefer not to have to worry about two ladies that are in the delicate way."

Then he looked at me and I glared back at him. Miles chuckled and slapped him on the back of the head hard enough to make the point that he was being impertinent.

Just then behind us there were sounds of a scuffle, Miles went back to see what the problem was and returned with Gabriel and Robert. Robert came straight to Mother while Gabriel stood back and glared at Dr Grimes. "Mrs Turner! Mr Hughes and my uncle are ready to storm the front of the house, they just need us to give them a signal."

Miles explained the current situation to them and that stealth was needed now. Robert didn't say a word but turned around quickly and soundlessly to make his way out the back. Gabriel looked torn as to which way he should go, "Where's Burley?"

Dr Grimes pointed upwards, he assumed like the rest of us that after the fire in the stable that Burley went to check on his prisoners. Gabriel pushed forward and before we could stop him he was marching out through the service door. There was a grunt then the sound of something falling to the floor, followed by two more in rapid succession. The doctor stuck his head out the door as Gabriel was striding down the hallway, the slumped forms of three men were laying in our path. Just as Gabriel reached the hallway to the conservatory, a man jumped out at him with a gun aimed at his chest. He smiled at Gabriel, at the same time that I felt a rush of air across my cheek, then a knife was protruding from the man's chest as he too slumped to the floor. Gabriel never looked back, he stepped over the man and continued towards the main foyer where two guards stood by the front entrance. The doctor pulled out another throwing knife in one hand and a pistol in another. One of the men recognized Gabriel and called him Cap'n, he stepped forward, but the other man watched him suspiciously. Gabriel put his arm around the man who knew him and spoke to him in Spanish. The man's eyes got very wide when he looked at his fellow guard. He stepped forward and clubbed is partner under the chin with his rifle stock, knocking him out and into Gabriel's arms.

As Gabriel pulled out a knife to cut the man's throat but Dr Grimes stayed his hand. "No, my friend, as little blood shed as possible please, people live here and the fewer bad memories associated with it the better." Gabriel looked glum, but he nodded. Dr Grimes turned to the other man, pulled the cook's cudgel out of his waistband and smiled at the other man. "Hello, Jose," and then he clubbed the man soundly on the head, catching him and easing him to the floor.

Gabriel looked at him and nodded saying. "I could never trust Jose either."

Dr Grimes clapped him on the back. "Neither could I, I should have killed him years ago. But I think he would be better off in an English prison." They both grinned at each other and turned towards the stairs without a backward glance. But Grimes stopped him and put his finger to his lips and pointing back our way.

Miles had moved forward and motioned for Mother and I to stay put. Then the maids came in with some of the women from the yard and started pulling bodies out of the hallway armed with ropes and gags to tie them up. Then they joined the men at the bottom of the stairs and ascended as stealthily as Dr Grimes. Gabriel stayed behind with Miles, Mother and me. They moved to the library door and once it was opened motioned for Mother and me to join them. Inside the air was stale with the odours of tobacco and brandy which permeated every surface. Gabriel opened the windows then went back out into the hallway. Robert climbed through one of the windows followed by several gypsies. There was a no noise anywhere until Dr Grimes came running down the stairs grim-faced. Mother bit her fist when she saw his face. Then he put up his hand. "No, no, Mrs Turner, your family and the Johnsons are fine. They didn't have time to hurt them, but Burley and his associate have escaped."

Gabriel yelled from the back of the house. The doctor, Miles and I went after him and found him standing over Mrs Rook, a knife protruding from her chest. Gabriel balled up his fist and punched the wall in front of him hard enough that he cracked the plaster. "They must have come down the service stairs once we went through to the main house."

Miles yelled. "The beach!" he started towards the yard running out the door followed by Dr Grimes. We all ran to the cliff side. Below a small boat was being rowed out to a waiting schooner. We stood and watched two people climb from the small boat onto the ship. Miles groaned, "We checked the beach, how did he hide a boat!"

Gabriel was staring across the water. "That ship was probably standing off behind those rocks waiting for a signal."

The doctor slapped his forehead. "That's why the seals were so active this morning someone or something had disturbed them. The bloody bugger gets away with it and we can't prove a damn thing."

We walked back to the house and found my father sitting by my mother in the large drawing room looking as green as the sea with huge knot on his forehead. The rest of our families and friends were arrayed about the room. Jibben was outside seeing to his people and of course the horses. The Assistant cook who lived in was sitting with Mrs Rook's body in the kitchen. Jibben had sent one of the gypsy women to Old Jessica to get word to Mrs Rook's family and fetch the real servants back. It wasn't long though before the assistant cook Bonnie Bell brought in a tray of tea and the drinks decanters along with some sandwiches and promised us something hot for later.

Mrs Rook's husband, son and daughter arrived within the hour with a wagon. Father, Mother and Uncle Samuel spoke with them privately. Aunt Mary joined us and when they were ready to leave, she promised to deed the land that the Rooks currently worked for the estate to Mr Rook and his family, saying, "It is poor compensation, Tom, for the loss of Sadie, but I should have done it ages ago." He thanked her then turned away to follow the cart carrying his wife with his son and daughter walking at his side. The horse led the way at a slow pace as if knowing the sadness that accompanied the burden he pulled.

When we came back in the Johnson family were congregated together at one end of room with Miles standing in the middle. Miles came to me and introduced me to Lady Jane, John, William and little Diana. All four of them seem to have no idea what had transpired or that they were on the verge of losing their lives. Lady Jane was just as Miles had described her, a very pretty, kind and socially acceptable woman without an original thought in her head. But it was obvious that she loved her children. When the Earl finally arrived, it was obvious too that Lady Jane was fond of him, but she showed no sign that he was her grand passion, while the children on the other hand worshipped him. Perhaps that's where her fondness for him came, that her children loved their father unconditionally. They sat together making plans for a grand vacation that eventually went from four months on the continent to three months in the lake district and then to just two in Scotland visiting the Earl's sister.

My own family sat together as if it was just another day and perhaps it was. Meg and Beth had returned, they had been with several young gypsy women leading the outside guards into the woods but instead of the men having a tryst with some comely young women they were met by Jibben and his men. In total, we had captured sixteen men not counting the one that the doctor had to kill. Jibben had them all securely bound and in the stables under guard. The local police constable appeared when he heard of Mrs Rook's death, but matters were settled quickly and he was amenable to calling out the local militia to escort the prisoners to London and into Sir Thomas's custody, especially now that the murderer had escaped, and he was assured that agents of the Crown were actively engaged in pursuing him.

Father was not at all pleased about the escape of Burley and his companion who from the description from the staff was Charles Brathwaite Burley's son-in-law and the son of a prominent London banker. But no one had ever heard the older man with Brathwaite referred to as Lord Burley. It was only our assumption that the he was his Lordship. This whole assignment of quashing the smuggling ring just kept getting more complex the closer we got to the leaders.

# Chapter 40
## *Return to London*

Later that day the gypsy caravan arraigned itself across the property and suddenly an impromptu fair popped up to the delight of the village people as well as the gypsies after they had received Aunt Mary's approval. Jibben had sent some of his men back with Robert, Dalton and with our coachmen to retrieve our carriages then they would collect the baggage which we had so precipitously left at a coaching Inn one night…it all seemed a lifetime ago. Gabriel spent the rest of the day questioning the servants and village folk about Ramsey, but no one had seen him. Once again it looked as if he had gotten away much to Gabriel's annoyance.

Two days later we all attended the funeral for Mrs Rook and after the service, my aunt presented Mr Rook with the deed to his land. Father contributed further by providing money for the daughter's dowry and at comparable amount for the son's future. The wake was provided for by my Aunt Mary and Uncle Arthur and to everyone's delight it eventually turned into a rather merry affair, a celebration of Mrs Rook's life which Mr Rook assured us his Sadie would have approved of.

During the time that we waited for our carriages to return, Miles was either off hunting with Jibben and his father or closeted with all the men reviewing what had been learned during his time with Dr Grimes, so I had very little time alone with him. It was on our last evening there that I found him in the garden looking over a stone hedge at the windswept cliffs. I walked up to stand beside him taking his hand. He did not turn or acknowledge me in any fashion other than by squeezing my hand. I stood there in silence with him for a time until he said as he continued to gaze out to sea, "It was a blow to the head."

I wasn't sure what he was referring to. "What?"

He then turned his head and smiled as he looked at me, "It was another blow to the head that restored my sight. Dr Grimes now believes that my brain may have been scrambling the signals from my eyes and the blow set things to rights."

Miles was scrunching up his eyes against the light from the setting sun. "You don't sound convinced."

He sighed. "I think it was a convenient explanation for something for which he had no other plausible excuse."

I shifted so that I could see his face more clearly. There were lines around his eyes and his brow that I had never noticed before, they were lines of pain and endurance. "And what do you think happened?"

He didn't answer right away but he turned away from the view to lean against the wall pulling me to him and turning me around so that the back of my head laid back against his chest and he whispered, "It was you. Or rather it was you not being there to guide me through my day, so I had time to think. Grimes is a nice chap, but he amuses himself with his own conversation, the result being he required very little from me. When we went out, he let me find my own way, he didn't ridicule me, nor did he aid me. I stumbled about a great deal making a damn fool of myself in the bargain. Then one day I fell off a cliff." He chuckled as I gasped. "It wasn't a very high cliff, but I was laid up for a couple of days. I'd hit my head rather sharply that day and I had some very graphic dreams about my time in Paris. I can remember every detail of those dreams, but I had the feeling that you were there listening to everything. I remember hearing Grimes' voice every now and then asking me questions, pushing me to relive my whole time in that hell but you were always there somewhere just out of reach. When he finally left me alone, I fell into a deep sleep and I dreamed of a life with you, first as if I was blind and then as if I had my sight and between them you never treated me differently, you never loved me differently. When I woke up I could see again, and I knew the truth. While I was an invalid in Paris my blindness was an excuse to keep you near me, I wouldn't allow myself to believe that you could love me regardless if I was whole. I realise now that it doesn't matter. You were right, I can't let what happened to me define who I am." I reached up and pulled his head down to mine and kissed him. Then we stood there just looking out at the scenery, the sea to our backs, no words were required, his arms were wrapped around me as I leaned against him watching the light fade and listening to the ocean pound on the shore below.

The next day our carriages arrived with our trunks and portmanteaus, along with messages from Emilie, Murphy and Sir Thomas. The prisoners had arrived, and we were being entreated to return at once to London. It was a relief in some ways to change into our own clothes again. I felt more like myself; but I missed the freedom of movement in the gypsy clothes.

We parted ways with our nomadic friends…they had decided with my father's blessing to spend some time in Cornwall, seeking out whatever profit and information that could be gleaned from the inhabitants. The Earl, Lady Jane and their children would travel with us only as far as their country estate where they planned to take a much-needed rest from London and all that had recently transpired. The Earl would be in London as soon as he was summoned by the King regarding his petition to legitimize Miles. Edward and Miles spent the first day on the road riding with the Earl to resolve family issues as Miles put it. At one point, they pulled over rather abruptly with Miles and Edward falling out the carriage door, yelling and screaming obscenities at each other. They removed their coats and stomped into an adjacent meadow.

I reached out to my father in a panic. "They aren't going to duel, are they?"

Father looked at them with an amused expression on his face. "No, I think they intend to beat each other senseless."

"WHAT!" I moved to open the door and jump from the carriage, but my father pulled me back.

He pushed me back into my seat and admonished, "You wait here. I think this has probably been a long time coming and it may help to clear the air."

I looked at my mother for an explanation, she simply shrugged "It's what men do." Father got down and looked like he was debating about taking James with him but when he reached for him, my mother refused to let him go. "Oh, no, Colin, he is much too young for that sort of thing yet." He nodded and joined the other men who had by now formed a loose circle around the two combatants that were earnestly trying to beat each other to death."

The Earl came to our window laughing so I ventured to ask, "What happened?"

He smiled at me then turned back to watch his sons. "Years of unrelieved sibling rivalry."

I couldn't believe that everyone was taking this so lightly. I couldn't watch the fight, but I was constantly shifting in my seat. Mother passed me James and got out, she came back shortly and pointed to a small rise covered with trees. "We'll picnic under those trees over there, it's far too warm to sit in this carriage. Besides the men will need some time to cool off and relax. It's near a brook and they can wash off their grime." The door was opened for me by Dalton, Mother took James and we walked towards the trees. Aunt Mary followed with Meg, Beth and Adele in tow who carried blankets to sit on. Dalton and Robert brought the hampers along and dropped them in front of the three maids then hurried back to join the other men. Finally, when neither Miles nor Edward could raise a fist, the fight was declared over and a draw by the Earl. He went up to each of his sons, patted them on the back and handed them each a bottle of ale. He then insisted that they shake hands which they did at first with reluctance and then with what appeared to be genuine appreciation if not exactly affection. Then they stomped off through the trees to avail themselves of the brook's cool running water.

When they returned they sat down beside me, splashing me with droplets from their wet hair, laughing and exchanging stories about how they had hated each other while growing up but truly wishing that they could change places with each other or at least be friends. They both had lonely childhoods and I could only watch them in amazement. James by this point had toddled over and sat down between them, offering them each a half of his soggy biscuit which they both took and popped into their mouths much to my disgust and James's delight.

Edward swallowed his portion of biscuit then picked up James, talking to him. "Tell me, old chap, how did my lout of a brother ever captured the heart of your sister. Was it magic, do you think? Did he cast a dark spell on her?"

James reached up and with one hand on either side of his face pushed his cheeks in to make his lips pucker and essentially stopped him from talking. Then he let go of his cheeks crowing. "NO! Mills not bad...I like Mills." Then he cocked his little head from side to side and laughed letting go of Edward's face. "I like you. You work like Mills, he yur brudder! I'm going to have a brudder too then you and Mills can play wiff us." Everyone burst out laughing including James. Any tension that had been in the air was gone now, even Gabriel was laughing with us.

My father argued Gabriel into staying with us rather than try to find Ramsey on his own after he convinced him that Ramsey wouldn't stay in Cornwall since we seemed to be his target. Besides he missed his family after having only just been reunited with them and the draw to be with them as strong, so he agreed to accompany us to London and would continue to accept our hospitality.

Aunt Mary and Uncle Arthur would stay with us a for a short while then continue onto Northumberland to Alford Manor. It seemed that Dyson had got himself into a spot of trouble over his attentions to one of Lord Fitzwilliam's daughters and he needed his mother to extricate him. Uncle Arthur's solution was to let him stew in his own juices. But Aunt Mary was a loving mother and Dyson was her only surviving child. She still held out hope that he would turn out to be more like her than his father in the long run. However, I think her faith on that count was misplaced.

Once we reached London, our party had shrunk considerably but we were met in the foyer by Lettie and Murphy. Lettie took charge of James to his squeals of delight at seeing his nanny. Father, Miles, and Edward adjourned to the study, Uncle Samuel and Gabriel set off to find their wives. Mother and I begged Mr Allan to ask the housemaids for a hot bath before he settled back into his routine. He agreed but as he went towards the green braise door he was already running his hand across the hall tables looking for any tell-tale dust.

Our maids and valets preceded us up the stairs. Dalton and Robert remarking that they'd be looking after Mr Johnson and Mr de Bearne now. Robert claimed Mr Johnson as his responsibility because of his connection with him in Dorset. Dalton just sighed, "So you leave me with the Spanish pirate, might I remind you that I have had a connection with Mr Johnson longer than you."

Robert just smiled. "It'll give you a chance to brush up on your Spanish, old man."

Dalton stopped. "What Spanish...look here, what has Beth been telling Meg? How do you know that I speak some Spanish?"

They continued in this good-natured fashion as they went ahead of us while Mother and I retired to our rooms to await our baths.

Dinner was an informal affair and we served ourselves from the buffet. Talk in general was about how exhausted we all were. Miles and Edward were both chewing gingerly and emitted several groans while they ate. They had both declined having Dr Jefferson attend to them and once they were done eating they excused themselves to retire for the night, each with a decanter of brandy and a book. Gabriel left with Charity to spend time with their boys. Samuel and Emilie retired to their rooms to just spend time alone. While we sat at the table I noticed Mother and Father touching each other as often as possible so I told them that I was going to visit James in the nursery and tell him a bed time story and that they should go and get some rest.

When I reached the nursery, Murphy and Lettie were playing with James and his toy soldiers. I suggested that they both take a stroll around the garden and get some air and that I would see James to bed. I swear that they had left before I had even finished making my suggestion.

I looked down at my brother who sat there with his mouth open, surprised to see Lettie and Murphy leave so quickly, I smiled and sat down beside him. "Well, little man, it looks like it's just you and me. Shall I get you ready for bed and tell you a story about King Arthur and his knights?"

James appeared to consider this, crinkling his baby brow. "No! I don't wanna go to bed. I's not sleepy, Issa."

I reared back in pretend shock. "What, no bed? How do you ever expect to grow up and be big and strong like Papa if you don't sleep?"

He considered my remark. "Papa seeps?" I nodded my head yes. It had never occurred to me that James had never seen our father asleep. Even when he was stretched out with my father on a settee or in carriage, my father was ever alert and would wake before James. "Ohhhhhh...big people seep too." He jumped up and ran for his cot throwing himself on it and squealing when I tickled him to get him into his nightshirt then under the covers. He asked for his stuffed bunny and rolled over watching me as I banked the fire and blew out all but two candles, then I came to sit by him to tell him a story. My brother had a vivid imagination, but he liked true stories, not ones based on fables, so I was at loss as to what I should tell him. I finally decided to share some of Miles' stories with him without using his name. James fell asleep quickly leaving me at loose ends once again.

I called for one of the nursery maids and retired to my room dismissing Meg. I could care for myself for one night at least and besides I wasn't a bit tired now, so I sat down at my writing desk and pulled out my journal, opening it to a blank page. I hadn't written in a journal since leaving the Abbey, so I decided to write down our adventures to this point.

As I wrote late into the night I could only wonder what the dawn would bring us. There were still Sir Thomas's concerns regarding the smuggling ring to attend to, Lord Burley had escaped along with Mr Braithwaite and Ramsey was still at large, possibly even watching us from the garden of the empty house next door.

# Chapter 41
## *November 1830*

Time was moving on and nothing happened after our return, so life settled into a routine. Emilie was in a rush to establish her own household and design a nursery, but Samuel was dragging his feet. He finally had a conversation with my mother as to why he seemed reluctant and he gave her permission to share with us. Samuel had never lived on his own, he grew up with my mother and he had always shared loggings with my father since they had both been at Harrow and then Cambridge together. It was always my father who had made sure that everything was looked after and accounted for rents, servants and the normal household tasks. It's not that my father was so very good at these things himself, but he had a knack for finding accommodating landladies, shop keepers and for hiring servants.

Emilie on the other hand had never run a large household, hired servants, furnished a home or kept accounts. The Abbey's expenses for economy's sake had to be reduced so the money saved there could be invested into improving the property and make it a profitable estate. But that left Samuel and Emilie with two estates to run and now he was being pressured to purchase a London town house. Some of the younger Abbey staff Mother was sure would agree to relocate to London for the adventure while others would choose to retire. The Burns would remain in charge of the Abbey with a skeleton staff while the outside staff and their duties would be increased under the direction of Mr Seamus O'Toole, an old friend of Murphy's who was well versed in estate management. He had a keen interest in bringing the Abbey back to its past glory and once the outside was a paying venture then the inside would be refurbished. In the meantime one of the wings in need of the most repair would be closed off.

The chateau in France was under excellent management by Monsieur Andre Dupont and Mademoiselle Bridgette Dionne and probably not too far off in the future she would be Madame Dupont if what Mrs Baxter had to say was true. They were doing a thriving business with the Embassy using it for additional quest quarters. And Mr Dupont was looking to establish a small winery first to serve the estate, the Embassy guests and then expand it later as a business venture that Samuel and the Marquis had been in discussions about.

Things eventually started to fall into place, with the machinations of my mother and Aunt Mary it was decided to the delight of all concerned that Samuel would purchase the house that the Clarkes had hitherto occupied. Their cook, Mrs Lamont, was very amenable to the kitchen there and loved being back in England. She had already formed a fast friendship with our cook. But without a housekeeper or a butler taking care of the staff it would fall to Mrs Lamont to manage the other staff, not an ideal arrangement. It wouldn't be long before it began taking its toll on her. Mother warned Emilie that until a staff came together cohesively it was like a fight in a hen house to establish a pecking order and she had better take charge soon or lose the staff she currently had, including Mrs Lamont. She had literally interviewed dozens of applicants, but the same issue applied to my uncle's household that applied to ours, the nature of my uncle's work required a flexible staff that knew how to be discreet.

It was while the garden gate was being removed leaving a beautiful archway in its place that led to Emilie finding her butler. We were in the garden one afternoon and the foreman was arguing with our gardener about how the demolition of the gate could not proceed without cutting back the espalier on our side of the garden wall. It was rather comical in that the volume of their argument continued to increase while it was obvious that neither of them was listening to the other. All the workman had shuffled off to lay back on the grass and watch the show. That is all but one middle-aged man who was rather well put together for a common labourer. He finally stepped forward and in a very quiet, educated voice that commanded attention explained how some of the branches could be tied back out of the way and those that could not could be pruned without ruining the espalier. Both protagonists in this argument had stopped yelling long enough to listen to him then looked at the wall and back at him. Just when I thought they were ready to embrace the idea, one of the itinerant day labours called out to the foreman, "Hey, Jock, you goin' let fancy breeches there tell you how to do yer job!" And that was it, both the foreman and the gardener started yelling at each other again.

Aunt Emilie stood there watching with me then a small smile began to creep across her face. She caught the eye of fancy breeches and motioned for him to join us. He hesitated looked around at his fellow workers who were intent on the argument that might soon dissolve into blows. He came up to both us and managed a very courtly bow then looked back over his shoulder and frowned. Emilie introduced us and he in turned introduced himself as Thomas Sproul.

Emilie hesitated for a bit then began, "Mr Sproul, I couldn't help but notice that you don't exactly fit the in with your fellow workmen."

He raised an eyebrow and smiled. "One takes work where one can get it, ma'am."

She closed her eyes halfway as if she was evaluating his worth. "I know that I've seen you somewhere before."

He nodded. "Yes, ma'am, I was the butler for Mr and Mrs Jamieson. You were giving private French lessons to Mrs Jamieson."

Emilie gasped. "That's correct! But why, Mr Sproul, are you now working in this capacity?"

He cleared his throat and bit his lip. "Mrs Jamieson absconded to Italy with a footman and several thousand pounds of her husband's money. Mr Jamieson took to drink and blew his brains out this past summer. None of the staff had any references so I did the best I could by them and saw that they all got places. Unfortunately, I was unable to find another position myself. People tend to remember the butler, and no one wants to be associated with scandal."

Emilie's mouth was hanging open in astonishment and then she began to laugh. Mr Sproul did not look at all amused. When she saw the look on his face she sobered up immediately. "Mr Sproul, I think you would be perfect."

He looked perplexed and annoyed. "Perfect for what, ma'am?"

She beamed then. "For me!"

Now Mr Sproul looked utterly aghast. "I beg your pardon?"

Emilie quickly ran a hand across her brow and laid a hand on her rapidly expanding belly, "How silly of me. As my…I mean our butler. My husband and I require the services of a butler and, Mr Sproul, I think you would be perfect!"

He looked completely gobsmacked and I was smiling now that the missing piece to her staffing puzzle was standing before her.

He looked perplexed. "But, madam, I have nothing to verify my character, I have come from a disgraced household."

Emilie put a fingertip to her lips then waved her hand around the garden. "Mr Sproul, this household and that of my sister-in-law are both unusual. Perhaps it is you who should be asking after our character."

Mr Sproul's eyebrows arched so high they were almost lost in his hair line. He looked to me and all I could do was nod. "My father and uncle work for a special service to the Crown and the staff need to be flexible and discreet. They can be coming and going at some very strange hours and be involved with some unusual characters."

He smiled at me and opened his mouth as if to say something but then his foreman yelled at him to get back to work. He nodded at us and turned to go. Aunt Emilie moved swiftly to stand in front of him and then turned to address the foreman. "I'm so sorry but I've just employed this man and he is to start at once or lose the position. I hope you understand." Then she took Mr Sproul's arm and walked back toward the house. With me following while she was chatting away about her household. I heard the gardener start to chuckle and the foreman yelled, "Here, what's that all about."

The gardener laughingly said, "I fancy that he's Mr Hughes's new butler."

The foreman started to laugh. "Shameful waste that is, he was a good worker, always on time and never lying about like these louts."

The gardener sighed. "Yeah, well, they do say that the cream will rise to the top." And that was the end of it, the men went back to work and the gardener started tying back the espalier just as Mr Sproul had suggested.

Emilie took Mr Sproul into the study immediately to meet my uncle even though he was begging to return to his lodgings and come back appropriately attired for an interview. My uncle made short work of the interview and much to Mr Sproul's surprise my uncle sent for the carriage to take him to his lodging to pick up his things and return with him. He would be introduced to the staff upon his return and could assume his duties the next day. Compensation was agreed upon then Ben, one of their footmen, showed Mr Sproul out. Aunt Emilie fell back onto the settee as if exhausted. "What a relief!"

In the days to come Mr Sproul became the backbone of the Hughes' London home and everyone including Mrs Lamont thought the sun rose and set on him. Finally, the household was settled and Emilie's education in household management began, Mr Sproul did not believe in taking charge of everything, he felt that his role was as a consultant and advisor to my brother and Emilie. He never presumed to know their minds. Though within a short time I swore he could read their minds. After a month, Emilie had a good grasp of household management under his tutelage and visitors once again began to sing his praises.

341

In my own home, Mother was advancing with her pregnancy, James thought the idea of having someone usurp his cot in the nursery a great idea since Papa had promised him a big boy's bed even though it would still be in the nursery. Emilie was anxious about wanting a son but was sure she was having a girl. Mother on the other hand just simply said that they were both having boys while Aunt Mary insisted they were both carrying girls.

Miles and Edward went to join their father on his country estate and he wrote to me every few days. It had been agreed that no matter the outcome of Lord Shellard's petition to establish Miles as his heir, he needed to understand Lord Shellard's business affairs and estates. Edward had no head for business and if the worst happened and Miles was not recognized, it had been stipulated in a contract between the brothers as well as in his Lordship's will that Miles would in fact oversee the running of the estate from which Edward would draw a substantial living.

Miles also took a couple of weeks and journeyed to Scotland with his brother to visit with their Aunt Millicent and so the brothers could get to know each other better now that they were equals in each other's eyes. The King was still mulling over the petition submitted by Lord Shellard and no answer was expected before spring. Humph...spring, the spring in which my mother had expected me to marry. But still Miles had not formally asked me nor given me a ring. It made dinner parties and balls rather uncomfortable with young men flirting with me constantly. Yet I could not claim an attachment hence I gained the reputation of being aloof and cold. I had no friends my own age for the simple fact I had nothing in common with my contemporaries. I was better educated that most of them, including the young men of my age. I had never been interested in gowns and parties to the exclusion of all else and I didn't swoon at every piece of titillating gossip. Therefore, I spent considerable time with our household staff continuing with my unorthodox pursuits and in the library with my head buried in a book. Father had promised us a holiday in the country at Christmas but subject as always to the needs of the Crown.

It was the early November when we heard that Lord Burley was back in England. As hard as my father and Sir Thomas had tried it was impossible to connect Burley with the smuggling ring or with the murder of Mrs Rook. But his henchmen were still incarcerated in Newgate for the assault on my aunt's home in Cornwall with the intent to extort ransom. None of the men arrested had said a word about Burley or Braithwaite, only that they had been hired by a young blond man. None of them claimed to have ever seen Burley. It was finally discovered that their leader who had the most contact with the gentlemen was the one that Dr Grimes had killed to protect Gabriel.

For the time being smuggling activities that had been attributed to Lord Burley seemed to have ceased. But Burley was by no means flaunting his return to England; he had rarely been seen in public since his return and was not accepting invitations using the death of his son Julian as his reason to retreat from society along with his daughter Arabella and her husband. Yet his oldest son Justin was often in town being very sociable along with his sister Marianne with her husband Charles Braithwaite. We had no idea if Lord Burley had retired from his life of crime or if he was just biding his time. Father was sure that he was still involved, it was only a matter of time before he became active again.

The time finally came for the de Bearnes to leave for Spain and be reunited with Gabriel's family and for them to meet his wife and sons. Father had helped Gabriel invest much of proceeds from his adventures in the West Indies and since he had targeted Burley's interests exclusively, Father did not wrestle with his conscience over aiding a pirate. His assets were considerable, and Gabriel had become without training an astute businessman when it came to turning goods into cash. Those proceeds were deposited with a reputable banking house in London and he hired our Mr Crenshaw to manage his affairs.

Charity and I never became friends, though she and Emilie had formed an attachment, so she was sad to see them go. Thankfully Charity had flourished under the tutelage of my mother and Emilie, she now knew how to dress to impress and for comfort. Her social skills had been polished, and Gabriel was as proud as any man of his beautiful wife in any social gathering. It had been a shock to society to hear the dreadful news about the de Bearnes. And while some aspects of their life had been glossed over such as the pirating and murder, the dowagers soon forgot that they had once paraded their precious sons in front of a married woman. That the family was now embraced by society was in large part due to Gabriel's forceful presence and charm and there simply wasn't a better story out there.

Lettie and Murphy were married in our home with Murphy's sister and her husband from Ireland in attendance to everyone's delight.

Shortly after that we had a surprise visitor, the widow of the partner who had defrauded Dalton and Lettie for so long. She had come to set right the wrong done to them. The company had continued to prosper in recent years and the dividends that were due to Dalton and Lettie were paid out in full. Dalton and Lettie in turn sold their shares back to the company and invested the proceeds with Mr Crenshaw's assistance. It was not immense wealth, but it gave them both a very comfortable nest egg that neither would ever have to work if they chose to retire. But it was the work they both said made their lives interesting.

Murphy, we discovered also had property in Ireland that he owned in conjunction with his sister that earned him a tidy annual income, but it was again the work with my father that made his life worthwhile. His sister and her husband managed their affairs there and their properties were doing well. But Murphy had no desire to leave and take it over. Besides there were individuals there that would take a dim view of his returning after working for the Crown, so he'd just as soon keep his distance. They took a short honeymoon to the Seaside and returned to us happy and refreshed. James did not like the fact that he couldn't go with them, but Father took him to see the menagerie in the Tower twice while they were gone to mollify him.

We were well into November now and plans were being made for a Christmas in Somerset. However, Emilie and Samuel had decided that they would stay in London and enjoy their new home. Miles had been invited to stay with us for Christmas but had declined saying that he was expected to visit with his father and family. But since our country home was not so far from his father's estate he asked us to join them for New Years. I was extremely disappointed to say the least and was rather petulant when out shopping with my mother, Aunt Mary and Emilie for the holidays.

It was at our last dinner party before the holidays when I met Justin Browne, Lord Burley's heir. He seemed to be everything that his two brothers Randall and Julian were not. He was polished and sophisticated. He did not appear to have much of an intellect, but he was a keen listener and therefore in my mind a keen learner.

He was handsome in a rather effeminate manner but not so much as to attract ridicule.

I sat across from him at table, watching and listening to him while I tried to maintain a conversation with a dean of one of the Cambridge Colleges and keep Lawrence Tillbury's hand off my leg. The Dean required little more than a conveniently placed nod or smile while Tillbury required good reflexes and few cracks of my ivory fan across his knuckles every now and then. I focused as much of my attention on the Viscount as I could when he mentioned that he was looking to purchase property in Cornwall. Apparently, he was interested in resurrecting several defunct copper mines that he hoped to make profitable once more with the new mining techniques now available. When pressed as to what methods he was referring to, he was at a total loss to explain so the discussion ceased. The Viscount eyed me over his glass as he took a sip as if noting that I had been paying attention. His eyes sparkled but not with merriment and he made me feel uncomfortable.

In an endeavour to forget his look, I turned my attention to Major Hopewood seated to Browne's right. He was lean with features that were neither appealing nor repugnant and he was impeccably dressed in dark clothing as if he was in mourning. He did not converse much and when he did, his answers were short and clipped. This was the retired Major that Father thought was possibly the father of our stable boy Billy Phipps. Hopewood had icy blue eyes but there was a sadness about him that clung like a second skin. I couldn't find anything of Billy in his features, but the boy was still young and might favour his mother. I only hoped that when my father spoke to him privately that both his and Billy's pervading sadness would be alleviated. In the meantime, I tried not to make eye contact with the Viscount yet still pay attention to his conversation that had now moved on to the latest gossip in town which did not interest to me.

When dinner was over, there was a musical evening planned but a card room had been set up for those that had no appreciation for the musical arts. I saw my father engage the Major in a conversation as he started for the card room, but I was too far away to hear what was said, but Hopewood's countenance had brightened considerably.

He and my father made a detour for the study. As I was about to follow, I felt someone grip my elbow tightly. Looking to my left I saw it was the Viscount, his fingers digging in and it hurt. His face was very close to mine and he was smiling but the smile did not reach his eyes. "Would you care to show me the conservatory, Miss Turner? I understand that your mother has a fine collection."

I decided to use bravado while looking for a rescue. "Which collection would that be, my Lord?"

He looked cross and confused at my response. "What?"

I repeated myself while trying to wiggle my arm from his grasp, but it remained firm and painful. "Which collection... What are you interested in viewing?" I saw Murphy conversing with the Cambridge dean at the entrance to the music room which was only a few paces away from me, so I continued. "I would gladly give you over to my father's secretary, Mr Murphy." I emphasised Murphy's name by raising my voice and tapping out help with my fan on the table next to me hoping he would hear me. "He has a wide range of botanical interest alas I can barely distinguish a rose from a daisy." Murphy came quickly to my side as I was finishing my last sentence. He eyed the Viscount's hand on my elbow, raising his chin and brow as he glared at his Lordship who dropped my arm. His fingerprints were noticeable in my flesh and sure to leave bruises, so I pulled my shawl around to cover the area. Mr Murphy was grinning widely at the Viscount and offered to give him a private tour of the conservatory. The Viscount declined, suddenly remembering a previous engagement and excused himself calling for his coat and left without even thanking my mother who had seen the exchange take place from across the foyer.

She came to my side and passed me some ice wrapped in a napkin. "Put this around your arm then wrap your shawl around it, it will help. Murphy, how did that odious man come to be invited? I don't recall him on my list."

Murphy raised a brow. "You mean you didn't invite him, ma'am?"

Mother was fussing with my arm. "Good God, no,! I hate even being around any of that family let alone having them in my home."

Father's study door opened, he stuck his head out and motioned for Murphy, who after speaking to him left I assumed to bring Billy Phipps from the stable. Hopefully that would have the happy outcome that everyone wanted.

I returned to the music room with my mother who was still fuming about the Viscount. I was restless and walked about the room…my arm was aching. Father came to tell us that Major Hopewood would be staying with us for a few days to get to know Billy better. He would consider formally adopting Billy since there was no way to prove his actual parentage and he admitted that he had loved Billy's mother, but she would not disgrace him by marrying him. Apparently, he had been devastated when he found out that she was dead, and that Billy had been thrown out onto the street.

But Mother and I were sceptical that he had made any concerted effort to find Billy. There had been several reputable witnesses that knew my father and saw him pick Billy up. It was from these individuals that Father had initially gleaned the bulk of Billy's story. When I saw Major Hopewood again, he did not look like a man who was happy to be reunited with a child he had considered lost to him. In fact, he looked disgruntled. Father for some reason that escaped me urged him to waste no time in returning to reside with us, Hopewood though tried to get my father to agree to allow him to take Billy to his lodgings instead. Fortunately, both Billy and my father refused his offer. Billy's things were moved from the stables into the house and he would have a room on the same floor as Mr Hopewood. I looked forward to seeing them interact at breakfast in the morning, Mr Allan had already informed the staff of the change and everyone was happy for the boy.

After Hopewood's departure I wandered through the card room and back out again. I thought about retiring for the night when Mr Allan came to me with a single rose in his hand, smiling as he presented it to me. "There is a gentleman in the summer room, miss, who asked me to give you this and requested that you please join him there."

I bristled at first thinking that it might be the Viscount returned and I almost fled to my room, but Mr Allan nodded his head to someone behind me and I felt a cool hand touch my shoulder. I tensed then turned around and there was Miles. He took the rose from Mr Allan presenting it to me, "I'm sorry, Mr Allan, I found that I just couldn't wait." I looked back for our butler, but he was gone. Miles took my hand and led me to the summer room. A fire was burning there, and the drapes were open so that we could see the stars and moonlight cascaded across the floor. On a low table by the fire was a bottle of Champagne with two glasses. He pulled me down to the hearth rug with him then reached out to touch my face with one hand while the other was clasped in a fist. His hand was shaking. "You're so beautiful! I never thought I would ever see your face again." Then he took my left hand and kissed it. "You are no longer my poppet, but I hope that I may call you my lady?" He opened his clenched fist and in the palm of his hand was a gold ring with a single blood red ruby.

He gazed at me waiting for me to say something. "Miles I...I thought...I...why..." I couldn't complete a coherent phrase let alone a sentence.

He looked hurt at first, then comprehension lit up his eyes. "I want you to marry me, Clarissa." I shook my head to clear it then put my fingers to my lips to stop them trembling. He swallowed. "I'm sorry for leaving you after Cornwall but I did go to Scotland, I needed to sort things out in my head and the Highlands are always good for that. But I didn't go to my father's estate, instead I went to Switzerland to meet my mother's family and to get this." He held up the ring so that the firelight made the stone blaze a molten red. "It belonged to my mother and had been given to her by her grandmother. The Marquis was going to bring it to England in the spring when he comes to visit but I didn't want to wait till the spring. I want to marry you now if you'll have me."

Tears were racing down my cheeks and I flung my arms around his neck whispering a simple "Yes" into his ear. He wrapped his arms around me and we sat there in utter bliss until my shawl slipped and he saw the marks on my arm, they were already turning from a deep red to an angry looking purple. He pulled away from me and lit the candle beside him then held it close enough to my arm that I felt the heat from the flickering flame, but the heat of the anger in his eyes was even more painful. "WHO DID THIS?!"

I was at a lost as to what to tell him, but I couldn't lie, it must always be the truth between us from now on. "Lord Burley's son Justin."

"That's why you hesitated when Mr Allan asked you to come to meet me, you were afraid it was a ruse?" I nodded, and he smiled. "Smart girl." In a half-amused voice, he said, "Now how do I make him pay for this insult, should I call him out or assault him in a dark alley...either way is fine by me."

I gasped. "No, Miles, you can't, please don't spoil this moment. I just want to forget about it and think of our future."

Miles grimaced clenching his jaw. "I understand, Lissa, but this will not go unanswered."

I took both of his hands in mind and pleaded, "Miles, please...don't."

He sighed pulling me back into his arms. "I will discuss it with your father but one way or another he will pay for this eventually." Then his lips descended in mine and we lost ourselves in each other.

# Chapter 42
## *A Knife to the Back*

Miles and I joined the family after the other guests left and told them our good news. Father was the first to congratulate us both and I silently said a prayer of thanks that Aunt Mary and Uncle Arthur had left so the planning for our wedding need not start immediately. Miles and I wanted to savour our engagement for at least the rest of the night before the juggernaut of planning took over.

Father opened a bottle of champagne to toast us and Mother sat quietly watching Miles and I as we openly held hands. I waited for any censure, but it didn't come. Because we didn't want to wait till spring to marry Mother suggested that a Christmas wedding might be perfect, where it would be held and how big it would be was up to Miles and me. The only thing Father insisted on was that it be a proper church wedding where he could walk me down the aisle. Mother's expression changed to one of concern when she nodded towards my arm knowing what was under the shawl. I sighed and let my shawl drop and everyone's eyes immediately focused on the bruises.

Father got to his feet with fists clenched glaring at Miles who put his hands up in surrender then my father turned to me. I tried to speak but all that came out was a squeak, "It was the Viscount." Father narrowed his eyes and crossed his arms. I cleared my throat then described what happened and that Murphy had intervened. Father reached out and rang the bell. When Mr Allan arrived, he requested that Murphy attend us.

"I'm sorry, sir, but Mr Murphy is not here, he left with Jacob to follow the miscreant who assaulted Miss Turner."

Father inhaled deeply and growled, "Without my permission?!"

Mr Allan nodded. "You were engaged with Major Hopewood and he didn't want to wait and perhaps lose sight of him, sir."

Father nodded. "Thank you, Mr Allan. When he returns have him come to me regardless of the hour. I'm not about to let such treatment of my daughter go unanswered." Then he turned to the rest of us. "If you'll excuse me, I think I'll send a note to Sir Thomas advising him of what happened. We need to start watching Burley's entire family closely from now on." With that he abruptly turned on his heel and followed Mr Allan out.

Emilie was seated by my uncle with her hand resting protectively on her very noticeable belly. Then her face crinkled up and she started to cry and between sobs she managed to say, "Will they never leave us alone!"

Uncle Samuel put his arm around her, kissing her on the forehead. "Darling, it will be alright, I promise you."

She looked back at him with tear-stained eyes. "You can't possibly promise that, Samuel. And I don't need to be coddled! I'm just emotional and irrational right now and I can't stop myself. But just once I wish we could have a normal life!"

She had put a voice to all our thoughts, I felt the same way and I could see from everyone's expression they did as well. Mother smacked her hands on the arms of the chair where she was sitting. "Well, it has been an eventful night, so I suggest that we all retire. Miles, you might as well spend the night, just not in my daughter's room if you please. I don't think Colin would be able to handle that right now."

I must have turned fifty different shades of red as everyone looked at us. Miles tightened his grip on my hand glaring at the assembly until Emilie broke into laughter that sounded like bells tinkling. "Oh, Irene, you do so amuse me. But I think it's Clarissa that you need tell to stay out of Miles' room." I opened my mouth and closed it several times, unable to collect my thoughts or my breath to rebut her statement. Finally, we all disintegrated into raucous laughter.

Miles walked me to the foot of the stairs and gave me a chaste kiss while we were watched by my mother, uncle and aunt. Then he stepped back. "I'm not going up yet, I need to speak with your father."

Samuel hung back and kissed Emilie. "I need to speak to Colin as well, darling, John will see you home, I won't be long."

Emilie lifted her shoulders and pursed her lips. "John needn't bother seeing me home for heaven's sake, I can go through the garden, Samuel!"

He looked down at her and sighed. "After what happened here tonight I'm not going to let you traipse around at night unprotected, you had better come with me."

Mother took a deep breath, she looked exhausted—she was huge with child—she sighed, "We might as well all talk to Colin, come along then." She walked back down the stairs and over to the study. When she opened the door, she took a step back and screamed. Miles and Samuel ran forward to catch her just as she fainted.

I raced to the door of the study and saw my father slumped over his desk with a knife in his back. Then I saw his hand move. I yelled at the top of my lungs, "GET DR JEFFERSON NOW!" I ran forward with Miles and took hold of his hand as he went to remove the knife. "NO, wait till the doctor comes." I leaned forward and placed my face as close as possible to my father, "Papa? Papa?"

He groaned and opened his eyes. "I feel terrible."

I smiled at him. "Don't move, Papa. Dr Jefferson has been sent for."

He grimaced. "Your mother…was that her screaming?"

I bit my lip. "Yes, Papa."

He smiled. "I promised her I would never go anywhere without her, ever again. Tell her I'm not about to start now." Then he groaned again and closed his eyes.

My uncle leaned out the door yelling for John who was there within seconds, "Take every available man, check all the doors, windows and the gardens."

I panicked. "Papa?!" I tried to rein in my emotions and do what the doctor had taught me. I watched his breathing, it was shallow but regular. I could see the pulse in his neck just where he must have loosened his neck cloth when he sat down.

Supported by my uncle, my mother came to my side, she appeared to have collected herself somewhat, so I stepped away for her to take my place. She kissed his forehead then place her hand on his cheek. "Oh, Colin…"

His eyes fluttered but didn't open. "I won't leave you, my love, I promise." Then he slipped into unconsciousness. Mother stood there leaning over my father with her head next to his, whispering to him.

It seemed like it was hours before Dr Jefferson arrived, bag in hand. He examined my father then looking up he waved me over when he saw me standing there with a brandy decanter in my hand. "Alright, the lot of you either clear out or be ready to do exactly as I say." Then he looked down at my mother. "Irene, you're in my way. I need you to sit on the other side of the desk but keep talking to him while I work." She looked up at him but didn't acknowledge him. "Irene?"

She seemed to be in a trance, but she answered him never taking her eyes of my father. "Yes, Matthew, whatever you say. I'll just talk to him while you work." Uncle Samuel came around the desk and took her by the arms, turning her around and walked her to the chair facing my father. She immediately reached out to touch him then withdrew her hand when the doctor shook his head no. So, she began talking to him about me from the time when I was a baby.

Dr Jefferson removed everything from the desk then took out his instruments. Allan arrived carrying two basins, another bottle of brandy and several towels followed by Richard, our new footman, with two pitchers of hot water and one of cold. The doctor threw his instruments, suture and needles into one of the basins and poured the brandy all over them leaving them to soak in it. Then he took off his jacket rolled up his sleeves and washed his hands and forearms thoroughly first in hot water with soap and then in brandy. He asked me to position the towels around my father and had Emilie light every candle in the room and place them on the desk. Uncle Samuel held onto a candelabra behind the doctor. He asked that Richard and Miles hold my father down and when they pushed on his shoulder, he groaned.

Father's breathing was raspy, and was become more laboured. The doctor listened to his chest, pausing, he looked up at the ceiling with his eyes closed before saying. "Damn…the lung has been punctured. I need to relieve the pressure first before pulling out the knife. Lissa, in my bag there are several small glass tubes and a jar of honey, bring them to me." I obtained what he asked for then he soaked the tubes with his instruments. Once he was satisfied he took out a fine thin blade from the basin and one of the slender glass tubes, laying it on the towel beside him and a suture already threaded through the needle. He then positioned the blade between the ribs and tapped the end soundly as it slid in then out followed by a hiss of air escaping along with some blood the doctor quickly dropped the knife, and picked up the glass tube which he pushed through the slit. Then he ran a suture through to either side of the tube and around it to anchor it in place. Then he took what appeared to be an animal's bladder and secured it over the open end of the tube and applied sealing wax all around it, making a tight seal.

Without missing a beat, he grasped the knife and pulled it out of my father's back then with another suture he stitched the wound close. "Quickly, Lissa, the honey." I opened the jar for him, he inserted a spoon from the basin then carefully smeared the honey over the knife wound and around the slit with the tube. Lastly, he pulled the tube out, quickly pulling on the sutures to either side tight then smearing more honey over the site. He applied a thick dressing over both, anchoring them with a strong linen bandage wrapped several times around his chest. He stood up stretched his back then took the bottle of brandy and drank from it passing it to my uncle who passed it off to Miles.

349

Mother had by this time stretched her hand out to rest it on my father's shoulder as tears poured down her cheeks. She looked up at Dr Jefferson. "Well, Matthew?"

The doctor sighed, stretched again. "If the wound doesn't become infected then he has a very good chance for surviving this, Irene. We'll know in the next few days."

Uncle Samuel stood there with a puzzled look in his face. "Why the honey, Matthew, won't that make things worse?"

Matthew laughed nervously but it helped to relieve some of the tension in the room. "Honey I've found has some amazing healing properties. A friend of mine discovered it in an old herbalist book when he was in Edinburgh. I've used it often this last year and it has proved to be most efficacious. Now what to do with our patient." He looked about the room pursing his lips and shaking his head. "We need to move him from the desk, but we can't risk carrying him upstairs." He stood there looking pensive.

Miles spoke in a whisper to Samuel then said, "Give us a bit, Matthew, I think we can move everything you need into here, just clear a space by the hearth." They both left the room while the rest of us helped to clear half of the room nearest the fire. They returned with Allan and Richard carrying two feather beds and of all things a door. Then Allen and Richard went out and came back in with my mother's large chaise lounge from her sitting room.

My uncle smiled at them and then took my mother's hand, "Allan knows you so well, this way you can stay here with Colin and still be comfortable."

Suddenly a tea trolley came jerking into the room pushed by Mrs Cripps. "Good heavens, I got up to set the bread to rise only to find the lot of you still up and Mr Turner near death. Well dying or not, you are all going to need something to keep up your strength. It's still the wee hours of the morning so I imagine you won't be to bed for hours yet. I made you something to eat, breakfast will be at the usual hour. I can't rush the bread rising nor the hens laying so this should tide you over till then." She parked the heavily laden trolley and shuffled out, sniffling and wiping her eyes with a huge handkerchief.

Father groaned again. "Will someone please tell the dear lady that I'm not dying." Mother choked on her own tears then giggled. She reached out and touched my father's head, smoothing his hair back, he smiled but never opened his eyes.

Dr Jefferson knelt beside him. "Colin, I want to give you something for the pain before we move you. You'll have to suck on this glass tube, I don't want to sit you up because you've lost a great deal of blood and your lung was punctured. But first I need you to take a deep breath for me while I listen to your lung."

Father didn't respond but he tried to take a deep breath and called out "CHRIST!" with the pain.

"That's very good, Colin, you're going to need to keep taking deep breaths every so often." Father cracked an eye open and grimaced. Dr Johnson added a few drops of laudanum into a glass of punch, inserted a clean glass tube and put it between my father's lips. "Suck on the tube, old man." Father automatically did as he was told then closed his eyes once more.

Major Hopewood came to the door and knocked. "Excuse me…" Then he saw my father. "Oh my god, what happened?"

Mother turned to look at him as she tucked a strand of hair behind her ear and wiped her face with the back of her hand. "Oh Major…I'm sorry. May I help you with something?"

The Major walked further into the room. "I should be asking if you require my assistance, dear lady."

Uncle Samuel rubbed his brow while looking at my father. "Actually, Lionel, we could use your help moving Colin to the makeshift bed by the fire."

Hopewood's mouth opened and closed, he looked annoyed but said, "Of course."

Miles, Dr Jefferson, the Major, my uncle, Allan and Richard then picked up my father following the doctor's instructions and laid him face down on the door that had been covered by the feather bed. Then Hopewood turned to my uncle. "Hughes, I'd like to speak to you about William…I mean Billy. I'm most perplexed, he's been telling me some fantastical stories about what goes on here. I'm concerned that perhaps he was damaged when Colin's carriage…or when he saw his mother…I ah…I thought that the doctor might be able to help him."

Samuel looked down at his toes then over to Colin and finally to Miles who merely nodded, both Miles and my uncle looked less than pleased. But if there is one thing I knew for sure it was that Billy would never tell anyone about Father's business or the talents of the other staff without his approval. "Why don't you join us here for a pre-dawn snack, Lionel, and we'll endeavour to answer your questions."

They satisfied the Major's curiosity enough without giving away the nature of their work or who exactly was involved in the business. The doctor assured him that Billy had not been damaged, that in fact he was a remarkably well-adjusted, intelligent and curious boy. He did warn him though that raising him above the station from which he had spent the last eight years would take time and patience. The Major dismissed these concerns and tried once again to ask questions about the family business. Samuel and Miles did not indulge him, so he left to retire somewhat disgruntled.

We were all exhausted from the previous night's events and those that took us through the early morning hours to dawn. Mother was asleep on her chaise lounge with one hand dangling off the side to rest on my father's shoulder. It was decided that we should all retire. Emilie and Samuel left to go to their own home. I climbed the stairs while Miles and Dr Jefferson decided to partake of one more nightcap. As I reached my own door, Beth came out of my parents' room looking perplexed and agitated, she was wringing her hands, so I motioned for her into my room. Once she was in I closed the door. "If you are concerned about my parents, Beth…"

She cut me off before I could continue. "Oh, no, miss, I'm so sorry. Robert told me what had happened. But that's not what's amiss right now, it's your parents' room! I went in to get your mother's shawl and a few pillows, but I found it all tops turvy. I can't for the life me understand who would do that or why!" I started for the door when she reached out. "Robert has gone to fetch Mr Johnson." I was unsettled to say the least, was this another attempt of Lord Burley's to scare my father and uncle into stopping their investigation?

I heard Miles' and doctor's voices and opened my door. Beth and I both stepped out to find Meg and Dalton standing outside of my parents' room along with Mr Allan. Miles and the doctor stood on the threshold of the room, taking it all in. I walked up and stood behind them, the room looked like a whirlwind had passed through with things knocked over, tossed about, pushed over or torn open. Books had been ripped apart, clothing was in shreds with linings pulled out and hems cut open. A trail of clothing led to their dressing room. My mother's jewellery on inspection was all there though her jewellery case had been destroyed. The same could be said for my father's things. In their dressing room the same level of destruction was to be found.

Dr Jefferson looked ill. "We'd better notify Sir Thomas about this."

Miles nodded. "In the meantime some of us have been up all night and need to get some rest. Beth, will you please go to Mrs Turner and stay with her. Robert, will you wake me as soon as Murphy and Jacob return. I'll send a message to Sir Thomas and Mr Hughes. Mr Allan, please lock the door to this room and the hallway entrance to the dressing rooms. I think perhaps the staff should keep their weapons of choice nearby as well. This is an act of a desperate person." He turned back to our butler. "Mr Allan, we need to search the house, find out where they entered or if they are still here." Miles walked me to my room and opened the door letting Meg precede me then he took me in his arms, hugged me close and kissed my forehead. "Try and get some sleep, my darling, and lock your door, Meg should sleep there as well." Then he let go of me and stepped back.

I looked up at him. "Miles, what could they have been looking for?"

He shook his head. "Honestly, I don't know, Lissa, maybe this was just a scare tactic."

"Oh my god, I have to check on James!"

"I'll do it, love." He walked down the hall to where the doctor stood waiting, but he said, "I'll go with Miss Turner, we'll check on James together. You need to send a message to Sir Thomas and Samuel." Miles nodded looking back at me and smiled before descending the stairs. Then the doctor came to me and we went off to check on my brother.

Lettie was with James, but he was sound asleep. She had not heard a thing, but I insisted that when we left that she lock the door. I knew that she would keep watch and wouldn't get much sleep especially since Murphy had not returned from tracking the Viscount.

When I returned to my room, Meg helped me prepare for bed. "I don't understand it, Meg, who could have gotten into my parents' room without anyone seeing them."

Meg bit her lip. "Well, miss, it was a large party with lots of people coming and going. There were ladies coming up here to find a place to rest or freshen up all evening. A there was that son of Lord Burley's, he was up here with a lady."

"What!? Where?"

"He was with a lady standing by the servant's stairs, he had his back to me, but I recognized his wine-coloured cut away and those breeches like he was dressed up for Almacks instead of a musical evening and cards."

"The lady, did you see who she was?"

"No, miss, he was standing in front of her." At which point Meg blushed and swallowed several times, I assumed by her demeanour that the couple were intimately engaged. Then Meg continued, "All I could see was the train of her gown, it was pale, but the light was poor, it could have been blue or maybe lavender."

"Thank you, Meg, would you be so kind as to tell Mr Johnson what you saw, he should be in the study or library. I'd go myself, but I'd rather not have to dress again and I'm exhausted…" just then I yawned in a most unladylike fashion, "ring for one of the footmen to go with you."

Meg smiled, rang and quietly gathered up my clothes as I sunk down under the covers and fell asleep.

# Chapter 43
## *The Great Strategy*

When I awoke, I knew that the day had slipped away from me. The light which usually brightened my room in the morning was gone and the shadows of late afternoon snaked across the floor. My head felt like it was stuffed with cotton wool as I sat up reaching for the water beside my bed, it was tepid but satisfied my parched mouth. I turned and rang the bell for Meg then sat there and waited and waited. Finally, I flung back the covers, slipped into a simple day dress and ran a comb through my hair, tying it back with a ribbon then slipping on my shoes I left the room. In the hallway all was quiet but the noise emanating from downstairs sounded like an army was camping in our entry hall. Just then Meg appeared at the top of the stairs blowing a stray lock of hair out of her eyes while carrying a tray of my mother's porcelain figurines and my father's snuff box collection. "Meg, what on earth are you doing?"

She looked up with a harassed expression on her face. "Mrs Turner ordered all breakables and pocketables to be removed and locked in the box room on the third floor."

"Whatever for? And what is all that noise down there, are we hosting a division of cavalry?"

Meg looked aggravated. "Not quite, miss, just a few of Major Hopewood's regiment are here along with Sir Thomas and some of his special men. It seems that someone killed Lord Burley and set fire to his town house."

"WHAT!"

"Yes, miss, that's exactly what your uncle said."

Then she shifted the weight of the tray and it almost overset so I urged her to set it down on one of the hallway tables. "Perhaps you'd better start from the beginning."

But before she could say another word Robert came the up the stairs equally burdened with items destined for the box room. He huffed and then said, "Oh, miss, glad to see you're awake. Mr Johnson and your mother would like to see you in the breakfast room. Dr Jefferson, your aunts and uncles are already there."

I looked from one to the other then at their burdens. "Is that the last of it?" They both just nodded. "Then just put them in my dressing room and go get yourself a cup of tea and put your feet up." They both smiled and lugged the trays into my dressing room after I opened the door for them. As they passed me I slipped the key into Meg's pocket. "You had better lock both doors just in case."

She smiled. "I will, miss."

I walked to the head of the stairs looking down on the organized confusion of strange men both in and out of uniform racing across the entry hall between the library and the dining room. I was convinced that I was in the midst of a counsel of war. Uncle Samuel was standing at the foot of the stairs looking up at me and it brought back memories of the Abbey and the many times he had waited for me just as he was now. He smiled up at me and held out his hand, "Come on, brat, don't dawdle. I'm starving. You've practically slept the day away. But that fiancé of yours wouldn't stand for you to be awakened."

I raced down the stairs and took his hand, smiling to myself at the word fiancé. "Why the breakfast room?"

"Ah. Well… Sir Thomas has seconded the dining room as his office and Major Hopewood has taken over the library with his men. Did you know that he was called back to his regiment last night on Sir Thomas's request?" He chuckled. "Next the old man will want to start a special branch in the military."

I pulled on his hand to stop him. "And Father?"

He fell silent and bit his lip. "He has a fever, Lissa." I gasped and could feel my lower lip tremble. "But Matthew says it's not serious, that it was to be expected and that he should come through it alright."

"He said 'should' and not will?!" I was breathing rapidly and felt sick, I couldn't move and closed my eyes trying to catch my breath.

Then suddenly Miles was standing in front of me with a hand on either cheek. "Poppet, poppet? You have to let go of Samuel's hand before you break it." I automatically released my uncle's hand as he whispered a quiet thank you. Then Miles' took my hand in his. "Samuel, will you get the doctor? I think Lissa is in shock."

When he said the word shock it was like a trigger that unlocked my limbs. I shook off Miles' hand and ran to my father's study. Lettie and James were there with him. James was laying down beside Papa and giving him kisses on the cheek as Lettie bathed my father's head with a cool cloth. She smiled at me when she looked up and James put a finger to his lips and in a loud lisp said, "Sssh, Issa, Papa sick and nees us be quiet."

As he finished his announcement my father opened one eye. "You tell them, son." Then he closed the eye and went back to sleep.

James got up and ran to me putting his arms up. Miles was there beside me and bent down to swing him up to eye level. James popped his thumb in his mouth and looked at us then at our father. He caught me watching him and pulled his thumb out and touched my cheek with his wet hand then with his darling lisp asked, "Is Papa gonna get bettar, Issa?" He caught the sight of a tear rolling down my cheek and his chin started to quiver when I didn't answer him. "Issa, is Papa…" and he choked on his own tears. I couldn't lie to him or tell him that I didn't know.

My father came to my rescue. "James…you're a Turner, just like me and Lissa and we don't give up. I'm going to be alright. I just need to rest… Now you take your sister and go get something to eat… Lettie will watch over me till your mama returns." He grimaced and closed his eyes for few seconds before saying, "I'll see you both later." Then he winked of all things…he winked at us! But this small interaction had exhausted him, and he was sweating more profusely but his eyes were closed again, his breathing was not deep, but it was regular. I looked to Lettie and watched her wring out the clothe yet again. She looked over at us and smiled then nodded that it was okay for us to leave.

In the breakfast room Mother sat in her usual spot, toying with her soup, she was pale with dark circles under her eyes. She had obviously slept very little and if this kept up it would not be good for the baby. James squirmed to get down out of Miles' arms and ran to her. "Papa is gonna be okay, Mama, he says Urners don give up!" She smiled at him and pulled a chair close to her, so he could sit beside her and share her soup. Miles and I sat down at the table then John and Richard served us.

I looked to my Aunt Mary, but she shook her head as if she could read my mind, so I decided not to state the obvious about my mother. Instead I turned to Emilie and asked how she was feeling. From her appearance, she was only marginally better than my mother. In fact, everyone looked exhausted. Sir Thomas came into the room followed by Major Hopewood, Murphy and Jacob. I raised my eyebrows at the state of Murphy and Jacob, they both looked like they had been beaten within an inch of their lives but they each managed a smile as I stared at them open-mouthed. Mother asked them all to be seated though Jacob tried to resist, but Sir Thomas insisted. John and Richard both gave him a nudge and a smile as they served the newcomers.

Sir Thomas ate his soup in silence and when he was done, and we were waiting for the next course, he looked pointedly at my mother. "Mrs Turner, I have talked to Matthew and he says that with great care Colin can withstand a trip to the country, therefore, I want you to move there as soon as possible."

Mother raised her head with a look of astonishment. "Sir Thomas, my husband almost died. He is still very ill, and you advise us to journey to the country?!" Then she turned and glared at Dr Jefferson who wouldn't meet her eyes.

Sir Thomas was not to be put off by her and continued, "Yes, I want you to go to Mr Johnson's home in Dorset."

Mother sat with a sour look on her face wringing her napkin. "Colin will not be happy."

Sir Thomas cleared his throat. "Nonsense, the country air will be good for him and I understand that the gypsies have returned to winter there and with them there it may be a deterrent to anyone planning any hostile action. Those old Tudor homes not only have character but conveniently thick walls and small windows plus the two floors make it adequately defensible." He seemed very pleased with himself as he looked around the table, but no one was smiling with him.

Mother straightened up and glared at Sir Thomas. "I beg your pardon, Sir Thomas, but I would like to know why you think you can order my family about on a whim. Is the investigation to be continued here in London?" Sir Thomas nodded in the affirmative. "Then I see no reason to impose on Mr Johnson. If I move my family, it will be to our country home in Somerset and only when my husband says so."

Sir Thomas smiled at her as he might at a child and I could see my mother setting up for a fight. At this point it was Miles who jumped in. "It's a trap, ma'am, if you go to Somerset that's what they want. They can't risk a major altercation in London, not with the resources available to us here. By bringing everyone to Dorset with the gypsies there, it should be a great inconvenience for anyone to attack your family…if that is their goal and so far, that's what all our intelligence indicates. He wants to eradicate the Turners and Hughes, ma'am, so we intend to give him a target that he cannot resist with everyone congregated in once place. My home is not a great entailed property and as such has been considered expendable." He turned and glared at Sir Thomas. "But as Sir Thomas has indicated it is very defensible and the gypsies will provide us with a decided advantage…that is if I can convince them to once again stand with us." Miles started to pace which was indicative of his unease and concern about this plan. He paused and taking a deep breath continued, "Therefore, the new Lord Burley, if it is him, will have to bring to bear all of his associates…if his goal is to eliminate you. The Crown will be sending some troops to support the effort. This could be the end of it, Mrs Turner, no more threats, no more unexpected attacks, it will be over."

Mother's shoulders slumped forward. "You make it sound like a siege, Mr Johnson." Then she looked at Aunt Mary and Uncle Arthur, both nodded as did Uncle Samuel and Emilie. Lastly, she turned her head to look at me and I nodded. She started to cry, and James reached up to catch a tear from her right eye before it could roll down her cheek. "Don' cry, Mama… Papa says 'Urners don' give up."

She smiled at his innocence, wiped her eyes on the back of her hand then sniffed and looked at Sir Thomas then Miles. "Miles, it's lovely of you to invite us to take shelter in your home, thank you. I'm looking forward to seeing the improvements you've made. Will your father and Lady Jane be there as well?"

Miles looked perplexed, "Well, ma'am, I…I'm not sure."

Mother smiled her most winning smile. "I should think that it would be a perfect time for a wedding and they surely wouldn't want to miss out on the festivities." I was as shocked as everyone else.

Then Mother stopped smiling and looked around the table. "Come now, if we are to set a trap in Dorset, doesn't it make sense to act like we are carrying on with life as usual and not burying ourselves behind fortifications?"

Sir Thomas puckered his lips, nodding, "Very astute, Mrs Turner, it will be easier to hide my men amongst your revellers." Then he turned to Miles. "Johnson, how amenable are the town folk to you?"

Miles was concentrating as if tallying up potential allies. "Well, the local vicar is a most persuasive man and Father did donate the money to repair the church roof and bell tower. Plus, I intend to build a larger school and hire more people from the local populace as the estate begins to show a profit. The Dawsons buy all our supplies and food stuffs from the locals and towns people and Dawson has been assisting with repairs to the vicarage. The gypsies even set to rights the graveyard after the last storm, though I'm not sure how he'll feel about the flowers they planted. I would say he's our biggest ally and can win over most of the village folk that are not impressed with my unconventional wandering tenants. With him on our side I would say that we could count on the general population to stand behind us or at least not side with our enemies." He grinned, "And the additional commerce of a wedding and the business from a house full of guests just before Christmas will be welcomed." He turned to my mother beseechingly. "But, Irene, I haven't much in the way of staff beyond the Dawsons."

Mother waved her hand. "Oh posh, Miles, I wouldn't think of depriving our staff of attending this event. I'm sure Mrs Cripps and our staff will manage quiet well with the Dawsons."

Miles grimaced. "One can only hope that Mrs Dawson sees it the same way." I giggled at the thought of Mrs Cripps and Mrs Dawson at loggerheads in his huge kitchen.

Mother then spoke up, "But I will not move Colin until Matthew agrees." She looked at Dr Jefferson who was deep in thought.

When he looked up, "I think we will need to invite some additional guests that Burley would be familiar with if we're to make this convincing. The new Lord

Burley is not stupid, he will be prepared for some sort of ruse. We cannot just play act at this. Therefore, Sir Thomas, I think you and Isabel should be there and Miles, your father at least needs to be there." Sir Thomas nodded.

Emilie touched Samuel's sleeve. He looked up from the glass of lemonade that he had been staring into, "Yes, I agree, Matthew. In fact, I think we should invite the de Bearnes. I had a letter yesterday to say that they will be back in London before the end of the week and you know Gabriel will want to be part of this fight."

Mother perked up. "Will Charity and the children be coming?"

My uncle smiled at my mother. "Yes, Irene, apparently, they will be living in London. It's something to do with setting up his wine business here with the Marquis' son Anton. It would seem that Miles' uncle and the de Bearnes will be partners in an endeavour to bring the best continental wines to England. Gabriel has better English than Anton and he understands English business practices. Anton has recently married, and his wife is not so keen to live in London, so the de Bearnes will be the London mangers and Anton will be the go between in Paris."

Aunt Mary and Uncle Arthur had been sitting quietly listening, then Aunt Mary cleared her throat, "I think we need to be precise about this gathering. It would appear that you have hijacked my niece's wedding for your convenience, Sir Thomas."

Sir Thomas looked perplexed. "Do you have another suggestion, Mrs Spencer?"

Aunt Mary looked at me. "It's your wedding, child, Lord knows this family tends to be eccentric when it comes to where and how they celebrate their nuptials. But what do you say?"

I looked at Miles and squeezed his hand. "Dorset is fine, Aunt Mary. I'd like it to be just family and close friends anyway. I'm sorry Sir Thomas but I think your men would be better utilized elsewhere."

Major Hopewood eagerly jumped into the conversation. "I agree with Miss Turner, Sir Thomas. But I can easily take my men on a training expedition to the Poole area, keeping my distance and move in when we're needed. If all goes well, the Turners and Hughes could be home in time for Christmas, that is if they are willing to relocate to Dorset by mid-week next."

Murphy was taping his fingers on the table and it was becoming louder and more annoying. Uncle Arthur finally stayed his hand. "Obviously, you have something that you'd like to say, Mr Murphy?"

Murphy moved as if to push his chair back. "I think all of you know what this family means to the staff of this house and where you go we go. But Jacob and I walked right into a rat's nest when we tried to follow the new Lord Burley. He is a canny man and has some of the worst dregs of humanity working for him. I agree that it would be best if the family left London, it will pull those men out of their comfort zone. But make no mistake, Burley's operation is spread wide. No one is going to be safe no matter where we go but I agree with Sir Thomas, Mr Johnson's place offers us the best opportunity to lay this business to rest." Then he looked pointedly at me then down at the table and resumed his taping.

His taping, oh my god, then my back went ramrod straight, I suddenly lost my appetite, but I forced myself to continue eating and answered Murphy back taping out one word, 'understand'. Miles watched my hand as I tapped when I looked at him, his brow was furrowed. I grasped his hand and wrote 'later' and he squeezed my hand in response. Conversation died down to the logistics of how to move Father, along with packing up an entire household. Miles became heavily involved in all of this since he was the only one who knew what repairs had been made to his home and how many people it could accommodate, let alone the supplies we would need to carry with us. Mr Allan was asked to sit in on these conversations and to pass on the information to the staff, especially Mrs Cripps.

I attempted to engage Major Hopewood in conversation, but he was intent on listening to Miles who thankfully seemed to have realised that discretion was required. He was delightfully ambiguous about the size of the house, its position and the status of the out buildings etcetera. It came to the point that I thought my Uncle Samuel was going to punch him if his responses continued to be so vague. "Good God, Miles, I know you've been out of the country but does that man Dawson not keep you informed about the builder's progress?!"

Miles chuckled. "It's not Dawson that has been overseeing the building, he has enough to do with working the fields and tending the orchards and gardens. Mrs Dawson and her grandmother have been managing the renovations and overseeing the builders."

Hopewood's jaw dropped. "My Lord...gypsies are overseeing your estate? You'll be lucky if they haven't robbed you blind!" I found it interesting how it registered with everyone in the room that the major had jumped to that conclusion that Mrs Dawson and her grandmother were gypsies since no one had told him. Uncle Samuel made a quick move as if to grab the Major, but Sir Thomas gave him some signal and instead my uncle dropped his napkin to the floor and bent to pick it up.

It wasn't until the next day that I could speak to Miles and he asked if I'd like to take a carriage ride, everyone else had gone off to run errands. Major Hopewood was apparently off to meet with his regiment and had left Billy in my charge. "Miles, I can't, I have Billy with me."

Miles whispered in my ear, "Bring him along, I need to talk to him privately anyway."

Billy had been sullen all day and I had thought it was because the Major was absent, but he brightened considerably when I asked if he'd like to come with Miles and me.

Once outside and ensconced in the carriage with Billy between us, Miles wrapped his arm around him and gave him a hug. "You've done a wonderful job, Billy, and I promise you will not have to pretend to be Major Hopewood's son once we go to Dorset."

My mouth fell open and both he and Billy laughed. Billy smiled up at me. "We really put one over on everyone, didn't we, miss! Only Mr Johnson and Mr Turner here knew that Hopewood weren't my father."

I was astonished and a touch angry. "But, Billy, you identified him as your papa."

Billy cast his eyes down. "Well, I did think it was him when I first glanced him, but I saw him from a distance and he was in ordinary clothes. But when I met him I knew right off that it weren't him. But Mr Turner asked me to pretend he was...he wanted to know why the Major would go along with pretending I were his son, so he set me to follow the Major and I saw him talking with the new Lord Burley in a coffee house like they were good friends. Mr Turner was suspicious when the Major had made a point of telling him that he didn't know the Burley family at all, which seemed odd to him seeing as how the Major's home is in the same county as the Burleys'."

I felt sad for Billy. "So the Major isn't your father? Oh, Billy, I'm so sorry."

"No, miss, he ain't, but don't feel sorry for me. I never expected to be as well off as I am after me ma died. Your da has promised he'll send me to school and then to university, so that one day I can be a doctor or lawyer if I want to so it were worth the few cuffins the Major gave me when I told him I didn't know nothing about what happens in the house."

Again, I was shocked. "Oh no, Billy! Did he hurt you badly? Did you really lie to him?"

Billy laughed. "He just rung me bell a bit, but I've had worse back at the house where my mum and I stayed. And I lied through my teeth, miss, never told him the truth about anything but I stuck as close to the truth as I could without being specific, Mr Johnson taught me that. He said it was easier to remember me lies that way."

I raised a brow and looked at Miles over Billy's head. "He did, did he?" Billy and Miles both chuckled and he gave Billy a squeeze.

I shuddered at what Billy must have gone through, so I changed the subject, "And what about your real father, Billy?"

He shrugged and looked at Miles who also shrugged. "Sir Thomas has a man looking for anyone in the army answering the description that Billy gave him. But only when he can spare the time, so it could take a while."

Billy became serious saying. "I suspect he's dead, miss, maybe in the war but then I'd be older, wouldn't I. So maybe he died in one of the Luddite riots over here." He was philosophical about it, but I felt his pain that he had not gained the father he so desperately wanted.

I took his hand. "Perhaps, Billy, but I have faith that Sir Thomas will find out at least who he was."

He smiled at me. "I have my memories of my ma and the stories she told me of the grand family she came from which always seemed like a fairy tale to me."

A thought came to mind that perhaps we could find out his origins and who his father was through his mother's family. "Phipps wasn't your mother's real name, was it, Billy?"

"No, ma'am, but she said we couldn't use our real name or bad people would come looking for us."

"If we promise not to tell anyone would you tell Mr Johnson and I?"

He stared out the window giving my request consideration before saying, "Her name was Mena Phillips and we are descended from the first King of Wales, Rhodri Mawr." He smiled at us both then settled back to enjoy the ride around the park. I looked at Miles and knew he was thinking the same thing I was. I suppose Billy could have been telling us a tale, but there had been a famous scandal or rather mystery about a Phillips family that was still talked about today. I remember hearing it gossiped about for months among the servants at the Abbey that the beautiful daughter of a wealthy member of the Welsh landed gentry had disappeared when she was out riding. Her horse had been found and her groom had been knocked unconscious. There had been signs of a struggle and though an exhaustive search went on for over a year she was never found. Her name was Philomena Phillips. This just added another layer of mystery to the Turner household.

When we exited the park, we found ourselves in front of my Aunt Mary's grand town home which apparently was the gathering place to discuss what we had inadvertently discovered the previous day and so Billy could tell everyone what he knew.

# Chapter 44
## *Secrets, Bequest and Travel*

When we entered the drawing room, everyone was there except for my mother who had stayed behind with father. His fever had broken last night but he was extremely weak, and Mother wouldn't entrust anyone else with his care at this point.

Sir Thomas was kind enough to ask after my father, though I'm sure he had already heard from the men he had stationed at our home. The preliminary investigations into his stabbing, the ransacking of my parents' room and the previous Lord Burley's death in the fire at his town home were still in progress. Sir Thomas's men were now out looking for the possible perpetrators with the aid of Bow Street and the Major Hopewood's regiment.

There was a commotion at the door as Miles' father and his brother entered. Both were grinning from ear to ear. Edward looked less put together than I had seen him in the past, assuming the casual dress of one of the romantic artists that were making their mark by placing an emphasis on emotion and individualism in their work. The look suited him. Lord Shellard on the other looked his normal well-groomed self except he was waving a paper like a school boy as he walked up to Miles, exclaiming, "We have it!" and he pulled Miles into a hug who was totally perplexed especially when he looked at his brother who appeared absolutely delighted! While everyone in the room except for Aunt Mary and Uncle Arthur looked bewildered.

The Earl handed Miles the paper then stood before him waiting for his reaction as he read it through. Miles suddenly dropped onto the settee beside me looking up at his father, he sounded totally incredulous, "His Majesty approved this? No discussion, no debate, he just signed it! Is he aware of what he has done?" He glanced up at Edward. "And Edward...why are you smiling?!"

The Earl looked down at Miles, his face solemn and serious with Edward standing beside him with an equally solemn facial expression. It was Edward that spoke to him. "Aye, brother, he signed it in front of me to my great relief or I might not have believed it myself. I imagine my mama will be rolling over in her grave since all her scheming was for naught." He turned to Aunt Mary and bowed. "And, thank you, ma'am, for your gracious assistance in procuring my audience." Aunt Mary smiled and bowed her head to him.

Miles looked askance. "An Audience?"

His Lordship nodded, "Yes, indeed." Then he glared at Edward. "It would seem there has been some scheming going on behind our backs. Your brother gained an audience with the Duke of Clarence by representing himself as an artist seeking a royal commission on Mrs Spencer's recommendation, she had sent the Duke one of Edward's paintings by way of whetting his interest. But Edward insisted that I accompany him, where upon your brother very eloquently laid before his Highness our quest to establish your legitimacy as my heir." He looked at Edward and clapped him on the shoulder. "His Highness was impressed and amused by the uniqueness of the request coming from the one that would be dispossessed. Then just yesterday we were called to the palace where we witnessed the King sign the document of legitimacy. You, Miles, are now my heir."

Miles sat with his mouth open. "But Edward, you were raised with the expectation of inheriting!"

Edward let out a breath in a huff. "Brother, that expectation clung to me like a curse! Thankfully I found out before too late that I'm more like my father than my mama, after all. As much as I loved her she was too imbued with her father's traits of scheming and manipulation, which I could never abide. Even though I miss her, I know that had she lived she would never have sanctioned my desire to be recognized as an artist. But Father has endowed me with a handsome annuity, a town house in Edinburgh and a cottage near Aunt Millicent in the Highlands. I have never been happier, brother!"

It was then that the Earl looked about the room. "We had the devil of time tracking you down, son." Then he turned back to face the room. "You must excuse our intrusion, from the looks on your faces when we entered you were engaged in a counsel of war."

He then noticed Billy behind our settee playing with one of my aunt's spaniels and raised an eyebrow. Billy caught his eye and gave him an impish smile. "Right you are, your Lordship...it's a dark tale too." Then he giggled.

Miles reached behind him swatting Billy lightly on the head. "Silence, you imp."

Sir Thomas had been sitting quietly watching this tableau then he rose and came to Miles reaching out his hand to shake it. "Congratulations, Lord Tinley, and to you as well, Mr Johnson, since you both seem amenable to this change in fortune."

Edward smiled and shook his hand with enthusiasm. "Thank you, Sir Thomas! I relish the change in my status. Then Edward arched a brow at Miles and pointedly looked at Sir Thomas's outstretched hand."

Miles was still stunned, finally reached out taking his hand. "Yes, thank you, Sir Thomas. I can honestly say that I can hardly believe it and I'm at a loss for words."

Aunt Mary in the meantime had rung for her butler and when Mr Douglas responded, she whispered to him and he retreated. Suddenly everyone was congratulating the brothers. Edward came to my side.

"Miss Turner, I owe you many apologies, I have been the worst kind of man and an insulting bastard if you will excuse my language."

I touched his arm as he looked at me beseechingly. "No need, Mr Johnson, I think I understand the pressure you felt not being sure of your place in this world."

"I think most of my irascibility and boorish behaviour was from the fact I felt like an imposter in my own life. And yet Miles never hated me, he accepted me for who was, and I know he will accept me for who I am now. I have never been happier in my life especially now that my brother will be part of that life." He paused with glistening eyes. "When we were boys, I thought he was remarkable and despite all that has happened to him he is still a remarkable person." He took my hand and kissed it.

I smiled at him. "Yes, he is, Mr Johnson."

Miles turned to me, taking my hand. "Really, you two are going to ruin my reputation. I thought I had always been irritating and incorrigible." The three of us were laughing as Mr Douglas returned with champagne and a tray of savouries with which to toast the brothers. The Earl was beyond happy for both his sons, it was obvious in his expression and his manner.

Eventually we returned to the topic of what had transpired since the party. We discussed what Billy had done for my father after discovering that Major Hopewood was not his father. How Hopewood knew that Mrs Dawson and her grandmother were gypsies and other inconsistencies regarding his behaviour since staying with us.

Edward was paying close attention and remarked on Major Hopewood. "You mean Lionel Hopewood of the Coldstream Guards?"

Sir Thomas leaned forward, "Why, yes, do you know him?"

Edward was silent for a bit. "I was introduced to him once, just let me think of where and when." He rubbed his hand up and down the side of his face. "Good God, I wonder but…"

Sir Thomas was getting impatient. "Yes… What is it that you think you know?"

Edward looked up with a look of disbelief. "Stanhope, Stanhope is the common thread."

We all sat back racking our brains for the name Stanhope.

Miles grimaced. "Richard Stanhope?"

Edward shook his head no. "No, Franklin Stanhope, his son."

Miles shook his head. "Who?"

Edward grimaced. "He is the natural son of Richard Stanhope. The old man has never recognized him, but he gives him an allowance and Franklin uses the Stanhope name, even though he has no claim to it. He's very adept at cheating at just about anything he puts his hand to. He has no scruples or morals whatsoever and because of that he's made a small fortune for himself. There is a country house just outside of London where he holds parties, the details of which shouldn't be spoken of in polite company.

"Lord Burley's sons were frequent visitors along with most of the dregs of the ton with singular appetites. I went with Julian only once; the place is little more than a trumped-up gaming hell and whore house out in the country. It was not at all to my tastes, in fact, I left after the first night. Julian spent weeks apologizing to me saying he had no idea what kind of place it was, and I was naïve enough to believe him. But since…well, since his death I started to hear whispers from some of our mutual acquaintances that Randall and Julian were heavily into debt to him. Stanhope's ploy is to ruin or blackmail those that attend his parties."

Sir Thomas looked delighted. "How does he blackmail them, Mr Johnson?"

Edward shook his head. "I have no idea. But when I was leaving…" he looked at me and Samuel, "I saw your father, Hughes, he was arguing with Stanhope in a small reception room as I waited for my hat and coat to be retrieved. The General was most distressed."

"Did you hear what they were saying?"

Edward shook his head no. "No, I'm sorry, I didn't. It was once I was outside waiting for my curricle that I met Lionel Hopewood and he had the audacity to introduce himself, he was coming, and I was going so I had little time for conversation."

Miles was deep in thought looking intently at his brother when I felt Billy pulling on my arm, he looked scared and whispered in my ear. "He was the one that run my mum over."

I turned to him. "Who…what do mean, Billy."

Then Miles crouched down to look Billy in the eye. "Billy, do you know this Franklin Stanhope?"

Billy's eyes were full of terror. "Mr Franklin, he wanted me mum to work for him, he'd come again and again and offered her a lot of money. But she always said no, saying that it wasn't a fit place and she wouldn't take me there. I wasn't supposed to know but I heard him say that he only wanted Mum, not me, unless he could use me for…things…" He started to tear up."

Miles touched his shoulder. "It's okay, Billy, I think we understand."

He sniffed. "It was him what tried to kill me, but he killed me mum instead."

"Why did you never tell anyone, Billy?" Miles spoke softly laying a hand on Billy's shaking shoulders then pulling him into a hug.

Billy was sniffling, trying hard not to cry. "No one was going to believe me. No one was going take my part against the likes of him. He's bad, milord; evil all the way to his heart if he has one."

Edward knelt down beside his brother. "I believe you, child, everyone in this room does. Mr Spencer?" He looked over his shoulder, but my uncle and Sir Thomas were both gone, and Aunt Mary had her hand to her mouth with a fearful look on her face. Emilie went and sat beside her as Edward addressed my aunt, "Mr Spencer knows him, doesn't he, but by another name?" She nodded. Edward looked at Miles. "Should we follow them, Miles?"

Miles stopped him, placing a hand on his arm. "I need you and Father to stay here with the ladies. Samuel, I think it's time we find the Major and have a chat. He's supposed to be at the barracks."

Edward grabbed his arm. "Miles, be careful! If he's working with Stanhope, he's no fool. Besides that, dear brother, I have no desire to be elevated to the peerage again." Then he chuckled and clapped him on the back. Giving his father a stern look, "Father and I will stay here as you request."

Miles turned to wrap his arms around me while not quite whispering in my ear, "Watch Edward, I'm still not sure I can trust him…with you." Then he chuckled.

Edward was laughing out loud now. "Dear brother, that is the only thing you need to fear from me that I may win your lady's heart…especially since you're always running off."

Miles clipped him on the ear then bent to kiss me. "Pay no attention to him, my love, these artist types are totally unreliable." The brotherly banter delighted me but personally I didn't trust Edward completely, so I would be keeping an eye on him regardless of his apparent delight in his change of status.

After they left Edward paced around the room like a caged cat. Aunt Mary and Emilie were looking over my aunt's latest needle work and Billy was playing with my aunt's Spaniel but since they started to get a bit rambunctious, my aunt had banished Billy and Buster to the garden. Edward finally flung himself into the chair across from the Earl who was studying a chess problem that my Uncle Arthur had set out. "Would you care for a game, son?"

Edward smiled. "No, thank you, Father, I'm too restless to concentrate. I feel like I should be helping Miles or doing something more constructive then just making polite conversation." But he remained seated in front of his father, gazing out the window watching Billy and Buster chase each other…all the while his one hand appeared to be making tracings on the table top.

I rose and walked over to my aunt. "Aunt Mary, do you have any drawing materials? I'd like to do something to take my mind off what Miles may be up to."

She smiled up at me then glanced at Edward and motioned to a cabinet at the far end the room. As I walked past Edward I touched his shoulder. "Come with me." I opened the cabinet and Edward immediately grinned from ear to ear reaching out for a tablet and some pencils. I chuckled. "It seems that you and I share the same problem when others are out having adventures and we're left behind. We both need a distraction, fortunately I can lose myself in my art. Is it the same for you?"

Edward nodded. "Since I was a child, I found another world in my art. My mother viewed it as a wasteful occupation and would rather that I was at the race course or out hunting. My father surprisingly supported me in whatever my interests were." He directed his gaze to the Earl concentrating on the chess board then he smiled and looked back at me. "But I failed to appreciate him for it and, so I pretended to distain anything he supported. It was only with my Aunt Millicent that I felt comfortable being me. She tried to tell me that my father only wanted me to be happy, but my mother was a good teacher. If I showed any interest or affection towards him or Miles, I was sternly and repeatedly chastised. When Miles went off to school I was totally at her mercy and Father started spending more and more time in London and abroad than at home. He would invite me to stay with him and Miles on school holidays, but I always refused. I wish now I had followed my heart. My mother loved me, but she hated my father and brother more." He had a wistful faraway look in his eyes. Then he grimaced. "That's how I became friends with the Brownes. Lord Burley was a childhood friend of my mother's, so we spent a great deal of time with his family whenever Father was away." He looked over his shoulder at his father and sighed. "I should have known that my mother and Lord Burley were lovers, it seemed to be the only time that she was ever happy." Then he looked down at the materials in his hand. "This is me, it always has been. I would have been much happier all those years perhaps if I had told my father that I wanted to be with him and Miles; but what do children know." He kept looking down then finally he rallied and smiled at me, but I could see his eyes were glistening when he asked, "Will you join me in sketching Billy?"

I looked at him with sympathy, picturing him as that confused and lonely boy torn between two parents then I thought of my own childhood. "It would seem, Mr Johnson, that you and I have a few things in common, an interest in art and a less than stellar childhood. I would love to join you in the garden to sketch Billy. It will give me a chance to get to know you better."

"Thank you, Miss Turner, I would like that." He stepped back taking my drawing materials then offering me his arm to escort me out into the garden.

Billy came rushing up to us asking what we were intent on doing. When we told him that we were going to draw him, he pulled down his mouth. "Okay, but I'm not sitting! Buster and I found an ole rabbit whole and we means to see what's living in there now."

Edward laughed. "By all means, young man, I prefer to draw people doing things, personally I think just sitting for a portrait is overrated." Billy looked at him like he was daft but then turned and ran after Buster who was jumping and barking at the rabbit hole. We didn't speak to each as we sat and drew whatever pulled our eye. It was interesting to see our individual visions of the same scene materialize. I stopped drawing after a while and mused over how complex the Johnson brothers were. He must have noticed my lack of attention to my sketch and put his aside. "I would understand, Miss Turner, if you didn't trust me; after all, I have done little to inspire your confidence in me."

I tried to appraise his sincerity from his expression as much as from his words before I responded with "I imagine that you're practiced in the art of keeping your true feelings hidden, Mr Johnson; you are very like your brother in that respect. So yes and no about your inspiring my confidence. I don't know you well enough yet, but I see much of your father in you and I trust him."

He chuckled. "I can only hope that I will eventually earn your trust and confidence. Perhaps one day I will be as lucky as my brother to find a woman like you."

Samuel and Miles eventually returned but they had been unable to locate the Major, in fact he had not been to the barracks in several days; despite having left my parents' home on multiple occasions pleading business there. Aunt Mary invited us to stay for dinner, but I wanted to return home as did Emilie, so we thanked her and prepared to go our separate ways. I invited the Earl and Edward to join us, but they had a prior engagement. Miles and Edward's aunt and uncle were in town and they had promised to join them for dinner. I encouraged Miles to go with them, but he declined. "I'll see my aunt more than both of us may want over the next while. Once she found out I was to marry she announced her intent to journey down to Dorset with us. So, I intend to keep my distance until I can no longer avoid it." He laughed out loud at the stern look he received from his father. "You know it to be true, Father, Aunt Millicent and I both enjoy a good debate and invariably we get carried away vowing never to speak to each other again. So, I'd rather put that off as long as I can."

I looked at Edward for confirmation. "It's true, they are both extremely passionate about certain causes. But never fear so long as we can direct the conversation away from those topics, all should be pleasant."

I wasn't sure that I was going to like Aunt Millicent, Miles was progressive but compassionate at the same time. "Do they disagree so much that it can cause such discord?"

The Earl laughed and answered, "Not at all, my dear, they both agree as to the end result, it's all about the means to reach the end that causes such a hullabaloo at family gatherings. If they would just stop before they started threatening each other, it would only be amusing. And if they could ever compromise and combine their efforts, I think they could move heaven and earth."

Miles scoffed shaking his head, "You have greater faith in us than I do, Father. I fully expect Auntie to haunt me to my grave disapproving of the way I died." Everyone laughed then.

Finally, Uncle Arthur returned without Sir Thomas. He was glowering and cursing under his breath when he entered the room and slammed his fist against the wall. Aunt Mary went directly to his side and took his arm surreptitiously looking at his fist then at the wall as Uncle Arthur continued, "Stanhope seems to have disappeared. He was not at his town home nor at his club or the other places is he known to frequent. Sir Thomas has sent some men to check out his country home and the docks and warehouses." Then he looked at me with a softer expression. "In particular the one owned by you, Clarissa."

I was shocked. "ME! I don't own a warehouse...do I?" I looked at my Uncle Samuel. He tipped his head to the side and looked uncomfortable, then it came to me, "Oh, the General's bequest... I forgot."

My Uncle Arthur smiled at me. "The place has remained as it was before you inherited it, all the goods are all still there. Your father had hoped that someone would try to empty it by now, but it hasn't happened yet." I grimaced at the thought of being the owner of anything belonging to the General but smuggled goods was even less appealing. "There is a small fortune sitting there and I can't see Stanhope waiting much longer, especially if he knows we're onto him."

I was stunned. "Onto him? Today is the first time I've heard his name mentioned. How long has he been a suspect?"

Miles took my hand. "Since your father first came back from France and was assigned the task of throttling the on-going smuggling. Sir Thomas knows just as your father does that it can never be stamped out completely, but he means to make the major players pay for their activities. For years, they have effectively been robbing the crown of significant revenue, disrupting honest commerce, ruining lives and livelihoods, all to line the pockets of a few select people."

Uncle Arthur was muttering to himself and finally spoke up with a bitter vehemence, "We'll get him and his associates, then hang them."

# Chapter 45
## *November 25, 1830*

Once we arrived in Dorset my mind was in a constant whirlwind. I had to worry about a wedding, a madman after my family, my father still recovering from a stab wound, my pregnant mother and several aunts fussing over everything. There were gypsies on the property and the townsfolk were all vying for our favour when word spread that Miles would be the next Lord Shellard and that I would soon be his lady.

This was my first visit back to the site where I had killed a man and Miles had almost died. I could see that to others marrying into the Turner and Hughes family would not be for the faint of heart. Since our first meeting Miles had been shot, tortured, temporarily blinded and if not for the timely intervention from my father and uncle, he would have likely been a victim of madam la guillotine all because he worked with my father. Yet Miles still wanted to marry me, he was a truly an amazing man.

It was obvious that Miles was in his element in Dorset, the villagers came to him from the district surrounding Poole to ask for his assistance in settling disputes and to act as a spokesperson to the other landowners on their behalf which suited the landed gentry just fine so long as nothing encroached on their own rights. But his father was concerned that he might be taking on too much and spoke to him about having the responsibility of managing two estates, Dorset albeit was a much smaller one but still needed a great deal of attention. And he still needed to refamiliarize himself with the management of the Johnson estates which included more than the ancestral home in Devon. The Earl was pressuring him to go with him to Devon for a few weeks after our wedding. He wanted him to become reacquainted with the residents in the district and to meet with the estate manager. I was terrified at the prospect, but I agreed with the Earl that he could not shirk his responsibilities, but now was not the time to resolve these things as Miles pointed out.

Mrs Dawson thankfully was unchanged when I met her again in the enormous kitchen. She and Mrs Cripps had sized each other up and decided to be fast friends but only after Mrs Cripps had tasted her pudding and Mrs Dawson had tasted her bread. Both assured me that they would be more than able to handle my Aunt Mary and Miles' Aunt Millicent with aplomb. Both Mother and Emilie had vowed to leave the menus up to my good judgement, so I intended to leave it up to the two cooks to their great delight.

The greatest surprise was Mr Dawson, he looked like a new man. He was sober, and sun kissed plus he had shed at least three stone of weight, he was muscular now and not at all sickly. Bita caught my look and jokingly said, "My Jack's a braw man again, just like when I married him, thanks to Mr Johnson." Then she smacked the side of her head "Oh the devil, I mean his Lordship...that will take some getting used to, miss. But my Jack does love working on this land again and even owning a wee bit of it hisself." She noticed my surprise and smiled. "Twas a gift from his Lordship for back wages, can you imagine! I swear it's made Jack twenty years younger."

Angel was nowhere to be seen so I asked after her. "Angel's about somewhere, you know that she married one of Magda's young men while you were in Paris, one whose pa was English and a school teacher." She smiled then snorted. "Set Magda right on her ear when he declared that he would follow in his father's footsteps and became a teacher. He and Angel have set up in one of the tenant cottages and use it as a school as well, she's so proud of him. Jibben helped Charles go to university before our people had a permanent winter camp here. When he came back, he took a shine to our Angel and there was no stopping them. He's running the school that his Lordship wanted for the gypsy children and he has just as many of the fisher folk's children attending as gypsy. Mark my word he'll be speaking to his Lordship soon about building a real school house. You might want to warn him that Charlie has his eye on a tumbledown barn near the church." She snorted again. "Strange ways these days, I never thought I'd see the mixing of folks like we have now. One of these days you'll come here and won't be able to tell one kind from the other that might not be such a terrible thing either." She bustled off when she saw Robert come in looking every inch a London valet. She clucked at him then hugged him, she was so proud she was ready to burst.

Miles came in from the yard and asked me to go for a walk to get away from all the madness inside. I told him about Angel and Charles and their desire to build a school in a tumbledown barn, he groaned but good naturedly, "I'll have my father speak to him, it was going to be his project anyway."

The Rambles as Miles called his home was like an old friend, despite the dark memories it contained. The wall that Miles had jumped from behind to rescue me when Randall intended to run off was still a tumbled wreck, some late roses were now climbed over it, making it an interesting feature. He noticed me studying the wall as we walked past. "I couldn't decide if I should pull it down, rebuild it or just leave it. But when I saw that the roses had made it home I left it as is." He laughed. "Edward said it was the best decision that I'd ever made, second only to asking you to marry me."

I kissed him on the cheek. "I agree with Edward."

He chuckled then held me close, kissing my forehead, "You know I've discovered something I never expected...I'm beginning to like my brother especially since he promised to broker a peace treaty between me and Aunt Millicent at least for the wedding."

We walked around the yard where he pointed out the outbuildings that for the most part had been torn down and rebuilt in the same brick as the house. The only original feature left was the old clock tower that had been part of the stables for as long as anyone could remember. The garden itself he said would need a woman's touch since he had left it to run wild. We'd have to hire more gardeners in the spring unless I wanted to make it my own project. I gave him the eye as I looked over the expanse of the gardens and lawn, he laughed at my look and then waved over an elderly man who was clearly starting to set things to rights. "This is Mr Jamieson, my dear, he and his grandson will be our permanent gardeners. In the spring he'll be better able to tell us how many helpers he'll need and how often. With your permission he intends to restore the Elizabethan Knot gardens and he and Mrs Dawson have plans to expand the kitchen garden as well as add an herb and medicinal garden."

Mr Jamieson nodded and gave a funny little bow. "Tis a pleasure to be back here, milady, I was the undergardener here a long time ago and my grandson is a natural with plants." He nodded again. "But If you'll excuse me I should get back to burning that scrub, I don't like leaving it untended. My felicitations on your forthcoming marriage, I only wish our gardens could be providing the wedding blooms." He sighed then knuckled his brow and walked away.

"I like him already, Miles…I believe we will get along very well."

We continued our walk around the old house, the façade was still the same warm red brick I remembered but the improvements and repairs made it truly a beautiful sight as it must have once been. The roof had been repaired and all the tall chimneys were now working at peak performance. The windows were a comforting mixture of mullioned, leaded and stained glass and they all gleamed when the light caught them. The kitchen had been untouched at Mrs Dawson's request, all she had asked for was some additional crockery, pots and pans and a new stove. She had said it was like Christmas when the crates had arrived from the London shops. She guarded the Wedgewood like it was the crown jewels, but it was the silver that was her pride and joy. She attentively listened to Mr Allan about the proper care and keeping of the silver, even taking notes which had impressed him.

But it was the inside of the Rambles that was a true wonder, all the mildew, rack and ruin was gone. Some of the Elizabethan charm remained, such as the dark wainscoting in the more masculine rooms like the library, billiard room and study. But elsewhere it had been whitewashed or changed out for a lighter oak. The walnut and oak throughout the house was now polished so that the deep hues within the woods captured the sunlight and reflected it back into the rooms. The intricately carved staircases remained as is and the slate in the entry hall was polished to a high gloss, showing a myriad of colours in its depth. The ceilings were still low in some places and the odd beam required Miles to bend his head at times but many of the doorways had been enlarged and a few of the smaller rooms had been knocked out to make for more spacious family and guest accommodation. All the rooms were now light and warm, being comfortably furnished in a mixture of beautifully wrought new and salvaged old furniture. I could see that this home would be our retreat like Cornwall was for Aunt Mary and my parents.

I started counting the rooms and the amount of work that it must entail to keep it up, "How can Bita and Angel possibly manage all this?"

He shrugged. "Bita manages, most of the rooms aren't open even when I'm here. Though she keeps them ready just in case. She has hired a few girls from the village and she'd like them to live here eventually but not with the current state of the servants' quarters."

"I would have thought it would be difficult to find staff in the area willing to live away from their place of employment."

Miles shrugged. "Most of them are untrained villagers just looking for work so Bita and Angel are training them as maids, cooks and other domestics, she'd apparently been corresponding with Mr Allan asking for advice." He chuckled. "He seems to be in his element teaching her, but he says she already has a firm grip on basic housekeeping in a country home. However, I'll need your help speaking to Bita later, she won't allow me to hire any footmen because in her words men in the house only cause trouble."

I arched a brow. "Really? How forward thinking." And I gave him an impish grin.

He merely rolled his eyes and continued, "Yes, she says the stable and farm hands are enough for her to deal with when the girls are here during the day. Angel corresponded with Mr Allan and he had sent Mrs Dawson books on housekeeping in a manor house. And from what I hear, Angel's been badgering Robert for details about the footmen and other superior servants in your parents' home. She wants to convince her mother that we need footmen."

I giggled a bit. "Poor Robert, Angel and Bita I imagine can be relentless. I know the letters I had from Angel before we went to Paris were very focused on the role of a lady's maid. I thought she might be looking for a position but now it makes sense. I had to beg Meg to tell me all about what she does so I could answer all of them and from what I've learned Meg deserves a raise."

Miles smiled. "Done!"

I slapped his arm. "Miles, you can't just give a person a raise like that. A wage must be fair and commiserate with their experience, you cannot be known to pay staff excessively, it causes jealousy and envy between different houses and your neighbours might cut you for it feeling that your trying to steal their staff away."

Miles merely arched his brow. "Incredible. I had no idea there was such politics involved in hiring staff."

I chuckled. "It's a very complicated system." He laughed and patted my arm. "But we can provide our staff with superior uniforms and accommodation and there are other perks that my parents provide such as a full day off once a month in addition to their weekly half day, arranging for holiday celebrations for them and their families and most especially providing aid to those that need our help. I would also like to allow our staff to marry if they so choose, just as my parents do. It may be difficult to find experienced staff they can be very set in their ways, so I think Mrs Dawson has the right idea of training our own staff. Just be prepared to be labelled eccentric."

Miles raised his hands. "The house will be your domain, my love, and I leave it to you. All I ask is that you keep me informed, I hope to run the Rambles at a profit eventually."

I held onto his arm as we leaned against the paddock fence. "How is that coming, my love?"

He took a deep breath as he looked over the paddock and the pastures beyond, a smile of satisfaction lighting up his face. "Dawson has hired farm hands from the village and like the maids most of them are untrained, having been fishermen, but he says they're doing well. It seems we are now the county's greatest benefactors since many of our neighbours in the area leave their properties to be run by managers, they rarely if ever visit nor take any interest in county affairs." He turned around looking back to the house and stable yard. "I need to improve the servants' quarters at some point and the sooner the better. Right now, even the birds decline to use the attics in the house, there're so cramped. The stable accommodation has been expanded for the horses as well as the grooms and the workers' cottages are being torn down and reconstructed, they should be ready before planting."

"Where are they living now?"

He sighed obviously not happy with his answer. "The single men are living in the loft in one of the barns and the ones that are married are still living in and around the village with their families. Don't worry, I've made sure that they have food to eat and fuel for their fires."

I squeezed his arm to reassure him. "You're a good man, Miles Johnson."

He beamed at my praise. "I have a mind to add a servants' wing to accommodate the in-house servants. What do you think? I like that idea better than having them scurrying around above our heads."

"I think that's a wonderful idea. I must admit that I'm surprised the Dawsons are so welcoming to outsiders and proving to be so competent in running things. But I wonder why they haven't hired any of Magda's people to help in the house and the fields?"

He shook his head leaning back pulling me to stand between his legs. He started to kiss me on the cheeks then the neck, "Magda...won't...allow...her people...to work as servants. They will help at planting and harvest for a portion of the harvest but that's all."

Then he claimed my lips and deepened the kiss and we were lost to each other.

His caress was my entire world so when I heard someone clearing their throat I was more than annoyed. Finally, a voice broke in, "Miles, let her go before one of her uncles finds you and puts a hole through you brain pan. She's not married to you yet, nephew."

Miles groaned while still kissing me, but I think it had more to do with his Aunt Millicent coming upon us than his passion. He looked up briefly, "Go away."

He bent his head towards me again, but I had come to myself enough to push him away and turned to look at her nervously. I refused to fidget or check my hair as was my inclination and Miles huffed as he pulled me back against him so that I was aligned with my back to his front. His intent I believe was for me to be aware of how close we had come to putting our wedding night before our wedding and so that his aunt would not be aware. His aunt rolled her eyes and crossed her arms. "Miles, you needn't hang onto the girl like she'll vanish. And if you think you are hiding anything from me, might I remind you that I have five children and I know what a man looks like when he's aroused." I blushed when I looked up into Miles' face, he had turned the deepest shade of red that I'd ever seen. Then he and his aunt both suddenly burst out laughing.

His aunt stepped forward and took my hands. "It's a pleasure to meet you at last, my dear. At least I assume you're my nephew's fiancée?" I was so embarrassed all I could do was nod. "Good, you and I must have a long chat sometime. But right now, you're needed for the final fitting of your wedding gown."

I felt the blood drain from my face. "What wedding gown?" There hadn't been time in London for me to have one made so Mother and I had picked out what we thought was a suitable dress from my current wardrobe.

She smiled at me, patting my hand then looked at Miles as if she was perturbed with him then back at me. "He didn't tell you, did he." I caught the exasperated look on Miles' face and so did she. "Oh, he's a canny one, our Miles. Did he never tell you that one of his many talents is that he likes to design all sorts of things? He's made several of the beautiful pieces of furniture about this house; our boy is very good with his hands." Then she giggled. "But I'm sure you'll find that out on your own." Miles groaned again and pinched his nose while she smiled in triumph and continued, "Not only does he design and make furniture, he has on many occasions designed costumes for several masque balls that I've hosted over the years." I noticed her smile had become rather smug; she seemed bent on embarrassing Miles even more. "Your fiancé took it upon himself to send me his design and the material for a gown though I didn't know at the time it was for your wedding gown." I must have looked puzzled because she went onto explain. "I know a very talented seamstress in Edinburgh, who used to live and work in Venice and worked in the theatre. She has always been able to take his designs and make them a reality no matter how fanciful; she's an absolute genius with a needle."

I glanced at Miles, he wasn't laughing anymore but he was giving his aunt a very stern look. I can only imagine what he might have said if I wasn't there. I had to admit I was intrigued, "When did you manage to do all that?"

He cleared his throat and stood out from the wall. "The furniture I have been working on for years, it helps me think and relax. The dress was some time ago."

I wasn't letting him off the hook. "How long ago?"

"Does it really matter…it was…before I went to France."

I tipped my head to the side gazing at him and saw how uncomfortable he was, "No, Miles, it doesn't matter at all."

His aunt looked astonished. "Well, Miles, you seem have your bride under your spell as much as she has you under hers. Well done, my boy…well done." Then she took my hand and pulled me along towards the house. I looked back over my shoulder and Miles was watching us looking like a little boy who had just had his favourite toy taken from him. I blew him a kiss and he brightened up. As I was dragged into the house I caught one last glimpse of him walking in the opposite direction and whistling. I couldn't help but love him even more.

The gown laid out on my bed was stunning in its simplicity, it was made of shot silk that shone like iridescent mother of pearl in the light. The design itself was almost medieval with long sleeves tight fitting from the shoulders down to my wrists, the neckline was scooped with a high waistline made discernible only by an embroidered girdle of the palest iridescent beading incorporating roses and ivy which was repeated at the neckline and the hem. Yards of material fell from gathers at the back, creating a train. There was no other ornamentation on the dress. I was in awe, it was simply the most beautiful gown I had ever seen. Just as the sun came through to shine on my bed the gown shimmered in a myriad of colours like a rainbow. The women of the household were all there in awe waiting for me to try it on.

I turned away from the ethereal confection lying on my bed to be confronted by a very tiny woman with jet black hair. She had come out of my dressing room carrying a sewing basket and had pins stuck in the bodice of her dress with a tape measure around her neck. She eyed me up and down then pronounced, "You'll do." She walked around me puckering her lips, "I'd say from the looks of you that Mr Johnson is intimate with your measurements." I was shocked by her forwardness, but she didn't seem to be bothered at all and the other ladies only giggled, before she gave them a withering look that silenced them. When she spoke, it was in a very clipped tone and from her olive skin and a hint of an accent it was obvious that she was not from Scotland, yet she introduced herself as Mrs Mactavish "If it had been anyone else but Mr Johnson that had wanted me to cut into that bolt of shot silk with the wearer sight unseen I would have refused and kicked them out of my shop. But

Mr Johnson has a good eye. Now let's see if he was right that the dress would suit you. I was sceptical of the sleeves at first, they're very severe and are never seen these days, but he insisted."

I followed her and Meg back into the dressing room, no one else would be allowed to touch the gown but Mrs Mac as she had asked to be called. Meg assisted me out of my day gown and into a new silk shift that was also courtesy of Mrs Mac. Then the wedding gown flowed over me like cool water. I had my back to the cheval glass, but I heard Meg's gasp as the dress settled on me and she did up the tiny pearl buttons in the back. The gown was as light as a feather and it fit perfectly. Mrs Mac walked around pulling here and there, then stepping back she walked around me, scrutinizing every angle. "Yes, it will do nicely." She stood back contemplating yet again with a critical eye. "You know he sent to France for that material and the beads." She had a hint of smile around her lips and her eyes glowed with pride at her work. "I wish he would let me copy this, but he wanted the pattern and drawings destroyed; no one else will have a dress like this, it's such a shame." She sighed. "This is some of my best work, but he paid me handsomely for it, so I shouldn't complain. I only wish that you were being married in London or Edinburgh. I'd have them lining up outside my shop within a fortnight." When she shook her head. "What am I thinking? I have enough work as it is, so it's probably for the best." She stopped fussing with the hem and sighed when she looked up at me, she smiled. "He is a rare man, miss." I could do nothing but nod in agreement. Tears were welling up in my eyes and threatening to spill over. She was quick to notice and had the buttons undone and the dress whipped up and over my head in no time as Meg passed me a handkerchief. I thanked Mrs Mac and allowed Meg to help me back into my day dress. When I returned to my room everyone appeared disappointed that they had not seen me in the gown. Mrs Mac came out with the dress, even Meg would not be allowed to handle it before the wedding. She looked at all the long faces. "Sorry, ladies, but Lord Tinley was very specific, no one sees her in the dress but me and her maid until the wedding."

Aunt Mary huffed. "Humph and since when is Lord Tinley in charge of this wedding?"

Mrs Mac gazed at the dress and her fingers caressed it. "He isn't as far as I know, ma'am, but this dress is his bride gift to Miss Turner, so I think he has the right to say when it will be displayed."

Millicent laughed out loud. "That sounds just like him, he's very much like his father; needs to have his finger in everyone's pie whether it's welcomed or not." She was admiring the gown and went to touch it, but she pulled back as Mrs Mac turned away with it. She was smiling, and her eyes sparkled. "He has his mother's aesthetic eye too; that dress is a work of art." Mrs Mac looked very pleased but only nodded.

Aunt Mary looked over her spectacles at Millicent then back at the dress as Mrs Mac wrapped it in paper and placed it in a box. "You're quite right about that, my dear, his mother would have been very proud of him."

Millicent went to my aunt and hugged her. "Maria was a kind-hearted soul…I only wish that she could have lived to see her son so happy and everything set to rights."

I smiled at their kind words and promised myself that I would convey them to Miles. Mrs Mac left with the box and Meg, Beth and Angel trailing in her wake. They were all talking at once and seemed bent on learning anything that Mrs Mac was willing to teach them. My mother sat down abruptly on my bed, arching her back. "If we lose my maid to Mrs Mac, I will hold your fiancé personally responsible." She made a half-hearted attempt to giggle as she looked up at me, she looked so tired, appeared to have lost weight in the last few days and her colour was sallow. "I think I shall go rest for a bit." I looked at Emilie who looked equally uncomfortable, arching her back but in contrast she was the picture of health.

Emilie sighed and nodded. "I wonder if Samuel is about, I'd would love to have…" She looked about her and blushed "…well, never mind, but you know, Irene." She walked to the door and opened it and my mother joined her, taking her arm. They walked out together as Mother was saying, "That's an excellent idea, Emilie, let's see if we can find him."

I looked at my Aunt Mary and Millicent. "What was that all about?"

Aunt Mary laughed. "Swollen feet."

I tipped my head sideways and stared at her, "And what of them?"

She was staring at the open door and smiling then snapped back to look at me. "Oh, Samuel apparently gives the most amazing foot massages; it has to do with him having such very large hands. It helps tremendously with swollen feet."

Millicent looked up at her. "Really? Oh my, I do wish I had known that; Angus has absolutely huge hands." and with that they both sailed from the room discussing the vagaries of their pregnancies and laughing.

I couldn't decide if I wanted to follow them, sketch, read or visit with my father. I chose my father and walked down the hall to his room. He was sitting up in bed with an abundance of fluffy pillows threatening to swallow him, "Oh thank God, Lissa, please, will you get rid of some of these confounded pillows. Two shall be sufficient for my needs." I assisted him to sit forward and removed no less than four huge soft feather pillows. I kissed him on the cheek then sat in the chair by his bed. He was healing remarkably well and attributed it to Mrs Dawson and Mrs Cripps' combined talents in the kitchen and the fresh air that Dr Jefferson insisted on. Even on the coldest days he was to have the window open no less than thirty minutes in the morning and afternoon. Dr Jefferson had not arrived yet, but he would be coming down with his fiancée, Isabel, and her father, Sir Thomas.

He looked at me with his hands cupped on a book in his lap, "Well, my dear, I understand that the unveiling of the gown has taken place, so what do you think of it?"

I found it hard to describe in words of how beautiful and happy I was with my wedding dress. He smiled and nodded as I tried fumbling with my words then I realised he was only humouring me, "You already knew about it, didn't you?"

He smiled and nodded. "Before he went to France we talked, and he showed me his designs, he didn't come out and ask me for your hand then, but we understood each other. I must admit I was surprised at his talent and perplexed that a man would know so much about women's apparel. He's a romantic like you, my dumpling, but far he's more pragmatic and sensible." I threatened to throw a pillow at him as he held his hands up in mock horror which caused him to gasp and grimace at the movement. I jumped up and rearranged the pillows behind him then offered him his medicine which he declined. "Stop fussing, Lissa, I was merely caught off guard when I moved my arms so quickly. I'm fine. Now, sit down."

I took my seat again and quickly examined him for signs of distress. He appeared to be his old self except for being a little pale. He smiled at me lovingly then whispered, "I want you to help me get out of bed. I intend to walk you down the aisle as long as it's a short one."

I heard the door open behind me. "Father, is that such a bright idea?" I was worried about his condition, we had come very close to losing him and I didn't want to journey down that path again.

My father looked over my shoulder and I heard Dr Jefferson's voice, "I think that would be a splendid idea."

Father snorted. "You are not at all like your peers, Matthew. No wonder you have so few friends among them."

I stood to greet the doctor, smiling as he bowed, "Well, they're fools for shunning my company merely because they're incompetent. But I still correspond with many of my learned colleagues in Rome and Paris. Believe it or not, Colin, a few of the younger physicians and surgeons in London have approached me to study my methods. I'm looking around for a promising surgeon that I can convince to become a physician. I'd like to have a partner in my practise that is willing to work as both."

"Really, Matthew, has your client list expanded to the extent that you need more help?"

He didn't answer right away but instead he came to my father's bedside and bent over to listen to his chest, once he was satisfied he said, "My partner has established his own practise in Brighton, so I am alone once again. But Isabel has been finding me new patients from all over London." He chuckled. "I had to tell her to stop, I need to find suitable rooms for an office now that I'm to marry. I can't continue to work from my lodgings. But there is a vacant property near to what will be our home that has potential."

Father chewed on his lower lip. "Does this mean that you will cease to work for Sir Thomas?"

"Good God, NO! And before you ask, Isabel is aware of my stance and is completely amenable. Now enough about me. Would you care to assist me, Miss Turner, in helping your father out of bed and perhaps to a chair? We have a bit of time before the wedding to help build up your stamina, Colin."

I walked to the bedside and positioned myself as Dr Jefferson requested. Father looked at me, "Not a word to your mother." Then he amended it, "Neither of you not a word! I want this to be a surprise not a disappointment if I can't do it."

# Chapter 46
## *The Guests*

Sir Thomas arrived later that afternoon but without his daughter, Isabel, he immediately went to my father's room followed by every man from in and outside of the house including the gypsies, field hands and stable workers, even the vicar had been invited and came puffing up the stairs. I stepped outside my room and watched the procession as the field hands gawked and remarked on the grandness of the house shyly nodding as they passed by. The last person to arrive was Magda, I walked along with her but as she passed through the door I was met with Miles' smiling face, he leaned forward to kiss me on the forehead, "Sorry, my love, not this time." Then he closed and locked the door in my face. I proceeded to the dressing room door but found it to be bolted shut. I huffed and walked back to my father's door and attempted to eavesdrop but doors here were solid oak and I could only hear mumbling.

Lettie came walking by with James holding onto her hand she looked at me then down at James. "Well, my man, it looks like Papa is busy right now. Would you like to go out to the barns then and see the animals?"

James was standing there looking at me with my ear plastered to the door then let go of her hand and twisted up his face in puzzlement and dropped to his knees to lay down by the door. And he quietly called out, "Papa?" his face brightened then he yelled "PAPA!" The door was opened by my Uncle Samuel who scooped James up and then summarily shut it in my face yet again.

I looked at Lettie and she burst out laughing, "Looks like you can never be too young to learn the family business." She walked off leaving me perplexed and irritated. I went back to my room and pulled a chair over to sit in the doorway but after having sat like that for a bit and having had two maids walk past giving me strange looks I pulled the chair just inside my room and pushing the door almost closed, so I could listen for my father's visitors leaving.

However, I didn't hear the approach of my mother who knocked on my door and spooked me to the extent that I fell unceremoniously backwards onto the floor with my apron flying over my shoulder and my skirts hoisted up to my knees. That's how she found me when she opened the door after hearing me fall. "Good heavens, Lissa, what on earth are you doing?"

I pulled down my apron and dress then blew some hair out of my face while scrambling to my feet. "There is a meeting in Father's room and all the women have been excluded." I pointed out my door, totally exasperated. "Even James is in there!"

Mother covered her mouth like she was trying not to laugh, "I thought Magda was in there as well."

I waved my hand in the air. "That's only because she rules her people like a despot!"

Mother took my hand and pulled me over to the window seat to sit down. "Lissa, you can't be involved in everything. If there is a role for us to play in whatever is coming our way, then your father or Miles will tell us."

"How do you know something is coming?" She turned my head, so I had to look out over the garden and into the fields beyond where troops could be seen marching off into the woods.

I was astonished. "Are we expecting an invasion?"

She smirked shrugging her shoulders. "I don't know, dear, but I don't think they're here just for the wedding. When Sir Thomas arrived, he called for all the men of the household to meet in your father's room." She pointed out the window. "And then they arrived, a very nice Captain Bruce came in an introduced himself to me and your aunts. It seems he's here at the behest of Sir Thomas but that was all he was at liberty to say and by the way he's Mile's cousin."

Unbelievable, my wedding was about to become a war zone. "Maybe we should just cancel the wedding."

Mother caressed my cheek. "No, my love, one way or another this wedding his going to happen! That was one thing that Miles made very clear to Sir Thomas when he arrived."

I sighed as I watched the line of men disappear into the trees. We sat there in silence for a while then Mother proceeded to discuss the menu for the wedding breakfast and supper devised by our two cooks. My only suggestion was that perhaps we needed to increase the quantities to include the other eighty or a hundred extra guests camping in the woods. She agreed so we made our way down to the kitchens to find that Mrs Dawson and Mrs Cripps were already sending to Poole for more fish, capons and several sides of beef. There were also plans to have Silas our hog wrangler butcher a few more pigs. I looked about the kitchen and thought that while the old hearth was huge, it would never accommodate it all. "How will it all be ready in time?"

Mrs Dawson smiled as she chopped vegetables without even looking up, "Now don't you worry, miss, my mother's people already have the hogs roasting in pits, the fowl we'll do here, and a nice army cook named Sergeant Bigelow has volunteered to look after the fish and beef. He's even brought some fresh spices down from London right off the boat. He seems to know what he's doing, so don't you worry. All he's asked for in return is some root vegetables and apples. He's even going to help with the cakes." My eyes got wide and I opened my mouth, but she interrupted me, "Now don't you be thinking I meant your cake, it's all done and is soaking in some good French brandy."

I sighed and smiled at her. "You both are a wonder. But the cost?"

Mother coughed. I look at her and she was very pale, "Really, Lissa, the cost is negligible to what a wedding at St James would have cost. Besides your father and I want everything to be perfect for you…as perfect as it can be, anyway." Mother leaned heavily against the table then sagged into a seat. Mrs Dawson looked at her motioning for Mrs Cripps to come over, both ladies looked worried.

While Mrs Cripps fixed us a cup of tea, Mrs Dawson continued, "And don't you worry about Grandmama's people. She may not be thrilled to have the soldiers so close, but I'm sure the people will make a great deal of money from them."

With that Magda came storming into the kitchen brandishing one of her knives and rammed it into the old butcher's block. Jibben and Miles followed her in then she turned on them and practically spit "Englishmen, SOLDIERS! On my LAND! NO! They must go!"

Miles was smirking but Jibben was enraged. "It's not your land, Grandmama! It belongs to Miles! The woodland was never part of our bargain and you know it!"

"I will not have those gadjos around my camp enticing our women!" Then she made as if she was going to spit at his feet but at the last minute changed her mind.

Jibben rolled his eyes then put his hand on his hips. "STOP! Right now! Enough, old woman! We are going to help Miles and the Turners and for once we're going to do something that will make people say our people are honourable and that we fought on the side of good without a thought to the profit."

Both Miles and Magda's eyes widened as they looked at him in shock. Magda shook her finger at him. "That's your father speaking!" She paused biting the inside of her cheek. "But you may be right." Now it was Jibben's turn to look shocked until she continued, "We can make it up by offering some entertainments to the gadjos." She took her knife out of the block in one swift movement then walked out the door to the yard.

Jibben hurried after her yelling, "Grandmama!"

Miles was laughing. "I bet he's glad that this will be his last season with Magda."

I looked at the door then back to him, "Really! And why is that?"

He smiled at me as he came and put his arm around my waist. "Jibben is to be married this spring to a very respectable young lady in his father's home district. She apparently comes from a fine family with some property that just happens to adjoin his father's and she is an only child, so she stands to inherit it all."

I stepped back and looked up at him with my mouth agape. "Is the family aware of the details of his family tree?"

He nodded. "Yes, but Miss Ashley's background is not pristine when closely examined. Her mother was a Parisian courtesan, Jibben found out while he was in Paris. It was a strong point in his favour when he negotiated the marriage contract."

"Oh my god, Miles, he didn't blackmail the girl into agreeing to marry him, did he?"

He snorted and shook his head. "No, my love, the girl is perfectly willing. It's a love match if that's what concerns you. Magda merely made it known to her parents that she had proof of the mother's background. He truly loves Miss Ashely, but he wanted no objections to their union based on family associations."

I leaned my head against his chest and chuckled. "I'll miss him."

Miles chuckled. "Oh, we won't be entirely rid of him, Matthew told me that Jibben has purchased a home in Mayfair not far from your parents' home. He's done very well as an independent information contactor and tinker." I laughed then.

Miles started to chuckle. "Now that I'm a Lord I think I'll sponsor him at my club, that is after I join one…just so I can have some decent conversation. I can't wait to see how we'll set the old guard on its ear and with Edward in tow we may have to form our own club."

Then he took my hand and walked towards my mother. "We need to talk, Mrs Turner." Mother looked at the kitchen staff. "Mr Dawson and Robert will be down to speak with them. Dalton, Allan and Murphy are already speaking to the other staff." We followed him out to the drawing room, Mrs Cripps came along behind us in with a tea trolley and a few decanters then returned to the kitchen.

Mother waved away the tea, but I nodded and took a cup from Aunt Mary, Emilie declined one and the gentlemen all went for the decanters while Uncle Samuel was handed his pomegranate juice.

Once we had settled Sir Thomas joined us and opened the conversation. "We have reliable intelligence that Stanhope has been collecting information on several prominent and wealthy people for several years and has used that information to blackmail these people to fund his smuggling activities. His endeavours had grown significantly with the involvement of the late Lord Burley. Though the new Lord Burley connection isn't clear, he seems to be a young man who is only desperately trying to save his family's fortune and reputation. But has been misguided as to who his enemies truly are, so he's targeting your family, Mrs Turner."

He sat back and took a sip of his drink before continuing, "With the assistance of Lord Tinley and Dr Grimes we discovered that Stanhope had been using a Coldstream officer to recruit an army of the disaffected and disenfranchised within the army or those that have had connections to the military, many of whom are deserters, while others that have been cashiered for one offense or another and some have worked as mercenaries abroad. I think it's safe to assume that officer is Major Stanhope." He paused then looked around the room.

Miles cleared his throat. "This time the Rambles won't be attacked by a collection of local smugglers and fishermen. These men have had military training and they have leaders who have been in battle. Ladies, we would like to remove you from the vicinity…" I bristled, and he noticed, "however…we don't have the luxury of providing you with a sufficient escort for a lengthily trip back to London or even to one of the neighbouring estates. Our greatest concern is that all of you would be taken hostage and we won't risk that. So, ladies, instead we need to enlist your aid in readying this house to withstand an assault."

Following his address there was total silence…no one said a word, no tears were shed, and everyone appeared to be wrapped up in their own thoughts. My mother was the first to move, she got up and walked to the decanters, selected Mile's best scotch and poured out a measure into each of five glasses and passed them around to the ladies. Then she raised her glass while she placed her hand on her belly. "Ladies, to our success. And gentlemen, this wedding damn well better come off without the smell of gunpowder." We all drank down our glasses and no one even blinked or coughed.

The men were stymied and in turn raised their glasses as Sir Thomas said, "To the ladies." We then broke apart and all went in different directions. Mother went to father, Emilie and Samuel escaped into the garden, Aunt Mary, Uncle Arthur, Aunt Millicent and Sir Thomas sat down to play cards.

I looked at Miles. "So when do your cousins and uncle arrive?"

He took my hand and pulled me towards the window pointing towards the woods. "That company is my Cousin Derek's from the 1st Regiment of Foot. Uncle Angus and my younger cousins were riding down with him."

"You never told me that you have a cousin in the army."

He laughed out loud and was shushed by his aunt. Then he whispered, "It's not something Uncle Angus is particularly proud of, having a son of his in the English army. Uncle Angus is a cousin to the 7<sup>th</sup> Earl of Elgin though they don't get along but he's fiercely proud of the Bruce heritage."

"So how does he account for Derek betraying the family trust?" Miles looked over his shoulder at the card players and then whispered in my ear, "Oh, that's my aunty's fault for being English even though the regiment is called the Royal Scots."

Aunt Millicent had obviously heard us for she piped up, "When Angus told the old bastard that he married me, the Earl said he must have been drunk and nay knew what he was doing." She laughed. "Angus was very drunk on our wedding day, but he was stone cold sober on the day he proposed." She looked back to her cards and played her trump without missing a beat.

Miles just shrugged then nodded towards the field beyond. "Would you like to go meet them? I can't say they're all harmless having grown up in the wilds of Scotland. But Maurice is the kindest soul you could ever meet even though he's the most like Aunt Millicent."

I looked at his aunt and she was smiling from ear to ear saying. "Georgina unfortunately will not be with them, she is awaiting the birth of her first child any day now."

Miles took my arm and led me out the door through the kitchen garden and into the yard to meet the horseman approaching us across the field.

One brash young man with the same red hair and brilliant blue eyes as the others jumped down just as his horse came abreast of us, taking Miles into a head lock and not even acknowledging me. "I told you you'd marry the English chit, now pay up, cuz!"

Miles extricated himself and straightened his jacket. "I can see that Cambridge has not improved your manners any, William, and my fiancée is not a chit!" He smacked the young man on the ear to get him to loosen his grip then turned his back on him to look up at an older mountain of a man who was still sitting on his horse and smiling at the exchange. "Well, Uncle Angus, are you determined to give me a crick in my neck or shall we serve you supper up there." The older man laughed and jumped down off his horse with an energy that belied his years and pulled Miles into a hug. Another younger man had dismounted behind him, but he didn't say a word…he just stood there staring at me.

A much younger man came around him and stopped in front of me. "You must be Miss Turner." I nodded. "I'm pleased to meet you and ask that you excuse the course manners of my father and brothers. May I introduce myself since my cousin seems to have forgotten his manners as well? I am Maurice Bruce." He bowed elegantly as his brothers whistled behind him.

The older gentleman stepped forward taking my hand, his eyes were as bright as his sons, in fact, they all looked like copies of the man in front of me just different ages. He noticed my eyeing them all and laughed. "Yes, my dear, I can nay say that my wife ever strayed on me. One look at these three and their other brother is like looking at my past in the mirror. Now my daughter Georgiana is all her mother thank God, at least I've been blessed there." Then he kissed my hand. "Angus Bruce at your service, Miss Turner. Miles' letters have not done ye justice for I can see that you are a rare English Rose, not one of those pale yellow-haired fortune hunters." I smiled and tried to supress a giggle. He caught me at it and snorted. "Aye, these bumbling arses of mine have brought home more than one of them thinking they're in love, but I soon showed them the door. You wouldn't happen to have any sisters, now, would you?" I shook my head no. "Ah, well, there's still time and all of Scotland for them to pick from."

He abruptly changed his tone and looked at Miles, "I need to speak to Sir Thomas, we heard a few things while we were passing through Hampshire about several bands of ruffians headed this way." Miles clapped him on the back and walked back toward the house with his uncle leaving me at the mercy of his cousins.

William came forward, introduced himself formally then bowed and kissing my hand for just a second to long. He was soundly thumped by his eldest brother, Douglas, who slapped William aside with his hat. "Please, don't judge us by William's conduct, he has been socializing with the wrong crowd at university and if he doesn't stop soon, I'll recommend that Father order him back to Glencoe."

Now I was perplexed. "But I thought...Miles said that you lived just outside of Edinburgh? Isn't Glencoe in the Highlands?"

Douglas nodded and smiled. "Aye, it is, Glencoe is our summer home. Edinburgh is where we go in the winter for the entertainments and when Mother needs to do a wee bit of shopping."

I knew immediately that they would be delightful additions to our party. I also noticed that they were casual about their weapons and comfortable using them. They all carried a brace of pistols as well as dirks and a sabre. Maurice even had a long bow attached to his saddle and William a crossbow. He caught my eye wandering in that direction. "Aye, Miss Turner, we've come ready for some fun. Poor Georgie will be nigh onto exploding when she finds out that she missed a fight, she is a fair shot with both bow, and rifle. Miles told us that you're a fair marksman yourself, Miss Turner, I looked forward to seeing your skill, providing our cousin doesn't wrap you in cotton wool and lock you in a closet." I was taken aback by his statement. "Aye, miss, we've heard of your adventures. Miles was beside himself to think of what kind of trouble you might find yourself in when he wasn't around."

It was then that I felt an arm slink around my waist. I jumped and glancing over my shoulder to see Miles glaring at his cousins. "Telling tall tales runs in this family, my love, especially if it will get anyone else into trouble." He leaned over and kissed my cheek. "Come, darling, I would like a few minutes alone with you before dinner." He took me to his study and closed the door then whirled me around against that door and proceeded to kiss me deeply and thoroughly, taking my breath away and making my head spin. Then he pulled back. Let's go down to the village and get married this instant, I've talked to the vicar and he's willing to conduct the ceremony any time we want. I don't want to wait a minute longer, before whatever is going to happen I want to know that you're mine.

I was speechless, all the reasons of why we should run away ran through my head. But then I saw my father walking across his room holding onto my arm and the smile on his face. "I can't, Miles." He looked hurt as he opened his mouth but before he could say anything I rushed on, "It's my father, he walked across his room today, he wants to walk me down the aisle. He's been keeping this as a surprise for everyone. He's had so little time with me, I can't deprive him of this."

Miles face softened, and he nodded as he bent down to kiss me again. "I love you, my sweet darling. And I know how he feels. I have loved and cherished every single moment that I've spent with you. I won't cheat him out of this moment." He leaned his forehead against mine as we stood there in peace with the knowledge that our commitment would be forever. Then he pulled me over by the fire, he sat in his favourite chair pulling me down onto his lap and we lost ourselves in our love.

That is until the pounding on the door rattled the windows. "Come out, cuz! Your Mrs Dawson is ready to feed us!"

Miles rolled his eyes. "Away with you, William."

There was a pause and then the pounding started again. "Edward has arrived!"

Miles propped his chin on top of my head and took a deep breath. I giggled and jostled him in all the wrong places, he groaned then kissed me quickly. "Up you get, you temptress, before I get us both into trouble."

I rose, smoothed down my skirts and checked my hair in the looking glass over the mantle while Miles watched me with a crooked smile. Then I offered him my hand and we walked to the door just as it burst open with William and Maurice tumbling in and falling to the floor. Douglas and a man in uniform were standing outside the door obviously amused at their siblings both being kicked then picked up by Miles. He caught sight of Derek and beamed. "Lissa, that person looking like a toy soldier is my cousin Derek. Captain Derek Reginald Lucas Bruce of his Majesty's 1st Foot."

The man in uniform came in and gave me a courtly bow. "Miss Turner, I am delighted to finally meet you." Then he turned smartly to Miles. "Well, cuz, I hear that you are now Lord Tinley! That must have made Edward the happiest man in the realm. I've never known a man who hated his exalted position more than he did." Derek seemed rather cool in his form of address, but his eyes were warm and friendly as he offered his arm to me. "May I escort you into dinner, Miss Turner?" All his brothers and Miles stood there looking at him mouth agape.

Miles recovered quickly and took my arm away from Derek. "He is the one that you really have to watch, my dear, or rather I'll have to watch. He fancies himself a lady's man and so far, no lady has proved him wrong." Then he looked at Derek and the others. "This lady is taken, gentlemen, so go find your own but leave the maids alone!" We left them flummoxed standing in the doorway of his study.

# Chapter 47
## *Preparation*

We didn't stand on ceremony at the Rambles, so dinner was served at country hours. Miles' father and Edward had arrived, the Earl looked weary and Edward was chewing frantically on his lower lip. Miles noticed immediately. "What's wrong? Are Lady Jane and the children alright?" The Earl smiled at the mention of his current wife and their young children. Edward answered, "They're splendid, Miles, and looking forward to meeting your bride."

Miles looked at the Earl. "Then what's bothering you, Father?"

The Earl's countenance changed. "I met young Burley before I left London. He was at my club and deep in his cups. He asked me to tell you that he was sorry, that he had no idea how far his father had fallen. Then he told me that hell was about to be unleashed and that I would do well to get you and Miss Turner out of the way. I questioned him, but he was unable or unwilling to give me any details before he had to be carried home by his friends. I found Edward and we left immediately." He glanced at Derek. "I assume that's why you're here with your men, it's not for the wedding."

Derek was eating like he hadn't seen a decent meal in months. "Aye, Uncle, Sir Thomas has a way with words and my regiment's commander sent me down here to help with the problem. One other thing I meant to ask you, Miles, where did those gypsies go that you've talked so much about?"

Miles swallowed. "Go? What do mean where did they go! They were here this afternoon."

"Aye, they were when we arrived but shortly after they decamped."

Miles sighed. "I'm sure they're nearby, they've committed to helping us. But Magda doesn't want her people too close to your troops."

Derek grinned. "That's good to know, I wasn't too happy to see them either. My men just got paid and I haven't had a chance yet to bully them into sending some of it to their wives and children."

Miles groaned. "Then I fear that you may be too late, cuz."

Derek shrugged. "I often am."

Dinner proceeded in the usual fashion except that the men didn't stay behind for port, instead they went about the house in tandem, reviewing the need to fortify it and the out buildings.

Once I was in bed I could sense that an uneasy peace had settled about the house, but I was too anxious to rest so I sat by the window watching the clouds scud across the moon. It was then that I saw a movement by the stables then a burst flame. I jumped to my feet and ran to Miles' room pounding on the door. When he opened it, he was partially undressed, "Miles, the stables!"

"I know, I saw it too. Rouse the house, will you… I think tomorrow just arrived."

I pounded on all the doors. rousing both guests and staff. Mrs Dawson and Mrs Cripps were arguing as they padded downstairs about who would load for who. Mrs Mac came up behind them with a brace of pistols and a rifle. They both looked at her shocked as they viewed her armoury, she smiled, "My work is valuable, ladies, and I travel a good deal. I've been robbed more than once so necessity has been my teacher," she continued as she brandished the pistols. "I never leave home without these lassies."

I hurriedly dressed and raced down the stairs coming up short when I saw the entry hall full of people. Captain Bruce was there with his aid and senior officers and Jibben was there with his most trusted people. Magda stood nearby taking in the scene through narrowed eyes and with a deepening frown on her face then she spied me on the stairway and nodded just before she placed two fingers in her mouth and let loose an ear-piercing whistle then yelled, "STOP!"

Gradually everyone stopped talking and turned to look at her as she came shuffling up the stairs to stand by me. Without preamble, she yelled, "You do not want to meet them on their terms by marching out and letting them attack you." She stomped her foot hard on the stair making it shake when the others started to talk again. An immediate hush fell over them again. "You must lure them into a trap of your making!" No one spoke as she went on. "They will not attack the house knowing that you are prepared. That little fire by the stables hurt nothing, it was made so you would know they are coming. They are hoping to draw you out and divide your forces."

She paused eyeing everyone and I noticed that Derek soon wiped the smug smile off his face along with his officers. It was obvious that he had planned to do just that and race off into the night to chase them down. Magda looked fierce with her knives in her belt and two pistol butts jutting out of the waistband of her skirt. She smiled, pointing her finger at Sir Thomas. "You need to ignore the fire. The wedding must happen tomorrow…to bait the trap. They must believe that you are not ready." She paused and still no one said a word. "Captain, some of your men will be an honour guard at the wedding, the rest will stay behind with Jibben's men."

She smiled, and it sent shivers down my spine, in the half-light she looked like a storybook witch. Then with a grin she added, "It will be like hunting wild pigs. My girls and some of our men have enough English clothes to dress like English gentry. The rest of you…do what you would always do…they cannot know we expect them. Keep your weapons hidden but within easy reach." She stood there with her hands on her hips looking at all their up-turned faces.

I heard a noise behind me and turned to see my father walking down the hall with Lettie on one side and my mother on the other. They reached the top of the stairs and all eyes locked on them. Then Sir Thomas came forward and kissed Magda's hand. "Excellent plan, dear lady, I wish I had you on my staff." Then he looked down at everyone in the hall. "Are there any objections gentlemen?" No one said a thing. "Good, then I think we all need to get some sleep." He turned to me, "Miss Turner, you will be married tomorrow after all. I'm only sorry that the reception might be during a battle."

I could do nothing but shrug. "It wouldn't seem like a family affair without some sort of drama, Sir Thomas."

I returned to my room and as I climbed into bed my door opened and my mother came in. "I'm sorry to disturb you, my dear, but your father and I have talked. We'd like you to postpone the wedding until this is over. You've had so much disappointment in your life that this hardly seems fair. They can find another way other than your wedding to lure these people in."

I smiled at her. "Thank you but no, Mother, I don't want to wait, and I would venture to say that Miles doesn't either. Sir Thomas and Magda are correct, it's the perfect lure. I want this over with, we all want it over."

Mother stumbled as she came to my bedside and kissed me goodnight. I was growing more concerned for her health as the days went by, it seemed as my father improved she declined. "Your father seems to know you better than I do now…he said you'd refuse our offer. I'll see you in the morning, my darling." She tried to smile and left my room moving slowly grasping at furniture nearby to lean on as she went. I would have to speak to Dr Jefferson about her and soon. I had half expected Miles to visit me, but he didn't, which was just as well. I don't think I could have resisted the temptation to start our honeymoon early.

Before dawn, the household was awake, and preparations were under way. Some of the Captain's troops had moved closer to the house while the rest remained hidden in the woodlands. There was no sign of the gypsies' camp at all. Meg informed me as I relaxed in my bath that many of their ladies and some of the men had been accommodated in the house looking and acting very much like ladies and gentlemen which had astonished her. But Angel had told her that gypsies were talented mimics and providing no one looked too closely they would appear to be who and what they pretended to be.

I met Miles in the breakfast room, he looked upset and was drumming his fingers on the table then glanced up and smiled when he noticed me. "I've missed you, poppet. I hope you got some sleep."

I only nodded having spent a sleepless night, I sat down and helped myself to some toast and tea. "You looked preoccupied when I came in, is everything alright and where is everyone?"

He grimaced biting his lower lip. "Everything is fine, and others are off doing things to prepare for today."

"But I thought everything was ready for the wedding."

He reached out and took my hand. "It is…this is about our potential unwelcomed visitors. Lord Burley arrived this morning."

He couldn't have caught me more off guard, my cup slipped from my quaking hand, hitting the table, the tea ran across the shining surface to drip down onto the floor just inches from my dress. "He's here? WHY?"

Miles wiped a hand across his face. "He says he's here to help. He knows Stanhope and says he has some information for us that could be helpful. But I don't know if we can trust him. He might be here to gather information for Stanhope for all we know. He is also looking for his sister, Marianne, she apparently has vacated her London home and surprisingly Burley who always seemed to be a self-centred prig is genuinely concerned." He reached out to take my hand, squeezing it reassuringly. "He's in my study waiting to be questioned by Sir Thomas and your uncles."

"And why not you?"

He chuckled. "That may have something to do with the fact that when Burley first arrived, Sir Thomas found me with my hands wrapped around his throat trying to choke the life out of him."

I was mildly shocked. "I take it that was in retaliation for him hurting me the night my father was stabbed?"

He smiled and looked at me through half-lowered eyes. "Hmmph…that might have had something to do with it; that and he's a pompous ass, he wasn't invited, and I don't trust him."

I squeezed his hand in return, trying to quell my natural fear where the Burleys were concerned. "Does he know what we have planned?"

He smirked. "Not when he arrived, but he was very surprised to see the small contingent of soldiers camped next to the garden."

I righted my teacup and poured myself some more tea after wiping up the spill. "Can he be trusted?"

Miles was looking out the window at the soldiers milling around their camp. "I seem to recall that the old laundry room was a very secure cell…well, except for Timber, he still likes it in there for some reason."

"Timber the cat?!" We both chuckled and were lost in thought about the last time we had made a stand in this house and the different conditions we faced then.

He avoided my question by leaning over to kiss my hand, "Now, eat something, I don't want you fainting at the alter which is being set up in the entry hall."

I looked at him like he had lost his mind. "Why?"

He sighed lowering his head as he if trying not to laugh, "A journey to the church has been overruled. To accommodate all of our additional guests, we will have to open the drawing room doors and the entry hall was the only space left for the alter." He looked back at me with a mischievous grin. "Remind me to add a ballroom or enlarge one of the barns before we hold another celebration here."

I was fine with being married in the house and the entry hall was so beautiful and ancient that it would suit my gown perfectly. But I was curious why the original plan had changed. "Why are we not using the church?"

"That would be my cousin Derek's doing, he says it's in consideration of your father. But in fact, it was also sound judgement, we won't be caught out in open spaces. He collected vicar last night to sleep here for his own safety. Surprisingly he was most amenable to the idea and is currently tucking into a good English breakfast under the watchful eye of Angel in the small breakfast room."

"Miles, what are we doing? It seems like all we do is go from one fight to another. What if Stanhope is just another person being used?"

He stood up pulling me into his arms. "Then we keep fighting, Lissa." He kissed me leaning me back against the table. We were lost in our own world until someone coughed. Looking up, Miles groaned. "Go away, William, and you too, Edward."

Miles kept me pinned to him until William said, "Come now, cuz, are we not entitled to breakfast? This is where we were directed to find the morning repast."

Suddenly the room behind us was full of noise as our other guests came in along with servants carrying additional platters of food to add the already burgeoning sideboards. I extricated myself from Miles and he proceeded to introduce me to the officers in Captain Bruce's company. Then an impeccably dressed gentleman walked in; he looked familiar, but it wasn't until he smiled that I recognized him. I gasped and clapped my hands, "Jibben!"

He leaned over me. "Shush, little one, it's Stephen today, Stephen Locke." He looked the perfect gentlemen, and most of the maids as well as many of the women of his own people followed him with their eyes, smiling with admiration as he passed, but it was useless, he ignored them all. "I'm afraid that once I'm married this spring my life will be that of a country gentleman living in seclusion surrounded by sheep. So, I need the practice."

I rolled my eyes. "Really, Jibben... I mean, Stephen? I had it from a very good source that you've purchased a home in Mayfair, that hardly makes you a poor country gentleman."

He gave me a cheeky grin. "I thought that anything you told a doctor was held in the strictest confidence. It was supposed to be a surprise."

Dr Jefferson came up behind him and slapped him on the shoulder. "It's only confidential if it concerns your health, my friend."

The room filled quickly so Miles and I decided to remove ourselves. We found his cousins Douglas and Maurice in the hallway arguing with their father while their mother stood by with a hint of a smile on her face. I gave Miles a look of concern but he only chuckled. "It's tradition, my dear. The day isn't complete for a Bruce without an argument of some kind."

"What could they possibly find to argue about so early?"

He tossed his head back and rolled his neck. "Just about anything. But with those two it's usually about Maurice wanting to move to Italy to attend university and study art. My uncle and Douglas, however, want him to go to university in Scotland. They're under the impression that you can't get a decent education anywhere outside of Scotland, the only exception to that is Cambridge in deference to my aunt."

I caught Lady Bruce's eye as we made our way upstairs and shook my head, she smiled and with the look of the long suffering interjected to support her son's choice of Italy. But before we had gone more than a few steps Robert and Murphy came crashing through the front door. Miles stopped, waiting for them to catch their breath, then they yelled in unison, "THEY'RE HERE!" Then Murphy crumpled at Miles' feet. He had been shot and blood was pouring down the far side of his face.

Miles grabbed my shoulder. "Lissa, get Jefferson." As I started to go after him Dr Jefferson came out of the breakfast room. "I'm here, Miles! We're going to need to use the drawing room for our hospital." Then he yelled, "MRS DAWSON!"

She came scurrying in, took one look at Murphy, "I know, I know, doctor. Angel and I'll get it all set up, you just tend to Mr Murphy." She looked up at me. "Will be you shooting, miss, or nursing today?"

Miles spun around and said, "Nursing! But she'll be armed to protect you as well." I smirked at him, he was trying to protect me without stealing my need to be involved, the clever man.

I nodded and raced upstairs to get my pistols. Father and Mother were standing in the doorway to their room, they both grimaced at the look on my face. "So it's begun?"

"Yes, Papa, and Murphy's been shot." Mother gasped and grasped my father's arm as I quickly added, "It only grazed his head, but he's lost a lot of blood." It was then that I noticed Lettie at the end of the hallway holding onto to James' hand. She had gone white as a sheet and tears were forming in her eyes. I whispered, "Lettie..."

My mother walked up to her and took James' hand. "Go to him." Lettie started to rush forward but my father reached out to touch her arm, "Do you have a weapon,

Lettie?" She nodded, patting her pocket. James was holding onto my mother's skirts, so he tugged on them looking distressed when he said, "Murph okay, Mama?"

She stooped with a groan to look into his eyes, saying, "He will be, darling. Now why don't you come with me and Papa into our room? We have to shoot at some bad men."

It stunned me that she told him as if it was the most natural thing in the world. But she had never lied to me when I was growing up and never sugar-coated anything. James kissed her cheek. "I be good, Mama, and not get scared."

I was so proud of my baby brother. But my mother worried me, she looked ill, "Mama. Do you need anything?"

She sighed as she reached out to my father, taking his hand. Both of my parents looked ill, but my mother by far looked the worse. Father was the one to answer me, "We have all that we need, my sweet. Take care of yourself and Miles, he tends to be reckless." Then he and Mother disappeared into their room, closing the door behind them. It struck me then that this could be the last time that I would ever see them again. It almost brought me to my knees, but I could hear my little brother saying in my head that Turners never give up.

I pulled myself together and found Meg with Beth in my room, they were setting out their crossbows with rows upon rows of bolts ready to be loaded as they fired. They both blanched when I told them about Murphy. Emilie's maid Gwen came rattling through the door carrying three rifles with shot and powder, huffing and puffing as she dropped them next to where Beth and Meg had set up. "It is just like Paris, *mon dieu!*" She blew a tendril of hair back from her face glanced up at the three of us staring at her then she beamed, "We fight…*oui?*" We all nodded and gave a nervous chuckle.

As I collected my pistols and changed into more suitable clothing I told them that my parents were across the hall with James. I asked for them to keep an ear out for the three of them.

Meg was staring at the doorway while clutching at her chest, "Robert?"

"He's fine, Meg, he brought Murphy home…he's alright." She took a deep breath and nodded before returning to help Gwen load the rifles.

Gwen smiled at her and winked, "Have you seen the Mr Bruces?"

Beth rubbed her eyebrow with one finger obviously trying to puzzle out what Gwen meant, "Which one?"

Gwen looked askance at the question. "All of them, of course! Mr Maurice, he is a romantic, Mr William is so…he makes me laugh, Mr Douglas will be a milord one day and Mr Derek I think he will not always be in the army, he has not the heart for it, he loves the land."

I was puzzled. "How do you know that about Captain Bruce?"

"I listen and watch him, he talks with Lord Tinley and his father a lot, and to Mr Dawson too. I don't think he will stay with the army for long." She smiled shyly, and I felt a knot in my stomach. I wondered if I should I warn her or Derek? Granted she was a perfectly respectable school master's daughter and had been raised as a gentlewoman. But I could see that Beth and Meg were astonished by her remarks, they had been born into the serving class, it only made sense that they would be surprised that she might set her sights so high. Gwen on the other hand had been forced into service for reasons of survival while Beth and Meg had risen above their parent's station. I decided to leave it, if we made it through today who knew what might be possible.

As I stood there contemplating a future that was by no means assured, a volley of gunfire could be heard coming from the vicinity of the stables and barns. I gathered my things and raced down to the drawing room. The windows were shuttered and bolted tight. The centre of the room had been cleared and feather beds now occupied the floor while the furniture was being used to barricade the many windows. Lettie sat with Murphy who was still unconscious, and Dr Jefferson had his instruments out of his bag placing them into a cauldron of boiling water on the hearth, nearby there was a stack of towels, linen and lint that Mrs Cripps was organizing for him. While Mrs Dawson and Angel were bustling about bringing in jugs and buckets of fresh water and bottles of brandy. As she passed me Mrs Dawson muttered, "Bless the person that thought of having a well inside the house, it must have been a woman." I smiled and agreed. I looked back out into the hallway, but Miles was nowhere to be seen. I went in search of him and made my way into the library where I found Lord Burley trussed up like a Christmas goose and lashed to a chair. I grinned at him. "I assume that they decided not to trust you after all, milord."

He grimaced at my remark. "It would seem so, Miss Turner. But may I say that I do owe you an apology for how abominably I treated you at your parents' home. I was very confused about things that my father had told me about my brothers and it went contrary to what I thought I knew myself."

I crossed my arms and glared at him. "Really, Lord Burley? I assume it was all just a mistake and you didn't order the attempted murder of my father?"

He looked like a beaten man until I mentioned my father then his head snapped up and he looked up at me astounded. "Never! I've known Colin since our days at Cambridge, he and your uncle were much admired upperclassmen when I was there."

I wasn't about to believe a word that came out of his mouth. "Jealous, were you?"

"No, on the contrary I was very grateful for your father on more than one occasion. I was not popular with my fellow students being rather bookish and I was ripe pickings for hazing, but your father would not have it. He was my saviour on several occasions, he even taught me how to fight for myself." He tried to move but flinched, his bonds must have been very tight. "Your father is a very patient man, unlike your fiancé who tends to let his emotions rule him especially where you are concerned. Yet for some unfathomable reason your father and Sir Thomas think highly of him."

I was angry and unsure that I could believe anything he said, so rather than speak my mind and say something that I might regret later I turned and left the room without another word or backward glance. I reached for Dalton as he walked past me coming from the kitchens. "Where is Lord Tinley?"

He sighed looking down at his feet then back over his shoulder. "He's with Captain Bruce, Mr Locke and some of the soldiers and gypsies."

I was losing patience. "And where might that be, Dalton!"

"The stables, miss." My heart plummeted into my boots and I had a tough time breathing. I started to walk towards the back hall and kitchen when he called out to me, "Miss, you promised him that you would guard the wounded, he told everyone to keep you out of the yard." I pulled up short as he reached out for me then pulled back before touching me. "You can't, miss! If he sees you there, you'll distract him, and he'll get hurt for sure."

That stopped me dead in my tracks; he was right, Miles could get hurt because of me. I needed to focus and do what I promised. I about-faced and headed back into the drawing room. As I entered I noticed that three more people had been added to the wounded. Lettie and Angel seemed to have it under control and Matthew was involved in digging a piece of shot out of the shoulder of a private from Captain Bruce's command, so I went to check the windows. All of them seemed to be sound until I came to the one nearest to Matthew. As I examined it I saw the barrel of a rifle aimed at a chink in the shutter. I jumped back and yelled at the doctor as it discharged. The shutter shattered, and I felt a piece graze my arm. I stepped forward and fired out the window into the smoke beyond and with some satisfaction I heard a grunt and hoped that I had at least wounded the bastard. Then I called for help to move a hutch to block the aperture created by the shot. After pushing it into place with the aid of young corporal I turned to find the doctor sprawled on his side with a piece of the shutter embedded in his right arm. While not life-threatening it would seriously impede his ability to help the wounded. I panicked until I saw that Maurice come into the room and rush to the doctor's side, immediately assessing the damage and calling for Mrs Dawson's assistance. I approached him. "Do you have any idea what you're doing?"

He never turned away from Matthew who was trying to direct him as to what should be done. "Aye, miss, you canna live in the Highlands six months out of the year and not have a fair understanding of surgery and physic. My mother I dare say is the equal of most university educated physicians and she made sure the lot of us at least knew the basics."

"Where is your mother, perhaps she could help?"

He chuckled. "Oh, she'll be along at some time, but she and my father were off to the stables before all hell broke loose." My heart was in my throat. "But, Maurice…"

"I'm aware, Miss Turner, that it started in the stables, but it wouldn't surprise me one wee bit if it was one them had fired the first shot. If I know them, they're in the loft shooting down at any sneaks trying to work their way in behind us. They'll be fine, miss, don't you worry."

The shooting, yelling and screaming continued for some time. Maurice was right, his mother and father did appear once the stables had been secured and they both stepped in immediately to aid the wounded which surprisingly only amounted to about ten and most of them were Captain Bruce's men. Mrs Cripps and Mrs Dawson started passing out soup and bread to the wounded and those in the various rooms about the house that had been sent in to rest for a bit. I decided to take something to Lord Burley but when I entered, I found him lying on his side on the floor. "Good God, are you hurt?!"

He chuckled. "Not for lack of trying, but no, I'm fine. Someone tried to gain entry by shooting out the window and shutters. Your father's young valet came in and took care of the bastard then pushed that bookcase in front of the casement. He decided it might be better for my health if I was lying on the floor rather than sitting up since being upright made me an easy target. I agreed with him, but he declined to release me and only pushed me out of the chair then left. Is that food I smell?" I righted the chair in which he had been seated and with the assistance of a passing maid got him back into an upright position leaning back against the chair. I was at first inclined to unbind his wrists but with the thought of the bruises he had left on my arm still fresh in my mind, I thought better of it. I dipped the bread into the soup and offered it to him. He thanked me and could reach up just enough with his hands to consume the bread as I continued to dunk pieces of it and hand it to him. "I suppose using a spoon might be dangerous?"

"Yes, I think it would be in my case, I still might want to hurt you, Lord Burley."

He laughed out loud. "You are your father's daughter." And grudgingly he added, "Johnson is a lucky man."

I looked at him suspiciously. "It's Lord Tinley now or haven't you heard." He looked furtively around the room and then glowered in my direction as I resumed. "You don't care for my fiancé, do you, Lord Burley. But perhaps you don't know the whole story of what your family has done to him since the day he was born."

He was able to reclaim some of his bravado. "To him! Really, enlighten me, Miss Tuner! What has my family done to the murderer of two of my brothers and my father. I would love to hear this work of fiction. I only hope that it doesn't make me sick to my stomach. Edward is the rightful heir and he can corroborate all that I've said about your precious fiancé."

Then from behind me I heard Edward's voice, "Afraid not, old chum. Though I must say that I'm surprised that you of all people are defending the family honour. After all, it was you that discovered my mother and your father were carrying on an affair…even before your mother was dead. I believe you said at the time that if you ever had the opportunity you would kill them both. As for your brothers, they got what they deserved whether you'd like to believe it or not. Miles killed Randall to save Colin Turner, but he did not kill Julian and as for your father no one knows who killed him and set fire to his house. However, now is not the time to have this conversation." Edward touched my shoulder. "Miss Turner, Miles has asked me to bring you to the breakfast room, we have a new guest that he'd like you to meet…it seems you know him."

"Is it Ramsey?"

He shook his head. "No, alas, we have not come across him yet."

With hope in my heart I asked tentatively, "Is it over then?"

He shrugged his shoulders while keeping an eye on Lord Burley's reaction. "For the time being. The gypsies and Captain Bruce are chasing the remnants towards Poole at this point. They will be trapped between us and the villagers who have apparently risen to fight with us. Miles has somehow managed to win their trust and admiration."

Burley only look bored with the whole discussion.

In the breakfast room Miles was seated facing the door, he was a bloody mess and looked exhausted, the three of the Bruce brothers were there with him and didn't look much better. Douglas had his arm in a sling and a glass of whiskey in his hand. Maurice was tending to William who was trying to push him away as he examined a nasty gash on his forehead, it was William who caught my eye and gave me a saucy smile. "Miss Turner, what do you think, if this cut leaves a scar would you find me as dashing as my cousin? Perhaps I could entice you to change bridegrooms?" I blushed and shook my head no. He grimaced as Maurice resumed his ministrations. "Oh well, it was worth the try, Mother has been on me about getting myself a wife."

Miles grimaced and punched his shoulder. "Then do the work and get one yourself and stop trying to steal my bride!"

Then I heard a voice say in a rasping whisper, "Is that you, Miss Hughes? Oh, I'm sorry, it's Miss Turner now, isn't it," followed by a grating chuckle that I remembered too well.

# Chapter 48
## *Prisoners and Victims*

I gasped when I heard the voice coming from the man tied to the chair in front of me. I walked around the table to stand behind Miles, leaning against his chair my legs felt like jelly. Facing us was my grandfather's valet Appleforth. When the General came back from India this man came with him. The general's previous batman had apparently died of a fever and Appleforth had stepped in to take his place. Once back in Northumberland I had often found him with the general, whispering to him. He was a weasel of a man, who seemed to always be spying on the family and servants, no one liked him. I never knew what had become of him after the death of the General and honestly, I had never even thought to ask, I loathed the man. Yet here he sat grinning from ear to ear like a maniac. "Sorry to interrupt your nuptials, miss, but I must say that I'm not sure the General would have approved of you marrying a bastard…"

Miles jumped to his feet leaning across the table. "Shut your filthy mouth, you murderer!"

I was shocked by the vehemence behind Miles' statement which must have been clearly written on my face as he bent to whisper to me. "He was the one that killed your grandfather and Lord Burley."

I glared back at Appleforth, though I had never loved the General I needed to know, "Why?"

Appleforth snorted. "Why…she asks." Then he laughed. "Good lord, isn't that a good one. Here I thought you'd be thanking me."

Miles threatened him with the back of his hand but Appleforth only sneered at him, so Miles grabbed his head and banged it against the table. "I warned you!" Then he called out, "Sergeant!"

A soldier came into the room followed by two subordinates. "Yes, sir?"

"Take him away and put him in the old laundry room," Miles waved his hand, but the soldier looked confused.

"Beggin' you pardon, sir, I don't rightly know where that would be, sir."

Miles was glowering then his face lightened, "Sorry, sergeant…just ask anyone in the kitchen, they'll have the key and you can lock him in."

The sergeant smirked when he looked at Appleforth. "Will he be needin' a guard then, sir?"

Miles had turned away but looked back at him. "What? Oh, no, it's very secure. But check for the cat first, he likes to hide in there."

The sergeant chuckled. "Right, sir." He motioned for the two soldiers with him to take Appleforth then they walked out with him between them. Appleforth yelled back at us, "Burley and your grandpa both grew a conscience in the end! Men with a conscience are a liability in our business." Then he started to giggle like a mad man as his voice faded away.

William was standing in the doorway with a look of total lethargy and lack of concern, but he pointed at Miles with the hand that was holding a glass. "You should have gone into the army, cuz, you're better at it than Derek."

Miles looked at him with bitter amusement. "You're really drunk if you think that any bastard son would have been welcomed into an officer's club."

Edward poured a glass for himself and Miles and handed it to him. "William, my mother did everything she could to make it impossible for Miles to succeed." He shook his head then threw back the contents of his glass smacking his lips and considering the empty glass. "She must be turning in her grave now that Miles is Lord Tinley…may she never find peace"

I was stunned. "Edward, what a terrible thing to say about your mother. Surely you loved her?"

Edward bit his lip shaking his head. "No, sister dear, I think not, it was more that I feared her displeasure, that's not love. My mother was not a woman that allowed people to love her. Aunt Millicent was more a mother to me than my own. Now for the first time in my life I can choose my own destiny and I find that extremely satisfying! So, I raise a toast to the old and the new Lord Tinley, may our lives bring everything that we've hoped for…finally." He leaned into me and kissed me on the top of my head.

I took a seat amongst these men that would soon be my family. "Now what?"

Miles sat beside me and took my hand, "Appleforth will be questioned by Sir Thomas, your father and Derek when he gets back. If Stanhope and his confederates get away, then we'll continue to look for them. But I doubt we'll find them among the rabble that ran. I expect they will make for the continent. Sir Thomas made it known recently that we have allies in both Spain and France, so I doubt they'll go there. That leaves Italy as the most likely place where they can start again." He sighed pulling me down onto his lap. "As we speak all the warehouses that Sir Thomas has been able to connect to Stanhope, Hopewood, Burley and your grandfather are being seized as crown property. I'm afraid though that even if Derek catches Stanhope, we will have only scratched the surface, there is more to this than meets the eye."

I was very concerned about what this would mean for my family and I gazed up at Miles with tear-filled eyes. Then I looked towards the open doorway, through it I could see my father slowly making his way down the stairs. Miles jumped up standing me on my feet and went to him as I followed, "Sir, should you be up and about?"

Father took his offered arm and laughed. "Probably not. I was saving my energy to walk my daughter down the aisle. But it came to me that you might want to look for Ramsey out on the moor before he gets away." He snorted looking at me. "Your mother winged him from our room and he staggered off in the direction of the bogs." Miles kissed me quickly then ran out the door calling for Michael, Jacob and Robert to follow him.

"Father, you need to rest, where shall it be, your room or somewhere down here?"

He smiled down at me leaning on my shoulder. "The nearest soft surface where I can recline will do." With twinkle in his eye he continued, "Tell me, do you think there will still be a wedding?"

I glared at him. "Come with me, there's a chase lounge in the library, I'll find you something to read."

When we entered the library, I had forgotten that Lord Burley was there until I heard him say, "Ah, the Turner patriarch and his offspring! To what do I owe the honour this time, Miss Turner?"

Father looked at him with contempt but moved to recline on the chase beside him. "Well, Burley, on behalf of my future son-in-law welcome to the Rambles. Sorry for your current treatment but I think you can understand his reasoning. In fact, I'm surprised to see you unscathed, let alone alive."

Burley looked daggers at my father then his face softened somewhat, "I would have done no less under the same circumstances. Be that as it may I came to offer my services which were refused, no doubt with good reason. I've been mostly ignored even though I have information that I thought could be of use to you and Sir Thomas."

Father gave him a rather sardonic look. "Really and what would that be?"

Burley looked at me assessing me, "It's rather sordid. Turner, are you sure you want your daughter to hear?"

Father looked at me then the door, but I crossed my arms daring him to order me out. "Well, perhaps you should…" Then he saw me bristle. "Alright, my dear, you've been a part of this all along but feel free to leave at any time."

He nodded at Burley who actually coloured as if embarrassed to be speaking in front of me, "Really, I'm surprised that more people haven't been aware of it, but society is very good at turning a blind eye to unacceptable behaviour as long as it isn't flaunted publicly. I'm referring to Stanhope's method of obtaining financing for his smuggling operations. He sought out and exploited people's weaknesses then blackmailed them. With the General…"

I spoke up. "I know it was his gambling."

Burley rolled an eye in my direction and laughed. "My dear Miss Turner, most of the Beau Monde gamble to excess, his weakness was opium. He became addicted after serving in India and the Far East. The rumours of his gambling were only a cover for his other appetite. The only person other than Stanhope that was aware of it was Lord Gromley. The old buzzard used that information to ensure that the Abbey would survive and as much money as he could weasel from your grandfather would remain intact for Hughes' inheritance. I never understood why he did that, he even forced the General to establish your inheritance and that it was to be separate and inviolate. You would think that the bunch of you were Gromley's progeny." He wriggled his hands and grimaced with disgust at how tight his bonds were. "Your uncle and mother's wealth was already untouchable under the bequest of your grandmother and that's why the General was so desperate for funds. Lord Gormley had him tie up much of what was left before he left for India, so he was essentially penniless when he died." He looked disappointed at our lack of reaction. "I assume from your faces that you were already aware of that."

Father I could see was sceptical that the General had indulged in opium and frankly I couldn't see it either. But he couldn't afford to ignore whatever intelligence Lord Burley had to share. "And your father? I don't see him as an opium eater."

Burley shook his head. "No, it was the family honour that was his trap. Once I was born my father's attention was focused on two things, moulding me into an image of himself and the other was Lady Shellard, nothing else mattered to him. But he continued to use my mother to assuage his appetites. The products of those unions being my brothers and sisters were irrelevant to him. My mother had influence over Arabella and Marianne and while they lacked a father's love my mother made every attempt to make it up to them. As a result, she also became rather indulgent of her sons. But once we were off to school she had no influence on us. When at home I was still under my father's thumb, constantly in his company, learning my responsibilities as the heir. Randall and Julian were cut loose on holidays with money in their pockets and a blind eye turned to their less savoury predilections. They both had a cruel vile streak in them, inherited no doubt from my father and his father before him. They used their lovers abominably and had in fact been banned from the better whorehouses in London. That was when they were introduced to the services of male prostitutes. They required only one thing from them, that they be of equal strength and would fight back. There were some murderous results from these encounters that came to the attention of the Bow Street Runners…my father had to hush them up. Yet Mr Spencer was exceedingly determined to trace the killers of these unnatural beings as if the world wasn't better off without them."

My father continued to indulge Lord Burley, but with a cold glare full of contempt for his opinions of his fellow man as Burley continued without a pause. "Stanhope found out about them after Randall and Ramsey Clarke had become lovers in the West Indies. Stanhope backed some of my brothers' smuggling endeavours between the Indies and America, it was there that he had been introduced to Ramsey Clarke who would whore for anyone willing to pay. Stanhope set him to seduce Randall, not a difficult endeavour and they became unnatural lovers. Seems after that Stanhope decided to move all his financial concerns to the smuggling operations between England and the continent. By then your friend de Bearne had been substantially cutting into his profits in the Indies, so he set Randall up as the face of the operation in England and with Stanhope's encouragement Ramsey became the exclusive play thing of first Randall and then Julian."

Father continued to sit back and for all intents and purposes looked like he was resting and while his face was devoid of emotion I could see the tension in his neck and hands when he asked, "How did my valet become involved?"

Burley wasn't surprised by the question. "Oh, that was through Hopewood, he knew Richards when you were in Belgian. Richards was already as you know involved in smuggling. That's why you recruited him, wasn't it, Turner? But it was gold that bought Richards' services, he didn't give a fig who was paying him, he wasn't loyal to you or Hopewood.

"Hopewood was still in the military and oversaw the docks watching for theft and smuggling at the time." He chuckled. "When he was assigned that duty, he truly was an honourable man. But Stanhope doesn't believe that a man can't be corrupted or isn't hiding something. He got Hopewood roaring drunk one night and married him off to a cooperative whore, all done with witnesses. Then the young woman was spirited away so Hopewood had no recourse but to indulge Stanhope's demands or risk a scandal particularly since he had his eyes set on marrying a young lady of the Beau Monde. He bought Stanhope's silence with a pledge that he would turn a blind eye on the docks if Stanhope would not reveal his marital status. Hopewood had been a pigeon just waiting to be plucked and showed his true colours when he didn't even ask for proof that his wife was even still alive." He shook his head and sighed. "Stanhope had slit her throat himself once he had her away from town and left her to rot in some ravine to be crossed off as just another causality of war."

He took a breath with a smug smile, "And that, Turner, is sum of my knowledge."

I could see that father was very tired, so I moved to his side ready to assist him if he needed it, "And why should I believe you, Burley?"

Burley chuckled. "My father was smart enough not to trust Stanhope, that's what cost him his life. The old man kept meticulous records of everything and any information he could glean of his operations in case anything happened to him, other than death by natural causes. Our solicitors were to deliver it to me and I was to decide what was to be done with it."

Father perked up. "And where are these documents?"

Burley laughed. "Not with me, Turner. I still intend to save my family's honour for my sisters' sake and our mother's memory, they deserve that at the very least. I will not let you destroy my family. If you expect my cooperation, you and Sir Thomas will need to meet my conditions."

Suddenly my father slumped. "Lissa, I think I need to lie back." I assisted him to raise his feet to the chase and he fell back, exhausted.

Burley looked at him with actual concern. "Is there anything I can do, Miss Turner?" I glanced at him looking pointedly at his restraints then he coloured. "Oh, yes."

I tried to keep my voice soft and measured and replied, "No, but thank you, Lord Burley."

My father sighed as I put a rug over his lap and he closed his eyes and I pulled a chair up beside him. "Lissa, when Sir Thomas is available, I think he needs to speak with Lord Burley."

Burley then chimed in, "Do you think that I might have these bonds removed?"

Both my father and I said "NO!" simultaneously.

Then Father nodded off to sleep and I took up a book pretending to read while I stared out the window. Lord Burley laid his head back and stared at the ceiling. "You know I believe that Miles will be a better Lord Tinley than Edward ever could be." He paused, then continued as if he had given the issue some thought. "I envy Edward. He is his own man now, rich enough to do what he wants, when he wants and with no obligations."

I couldn't for the life of me think of why he felt the need to talk but it would be rude not to respond. "Really? You're young, rich and not married, what possible impediments do you have to leading any kind of life you want."

He looked directly at me. "I have responsibilities, Miss Turner, that I take very seriously. I am responsible for my younger brother and to make sure that my sisters remain happy in their marriages. Then there are my tenants and the staff on my country estates and in London. There are many people who rely on me for a living and look to me for answers and assistance. My father always said it was my duty! In fact, I'm sure my father's family are waiting for me to fail, then they will swoop in and pick at my bones." He sighed and look very unhappy.

I considered that then told him what I saw as his duty, "Is it really required that you have all the answers or is just that you need to help others find the answers.

You're not a feudal lord whose every word is law. There is no need to put that kind of pressure on yourself. My father and Lord Shellard, even Miles have said it's about surrounding yourself with the right people. Those that are intelligent and trustworthy that demonstrate it through loyalty and hard work and are rewarded appropriately and those that aren't will have to seek employment elsewhere."

He laughed. "Miss Turner, may I hire you as my steward? No, that wouldn't be proper but perhaps I could have you interview my staff and tell me who to keep and who to sack."

I couldn't help but smile at him. "I should think your sister Arabella would be a good person to assist you with that. Though I have never met her, I understand that she is an intelligent woman and a good judge of character."

His face softened. "Arabella is the most like our mother. I think you're right, Miss Turner, she would be an excellent choice to help me sort the wheat from the chaff. In fact, she's been hinting at visiting to help me go through our father's things and in her words 'set things to right'. Thank you, Miss Turner, I shall take your advice…" he looked at his bonds and chuckled, "…eventually."

Mother finally came downstairs and found us. Lord Burley appeared to be napping or resting his eyes, I couldn't tell which when she came in. "Mama, you're very pale, are you alright, should I fetch Maurice?"

She raised a brow at me and smiled. "Maurice? Is there something wrong with Matthew?"

I nodded. "Yes, he was injured in the crossfire, it's not bad but his right arm is of little use right now, so Maurice is helping. Apparently, it's a requirement of living in the Highlands that you understand more than just the basics of medicine."

She nodded and pulled up a chair beside my father. "No, I'm fine, my dear, just tired. Shooting someone is emotionally exhausting." Then she chuckled and turned to look at Lord Burley. "Has he been behaving himself?"

I nodded. "I think Lord Burley is less of a devil and more of a lost boy."

With his head still tilted back and his eyes closed, "I heard that, Miss Turner." He said nothing else and proceeded to snore as did my father at that moment.

Mother shook her headed and nodded towards the door. "I'd love a cup of tea, would you care to join me?" I agreed, and we went to the kitchen in search of a hot cup.

Michael and Jacob came back soon after we had finished our tea. They were muddy, wet and exhausted. Mrs Cripps buzzed around getting them out of their wet clothes, wrapping them in warm dry blankets then shoved bowls of hot soup and fresh bread into their hands. Michael began eating immediately while Jacob sat just staring at his, he looked up and nodded. "Mrs Turner, Miss Turner."

I waited for him to tell us what had happened, but he said nothing else, so I prompted him. "Where are Lord Tinley and Robert?"

He shook his head as if to wake himself and looking at me with sad eyes. "His Lordship asked me to tell you that they're fine and will be back later."

This puzzled me since Jacob looked so sad. "What are they doing that they couldn't come back with you?"

Michael stopped eating to look up at my mother then at Jacob, he swallowed hard, "They're with Ramsey Clarke, he's ah…dying."

My mother gasped. "I only wounded him in the arm! How could he be dying?"

Jacob looked at Michael who shook his head no. But Michael ignored him and sighed before he continued, "He's trapped in the bog, miss. Lord Tinley and Robert are watching him sink or rather Lord Tinley is. His Lordship sent Robert away with us, but Robert stayed behind to make sure that his Lordship could find his way back."

My mother looked horrified. "He's just going to let him drown in the bog?"

It was Jacob that answered this time. "Yes, ma'am, we discussed it and, well, beggin' your pardon, it seemed fitting considering all the pain that he's caused in this world and not just to this family."

Mother's eyes glistened. "But for Miles to stand there and watch, why?"

Jacob sighed. "Someone had to, ma'am, for the record, so we could be sure he was gone. 'No loose ends', his Lordship said. He felt that the de Bearnes deserved no less than an eyewitness account, ma'am."

One of the maids poked her head into the kitchen. "Mrs Turner? Mr Turner and Sir Thomas are asking if you and Miss Turner would please join them in the library."

"Thank you, Daisy, would you please tell them I will be right there. Is there anyone else with them?"

She nodded. "Lord Shellard, Lord and Lady Bruce, their sons, Mrs and Mr Hughes and your Aunt and Uncle Spencer, oh, and the gentleman what's tied up."

She nodded then patted my hand saying to Mrs Cripps. "Could you please see to it that some refreshments are brought into the library, Mrs Cripps?" She nodded and scurried about with Mrs Dawson to collect what would be needed. Then Mother turned to me as I sat in despair thinking of what Miles must be going through. "Lissa, you needn't come along." I made to rise but she put her hand on my arm as she stood. "No dear, you stay here and wait for Miles…he'll need you."

I sat and watched another cup of tea grow cold and waited. People came and went while I sat staring at the door to the yard. It was turning dark outside before I heard the horses arriving in the yard. Captain Bruce came in with some of his men, he was soaking wet and looked bereft. I opened my mouth to ask if he had caught Stanhope, but he refused to make eye contact. Jibben came in behind him, his beautiful clothes were a muddy mess and two equally bedraggled gypsies dragged in a wounded and barely conscious Major Hopewood. Jibben motioned towards the laundry room but Mrs Dawson shook her head. "Already occupied." He moved towards the yard door again when Mrs Dawson sighed, shaking her head. "No need to go back out in the wet, Jibben, my second pantry is dry, and the door is solid with a sturdy lock. Then you men sit here in the kitchen and get warm but try not to drip all over my floor." She handed Jibben a large key and nodded towards the door. He turned with his men and deposited the Major none too gently just inside the threshold, slamming the door and locking it.

I decided to speak up. "Mr Locke, don't you think that the doctor should have a look at him."

Jibben scowled at me. "I don't, he can rot in there for all I care. I lost a good man chasing him down. It had better have been worth it or I'll take care of him myself, he'll die a long slow death at the end of my knife and I'll enjoy every minute of it." Everyone had stopped to listen to him in fear and sympathy.

Captain Bruce produced a silver flask from inside his coat and offered it to him. "Here, you need this more than I do." He placed a companionable hand on Jibben's shoulder as they sat down on the settees by the fire. "You have more guts than all of my men and I put together. Once we shot him in the leg then lost him on that moor I would have left him to hell, but be damned if you didn't track him down. Why?"

Jibben took a long pull on the flask then wiped his sleeve across his mouth. "What do you mean why? Isn't that what Sir Thomas wanted?"

Captain Bruce slapped him on the back. "Now I see why you left the army, they would have hated your dedication to duty."

Jibben cracked a hint of a smile then took another swig. "You lost men tonight as well, Captain."

Derek nodded. "But not as many as I might have without your men working with us. They sat on the settee by the fire passing the flask back and forth, not saying another word, just staring into the fire. They took the soup and bread Mrs Dawson handed them, eating it mechanically and ignoring the rest of us."

I watched them and was hypnotized by the fire flashing off the flask being passed back and forth. Then the yard door opened, Miles and Robert entered, totally spent. Mrs Dawson took over immediately and where the Captain and Jibben had at first refused her ministrations, these two listless men surrendered to her. Finally, she shooed Robert off to find his bed or I imagine to Meg, whichever came first. Then Miles came to me. We said nothing to each other, I just took his hand and walked with him out the door, up the stairs and to my room. I helped him to undress completely and urged him to get into bed. In turn I undressed in front of him as he watched. As much as I thought I would be self-conscious with his eyes on me I wasn't. The only light in the room came from the moon shining through the window and from the blaze in the hearth.

Meg knocked at my door. "Do you need me, Miss Turner."

Meg had never spoken through the door before, her usual action was to just knock and enter. She knew then that Miles was here with me. I smiled at Miles. "No, Meg, I'm fine, thank you, but I know Robert is looking for you."

"Yes, miss, thank you, miss," and I heard her run off down the corridor.

I turned back to Miles, he was still watching me, then he opened his arms to me and I went to him.

# Chapter 49

## *A Wedding and a Funeral*

When I awoke, I was alone, not that I was surprised. Miles and I had consoled each other last night, I found him to be a vulnerable, yet patient and passionate lover. My passion had equalled his, but he was my teacher, he led me down paths that I had never dreamed could even exist between a man and woman. We had bonded in more ways than just the physical. Our spirits touched when we wept for those that had died and were injured, all because of one man's greed.

I rose and rang for Meg. She came in beaming from ear to ear and I smiled at her. "I take it you and Robert had a good night?"

She blushed. "Not like you might think, miss. But we have come to an agreement. We'll marry when he feels confident in his skills as valet and when we've put aside a bit of money."

I hugged her, she was the happiest I had ever recalled seeing her. "Congratulations, Meg! And if I can help in any way to speed that up, please let me know."

She bit her lip and lowered her head. "Well, miss, there will be the issue of Robert and I belonging to two different households once you and his Lordship marry." I squeezed her hand. "Miles and I have already talked about that, he intends to steal Robert away from my father and I think Father will be amenable to it."

Meg looked stunned. "Oh, miss, that would be grand, but would he still be able to work with your father in his other capacity?"

"I don't see why not; Lord Tinley intends to continue his work with my father and Sir Thomas."

Meg just glowed with happiness as I sat at my dressing table and she worked on untangling my curls. I was afraid to ask what it was like in the rest of the house. "How are things downstairs, are Murphy and the doctor alright?"

She nodded. "They both be on the mend, miss, but..."

She had paused, and her face crumpled. "What happened?!"

She bit her lip and tears started to run down her cheeks. "Tis Mr Allan, miss, he was helping to clean up the barns late last night in preparation for the wedding party when he came across one of the rabble that had attacked us. He shot our Mr Allan in the chest." She started to cry outright now in shuddering sobs. "He died this morning, miss."

I felt my lip tremble and tears welling up in my eyes. "Does my mother and father know?"

"Aye, miss, they were with him as he passed on." Then I felt the tears rolling down my cheeks. I hugged her as we both cried. I thought back over the time that I had known Mr Allan and how valuable he was to my father and all the things that he had done for Mother and me without ever being asked. Meg and I talked about him teaching us both about etiquette and history. How he never chastised us when we yawned, he would merely point out that this was the foundation of English society, what raised us above the beasts in the field and the French, which never failed to make us laugh. He had thought of us all as his family. I knew he would be mourned by all of us as a beloved friend and family member.

We had just starting to pull ourselves together again when there was a knock at the door and my mother entered. She looked tired but there were some roses in her cheeks that had been absent for some time. "What's this, tears on your wedding day? Mr Allan would not have approved, my dear." She sat down and took my hand. "He told your father and I how much your marriage meant to him, he highly approved of Lord Tinley even before his elevation to Viscount." She sighed deeply, and her eyes glistened, yet I could see that she had already shed her tears for Mr Allan, these were tears of happiness. She smiled then and squeezed my hand. "His last wish was that you marry today as planned so that his death wouldn't go for nought." I could hear the emotion behind her words. She sniffed dabbing her nose with her handkerchief before going on, "Mr Allan was a most intelligent and caring man. I only wish that I had had the opportunity to get to know him better."

I sighed then wiped my eyes. "I suppose Papa will want to take Mr Allan back to London soon."

She moved to ease herself into a nearby chair. "On the contrary, he asked if he could be laid to rest here. He was very taken with the Rambles, said it reminded him of a place and a person that he had once loved. But she was above his station and couldn't marry him. He had a letter from her brother not too long ago apparently, he had felt guilty at what his parents had done to keep them apart. He explained that she never forgot Mr Alan. In fact, after he had left for London, she went to live with him and his family. But she was only with them a fleeting time…she wasted away and finally died from a broken heart, so don't be sad for him, Lissa, I believe he was happy to go in the end. I would like to think that he's joined her now and that they will be together. He didn't fight death, so I knew he wanted to go."

Then we were all crying once again. Father stepped into the room and looked around. "Oh, my word…Irene, I didn't think you had anymore tears in you. Come now, my love, we have much to celebrate and to be happy for!" He was trying to be cheerful, but I could see the underlying sadness as he choked on his next words. "Mr Allan wouldn't want it any other way." He sighed and continued, "Miles has carried him to the icehouse and the wedding will take place today in the church according to Mr Allan's wishes. Murphy and Lettie are speaking to the vicar about a final resting place for him and it will all be taken care of in a style that he would want tomorrow. But till then today is your day, my darling daughter, put away your tears." He came over and caressed my cheek then extended the same hand to my mother. "Come, Irene, help me dress then we can both rest before walking our daughter down the aisle." He turned around slowly looking back over his shoulder. "Meg, would you check with Lord Tinley about moving Lissa's things. I suggested to Miles that he might like to relocate your room until your journey to Devon. You two kept your mother and I awake half the night."

I turned a bright red as I looked at his reflection in my mirror, but he had an impish grin on his face until I remembered that he and Mother had been with Mr Allan last night. Then my mouth flew opened and I covered my face with my hands.

Mother just laughed and between my splayed fingers, I saw her walk to my father who was also laughing and as they left she said, "I thought that was the way of it. Miles was far too content this morning."

I looked up at Meg who had her mouth open, staring at me as if I had mutated in front of her. Finally, I just said, "What!?"

She smirked. "Nothing, miss, nothing at all." How could I face anyone in this house now? My shoulders slumped. I crossed my arms then laid them down on the dressing table and hid my face. I heard Meg's voice, "You'll be fine, miss, don't let it bother you. Honestly most people had thought it had already happened when we were in France and you two would go off for those long walks." Now I just groaned, I was mortified.

I sat up to let Meg finish getting me ready. "Well, I suppose I had better go down and eat breakfast, so I don't pass out in the church." With that just out of my mouth, Angel came bouncing through the door with a tray loaded with enough food to feed an army. "I can't eat all that!"

Angel beamed. "Oh, you won't be, miss, Beth, Meg and I are to stay with you. Mrs Turner asked us to stand guard, it seems that your bridegroom wants to see you before the wedding and your parents have forbidden it." I was astounded at my parents forbidding Miles after knowing what we had done the previous night. My god how could I show my face at the wedding. Angel was nibbling at a piece of toast before she continued, "By the way, miss, the guest list has increased somewhat to include everyone that aided us yesterday, so the village folk and the people from Poole will be here as well. Mr Johnson... I mean Lord Tinley is having the big barn cleaned up for all the extra guests and there'll be dancing! My Charles plays the fiddle and the gypsies will be singing and playing as well." Then she blushed. "Come on now, eat up so we can get on with dressing you. I'll go tell Mrs Mac that we'll be ready for her in about an hour. She hasn't let that dress out of her sight since the fighting ended last night."

As she left Lady Bruce came in carrying two boxes, she smiled at me as she set them before me. "They're from the family, my dear." I opened the first, it was a veil of the sheerest material I'd ever seen. Her eyes were glowing. "It's Chinese silk. My great grandfather brought it back from the Far East and brides in the Shellard family have worn it ever since, all except for Maria." She frowned and looked sad just then. "My father was terrible to her, I wish I could have made it up to her, but I never really got a chance. I always seemed to be pregnant and unable to travel." She brushed her hand down the length of the silk. "I had meant to return this after I married Angus, but I held onto it. I thought that Georgina might wear it when she married but she's a Bruce and not a Shellard as she told me, and the Bruces have their own traditions, so I never got around to returning it. But it belongs to a Shellard bride and you're the first in some time. I guess it's not strange that William never asked me for it when he married Carolyn, she even asked for it, but he told her that it was lost. He never even mentioned it to Jane, though he knew that I had it and he could have sent for it at any time."

She passed me the veil, it was cool and smooth to the touch as it cascaded across my hand like water. She watched me smiling then she pushed the second box towards me. I opened in and seated in a bed of black velvet rested a silver circlet of woven ivy leaves and roses, just the size to wear as a tiara. Lady Bruce had tears in her eyes. "This was delivered to my brother by courier just before we left London, he asked me to give it to you this morning. It's from the Marquis Du Quenoy, he was so sorry that he couldn't be here, but he wanted you to wear this; Miles' mother wore it at her wedding, he said you could return it when he comes to visit in the spring."

I took a deep breath as I stood up and gave her a hug of the purest joy! Then she let go of me, turned to the tray lifting the covers and inhaled. "Mmmmm, I'm starved!" She picked up one of the forks and began to eat.

My life was complete. I had a family, friends, an exciting future and a man that I adored above all else. Still there was much that needed to be explained and dealt with; but today was my day, mine and Miles. Mr Allan had ordered it so and Mr Allan had never been wrong.

PROUST, BLANCHOT AND
A WOMAN IN RED

| Ven | |
| Sam | |
| DIM | 7 |

| Lun | 8 |
| Mar | 9 |
| Mer | 10 |
| Jeu | 11 |
| Ven | 12 |
| Sam | 13 |
| DIM | 14 |

| Lun | 15 |
| Mar | 16 |

# Proust, Blanchot and a Woman in Red

LYDIA DAVIS

The Cahiers Series

CENTER FOR WRITERS & TRANSLATORS
THE ARTS ARENA · AUP
—

SYLPH EDITIONS

# CONTENTS

*Preface*

The three pieces collected in this cahier relate either directly
or indirectly to three writers who have been very important
in my career as translator: Marcel Proust, Maurice Blanchot,
and Michel Leiris. Although any narrative of one's progress
as translator or writer will be neater than the actual course of
events, it would not be false to suggest that, taking the three in
chronological order: I learned to adhere closely to the original
text in my work on Blanchot (practicing an extreme fidelity that
was not always necessary or even desirable in some of the work-
for-hire translations I had to do before and after); in my work on
Leiris – his *Brisées* (*Broken Branches*) and the first three volumes
of his *La Règle du jeu* (*Rules of the Game*) – I learned to preserve the
syntax of sentences which, unlike Blanchot's, were very long and
almost wilfully complex; and in my work on Proust, I tried to take
that close fidelity a step further, reproducing, when I could, even
the sounds and punctuation of the original, and in the process
often exploring the remote history of a single word.

I will lead off this cahier with descriptions of a few of my
Proust translation struggles. I will then describe my endeavor
to summarize a novel of Blanchot's, an endeavor which led me
into a fascinating but perhaps doomed attempt to articulate the
many different levels and forms in which action takes place in
this novel.

The third element is a recent sequence of dream narratives
that illustrates the way in which a work of literature or even
merely the idea behind a work of literature (in this case, Leiris's
*Nuits sans nuit et quelques jours sans jour*) can exert an influence
that produces a concrete result only years later.

become a simple phrase they used without
they wanted to signify the act of physical pos-
possesses nothing—lived on in their lan-
after that forgotten custom. And perhaps
"make love" did not mean exactly the
Even if one is tired of women, even if
session of the most various women is always
beforehand, this possession becomes a new
women difficult enough—or believed to be so
to make it happen as a result of some episode
foreseen, as had been for Swann, the first

*A Proust Alphabet*

My version:

> What needed to move, a few leaves of the chestnut tree,
> moved. But their minute quivering, complete, executed
> even in its slightest nuances and ultimate refinements,
> did not spill over onto the rest, did not merge with it,
> remained circumscribed.

I had gone over the entire passage many times. But I was stuck
on *baver*, which was most familiar to me as 'drool'. I could not
seem to find a good equivalent. I was puzzled by Proust's choice.

Then I saw it: the extended metaphor here was one of drawing
or sketching: the shivering of the leaf was the subject of the
drawing. What Proust was saying was that the lines with which
it was sketched did not *run* or *smudge* or *bleed* over onto the rest.
I understood, but was still stuck. 'Run' would be confusing;
'smudge' would be clumsy and not quite right; the sense of 'bleed'
was right, but, of course, I could not use that entirely different
metaphor, one which would introduce such violence and color
into the quiet moonlit scene. *Baver* is very wet: 'spill over' was the
closest I could get, still a compromise, since it does not sustain the
drawing metaphor. (Scott Moncrieff changes metaphors entirely,
to a musical one, with 'made no discord'. The Kilmartin-Enright
revision replaces that with the far more abstract 'did not impinge'.)

# C

The word 'contiguous' occurs five times in *Swann's Way*, or maybe it would be more accurate to say that the word *contigu* occurs
at least five times in *Du Côté de chez Swann*; I decided after some
debate to use the closest equivalent, the cognate, in each of these
occurrences in my English version. I like the word, although it
is a little chilly or prickly. It has nice crisp sounds in it – the hard
*c*, *t*, and *g* – and a good rhythm – four syllables with the accent
on the second. In translating Proust, I attended closely to just
such details of sound, mainly because he himself did, but also
because, beyond the meaning of the prose, I wished to translate,
or try to find an equivalent for, its sound. It was necessary to pay
attention to syllable counts, internal rhymes, good alliteration,
clumsy alliteration.

'Contiguous' is applied, in these five occurrences, to: states of mind; houses; houses again; the details of a true story that fit together like jigsaw puzzle pieces; and the impressions that, together, make up one's memory of one's life – that is to say, to three abstract ideas and two concrete objects. Here I will discuss just two occurrences of 'contigu', the first and the last. The first:

> Et de la sorte c'est du côté de Guermantes que j'ai appris à distinguer ces états qui se succèdent en moi, pendant certaines périodes, et vont jusqu'à se partager chaque journée, l'un revenant chasser l'autre, avec la ponctualité de la fièvre; contiguës, mais si extérieurs l'un à l'autre, si dépourvus de moyens de communication entre eux, que je ne puis plus comprendre, plus même me représenter dans l'un, ce que j'ai désiré, ou redouté, ou accompli dans l'autre.

I translated this as follows:

> And so it was from the Guermantes way that I learned to distinguish those states of mind that follow one another in me, during certain periods, and that even go so far as to divide up each day among them, one returning to drive away the other, with the punctuality of a fever; contiguous, but so exterior to one another, so lacking in means of communication among them, that I can no longer understand, no longer even picture to myself in one, what I desired, or feared, or accomplished in the other.

It may be that part of the attraction of using 'contiguous' in this passage, rather than the more familiar 'adjacent', derives from the close proximity of 'fever', and thereby the association of 'contiguous' with 'contagious' (which would work similarly in French as *contigu* is close in sound and appearance to *contagieux*). The last phrase of the passage offers a very good example of Proust working with parallel structure, and with pairs, something he does quite consciously throughout the novel.

The last instance comes at the very end of the book, which is why I paid particularly close attention to this word, and probably why I went back and looked at all the other occurrences of it.

> La réalité que j'avais connue n'existait plus. Il suffisait que Mme Swann n'arrivât pas toute pareille au même moment,

pour que l'Avenue fût autre. Les lieux que nous avons connus n'appartiennent pas qu'au monde de l'espace où nous les situons pour plus de facilité. Ils n'étaient qu'une mince tranche au milieux d'impressions contiguës qui formaient notre vie d'alors ; le souvenir d'une certaine image n'est que le regret d'un certain instant ; et les maisons, les routes, les avenues, sont fugitives, hélas, comme les années.

I translate this as:

> The reality I had known no longer existed. That Mme Swann did not arrive exactly the same at the same moment was enough to make the avenue different. The places we have known do not belong solely to the world of space in which we situate them for our greater convenience. They were only a thin slice among contiguous impressions which formed our life at that time; the memory of a certain image is but regret for a certain moment; and houses, roads, avenues are as fleeting, alas, as the years.

One thing to note here is the variety of different verb tenses and moods Proust uses in these sentences, as though running through them again, at the very end, to reflect the mix of varieties of past and present in his novel and in his very approach to the experience of life in time. In sequence, they are: past perfect, imperfect, imperfect, subjunctive, subjunctive, perfect, present, present, imperfect, imperfect, present, present.

Now in choosing 'contiguous' over 'adjacent' and 'adjoining' I was guided in part by the sound of the word, in part by reaching for a cognate whenever appropriate, and in part by searching for the most exact equivalent. And part of my search is always into the etymology of the word – the deeper layers of it, often the concrete metaphor from which it evolved. In this case what I found for the three choices was:

adjacent:    from the Latin *ad-* and *jacent*
             meaning 'lying near'
adjoining:   from the Latin *ad-* and *jungere*
             meaning 'joining with'
contiguous:  from the Latin *contingere*
             meaning 'having contact with'.

interacting and effecting emotional changes in the narrator and between the narrator and his companion.

Throughout the novel, this companion presses the narrator with the question 'Are you writing now?'. What the novel sets out to explore in the most astounding detail, from within the very center of the narrator's almost desperately heightened consciousness, is his hesitant approach to the idea of writing, his consideration of the possible effects of his writing, and his relationship to his own words, which themselves become active, concrete presences in the novel, sometimes flying gaily and violently through the house, and sometimes closing about the narrator in a suffocating circle.

In this narrative, in which paradox, and impossibility, are incorporated as perfectly natural elements of the action, an attempt to identify actors and types of action, to separate out concrete actors from abstract and permutations of both, yields these notations:

1   There are concrete actors, such as the narrator.
2   There is concrete action in concrete space, and the narrator declares it positively: e.g. 'I moved'.
3   There is possible concrete action in concrete space; the narrator qualifies it: e.g. 'I think I moved'.
4   There is a possible concrete situation; the narrator is even more tentative about it: e.g. 'I had the feeling someone was sitting in the armchair'.
5   There are actors who are possibly but not certainly imaginary, such as a figure, possibly of the narrator's invention, who may be sitting in the room.
6   There are abstract qualities which perform as actors, such as the narrator's desire or immobility.
7   There is a concrete interaction but it takes place between one concrete entity and one abstract entity: e.g. 'I was stopped by my own immobility'.
8   There is 'concrete' interaction between things that do not concretely exist, that exist only in the narrator's mind or imagination – thoughts, sensations, illusions.
9   There is no interaction between the narrator and, say, an imaginary figure; but there is interaction between the narrator and the effect, on the narrator, of that lack of interaction.

This list is probably not exhaustive.

*Swimming in Egypt:*
*Dreams While Awake and Asleep*

And here I discovered that in fact 'contiguous' and 'contiguous' derive from the same Latin root, *contingere*. I further discovered, looking in the handy comparison of synonyms provided by my dictionary (an old *Webster's New Collegiate*), that whereas 'adjacent' does not necessary imply touching, and 'adjoining' does imply touching but not necessarily at more than a single point, 'contiguous' implies 'having contact on all or most of one side', so that in each instance, but especially in the case of the house or the jigsaw puzzle piece, this word really is the most appropriate and the most exact equivalent of Proust's term. And the possible association (either conscious or unconscious, in Proust's mind) of 'contiguous' and 'contiguous' confirms another of my reasons for trying to keep as close to Proust's original as I can: not every reason for his choices has yet been discovered. I want to preserve these choices as nearly as I can, for further investigation.

# D

About two-thirds of the way through *Swann's Way*, in the part of the novel entitled 'Swann in Love', the jealous Swann, after going home from his beloved Odette's house, becomes suspicious and returns to see if she is with another man. He walks around to the street behind her house onto which her bedroom window looks out. He sees a light through the closed shutters and hears voices.

> Il se haussa sur la pointe des pieds. Il frappa. On n'avait pas entendu, il refrappa plus fort, la conversation s'arrêta. Une voix d'homme dont il chercha à distinguer auquel de ceux des amis d'Odette qu'il connaissait elle pouvait appartenir demanda :
> « Qui est là ? »

My translation:

> He raised himself on his tiptoes. He knocked. They had not heard, he knocked again more loudly, the conversation stopped. A man's voice which he tried to distinguish from among the voices of those of Odette's friends whom he knew asked: 'Who's there?'

The sentence whose construction so frustrated me is the last, long one, the one that takes what I always consider unfair advantage of the maddening *dont*, so handy in French, so cumbersome to translate into English – of which, from which, with which, by which, about which, concerning which, etc. This sentence is a highly complex hypotactic one of the 'Russian-doll' type – one clause enclosing the next, which encloses the next, etc. – though it is not very long.

There are no punctuation marks in the sentence at all until the colon before the question. In addition, Proust has constructed it in such a way that, of the five words at the end of the sentence, before the colon, four are the closing verbs of clauses he has begun earlier – because the main clause, 'A man's voice asked', encloses the second clause, 'concerning which he tried to distinguish', and a third clause, 'to which … it might belong', which in turn encloses a fourth clause, 'of those of Odette's friends whom he knew'. This is the sort of stylistic manoeuvre which Proust performs that is so tricky and delightful you have to think Proust enjoyed writing it as much as we do reading it. Mapped out, the clauses look like this:

> [1] Une voix d'homme
>    [2] dont il chercha à distinguer
>       [3] auquel de ceux des amis d'Odette
>          [4] qu'il connaissait
>       [3] elle pouvait appartenir
> [1] demanda :

And so I wanted to have no punctuation at all until the colon, jam up as many verbs as possible at the end, and preserve the order in which the sentence unfolded. If you do not try to create a very pleasing sentence, it can, grammatically, be done, and doing it is rather fun:

> A man's voice concerning which he sought to distinguish
> to which of those of the friends of Odette whom he knew
> it might belong asked: 'Who's there?'

This retains the string of 'of's – 'of those of the friends of Odette' – and the logjam of four verbs at the end: 'he knew it might belong asked'. But 'concerning which' is no good and can't substitute for the elegant *dont* – that blasted French *dont* which creates the problem.

After a lot of fiddling, my final version did some but not all of what I wanted it to do: it had no punctuation until the colon and it unfolded in the same order, but it had only two instead of four verbs at the end, sacrificed the string of 'of's, and left out the phrase 'it might belong':

> A man's voice which he sought to distinguish from among those of Odette's friends whom he knew asked: 'Who's there?'

Returning to this solution after some time, I realized that the word 'those' was ambiguous, trying to refer both to 'voices' and to 'friends', and I decided that although it contains a repetition not in the French, a better choice might be:

> A man's voice which he sought to distinguish from among the voices of those of Odette's friends whom he knew asked: 'Who's there?'

# F

The lovely word 'flensed', which I could not use in my translation, would have occurred in a passage that describes the young narrator's outings to the Champs-Élysées, where he goes faithfully day after day, when his mother lets him, in hopes of meeting the object of his infatuation, the red-haired Gilberte. The weather becomes important to him: if it is too unpromising, his mother may not allow him to go out or Gilberte herself may not appear. (A paragraph or two before the passage in question, for instance, he has been watching anxiously for the clouds to pass, and is overjoyed when he sees on the stone of the balcony the shadows of the elaborate wrought-iron support of the balustrade at last alight like birds, 'pledges of calm and happiness'.)

On his outings to the park he is always, though he wishes he were not, accompanied by the servant Françoise. On this particular day, he has little hope of seeing Gilberte on the snow-blanketed lawns and paths, but by the end of the day will be happily surprised. 'Flensed', if I had used it, would have occurred early in their outing, while Marcel is still struggling with his disappointment over Gilberte's probable non-appearance.

> Françoise avait trop froid pour rester immobile, nous allâmes jusqu'au pont de la Concorde voir la Seine prise, dont chacun et même les enfants s'approchaient sans peur comme d'une immense baleine échouée, sans défense, et qu'on allait dépecer.

My version runs:

> Françoise was too cold to sit still; we walked to the pont de la Concorde to see the frozen Seine, which everyone including the children approached without fear as though it were a beached whale, immense, defenseless and about to be cut up.

This sentence interests me because of the pair of rhymes in the French, which can be reproduced in English (as is the case more often than one would think), and a third rhyme in English that would have been so perfectly apt and yet could not be used for a couple of reasons. But there are other features of the sentence to look at, involving two more instances of the inevitable compromises involved in translation.

First, the rhymes: they occur near the end of the sentence. The whale to which Proust compares the Seine is described as '*immense*' and '*échouée, sans défense*'. The rhyme of *immense* and *défense* is clearly audible. It is also easy to echo in English: 'immense, defenseless'. Now we come to the third qualifier for the whale, which Proust has rather awkwardly tacked onto the end of the sentence, as he sometimes does, almost as though to disrupt his own lyricism: '*et qu'on allait dépecer*', 'and that they were going to cut up', or 'and that was going to be cut up'.

*Dépecer*, from the Old French *pèce*, piece, means to cut to pieces or dismember, when applied to an animal. A butcher may *dépecer* a lamb for Easter dinner, or a lion may. Here is the word in a sentence of Flaubert's: '*Ils tiraient à eux les morceaux de viande . . . dans la pose pacifique des lions lorsqu'ils dépècent leur proie*'. 'They drew the pieces of meat towards them . . . with the peaceful mien of lions dismembering their prey.'

Now, when *dépecer* is applied specifically to a whale, says my *Harrap's French-English*, our word for it would be 'flense', even though, as I discover when I check it in my *Webster's*, 'flense' means more exactly to cut the blubber from a whale. But this

would be an apt enough equivalent and a fortuitous rhyme for 'immense' and 'defenseless'. It might have been one of those happy accidents the translator encounters less often than the impossible cruxes. Yet there are two problems with writing 'immense, defenseless, about to be flensed'. The word is not familiar enough to English readers to be comprehensible, even with the help of the context; and – perhaps in part because of the unfamiliarity of the word – the rhyme would have been excessive and intrusive, more appropriate for humorous verse than for a lyrical description of a frustrating winter afternoon. And so I abandoned 'flense', though it continued to haunt me as being an unusable perfect solution.

As for the compromises, the first is: 'which everyone including the children approached without fear'. A better alternative would perhaps have been 'which everyone, even the children, approached without fear'. 'Even' would have been closer to *même* and it would have sounded better, echoing 'everyone' and being a nimbler, less pedestrian word than 'including'. But at the time I opted for it, I had only recently discovered, by looking specifically at Proust's punctuation, how sparing he was with his commas and how often I could reproduce that light touch in English. Fresh from that discovery, I wanted to avoid using the comma pair there, so as not to slow the sentence more than Proust does. (Already, my semi-colon in place of his comma in the first line had stopped the forward motion.)

The second compromise is the order of images in 'beached whale, immense, defenseless...'. 'Beached' comes first in English; 'immense' comes first in French: the French gives us *immense baleine*, 'immense whale', then continues with *échouée*, 'beached' or 'stranded'. (Though 'beached' and 'stranded' are both correct for the image, we in English tend to use 'stranded' metaphorically so much more often than literally that it has lost some of its concreteness. I therefore opted for 'beached'.) I preferred to keep the rhyming words side by side: 'immense, defenseless'. If I had chosen to follow the French order of images, I would have written 'immense whale, beached, defenseless', which would have been perfectly good. As often, it was something of a toss-up.

# S

Proust's syntactical structures: so often, the more elegant they are, the more problematic for the translator. One which deploys inversion in a manner almost impossible to reproduce occurs about one-quarter of the way through *Swann's Way*.

> De grilles fort éloignées les unes des autres, des chiens réveillés par nos pas solitaires faisaient alterner des aboiements comme il m'arrive encore quelquefois d'en entendre le soir, et entre lesquels dut venir (quand sur son emplacement on créa le jardin public de Combray) se réfugier le boulevard de la gare, car, où que je me trouve, dès qu'ils commencent à retentir et à se répondre, je l'aperçois, avec ses tilleuls et son trottoir éclairé par la lune.

I translated this:

> From gates far apart, dogs awakened by our solitary steps sent forth alternating barks such as I still hear at times in the evening and among which the station boulevard (when the public gardens of Combray were created on its site) must have come to take refuge, for, wherever I find myself, as soon as they begin resounding and replying, I see it, with its lindens and its sidewalk lit by the moon.

I will compare my solutions with those of Scott Moncrieff and of James Grieve, the second translator, whose *Swann's Way* was published in Australia in 1982. Scott Moncrieff's version:

> From gates far apart the watchdogs, awakened by our steps in the silence, would set up an antiphonal barking, as I still hear them bark, at times, in the evenings, and it is in their custody (when the public gardens of Combray were constructed on its site) that the Boulevard de la Gare must have taken refuge, for wherever I may be, as soon as they begin their alternate challenge and acceptance, I can see it again with all its lime-trees, and its pavements glistening beneath the moon.

Grieve's version:

> From garden-gates, set far apart from one another, dogs
> which had been wakened by our untoward footsteps in
> the silence began their antiphonal barking, the like of
> which I still hear some evenings, and which must have
> become the last refuge of that avenue leading from the sta-
> tion when it was abolished and converted into Combray's
> public park, because, wherever I happen to be when those
> alternating barks start to sound and answer each other,
> I always glimpse that old street with its lime-trees and its
> moonlit pavement.

The main problem, as so often in Proust, is how to keep the
complex syntax of the original, with its dependent clauses, and
still write a sentence that sounds natural and pleasant in English.

1   The first part of the problem is the barking of the dogs. The
    literal translation is: 'dogs awoken by our solitary steps caused
    to alternate barkings such as I etc.' Most natural and vivid in
    English would be something like 'barked alternately' or 'took
    turns barking' or 'barked back and forth', but if you want to
    retain the structure of the sentence, two clauses – 'such as
    I still hear etc.' and 'among which the station boulevard etc.'
    – both need to hang off *barks* or *barkings*, and so you have to
    keep the order somehow, you have to keep *barkings* or *barks*
    as a noun following the verb.
        Scott Moncrieff has: 'set up an antiphonal barking'. *Antiphonal*
    is tempting, but it carries with it an ecclesiastical association
    not present in the Proust: the plainer idea of *alternating* is what
    Proust intended. For dogs to 'set up' an antiphonal barking
    is also a little clumsy, although Proust's 'cause to alternate'
    is equally undoglike. Scott Moncrieff's choice of the singular
    *barking* means that he can't refer back to it later in the sentence
    with *they* but, in order to give that *they* a referent, must insert
    material: 'as I still hear them bark, at times, in the evenings'.
    My solution – 'sent forth alternating barks' – doesn't sound
    much better, especially when read out of context (context can
    be very protective), but was the only way I could see to end
    with the plural needed to become the referent for *they* later in
    the sentence.

Grieve's solution is to adopt Scott Moncrieff's *antiphonal* – 'began their antiphonal barking' – which is all right, though there is the same problem of the singular *barking* which means that later in the sentence he must repeat material: 'when those alternating barks start to sound and answer each other'. Proust tends to construct a sentence very tightly and avoid repetition.

Note that Scott Moncrieff has *watchdogs* instead of *dogs*, which changes the French but does add a nice alliteration with *awakened*. Note also that he has changed 'our solitary steps' to 'our steps in the silence'. Grieve has expanded the phrase: 'our untoward footsteps in the silence'. Both are interpreting the original rather than translating it more directly: Proust implies but does not mention *silence*.

2  The next syntactical problem is the conceit of the boulevard taking refuge among the barkings of the dogs so that although it has physically disappeared it lives on in the narrator's memory. Proust, typically, delays revealing the subject of the clause by inverting the word order and inserting a parenthesis: *et entre lesquels dut venir (quand sur son emplacement on créa le jardin public de Combray) se réfugier le boulevard de la gare* – we don't reach the subject until the very end of the clause. (And part of my motive for wishing to follow Proust's word order so closely has been to offer information in the same order he did, to let the images and ideas unfold and reveal themselves in the same sequence.) Literally, this would be: 'and among which must have come (when on its site they created the public garden of Combray) to take refuge the station boulevard'. Whenever possible, I retained Proust's delaying tactics, but English can't invert word order as freely as French. I wanted to put 'the station boulevard' on the far side of the parenthesis but couldn't think of a way to do it that didn't sound hopelessly awkward or didn't lose the idea of 'take refuge among them' or didn't sacrifice the structure of the sentence, as Scott Moncrieff does: 'and it is in their custody (when the public gardens of Combray were constructed on its site) that the Boulevard de la Gare must have taken refuge'. Grieve changes the function of the word *refuge* and does not try to duplicate Proust's order.

Now some lesser problems:

3  I wanted to echo the alliteration in *retentir et se répondre*, which also has a pleasing rhythm. There were, conveniently, several possible *r* choices for both words: *resound, reverberate, resonate* for *retentir*; and *respond, reply* for *se répondre*. I thought the best choices, for meaning and rhythm, were 'resounding and replying'. Scott Moncrieff loses the alliteration with his 'alternate challenge and acceptance', also reduplicates the *antiphonal* idea with his *alternate*, and adds, with *challenge and acceptance*, an idea not in the original. Grieve stays close to the French but loses the alliteration with his 'sound and answer each other'.

4  I wanted to end the paragraph with the word *moon* as Proust does with *lune* – Proust takes great care with his choice of end-words to long sentences and paragraphs. Hence my choice of 'lit by the moon', and Scott Moncrieff's 'pavement glistening beneath the moon'. Scott Moncrieff likes to be faithful to Proust's word-order, often using great ingenuity to achieve this, but he is not opposed to adding ideas and images not in the original, as here: there is no *glistening* in the French, only *éclairé*, meaning *lit* or *illuminated*. His *glisten* adds the idea of sparkle or luster. As for Grieve, he retains the simplicity of *lit* but sacrifices Proust's word order: 'with its lime-trees and its moonlit pavement'.

5  In Proust's original, that last phrase contains another instance of alliteration: *avec ses tilleuls et son trottoir* (the parallelism enhanced by the fact that each *t*-word also contains two syllables and is preceded by *ses*). I could not find a word for *lime-tree* or *linden* that alliterated with *pavement* or *sidewalk*, but the head-rhyme of *linden* and *lit* are at least audible.

It takes much longer to write out the debates that go on over these translation problems than it does to think them through to oneself, but then, one's thoughts are more repetitive than this writing: often I can't accept the fact that there isn't a way to solve all the parts of a problem successfully, so I go over them again and again.

*The Problem in*
*Summarizing Blanchot*

IT WAS WITH MAURICE BLANCHOT'S *L'arrêt de mort* (*Death Sentence*, 1978) that I had my extended initiation into translating closely and exactly – it was my first experience of translating his work, and in the case of his words one would not dare to paraphrase, to normalize, to recast a sentence; every word and its placement had to be respected. In the years after, until 1991, I translated three more of his novels; a novella; and the selection of essays that went to make up *The Gaze of Orpheus*.

The experience of translating the essays was one of the most difficult I ever had, in translating. As though the experience were, in fact, a piece of fiction by Blanchot, the meaning of a difficult phrase or sentence would often become a physical entity that eluded me, my brain becoming both the pursuer and the arena in which the pursuit took place. Understanding became an intensely physical act.

It was during this translation that I experienced another sort of struggle with understanding: although, in a simpler paragraph, I might be able to follow the thread of Blanchot's argument from one sentence to the next, I found that I could not summarize, at the end of the page or even at the end of the paragraph, what I had just read. I thought this was my own weakness, some sort of mental deficiency; but when I described it to others, I found that it was true for them as well: it was in the nature of Blanchot's argument to resist summary. The experience of reading had to take place moment by moment; one's understanding proceeded like a guide's flashlight, illuminating one by one the animals painted on the wall of an ancient cave.

The following description portrays a different kind of difficulty in summarizing Blanchot.

\*

)97 and contin-
)n in 2002
tle being a story
hen being called
004 softcover. In
nsider even the
llightenment in
mething I had
d me, and I noted
debate with
vy was turning
nn's Way*; the
the umbrels and
ntually, I began
of an *Alphabet of
ntries.

roust is describing
scribing a stained-
r quelque aurore*,
d by some aurora'.
s novel was C. K.
n 1922 and 1930. He
e'. Scott Moncrieff's
and D. J. Enright
eing with 'sunrise',
light of dawn'.

31

II

I consult the *Petit Robert* because *aurore* seems to me an unusual choice for 'sunrise' or 'dawn' – why didn't Proust use the more common *aube*? – and find a differentiation that surprises me: *aube* is the first light that begins to whiten the horizon; *aurore* is the brilliant pink gleam that appears in the sky following *aube*; and then the sun itself appears. As I must do often when translating Proust, I look up the English words, to make sure I know my own language. In English, 'dawn' and 'daybreak', too, mean the first appearance of light in the morning, and would be the equivalent of *aube,* whereas the English word 'aurora', in fact, means the same as the French: the redness of the sky just before the sun rises. We tend to be familiar with the word only in the term 'aurora borealis', which means, literally, 'northern dawn'.

The perfect equivalent of *aurore* is therefore 'aurora'. But 'aurora' will not be very expressive; it has not accumulated the same emotional and metaphorical associations as 'dawn'. For some time, I think I will compromise: the perfect equivalent exists, but it will mean less than something more approximate or more wordy; perhaps I will put: 'snowflakes illuminated by some rosy dawn'. But in the end I am not willing to give up the perfect equivalent, and I opt for 'aurora'. If a less familiar word may be less immediately evocative, it does add something else of its own to a text – its surprise, its novelty, and of course its perfect match to the French original.

# B

The sentence containing the problem word *baver* occurs in a passage in which the narrator runs a serious risk of punishment by waiting up for his mother, in his bedroom, to demand the kiss that she has not given him downstairs. He opens the window and sits at the foot of his bed. He is very still, and outside, things seem frozen in mute attention also.

> Ce qui avait besoin de bouger, quelque feuillage de marronnier, bougeait. Mais son frissonnement minutieux, total, exécuté jusque dans ses moindres nuances et ses dernières délicatesses, ne bavait pas sur le reste, ne se fondait pas avec lui, restait circonscrit.

ce Blanchot's novel *Celui qui
as Standing Apart from Me*)
or publicity copy – in other
hensible to a larger audi-
comprehend. Being forced
dentify precisely what was
ed the action forward. This
novel. Here is one perfectly
e: 'In a house in the south-
from room to room being
ow?' by another character
mary would not be appro-

e conventionally acceptable:
nly as somewhere in the
hange from autumn to win-
ly, at long intervals, from
arden he remembers with
glass of water, he stands by
rs room in which he says he
rge ground floor room which
a large disordered bed, a
the narrator – for whom the
quality that causes them to
it might not be a bed after all,
he hesitates to lie down on it,

f the room into the garden
ay not really be there stands
man does not seem to see the
out the house, the narrator
companion", who may or
lf, and may or may not exist
he is not moving or speaking,

ppens', in a sense. Yet between
within the mind of the nar-
terious level where abstrac-
me strong concrete presences

IN HIS « Rêver, écrire » ('Dreaming, Writing'), an essay on Michel Leiris's *Nuits sans nuit et quelques jours sans jour* (1961) that was reprinted as a foreword to the English version which appeared in 1987, Maurice Blanchot makes a general comment about dreaming: 'Do we not frequently get the impression that we are taking part in a spectacle not meant for us or that we are looking over someone's shoulder at some unexpected truth...?' (translation by Richard Sieburth). Then, as so often happens in his essays, he goes on from this point, with which we can easily agree, to create an elaborate construction of his own that retains its own inner logic but leaves us in a strange place: 'The fact is that we are not really there... One could almost say that there is nobody in the dream and therefore, in a certain fashion, that there is nobody to dream it; hence the suspicion that when we are dreaming there is also someone else dreaming, someone who is dreaming us and who in turn is being dreamed by someone else...'

I acquired *Nights as Day, Days as Night* many years ago, soon after it was published in Richard Sieburth's translation. Leiris's project was to record his dreams; to record waking experiences that resembled dreams; and to put them together in sequence as they had occurred. Some two decades later – just recently – I had a waking experience that was inescapably dreamlike: I was driving along a well-maintained road which I had never taken before and which, according to my map, seemed to lead straight to a busy town. But the road became narrower and narrower, its surface rougher and rougher, until it was a mere rocky track winding through thick woods. With difficulty, I turned back before the road disappeared altogether.

This experience caused me to contemplate Leiris's book with fresh interest and devise a project of my own, slightly different:

I would record actual dreams and I would record waking experiences that were like dreams; I would group them together, but, unlike Leiris, refrain from identifying which were which and sequence them according to a logic that was not necessarily chronological. I would also select from the raw material, shaping the dreams as I liked and even, sometimes, combining elements of different dreams. Part of my interest in not identifying which were actual dreams was to allow all the pieces to remain in the same dreamlike territory, that zone in which our life experiences are sometimes stranger than our sleeping experiences – though of course one striking aspect of our role as protagonist in our dreams is, it seems to me, that we are not surprised by the surprising things that occur, even though, usually, we believe that what we are experiencing is real.

*Swimming in Egypt*

We are in Egypt. We are about to go deep-sea diving. They have erected a vast tank of water on land next to the Mediterranean Sea. We strap oxygen to our backs and descend into this tank. We go all the way to the bottom. Here, there is a cluster of blue lights shining on the entrance to a tunnel. We enter the tunnel. We swim and swim. At the far end of the tunnel, we see more lights, white ones. When we have passed through the lights, we come out of the tunnel, suddenly, into the open sea, which drops away beneath us a full kilometer or more. There are fish all around and above us, and reefs on all sides. We think we are fly-ing, over the deep. We forget, for now, that we must be careful not to get lost, but must find our way back to the mouth of the tunnel.

*The Moon*

I get up out of bed in the night to go to the bathroom. The room I am in is large, and dark but for the white dog on the floor. The hallway is wide and long, and filled with an underwater sort of twilight. When I reach the doorway of the bathroom, I see that it is filled with bright light. There is a full moon far above, overhead. Its beam is coming in through the window and falling directly onto the toilet seat, as if sent by a helpful God.

Then I am back in bed, and I have been lying there awake for a while. The room is lighter than it was. The moon is coming around to this side of the building, I think. But no, it is the beginning of dawn.

*The Schoolchildren in the Large Building*

I live in a very large building, the size of a warehouse or an opera house. I am there alone. Now some schoolchildren arrive. I see their quick little legs coming through the front door and I ask, in some fear, 'Who is it, who is it?', but they don't answer. The class is very numerous – all boys, with two teachers. They pour into the painting studio at the back of the building. The ceiling of this studio is two or even three stories high. On one wall is a vast mural of dark-complexioned faces. The schoolboys crowd in front of the painting, fascinated, pointing and talking. On the opposite wall is another mural, of green and blue flowers. Only a handful of schoolboys is looking at this one.

The class would like to spend the night here because they do not have funds for a hotel. Wouldn't their home town raise the money for this field trip? I ask one of the teachers. No, he says sadly, with a smile, they wouldn't because of the fact that he, the teacher, is homosexual. After saying this, he turns and gently puts his arms around the other teacher.

Later, I am in the same building with the schoolchildren, but it is no longer my home, or I am not familiar with it. I ask a boy where the bathrooms are, and he shows me one – it's a nice bathroom, with old fixtures and wood panelling. As I sit on the toilet, the room rises – because it is also an elevator. I wonder briefly, as I flush, how the plumbing works in that case, and then assume it has been figured out.

## The Woman in Red

Standing near me is a tall woman in a dark red dress. She has
a dazed, rather blank expression on her face. She might be
drugged, or this is simply her habitual expression. I am a little
afraid of her. A red snake in front of me rears up and threatens
me, at the same time changing form once or twice, for instance
acquiring tentacles like a squid. Behind it is a large puddle of
water in the middle of a broad path. To protect me from the
snake, the woman in red lays three broad-brimmed red hats
down on the surface of the puddle of water.

## The Dog

We are about to leave a place that has a large flower garden and
a fountain. I look out the car window and see our dog lying on a
gurney in the doorway of a sort of shed. His back is to us. He is
lying still – he is probably dead. There are two cut flowers placed
on his neck, one red and one white. I look away and then look
back – I want to see him one last time. But in that one moment he
has vanished: the doorway of the shed is empty. A moment too
soon, they have wheeled him away.

## In the Gallery

A woman I know, who is a writer, has created a piece of visual
art. She is trying to hang her work for a show. Her work is a
single line of text pasted on the wall, with a transparent curtain
suspended in front of it.

She is at the top of a ladder and cannot get down because she is
facing the wrong way – out instead of in. The people down below
tell her to turn around, but she does not know how.

When I see her next, she is down from the ladder. She is going
from one person to the next, asking for help in hanging her artwork. But no one will help her because, they say, she is such a
difficult woman.

*The Piano*

Our piano has a crack all the way across the soundboard, and
other problems. We will have to go to the piano store and buy
a new one. We would like the piano store to take our old one and
resell it, but they say it is too badly damaged to be resold. They
will have to get rid of it by pushing it over a cliff. The way they
do it is this: two drivers take it out to a remote spot with a high
elevation. One turns his back and walks away down the lane.
The other pushes the piano over the cliff.

*The Piano Lesson*

I am with my friend Christine. I have not see her for a long time,
perhaps seventeen years. We talk about music and we agree that
when we meet again she will give me a piano lesson. In preparation for the lesson, she says, I must select, and then study, one
Baroque piece, one Classical, one Romantic, and one Modern.
I am impressed by her seriousness and by the difficulty of the
assignment. I am ready to do it. We will have the lesson in one
year, she says. She will come to my house. But then, later, she
says she is not sure she will be returning to this country. Maybe,
instead, we will have the lesson in Italy. Or if not Italy, then, of
course, Casablanca.

*The Grandmother*

A person has come to my house carrying a very large peach tart.
He has also brought with him some other people, including a
very old woman who complains about the gravel and is then
carried into the house with great difficulty. These people sit
down with us to some sort of a meal. At the table, the old woman
observes to one man, by way of conversation, that she likes his
teeth. Another man keeps shouting in her face, but she is not
frightened, she only looks at him balefully. Later, she has been
eating many cashews from a bowl, and she has also eaten her

hearing aid. She has chewed on it for nearly two hours, but she cannot reduce it to particles small enough to swallow. At bedtime she spits it out into the hand of her caregiver and tells him this nut was no good.

*In the Train Station*

The train station is very crowded. People are walking in every direction at once. Some are standing still. A Tibetan Buddhist monk with a shaved head and a long wine-colored robe is in the crowd, looking worried. I am standing still, watching him. I have plenty of time before my train leaves, because I have just missed a train. The monk sees me watching him. He comes up to me and tells me he is looking for Track 3. I know where the tracks are. I show him the way.

*The Churchyard*

I have the key to the churchyard and unlock the gate. The church is in the city, and it has a large enclosure. Now that the gate is open, many people come in and sit on the grass to enjoy the sun.

Meanwhile, girls at the street corner are raising money for their mother-in-law, who is called 'La Bella'.

I have offended or disappointed two women, but I am cradling Jesus (who is alive) amid a cozy pile of people.

COLOPHON

THE CAHIERS SERIES   ·   NUMBER 5
ISBN: 978-0-9552963-5-2

Tritone printing by Principal Colour, Paddock Wood,
on Neptune Unique (text) and Chagall (dust jacket).
Set in Monotype Dante by Giovanni Mardersteig.

Series Editor: Dan Gunn
Design and photography: Ornan Rotem
Additional photography: Lian Stibbe

The French quotations in 'A Proust Alphabet' are
taken from *Du côté de chez Swann* (Editions Gallimard,
1987). The quotations from the English translation
are taken from *Swann's Way*, trans. Lydia Davis
(Viking Penguin, paperback edition, 2003 and 2004).
'C' from 'A Proust Alphabet' was originally pub-
lished in *Parakeet* 1: Syracuse, 2004. 'S' from 'A Proust
Alphabet' was originally published in a slightly dif-
ferent form as 'A Problem Sentence in Proust's *The
Way by Swann's*' in *The Literary Review,* Vol. 45, No. 3:
Madison, Spring 2002. Portions of 'The Problem in
Summarizing Blanchot' first appeared, in a slightly
different form, in 'For Maurice Blanchot,' *Nowhere
Without No: In Memory of Maurice Blanchot* (Vagabond
Press: Australia, 2003). 'The Moon' and 'In the Train
Station' from 'Swimming in Egypt: Dreams Awake
and Asleep' were originally published as a broadside
by Kore Press: Tucson, 2007.

CENTER FOR WRITERS & TRANSLATORS
THE ARTS ARENA
THE AMERICAN UNIVERSITY OF PARIS

SYLPH EDITIONS, LEWES │ 2007

THE ARTS ARENA

center for writers and translators

SYLPH
EDITIONS

www.aup.fr    ·    www.sylpheditions.com